JAGO

Kim Newman

D1354582

POCKET
BOOKS

LONDON · SYDNEY · NEW YORK · TOKYO · SINGAPORE · TORONTO

First published in Great Britain by Simon & Schuster Ltd, 1991
First published in paperback by Grafton, 1992
An imprint of HarperCollins*Publishers*
First published by Pocket Books, 1997
An imprint of Simon & Schuster Ltd
A Viacom Company

Simon & Schuster
West Garden Place
Kendal Street
London W2 2AQ

Simon & Schuster Australia
Sydney

A CIP catalogue record for this book is available from the British Library.

0 671 85580 8

Printed and bound in Great Britain by Caledonian International Book
Manufacturing Ltd, Glasgow

For the people of the village of Aller, in Somerset. A much nicer crowd than the inhabitants of the village of Alder, in the strictly imaginary county of the same name.

'I've heard all this stuff about consensus reality, and you honestly expect me to believe that we've just been maintaining this fragile structure of reality based on an agreement between people who can't agree upon *anything*?'
Lisa Tuttle

Prologue

U NDER BLOOD-RED clouds, the Reverend Mr Timothy Charles Bannerman touched a lucifer to his sexton's torch. Flames curled like instantaneous ivy about the pitch-clogged cotton. When Old Jerrold held it up, wind-whipped fire was briefly transparent against the sky.

'Quickly,' said Bannerman, 'before it goes out.'

He pulled his ulster tight against the ice caress of winter, and wished he had thought to save his gloves. A pile of combustibles towered three times a man's height in the centre of the clearing. Jerrold thrust the torch between dead branches into the straw, cloth and paper heart of the structure. Bales in the middle – good hay which in other years would have lasted until spring – caught easily. Epileptic flickers lit the insides, and dancing black bars of shadow were cast upon the villagers. Deep in the belly of the fire, wood began to crack and spit. The burning heap shook, and settled for the first time.

'It would be as well, I think, if we all stood a little back.'

Others followed the vicar's lead, but the heat reached further, unwilling to free them. Bannerman's hands were pleasantly warm now. He admired the bonfire. The vicarage library was in there. The collected sermons of his predecessors could serve no better use, and there would be little further call for novels, tracts or bound periodicals. His flock had looted their homes, scavenging anything that would burn. Clothes and books were easiest to bring up the hill; but those whose households were equipped with neither had taken axes and split doors, beds, tables, fences. The sparse furniture of a double handful of lives was cast away, leaving souls the purer for the sacrifice.

They had been gathering fuel for some weeks now, with the enthusiasm usually reserved for Guy Fawkes' Night. Neighbouring villages had mocked over mulled wine and mince pies on the 5th of November. The story had been that the

people of Alder proposed to set light to their own houses by
way of honouring the failure of Gunpowder Treason. There
had doubtless been no little measure of disappointment in the
taverns and taprooms of Achelzoy and Othery when this had
turned out not to be so. Bannerman's flock had its ambitions set
higher than the preservation of Parliament. No effigy in a tall hat
perched atop this fire. The clothes crammed into it were Sunday
best or workaday sturdy, not worn-through scarecrow castoffs.

'How the stuff of this world burns, sir,' said Jerrold. 'How
the things that are dear to men and women are as nothing in the
sight of the Lord.'

'Quite,' Bannerman replied. 'Should it be deemed necessary
that we pass through the eye of the needle, we shall have no need
of Mr Lewis Carroll's fabulous elixir.'

'Indeed not, vicar,' replied the sexton, who (Bannerman at
once realized) could have understood but half his allusion,
'indeed not.'

The faithful of Alder had begun to gather on the hillside in
the middle of the afternoon. Now they stood about, uncertain.
Most were quiet, some doubtless inwardly afraid, some radiant
in prayer. All were wrapped in the solemn business of putting
away from themselves everything they had known. Fields had
been neglected for days, tools abandoned on the bare earth,
bewildered livestock left to wander. Down in the village, a
dog was howling for its supper. A few had brought house
animals with them. The Graham child struggled with an armful
of kittens.

Bannerman turned away from the fire. He saw the familiar
view as if for the first time, knowing this was his last look at the
Somerset levels. The red in the sky spilled across the horizon,
staining the wetlands as they had once been stained with the
blood of the Monmouth rebels and King's men who fell at
Sedgemoor. Until tonight, that had been the last battle fought on
English soil. An older rebellion, Bannerman thought, was about
to be put down. Out on the moors, just visible from the clearing,
a lone farmer stood with his cattle. Jem Gosmore had chosen to
be with his beasts at the last, not his wife and children.

Occasionally, a ripple of talk would run around, as of the
crowd clearing its shared throat. But mostly the flock was quiet.
Quieter even than they were wont to be of a Sunday morning,
during Bannerman's sermons. He sensed barely suppressed

elation among them, but also unconquerable unease. The widow Combs was silently weeping. He could not tell whether her tears were for Geoffrey Combs, dead three weeks too soon to be here, or for her front curtains, reluctantly yielded and just now crumpling in the flames.

He had assumed they would sing hymns, but did not think it ought to fall to him to propose the notion. Bannerman could feel the strength of his congregation's faith when their voices were raised in 'He Who Would True Valour See' or 'How Amiable Are Thy Tabernacles, O Lord of Hosts!' Granver Shepherd had brought his fiddle, but seemed undecided whether to play an air on it or pitch it into the fire. Often, after a strenuous bout of bowing, Shepherd remarked wistfully, 'I don't know, when the time comes, as I should care to exchange this old instrument even for a harp.'

Shepherd tossed first his bow, then the fiddle itself, on to the fire, and stood back. As the wood buckled and smouldered, the catgut snapped with eerie, high-pitched sounds. Granver backed into the crowd and received the sympathy of those who had likewise surrendered their dearest possessions. Many had given up the tools of their trades, thus their earthly livelihoods. Despite the heat, Bannerman shivered. His first doubt worried gnatlike at him; he hastily brushed it away.

The people of Alder were not wrong. He was not wrong.

There was an outbreak of chattering as the Misses Pym, pretty Alice and prettier Grace, arrived, trailed by their father. Tom Pym was bent double under a wicker hamper. Several younger men came forward to relieve him, and, opened, the hamper gave testimony to his daughters' well-proven talent for the manufacture of cakes, tarts and sundry sweetmeats. In a burst of excitement, suddenly hungry queues assembled, and the Pym girls began to distribute their produce.

Alice came to him, bearing a fat cream horn, and smiled with deliberation. She was trying to show her dimple to its best advantage.

'Mr Bannerman, would you care . . .?'

'Thank you, Alice. I believe I would.'

He took the confection out of politeness, but found it disappeared in three bites. His normal appetites, which he had thought reduced to insignificance by the momentousness of the occasion, were running strong. Of late, he had neglected the trivial necessaries of a life soon to be abandoned. Now he rather regretted his absent-minded abstinence from the honest pleasures of the table. Other abstinences, not quite thought of, bothered him too, but . . .

Alice fluttered around, inquiring after the cream horn. He rewarded her with a kind word, which he instructed her to halve and share with her sister. When she gave no sign of practising the prescribed generosity, he called Grace over and bestowed the demi-compliment in person. Miss Alice shone a little less than previously, and Miss Grace's habitually pert expression shaded microscopically into smugness.

There was no doubt but that the Misses Pym were the local beauties. Attentions, thus far unrewarded, had been paid to them by young men from as far away as three parishes. Had things been otherwise, Bannerman might have been disposed to consider either as a suitable match himself. In addition to his living, he had holdings from his late father. The girls could not find a more marriageable prospect within the county boundaries. Tradition would seem to indicate that he pay his attentions to Alice, the elder Miss Pym, but he suspected that his inclination would be rather towards Grace, the younger. But things were not otherwise.

He caught Jerrold frowning disapproval as the Misses Pym pressed more food upon him. The sexton had lived sixty-six years and never married.

The girls let him be, their father having summoned them elsewhere to be praised for a particularly successful jam pastry. Bannerman wiped traces of cream from his moustache with his handkerchief, and threw the balled linen into the flames. It was alight and gone like a mayfly. He tried to think about anything but the Misses Pym, and found it easy. The coming events bulked large in his mind. He could not help but regret in some small way the need totally to abandon the life he had made for himself. He tried to compose himself, to lose the tautness in his throat. He stepped away from the heat that excited his exposed skin and warmed his clothed flesh.

As the sun dipped below the horizon, he consulted the half-hunter his father had presented to him upon his graduation from Lampeter College. 'Make something of yourself,' he had exhorted. He snapped the watch shut and pocketed it. From this moment onwards, he would have no more use for his father's gift, but he did not think to toss it to the fire.

The almanac entry for the day – Tuesday 8th November 1887 – had been proven correct. The sun had gone down at precisely eighteen minutes to five o'clock. The book was in the fire now, never to be right again. By its reckoning, the sun would rise again at fourteen minutes to seven tomorrow morning. In this, Bannerman knew the almanac to be wrong, for tonight was the Last Night of the World.

Throughout his short career in the Church, Timothy Bannerman had thought of himself as a 'modern'. Given a choice between the account of the Creation set out in the Book of Genesis and that which might be inferred from *The Origin of Species*, he was apt to agree with the bishop who remarked that the one was dictated to Moses by the Lord God, while the other was the work of a far less distinguished gentleman. However, he was willing, more willing indeed than the majority of his parishioners, to concede that a literal interpretation of the Bible led to arguments more troublesome than those into which he cared to enter. And he was of the decided opinion that miracles, visions and angelic visitations were the province of the Roman rather than the Anglican Church. Bleeding statues, portents in the skies and nuns speaking in tongues he believed the province of sensational romances of an earlier century, not of current religious thinking.

Therefore, when Jas Starkey – hardly the most devout of his flock – wakened half the village with hysterical tales about a burning man in the woods, Bannerman had not instantly deduced that his parish was regularly playing host to the Angel Raphael. Indeed, his next sermon had been a largely humorous warning against the evils of strong drink, in which Starkey's fable was instanced as an unfortunate result of inordinate fondness for the rough cider brewed in the locality. Those who had spent a fine summer night dashing up and down the hillside paths with pails of water, drenching perfectly good trousers, had laughed appreciatively. It still seemed singular that the Angel should choose to reveal himself first to a tosspot who would greet the Apocalypse with a head befuddled by scrumpy from the bed of a woman not his wife.

And yet, that was precisely what had happened.

The village stopped laughing at Starkey when others began to see the burning man, and to give more detailed descriptions of the apparition. It was not easy to discount the testimony of Thomas Pym, lifelong abstainer and church warden, or Geoffrey Combs, farmer and respected local sage. Nor could they deny the account of Louisa Gilpin, a girl whose eagerness to talk about the Angel that had come to her exceeded her reluctance to explain the nature of her nocturnal excursion into the woods with Jem Gosmore's second eldest. Finally, no one could doubt the word of the Reverend Mr Bannerman, vicar of the parish and *soi-disant* 'modern'.

Bannerman had been with the first party deliberately to enter the woods by night in the hope of seeking out the apparition. It had seemed larkish, accompanying superstitious locals to chase the resident ghost. With others more credulous, he thought, than himself, Bannerman waited in the clearing where the figure had most often been seen. He examined the burned patches that bore witness to the spectre's late presence, and personally put them down to careless handling of night lanterns. His own light burned low, needless under the unclouded, new-shilling-bright half-moon. He took the odd nip from Dr Skilton's hip flask.

Dr Skilton of Yeovil, Bannerman's frequent dinner guest and conversational companion, was the sole outsider on the expedition. The medical man had lately returned from the interior of China, and was full of amusing accounts of the superstitions he had met there. Tom Pym viewed Skilton with open suspicion, especially when the brandy was in view, but the rest of the company were by no means against a brief suckle at the little silver bottle. The best of the village was there, Bannerman supposed: Pym, Granver Shepherd, Combs, Winthrop of the Manor House, and two or three of the 'newer' landowners, whose families had farmed their acres for less than three generations. Although still September, the night was cold. Skilton was joshing Bannerman with facetious comments about looking up the rites of exorcism when . . .

. . . when the burning Angel appeared.

The heat was tremendous. All present were browned as if from the summer sun for days afterwards. Bannerman covered his eyes, then forced himself to look . . .

. . . at the beautiful form of the man in the halo of fire. White vestments hung from perfect limbs. His hair was a smooth sheet of flame. His outstretched arms were tipped with blazing balls in which fingers could barely be discerned. Bannerman knew at once this was an Angel.

The apparition opened his mouth, and a tongue of fire flickered. His eyes, too, were ablaze. And the Angel spoke, 'Babylon the great is fallen, is fallen, and is become the habitation of devils . . .'

The Angel continued, but Bannerman knew the words anyway. The words of Chapter 18, Verse 2, of the Revelation of St John the Divine.

'. . . and the hold of every foul Spirit, and a cage of every unclean and hateful bird.'

Skilton went forward to touch the Angel, and, in an instant, burned the flesh from his hand.

Bannerman did not hear the doctor scream or smell the cooking of his meat. The clergyman was on his knees in worship, in wonderment. This was the moment he had been awaiting in ignorance all his twenty-seven years. His mind stretched like a balloon, expanding with the revelation that had been granted to him.

To *him*! Not St John the Divine, but Timothy Charles Bannerman of the parish of Alder in the county of Somerset!

As one entranced, he saw it then. He knew without doubt that the Day of the End was at hand, its very date burned into him by the glance of the Angel. He felt it raise in fire on his forehead, then sink into his brain. The 8th of November. Had he lived, it would have been his father's sixtieth birthday.

Day of Judgement. Day of Atonement. Day of Armageddon. Day of Apocalypse.

When the Angel was gone, his image danced before Bannerman's eyes, burned into his sight as if his retinae were photographic plates.

Bannerman knew his Bible and his history well enough to gather that being the Chosen People could be uncomfortable, and he acted accordingly. Knowledge of the privileges due to his parish was to be kept within its bounds. He preached no sermons on the Angel's announcement, and did not alert his bishop to the divine manifestation. He believed the revelation to be for the benefit of his parish only. Or else, why grant a foretaste of it to Jas Starkey who had nothing, apart from his theoretical membership of the Alder congregation, to recommend him?

Bannerman abandoned the scheduled services. He did not need to spread the word. Within days, everybody in the village knew. Others saw the Angel in the clearing, others received the news. He had no trouble convincing his flock when the burning Raphael could be seen every other night in the shimmering flesh. Only Skilton, his useless right hand baked through, disbelieved the divinity of the apparition, and he retreated to London in search of a doctor who might give him back his fingers. The doctor was not disposed to spread the news.

In Bridgwater and Taunton, there were distorted tales of an Alder ghost and a parson gone mad, but when they reached Bath and Bristol they seemed to blend in with other, similar stories. There was no need for another Spirit presence or another crazed cleric in a half-century already overstocked with both commodities. Bannerman's bishop wondered if he should do anything about whatever was going on in Alder, but decided to wait until after Christmas on the assumption that it would blow over long before that. A few – very few – people vanished from their homes and went to stay indefinitely with relatives in Alder. Others with kin in the village were either not offered, or refused, the chance of salvation.

The flock were at first bewildered, then frightened, then delighted, then bewildered again by the knowledge that the End of the World was due directly, and that they alone of humanity had been vouchsafed a definite absolution for any and all sins and selected to sit at the right hand of God. But they respected their young vicar, who had never before misled them, and most followed him. Some who had not hitherto been overly dedicated became sudden converts. The more devout put aside their daily toils and spent their time in and around the church, singing, praying, contemplating.

Louisa gave up whatever functions she performed on her parents' farm and transformed into Bannerman's unofficial maid-of-all-work. Wherever he was, she could be found a respectful fifteen yards behind, hunchbacked by the huge family Bible she carried everywhere in a shawl slung around her shoulders. As she prepared the parson's occasional meals or desperately sought to see some pattern in the letters that made up the words of the Book, several young and not so young men of the village felt cause to regret her current distraction. Bannerman was amused and moved by the girl who thought she had been given a free pass to Heaven, and was trying to scrape together in good works enough coin to pay her way above board.

The idea of the bonfire came from nowhere. Perhaps it had started as the usual Guy Fawkes' celebration but been taken over by the more significant event. In any case, Bannerman approved, and what Bannerman approved was as close as spit to the will of the Angel Raphael.

So it was that the Righteous gathered on the hillside, sure of a good view of the devastation of the rest of the world. They could see at least as far as Glastonbury Tor from the clearing, and the spectacle was bound to be magnificent. Word had spread of the desolations to be visited upon the unrighteous, and opinion was divided as to whether the sinners of blighted Bridgwater – whose lights could be seen on the horizon – would be burned up by a rain of fire and brimstone or swallowed down by the opening of the earth. Either calamity would be no more than the harlots, swindlers, gin dogs and municipal thieves of that notorious town deserved.

So it was that the End was near.

The fire swept upwards, fifty feet or more. Embers funnelled towards Heaven like mad stars. None could endure the heat within ten feet of the blazing pile. Bannerman's underclothes were sweated through. His face was grimed, and his heavy ulster had a fine dusting of ash. Withal, he was jubilant.

The hour of the Angel was approaching. All the hosts of Heaven and Hell were soon to be let loose in this place.

He stripped his cape and twirled it from his hand. It sailed on the hot wind of the fire, an albatross taking wing. In the flames, it writhed like a man afire and was gone in seconds.

Bannerman was giddy.

The flock followed his example, and ventured nearer the fire, pulling off winter coats and woollen shawls that would never again be needed. It was warm enough. Hands helped Bannerman with his frock coat. He was comfortable in his waistcoat and shirtsleeves, able to feel again the not quite dispelled bite of November night. He wiped his face with his hands, and wiped his hands on his trousers.

Some of the men were stripped to the waist, dark streaks of soot on white skins. The Misses Pym wore only cotton shifts and stockings. They were without sin. The whole flock was without sin.

Someone was quoting, 'Naked you came into this world, and naked you shall pass into the Kingdom of Heaven.'

Bannerman clutched his throat, and twisted away his white collar. He felt freer without it, better able to breathe.

On the other side of the flames, Louisa Gilpin danced. She was naked as a newborn child. 'See, oh Lord, how we have put aside the things of this world,' she shouted.

Somehow, Bannerman was still shocked. He understood, and tried to purge himself of feelings he knew to be a part of the world well lost. He had never seen a woman naked, and Louisa was not like his imaginings. The phantoms of his night thoughts were cleaner, more like classical statues than this substantial, galumphing girl. He wondered whether he should take steps to curb the faithful lest joy give way to licentiousness.

But there was no sin.

'It don't matter any more, do it?' asked Jerrold. He was naked himself, his body like sourdough hung in lumps on a skeleton. 'We're saved?'

Bannerman hesitated, but the Spirit of the Lord was within him and guided his words.

'We're saved, Jerrold! We of all are Chosen! We are without sin!'

'Without sin,' echoed the sexton. The cry was taken up, and became a sing-song chant. 'Without *sin*! Without *sin*! Without *sin*!'

Clothes flew to the fire and were consumed. Shirts danced in the updraft and flamed like crepe paper. The chanting went on, and there was dancing. It might have been a festival of the South Sea Isles, but Bannerman knew true Christianity when he saw it. Flesh glowed in the firelight.

Bannerman backed away from the dancers, but the Misses Pym came to him, breasts bobbing, and tugged at his remaining clothes. He helped the Pym girls, plucking buttons, shrugging out of his waistcoat, kicking his boots away. Finally, he stood naked as Alice and Grace, close to them. Beneath the warmth of the fire, he could feel – even without touching – the warmth of their bodies.

They had kisses for him. He touched the secret places of their bodies, and felt their flesh pressed close against him.

First one, then the other. Alice, then Grace. Then he could no longer tell which was which. Inside his head, he heard the Angel Raphael whispering. More familiar words. 'Let him kiss me with kisses of his mouth, for thy Love is better than wine . . .'

His knees buckled, and he sank to the ground, the Pym girls with him. A sister – which one? – rolled apart, and the other was beneath him. They joined with strange ease. By the red light on her face, Bannerman saw it was Grace. Prettier Grace. His head close to hers, he could hear her whispering a disjointed, distracted prayer.

Still moving with the girl, he looked up. In a series of photographic flashes, he gathered that Grace and he were not the only ones among the flock who had taken this last opportunity to pleasure in the flesh they would soon leave behind. There would be a resurrection in the flesh, but it would be better, cleaner stuff than this.

The Angel was smiling upon all: Granver Shepherd fumbling with the widow Combs; Tom Pym – Tom *Pym*! – kneeling behind Louisa Gilpin, the girl on hands and knees, her hair over her face, his hands working her hips; Jerrold and Jem Gosmore's youngest son, conjoined in an unimagined act of love; Winthrop, still in his breeches, kissing Jem Gosmore's wife, his hands on her breasts; Bannerman and Grace . . .

Grace!

She grasped under him and collapsed, crying his name as he spent. They lay cooling together for a minute, and then she rolled away. He lay on his back, grass and earth beneath him, stung all over from the spark-spitting fire. He sucked in great gulps of cold air, and tried to shake fevers from his brain, but a Pym girl – Alice, this time? – came to him, hot hands stroking, and he was lost . . .

Bannerman woke up warm between bodies. A blanket or something had been thrown over them.

A horror came upon him.

He sat up, elbowing one of the Misses Pym in the process. She groaned, and pulled the blanket.

Bannerman was cold now.

'Have I . . .?'

'Missed it?' came a voice. 'No, vicar.'

He looked around. The voice had been Jerrold's. The verger was cross-legged by the fire. Jem Gosmore's boy slept with his head in the old man's lap. Bannerman got his eyes to focus. Few of the faithful were standing, most were dozing. The fire had collapsed and spread, but still burned fiercely. Louisa Gilpin squatted, her unbound hair tented about her. She held out a cloth-wrapped arm.

'I burned myself, Mr Bannerman.'

'You must have it seen to, child.'

'No point to it. I won't have no use for this poor carcass when the Lord comes. He's a greater healer than you'll find in Yeovil. Or in London either.'

The clouds had gone, and the moon illumined the hillside. The firelight was dimmed by comparison. The night was half over. He had no way of knowing the exact time. His watch was in his waistcoat, and his waistcoat was gone to the fire.

Someone was sobbing. It was Tom Pym, wrapped in someone else's coat.

'What happened to us, Mr Bannerman? To be so close, and yet to throw it all away . . .'

Others looked at him. Other unhappy faces. Bannerman stood up, confused for a moment. What had happened?

Then he remembered.

'This is only flesh, Tom, and of no consequence. You know that. You all know that. We have been taught well. There will be no shame, for there can be no sin among us. We are the Chosen of God. The old ways are hard to put aside, but we must.'

Bannerman was not sure the words were right, but the Spirit was still strong in him. He cloaked himself in the blanket. The Misses Pym, awake now, shook in the cold, and huddled together. He saw the dirt on their bodies, in their hair; and the blood . . .

He opened the blanket, and invited them to the warmth of his body. Grace slipped in quietly and was enveloped, but Alice drew back. She was pouting, not playfully. She did not make a dimple.

She touched herself, and her fingers came away bloody. 'I'm hurt.'

'No, Alice –'

'*Yesssss!*' It was a cat's hiss, venomed with loathing. Alice darted lithe as a naked Indian into the bushes. He heard her fighting branches and thorns. Then she was gone.

The fire crackled and burned lower. It would have been perfect for baking potatoes. For a long while, no one said anything.

'Daughter,' said Tom, 'let us go home.'

Grace, snug next to Bannerman, pretended not to hear. She pressed herself to him, kittenish and coy. Tom looked death at his vicar, then turned and left. He found a path from the clearing and trudged after Alice.

It was as if Bannerman had been slapped, hard. He knew this was the Last Night, yet the faithful were divided among themselves. They had been Chosen, but they imperilled the privilege, spurning the Lord's favour. It would be a tragedy to suffer eternal perdition because of a lapse of belief scant minutes away from the sure and certain hope of . . .

Alice and Tom had not been the first to leave. Others had crept away while he slept. Winthrop was gone, taking Jem Gosmore's wife – whose name was Katy or Kitty, one or the other – with him. There were more than a few faces missing, and those that remained were shadowed with despair. Shame, even.

The faithful were sadly depleted. He began to preach to them, to recite rather, taking the Revelation as his text. He had most of it by heart, and his voice was good. The words came easily. He had read them so many times at Lampeter, and they had been given new fire by the Angel. He sounded strong. But his flock still drifted away in ones and twos.

Hastily, shamefully, defiantly, in disgust, in anger they left. Many cursed him out loud. Others were too exhausted to say anything. Still, he preached. Until there were only three beside him, and his voice faltered. Old Jerrold, pity in his eyes; Grace, asleep on her feet; and Louisa, face shining with madness, he realized, not divine light.

The fire was a circle of ashes. The sky was light in the east. The moon was low. It was nearly dawn. A dawn that should not be, but was.

The Reverend Mr Timothy Charles Bannerman wept for all he had lost. Even Jerrold was gone now, to face the things he had found within himself. Grace was curled up, an unburned dress over her like a bedspread.

Only Louisa was there to witness the very end. The End of All Things. She knelt, adoring the Lord, adoring him, waiting with him, aching for his dreams to be the truth . . .

'I seen him too,' she said. 'Raphael. Angels tell no lies.'

He had nothing more to say. There was a half-circle of sun on the horizon. His eyes watering, he kissed the girl on the lips. Perhaps, underneath everything, she was prettier even than the prettier Miss Pym. Maybe madness made her beautiful.

Gingerly, Bannerman stepped over the fireline and felt soft hot ash under his soles. He half knelt and scooped up a handful of cinders, rubbing them into his skin, smearing chest and limbs and face. There were a few hot coals. He ignored them, feeling burns less than itches.

He straightened and walked towards the centre, the last of the flames nipping at his ankles, scorching the hair off his shins. He did not know where he was going.

. . . but when he got there, Raphael was waiting.

Bannerman was closer than he had ever been to the burning Angel, and in daylight. He saw the dead cores of its flaming eyes.

He opened his mouth to ask a question, but the Angel – light dimmed by the dawn – took him in his arms and kissed him. The eternal fire bit deep into his back and spread over his body, raising great blisters as it spread in irregular patches. Hot breath crept down his throat.

The Angel's empty face was near, and Bannerman's eyes popped with the heat. He felt himself being burned alive, and was not sorry . . .

Louisa watched him until he fell in pieces from the Angel's embrace. The burning figure stood over the pool of stinking, steaming oil that had once been a man, and faded in the sunlight. To a yellow ghost, then to nothing. She found rags to cover herself, and went back to her father's farm.

Grace Pym slept until someone came for her.

I

One

WHEN THEY first came to Alder, the big heat had already been on for over a month. In the daytime, the house, built to weather centuries of winters, was like a Casablanca gambling hell. Paul had tried working upstairs and almost come down with heat stroke. Luckily, there had been a wobbly rolltop desk on the verandah. Hazel helped him set it up surreally on the lawn, under the fairly constant shade of a survivor elm. He replaced the missing foot with a nonessential book – William LeQueux's nigh-unreadable *Great War in England in 1897* – and now had a decent workspace. The extension cord of his IBM electric snaked back into the house through the kitchen window. Papers flapped under makeshift weights, which was irritating, but even the slightest breeze was better than still heat. The typewriter hummed, but he didn't even have a sheet of paper in the roller. This was one of his 'thinking' sessions, which meant he was stalled, letting his mind wander until his unconscious sorted out what he should do next and passed the message upstairs.

The converted cow sheds had big folding doors that opened to turn the studio into a cutaway diagram. Hazel was hunched over her wheel, working a lump of clay. She pushed her longish hair out of her eyes with a dry wrist, then got her wet fingers back to the emerging pot. Clay rose and fell, a mushroom cloud, a vinegar bottle. Throwing pots was hypnotic, almost erotic, to watch. Sometimes the process appealed more than the result. Paul knew nothing about ceramics but could tell Hazel relied too often on what her tutors told her. In the shop attached to the studio, her pots were distinct from the Bleaches', wax fruit among the real. But she was improving. Certainly, she had been the more productive of them so far this summer. She applied herself with enviable concentration, a strength he hadn't expected.

He had been going out with her since Easter, and it was now mid-July. Paul supposed he loved her, although he was always uncomfortable with the 'l' word. She was named Hazel for hazel eyes, naturally. In fact, almost almond eyes. She had very slight epicanthic folds. Her father had been in the Navy. Maybe a sea-faring ancestor once took a Chinese wife. Otherwise, he guessed she was just pretty. She was Paul's first major affair since Sally the Psychotic – *she* had liked skunk music and torn up T-shirts for a rock-merchandising company – and they had arranged to spend the summer together before deciding whether she should move into his flat back in Brighton. He'd thought this a formality, but now the possibility of it not working out was starting to tickle the back of his mind. While the countryside was very obviously burning up, they were almost imperceptibly cooling off.

The crisis had been official since spring, and the harvest was set to be a disaster. The land was ailing. Around him, the grass was piss-yellow. Up in the orchard, the property was a post-holocaust wasteland. The apples had ripened early, but under shiny skins the fruit had been sour and hard. This morning, Hazel had had to get up at six to phone the Bleaches, on their lecture tour in Canada until September, and break the bad news. Their garden was suffering a slow, lingering death. Mike and Mirrie were understanding. The instructions were to do the best to limit the damage. Paul had only met the couple once, but liked them very much. Mike was external assessor for the polytechnic, and one of Hazel's tutors recommended her as a working caretaker for the summer. The Bleaches were right not to shut up shop while they were away; agriculture might be down, but tourism was up. The shop was so busy some mornings that Paul had to fill in for Hazel with customers so she could get a few uninterrupted hours at the wheel.

The bell by the showroom steps jingled. He looked across the lawn. Hazel was sliding off the seat of her wheel, brushing off her apron. The visitors weren't customers. They hadn't gone into the shop. Hazel joined them on the steps. Paul realized immediately they were a pair of Jago's peace-and-love zombies. In their Woodstock-era outfits and beatific living-dead expressions, they were unmistakable. He'd seen a few of the species around the village, but had never had to speak to any of them. Until now. He'd heard of Alder before this summer, of course. The Village Where God Lives. There'd been a piece on cults in the *Independent*, and an acid profile of Anthony Jago in *The New Statesman*. The Agapemone was well away from the village but could be seen from the moor, a prime sample of early Victorian megalomaniac architecture halfway up its own little hill.

'Hi,' said the broad-hipped woman, 'my name's Wendy, and he's Derek. Welcome to Alder. We'd have been round before, but it's been hectic.'

She had brought flowers, miraculously unshrivelled, and handed them into Hazel's arms carefully, as if passing a baby. The Lord God evidently outranked the parish council when it came to water regulations. Paul had been yearning to violate the local authority's sprinkler ban and give emergency aid to the lawn, but water laws were being enforced with the zeal eighteenth-century revenue men had employed sniffing out lace smugglers.

'Hello, I'm Paul Forrestier.' They'd come over to his desk. Hazel had provisionally put the flowers in a vase in the showroom, and was wiping clay-grey hands on her caked apron. 'This is Hazel.'

'Chapel,' she added, smiling. Her name was Chapelet actually, but she didn't like it. 'Hi, thanks for the flowers.'

'We're from the Agapemone,' said Wendy, 'that means –'

'Abode of Love,' said Paul.

'Right. I'm impressed. I heard you were a brain of some sort. Are you a Greek scholar?'

'No,' he said, embarrassed. 'English Lit. I read an article . . .'

'Oh.' Wendy dropped a hint of defensiveness. 'Well, never mind. Don't be put off. Jesus Christ didn't get a good press either. We're not really like the Manson family, honest.'

Wendy's cheeriness was suddenly unconvincing. *The New Statesman* had compared Jago with Sun Myung Moon, L. Ron Hubbard and, tactfully, Jim Jones, but Paul let it pass. He didn't want to go into a discussion of the tenets of the Acid Gospel. He had Wendy and Derek pegged as old hippies, but Wendy's conversational daintiness was almost conventional. She wore CND, Animal Rights and Legalize It patches on her embroidered waistcoat, and her grey-touched hair was frizzed and long. However, she'd have been as happy representing the Women's Institute as a fringe cult which worshipped God in the flesh. Under multicoloured skirt and tie-dyed blouse, she was creeping chubbily into middle age.

'Tony's amazing,' said the man, Derek. He was thin and worn, his Midlands-accented hesitance suggesting he did little of the talking. 'He's got the whole world sussed.'

'Oh yes.' Wendy took over again, digging leaflets out of her Rupert Bear shoulder bag. Hazel took one. 'He's helped us sort ourselves out. We used to be really screwed up.'

Paul cringed inwardly. He was afraid Wendy was going to ramble on about their Messiah.

'He's far out,' said Derek, without apparent irony. If this went on much longer, Paul was going to have trouble keeping a straight face.

Hazel sat in one of the garden chairs and picked through the handout. Wendy and Derek sat on the ground, cross-legged. Derek plucked a few straw-coloured blades of grass, and started braiding them. 'The earth is dying,' he said. Or was that 'The Earth is dying'?

'Yeah,' said Paul. 'Time for the big red sunset and the giant crabs.'

'*The Time Machine*, right?'

'Yes.' Paul was surprised. He would assume Derek was remembering the film, but Hollywood had left out the giant crabs.

Hazel was excited, brighter than he had seen her since spring. 'Can we go?' The tiny overlap of her front teeth, which she hated and he quite liked, showed, as it did whenever she forgot not to smile broadly. She handed him a leaflet. It was for the summer festival. He did not realize how big it was going to be. Hazel pointed out the names of several groups he had never heard of. One of the headline acts was Loud Shit, a skunk band Sally had taken him to last year. He didn't think they'd get involved in anything remotely religious, and grinned at the idea of how well they would go down with the Tory-voting farmers of Alder. The nearest they came to a love song was a number called 'Fuck Off and Die'. He'd broken up with Sally shortly afterwards, when she'd had one of her breasts tattooed.

'We were going to ask you . . .'

'(Because you make pots)'

'. . . if you'd like a stall to sell stuff from. We've got all sorts of crafts people. Weavers, woodturners, jewellers. And some really good theatre groups. And things for kids. We've been scheming for months. It'll be even better than last year.'

Hazel went 'umm'. She was unhappy with her recent work.

'I've only had one gloss firing, and there was a hiccough with the glaze. Too many things came out dingy brown. I haven't got much sellable stuff. A few things from last term.'

'I'm sure it'll be lovely.'

'Most people will be stoned anyway,' said Derek, nearly giggling. 'They'll make up their own colours.'

A pause. Wendy's lips thinned momentarily. Derek would get a reasonable talking-to later, Paul was sure. He felt sorry for the man, intuiting that he'd been dragged by his girlfriend into Jago's sect and was liable to be stuck with it. Until the Reverend gave the Beatles' *Double White* one spin too many and called for a bloodbath, or, depressed by an income-tax investigation, decided it was time to try out the Kool-Aid and cyanide cocktail on his congregation.

'But I'm firing again tonight. I think I know where I went wrong. I'm not used to this big kiln. If it turns out okay, I'll have some pretty things. I hope. I've also got a couple of boxes of Mike and Mirrie Bleach's pots. They're supposed to replace the work that sells from the shop, but nobody will mind if they go during the festival.'

'That's great.' Wendy clacked her beads. 'We'll put you down for a table. Come over to the Agapemone when you can, and pick a site. We don't lock up or anything. We try to be really open, and anyone can come to one of our meals or Tony's services. There's no real mystery. We'd like to have you. Both.'

'Thanks, I'm a bit busy with my thesis, but –'

'We'd love to drop over,' said Hazel. 'There's blow all else to do out here.'

Hazel took Paul's hand. Hers was dry, and he felt slip-clay powder between their palms.

'You must come. He'll like you. And you'll like Him. Tony.'

Paul had known whom Wendy meant. The Reverend Anthony William Jago. In photographs, he had eyes like Robert Powell as Jesus and the three-weeks-dead expression Paul associated with William S. Burroughs. Post addressed to 'The Lord God, Alder' was apparently delivered to him.

'We must be going,' Wendy said. 'So much to do, so little time to do it in.'

When Wendy and Derek had gone, Hazel got a different vase for the flowers and filled it with precious water. Then she went back to work, and Paul was left to his books.

Two

Leaning on his cherry-wood stick, Danny Keough rested. Not wanting to strap himself into his old Volkswagen because of the heat, he had decided to go round the outlying farms on foot. Inside, the car smelled like burning tyres. Still, it might have been better than punishing his trick knee on this long hike. The old wound was playing up, and a permanent haze had settled on his brain. He had not been smitten by the sun like this since 1947, his stint in Palestine.

Maybe somebody would give him a lift to the Maskell farm. It was unlikely. On the levels, you could see cars coming from a long way away. There was nothing in sight except a blue van pulled up on the verge a hundred yards down the road. This was a B-route anyway, not wide enough for two vehicles to pass each other without one having to back up into a lay-by. It was only here to serve Maskell and a few smaller farmers. The tarmac was springy, the patches laid down in spring to fill in potholes were bitumen black and tacky. Across the ditches, rubbery fields were moistened only by rancid remains of long-dead grass. The ditches were mainly muddy depressions streaked with pale, cracked earth. Although these were the wetlands, there wasn't much wet this year.

It would be a bad year. And Jago's jamboree would only make it worse. Last Christmas, they had sent him an anonymous present. Inside the thin square parcel was a gramophone record. 'Don't Stop the Carnival' by the Alan Price Set. He should have laughed. This was not a carnival, this was a zoo. The hippies were animals. Despoiling the countryside, breaching the peace, disturbing the livestock, interfering with people, raising a racket.

He was late with his petition because he'd been laid up by the heat, but he had hopes it would be longer than ever. He mightn't stop them this year, but he was making a dent. Next year, or the

year after, maybe. He didn't care if he was grappling with the
Lord God. Danny Keough had dealt with a campaign of terror
before, and this time he would brave it out. His country had let
him down in Palestine, running away from the Jew-boy killers.
Things were different now. It was all up to him. There were no
politicians to chicken out when things got hairy.

Four years ago, he'd been sweet-talked along with the rest
of the village. But when he saw the first carload of teenage
tearaways come up the road, he knew what it would be like.
They didn't call themselves hippies any more, but that was what
they were all right. And hippies were no different from gypsies,
savages, vermin. Nomadic trash with no hopes, messing up one
place and going on to the next.

It was an invasion. An occupation. A week of unrelieved
din, litter, harassment and degradation. Naked and painted kids
using the street as a toilet. Drugged freaks running riot. And
the noise. It wasn't music, any more than a plane crash was
music. Afterwards, Alder looked as if a Panzer division had
rolled through, followed by an Apache war party.

The next year, and every year since, Danny had been making
a din of his own, trying to put a stop to the festival. He began
with letter writing. He remembered with pride the headline the
Western Gazette printed over his first published letter, '"Hippies
Should Be Stopped" Writes Decorated Veteran'. He sent copies
to the district council, the county council, the Sedgmoor and
District Preservation Society, his Member of Parliament and
the bishop of Bath and Wells. He'd been in the *Gazette* again
regularly, also the *Bridgwater Mercury*, the *Western Daily Press*
and the *Bristol Evening Post*. HTV West came and interviewed
him in his front garden, but they had cut up what he said and
also had on some posh-voiced drop-out from the Agapemone to
make him look an intolerant old fool. Even then, the television
station had letters in support of him.

But the festival happened again. And it had been even worse.
Every year, it got worse. Five weeks before the second festival,
the last of his cats had been run over in the road. Danny was sure
the car was from the Agapemone. It was part of some obscene
rite which demanded sacrifice. Over the years, indignities had
mounted up. His front garden had been trampled over, his
stretch of white fence pissed on and spray-painted. The side of
his house had been flyposted with so many advertisements

for groups with disgusting names that it looked like a modern art collage when he tried to rip it down. He wasn't the only victim. Mrs Graham, who lived alone, had been terrorized by young thugs who pitched a tent in her garden with not so much as a by-your-leave, and had passed away the next winter. Mr Starkey's youngest, Tina, had been lured into the festival; she had come back half-naked, doped up to the eyeballs. The family had to send her away to an approved school, and Danny heard she had to get rid of a baby. There was also damage to crops, animals, roads and private property.

It had to be stopped.

This used to be beautiful countryside, but since Jago came to the Manor House it had turned, like milk left in the sun.

He started walking again, trying to keep the weight off his knee. There was pain in each step. Lately he was more aware of his old wounds, and thinking of how he had got them.

It must be the heat, taking him back. During the Gulf War, he had grudgingly raised a brandy in salute every time one of Saddam's Scuds got through to the Jew-boys. Every time he read in the *Telegraph* about the PLO blowing up people in Israel, there was a little holiday in his heart. That was what an American writer had said about Palestine, 'Every time a British soldier is killed, there's a little holiday in my heart'. The Jews invented terrorism and he relished the thought of them choking in Tel Aviv on their own medicine. Some time soon, when he'd stopped the festival, Danny was going to get back on their case. He'd been prodding the army and government for years. He had a scrapbook. He knew how many Irgun killers held high office in the Israeli government. They hadn't paid their debt to Britain, their debt to Danny Keough, yet. But there was time.

He'd walked as far as the blue van, and was in sight of the Maskell house. There was a group of people in the nearest field, standing among some skinny cows. One of the animals was down, and a man knelt by it. Maurice Maskell stood over them, eyes shaded by a tweed cap, hands on hips, listening. The farmer looked now as his father, Major Maskell, had done in the 1950s, weathered and authoritative. But he wasn't the man the Major had been. He had never been to war, never faced the enemy.

Danny found a concrete bridge, not that he needed one to get across this ghost ditch, and walked into the field. He waved his stick, but no one turned to take notice. He joined the group.

The kneeling man was Donal Goddard, the local vet. Danny had taken his cats to him. Goddard was finishing a depressing diagnosis, which Maskell was doing his best to take on board.

'It's the heat,' Goddard concluded, standing up, brushing dry dirt off his knees.

'Umm,' Maskell was thinking. The two other men in the group looked at the tall farmer. They were farm labourers, Reg Gilpin and Stan Budge. Everyone was worried.

No one said anything, so Danny piped up. 'Maurice, if I might have a word?'

Maskell looked as if he didn't recognize him for a few seconds, then snapped out of it. He grasped Danny's hand and took hold of his shoulder, steering him slightly away from the others.

'Danny, hello, good to see you. I've got something on right now. I'll be with you in a moment. Go up to the house, and Sue-Clare will get you something cold. Okay?'

'Righty-ho.'

Maskell gave him a slight push, sending him across the field, toward the house, keeping him out of the group. Danny heard the vet talking. 'There's not much more I can do here, Maurice. Keep on as you have been, and I'll give you a ring tomorrow.' Maskell mumbled a goodbye, and Goddard started toward his van. When Danny got to the gate that separated Maskell's concrete yard from the fields, he looked back.

Maskell was talking to the men. Budge gestured angrily. Voices raised. The workman spat on the ground. It was obviously a rough day all round.

In the yard, Maskell's wife was greasing a saddle. She dressed like the land girls Danny remembered from the war, tight trousers and a loose man's shirt. Her eyes were covered by beetle-black glasses. She smiled to see him coming, and waved a cloth.

'Good morning, Mr Keough.'

'Is it?'

She ignored the comment. 'Maurice sent you over, eh? I've got a jug of lemonade chilling in the fridge. Join us.'

'I shan't be stopping long.'

Sue-Clare Maskell had her top two buttons undone. In the sticky heat, her shirt outlined her breasts. She wasn't wearing a bra. Danny found it hard to understand. These days, this was the way a respectable woman dressed.

'I've more calls to make,' he said, holding up his new folder. 'The petition.'

'Excuse me, will you. I'll get the juice. Maurice is coming. Be right back.'

She went indoors, to her kitchen. Danny watched the seat of her riding trousers as she walked. She must be years younger than her husband. Their children, a weedy boy called Jeremy and a robust girl named Hannah, were barely old enough for school. Jeremy was the beginnings of a nuisance, wandering around in a dream, falling in ditches, having tantrums. Danny had heard that Sue-Clare Maskell had strange interests. Crystals and acupuncture, stargazing. She wasn't from around here.

He remembered the girls in Jerusalem who crowded the barracks, bodies like ripe fruit. One of them had brought in the bomb. Perhaps one he'd been with? The heat had been driving everyone crazy. It was almost a relief to be in the fanned cool of the hospital. And he remembered the other woman from the other war. The German parachutist. No one talked about her. Danny might even be the last man alive who had been there the night the Nazis tried to bomb Alder.

Maskell was right in front of him, talking. '. . . brings you here?'

'Pardon?'

'Danny, you were miles off. Somewhere cool, I hope.'

'Uh, sorry.' Danny drew breath, preparing to say it all over again. 'Maurice, it's about the –'

He had to swallow his speech. Sue-Clare Maskell was back, with a tray. Maurice took a glass of thin green drink and forced it into Danny's hand. The glass felt like a thick icicle. He took a swallow. It was bitter, not the sweet fizzy stuff he called lemonade. Maskell rolled his glass between his palms, then put his chilled hand to his forehead.

'Wonderful, Suki. Just what I needed.'

'Was it bad?' she asked him, setting the tray down on a broad windowsill. The side of their house was thickly covered with none too healthy ivy.

'Uh-huh. Donal thinks we've lost more of the herd. It's not a virus, really. Just rotten grass, and the heat.'

'Oh no . . .'

'And I had to let Gilpin and Budge go. Budge hollered "union", but there's no case. We can't keep them on the roster.

There's nothing for them to do. Still, it wasn't any fun.'

'Shit.'

Danny flinched. It was wrong, a woman using language like that. A respectable woman. He opened his folder.

'What about compensation?'

'Nothing doing,' Maskell said. 'At least, not yet. It's not a real disease, Donal says. Just the heat.'

The woman frowned, brow wrinkles above her sunglasses.

'By the way, he said to keep giving Fancy the horse pills, and hope for the best.'

'Terrific,' she said acidly.

'It's not his fault, Suki.'

Sue-Clare Maskell drank her lemonade.

From the house, Danny heard a dog whimpering and children arguing.

'Stop it, you two,' Sue-Clare shouted. 'Hannah's been frightening Jeremy again,' she explained. 'She keeps telling him Jethro's got AIDS and is going to die.'

Jethro was the dog.

Maskell glowered. 'We'll have to see about that,' he said. 'Sounds like too much television.'

Danny saw Jeremy, a large-eyed little boy of about seven, in the kitchen door, lurking. Realizing the visitor could see him, he vanished inside.

'Maurice,' said Danny, 'I'm trying to put a stop to all the trouble.'

Maskell stared again, as if looking at a madman. 'What?'

'The trouble. The hippies. The festival.'

'Oh, *that*. Sorry, I thought you were going to do something about the drought.'

Danny's knee started to throb.

'If you and your wife would sign this . . .'

Maskell took the folder and cast his eyes down to the statement taped to it. Danny knew it by heart. He had spent a lot of time experimenting with different wordings.

> We the undersigned, year-round residents of Alder, take objection to the so-called festival organized by the Agape-mone. We charge A. W. Jago with failing to properly keep order at said event, and protest the considerable hardship, nuisance and financial loss it causes us. We entreat the

authorities to prevent the festival from taking place on the
grounds of flagrant violations of the law.

On an attached sheet, Danny had put details of the specific
laws broken over the years. It was an impressive and frightening
document, the upshot of long days in Bridgwater Library with
newspaper files and law books, and an expensive half-hour with
a Langport lawyer.

Maskell took a long time reading the basic proposition. His
wife leaned over, sunglasses up in her hair, and read too.

'Maurice,' she said, 'we can't.'

'I beg your pardon?'

'No. Suki's right. I'm sorry, Danny.' He gave the folder back.
'This year, we can't sign.'

'But the noise, the litter, the damage . . .'

'It's the heat, Danny. It's throttling us. If we harvest early,
we'll save something. But it won't be enough. The animals are
beaten. There's no grazing, no hay to be had at any price. We've
got insects, blight, everything.'

'I don't see what that has to do with it.'

Maskell sighed, and put his arm around his wife's waist. They
were presenting a united front.

'I've been talking to Jago's people at the Agapemone. James
Lytton, who does most of the organizing, is a reasonable man,
not a religious loony. In the past, he's made sure that everyone
has been recompensed for everything. You know that.'

'It's not the same.'

'No, but it's something. The festival is very profitable. This
year, it might just keep us all out of the poorhouse.'

'But it's a damned menace.'

'It makes money. Lytton says Jago wants to put some of it back
into Alder. The fields aren't much good for anything this year.
I'd rather keep going as a camp site than be broke as a farm. I'm
letting them use the place for a lot of things. Camping, parking,
a rec area. We're even having some music.'

'It's a godsend,' Sue-Clare said, resting her head on Maskell's
shoulder.

'Sorry, Danny,' Maskell said. 'That's the way it is. It's the
heat.'

'The fucking heat,' said Sue-Clare Maskell.

Three

WHEN THEY passed under the big WEST sign and started towards the motorway, Ferg slotted *Easy Rider* into the deck. It was great driving music, even if he had borrowed the tape from his hippie dad. 'Head out on the highway, looking for adventure . . .' By now, everybody else was already on their holidays. There was little traffic about, but what there was found it easy to overtake Dolar's camper. Ferg put that out of his mind. If he put his foot down hard, he ought to be able to get this wreck of a Dormobile up to sixty. This should be a breeze.

Then the player chewed up the cassette. It whirred, feeding tape into its workings.

'Careful,' Ferg said as Jessica stabbed Stop/Eject.

She pulled out the tape. Brown spaghetti strings pulled taut. 'Watch it.'

The tape snapped, leaving a snarl inside the machine.

'There goes the music,' said Mike Toad from the back of the camper.

Ferg glared sideways at Jessica, who was squirming, trying to shove the evidence into an overfull glove compartment. The catch sprang and the cassette fell between her feet. Plus half a bag of sweets, a fistful of tissues, a road map and some garage competition cards. She put her knees together, obscuring his view of the mess.

'No music, eh?' said Dolar. 'You forget I've got my trusty guitar.'

The first twangs filled the camper. And the first complaints.

'Perhaps you should save it for the festival,' suggested Syreeta.

'Perhaps we could fix the cassette player,' suggested Jessica.

'Perhaps Dolar should consider a career in silent meditation,' suggested Mike Toad.

The twangs took on a tortured and hurt tone. 'Come on,' Dolar wailed. 'You're supposed to be my loyal roadies. Where's the support I count on you mob for?'

Mike Toad, who was always trying to be supercool and cynical but was usually only rude, had the answer. 'We're mainly your roadies so we don't have to listen to your concerts.'

'And we get into festivals free,' Jessica added.

Ferg thought they were pushing Dolar a bit far, but kept his mouth shut and his eyes on the road. Getting on to the motorway here could be tricky.

'What smells of pork, fish and frog at the same time?' asked Mike Toad, who knew lots of jokes. After a pause, he finished the riddle, 'Miss Piggy's cunt.'

Dolar laughed, but he was the only one.

'Hitchers ahead,' Ferg said.

They all looked. Just before the roundabout, a scraggy line of people stood by the road. Most had duffel bags and number plates. But one couple had a cardboard square with ALDER FESTIVAL printed on it.

Ferg slowed down. 'Dolar?'

'What?'

'It's your van. Do we pick them up?'

'Sure. We're on the road. And you're road captain, remember?'

Ferg pulled over, and Syreeta had the back doors open. She leaned out and called to the Alder Festival sign-holders. Bundles were thrown in and the hitchhikers hauled up. Ferg was off again before the doors were shut.

'Batten that hatch,' Dolar snapped.

Someone saw to it. Everyone else turned to examine the new people. Ferg glanced up at the rear-view mirror to see what they looked like. They were teenagers, probably about his and Jessica's age. He was Asian, and dressed in expensive jeans and a casual cardigan. She was a goth, small, red-headed, all in black.

'I'm Pam and this is Salim,' the girl said. She had white make-up and red lipstick.

'Are you prepared to work your passage?'

'We can pay,' said Salim. He took something out of his bag. Ferg couldn't see, but there was a commotion.

'He's got some gear,' said Jessica.

If it had been Ferg getting into a vanload of strangers with some dope, he would've waited a while before offering it round. Then again, he supposed not many undercover policemen had mohicans.

'Welcome aboard, shipmates,' said Dolar, enthusiastically. 'I'm Dolar, and this is my crew. That's Ferg up front driving, with his lady Jess by his side. This is Syreeta. She's from Crouch End. And that's Mike Toad trying to look macho, mean and moody like a Levi's advert. Don't mind him, he's a prat.'

'Are you a band?' Pam asked.

'No, I'm a solo act. These people are my combination road gang and claque.'

'He was threatening to play,' said Mike Toad, 'so I'd roll a joint and quiet him down if I were you.'

'Oh, wow,' said Jessica, who could be very irritating when she tried.

They hit the motorway, and Ferg put his foot down. He wanted to be in Alder well before nightfall.

Dolar sucked the first puff out of Salim's joint and passed it on. He started in on one of his joke songs, a version of Roy Rogers' 'A Four-Legged Friend'. Ferg sniffed sweet smoke, and tried to ignore the horrible noise. This could turn out to be a long drive.

Four

Sister Jenny brought her a pot of Earl Grey and some fruit at three. It was one of the child's duties to organize the afternoon tea break, and she was punctilious about it. She had the Agapemone divided into coffee-drinkers and tea-drinkers, biscuit-eaters and fruit-eaters, and knew who took milk and/or sugar with what. Most of the Brethren were with James down at the festival site, so the girl had an easy job of it today. She lingered, drinking her own tea. Susan gathered she and Jenny were the only ones left in the house.

Apart from *him*. Beloved. Anthony William Jago.

She could feel his presence always. Blocking him out was a constant struggle. And Susan found it increasingly difficult to hold back. The Brothers and Sisters of the Agapemone were all so wrapped up in their spiritual wrestling matches. It gave her headaches to be around their emotional fallout. She couldn't be more than a few seconds in the company of Wendy Aitken without sensing the ghosts pressed around the large, energetic woman. Susan saw desperation behind all Wendy's activities, felt all too deeply formless yearnings, dangerous desires. Something had happened to Wendy once, something that left her in a permanent fug of shame, anger and dread. Throw in the usual religious fanaticism, and you had a powerful mix. Bad vibes, Derek would have said. Susan knew better than anyone what that meant. And the others were as strange: Mick Barlowe, all ambition and barely leashed lust; Derek, trailing after Wendy like a wounded dog, rarely acting on his own; Sister Marie-Laure, ticking away inside her burn-out zombie shell; Gerald Taine, silently awaiting his Beloved's orders, ready to die or kill for the fountainhead, flashing back to the Falklands. And the women, the Sisters: Janet, who'd been initiated at the same time as Susan; Cindy, Kate and Karen. All comely, to use Jago's expression, all looking for love, all trailing ghosts. Groups like Jago's were a lodestone for the neurotic, the disturbed, the disaffected.

The library was the largest room on the second storey, an irregular octagon with a wide door, two thin windows and five floor-to-ceiling bookcases. There were as many colourful paperbacks on the shelves as dusty embossed books. When the Brethren had moved in, they removed most of the Winthrop-Kaye books and papers to a storeroom, which was why it had taken Susan so long to get to them. Valuable material had been replaced with an assortment of the expected: three different sets of *Lord of the Rings*; plenty of Carlos Castenada, T. Lobsang Rampa, Erich von Daniken, John Lennon and *Love Is . . .*; an odd selection of religious commentaries, mostly Christian and mostly cracked. There had been one shock, in with the books about psychic powers, astrology, druggy mysticism and flying saucers. *The Mind Beyond* had been remaindered shortly after publication and this copy had the tell-tale groove sawn across the top. Susan had looked with a *frisson* at the young girl on the cover, and made sure the book disappeared. It seemed unread, but she'd felt more than usually uneasy for days and still had moments of irrational panic. There was such a thing as being too bloody sensitive.

Jenny ambled around the room, fingers brushing the spines of books. Susan wasn't getting anything off the girl just now. Jenny was too simple to be readable most of the time. Too young to have many ghosts. That said, Susan got the impression of great strength, a great sense of purpose. Both were unusual among Beloved's flock. The child, Jago's latest Sister-Love, was relatively new to the Agapemone. Maybe she would change. Jenny was a focus, the calm in the heart of chaos. Susan hoped she could protect her somehow. At least, she could try to limit the damage. Jenny should be young enough, resilient enough, to come through in one piece. Unlike some of the others: Wendy, for instance, or Marie-Laure, or Taine. Susan saw death in their faces, smelled it on their breaths.

Luckily, her duties kept her apart from the others, usually well shielded by the stacks of books. The Agapemone was like the army: they found you a job based on what you had done before. Her library and publishing experience made her the wordsmith. She supervised the Agapemone's publications, its occasional press releases, its work with local evangelical and historical groups. Like James, she had a welcome excuse to get out into the real world.

Otherwise, she would not be able to keep in touch with IPSIT, with David. IPSIT, pronounced 'eyesight'. So many masters, so many callings. No wonder she had trouble with migraines. She'd taken to using aspirin again. David claimed it should make no difference, but it seemed to cut down background noise. Probably a placebo effect.

She swallowed two pills with her first mouthful of tea. They stuck briefly in her throat, then washed down. She drank more tea and licked the roof of her mouth to make the bitter taste go away. Jenny asked after Susan's headache, and she gave a noncommittal reply. Sooner or later, she'd be called about her habit, but she'd deal with it then. Anything to stay sane.

The girl hovered, waiting for Susan's cup. Her long blonde hair was centre-parted, swept back behind slightly prominent ears. When she first came to the Agapemone, she had worn only black, with a gypsyish load of bracelets, earrings and bangles. Now she favoured white, and a small crucifix around her neck, usually under her dress. In her late teens, she looked younger. Susan remembered the fix she'd been in at that age. She had been Witch Susan, not Queen of the May. That was long gone now, and forgotten. Except by David. Jenny picked up a heavy book and stroked its binding. She opened it and paged through, looking for photographic plates. Susan bit a tiny hole in the bitter, purple skin of a plum, and sucked the sweet flesh.

Almost nobody else used the library, which alone made it ideal for Susan. During the last few weeks, she'd spent most of her waking hours at the desk in the middle of the room, spreading books and papers on the broad expanse of aged oak. She read, made notes in shorthand, cross-referenced volumes that had gone unopened for half a century. She was supposed to be here to build up the big picture. David should never have let it go this far, should never have let the project get so out of IPSIT's control. Now it was up to her to make him understand precisely what was going on out here in witch country. She rolled the sour stone around her mouth, tongue scraping away the last threads of plum. Finding nothing of interest in her book, a theological tract from the 1860s, Jenny put it down and looked at one of the Winthrop-Kaye scrapbooks. It had '1924' scrawled in watery blue ink on a paper plate pasted on the front cover, but the brittle newspaper cuttings inside came mainly from forty years earlier. At first, Susan had thought it was just someone's collection of juicy scandal.

The first few pieces related to a gruesome murder spree of 1887. Jeremiah Gosmore, a farmer, had killed Martin, his son, and Jerrold Hogg, the local verger. He had also attacked his wife, whose name wasn't recorded, and a Colonel Edward Winthrop before being captured, tried (incredibly enough before Winthrop, a magistrate) and hanged. The murderer's pitchfork had been bought from the widow by Madame Tussaud's waxworks for their Chamber of Horrors. Lurid, Susan supposed, but not very relevant.

Jenny was absorbed. 'Gosmore must have lived at Gosmore Farm. The Pottery as now is. The chief witness was called James Starkey. My nana was a Starkey. James must be some great-great relation. There've always been Starkeys in Alder. Funny how you never hear about these things. I thought Alder had a dead boring history. Year after year of harvests and floods. They must all be buried in the churchyard.'

'Except Jeremiah. They don't put murderers in hallowed ground.'

Next came a tiny scandal: the birth on 3rd July 1888 of a daughter, Mary Elizabeth, to one Alice Frances Pym, aged fifteen, who would appear to have been unencumbered with a husband.

'This doesn't sound very Victorian.'

'It wasn't all hard work, happy families and muscular morals. The age of consent was twelve or thirteen. Old newspapers are full of pieces like that. The mystery is why the man who put the scrapbook together thought it was worth clipping this particular one.'

Jenny looked back at the date in the front of the book. '1924. Mary Elizabeth would have been grown up. Perhaps he married her.'

'Oh no. Edwin Winthrop was otherwise engaged.'

The tenor of the items in the scrapbook changed. The headlines became unusual by the standards of any age. 'Miraculous Apparitions', 'Psychical Researchers Investigate', 'Poltergeist Phenomena on Haunted Hillside'.

'What's this?' Jenny asked.

'Ghost stories, I think. The man who lived here in the 1920s was interested in psychic phenomena. He wrote books about ghost hunting and local folklore.'

'"Burning Man Sighted in Somerset"? Sounds like the *Sunday Sport*.'

All this had been in the library, undisturbed, long before the founding of the Agapemone; long before, even, the birth of Anthony Jago. Susan shivered like the damn fool in a ghost story who, poring over manuscripts recounting obscure and bygone atrocities, feels the lengthy, many-jointed fingers of the unquiet dead reaching out for her rapidly beating heart.

'Alder is a very haunted village, Jenny. Whatever is happening here has been happening for over a hundred years.'

Jenny chewed her knuckle and turned a creaking page. A newspaper article, folded in on itself because it was too large to fit the book, flopped open.

'And something *is* happening, isn't it?'

Susan nodded.

'Beloved knows, doesn't He?'

Careful, Susan. Whatever else this girl is, she's also a Sister of the Agapemone. Jago, or Brother Mick, could have Taine break your neck.

'Beloved will tell what He knows in time, Sister. I'm just clearing the way for His revelation.'

Deep in the house, something vast stirred. Susan tried to blot it out of her consciousness by concentrating, visualizing the newsprint of the clipping Jenny was looking at. The article was a long interview, dated '13–11–87', with a Dr Joseph Skilton who, in a faded photograph, was displaying a bandage-mittened hand like a rabbit paw. The thing still moved. She felt the ripples. A swallow of cold tea did not help. Fear stabbed her. This could be an attack. She held her breath, shut her eyes, pressed her knees tightly together, and laid her hands on the table. Inside her head, she put up shutters, trying to conquer the fear. She was a minute creature of the deeps, caught up in the current as an unimaginably huge whale swims by, blind but full of purpose. With relief, she gathered it wasn't hostile specifically to her. But that didn't make it any less dangerous.

Then, the giant was gone.

'Are you all right, Susan?'

'Just more headache, I'm afraid.'

'You should get that seen to. Mum gets migraines. She says they're crippling. Who did you say collected these?'

'Edwin Winthrop. The son of the man who hanged his mistress's husband. He wrote books too, mostly in collaboration with his wife, Catriona Kaye. Well, actually, I think they weren't married. That would have been unconventional then.'

Susan wondered again about Edwin, who had apparently trod
the same scholarly path back in the 1920s. He had come out of
the First World War with some funny ideas and an even funnier
set of associates. She hoped to find more of his books in the
still-unopened Winthrop trunks upstairs. They were her link to
the past.

'Here, this is him.' Susan stood, and turned the pages of the
scrapbook. In the photograph, Edwin, dapper and Gatsbyish in
evening dress, was accompanied by two women. A veiled beauty
with black feathers and what had then been an unfashionably deep
décolleté, and a smiling girl in a light dress with bobbed hair and a
tiny hat.

'The dark woman is Irena Dubrovna. Her real name was
probably Irene Dobson. She was a medium. I imagine she
was a con artist and what they called "an adventuress". But
she had something, a Talent. She was good at what she did.
Very theatrical. She knew Arthur Conan Doyle.'

'The Sherlock Holmes man?'

'Yes, he was interested in spiritualism. He had a row with
Winthrop, actually. Edwin called him a "credulous fool" for
believing in fairies.'

'And the other woman?'

'That's Catriona. Catriona Kaye.'

'She was pretty.'

'She probably still is. Jago – Beloved – bought this place from
her. She inherited it from Edwin. I've not heard of her dying, so I
assume she's still about, revising her old books or whatever. She
wrote these.' Susan indicated a pile: *Where Women Go Wrong*, *Ghost
Stories of the West Country*, and, famously, *An Introduction to Free
Love*. 'They had strange enthusiasms, Edwin and Catriona.'

The Winthrop-Kaye book collection was much more arcane
than the psychedelia and charlatanism favoured by the current
occupants of their house. They had Crowley in the original
editions, also Harry Price, Arthur Machen, A. E. Waite, Madame
Helena Blavatsky. A glance at *The House of the Hidden Light*,
which she had never heard of, by Machen and Waite, revealed a
personal dedication from Machen, 'To Edwin and Catriona, for
Shedding Much Light'.

Really, Susan ought to feel at home. After all these years of
anonymity, she could be Witch Susan again.

'Why are you looking all this old stuff out?'

Susan rehearsed her excuse. 'Beloved chose Alder as the site of His community. It wasn't a random decision. This is a place of power. He wants to make us all aware of that. Brother Mick has asked me to prepare a dossier on local hauntings, psychic phenomena, spiritual things . . .'

'But what have ghosts got to do with Beloved?'

'Look again at the burning-man pages, Jenny.'

The girl flipped back.

'It's a local story. Most of these clippings are from the 1880s, but Winthrop found other records, going back earlier. Alder has its ghosts. But the burning-man isn't usually classed as one.'

Jenny found a line drawing, an artist's impression based on Dr Skilton's testimony. A beautiful man in a loincloth stood in flame, a circle of fire around his head, crudely sketched wings spreading behind him.

'He was supposed to be an Angel.'

For a moment, Susan thought she sensed a trace of recognition in the girl's mind.

'Not just any ghost, Jenny. A Holy Ghost.'

Five

H E HAD TYPED 'The Secular Apocalypse: The End of the World in Turn-of-the-Century Fiction by Paul Forrestier' at the top of too many sheets of A4. He used to put '*fin-de-siècle*' rather than 'turn-of-the-century', but now rejected that as a frenchified frill. Five variant opening paragraphs and more than forty complete or incomplete first sentences on folded pages were now in use as bookmarks. Large chunks of the thesis were written, waiting to be cannibalized from the last three years' worth of essays. He just needed to join them up and smooth over the cracks. But there were always ways of putting off real work: books to be read and reread and annotated; the shop to be looked after when Hazel was too busy; telephone calls to be made to parents and friends; the desk to be kept tidy and usable; Hazel to be lived with, however remotely . . .

The sun ground down, making the blank page in the IBM painfully bright even through shades. Hazel had started a tan in Brighton, and sunbathed in her lunch break and after work. He traced her bikini marks in bed. He hadn't brought sunglasses, and the only pair he could find in the house were antique mirror goggles that made him look like the Man with X-Ray Eyes. Hazel said they were creepy, but he got used to them. He thought she thought he used them to hide what he was thinking.

Yesterday, he had done real work. Vaulting over his sticky opening, he whipped the conclusion into shape. Discussing Arthur Machen's *The Terror* and Haggard's *When the World Shook* in the light of the religious revival that came during the Great War, he pointed out that post-1914 fictions return the responsibility for the end of the world to supernatural forces. His central argument was that after Darwinism, writers of scientific romances saw the apocalypse as a result of evolutionary decay (*The Time Machine*), virulent diseases (Shiel's *The Purple Cloud*, London's *The Scarlet Plague*), high-tech weaponry and global war

(*War in the Air*, Shiel's *The Yellow Danger*), passing comets or cosmic phenomena (Flammarion's *La Fin du Monde*, Doyle's *The Poison Belt*), invading Martians, or other natural or man-made forces. But while the Age of Doubt was going at full sceptical blast, there were still plenty of religious maniacs running about between 1875 and 1900 proclaiming the End of All Things. It always happens as centuries close. He could guarantee that before 2001 there would be a lot of Armageddon nuts about. If, as it sometimes seemed, he got *The Secular Apocalypse* out around the end of the century, he would be able to cash in on the furore.

'At most, terrestrial man fancied there might be other men on Mars, perhaps inferior to themselves, and ready to welcome a missionary enterprise,' Paul read again, consulting his much pencilled-in *War of the Worlds* paperback, with the album-cover artwork. 'Yet across the gulf of space, minds that are to our minds as ours are to the beasts that perish, intellects vast and cool and unsympathetic, regarded this earth with envious eyes and slowly and surely drew their plans against us. 'Wells was the key, and no matter how many intriguingly obscure and unread contemporaries – Garrett P. Serviss, Grant Allen, Matthew Phipps Shiel – he exhumed, he still found himself drawn back to Herbert George. His short-sleeved shirt sweated through, he could not help but think he was living in the days of the comet.

Hazel was struggling with the clay, more often than not mashing her finished work back into a lump and starting all over again. The board on the lawn was barely half-covered with drying bottles. She had been briefly enthused by the visit of the couple from the Agapemone, but now she was closed like a flower that shows itself only to the noonday son.

They had met on Easter Sunday, at the Brian-Alex-Eugene party, for which they'd coopted a large garden from a lecturer. The first weekend of the big heat. Sally and her new boyfriend had made an entrance, dressed like Betty Boop and Tin-Tin. Paul remembered people not much older than him, even a few of his university contemporaries, were being dragged around by small children, murderously intent on ferreting out hidden chocolate eggs. Vaguely fed up, he noticed Hazel, with a crying little girl who hadn't found a single egg, and rescued her by pointing to a foil-wrapped sweetie lodged in a cracked plant pot. The child belonged to one of her tutors, and she'd been given charge of her. Hazel was doing ceramics part-time at the polytechnic. She wore a lavenderish dress that left her legs bare, and a wide-brimmed straw hat. They talked, or were together, for most of the rest of the afternoon. Of course, he noticed she was a pretty girl. She was also, apart from little Amanda, unattached. They kissed goodbye twice. The first time was politely passionless, at about six thirty. Then they found themselves not parting after all. A parent claimed Amanda, but suggested Hazel stay on for the slimmed-down evening version of the party. Brian found a piano and started being Hoagy Carmichael, while Eugene impersonated the Battle of Britain with vocal sound effects and Alex sang cricket statistics to hymn tunes. Hazel didn't stay long – her parents lived in Hove, she was expected for a meal – but a difference was made. They exchanged telephone numbers. The second kiss was different, with a hint of moving tongue. She left him something to think about.

Under a fortress of books, the remote phone buzzed. Paul sorted through the desk until he found the receiver.

'Station Six Sahara,' he answered, a giggle at the other end identifying the caller. 'Hi, Patch.'

'Yo, Paul.'

'Haze,' he shouted, 'it's your sister.'

Hazel, having just let another bottle pass inspection, straightened up from the board and said, 'I'll just wash my hands.'

Paul told Patch – Patricia – Hazel was on her way, and they chatted. Patch was the only other human being in the large Chapelet family. In the bad moments, he even wondered whether he had picked the right sister. Younger than Hazel by a year, she'd gone straight from school into a junior admin post at the Arts Centre, and gained a power base as their head of publicity and promotions. Since the AC was on campus, she sometimes joined Paul for lunch in term-time. He wondered if Hazel were jealous of her sister. In her position he thought he might be, but the girls seemed to have a good relationship.

'Work going well?' Patch asked.

'Pass.'

'How's married life?'

'Um,' he thought aloud, 'here's Hazel now.'

He heard Patch laugh as he handed over the mobile phone. Patch was sharp.

Hazel wandered off into a corner of the garden, by the kiln shed, and talked quietly into the phone. Patch would not have called in the daytime, interrupting work, unless there was some problem.

The week after the party, he had nearly phoned Hazel several times but couldn't think of a casual enough excuse for getting in touch. In the end, she had called him, inviting him to a private view at the crafts shop where she worked half the week. There, he had been introduced to her elderly parents. Her father took an instant dislike to him which had since grown. Hazel only had three small pots among the new work on display, but he bought one. It was on the desk now, pens and pencils in it. She had since told him that her tutor helped with the glaze, but he still thought it one of her best pieces. At the end of the evening, before she went off with her family, they kissed seriously . . .

'Come on, Patch,' Hazel said, louder than her normal level, 'you know what Dad's like!'

. . . and eventually, after meals and movies and weekend afternoons, they were in bed in his flat with nothing else to do but make love. It was rather tentative at first, but became more rewarding as spring faded into summer and the flowers dried up and died. Apart from a brief getting-it-out-of-the-way talk about contraception, they had not discussed their sex life much. Recently, it hadn't been much to talk about.

Hazel was laughing now, and had come out of her corner.

'Yes,' she said, looking at the sickly garden, 'it's lovely here.'

When they had finished talking, Hazel gave him back the phone, compressing the aerial with a deft push.

'Well?'

Hazel bit her lip. 'It's Dad again, you know . . .'

'The same thing?'

'Uh-huh.'

'I don't see what the fuss is. Patch left home years ago.'

'Patch is Patch, I'm not. She says Dad says Mum's having angina twinges.'

'And you're to rush to the bedside?'

Hazel shrugged. 'Patch didn't say Dad said that.'

'Of course not.'

'You shouldn't take against Dad, Paul. He's only concerned.'

Hazel walked back to the studio, and Paul looked up the hill at the trees beyond the property. Sunlight reflected on something, and he half imagined an enemy, spying.

Six

As soon as his brother said, 'I'd shag her if she had a paper bag over her head', Teddy knew he was going to get bashed. As certain as night follows day and flies swarm on cowshit. There was nothing he could do about it. Whenever Terry said something stupid, a clever answer popped into Teddy's head and he had to let it out. If he had to be thumped a certain number of times in his life, this was as good a way as any to use them up.

'I reckon,' Teddy began, pausing to catch his brother's attention, 'I reckon youm'd have more luck with girls if youm wore the paper bag.'

There was a pause as it sank in. Terry always took a few seconds more than a normal person to get the funny. Teddy listened to flies buzz, and waited for the thump. Terry looked at him, nearly cross-eyed, and, quick as a snake once he had worked it out, leaned over to get him. Teddy took the casual but knuckly backhander on the ear. It hurt, but it could have been worse. If they were out with Terry's mates and Teddy showed him up, his brother used closed fists. After sixteen years of sharing a room, Teddy was an expert on what his brother would do if provoked. It had taken him a long time to realize not everybody acted like a caveman.

'You'm stupid!'

Whenever Teddy proved he was cleverer than his brother, Terry said he was stupid. Teddy sometimes reckoned he *was* stupid; for not keeping his mouth shut. But it was a waste not to use a funny when one came along.

Her name was Hazel, and Teddy couldn't see anything wrong with her face. Especially not from three hundred yards away, using a pair of binoculars that didn't really work. Terry wanted women to look like the glossy tarts in the magazines under his bed.

They had been watching her from the top of Gosmore Farm

orchard for over a week now. Neither she nor her boyfriend had climbed that far up the hill, so they hadn't been found out. So far. They would be in the end. If Terry was in it, they always got caught. That was another of the laws of nature. When they were seven and ten, Terry had masterminded the theft of three giant-sized bottles of Coca-Cola from the garage shop. Jenny Steyning's dad had caught them, and their own dad had taken their shorts and underpants down in front of everyone at the garage (in front of *Jenny*, Teddy remembered with a flush of embarrassment even after ten years) and taken his belt to their backsides. Since then, Terry had been caught for almost everything: bunking off school, knocking off records from the market in Bridgwater, snogging superhag Sharon Coram, smashing windows at the back of the village hall.

They were supposed to be out after rabbits, but even trigger-happy Terry hadn't fired a shot in days. Hunting was bad this year, like everything to do with the land. It was the heat. The undergrowth was yellow and rotting. The rabbits must all have had their brains fried, or tunnelled to Iceland. At first, the summer had been great: being outside, getting a tan, earning an extra tenner picking plums. Now, it was a pain. Teddy's back itched where his sunburn peeled. There was nothing to do. At least, not until the festival.

'Meeting's at six, Einstein,' he reminded. 'If we'm not there, James'll cross us off the lists. Youm know he don't like you.'

'Six's not for hours, thicko.'

'This's *boring*.'

'No, 't ain't.'

That was it. No more discussion needed. Terry wasn't bored, so there was no shifting him. Terry fiddled with their dad's binoculars, trying to get them in focus. The little wheel was missing, so he had to get his finger in and work a cog with a nail.

Teddy didn't care either way about the Gosmore Farm people, but Terry fancied her and hated him. Terry said he must be a poof. Hazel wore shorts and a halter most days, and had good legs and a flat stomach. For a week, Terry had been thinking aloud, laboriously trying to come up with a scheme to get the boyfriend out of the way so he could have a crack at chatting Hazel up. Some hope. It was difficult not to laugh at Terry when he was plotting. His plans were so stupid, like the time he wanted

to steal a barrel of beer from the Valiant Soldier. They wouldn't
have been able to lift it, let alone drink it.

Watching Gosmore Farm really was boring. Hazel was mostly
out of sight in the old cow shed making pots. She only ever came
out for meals and an hour or so of sunbathing in the late afternoon.
The sunbathing was what got Terry worked up. Sometimes, she
lay on her front and untied her halter. From the top of the hill,
Teddy didn't find it much of a thrill. When they first started to
watch Hazel and her boyfriend, Terry had reckoned they'd take
drugs and have it off in the garden. Terry said Hazel was probably
a nympho. Terry had a thing about nymphos. According to
Knave and *Fiesta* and him, nymphomania was as common as
hay fever. Considering most of Terry's ideas about women came
from the times when Sharon couldn't find anything better, Teddy
supposed his brother's delusions were understandable. However,
he still considered nymphomania a mythical condition, like the
curse of the werewolf.

It occurred to Teddy that his brother might be a werewolf.
Terry had a thick pelt on his legs and chest, his eyebrows joined
over his nose, and he did a lot of growling. Any hairs on his hands,
however, Teddy put down to something else Terry did a lot of.
Terry growled now. Hazel and her boyfriend were out of sight.

'Bet they'm going to have it off tonight,' Terry said, pointing
his shotgun at the house, taking an elaborate sniper's aim.
'Pow!'

'Le'ss go, Einstein.'

Finally, Terry stirred.

'I know a short cut,' he said, and Teddy's heart took a high
dive. For someone who'd spent his whole life in Alder, Terry
was incredibly unable to find his way around the woods. But he
always tried to come on like Indiana Jones.

Teddy had only come out with his brother because it was
even more boring at home. Dad was off working for Old
Man Maskell, and Mum just wanted to watch soap serials
or quiz programmes on the telly. This summer, Teddy was
waiting for his exam results. His teachers said he'd have no
trouble getting into college. Terry had left school as soon as
he could and never taken exams. Even the army wouldn't take
him, and the farmers all knew enough about him to give him
only seasonal work. He got his booze, fag and rubber-johnny
money from under-the-counter jobs.

'We'll be there in five minutes,' Terry said, pushing into the undergrowth, Teddy unenthusiastically at his heels. As it turned out, the one thing that thrived on this year's weather was the common bramble. The footpath was clogged with a tangle of vegetable barbed wire. 'C'mon, thicko,' his brother ordered.

Teddy had tried to be as mean and stupid as Terry, but couldn't carry it off. He got interested in his lessons and was pleased when he did well. Most of the things Terry and his mates did or wanted to do struck Teddy as being boring as well as stupid. Terry sometimes said he could set Teddy up with Sharon, and *that* wouldn't be boring. Teddy did not doubt it. The problem was talking to her before and afterwards. Secretly, Teddy still fancied Jenny Steyning. No one had seen much of her since she got religion.

Finally, after much scratching, they reached the Agapemone property, only to find a recently reinforced hedge too high to climb and too thick to breach. With some ill feeling, Terry let them give up and double back to the road. By the time they arrived, the meeting had started. On a dead patch of grass just by the Gate House, about twenty teenagers from Alder and the surrounding villages were sitting, cross-legged or sprawled out, paying attention as James Lytton addressed them. They were mostly lads, with two or three girls mixed in.

The man from the Agapemone paced, ticked off points on his fingers, repeated himself to add emphases, and made pointed jokes as if explaining the ins and outs of the D-Day landings to a roomful of army officers. He sounded like someone from a war film as well, his accent not really posh but not normal either.

Everyone else had cans of beer. James had laid on refreshments for the meeting, but they had run out before Teddy and Terry got there. Terry took this badly, and thumped his brother's arm to establish whose fault it was.

'Settle down at the back there,' said James, like a teacher.

Terry unshouldered his gun and squatted in sullen silence near Kevin Conway and Gary Chilcot, and Teddy had to take some ground near Allison, Kev's creepy, skinny sister. At primary school, Allison had bullied all the boys and, once or twice, had slapped Teddy until he cried. Now, she had long black hair, big black eyes and a worse reputation than any boy in the village. Terry said Allison fancied Teddy, and would torment him with it. Allison crept into his nightmares sometimes.

'What have we missed?' asked Teddy.

'Nothing,' said Kev. 'Same speech as last year.'

'Would the neanderthals who've just discovered the power of speech kindly refrain from using it while I get through this, please? Then we can all get in the pub earlier.'

A beery cheer went up, and everybody looked dangerously at Teddy and Terry.

'Thank you very much,' James said. 'Now, back to the agenda. Item nine: the weapons policy. By now, you should know this one. There are a lot of dickheads in this world, and plenty of them turn up here with nothing better to do than make trouble. We try to weed them out, but we can't eliminate them altogether. What we can do is ensure they aren't lugging any heavy artillery. Look for knives, baseball bats, suspiciously sturdy walking sticks, catapults et cetera. We've never had hassles with firearms or crossbows before, but be on the lookout. There's always a first time. No one turned up with a stun gun until last year. There will be various people who, for one reason or another, will be in costume. All the legitimate theatrical groups will be blue-badged. They've promised us that any swords will be cardboard and rayguns nonoperational. As for anyone else, Vikings will be relieved of their axes, ninjas of their chain sticks. There is no negotiation on this issue. If you see anyone violating our weapons rule, come to me or any of our security people, and we'll deal with the offender. Don't try to be a hero and handle the confiscation yourself. As Gary will tell you, it just ain't worth it.'

Gary Chilcot rolled up his sleeve and traced his scar with an index finger. The year before last, he'd tried to take a sharpened screwdriver off some paranoid kid and wound up with a tetanus infection. There were some humorous expressions of disgust around him.

'Joking aside, be on the watch,' James continued. 'We've got a secure area marked in red on your maps, where all the little cowboys can hang up their gun belts. We were lucky last year, electric shocks aside, and had relatively little trouble. Let's not let things slip. Item ten: entry points. We've heavily pre-sold this year to take the pressure off the gates, but we'll still be taking plenty of admissions in cash. Now, off the record, I'd far rather a few canny punters sneaked in for nothing than have two-mile queues tailing back through the village. The order of the day is to keep things moving. We've got five entry points to the estate, if you'll look at your maps . . .'

Teddy and Terry didn't have maps yet, but Allison let Teddy share hers. He was only half listening anyway, since he'd heard most of it last year and it didn't really apply to him. He assumed he'd be working in the crèche again. It was a laugh, and the kids liked his funnies.

The Gate House was a squashed cottage by the estate wall. James Lytton lived alone in it, well away from the Manor House and the loonies. Teddy couldn't understand why such a straight-up bloke was with Jago's crew. There were a few of *them* at the meeting, smiling placidly without apparently hearing anything, dressed smartly but out of style. He recognized Derek, who'd been in charge of the crèche last year. Teddy had got on all right with him, but there was something missing. They weren't quite zombies, like most people said, but they weren't living in the real world either. Derek was with his girlfriend, a loud and matronly woman, and two others, a muttering girl whose head was always bowed in prayer, and (his heart clutched) Jenny Steyning.

Her parents were up in arms about Jenny joining the Agapemone and had called in a lawyer, but she was over sixteen and could do what she liked. She didn't seem to have changed much, but then she had always been cool. In a long white dress, she looked like a sacrifice waiting for a hungry dragon. All she needed was a floral headband.

'. . . so, any of that, and we're empowered to take their badge, give them a partial refund, and kick them out. And I do mean *kick*. Item fourteen: the Manor House. It's off limits. No arguments, no special circumstances. Most of the Brethren will be involved in one way or another with the festival, but Mr Jago doesn't want the event to shake up his routine. You may not share his beliefs, but this is a religious institution and that demands some respect. The general public are to be kept away from the house, and from all buildings on the estate not designated festival facilities. That includes where I live, by the way. Item fifteen: our old favourite, the bogs. We had a fiasco last year, so we've been rethinking our whole lavatorial setup, and . . .'

Each year the festival grew, and the preparations for it became more elaborate. Organizing it *was* a lot like setting up the invasion of France. At first, the Agapemone had tried to make

do with the Brethren, but they hadn't even been able to cope
with the much smaller event it had been. Now there were maybe
a hundred local people involved, and professionals from outside
were being brought in to handle everything from food to first
aid. There must be a lot of behind-the-scenes work going on.
Teddy wouldn't be at all surprised if the festival was making a
lot of money for a few people. With this year's lump of cash, he
ought to have enough to buy a moped, and if he, a minor cog
in the machine, was being so well oiled, the higher-ups must be
bathing in it.

No one in Alder said much about the Agapemone itself any
more. These days, the festival was much bigger news than the
people behind it. A lot of the old farts were against the event,
but it went ahead every year because it was too sweet for many
local businesses to turn down. Douggie Calver, who owned the
apple orchards and cider presses out on the Achelzoy road, made
the bulk of his annual profit during festival week. His stall was
always the busiest on the site. When Jago first came to the
village, opinion had been split as to whether he was daft or
dangerous. Now, people had got used to the Agapemone. Jago
himself was so seldom seen he was almost forgotten. When Jenny
joined the Brethren (Sistren?), Teddy had thought a bit about it
and more or less decided there was something scary about the
Agapemone. What disturbed him was that too many of the
people connected with the place were obviously not crackpots.
If someone like James was involved, he couldn't write the setup
off as a congregation of God Squad nutters. And the festival was
run too smoothly to be the work of a bunch of loonies.

Usually, with the locals, the Brethren didn't even mention
their beliefs, but if pushed they'd come out with some serious
strangeness. Last year, Derek had tried to explain it during a lull
in the Lost Child season, but clammed up when Teddy asked
him for his personal feelings. One thing he'd gathered was that,
although they tried not to with outsiders, among themselves
the Brethren of the Agapemone referred to Anthony Jago as
'Beloved'. That had a nasty ring to it.

Maybe Jago was related to God after all, he thought, something
between a shiver and a shrug shaking his shoulders.

'. . . finally, the specific jobs. You've all been given assignments based on the questionnaires you filled in and your
performances, if any, in previous years. No arguments please,

my decision is final. I've had the job lists word-processed, and Sister Karen will now distribute the print-outs. So, let's do it to them before they do it to us.'

There was dutiful laughter from the four or five people who remembered *Hill Street Blues* while a pretty girl fussed with the hand-outs. She slit open a taped cardboard box with a scalpel and took out an armload of papers, which she passed in wedges to the other Sisters. Quickly, the stapled documents were scattered among the crowd.

Jenny gave the papers to the little group Teddy was in. He said hello to her, and she smiled back without saying anything. He knew she'd heard, but she was treating him as if they'd never met.

'No one home,' Allison said, tapping her forehead as Jenny went on to the next group. 'Jago's been fucking her brains out. They're all gone.'

It was as if Allison had started slapping him again; and he was turned back into a little crying kid, snot moustaching his face, hot tears on his cheeks. He recovered, and made himself look at the paper.

He was in the crèche again, but not with Derek. Jenny was also (his heart clutched again) down for the duty. He looked up and James was there. Everyone was standing up, comparing jobs, moaning or crowing.

'You did a good job last year, Teddy,' said James. 'You should be able to handle the whole thing this time. You'll have a full roster of volunteer mums under you. You might talk with Derek in the pub later, and get the benefit of his experience.'

'Thanks, James. I 'preciate this.'

'That's okay. You're good with kids. Just don't let your idiot brother screw it up for you again.'

Loyally, he didn't say anything. Terry was bitching because he was a lowly member of the car-park crew, which would keep him away from the music and whatever else was going on. Mainly, he would miss the drink, the dope and the nymphos. He'd done some pilfering last year. He hadn't been found out for a change, but Teddy reckoned James must've had his eye on Terry and made a few good guesses. The news made Terry feel mean, and he wanted to take it out on Teddy.

'Youm with they stupid kids, then?'

'It's okay, it's a good laugh.'

Terry tried to sneer. 'Raaahh! You'm a clown, my boy, a stupid clown.'

Last year, the kids had got into face-painting, and had coloured Teddy like a clown.

'Leave off him, Car Park King,' said Allison, which shut him up instantly. 'You're a one to talk. Everyone knows you're thicker'n two short ones, an' twice as dense.'

Terry tried to laugh but it turned sour in the back of his throat. His brother was scared of Allison. She had once done *something* to him in the copse by the primary school, something that still made him go white and treat her with respect. They had all grown up since primary school, but some things never change.

'We're off down the Valiant Soldier,' said Kev. 'You boys comin'?'

'Might as well,' said Terry.

Teddy was looking around, looking for someone.

'Teddy?' asked his brother. 'You comin' or goin' or what?'

'What?'

'Pub. You comin' or goin'?'

'Oh, yurp. Comin'. I was just thinkin'.'

Kev laughed. 'Your brother'll go blind if he keeps up all this thinkin', Ter. Gonna bust his brainbox proper.'

They left in several groups. Teddy looked back. Through the gates of the Agapemone, he could see the lawns in front of the Manor House. Jenny was crossing towards the huge doors. She was with people, but he could recognize her by the white dress and blonde hair.

In his head, he kept hearing Allison. 'No one home.' His memory added spite to every syllable. 'Jago's been fucking her brains out.'

His mind made up pictures to go with the words. Jenny, in and then out of her white dress, flowers falling from her hair. And Jago, half the darkly handsome man Teddy had seen several times, half the leather-winged dragon he had imagined earlier, folding her in his long, skin-sleeved arms, piercing her with a scaly, red-tipped cock. As they rutted, the life in Jenny's eyes dimmed.

'Jago's been fucking her brains out,' Allison had said. 'They're all gone.'

Seven

THE MAIN hall of the Agapemone was both chapel and dining room. The Brethren were assembled for the evening meal, but the great space felt empty. It was as if a light source had been removed; the absence of Him was as tangible as His presence. When Wendy was out of His gaze, the darkness crept in. Old panic stirred in the depths of her soul, waking like Leviathan, preparing to strike for the surface. They were very close to the End of Things, and she must be strong in her faith in the Beloved Presence. Sometimes she dreamed she was on an island in the mists, surrounded by strange shapes, and He was far from her. It was so easy to lose her hold.

She had come to the meal direct from the meeting, with Sister Marie-Laure and the new Sister, Jenny. She was struggling to put down the pique she felt at Derek's desertion. He hadn't needed to go to the pub with Lytton and the outsiders, but it wasn't her place to instruct him in the path of perseverance. And his was not the absence she felt most keenly.

'Beloved won't be joining us this evening,' Mick Barlowe announced as she took her place. 'He's tired, and is having His meal in His room. I've been asked to read His lesson.'

Wendy looked at His chair, no place laid before it, and at the wings of the altar which stood in the darkness beyond. In her memory she saw Him as a golden shadow presiding over the meal, Loving everyone through His words. The memory flashes were brief, and instantly gave way to the dark. When she was away from Beloved for even a few hours, Wendy found it hard to remember His face in detail. In her mind, He receded into His light and became indistinct.

Upon hearing the announcement, Marie-Laure swallowed a sniffle but did not look up from the carpet. Brother Mick led the girl to her place, touching her intimately in a manner he must think surreptitious. Wendy guessed that he must find it harder than most to forget the flesh . . .

Forget the flesh; for Beloved, the flesh is a temple, or else it is nothing
. . . but not as hard as she herself found that forgetting. She knew
things about the flesh that most did not. Things as inescapable as
the taste of water in her mouth.

*In fire, flesh can blacken and crackle and shrivel from the bone, and
flesh can scream . . .*

There were many unfilled places at High Table this evening, as
if the congregation were sundered and lost. With Beloved gone
from his proper position at their head, an air of purposelessness
had settled. Other absences went unnoticed. Everyone seemed to
be sitting alone. Wendy was sitting alone; not only was Derek not
in his place to her right, but Susan Ames was off somewhere as
usual, ploughing her own peculiar furrow, leaving a vacant chair
tucked under the table to her left. Beyond that were others, but
she felt nothing in particular for them. The Love could never be
constant, as she had imagined it, like a current in the third rail;
rather, it ebbed and flowed like a tide, pulled and pushed by His
light.

Marie-Laure sat opposite, between that bubble-headed Sister
Karen and the quietly spiky Sister Janet, head down even before
Mick began to read, curtains of hair hanging over her cutlery. She
was muttering noiselessly, Ophelia trying not to make a scene.
Under the table, her hands would be gripped in a prayerful death
lock.

'Brothers and Sisters, by the grace of our Beloved Lord and
Benefactor,' began Mick, flatly reading from a handful of stiff
cards that he dealt from top to bottom as he worked through the
lesson, 'we break bread and take wine not only for the sustenance
of our bodies but also for the fortification of our souls.'

Mick had been a performance poet before. He read well, but
he wasn't Beloved. Wendy reached into her head and turned
down the volume control on her hearing. Mick's voice faded
to a backing track. Without Beloved, the familiar words were
as meaningless as the school assemblies she had endured in her
early teens, knees aching, head full of boys and pop music. That
was more than years ago; that was decades ago. This wasn't the
life she had expected.

The hall hadn't been built with electricity in mind. It needed
a row of burning candelabra on the table, and candles in sconces
in the many corners. The feeble overhead fluorescents barely

established twilight, and the freestanding lamps were lost like streetlights in thick fog. With the altar lights off, the darkness was real.

Wendy's sphere of concentration shrank. The walls, the altar and the ends of the table were lost to her. Beyond her field, white face-blobs spooned blood-red soup into mouth holes. Their conversations were muffled like the whispers of ghosts. If she looked up from her soup, she wouldn't be able to see Marie-Laure as any more than an animated sketch.

She was tired, but she had to go through with the business of eating. If she neglected it, she would die. Although her perception of the world beyond was vague, everything within her reach was spotlit, as super-real as an IMAX image. Her knife and fork shone silver and were warm to her fingers. A herbal vapour rose from the bowl under her face, curling into her nostrils with stinging strength.

Could she smell meat? Roasted, burned, charred meat? It was impossible; the communal meals were vegetarian. Here, carnivores indulged a secret vice. There were unidentifiable black bits in her soup. One burst like a hot pepper between her teeth, and taste exploded. For a second, she was sure her shrunken gums had burst. She was harbouring a mouthful of hot blood. A spot of red on the blue tablecloth sizzled and sank in, a dark Rorschach stain spreading. Wendy spat out her soup and took a swallow of iced water. Her mouth chilled, but the stink of meat remained. . . . the stench of burning flesh, the hiss of boiling fat. The memories would always be with her. They had fastened on her brain like black rats, and would not be shaken. Only Beloved could make her forget, His radiance soothing away the fears.

Before she could work up the nerve to take another spoonful of soup, the bowl was taken away and replaced with a plate of vegetable mix. Jenny was serving this evening. In the Agapemone, there were no novices, no ranks. All were equal in His sight. But Wendy couldn't help but think of the girl as a newcomer. She envied Jenny her uncomplicated fervour, and felt keenly any instance in which she seemed to get preferential treatment. Everything – Revelation, Salvation, Servitude, Elevation – came so easily to the girl. She was the youngest of the Sisters.

The accidental touch of her sleeve on Wendy's face was like sandpaper. As Jenny apologized, Wendy flinched. She tried to

compose herself, rubbing out any evil thoughts in the ledger of
her mind. Unless she was perfectly serene and without blame,
the ceremony of breaking bread would be tainted. Jenny didn't
even need a moment of reflection: she was either virgin-pure to
her soul, or else so unthinking in her errors she didn't recognize
them as such. Wendy wondered if she had ever been like that,
even in the distant Eden of childhood.

The food was warm and mercifully tasteless. But it was like
a filling with no piecrust, generic food for those who thought
eating no more a pleasure than brushing their teeth. Without
Beloved, there was no real conversation. Private businesses were
being settled by groups of two or three: festival arrangements,
decisions about which channel to have on in the television room.
Sisters Cindy and Kate were off together as usual, gossiping.
But there was no communion. The Brethren could have been
strangers sharing a restaurant. Wendy missed the feeling of
community.

It was no surprise they should feel His absence. Beloved
worked so hard, and there was no one who could take His
place. He had to take three quarters of the responsibility on
His shoulders. Beloved needed devoted disciples, but there were
many things a disciple couldn't do. Even Mick must have the
humility to realize he couldn't hope to be a genuine substitute.

Wendy was fiercely humble. She'd been torn apart too often
to be certain of much, but she knew with a desperate surety
that the Agapemone was her only chance. The Agapemone
was Anthony Jago or nothing. Sometimes, she thought she
was nearly there, the baggage of the past left behind, but there
was always something to remind her.

A tone of voice, a swastika on a paperback, the smell of petrol in
a garage, a motorcycle passing in the night, the creak of stiff black
leather. A detail would swim out of a formless background, and
she'd be fighting nausea. It happened, *was happening now*, even
when she was safely surrounded by friends.

Black leather.

Someone at the table was wearing a black leather jacket, some
Judas among the Apostles. An arm reached for a pitcher of water,
a useless zip fastener dangling from a gash in the sleeve. Who was
it? The face was a liver-lipped blur. There was a retch of laughter
from the people around the figure, and Wendy looked away,
fixing her eyes on the high back of Beloved's chair, hoping He

would manifest Himself.

It could not be . . .

It was not. It wasn't anybody. When she looked back, there was an empty place. There had been no laughing. She'd been the victim of another stubborn memory gobbet.

She dared hope Beloved would see her later. She needed to talk with Him, to receive His counsel, to find safety in His Love. She shouldn't make demands on Him. But He always had time to Love, time to help.

Wendy couldn't finish her food. It had gone cold in her mouth. She spat a shapeless lump quietly out, and it settled on the already crusted mass on her plate. She pushed it away and poured herself more water. She drank, but her head would not clear.

After the evening meal, there was a period of prayer. Like all women present, Wendy had to cover her head with an appropriately anointed cloth. She always kept her scarf with her, in case she felt the need. When Beloved spoke, prayer was the gem-shining high point of the day, the one time when she could forget, *really forget*, the flesh. Without Him, the ritual was futile, an alarm clock sounding in a tomb. Mick droned, reading without real fire from one of Beloved's texts. Wendy tried to listen for the truth behind the voice, but her thoughts kept skittering off the lesson like a breadknife off a coconut. Rather than be taken out of herself, she was plunged back into the pool of her memories.

The crime had been her idea but, as in everything, Derek had gone along with it. He'd been her unquestioning instrument and, once set the task, had worked out the practicalities. Sometimes, lying awake while he slept in untroubled quiet, she came near to hating him for his acquiescence, for his guiltless complicity. Afterwards, they'd been together but adrift. Until Beloved.

She told herself she had no special claim upon Beloved. She was one among many. But she and Derek had been nearly the first, and she'd been with the Agapemone since its founding. In her secret, selfish heart, she felt those things should count for something. Her mind and body were vessels for His Love, had been since the stormy conversion in that semi-derelict Brighton chapel. She *had* been chosen. She had an important part to play in the visitation that would shortly be upon the world.

She needed at least part of Beloved for herself, for her particular troubled soul. It wasn't a humble thought, and she must have humility or else all her Love was spent, wasted on herself. She prayed hard, pain in her fingers and temples. The pain fuelled her prayers, forcing her thoughts heavenward, thrusting daggers of purity through the red fog of frustration. If Beloved were here, things would be different. Prayer wouldn't be such an effort. It was easier to be humble in His presence. The shade would be dispelled. Beloved, with His hawk face and angel eyes.

Marie-Laure looked up and smiled as she had been taught. Her mouth opened. 'I Love,' she said, 'I Love . . .'

The statement was enough. The sentence needed no object. Marie-Laure Loved. It was enough.

'We share Love,' said Sister Cindy. Marie-Laure trembled.

'We share Love,' Janet joined in, touching Marie-Laure's arm.

When she straightened up, Marie-Laure was a fairly pretty girl. But when her head was down, as it almost always was, her chin squashed into her soft neck and creases marked her cheeks. Her face was perpetually in shadow. It was a miracle she wasn't always walking skull-first into walls and closed doors.

Wendy tried to Love back. Usually, with Beloved there, she could channel herself into the feeling. It was one way of fleeing from memories, fleeing from the flesh. But now all she could manage was an uneasy wellbeing. She could not Love, but she could long. She longed (ashamed and disgusted) for the flesh, and the joys beyond. She longed for the Beloved.

Marie-Laure's sleeveless blouse left her arms bare. Old scars traced her like a join-the-dots puzzle. She'd been an addict once, and a prostitute to support the habit, and, at another time, for other reasons, a novice nun. No one could remember the order of Marie-Laure's traumas, least of all the girl herself, and when she was encouraged to talk out her unpleasant experiences in the community's regular discussion meetings, they tended to get mixed up. She remembered a brothel and a convent as one institution, and her progress from ecstatic religion to heroin as one long period of pain and suffering.

Pain and suffering.

At the last moment, long after she had given up trying, Wendy felt a brief flare of Love (mostly fuelled by pity, but love all the same) like the flickers of orgasm she had once derived from sex. Wendy's fingers, interlocked in a worshipful lattice, would not come apart easily. Her knuckles were meshed like gears, her rings scraped together. She pulled her hands apart. White pressure points faded on their backs, and the aching in the bones slowly died away. She reached out and held Marie-Laure's shaky hand, gripping harder than she had intended, as if to still her tightening of desire.

'We share Love,' she said.

Marie-Laure looked up, and Wendy saw twin red flames reflected in the girl's eyes. Involuntarily, she darted a look over her shoulder. There was nothing in the doorway behind her, but in Marie-Laure's eyes she had doubly seen the figure in the fire.

She'd seen him dwindle to cinders and ash, and scattered his still-warm bones the length of a Welsh valley. Long ago and far away . . .

Badmouth Ben was buried and dead, there was no doubt about that. But for Wendy, he'd never be gone.

Eight

IT WAS Hazel's turn to make supper. She warned him it would be leek soup, so Paul had a few hours to get used to the idea. He tried not to feel as hungry as he was. The sun wasn't down yet, the air thick with midges. His bare arms were badly bitten. Several varieties of cream had been no help.

Toward the end of the afternoon, he had done structural work. He cut up three photocopies of his Wells essays and stapled the paragraphs together in a new, reshuffled, order. The bundle had some repetitions, but they could easily be snipped. Strangely, he felt he'd achieved something. Retyped, with a bit of tinkering, these pages could account for over a third of *The Secular Apocalypse*.

Finished, he lay on the orange blanket spread out by the wooden garden table. There were no clouds. The sun was behind the house, but not below the horizon. The Pottery was fringed with what looked like an orange matte line in a cheap superimposition. It was a still, End-of-Time evening. The birds hadn't yet shut up, but he heard no cars on the road.

Hazel, he gathered, was still rattled by her trouble with bottles and the rumblings Patch had relayed to her. She came out of the house with two trays, and disconcertingly was different again. She put the trays on the blanket, and Paul saw bowls of steaming grey-green liquid with broken-off lengths of French bread and thick smudges of butter on side dishes.

Hazel sat near him, and inclined her face to be kissed. It was awkward at first, their necks not stretching the right way, and she tasted slightly of insect repellent. He eased closer and put a hand on her ribs. He licked her lips and sucked her tongue into his mouth. In his vision, her eyes shut.

'I love you,' he said.

'Thank you,' she said.

Wrong answer, but never mind.

It was still quite uncomfortable. His neck ached slightly, and, with their legs crossed, they found their knees got in the way. She twisted away from him and got comfortable. He picked up his bowl, cupping its warmth in his hands, suddenly aware of the semi-cool.

He gulped down large, lumpy spoonfuls. To get it over with. He tried to soak up and deaden the salty, nothingy taste with the bread. For dessert, they would have ice cream from the freezer and the blandness of the main course would not matter.

Individually, they were indifferent cooks. The only decent meals Paul could remember them preparing had been collaborations. That had been nice, with her giving serious orders and him making silly jokes, and having to improvise the ingredients the books said they needed but which they did not have. Recently, they hadn't had the time to devote to cooking as a joint exercise. They both had work to do.

Leek soup was easy, and the larder well-stocked with leeks and potatoes. Hazel had made a huge vat a week or so ago, and was doling it out whenever nothing else occurred to her.

Crack!

He spat soup. A caterpillar-shaped stain crossed the edge of the blanket and sank into almost bare earth. He tongued his teeth. It had been at the back, one of the grinders. On the upper left side.

'What's wrong?'

He licked a chip of enamel on to the back of his hand.

'A tooth. There was a stone in the soup. A bit of grit.'

She spooned in her bowl. Nothing came of it.

'It must have been in one of the leeks. Sorry.'

'It's okay.'

'You'll have to get it seen to.'

'I suppose so,' he said, still poking his tongue into the rough break. 'It doesn't hurt.'

Much.

Nine

'A T LAAAST,' said more than one person as they drove into the village. Jessica kept quiet; her mapwomanship had turned a two-hour drive into a full afternoon of touring the countryside. Outside the city, everywhere was the same: fields, trees, hedges, cows. Signposts bore three or four unfamiliar names and contradicted each other. It was as if, within the county boundaries, Somerset had decided to repeal the laws of space and time. For the last twenty miles, they'd been able to follow bright-yellow special signs for the festival. Otherwise, they'd be well on their way to Cornwall.

Alder was built around a Y-junction: right fork curling up over the long, loaf-shaped hill; left trailing off across the moor. At the parting of the roads stood a large dead tree straight off the cover of a horror paperback, and across from that was the Valiant Soldier. On the coffin-shaped sign, a redcoat stood to attention, musket on his shoulder, demonstrating the raw courage that had put the wind up Bonaparte and lost the American War of Independence.

'Pub,' Dolar burped, trying to hold in a lungful of dope smoke.

'We should find a campsite first,' said Syreeta.

She was disagreed with loudly. At least by Dolar, Mike Toad and the girl hitchhiker, a friend for life after the smoky afternoon. Ferg, head thick from sweet fog, would have gone for anything that got him out of the enclosed space. At a nod from Dolar, he pulled the wheel over hard, circling the tree on its asphalt island, and bumped across the low pavement into the pub car park. He was sure he heard the exhaust pipe scrape ground, but kept quiet. If Dolar's van got them back to town in a week's time it'd be a miracle, but that was an unimaginably distant future. And someone else, he'd decided round about Andover, would be driving.

The double doors at the back were opened and everybody piled out. Cool air filled the van. Ferg braked, switched off the engine, and pulled the keys. Outside, he could hear groans and creaks as his passengers straightened out after the long trip and got their limbs used to working again. Jessica sat in the front passenger seat, not making a move.

'You all right?'

'I'm a bit carsick. Are we there?'

'Yeah. This is the place okay.'

She coughed violently, almost retching. She had only been smoking gear for a few months, and wasn't as happy with it as she pretended to be. After an afternoon straight at the wheel, surrounded by the stuff, he could understand how she felt. Their clothes must be stale with the smell.

'Come on,' he said, wrenching his slide door open, 'let's get a drink. Then we'll find somewhere to crash.'

She followed him, slipping across the gap between their seats rather than open the door on her side. She was unsteady and leaned against him. Her hair smelled of dye and tobacco. He gave one of her tits a friendly squeeze. By the time she was twenty or so, Jessica would be fat; now, just the right side of sixteen, she was juicy. For the first time since they'd left London, Ferg remembered what this holiday was supposed to be about.

So far, Alder wasn't the magical kingdom of sex 'n' drugs 'n' rock 'n' roll he had been sold on. This was a typical pub car park, with dented litter bins as a reminder of long-gone drink-and-drive merchants, faded white letters that didn't add up to words stencilled on the tarmac. At this time in the evening, it was nearly empty. The Dormobile was badly parked, taking up a space that could have accommodated two or more cars. But that didn't matter: one drink, and they'd be out. There would be plenty of drinking time.

Ferg and Jessica followed the others, arms around each other's waists, and pushed into the public bar.

'Look at that,' said someone with an unfamiliar accent. 'Which d'you reckon's the girl?'

'Neither,' said someone else.

Dolar and Mike were already pressed up against the bar, negotiating a round of drinks with a flustered barmaid. In his electric-blue jump suit, polar-bear shades and panama hat, Mike Toad looked, considering it objectively, the complete prat. And

Dolar, embroidered muslin smock, beard and tangled hair, might have time-warped from 1967. Ferg foresaw trouble.

Two old men with seamed faces, big rubbery guts and elbow-patched jackets were perched like garden gnomes on bar stools, moaning to each other and the smooth, balding barman. They must be the comedy act, Ferg supposed. They radiated unfriendliness and misery. One drink, Ferg promised himself, and out . . .

'Hey, Ferg boy,' said Dolar, his eyes alight, 'have you seen the price of beer out here in the backwoods?'

'It's twenty pence a pint cheaper than London,' the Toad gasped, rattling a fistful of pound coins.

Salim and the girls had taken over a table by a window seat, and were collecting enough stools to go round. With twenty pence a pint off the price of beer, Ferg knew they wouldn't be looking for a campsite until at least after dark and probably after closing time. He wondered if the Dormobile could sleep seven. Probably, he concluded, but definitely not in comfort. His back, neck and hands ached from the drive, but the rest of the crew were in a boozing mood and his vote, even if he could get Syreeta and Jessica to back him up, wouldn't count.

While Dolar got the first round in, Ferg and Jessica squeezed behind the tables. It was good to get proper upholstery against his spine. Mike Toad helped unload the drinks on the tables, and started telling, 'the one about the farmboy with the eleven-inch cattle prod'.

By the punch line of Mike Toad's fourth or fifth 'animal husbandry' joke, Ferg could feel hostility in the pub boiling up like coffee in a pot. The bar was crowded now with clones of the two yokels who'd been there before. The combined mutterings of the drab old men were as loud as a constant rumble of thunder. Even if he listened, he couldn't make out more than the odd word. Their accents were strange, not the mangelwurzel caricature Mike used in his jokes, but something more primitive, more suggestive. It was like Welsh or Gaelic, a different language, an expression of contempt for English-speakers. When these men laughed, it was in bursts that came out like hawked phlegm, and Ferg knew something had been said about his haircut, Mike's outfit or Pam's pasty face.

Jessica and Salim were quiet, and even Dolar had calmed down with the beer on top of the gear, but Mike Toad just went on and on, sending people off to buy rounds and quoting country lore from *Gardener's Question Time*. Syreeta pushed her way through the crowd, exciting ribald gulps as she returned from the bar with an armload of assorted-flavour packets of crisps. She dumped them on a glass-crowded, ash-speckled, beer-puddled table.

'When are we going to eat?' Jessica moaned. 'Properly?'

No one answered, but Ferg felt he had to pay some sort of attention. He picked out a packet of salt and vinegar, her preferred flavour, and gave it to her. Gloomily, she bit the corner off and spat cellophane into an ashtray. Someone in the crowd said 'disgusting'. Ferg couldn't see who it was, but it probably didn't matter. Three-quarters of the people in the bar were naturally pissed off with them, and the rest were scratched the wrong way by Mike's routine. It wasn't the real world here, and the rest of them had better realize that before they wound up at the wrong end of a pitchfork.

Mike Toad was laughing like a camel. 'Do you remember that Burt Reynolds movie where the businessmen go canoeing in the forest?'

'*Deliverance*,' Salim put in.

'Yeah, *Deliverance*. Where the fat chap gets bummed flat by hillbilly strawsuckers . . .'

'Oh, right,' said Dolar. 'That's the one with 'Feudin' Banjos' in it. I tried to work it out once, but that fast-picking stuff is a bitch to do right. Your fingers get cut up.'

'What about it?' said Ferg.

'Nothing. Just to go by the looks that the barman has been giving you all evening, you'd probably do well not to drop your jeans and bend over while he's got his dipstick out.'

Mike laughed too loud. He talked too loud, too. Ferg didn't laugh. From where he was sitting, he could see angry blotches appearing like sores on the barman's face. The man wiped his hands on his cardigan, and made and unmade fists.

'Your round,' Mike said.

'I've had enough,' he replied.

'It's still your round.'

'I'm stuck back here. I'll give you the money.'

'So, just because I'm sitting on the outside I'm a waiter?'

'I'll get them,' said Dolar. 'I've got to get up to piss anyway. Is there a gents' around here or do we do it out in the streets?'

Ferg cringed, and a couple of locals shook their heads.

'Same again, everybody?'

There were enough nos in there to mean he got change from a fiver. Syreeta was wearing out too, and Salim hadn't said much in the last half-hour. Jessica was into her third packet of crisps, and had been forced to stoop to prawn-cocktail flavour. Dolar was getting mumble drunk. Only Pam was keeping up with the Toad, and she was gone enough to be permanently on the verge of uncontrollable giggling. When she laughed, she stretched lines in her face that put cracks in her make-up.

Pam was a very noticeable girl, more than Jessica or Syreeta. When she went up to get her round, the locals had paid close attention to the roll of her bum under her tight black skirt. And her shirt buttons came undone at the rate of one every half-hour. If Mike didn't keep his fingers off Pam's black nylon knees, Salim might be signing up with the local lynch mob and dusting off the ducking stool for unfaithful spouses.

'I wonder how they're getting on back in town?' Jessica asked. She'd had a row with her parents over this holiday, and diplomatic relations were temporarily severed. 'Is there a phone? I should call Mum and tell her we've arrived.'

'They're all dead in London, Jess,' said Dolar. 'Everything behind us is dead. We're at the Dawn of the New Millennium.'

'Too right,' said Pam. 'All change for the next thousand years . . .'

Things did change. The doors opened and a new group came in, raising the noise level again. They were mainly younger than the drinkers who had been in until now. If Alder had a youth scene, this was it.

They wore work shirts and unpatched denim. A few had cowboy boots. One had a shotgun slung over his shoulder. Ferg had never seen anyone routinely carry a gun before. Even here, it seemed out of place. He got the impression this bunch wasn't too popular with the regulars either. Newcomers swarmed to the bar, forcing gaps between the stool conversations, confusing the barman and his two chubby girlies with multiple orders. The Hole-in-the-Wall Gang had just hit the saloon. Someone kick-started the jukebox, and it cranked out one of last year's minor hits.

'Why do Somerset farmboys get married?' Mike asked, too loud.

Pam couldn't stop laughing.

'Because sheep can't cook.'

'We've got to go and find a campsite,' said Syreeta, hours of accumulated irritation giving her voice a squeak. 'We can't put up tents in the dark.'

'It's summer,' said Dolar, 'it doesn't get dark 'til late.'

'It's already late. Look out the window.'

Ferg was about to get into the argument and back up Syreeta when the disturbance started.

There was another newcomer in the pub, an excited little grey-haired man with a stick and a bulging neck. He was waving his stick and saying, 'Give me that back, you hooligan!' One of the local lads, the one with the shotgun, had a sheaf of papers in his hand. He was waving it in front of the small man's face like a makeshift fan.

'Give me that *back*!'

Ferg noticed a couple of men at the bar turning round to take an interest. They were in their forties, but they had come in with the younger crowd. One was, even more than Dolar, the stereotypical old hippie, a cringing reed with watery eyes and a sparse beard. But the one who counted was sharp-faced and commanding; a tough, smart man. Ferg somehow expected him to step between the disputants and sort out the trouble. But he didn't make a move, just kept his eye on the developing situation.

The smaller man was appealing to the bulk of the crowd. 'You've all got to sign. This is what it's all about, don't you see. Filthy hippies. This village is becoming a jive joint for weirdies!'

There were grunts of agreement from some quarters, but the sheaf had been passed from hand to hand among the teenagers while the owner played pig in the middle. Dolar and Mike Toad and the rest were laughing, but Ferg didn't think it was that funny. It was too late and he was too tired to get involved.

'If it's signatures you want, Danny,' someone said, 'we'll get 'em.'

The speaker was a thin girl with long, dark hair and large, dark eyes. She had the papers now, and was laughing as if she didn't mean it. She had a look Ferg had before seen only on the faces of the three leather boys who had taken him out into an alley during a school disco and beaten the piss out of him when he was fourteen. He didn't look forward to meeting her.

'Hey, you,' she said, singling him out as he'd known with a turning gut she would, 'last of the mohicans. You want to help keep this a filthy-hippie-free zone? Protect the rural heritage? Sign this.'

She tossed the papers across the table. They fell into his lap ruffled, like a dead pigeon. Dolar picked them up and read aloud from the top sheet. '"We, the undersigned, year-round residents of Alder, take objection . . ." Hey, crew, they need signatures on this petition to stop the vile, unspeakable, lice-ridden festival. Let's oblige the lady. This is a democracy and everyone ought to be heard from. Who's got a pen?'

Jessica gave him a ballpoint, and Dolar chewed the end while thinking of something to write. Finally, he signed 'Mickey Mouse' with a flourish, and passed it round. Mike Toad put down 'Bilbo Fuckoff, OBE', Pam 'Edwina Currie', Salim 'Bruce Wayne', Syreeta 'Betty Rubble' and Jessica, in a meek and neat hand, 'Minnie Mouse'. They all thought it was funny.

Ferg would have passed, but the little man looked at him with narrowed eyes and spat, 'Vermin.' Danny was obviously the local bigot. Ferg took the pen and paper and scribbled 'James T. Kirk' so nobody could read it. The others had left the address column blank, but he wrote in, 'Space, the final frontier'.

None of this was as funny as it ought to be, although the local youths were joining in the laughter as their girl told them what was being written. The petition passed back to them, and they competed to think up funny or silly or obscene names. The angry man was getting angrier, but no one was supporting him. Veins in his neck pulsed like firehoses, his eyes rimmed with water. He was taking this seriously. Ferg wished they'd skipped the drink altogether.

Mike Toad was getting on with the Alder girl, whose name was Allison, and he introduced the rest of them. She named all her friends, but none of it sank in. Ferg was fixated on Danny and his tantrum.

Suddenly, the little man swung his stick at the kid who had taken his petition. The wood didn't connect properly, but the boy took what must have been a painful knock on the shoulder. He reached for the swinging stick, but couldn't catch it. Danny grabbed for the kid's shirt, and spittle flew in ropes from between his teeth. He was shouting abuse, clinging to the boy. A few buttons fell to the floor. The boy couldn't react. He put his hand behind him, but didn't get a grip on his gun.

Ferg had a fantasy flash of the mess a shotgun blast would make. It would redecorate the whole bar with party strings of red on the beams, the brasses, the tables and the customers. He imagined Danny turning to look at him with eyes that were no longer there, the wall behind him visible through a great ragged hole that filled his head from brow to chin.

The boy's fingers touched the stock of the gun. The man at the bar stepped in and broke the fight up. He worked like a cop, detaching the combatants from one another and forcing them apart at arm's length. When he spoke, his voice was heavy with authority.

'That's enough. Danny, calm down. You're not that stupid, Terry. You're off the roster. Go home, hang up your gun and have your tea. You understand?'

'Fucker!' spat the boy, Terry.

The man slapped him. It was an instant, apparently unthinking response, like a trainer punishing a miscreant dog. The boy stiffened, fist halfway up, and backed away. He knew he couldn't handle the man.

Danny, yelping with frustration, had gone, ignoring the peacemaker's offer of a drink. Terry went after him.

'Teddy,' the man said to one of the boy's drinking friends, 'go after your brother and make sure he doesn't do anything really stupid.'

'Yes,' he gulped. 'Okay. Thanks, James.'

Teddy took off after his brother. Outside, it was fully dark.

'Welcome to Somerset,' said Allison, sitting down with them.

Ten

HALFWAY BETWEEN the Valiant Soldier and his cottage, Danny Keough slumped against the rust-eaten concrete and metal shelter left over from the distant past when Alder had a regular bus service, and cried in the dark. He punched graffiti-etched metal plates with a soft fist, and tried to hold the sobs in his throat like choked-back vomit. He was shaking violently, uncontrollably, from the shoulders down. He pushed himself away and sat down with a thump on the grass-and-earth verge that separated the pavement from a dusty, whitewashed wall. He hugged his petition folder to his chest, further crushing the papers jammed into it. It was ruined. All his work, ruined.

He had knocked his knee without noticing, and it was a useless knot of pain. There was dirt on his clothes, his petition, his face. Someone had spat in his hair. His eyes leaked like wounds. He ground his dentures, relishing the ache in his gums, and made fists so tight his palms bled. The memory of a painful erection tingled along his urethra. He felt the longest-lived of his needs, the desire to hurt somebody, to destroy something. To wipe out the humiliation of the last fifteen minutes.

They were after him, and he was standing alone. Everyone in the pub had looked into their pints while the kids crucified him. They had got everywhere, creeping behind faces he had known for thirty years, eating away even at the heart of England. The boy with the gun was Reg Gilpin's son, the girl who had thrown the petition to the carnival freaks was Bob Conway's daughter, Bernie Conway's granddaughter. They belonged to the village, just like him, but had gone over to the other side.

It was a clear night, a heatwave night. In the sky, the rind of the moon shone like an obscured face, blind and uninterested.

He had been assaulted. By the Gilpin boy and by Lytton, Jago's man. If he only had the money, he would sue. If there was anyone with the backbone to support his side of the story, he'd call the police in. But he realized he was alone. By tomorrow morning, no one in the pub would remember the way it had really been. They were either with the enemy or completely duped. The Gilpin boy had a gun, and Lytton acted as though he could kill with his hands. They had dropped their cover and gone for him. The next assaults, he knew, would be from another direction. They were clever, and he'd have to be continually alert.

Even before this, he'd suspected a concerted campaign against him. He had trouble with the petition. After the Maskells, several others had point-blank refused to sign; and more put their names down in completely illegible handwriting and fudged when it came to listing their addresses. They were gutless fools, afraid of reprisals. That was the kind of behaviour that left the country open to the enemy. He would have to start all over again. The now battered folder had been new this morning. By the moonlight, he saw that his name and address, which he'd inscribed in a proud copperplate, were smudged. The petition was unpresentable as it was. The freaks had marred it with obscenities and false names, and it had been abused in the tussle. He couldn't present this to his MP. He wept for the despoliation of his handiwork.

Finally, there was no more crying in him. He wiped his cheeks with the back of his hand, rubbing grit into wet skin. He found a handkerchief in his jacket pocket and blew his nose until his sinuses hurt. Then he stood up. He felt in his bladder the weight of the tea he'd been given as he went round the village. He unzipped his fly and, still feeling a ghost urge in the head of his cock, pissed in the gutter. He imagined the closed, mean face of the Gilpin boy grinning in the asphalt under his stream. It was no worse than he deserved. He got into his flow and, just as he passed the fail-safe point, was caught in the headlights of a passing car. Danny shrivelled, feeling a lance of pain inside his tool as his piss came and went in spurts. Hastily, when the car was gone, he finished his burst and zipped his fly, the last drops seeping through his underpants, running down the inside of his trousers.

He picked up his petition and began to trudge home. To discourage burglars he always left the hall light on, and he could see it from a hundred yards away. He slowed his pace to a halt, and remembered his precautions. Tired and upset, he still knew the importance of precautions. He had seen what

happened when those who should be vigilant got slack. Danny
had no intention of joining the failures buried in a jumble in
some military graveyard, their individual name markers a lie.
The bodies had been so scrambled it was impossible to sort out
who was what.

He tucked the folder into the seat of his trousers like a
schoolboy expecting a caning, and went down on all fours,
stick in his right hand, ignoring his protesting knee. Slowly he
crawled, stick sweeping the pavement in front for obstructions,
trying to keep his body in the well of shadow made by hedges
and fences.

He passed his neighbours' houses, alert to the slightest unusual
sound. The Cardigans, the young couple who had moved into
Mrs Graham's cottage, were in their front room, cuddled up in
front of the television. Danny was not sure of the Cardigans.
They put up Labour Party posters during council elections and
had a painting of two naked bodies twisted together hung over
their mantelpiece. They had the lights off, so their window was
dimly lit by the shifting colours of the television. He heard
a newsreader's voice talking about nuclear power stations.
Television was such rot these days; even the BBC had gone over
to the enemy. Sometimes he dreamed the real programmes came
through if you twiddled the dial, wireless programs: *ITMA, Dick
Barton, Special Agent, Much Binding in the Marsh*. Danny stood up
slowly and peered into the Cardigans' window, just to make sure.
On the sofa, Mr Cardigan had his hand inside his wife's blouse,
working away at her breasts. Not much of a threat, he supposed,
but they ought to draw their curtains. They were lax, like all
softie lefties. They wanted to give away all Britain's weapons,
but would be the first to moan when the enemy walked in. He
left them fumbling in their ignorance, and edged nearer home
ground.

He remembered the first time he'd been made aware of the
enemy. In the war, when the parachutist came to Alder, and the
knot inside him had first been tied . . .

All was quiet at Gosmore Farm as he crept past, in a crouch
now, stick ready. The pottery sign hung unmoving by the front
gate. He took care not to disturb the display on the verge. The
pots were ugly, strange-coloured things, not at all like his own
floral-patterned plates and royal-family mugs. But he was still
careful. The people who had the place over the summer would

check in the morning. Certain *they* were with the enemy, he had not even bothered to take his petition to them. The man was supposed to be a writer. They were the worst, the so-called intellectuals, listening to violin music while they beat you with lead-filled hosepipes, wiping their arses with Union Jack toilet paper. When he was a kid, they had had real writers: Sapper, Captain W. E. Johns, Edgar Wallace. They had not written about slackers.

The Conway house was quiet too. Bob and his wife were in bed; he could see an upstairs light. They probably didn't care that their children had gone over to the enemy and were out terrorizing the countryside.

His light was only a few houses away. His cock shifted, stiffening as his sureness grew. *They* were in the darkness somewhere, lying in wait. He was certain. He could picture them: olive-faced youths, tattooed numbers in the crooks of their elbows, oil on their skins, skeleton rifles at the ready. They would have someone on the garage forecourt, hiding behind the petrol pumps, rifle sighted on his front door. On some nights, they took pot shots at his greenhouse, shattering panes with silenced bullets for sport. They wanted him to know they were there, that they could come for him any time. They had all the modern equipment: sniperscope night sights, hair-trigger tripwires, body-heat-sensitive anti-personnel mines, brain-scrambling UHF transmitters.

But he had the edge. They had trained on poxy A-rabs and bum-boy bombslingers. Easy meat. He was British, and this was Great Britain. He would outwit them. He would show the stuff that would make Dick Barton and Bulldog Drummond proud. He grinned, sucking in his teeth, fixing them tight in his mouth. He knew eight different death blows that could be struck with his cherry wood. He had practised on an old tailor's dummy. The enemy was as good as dead.

He passed the village hall, clawing uselessly at the festival posters. They wouldn't come free. The Gilpin boy would be with *them*, of course, and Jago's crowd of crazies. Killers all. It was easy to see where Allison Conway came in. She'd do for the whole troop every night. They would have her two or three at a time, getting into her from every angle while Bob and Nicola brewed them tea in the kitchen. They'd have taken over several families by now, just to get near him.

He slipped into a narrow passage between two cottages, and squatted among the Starkeys' dustbins. The folder made his waistband bite into his gut. He smelled rotten food. He had no reason to suspect the Starkeys, but it would be best not to bring them into it. They'd be a danger to themselves as much as to him. He went into the garden of the other cottage. It belonged to the Starkeys too, but had been gutted and was being refitted for sale. The piles of bricks, bags of unmixed concrete and stacks of wooden planks made ideal cover. He found a spot shielded from all sides, and paused to take stock.

Peering over the top of a heap of rubble, he saw two tiny red dots up on the hill. They moved independently, occasionally vanishing behind trees. They were like the lights on his wireless that proved the batteries were working. The killers up in the woods had electronic equipment, obviously. It was so quiet he could hear a train rattling across the moor over five miles away. He breathed in silent gulps, nerving himself up for the final moves of the night. He'd be inside his house in ten minutes, the watchers beaten again.

There was another narrow gap between the empty cottage and his own. From his kitchen window he could see through the hole in the wall where a similar frame would be put. Belly to the ground, Danny crawled through the doorless doorway into the enclosed dark. He stood up and leaned in a corner, out of the window lines of fire. He brushed dirt and wood shavings off his clothes. A bath would do him good. His knee flared up again, and he leaned hard on his stick. In the hot darkness, he discovered he'd been sweating freely. For an instant, as the blood went to his head, he was on the lip of blacking out. He pulled himself sharply back. Nearly home safe, he mustn't let himself slip now. He stepped into the room that was once, and would soon again be, a kitchen. Glass crunched under his shoes. He tensed, stick up, ready for an attack. None came.

He had the Jew-boy cowards on the run.

The sink was tapless and dry. He climbed into it, and crouched, looking into his own house. The hall light seeped under the kitchen door, and he could make out the newspapers laid out under the cats' bowls. He was sorry about the cats. They'd been company. But they'd got careless, and been casualties. The animals were unfit for the war. One, he was sure, had turned traitor. He'd caught her in a forbidden place and hanged her with all due ceremony. She wasn't buried with the others. He'd put her in the dustbin.

He braced his hands against the brickwork where the window frame would be, and lowered his legs. His back rubbed over the sharp ledge. His shirt came untucked, and his file shifted into an even more uncomfortable position. It'd be over soon. His feet touched the concrete of his own side path. He sagged between the cottages, hugging his own property. He listened for noises from inside the house. His ears were sharper now than they'd ever been. Breathing would give the bastards away. They could not hold their lungs for ever.

There was nothing.

Anyone would think the kitchen window was conventionally locked. The arm was in place and wired, but it was a dummy. Danny had hacksawed it through and glued it back in position as a blind. His whole house was like that; secure, but offering anyone who knew the secrets immediate emergency entry or exit. Only Danny knew the secrets. He looked both ways. The red lights were gone. They must be on the move. He didn't have much time. He pushed the window inwards, and eased it gently to the right until he heard the hidden catch click free. Then he pulled, opening a crack at the bottom. He felt under the frame, probing for a pull wire. That was the most favoured detonator. He couldn't find trace of any infernal device.

Silently, he yanked the window open and dragged himself into it. He nearly got stuck halfway, but managed to struggle free. Using the taps as handholds, he hauled his lower body into the house.

Home free!

In the dark, he sat on a tall stool by the draining board and pulled the window shut behind him. He secured it with the real bolts.

His stick was still in the empty cottage, but he'd be able to get it back in the morning before the workmen began. The enemy could not operate in daylight. It was over for the night. They could huddle in their camouflage gear or take their turns with slag Allison. He was going to have a bath, then go to bed.

He pulled the folder out and dumped it on the kitchen table. Then he turned the lights on. The writing on the folder was a livid red. It hadn't been there when he left the Valiant Soldier. It was in Hebrew script; he couldn't read it, but recognized a death threat.

The bastards! They must have someone in the house.

He took a carving knife from the rack. The blade was keen enough to cut hair. Every week he gave it a hundred passes through the sharpenener. They knew he was in the kitchen, but wouldn't come to him. He'd have to draw the killers out. He opened his kitchen door and stepped into the hallway.

Nothing happened.

Then he saw it. The wire was almost spiderweb thin, stretched across space from the corner of his framed British Empire map to the overburdened coat rack, back again to the front-room door, then to the thermostat. He bent under the wire, which would have been about neck height, and went to the staircase. He lay full-length on the steps.

Upstairs. The Irgun assassins were upstairs.

Clocks ticked in the house. He had a silent digital on his bedside table and an ordinary mechanical clock in the front room. Otherwise, there was only his wristwatch. There were more tickings in the house than he could account for. Some of the bombs must be on time fuses. He had to deal with his human enemies quickly, then devote his energies to rooting out and disarming the devices.

He crawled up his staircase, eyes up, expecting another taut wire to appear in front of his face. He wanted to piss again, or maybe just to touch his cock. In his peril, he was aroused. It had been a long time. Perhaps the enemy would have sent one of their killer whores for him, like the murderess who'd come to the barracks in '47, a fat-titted slut with a switchblade taped inside her thigh. Or like the parachutist in her tight black suit, a swastika around her throat. He'd be well within his rights to give her a shafting before he snapped her spine. It wouldn't be rape; it'd be an example to the others, a symbol of his contempt for the enemy.

The tickings were louder. He heard his own pulses and the master pulse of his heart. His mouth was dry. There was sand on the stair carpet. Lower down, it was a fine dusting, like the prints of someone barefoot from the beach. Towards the landing, it became an inches-thick layer that shifted and cascaded as he climbed. Sand got everywhere: in your clothes, your eyes, your food, your foreskin. You had to be careful. Sometimes there were scorpions. And it retained the heat of the desert sun. You could burn your hands in it as easily as in scalding water.

On the landing, his broken-necked cat waited for him. She miaowed askew but couldn't do him any harm.

He was expected in the bathroom or bedroom. They liked to take their victims while helpless – naked in the tub, hunched over a bowel movement, asleep in a guiltless bed. Bathroom or bedroom. One or the other.

Bedroom, of course. In his bed, in fact. That was where his killer would be waiting.

Danny crashed through his bedroom door, lurching into a net of sticky wires that cut him. He dropped his knife, which slithered down the net, where his fingers couldn't reach. His digital clock alarm sounded, and the killer under his blankets stirred, stretching out a serpentine, perfumed arm. She shut off the alarm. Red jewels glinted on her rings. She pushed a mass of glossy black hair up, clearing her ancient, smooth face. Her eyes were darkest brown, with cat-slit pupils.

'Hello, Danny boy,' she purred.

Bedclothes fell from ballooning brown breasts. An eye-jewel shone in her navel like a button in the cushion of her stomach. She was naked but for her jewels. She had a necklace of cartridge cases, and silver snake armlets. The hair on her arms and legs was oiled flat against her skin.

The wires around him were getting tighter. A pair across his chest were cutting through his clothes, drawing lines of blood on his skin. Lower down also, he could feel sharp threads drawing tight. His ruined trousers fell away in sections. He was still erect. Strangely, in his pain, he felt younger.

She spoke again, Hebrew gibberish this time, and came for him. Her right forefinger was a lacquered gun barrel, and a revolving cartridge chamber stood out in her wrist, balanced on bone.

They had him.

The killer whore took his underpants down and squeezed his balls. Gently, at first. Not-quite-pain flooded him. He was drowsy, and dying. She stroked the length of his cock with her cold gunfinger. It stood to attention and she forced it down, jamming the head into herself. She slid smoothly over his erection, burying him. The whore ground against him. He opened his mouth for a death kiss, but her gritted teeth held back. Still thrusting with her wide hips, she reached up with one hand and held him by the back of his neck. The wires

didn't get in her way. Her gunfinger crooked as she touched it
to his lips, then straightened stiff again. The metal tube forced
its way into his mouth, displacing his dentures. His breath came
in gargles as the first flashes of orgasm made him shake. The
chamber in her wrist began to roll. Inside his head, something
exploded.

Interlude Seven

THERE WAS a plaque up in the church to mark the time when the village was the capital of Wessex, which was all there was of England in those days. 'In 877, King Alfred made his winter court in Alder, and, in the church that stood upon this site, King Gudrun of the Danes, lately defeated in battle by the armies of Wessex, was baptized into the Christian faith.' In 1944, Jenny's granddad, an American soldier who had come over for the war, had scratched, 'and damn all has happened here since' just under the plaque. When he told the story, Granddad always chuckled in a coughy way like an old cowboy on television and finished by saying, 'Only, I didn't exactly write the word "damn".' Actually, Jenny thought, something had happened to Granddad Steyning in Alder during the war, or why else would he stay? It wasn't a subject her parents brought up at all, and she had one of her feelings that there was something they didn't want to talk about tied up in it. Granddad Steyning had gone to Heaven when Jenny was small, but she could remember him well.

On the day they heard on the radio about John Lennon being shot, the Lord God came to live in Alder. It was the Christmas holidays, and Jenny didn't want to be in the house with Mum while she was crying over the dead Beatle. In all the years their house had had advent calendars, this was the first time no one remembered to open a window on the day it was supposed to be opened. When Jenny was only little, Mum had taught her the words to 'Yesterday' and 'She Loves You', playing along on the guitar which was in the loft now. Jenny bet Mum must have known John Lennon before she met Dad, and that was why she was so sad about him.

Jenny played with her toy cars on the forecourt of Dad's Shell station until Terry and Teddy Gilpin told her the Lord God was coming. She knew all about the Lord God, whose real name was

Anthony Jago. He called himself 'Reverend', just like the vicar.
He had bought the Manor House for himself and his disciples to
live in. All the other people who had lived at the big old place had
called it the Manor House, but Jago had put signs up changing its
name to the Agapemone. She had tried unsuccessfully to put the
syllables together in her mouth. Mum said that it sounded like a
kind of fruit, but Dad, who had read about it in the paper, said
agapemone was Greek for 'abode of love'. Dad said Jago was not
the Lord God at all, but a dangerous weirdo. Jenny decided she
would make up her own mind.

Her parents didn't much like the Gilpin brothers either, but
none of Jenny's school friends lived in Alder and there were
only two buses a week to town, so she had to play with
them during the holidays or watch boring television. Terry,
the older, kept saying horrible things to her and trying to
take her knickers down when there were no grown-ups
around. She had called him a git once, and hit him with
a biggish stick. She knew he hadn't forgotten that. Terry
was going to grow up to be like a baddie in a cowboy
film, the kind who rustle cattle and try to shoot the goodie
in the back. One day, he'd probably try to shoot her in
the back. She was practising her hearing, so he would give
himself away by stepping on a twig and she would get him
first.

Terry wanted to go and watch the Lord God and his
disciples, 'thick bunch of townie loonies', move into the
Aga-thingie. With Doug, the Gilpin dog, sloping along,
they took the short cut across the soggy fields, getting
over the ditches on planks although Terry wanted to jump,
but staying away from cows. They found a place near the
Manor Gate House and waited. It was not too cold, but the
sky was cloudy and dull. Terry and Teddy threw stones in
the ditch, making holes in the duckweed and watching them
fill in. Teddy found a wedge of concrete he could barely lift,
and heaved it into the water. There was a big splash, and
Jenny got little green spots on her skirt. The Gilpin brothers
thought that was funny, which just showed how stupid they
were.

When he had stopped laughing, Terry took his stubby thing
out and piddled in the water. Jenny thought he was disgusting,
and said so. She had learned the word 'grotesque' from a comic

last week, and was tempted to use it. But God's Volkswagen bus turned up.

Actually, it was the disciples who arrived in the minibus. Dad said the disciples were stupid people who had given all their money to Jago. The men mostly had long hair and beards, which made them look like the real disciples in her Scripture book.

A lady in a long skirt with an armful of red flowers came up to them.

'Have a flower, it's as pretty as you are,' she said, handing her one. The lady also gave flowers to Terry and Teddy. 'And as handsome as you, and you.'

The lady had long hair, a headband and lots of beads. She was floppily fat. Jenny got the idea she was the same age as her parents but wanted to pretend she was younger. She didn't know whether that was stupid or not.

Jenny said thank you. Terry and Teddy didn't want their poofy flowers but had to take them anyway. Jenny thought that funny but didn't laugh out loud. When the lady went away, Teddy started pulling the petals off his flower and Terry said something rude about her teats. Terry was stronger than Jenny and thought he could boss her about even though he was thick.

They sat on the lawn and watched the disciples. The man who had lived in the Manor last had chased them away once, but the God people didn't know they weren't allowed in the garden and let them stay. A big lorry came, and the disciples took lots of things out of it. Furniture, boxes of books and records, cooking stuff, gardening tools, bright-coloured clothes. The disciples were happy and nice to each other, which seemed sensible rather than stupid.

Terry got bored, and went away to let off some rook-scarers near Mr Keough's cats, but Teddy stayed, with Doug. When Terry was there, Teddy was just as horrible as his brother, but on his own he was almost nice. She knew he'd sent her a valentine card this year. She didn't fancy him, though, because he picked his nose and ate it.

After the big lorry had gone away and it was getting near lunchtime, a Saab came down the road. There were three men on motorbikes with the car. They wore leather and had Jesus slogans on their crash helmets. She knew who Jesus was. Jesus H. Christ. Granddad had said his name

lots of times, usually when he banged his toe or something.
'Jesus H. Christ on a bicycle.' The people who drew the
pictures in the Scripture books always left the bicycle out,
and when she put it in with her blue biro the teacher told her
off.

The motorbikers stood in a line when Mr Jago got out of the
Saab. He didn't look much like the God she'd heard about. He
had no long white beard and wasn't shining like the sun. He
had a TV-star type face, and a collar like the vicar's. He had
on black jeans, a long purple coat, and a white hat that did
look a bit like a halo. The lady with the headband gave the
rest of her flowers to him, and he gave her a squelchy kiss.
Teddy had run away with Doug, leaving the bits of his flower
behind.

She watched God some more, but knew Mum would have
cooked by now. She was hungry, and Mum would be mad if
she was late for lunch. She hoped Mum had stopped crying. It
made her tired when Mum cried. When she left the Agapemone,
the disciples were gathered around Mr Jago and he was talking
to them. They looked very happy. She wondered if they'd be
having loaves and fishes for lunch. That sounded like an odd
recipe, especially with no butter or chips or tomato sauce, but
it was God's favourite food.

Just down from the Gate House, she saw another girl, hiding
in the bushes. It was Allison Conway, the dark-haired fright
with big eyes who lived over the road. Jenny was afraid Allison
would jump out and chase her, which she did sometimes, but
the girl shrank back further into hiding. She must be spying on
God, too, and be worried about being caught. Mum and Dad
mightn't like Terry and Teddy Gilpin, but they'd actually told
her not to play with Allison. Mrs Yatman had told Mum about
something Allison had done to her daughter Elizabeth at a fête,
which Elizabeth wouldn't talk about. It must have been very
bad.

Jenny walked past Allison, pretending not to have seen her.
On the way back to the garage, Jenny had to go down a path
that was paved but too narrow for cars. It had high hedges on
either side, and was scary at night. It was all right in the daylight,
though. There was a sign prohibiting cyclists, but Jesus must not
have seen it. He was riding a lovely bike. She bet angels polished
the metal parts every day. They shone like the sun.

Jesus H. Christ stopped and talked to her for a bit. He was nice. He wanted her to follow him. Not follow like Mary's little lamb, hanging around wherever He went, but follow like being kind to poor people and doing all the things He liked you to do. She said she would, and gave Him her flower. He was pleased.

II

One

Syreeta was right: putting up tents in the dark wasn't easy. It especially wasn't easy when most of the workforce were wrecked.

They weren't in any of the official sites. On Allison Conway's advice, they'd driven up the hill and off the narrow road into the woods. There was a hard earth track, and Ferg had had to manoeuvre the Dormobile carefully to keep its wheels out of deep tractor ruts. In the pub, the local girl had given precise directions. According to her, there was a part of the woods that was common ground where anyone could set up a camp. He wasn't sure he was convinced. He expected they'd wake up tomorrow to find the area full of KEEP OUT and TRESPASSERS WILL BE SHOT placards, with dead animals nailed to trees as explicit warnings to the foolhardy.

It was a clear night, but the clearing, surrounded by tall trees, was thick with shadows. Ferg left the headlights on, which gave them a semicircle of visibility to work in. Dolar, who would be sleeping in the back of the van with Syreeta, wanted to crash out immediately, leaving the rest to it. She persuaded him with threats to help the others. The gesture would have meant more if he had been in a condition to be of actual use rather than just get in the way and trip over guy ropes.

It should have been easy. There were no wet patches to be avoided, and the dry, solid earth was ideal for hammering in skewers. Pam and Salim got their tent pitched first. Although it sagged in the middle, they did a good job. Ferg, working on his own since Jessica was off gathering sticks for the fire, came second. His tent wasn't straight either, but would do for tonight. Mike Toad, who had the biggest tent all to himself because he'd borrowed it from his sister, was waving his arms under floppy canvas pretending to be a ghost, while Dolar was hammering a skewer out of shape with a mallet. Ferg and Pam took over

from Dolar and eventually, despite Mike, the tent was put up.
It was collapsed at one end, but since Mike wouldn't come out
they assumed he must be satisfied. Pam looked in to make sure
he was breathing, and they left him alone.

Jessica had made a real Girl Guide's fire, with stones piled in a
circle around a teepee of broken twigs and twists of newspaper.
However, she was the only one interested in a barbecue. They'd
brought down sausages and frozen hamburgers in a cool box,
and Jessica was hungry. Ferg was hungry too, but in a vague
way that was a part of a larger discomfort. He already had the
hangover he'd expected to wake up with, and his back and neck
still ached from the drive.

Mike Toad was snoring like a chainsaw. Pam and Salim had
already crept into their tent: their shadows wriggled in torchlight
as they tried to get out of their clothes in the wardrobe-sized
space. Dolar came back from taking a leak in the woods; he
staggered sideways into a thorny shrub and made a lot of noise.
Syreeta pulled him out and pushed him towards the van. He
rolled his eyeballs and let her put him to bed.

'Where's the food?' Jessica asked.

Ferg was dead on his feet. This morning, he had thought to end
his day making love in a tent. It had been a pleasant fantasy, but
one he'd returned to with less and less enthusiasm throughout the
gruelling afternoon and unnerving evening. Now, his ideal was
to cocoon himself in a thick sleeping bag and never wake up.

'The food?' Jessica reminded, irritated. She would not be put
off. She probably felt as much like eating as he did, but had made
such a thing of it she had to keep up or be seen to back down.
Even if there was no pleasure in it, she'd have her barbecue.

'Can't it wait until tomorrow?' he said, knowing immediately
that he shouldn't have bothered with the suggestion. Her eyes
bled dry of expression, her lower lip curled out. If he pushed,
they'd get into a row that could last for days, seriously ruining
his holiday. The simplest course was to go along with her.

'Okay, okay. It's here somewhere.' He hauled his rucksack out
of the tent, and found the plastic kitchen container. She had her
lighter out. A snake-tongue of flame licked newspaper, and, in
seconds, twigs crackled.

'There's been a fire here before.'

She could be right. The flames lit up the ground, and he saw
a ragged circle around the fire, bare of grass. It was earth and

loose shale, and did look as if, a long time ago, it had been charred.

'Maybe a flying saucer landed here.'

She huffed and took the two-pronged barbecue fork from him. He had speared a pair of fat sausages on it. She held them in the flames. He knew she should wait for the wood to burn down to charcoal, but didn't say anything. He didn't want to drag this out. His eyes felt weighted. He opened two rolls with his thumb, and smeared in butter and ketchup. As far as he was concerned, Jessica could have both.

Inside their tent, Pam and Salim started breathing asthmatically in rhythmic union. The canvas shivered as they moved. Obviously, *they* weren't too tired.

Jessica's sausages went black and then split. Pink wounds opened and gristle dropped into the fire, which hissed like a kicked cat. Sitting by the fire, Ferg shut his eyes and looked forward to sleep.

Two

Hazel was out with the kiln. At different points during the firing, the temperature had to be changed. She was obviously nervous. In Brighton, her tutor supervised the process. Here she was on her own, except for a tatty, clayey exercise book filled with Mike Bleach's secret tips.

Paul was sitting up in bed, looking over notes for his imaginary war chapter. By tomorrow afternoon, he hoped to have a solid, closely argued 7,000 words on Chesney's *The Battle of Dorking*, Wells's *War in the Air*, Shiel's *The Yellow Danger* (ugh!), Saki's *When William Came*, with a footnote on the turn-of-the-century genre's best-selling last gasp, Hackett's *Third World War*. Invasion fantasies for an island nation. He wondered if he should consider the various if-the-Nazis-had-invaded fictions – Deighton's *SS-GB*, the films *Went the Day Well?* and *It Happened Here* – an offshoot of the form. All very respectable, and it got a lot of boring books out of the way without his actually having to read – or reread – all through them. *The Battle of Dorking* was short, and the Wells and Saki good enough to be painless. The rest were mainly hysterical, and got in as second-rank filler to prove he was being really comprehensive here.

Hazel was improving; after supper, she'd finished packing the kiln, which was fiddly and demanding but a change from being bent over the wheel, and started her firing. That done, she'd been almost satisfied with her day. For the first time in nearly a week they'd made love, finishing almost together. For a while, they were as they used to be. The Alder festival had encouraged the change in Hazel's spirits. She'd been working up enthusiasm ever since the couple from the Agapemone came round. He realized the recent upsurge in customers was probably due to the influx of festival-goers. In fact, he was about to start worrying about shoplifting. This was obviously how to turn into a reactionary before he was thirty. The local paper was full of awful warnings about a convoy on the way, laying waste to everything in its path, leaving desolation in its wake. This year, they probably couldn't make much difference to the countryside.

Earlier, Hazel had called the Agapemone and confirmed that she wanted a stall. Paul suspected he'd be drafted into looking after it. However, he didn't think he would find much joy in Christian heavy metal, or whatever Jago's followers were pushing. The festival was well organized and extensive enough to suggest behind-the-scenes muscle. The profits weren't going to starving Africans or endangered whales, but something must be making all these rock stars want to traipse to the West Country. He'd thought it unfashionable to be into spirituality these days. It had been a long time since pop groups went to maharishis or sang 'Atlantis will rise, Sunset Boulevard will fall'. But the shadow of the Sixties lay on the county. Glastonbury wasn't far away, and some of the landscape was decidedly hobbitesque. Maybe New Age was catching on.

'More homework?' asked Hazel, coming in.

Paul started. His mind had been wandering.

'Yes. I should give it a rest, I suppose.' He shut the notebook and shoved it on to the bedside table.

Hazel had gone out to the kiln shed in jeans and a dressing gown. She skinned her jeans off, dropped the gown, and slipped under the duvet.

'How are things out there?'

A pause. 'All right . . . I think. The glaze tests have melted properly. I've been following Mike's instructions.'

He slid his arm round her as she wriggled deeper into the bed. 'I'm sure it'll be okay.'

'Hmm. Maybe.'

She was cold, surprisingly so. It was a warm night, but Hazel had goose flesh. She was almost shivering.

'It's spooky out there,' she said. 'And I've got a whole night of it. It's darker here in the country.'

'Of course. There's no streetlight. You can see the stars better.'

She set her travelling alarm clock for her next visit to the kiln. 'Paul, are you sure you don't want me to sleep downstairs on the sofa? I've got to be out again at three and five.'

'I always sleep through your alarm anyway,' he lied. 'Just don't tread on me getting up.'

She put the clock back, and he snuggled closer to her. She was warming up, but still distracted. He kissed her neck, and she gently shoved him away, mumbling. He turned the light out. He fell asleep, lulled by the distant roaring of the kiln.

Three

EVEN IN the dark, *especially* in the dark, Allison knew the woods. There were the footpaths and rights of way everyone knew, and she used them from time to time. But her woods were mapped with secret runs she travelled alone. She was mistress of paths you couldn't see unless you knew exactly where to look, bushes that could be pushed aside like gates, fences where wires were loose, hollows that were tunnels under thick bramble, long-branched trees that made bridges over walls. Left alone by her parents and the other children, she had made the woods her own years ago.

She watched the kids from London sit by their dying fire, eating sausages. She had sent them to the clearing they called the Bomb Site, but which the oldest villagers called Bannerman's Bonfire Site. There'd been burnings here. Some nights, she could see its ha'ant, a faint firelight in the shape of a man. She was the only young person in Alder who appreciated the spot, who understood its importance. She wanted people there, in case they were needed. It was one of the several sites around the hill where the power could be felt. Moonglow Paddock was another. Burrow Mump, to the west. And an attic room she had never been in, high up in the Manor House, where there was a machine she didn't understand.

The goof-faced boy with the mohican and the plump, sulky girl with dyed hair and deliberately ripped clothes didn't talk to each other, just ate glumly. There was nothing to be gained from watching them further. She knew enough. On her knees, she crawled away from the kids' camp, feeling earth through torn jeans, and squeezed into one of her runs, forcing herself against the ground as she wriggled under a thorny mass piled thick against a fence marking the edge of the Starkey property. She'd dug a way under the fence a few months ago, and kept it open ever since. Her breasts rubbed against the ground, and she felt aroused. She was used to it. When she was in heat, she was more powerful, could see more things. Soon she would take care of her body's needs. At the festival, there'd be plenty of people to fuck.

She emerged into the Starkey orchard and stood up. Earth fell from her clothes. She stretched out, feeling strength in her muscles, and ran fingers through her hair, brushing out twigs and dead leaves. Pausing by a particular tree, she remembered making Tina Starkey cry by bending back her hand until the wrist popped. They were ten years old. By the end of primary school, she'd made all the children in her class cry or bleed. She had only needed to do it once or twice to each child to establish a pattern. She hadn't had to hurt anyone for years now, but she knew the time would come again. She felt it coming, felt it in her nipples, her guts, her clit.

Working her way through orchards and back gardens, she made it to the road, a mile or so outside the village. She had a drop in a lay-by, hidden under three flat stones. It held a black-handled Stanley knife with three fresh blades and a tube of mints. She flipped up a stone and pulled out the mints. She squeezed one into her mouth and replaced them. Also in the drop was her single heirloom, a small swastika. Her granddad, the only relative she'd ever had who understood her, had given it her, claiming he'd got it in the war after killing a German parachutist. That had to be a lie, because she knew Granddad never went to the war. As a farmworker, he was let off. She picked up the swastika and gripped it, trying to feel the power inside the symbol. Once, it had been studded with fake emeralds, but only two remained in their dents. She gripped the swastika, feeling she was drawing strength from it, and slipped it back into the drop.

It was quiet, but in the distance she heard a motorcycle. Someone was coming towards Alder from the Achelzoy road, swerving with its bends. She crouched in shadow. The noise got nearer. She scooped dry earth from the verge and camouflage-smeared her face, rubbing it in around her eyes. The bike was just around the corner now, engine loud as a pneumatic drill. She could smell petrol. She sucked the mint thin, then crunched it to powder. The rider came into view, leaning as he took the corner. He stuck his boot against the road and skidded in a circle. He wore a helmet with a dark mirror visor. He looked straight at her and she stood up, wiping earth from her face. He gunned his engine, making it roar, and let it die. He reached for a tag at his neck and pulled a zip that split his black leather jacket from neck to waist. He was naked underneath. The meat smell hit her, and she was fascinated by the whorls and ridges of hardened flesh on his chest. With a heavily gauntleted hand, he raised his visor. Another girl might have screamed at the face of Badmouth Ben, but Allison loved him at first sight.

Four

THE KITCHENS were the oldest part of the Agapemone, vaulted caverns at the back of the building. On the ground floor, they were robbed by the rise of the hill around the foundations of all windows but a row of glassed horizontal slits near the ceiling. If Beloved ever had to feed a multitude, he would have earthly facilities to back up His divine powers. Brass pots hung on one wall, arranged from largest to smallest like a percussionist's fantasy. Fine china, some of it over a hundred years old, was stacked and locked away in a huge, much-beaten dresser. There were enough deep sinks to service a morgue, and a yardage of work surfaces that could accommodate an attempt to break the world record for sequentially knocking over dominoes.

It was well past the ghosts' high noon, but Jenny was still working. Being able to serve made her content. Her days were full now, with not a moment wasted. The confusions she felt only a few months earlier were as solved and remote as the teething and toilet troubles of her babyhood. Exams, rows with her parents, universities, jobs, boys. That was over; now she could get on with things. She'd found the faith to realize that the choices which had bothered her were false. She could only do what was right. Nothing else was possible. She suspected some of doubt, but their feelings were as mysterious and unfathomable to her as her certainties now were to her parents.

She loved her parents as she Loved her Brothers and Sisters in the Agapemone, as she Loved the Righteous who would be Saved, as she Loved the Unrighteous who would be Cast Out, as she Loved, most of all, Him. Despite Love, her parents were lost to her. She could not waste time on regrets. It was the way it was to be. She hoped, in the end, they'd see truth and join the communion. He was infinitely merciful.

As she ran the cold taps to get the rust out of the water, she hummed to herself. When she had first learned the tune, at school, it had been called 'Lord of the Dance', and the words had been about Jesus (H.) Christ. Now, as she hummed, she thought of the older, lovelier lyric. Susan told her the song was associated with an American sect of the last century who believed dance a sacrament, that the expression of joy was the worship of God.

> 'Tis the gift to be simple, 'tis the gift to be free,
> 'Tis the gift to come down where you ought to be,
> And when you find yourself in the place just right,
> It will be in the Valley of Love and Delight . . .

The Valley of Love and Delight. She touched herself, feeling the heat of her body through her dress. She was learning, all the time, about the Gift. She was fortunate to have so many Gifts.

The water ran pure. She shut off the creaky tap to lift the bucket from the sink. She put it down by two others, full of the washing-up slops. In the drought, water was precious. It could be used in the garden or to flush the toilets.

She slid the big enamel basin into the sink and twisted the tap. Noisily, the oval bowl began to fill. There were echoes in the pipes. The basin was soon brimful with water, as she was with the Love of the Lord. It was good to be a sound vessel. She looked at herself in the mirror of the water, and seemed to feel her face waver as a ripple disturbed it. She turned the tap again, stopping the drip, and lifted the basin out of the sink. Water shifted but did not spill. She did not feel the weight. Strength of the spirit had a way of making up for the weakness of the body.

She put the basin down on a table by the door, flicked the light switches off, picked up her burden again, left the kitchens and steadily walked to the staircase. As long as she kept to her preordained path, it was like floating. The basin was insubstantial. Her feet hardly touched the carpeted stairs, though her long dress dragged a little. If she were to let go of the basin, she felt it would bob slightly in the air but remain more or less where it was, drawn as she was upwards, towards Beloved. But if she were to suffer, as Sister Wendy did or even the self-possessed Susan, from the slightest of doubts, the basin would fall, soaking her from the waist down, waking the household. Then, she might have to face the man in the leather jacket who stood in Wendy's shadow, waiting to take advantage. But, of course, her faith was unshakable.

The house was quiet. The library door was not showing lines of light, so Susan must have gone to bed. Everyone else who had no duty would have turned in at eleven o'clock. She should be the only person awake except for Beloved, who was always watching over His flock. He was on the top floor, up three flights of stairs. In one windowless room under the roof, there was a strange apparatus inherited from the house's former owner, a camera obscura. Jenny had been allowed up there once. With the device, Beloved could create in miniature an image of the house and the village. Even without it, He knew most things. Otherwise, His rooms were sparsely furnished. He had no need of luxuries.

With an extended foot, she pushed His door open, managing not to spill the water. She stepped inside and gratefully set her burden down on a stand. The gable windows were uncurtained and let in the thin moonlight. Beloved lay on a wooden pallet on the floor. In the pale light, His skin shone. His eyes were closed and He was still but Jenny knew He wasn't asleep. He never really slept. He shifted His head as if to look at her, but His eyes didn't open.

She took a fresh flannel and dampened it in the cool water. Kneeling, she began to wash Beloved, starting with His feet. He'd bled a little again, from the ankles. She had to be gentle, taking care not to rub too roughly the many times healed and opened wounds. The dry blood came away easily. Reverentially, she tried to touch Him only with the flannel. Whenever she failed and her fingers met His flesh, she felt a little start of joy deep inside. When she reached His face, His eyes were open. When she dabbed near them, He didn't blink. Beloved was beautiful.

The first of her ministrations complete, she stood. There was a damp patch on her dress, clinging to her stomach where the fabric was wet. She looked the Lord God in the face she had known for ten years, mainly in secret. The face He had worn the first time they had met. He had changed His name and was not bothering with the beard and long hair now, but He was otherwise eternally the same. She undid the drawstrings at her neck and waist, and loosened her dress. The wet patch peeled from her skin. She pulled the garment over her head. Her hair was caught, and swept upwards over her face as the dress turned inside out. Then it fell back into place, lying lightly over her shoulders. She felt strength in her body, aware that she was becoming a temple, a vessel for the Love of the Lord. Naked, she knelt on the floor by Him, and waited for the coming of His touch.

Five

THERE WERE huge, tentlike canvas sheets tethered over the three main outdoor stages to protect the sturdy iron and wood structures from the elements. Bleached almost white, they'd been bone dry since early spring. To Lytton they looked like knocked-over chalk monoliths. Surrounded by circular arrangements of lesser lumps, also part of the permanent skeleton of the festival, the stages were the ruins of a pre-Christian temple. In a sense, these were the post-Christian altars, upon which the high priests of rock would perform their rituals, sacrifices and fed-back blasphemies. He didn't even like that sort of music, but had long since given up wondering how simple surveillance had sprouted into the guardianship of a houseful of incomprehensible fanatics and the organization of a pop festival.

He had put in ten years on this posting. Started as a combination of sorry-we-fucked-you-over sinecure and second chance, it now threatened to become a life. His last assignment had ended through a press exposé allowed by his superiors as a trade for the paper not running an extremely damaging titbit about snake activities during the Wilson government. They had to sustain some acceptable damage, and he was elected. The hell of it was he had been getting interested in his journalism, just as he was now interested in the business of the festival. The same paper that stripped his snakeskin had commissioned an in-depth piece from him about the Québecois liberation movement. It wouldn't have been so bad if he'd been a snake in Hungary or an emergent African nation or somewhere neutral like Norway. It was just that Britain was not supposed to have an intelligence presence in Canada.

For him, the chief pleasure of the Alder festival was the opportunity to deal with people not from the Agapemone. The musicians and their complex entourages might not be the most sane and dependable individuals he had ever met, but compared to Jago's crew they were refreshingly normal. Despite some of the daffier statements they made to the *New Musical Express*, none of them really believed they were on a mission from God.

Lytton had been found at Cambridge, and delicately offered a career opportunity in a vague department of the Foreign Office. When he accepted, the snakes wove a skin for him. Articles were carefully planted in the right intellectual and student publications, and he'd had to take a crash course in genuine journalism, including two months on a provincial paper, in order to be able to write the pieces printed under his name. The secret of a snakeskin was that it had to fit comfortably, as if it, not the thing underneath, were the real person. A generous subsidy, routed through several banks, allowed him to set up as a freelance in Montreal. Then, all he had to do was keep an eye on things and make his monthly reports to a man in the local office. It was mostly harmless. He didn't know what was done with it, but he assumed his Québec Libre findings were fed back to the Canadians as part of a share-and-share-alike scheme, in return for tips about IRA activity in North America. He was fairly sure people high up in the Royal Canadian Mounted Police knew what he was and let him get on with it. The British Commonwealth was chummy like that.

Away from the house, in the fields with the stages, Lytton felt the claustrophobia he'd learned to live with evaporate. He was beyond range of Jago's camera obscura, so he knew the Lord God wasn't snaking on him. At least, not conventionally. Derek and his team of trustworthies should have recruited sufficient early arrivals to assemble a workforce strong enough to start tackling the bigger jobs. He wanted the stages uncovered and checked out this morning. With a few screws tightened and planks repainted, they'd be ready for the specialist crews with their skyscraping ranks of amplifiers. In previous years, bands had played with lasers, holograms and an assortment of unwieldy, spectacular and (sometimes) disastrously disfunctional stage effects. This year, the Heat, a reformed Seventies supergroup making a comeback near the top of the bill, wanted to have a full-size, completely articulated mechanical Godzilla airlifted in to add a bit more punch to their opening number, a reworking of their monster hit – ha, bloody ha, Lytton thought – 'Leaping Lizard'. He remembered hating the song when it'd been in the charts for what seemed like fifteen consecutive years.

The Montreal exposure had been embarrassing, and head office hadn't had the decency to warn him. The detective who came to his flat was accompanied by a pair of Mounties in full dress uniform. The red tunics couldn't help but alert the neighbours, and were obviously intended to rub it in. While he was in jail, awaiting charges or a negotiated release, there were protests of lynch-mob proportions outside. Francophones sang songs and waved placards. Anti-monarchists burned Union Jacks and effigies of the Queen. The Canadians got rid of him on a late-night flight, handcuffing him to the fold-down table for a bladder-abusing seven hours, and an insincere diplomatic row dragged on. He then spent years in a decommissioned safe house in Putney Bridge Road, waiting for a call from Garnett, an associate of Sir Kenneth Smart. His new snakeskin, the minister's man finally told him, would represent Lytton as a burned-out, cynical former intelligence officer with unfulfilled spiritual yearnings. It was a tighter fit than ever, although his subsequent ten years with the spooks had convinced him that whatever Jago was, he was far more of the flesh than the Spirit.

Derek was waiting at the gate that fed into the main field. He was twitchy and, as always when separated from Wendy, seemed lost. He wore a Mr Spock T-shirt with a Vulcan platitude on it.

'James,' he gulped, 'we've got a problem.'

That was a catch phrase during the run-up to the festival. Lytton was getting tired of it.

He strode across the field, Derek stumbling to keep step beside him. There was a ragged crowd of kids in front of the main stage, milling about aimlessly as if waiting for the acts who would not be tuning up for days. Or maybe this was what a Mongol horde looked like the minute after Kublai Khan decreed the immediate erection of a stately pleasure dome. Gary Chilcot was doing samurai sword excercises with a crowbar, providing swishing whistles to augment the sound effects. When he saw Lytton, he stopped and grinned like a clod.

'That's how people get hurt, Gary.'

The boy mumbled an insincere apology. Lytton gathered Gary had been showing off for the benefit of one of the new girls, the petite redhead who'd been in the pub last night when he had had to separate Danny Keough and Terry Gilpin. Well, no real harm in that. It might even do Gary good to be thumped by an irate boyfriend at some formative point in his romantic

career. It could save him grief later on. Several of the kids –
some older than kids, actually – who'd been with the girl last
night were also there: a junior macho man with a red cockatoo
cut, a posy prat in a bright-blue jump suit and a panama hat, a
glum girl with several sets of cutaway clothes overlapping enough
for decency, and some Sixties hold-outs. Most of his locals were
there too, nothing better to do thanks to school holidays or rural
unemployment. The Gilpin brothers were missing. He could well
do without Terry, and would have ordered him off the site if he had
turned up, but he'd like to have Teddy around. Partly because he
was a good lad, partly because it would mean he wasn't off being
dragged into trouble by his dead-loss brother. Some kids have
it stacked against them from the start and Teddy, following in
Terry's dreadful wake, had a lot to overcome.

'James,' said Derek, tugging his sports-jacket sleeve, 'look at
this.'

Someone had attacked the main stage with a knife. The canvas
would be easier to get off this year because it was in pieces. Several
patches had been slashed into tatters, and all the guy ropes had been
hacked through. A stretch of matte-black hardboard fronting had
been exposed and brutalized. There were brown asterisk cracks
where it had been kicked with heavy boots, and a foot-high FUCK
scratched into the paintwork.

'It must be one of the few words he can spell properly,' said
Lytton.

'Who?' asked Derek.

'Bloody Terry Gilpin, of course. He might just as well have
scrawled his signature at the bottom while he was at it.'

'What should we do?'

'Fix it, of course. We were going to have to replace a couple of
these hardboards anyway. Lucky for him there wasn't anything
more expensive lying about.'

'Lucky for us, you mean.'

Lytton snorted. 'No, *him*. At least, this way I'll let him live.'

Six

Paul was squatting by the pond, which was behind the kiln shed. It was green and unhealthy, evaporated down to a Second World War British bath level; nothing moved in its depths, and it was beginning to smell. Plants flopped listlessly in the murk. It was mid-morning and Hazel had gone for a walk, the first time she'd done that during potting hours. He guessed he wasn't the only one having trouble with self-set work assignments.

Their first week, she'd started at 9.00 sharp, barely took time off for coffee (11.00 a.m.), lunch (1.00 to 1.40 p.m., back to the wheel in time for *The Archers*), or tea (3.30 p.m.), and worked into the evening. After a waning of initial enthusiasm, and a few delicate complaints about how hungry he got waiting for her to be available for supper, she'd decided to stick to a knocking-off time of 6:00 p.m. That advanced to 5:00 and lunch expanded to an hour so she could take advantage of the sun. In retrospect, it sounded like creeping indolence, but actually she was diligent. Until now, she'd always kept to her preset rules, weighing each revision carefully before putting it on the statutes.

He couldn't work while Hazel was off in the woods. After an hour or so, he was getting concerned. This was the real country, not the Sussex Downs. She'd had to keep getting up in the night to check the kiln. The cycle took about thirteen hours. She had cut it off early this morning, but the bricks and the pots wouldn't be cool enough for her to unpack until late afternoon. It must be like opening a pyramid, to find treasures or grave robbers' leavings. Maybe she needed the break before she could face her handiwork. He had just come from the kiln shed. It was like an oven in there, and he could hear little tinkling and shifting noises from inside the kiln as the temperature came down.

The bell in the showroom rang and Paul straightened up, feeling the strain in his knees. He brushed a bush that overhung the pond, and noticed a strange fruit hanging from a grey branch. Looking closer, he saw it was a dead goldfish, bloated and still wet. He plucked it, feeling the suckerlike stem break, and dropped it into the brackish water. The fish sank, raising a cloud of mud as it touched bottom.

The bell jangled again. Paul looked around the shed, seeing the garden dark through his sunglasses. There was someone in the shop, and a girl by his desk, coming across the dead lawn towards him.

'Hi,' he said, walking to meet her. 'Can I help you?'

She had waist-length dark-brown hair. With the sun behind her and through his dark glasses, she had an eyeholed shadow for a face. Her eyes shone like those of an M. R. James ghost, liquid and unhealthy.

'It's Allison,' she said, accent instantly marking her as local. 'From next door.'

The way she said it sounded like the name of a tacky brand of chocolates, *nest d'or*.

Allison Conway. Mr Friendly's dark and usually silent daughter. She was often about, haunting the village like a junior spook. They had not spoken before. He guessed she was slightly retarded, or bright enough to pretend to be.

'Hi, Allison. What can we do for you?'

She half turned, brushing her hair out of her face. Sunlight fell on pale skin. She had adult lips, thick and sensual.

'Just looking, Paul. If that's okay?'

He felt uneasy at the use of his name, as if she'd stolen part of his soul. 'Sure,' he said, trying to sound normal. 'Do you get a discount?'

She smiled, pouting just a little. 'Never have before.'

Safe behind his shades, Paul looked at her. Allison was between seventeen and twenty, and thin. Not thin: lean, agile, a feral child. Her filthy jeans had burst, not trendily, at the knees. She wore sturdy boots that could be registered as offensive weapons, and a fringed, worn-ragged Shane jacket a size too big. Not exactly a Thomas Hardy heroine.

She was examining him too, not bothering to be subtle about it. Suddenly she looked away, up toward the orchard. 'Youm got hippies up the hill,' she said, 'they come last night.'

'It's not my hill.'

'Just thought you'm want to know.'

Behind Allison, Paul could make out someone in the pottery, moving between the tables. He was far enough back to be indistinct. It must be a boy, he guessed, wearing a shabby leather jacket.

'Sometimes hippies take things, chickens and that. Dad says they'm a menace.'

'We don't have any chickens. Just pots. And books.'

'Ah.' She smiled with a hint of malice. '*Books*.'

She picked up *The World Set Free* from a pile of volumes on the desk, and handled it strangely. Her wrist did not work properly as far as holding a book was concerned. Surely, she must be able to read. She made a face at the cover and put the Wells down again.

'Not much use in books, if you ask me,' she said.

'Well, if things get bad you can eat them.'

She grinned, her teeth not good. 'That's true enough.'

He couldn't tell if Allison was trying to flirt or pick a fight. Neither appealed. She took a strand of her hair and chewed it. It could have been Lolitaishly sexy, but her busy eyes made her seem the stereotype yokel strawsucker. She heaved her shoulders like Cagney, hitching her jacket open in front. Underneath, she wore only a black bra, the skin over her sternum dotted with blackheads. Madonna had a lot to answer for, he thought.

'Who's your friend?' he asked.

She turned to the pottery and, for a moment, he thought she was going to claim not to see anyone. It was an M. R. James day, he decided. He had a maggoty writhing under his shirt, a mix of goose flesh and sweat.

'That's Ben,' she said, after consideration. 'He's just come up.'

'Oh, for the festival.'

'Arr, that as well.'

He had the idea that Allison was teasing him. 'As well as what?'

'Other things,' she said with a secretive smirk.

There was no sexiness in Allison's pose now. If anything, there was menace. Paul wished her away, and started examining papers on his desk.

She got the message. 'Must be going now,' she said, trying to drop her accent and enunciate every syllable like Princess Di. '*So* delightful to have this little chat and all that, haw-haw. T T F N.'

She shrugged and walked away, rolling her hips, swinging her hair. He considered his quietly threatening typewriter. Glancing up, he saw Allison and Ben disappearing towards the road. He only got a glimpse of the boy's face, and he had wild hair and large goggles to cover most of it. But one quarter-look was enough to give a lasting impression. Whether through birth, accident or design, Ben's face was melted and set. That, he thought, was one ugly bastard.

Seven

T HE MASKELL farm had survived bovine spongiform encephal-opathy, 'mad cow disease', in 1990, through a savings lump that tided the business over the dip in the price of beef. Maskell could remember the Major, his father, battling foot-and-mouth in the 1960s, hard-facedly supervising the destruction of a fortune in cattle, his quirt dangling from his wrist. Even thirty years later, he couldn't hear wind-carried gunfire without remembering that mass execution. After defeating plagues, it hurt to see the farm crippled not by an agricultural disaster but by a conglomeration of nothings in particular.

Figures scrolled up on his computer as he tried to hedge his way around the economic crunch. The dead cows, six so far, had collapsed with differing symptoms. Malnutrition, festering bites, dehydration, heat prostration, mystery bugs. Mainly, the cattle just upped stumps to get out of the sun. Fancy, Sue-Clare's horse, was down with some weakening ailment, too. And Jethro, the Maskell dog, had taken to sleeping most of the time, hiding under a blanket in his basket. Jeremy blamed it on the Evil Dwarf.

And here he was, indoors, staring at a screen, struggling with the books. There was nothing he could do outside. The rump of his workforce were trying to limit damage, clearing the way for the Agapemone people to move in over the next few days. After that, he might as well take a holiday and wait it out. Eventually, it must rain. Then, maybe, he could start all over, scratching the land.

He had all electric fans on, but they were not helping. His face was hot and damp, his shirt stuck to his back. He had drunk an entire bottle of Perrier water and not needed to use the toilet.

The summer was a write-off. New diseases kept cropping up. Whole herds were being slaughtered in neighbouring counties. The price of British beef was at an all-time low, worse than in 1990. Because a few kids in Northampton had developed a new allergy, British milk was suspect, too. People up and down the country were nervous about eating anything with 'Produce of Britain' printed on it. The minister of agriculture tried to show his confidence in British foods by demonstrating he could feed his extended family on an all-British menu for a traditional Sunday dinner. The farming industry reeled when the Sunday newspapers ran pictures of the minister's twelve-year-old daughter sicking up British milk pudding down her best photo-opportunity frock.

His only hope for survival was the Agapemone, no matter what Danny Keough might say. In previous years, he'd remained neutral on the festival, fence-sitting while Danny got up his petitions and the outsiders rushed in. Sue-Clare and some of her New Age friends had dragged him along last year, and it had not been so bad. Not all the music was godawful shite. And Douggie Calver, the cider king, swore by the profits he could reap over the week. Before throwing in with the festival, Maskell had a long talk with Douggie. He'd been astonished, and a little appalled, to realize how much money floated around in ragged jeans pockets. Some of it might as well come his way, even if it meant Danny never spoke to him again. That wasn't much of a loss. The old soldier was getting ever more cranky, and was bound to burst a blood vessel soon.

In the corner of the office, a pyramid space that had once been a hayloft, Jeremy sat with a book, uncharacteristically quiet. Sue-Clare was off in Taunton with her crystal therapist. Since it was the long school holidays, Maskell was stuck with the kids. Hannah was no trouble at all. Stick her in front of the video with *Teenage Mutant Ninja Turtles 2* and she was content on her own. But Jeremy, who became bored with deadly ease, was working up to trouble. Now he was fine, but Maskell sensed harassment coming. His son had a concentration problem. Then again, he himself could hardly keep his mind on his home computer's columns of figures. In this weather, it was hard to think about one thing for any length of time.

At first, the heat had been pleasant. He had gone about with his shirt off, and Sue-Clare complimented him on his tan. Unlike some of his labourers, who had permanently bark-textured brown necks and fishbelly-white backs and chests, he did not burn. They ate long, picniclike meals in the open, and stayed outside late into the evenings. Sue-Clare enjoyed herself, browning her stomach and sipping cooled white wine or riding across the moors on Fancy, and patiently shushed his dark grumbles about the weather not being good for the farm. One day, everything had gone beyond ripe and started to rot. Since then, it had been Hell.

Maskell exited one file and entered another, checking running totals. The shortfall between expected and actual income was dangerous.

Jeremy sighed and put down *The Lion, the Witch and the Wardrobe*. Officially, he was a gifted child, but somehow that wound up being an affliction. He had a relationship problem, which meant other kids at his school did not like him. Two or three times a week, they formed a circle around him in the playground and jeered at him until he cried. Lisa Steyning, the angelic tyrant who owned the dinner break, was the ringleader. Maskell couldn't remember much of his own primary-school days, but was certain he had never been such a drip. If anything, he'd have been in the ring, linking arms with the others, chanting 'Jerm, Jerm, Jerm, Swallowing Sperm' at the cry-baby twerp.

Jeremy zigzagged slowly across the room, fiddling with things. Maskell knew he was about to need attention. He tried to stop himself getting angry before the boy had done anything. Jeremy was demanding more and more adult attention. Sue-Clare was dropping the phrase 'special school', but Maskell thought Jeremy's inability to make friends with kids his own age was not just a matter of differing levels of intelligence. In many ways, he seemed a lot *less* intelligent than the rest of them. He was so clever he had to do really stupid things to keep up. Like the time he smeared garlic on his windows to keep away the Evil Dwarf.

Jeremy was behind him, visible dimly as a reflection in the screen.

There was the concentration problem. The relationship problem. The night-time bladder-control problem. The coordination problem. The bad-dream problem. And the Evil Dwarf problem. The Evil Dwarf was Jeremy's bogeyman, a creeping malevolence who sucked out the minds of little boys, turning them into human sheep. It was hard to tackle the things that scared Jeremy. Controlling his reading and viewing didn't help, because Jeremy could take it into his head to be scared of almost anything. When they took the kids to see *Snow White*, Maskell had predicted trouble with the Wicked Queen but Jeremy had taken it into his head to be afraid of Dopey. Maskell could not remember now whether the Evil Dwarf had showed up before or after Dopey, but they were now the same monster. No wonder the other kids, including five-year-old Hannah, gave him a hard time. Anyone afraid of Dopey had a serious chicken streak.

When he was a boy, they'd had *really* scary monsters, like the Quatermass Experiment and the Trollenberg Terror. And he'd never shown his fear of them before his father. If he'd refused to go alone to bed in the dark, the Major would have given him a memorable quirting and banned him from the television.

Maskell was struggling anyway. Since the books had gone from paper to disc, things supposed to be simple had become complicated. He trawled around in the accounts, trying to find enough to meet the tax bill. He was required to pay for last year's profits while the farm was in its worst-ever slump, but he had been digging for two months into the set-aside tax money to keep up with the wage bills. Losing Budge and Gilpin helped – although their union rep had already left a curt message on his answering machine – but not much. He had no casual labour left to trim from the budget. Gilpin and Budge hadn't been fat, they'd been meat; and their loss left a bloody hole.

To top it off, his accountant of eighteen years had retired, and Maskell resented and mistrusted the ponytailed youth who inherited his business. He did not like the way he looked at Sue-Clare's chest and constantly flexed his fingers, and could not understand the manual that came with the software the sharp-faced creep had lent him.

'Dad,' said Jeremy in the whiny voice he always used when he was about to ask an unanswerable question.

Maskell entered the housekeeping account, hoping Sue-Clare had left something he could use to fill in a financial crack.

'Daaaad?'

'Yes, Jeremy?'

'Dad, what's scary for you?'

It was a favourite question. Since so many of the child's problems had to do with what scared him, he was fascinated by the subject. Hannah was scared of spiders, things Jeremy recognized as harmless animals. After all, why bother being afraid of nonpoisonous creepy-crawlies when you had an Evil Dwarf to worry about? Realizing scariness was inherent in people who were scared, not in things that were scary – just like the

varying taste in foods that made him love parsnips, which his
sister would rather go hungry than eat – he was interested in
what was scary for other people.

Maskell had been asked before, many times, and settled on
an answer. 'Jerm,' he said, 'the only thing that scares me is
stupidity.'

'Um,' said Jeremy, thinking. 'Um.'

Eight

S HE HAD LIVED in south London until she was ten, and in Hove
ever since. Used to streets and seafronts, this was the first time
she'd been away from buses every ten minutes, shops round the
corner, cinemas and parties and clubs within walking distance, and
being able just to go into the town centre and run into people she
knew. Here, apart from Paul, she was on her own. Her ideas of
the country had come from *The Archers* and television serials about
bodice-ripping in olden times. The reality was heat and insects, the
whiff of silage, dusty earth that got tracked everywhere. And the
quiet: you heard every car that passed, but there was no constant
background buzz of traffic. Even the birds were less raucous than
the seagulls which flocked on Brighton beach.

Hazel was surprised it was easy to find her way over the hill
back to the Pottery. The directions she'd been given were vague,
but the paths were clear. She'd expected to get lost in a jungle, but
this wild wood was open and sunny. Until now, she'd been too
busy to explore. Up here she could get an idea of where places in
the village were in relation to each other. This might be her only
chance in all her life to live in the country; she shouldn't waste it
all bent over a wheel or complaining about the lack of a Chinese
takeaway. From some of the hillside clearings, the views were
pretty. There was a bump on the horizon, sticking a finger into
the sky, Glastonbury Tor. Paul said it was one of the places King
Arthur was supposed to be buried. Nearer, she saw the Church
out on the moor, cows standing like toys in yellow fields. With
straight ditches and winding roads like lines, it was like looking
down on a map.

She'd given herself a turn or two last night, on her way out
to the kiln shed with her torch, imagining strange shapes in the
shadows of trees and the outbuildings. It was a different dark,
with no underglow from street lighting. Now, with the sun
high, that was a distant memory. It was cooler up here, with

shade from the trees and a slight wind. No wonder those kids camped up here. It was like being above the world.

It had done her good to get away for a morning and most of an afternoon. Paul was right, she'd been working too hard, knocking herself out. If she was tense, she messed up her pots. After only a few hours of wandering, the pains in her lower back faded. Backache was an occupational handicap for a potter, for ever bent over a wheel, humping heavy boards of work about. Was that really something she wanted to take on for life? Was she really good enough to make it worth the effort? Yesterday, last night, this morning, she hadn't thought so. It wasn't too late, she knew, to change; move into the teaching stream, even switch completely and take computer courses. Today, with the sun up, the bottles abandoned and a kiln waiting to be unpacked, she was beginning to feel good about it again. Her hands felt competent. She was even looking forward to unpacking the kiln this evening. It would be a discovery.

There weren't so many insects up here. She hadn't been bitten all day. She found herself a spot that overlooked the Pottery. She could see Paul. A few people (customers?) came and went. Paul saw to them. Someone had left a pair of old binoculars hanging on a dead bush. She tried them out, but all she saw through them was a fuzzy blur.

She'd been moody lately. Paul was scratching against her, getting sarky when she didn't need it, making half-apologetic demands. They shared the cooking equally, but she always ended up loading the dishwasher. And she did the ironing. Patch had wanted her to join a women's group this spring, but she had been busy, been sidetracked, with Paul. Maybe when they got back, she'd have time. Hazel wasn't sure Paul would last through the autumn. It wasn't that she didn't love him, it was just . . . She didn't know, just he could be so miserable at times.

He looked small now, working at his desk. His typewriter chattered like a tiny woodpecker. Every so often, he would stop tapping and rummage through his piles of books. There were more things than books, Hazel thought. More things to do. This was the first relationship she'd been in where she'd had to think beyond the next stay-over, the next day out. But that wasn't necessarily a sign *this* was the Big One. She didn't believe in life-long love affairs, anyway. When Paul had been away lecturing in Manchester last term, she'd missed him

fiercely, had read and reread ragged his letters. She hadn't wanted
to do much of anything, go out with Patch or her friends. She'd
even read some of Paul's books, to try to get close to him. But
she'd caught a bug of some kind and felt nauseous. Then her
period was late, and she'd known, with a terrible certainty, that
she was pregnant.

She waved to Paul. He didn't notice.

During the Week of the Baby, she'd thought through the life
they might be stuck in. Paul would want the child, would insist
that he could help her, and she'd give in. But he'd go forward
while she'd come to a halt. She'd take time off to have the baby,
and never get back to her courses. Maybe they'd get married.
Dad would give them both what for if they didn't. Then they'd
find they didn't have the money to get a mortgage on a house or
flat big enough for a family. And childbirth, she knew, would be
an agony. She loved Paul, yes, but did she love him enough to
fit into that kind of life? Did she love him enough to end up like
Mum, stuck with order-barking Dad?

There wasn't a gate proper, but there was a gap in the hedge
with the slatted top of a packing case wired into it. She undid
the wire and pushed the wooden square aside, then refastened it
behind her.

The day before Paul was back, she had started to bleed. For
the only time in her life, she was jubilant to get her period. No
baby. However, it had still been a reprieve rather than a not-guilty
verdict. She'd seen the future, a future, and not liked it.

Paul saw her. She waved again. He stood, and waited for her
to come down. The slope was steep and the basket heavy, so
she had to be careful.

'Plums,' she said to him, tilting the basket to show off the fleshy
yellow fruit. 'It's a good year for plums.'

Paul looked nervy, a little annoyed. She would have missed
lunch. Paul was as keen on routine as her ex-Navy dad, and
always wanted things on time or not at all.

'Where've you been?' he asked, speaking evenly, ready for the
debriefing. 'You didn't say when you left.'

'It was just a walk.'

'What about your work?'

'I was up all night. And I'll be unpacking the kiln after teatime.
I deserve a morning off. I've more than made up the time. Have
a plum.'

She picked one out, and took a bite. Juice squirted through her fingers. She giggled, chewing the sweet meat, and put the basket on his desk. He took a plum too, and bit it. He spat out a mouthful on the ground. The half-plum in his hand was mostly brown.

'This is rotten.'

'There's always one. You should look before you eat.'

He tried to lick the taste off his teeth. She finished her plum, and dropped the stone into a used cup on his desk.

'Tea?' he asked.

'I've just had some, thanks.'

Hazel noticed the jam-jar wasp trap she had put on the low stone wall of the verandah earlier in the week was full. Yellow-black corpses clogged the inch of greasy water in the bottom. There was a nest nearby. The killing jar wasn't making much of a dent in the local insect population, but there still ought to be a queue at the doorway to Wasp Heaven. Paul had made a joke about insect angels sharing cloud space with California surfies, Bible-thumping bigots and US presidents, and suggested they should dedicate a special Hazel Chapelet wing. His jokes were all like that, long and complicated and hardly worth the effort.

'Tell me about your walk,' he said, obviously digging.

She wasn't stopped. 'Later, Paul. I want to wash. I'm all sticky.'

'Okay,' he said. '*I'll* make some tea. Do you want any lunch? I can nuke the rest of the spaghetti in the microwave.'

'I've eaten, thanks,' she said, walking towards the house, cutting short further questioning.

He followed her into the house, and took a detour into the kitchen while she went upstairs to the bathroom. She ran the cold tap on to a flannel and wiped her face. Then she did her arms and legs. Some of her bites were inflamed, but the stinging was going away. She must have developed immunity. She had a pee, and took a brush to her tangled hair. It was getting long. Back in Brighton, she might have it styled shorter, like Patch's, but in the meantime, she'd better wear a headband. It kept falling into her work while she was throwing. She changed her shorts and shirt for a fresh-smelling loose dress.

She went out to the verandah, feeling cleaner, and Paul brought a teapot and some mugs. The teapot was Mike Bleach's, but the mugs were hers. They'd been using them all week, but Paul hadn't noticed. She decided to have a cup of tea after all. Paul made it too weak as usual, but she didn't complain. He kissed her. He was good at that. He didn't kiss like anyone else she'd gone out with (the list was into double figures by now) and she was always surprised at the variety he brought to basic tongue-wrestling. They sat in basket chairs, shaded from the sun. She drank her tea.

'Well?' he said after a while.

'Well what?'

'Your walk. Where did you go?

She smiled and leaned back. 'A long way. Out over the moors, up through the woods. It's lovely up on the hill. You can see for ages. There are kids camped up there, a bit beyond our boundary, in a clearing.'

'I know. Someone told me. Were they the people who gave you lunch?'

'No. There was someone asleep in a van, but no one else about. They've got tents set up, and there was an ashy campfire place.'

'Silly buggers. They're warning about forest fires on the radio.' He couldn't hold out any longer. 'Where *did* you eat?'

'I went round to see Wendy and ask some more about the festival.'

'You went to the Agapemone?'

'It's a beautiful old house, Paul. Like something from an Agatha Christie book, and –'

'Hazel,' he said, 'you should be careful with those people. You know, they're not . . .'

He was reacting just as she'd known he would. She had a spark of anger. 'Come on, Paul, they're really nice.'

'It's not that.'

The whine was creeping into his voice, the I'm-cleverer-than-you-so-why-don't-you-listen? whine. On the verge of one of their almost-rows, Hazel didn't want to go further. But there was no avoiding it.

'What is it then, clever-clogs?'

'You know what these cults are like. The Moonies . . .'

'You think I've been brainwashed, then?'

'No, but . . . but you shouldn't get too involved. They're very clever at what they do. They've got all kinds of techniques. Some of their methods are sophisticated, very nasty.'

'I'm not about to join up or anything. I'm not religious. I hardly think they're going to slip me the Queen's shilling in a basket of plums.'

'I don't think they want to go to the bother of kidnapping you –'

'Thank you very much, I'm sure!'

'That's not what they want, Hazel. It's this festival.'

She was angry now. 'That's got nothing to do with the churchy stuff.'

'Hasn't it? Some people get very rich being the new Messiah. It's big business, like TV evangelists in America. God doesn't have anything to do with it. But the festival isn't just there to raise cash. It's supposed to make you forget what the Agapemone is really about. It's to make Jago respectable. And by associating yourself with it, you're associating yourself with him.'

As he was talking, she saw another wasp going headfirst to its doom in her trap. It landed on the tracing paper fixed to the jam jar with a rubber band, and poked its head at one of the holes she'd made with a pencil. The head went through, and the wings, and the whole body.

'So you think I shouldn't have a table at the festival.'

'You ought to be bloody careful.'

'It's not like you think, Paul. There aren't any hooded devil monks or slaves in chains. They're just people who live together in an old house. They're no different from your friends in the Montpelier squat.'

'Yeah, well, I never said Brian, Alex and Eugene were normal, Haze.' Inside the jar, the wasp had caught on and was buzzing furiously against the smeared glass. 'So, what was it like, then?' He couldn't help being curious, she noticed. 'Did you see Jago?'

'No. He stays in his room, apparently. He's very busy. I helped pick plums, and they let me keep a basket –'

'The rotten ones.'

'. . . to bring home. Wendy and Derek were there, and some others. Young people, mostly. And just ordinary. They didn't talk about religion all the time. They told jokes. Paul, they were *happy*. There's nothing wrong with that.'

'Yeah, well, happiness can't buy you money.'

'I'll bet you got that from a film.' A lot of things he said he did. 'There was a girl called Marie-Laure. She was a bit funny, looked at the ground all the time. And there's Mick, who used to be a rich poet.'

'Until he gave it all away to the rev, I suppose?'

'He didn't say, but he did say he was happier now, sharing with others. That doesn't sound sinister, does it?'

'Well . . . I suppose they all smiled a lot.'

'What's wrong with smiling?'

'You have to do it with your eyes as well as your lips. You have to mean it. You have to have the choice not to, or it doesn't count.'

'You're just being nasty because I'm interested.'

'Okay, Haze, you know what you're doing. But be careful. Never trust anyone who claims to be on speaking terms with God, especially if they've got collecting tins. I love you, you know that, and I'm not just saying this to whip up an argument. I hate pointless arguments, you know that too. Just be careful.'

She knew what he would say next, felt ground crumbling under her, and had to be ready to put up a defence. 'The money? You're not giving them anything from your sales at the festival?'

She looked down at her tea, reading her fortune in the dregs. 'No, I pay a flat fee for the table.'

'How much?'

'Twenty pounds a day.'

'That's a hundred pounds for the whole week!'

'There's a reduction.'

'Still . . .'

'It's reasonable, Paul. I might sell out.'

'Watch out. I don't want you taken advantage of.'

'By anyone else, you mean.'

'That's not fair.'

The wasp gave in and died. Hazel could chalk up another victim. She left her cup on the freezer and walked away from the verandah, back to the pottery. In the trap, nothing moved.

Nine

ALONE IN THE kitchen, Susan filled a kettle and set it on the cooker. She turned on the gas and pressed the ignition. The ring hissed, but no flame appeared. She tried again. Nothing. The device always was untrustworthy. Rather than root through drawers for matches, she lifted the kettle and held her right forefinger a few inches from the escaping gas. She *thought*, and a spark danced from her fingernail. The gas caught with a rush, and she pulled back her hand swiftly. Setting the kettle on the ring, she felt a tiny satisfaction. Using her Talent in small, useful ways made her feel harmless and empowered.

There was enough earth and stone between her and Jago to damp the interference. Susan knew she was only here, probably only *alive*, because Sir Kenneth Smart, the minister with responsibility, saw 'defence applications'. During the two minutes of the Gulf War, he had asked David to run a scenario whereby a Talent could be used invisibly to stop the heart of an unnamed subject whose physical profile happened to match exactly that of Saddam Hussein. David dithered until the crisis passed, his file presumably picking up a black asterisk. At the time, Alastair Garnett, the minister's liaison with IPSIT, was around the complex more often, assessing the project's ten-year performance. David, she knew, was worried almost as much by all this as he was by knowing Jago was still out there.

She had been introduced to Sir Kenneth at various functions, but the constantly updated file on her relayed to him through Garnett was watered down, making her seem little more than a human toy, a barometer that sometimes produced results. Finally, she'd been given this position almost as much as a way of keeping her out of Smart's clutches – David thought he wanted to slap a uniform on her and train her to dismantle missiles in midair – as of getting near Jago.

Inside IPSIT, Jago was a legend, file restricted to all but the Big Three. Susan heard rumours from the other Talents that Anthony Jago was gifted to such a degree that he couldn't even be classed as human. The man, she'd been given to understand, was something between a god and a monster. The snakes had Lytton with the Agapemone almost from the first, and pored over his reports. From Sir Kenneth's point of view, Jago was like the chemical weapons Britain had stockpiled. There was no point in making even tentative steps towards deploying him until he could be controlled; in the meantime he was watched but generally left alone.

It was David who decided Susan should be assigned to Jago. He turned her over to the snakes for a few months of training. They had taken her past, with its gaps and aimless drifts, and woven a close-fitting snakeskin, characterizing her as a restless neurotic, given to alternative religions. She was disturbed at how little they had to make up to make her convincing as a potential Sister of the Agapemone. Now, she often measured herself against Wendy Aitken or Jenny Steyning, asking herself how she was different from them, and how she was the same.

She found loose tea in a tin and snagged a teapot with a mentacle, pulling it down from a shelf she couldn't reach with her hands without using a stepladder.

In the early days, Jago made a few conversions that did not completely take. Most of those would-be disciples were institutionalized or dead, but one or two had been deprogrammed and were staggering towards normality. Susan took part in debriefings, and learned what to expect within the walls of the Agapemone. She wasn't shocked, although the Great Manifestation sounded like a service she wouldn't be keen on participating in. With due consideration, the snakes tailored her skin to characterize her as a joiner *and* a loner, hoping she could get into the community but remain isolated within it, free to report back, safe from the more obvious dangers.

Finally, she'd been allowed to examine the Jago file. David talked her through it. 'Born London, 1942. Not a very comfortable place and time. Both parents dead when he was an infant; raised by his grandmother, an elderly, superstitious woman. Schools, university, church activities, various unspectacular livings. A few odd little scandals. Likes the ladies, I suspect. A pretty standard ecclesiastical CV, I'm told.'

'Jesus Christ,' she'd blurted, finding the newspaper clippings.

'Quite,' said David. 'Twenty-eight people dead. A few "accidents", four murders, the rest suicide. The incidents took place between March and April 1975, within an area of no more than a few square miles.'

'Inner-city decay?' she ventured.

'This was a prosperous suburb. They all went to his church. They were his parishioners. And they died. They weren't manic-depressive pensioners on the dole, they were middle-class, mostly middle-aged, mostly secure. The man who strangled his sister-in-law was an alderman and on the board of Leeds United. No history of mental problems or violence. He killed her because they were waiting for his wife to come home and she wanted to watch the gardening on BBC2 while he was in the middle of *Morecambe and Wise* on BBC1. They were all like that: one minute, Mr or Mrs Boring, the next Jack the Ripper, Molly the Maniac. Until we came across them, the deaths were down as a blip on the statistics. "Something in the water" was the local scuttlebutt.'

'You think it was projection?'

'Right, Susan. Consider the report from his parish council. It's obvious that from March through April 1975, he was going through a crisis of faith, I suppose you'd call it. The only way he could cope was to spread the load, dissipate some of his agony through the pulpit. The text of one of his sermons is in the file. It's pretty cracked. The earth breaking open to disgorge clouds of wasps. Another man might have reached for paracetamol, but he had options not open to another man. If you want some light reading, there's a sheaf of suicide notes in there. Mostly God-told-me-tos, but some are peculiarly elaborate. It's not just Goodbye, cruel world. There's visionary stuff. It compares interestingly with the sermons. We've always known a Talent like this could come along.'

She'd been impressed, and suddenly understood why David went along with Garnett's D-notices and cover stories. Jago could bring bad publicity for the field. The last thing they needed were fearless vampire killers hunting out Talents.

'We first turned him up as we turned you up, random applications of Rhine tests to students. He was told he was a Talent, but that's not the interpretation he's chosen. He has followers. Disciples. It's well within his power to perform what might easily be classed as miracles. What do you think he thinks he is?'

The kettle whistled, and she poured boiling water into the teapot. She was shaking, remembering the cold seriousness David had radiated.

From somewhere, Garnett found Janet Speke, a fellow traveller with the Agapemone who was, after a traumatic childhood and a nightmare marriage, gradually jumping through the hoops that would turn her into Sister Janet. She was living in Achelzoy, attending services at the Agapemone, her petition for initiation obviously under consideration. Garnett arranged for her to be Janet's upstairs neighbour and Susan did the rest. It was guilt-makingly easy to get close to the woman, and, through her, to pick up a crash course in the beliefs of Anthony William Jago. She was introduced to Mick Barlowe, who acted like Jago's appointed representative on Earth, and attended some of Jago's services, feeling power welling as he spoke. She'd met other Talents, but Jago was giant, a monster.

Janet was guaranteed a place at the Agapemone by virtue of her sincere belief in the Beloved Presence. Susan could only counterfeit so much, and Garnett thought it best she not appear too fanatical. To get even with her Sister, Susan had to have something else to bulk out her obviously shadowy faith. That was simple. Susan slipped to Janet, who most certainly revealed to Mick, that she'd recently realized a substantial sum through the sale of her dead parents' house. The Agapemone practised sharing of communal property, so her savings were even more welcome than she was.

Sister Janet was selected by Beloved for a Great Manifestation, and Susan wondered gratefully why the honour had passed her by. How far could Beloved see through her? He must be able to read her to some extent, although he always gave the impression he was so close to Heaven that earthly matters were miles beneath him. Jago never took an interest in Susan, not in the way he took an interest in some of the other Sisters. Of course she was relieved, but at some level his inattention peeved her. What did the others have that she did not? She liked to believe the factor the Sister-Loves shared was a lack, not a quality. Jago towered above his devotees, but of all the Brethren only Susan could measure herself against him. He saw her, if at all, as furniture or an ornament, never speaking directly to her. Her dilettante researches into the house's store of books and papers were tolerated so blithely that Susan assumed word must have come down from on high to let her get on with it. Despite everything, she knew Jago was watching her.

She poured her tea and added milk. She raised the steaming cup cautiously to her mouth. When she sucked in a mouthful, it was cold as ice. The heat had drained away somewhere.

Ten

IT WAS THE hour of the wolf, between sunset and night, dark enough indoors to have one or two lights on. They had not exchanged more than a few words since the afternoon, but Paul felt he should be here for the unpacking. It was important to Hazel, and he needed to understand her work better, to get back close to her. She didn't complain about his being there, but she wasn't welcoming either. The bricks were pleasantly warm to the touch, but there might still be dangerously hot spots. Hazel slipped on the large gauntlets. She made and unmade floppy fists and scrabbled at the top of the kiln, pulling the key brick out of the arch. She worked quickly and precisely, like a film of someone building a wall run backwards, pulling out the outer bricks and stacking them. Rapidly, she stripped away the bright orange outer layer, baring the core of white firebricks.

The clay-stained portable radio was tuned in to a Top Twenty show. She hummed along with bland, repetitive pop. She was trying to be matter-of-fact, but he could read her well enough to know she was wound tight. There was tension between them from the afternoon argument and other as yet unspoken grievances, but mainly she was worried about this kiln. Paul had the idea this was crucial for her, the one that decided whether she stuck with pottery and made something of it, or wrote it off as a passing enthusiasm and decided to do something else. He hoped the kiln would turn out well, not just for Hazel but for himself. If she were jogged out of her mood, he might have a chance of smoothing over the fracture between them.

Both were sweating. The double doors were wide open and the comparative cool of the evening had come, but the kiln shed was heavy with retained heat. He felt a headache coming. In her tatty jeans and clay-caked T-shirt, Hazel looked very gamine. She crouched on the box in front of the kiln door, easing out the first of the firebricks. As she went up on her toes, callused

heels rose from flip-flops. Paul squashed the impulse to hug her
from behind. The news was on now, and she wasn't humming.
Somerset was mentioned: the hippie convoy had been moved on
again. Bricks piled up. The interior of the kiln was in shadow.

'The torch,' she said.

He handed her the rubber-coated torch, and she shone a
beam into the cavity. Pots glistened and, as he looked over
her shoulder, he saw unusual colours. Blues and greens. Not,
thank God, browns.

'It looks okay,' he said, wishing it so.

She made a noncommittal noise, and passed back the torch.

'Let me help.'

'All right,' she said, 'but be careful to stack them in order.
They're numbered and lettered, see.'

He took hot bricks from her with bare hands and put them on
the pile. She had laid out boards earlier to receive pots as they
came out of the kiln.

Finally, the kiln was open. Hazel slid back off the box and stood
away, staring in with an unreadable expression. Paul looked, too.
A wave of invisible heat struck his face. It looked as good as
anything she had ever done, and better than most of her output.
He reached for a cup near the front, but she took his hand before
he could touch it.

'Fingers,' she said. 'Be careful. It's hot.'

With a gauntlet, she pulled the pot out and held it up. An
intricate design ringed the rim, vaguely Greek, white on blue.

'It's a success, isn't it?'

She smiled tightly. 'Yes, better than expected.'

She was puzzled, though. She put the cup on the nearest board,
and started taking out other pots.

Paul knew she was better at throwing than glazing, that she
always had problems with her gloss firings. Her usual complaint
was that everything she did came out brown, no matter what it
was when it went in. Now, as he saw from the cups, plates, jugs,
bottles and bowls on the boards, she'd got it right. Her design
was more imaginative, more richly coloured. It was as if she had
finally discovered how to do the trick.

Boards filled up, but Hazel stopped before the kiln was even
half empty. She took off her gauntlets and ran her fingertips
over a large plate, tracing the image of a girl's face drawn there
with a few simple strokes. Then she left the kiln shed, and was

silhouetted in the doorway. Paul realized she was crying. He went to her and embraced her. She was hot and squirmed ineffectually in his arms.

'What's the matter, darling? These are terrific.'

Hazel freed herself and turned. A tear cut through the dust on one cheek. She was having trouble speaking, but finally she managed. 'I didn't do anything different. This just happened . . . on its own. I don't know if I can do it again.'

'Of course you can, Haze. Don't underestimate yourself.'

'No, it's not . . . some of those designs I don't recognize. The face in the plate. I don't know where it came from. I don't think I put it there.'

'You're being silly.' He kissed her cheek. 'You're just going to have to put up with being talented. Come on, I'll help you finish.'

She followed him back into the heat, and together they emptied the templelike kiln of its treasures. Outside, it started to get dark.

Eleven

H<small>E WAS SUPPOSED</small> to call his mummy and daddy Sue-Clare and Maurice, but kept forgetting. Everyone told him he wasn't a baby any more, then jumped on him when he tried to be grown up. Jeremy knew that wasn't fair, but didn't complain. His sister sometimes moaned that things weren't fair, but it never got her anywhere. Earlier, when Daddy quirted her for ruining a tablecloth by poking her coloured pencils through it, she'd said it was not fair. But she had still got a quirt. It was a smack, really – not even a hard one – but Daddy called it a quirt.

That was forgotten now, and Hannah was on the sofa with Mummy and Daddy, watching the video. He was in the chair by Jethro's basket, attention split between the screen and the sleeping dog. He was worried about Jethro. He wasn't awake much these days, and when he was he whined and drooled thin spit. Hannah told him, spitefully, the Evil Dwarf had given Jethro AIDS, knowing, even though she didn't believe in Dopey herself, it would upset him.

Hannah clapped as James Bond's boat turned into a hang-glider and saved him from a waterfall. There was a tall man with steel teeth in the video. Jeremy knew the man was in with the Evil Dwarf. They had the same rotten-egg eyes. When he grinned, which he did often, his steel teeth shone, gnashing like rows of bullets.

When the video was over, Mummy told the children to go up to bed. They'd been downstairs in their pyjamas, watching the video as a treat. Their teeth were brushed.

'Come on now,' Mummy said again, 'off to bed.'

Jeremy looked at his parents. Daddy was practically asleep himself, slumped eyes shut, shirt open to show his brown chest.

Hannah looked at him, smiled nastily, and got up.

'Good-night, Sue-Clare; good-night, Maurice,' she said, exaggerating like an angel, and scampered off towards the door, passing into the dark corridor, up the dark stairs, across the dark landing, and into her dark room. He heard the click of her light-cord and the thud of her shutting door, then imagined her mean giggle.

Two and a half years younger, she was proud of her courage. The dark didn't matter to her. She didn't understand about the Evil Dwarf. Hannah was stupid and didn't understand much. She was making a show of going to bed to get back in with Mummy and Daddy, to prove she was forgiven her pencil rampage. One of the kids always had to be out, and it was usually Jeremy. Hannah was only out when she did something like making holes or setting fires. And often the blame could be passed on to her best friend, Lisa, who was usually the one to propose the actual mischief. Lisa was mean enough to be the Evil Dwarf's girlfriend. After her quirt, Hannah was always given a cuddle and brought back in again. Jeremy was out most of the time, without it actually being his fault.

'What are you waiting for, Jeremy?'

Mummy's smile had gone hard, like a woman advertising toothpaste. She was pretending she didn't know what the problem was. Grown-ups said they didn't pretend like children, but they did. All the time.

'Come up with me,' he said, experimentally. 'It's dark.'

The corridor wasn't the problem, the stairs weren't the problem, and the landing wasn't the problem. He could reach the light switches easily, and banish the darkness. He could know the Evil Dwarf wasn't there. Wherever was lit up, Dopey couldn't go. Jeremy thought that if he caught the Evil Dwarf with a beam of light, then he'd shrivel up and melt to a pile of sizzling goo.

'The dark,' Jeremy said.

But in the dark, the drooling idiot could come for him, tongue extended to puncture his head and scoop his brains, to make him a mindless moron.

'Jeremy,' his mummy said, V-lines between her eyebrows, 'you know there's nothing.'

Daddy was sitting up straight now, paying attention.

'Off you go, Jeremy,' he said, pretending to be cheerful. 'Suki and I need to be alone. We've grown-up things to do.'

'It's not actually dark yet,' Mummy said, 'just dusk.'

Jeremy looked at his parents, tears creeping behind his eyes. Daddy put a hand on Mummy's shoulder, and his fingers dug

in, kneading around her neck. She angled her head like a cat's
and rubbed his hand with her cheek.

It was his room that was the problem. It was a funny shape,
and in the oldest part of the farmhouse. Built before the electric
light was put in properly, that part of the house didn't have light
switches by the doors, where they should be. There was a lamp
by his bed, for reading. But he'd never cross the room in the dark
and find the switch by fumbling. Not before the Evil Dwarf's
tongue displaced one of his eyes and bored into his brain. There
was a light-cord, also by his bed, and he'd have to try for that.
If he couldn't get Mummy or Daddy to come with him and go
into the room to turn on the light, then he'd have to run across
the room, zigzagging to avoid Dopey, and make a grasp for the
cord. He'd done it before, but he didn't want to try again. This
time, his fingers might miss, and the Evil Dwarf would have him,
tongue snaking into his mind.

'Mummy, can you come with me?' Jeremy said, hating his
whiny voice. He was determined not to cry. 'Mummy?'

He wasn't simply scared. He was sensible. His teachers told
him it wasn't stupid to be scared of dangerous things. Everyone
should be scared of big lorries travelling too fast, or electric cables
that could turn you to a skeleton. Being frightened of those things
wasn't being scared, it was being sensible. And the Evil Dwarf
was as actual and dangerous as a two-ton truck or a megavolt
current.

He *knew*.

'Jeremy, you know what we've said. You've got to learn to
do it on your own.'

'Oh, Muuum,' he said, tears beginning.

Mummy would give in first. If she were on her own, she
always gave in. The only times he lost this game were when
Daddy was with Mummy, and in a grim mood.

Like tonight.

'Please . . .'

Mummy bit her lip and chewed, slipping a glance at Daddy.
He sat stone-faced, not giving anything away, hand still on
Mummy's shoulder.

He'd tried leaving his lamp on all day, so the light would be
waiting for him when it got dark outside. But it was always
turned off by someone. Daddy warned him about wasting
electricity, and Hannah liked to tease him, but Jeremy suspected

the Evil Dwarf was behind it more often than not. It was an Evil Dwarf sort of thing to do.

Mummy sighed and looked annoyed. 'Maurice,' she said, pleading a little.

'No,' Daddy said, 'he has to learn.'

Daddy looked at him.

'Jerm,' he said, the name like a stab, 'up to bed. Now. No nonsense.'

'But Daddy, Dopey . . .'

Daddy clapped his hands and nodded towards the sitting-room door. 'Jerm, you're close to a quirt.'

Jeremy didn't want to be made stupid, like a sheep or a vegetable. He knew it was only being clever that made him what he was. If he were stupid, if the Evil Dwarf ate his brains, he wouldn't be himself. He'd be dead, like the cows. Worse, he'd be pretending to be alive, like Jethro, but nothing like his old, actual self. Daddy ought to be able to understand. He admitted the thing that scared him was stupidity. Dopey was stupidity, infected with it like the measles, mindlessly bent on spreading the plague wherever he went, wherever his tongue probed.

Jeremy's chin wobbled, tears dripping from his eyes. 'Muuum,' he said, 'please . . .'

'I'll come,' said Mummy, giving in. Daddy was quiet.

Mummy turned on the lights in the corridor, on the stairs and on the landing.

'See,' she said, 'nothing.'

She opened Jeremy's door, dipping her hand into the darkness. Daddy was at the bottom of the stairs, disapproving. Mummy disappeared into the dark. She was safe, Jeremy hoped. The Evil Dwarf was only after him. The moment extended, and Jeremy felt himself building up to a panic. Inside, he was trembling. He imagined the Evil Dwarf pinning Mummy down on his child-sized bed, gripping her with his bony knees, quieting her cries by filling her throat with his bulging rope of tongue, so he could puncture the roof of her mouth, thrusting into her brain from below.

There was a click, and the light came on. Jeremy, quiet, crept into the room. It was undisturbed. His posters and models were where they should be. His Narnia books were on the shelf in proper order, *The Magician's Nephew* first, *The Last Battle* last.

Mummy was all right. She drew his curtains, shutting out a faint red somewhere in the night.

'Happy?' Mummy said, still annoyed.

Jeremy nodded.

'Get into bed, nuisance,' she said, smiling a little.

Jeremy leaped under the covers and pulled them tight up around him. The covers were protection. Even if it was dark, the Evil Dwarf couldn't get through the covers.

Mummy sat on the bed, and Daddy loomed in the doorway.

'It was only a film, you know,' she said.

'The man with steel teeth?'

'An actor. He takes out his teeth and goes home. He's not actual.'

Jeremy nodded, agreeing. He knew better, but agreed.

'Mummy,' he said, 'can I have the landing light on?'

A thin line of light under his bedroom door was more protection.

'You know you won't be able to sleep.'

'I will.'

Mummy looked at Daddy, and Daddy shrugged. He was past complaining.

'All right, but it's the last time . . .'

Safety!

'Good-night, Sue-Clare; good-night, Maurice,' he said, trying very hard.

His parents left, shutting the door behind them. He heard them going downstairs. The landing light was still on.

Jeremy reached out for the light-cord. This was the trickiest part. He had to wrap the covers around his arm, so nothing would be left uncovered in the dark the moment the light went off, and keep his head under the blankets, eyes tight shut. He couldn't see the light under the door but knew it was there. That made a difference. He pulled the cord and whipped his hand in, too fast for the Evil Dwarf.

Curled up into a tight ball under the covers, he waited. Nothing happened, so he relaxed, stretched out, and slept.

Twelve

PAUL CHANGED into his robe and slippers. He had let her have the bathroom first and, by the time he was ready to come downstairs, Hazel had laid out supper in the sitting room. Biscuits, cheese, salad, white wine and newly washed fruit. Some of the plums from the Agapemone were fine. She had put music on, apparently at random since it was something he liked, Louis Armstrong. 'What did I do to be so,' Satchmo sang, 'black and blue?'

Hazel wasn't quite out of her afternoon mood yet, but was changing. At least she was talking, mainly about the kiln. She was getting over her puzzlement, starting to be pleased. Paul was too relaxed to pay complete attention to her when she got technical, but was warmed by the recurrence of her old enthusiasm.

The large plate with the girl's face, still warm, was on the coffee table. Hazel was especially pleased with it, and now thought she could remember tracing the design in hot wax during the glazing session. It had a simplicity which reminded him of a Saul Bass poster. The girl's lips were a cupid's-bow smile, but the one exposed eye – the other was covered by a wing of hair – seemed pregnant with a soon-to-be-shed tear. The face didn't look like anyone they knew.

'I think I'll keep her,' Hazel said, 'as a showpiece. I might try to slip her into my coursework next year.'

She couldn't stop running her fingers over the design. Nine lines, two dots. She wasn't usually so pleasingly simple. Most of her patterned pots, he thought, were scruffy because they were too cluttered.

'It's the best thing you've ever done.'

'Thank you,' she said, raising her wine, 'I think so too.'

'And the rest of the kiln is good, too, isn't it?'

'Yes. Almost all of it. Some of the saucers are speckled. They'll be seconds.'

'I love you.'

'Mmm.' That was an agreement, he gathered, not a reciprocation. Still, she bent sideways on the sofa to kiss him, brushing her lips to his.

He wore his bathrobe and slippers; she had on a thin shift that hiked up when she sat down. He put his hand on her knee and responded to the kiss, gently poking with his tongue. He stroked her side, smoothing cotton over her ribs. Her hand came up and cupped his chin, prolonging the kiss. He fumbled with her buttons and held her breast, thumb teasing a nipple. She took his wrist between thumb and forefinger, and unstuck his hand from her body. The kiss broke.

'Let's go upstairs,' one of them said.

'Okay.'

They left the supper things and the girl plate in the sitting room, and clung to each other on the stairs. His robe had fallen open, cord dragging behind him like a mummy's loose bandage. They paused halfway up the stairs to lean on the banisters and kiss again. He felt warmth as his erection started. The sooner they got to the double bed, the better. Hazel sucked hungrily at his tongue, playfully biting. Then she drew away and went up ahead of him, tugging his hand. Downstairs, Louis was playing 'All of Me'.

On the landing, Hazel paused to pull her shift over her head and drop it on the rush matting. Naked in the dusk, in front of a window that afforded a view of the orchard, she was almost nymphlike. Her still-damp hair shone faintly with the last traces of red in the dark-grey sky. Goose-pimpled bikini marks were distinct against her tan.

He cuddled her and kissed her neck, his hands stroking the small of her back and working down. Then, he looked out of the window as he opened his mouth to nibble her ear, and had a premonition his life was about to go to hell. A black cloud mushroomed over the horizon, hanging in the air like a Montgolfier balloon.

'Shit,' he said, pushing Hazel away.

'What?' She was startled, her eyes alive, suddenly shivering. She hugged her shoulders, crossing her arms over her breasts.

'Look.'

She turned, and said in a whisper, 'Fire.'

'Yeah,' he said. 'Those kids and their camp. The arseholes.'

Another uprush of dark smoke joined the first, making an asymmetrical blot above the treeline.

'I'll go,' he said, 'you call the fire brigade.'

Still naked, Hazel dashed downstairs to the telephone. Paul stepped into the bedroom to pull on a pair of trousers. He heard her dialling the emergency number. She was talking with the operator as he shot through the back door. The lights of the house receded behind him as he jogged up through the garden towards the orchard. There were shadows all around.

He had never been to the top of the Bleach property. He'd meant to, but been busy. The hill was steeper than it looked. His lower legs hurt before he was even halfway up, and he had to slow down because he could not see far enough in front of him to keep out of potentially ankle-twisting depressions and thickets.

Among the trees it was darker than in the open garden. It was night here already. He couldn't see flames ahead, but the tangy smell of wood smoke was all around. It had turned cold, and he had trouble drawing breath. There might be droplets of ice in his lungs.

He wasn't at all aroused any more.

The local fire brigade had better be equipped for immediate action. Dead bushes and fallen twigs snapped under his feet like ancient bones. Alder was in the middle of twenty-five square miles of tinder. This could be the summer's big forest fire.

He weaved in and out of the trees. Where was the fire? He'd thought it was fairly near, even on the property, but perhaps he'd misjudged distance. Suddenly he hit a pocket of warmth. Ashes crunched under his feet. He stumbled, and landed heavily on his hand and one knee. He pushed himself upright, his hand black and stinging. He wiped it on his robe.

He was near the edge of the orchard. Beyond the top fence, the woods were denser. If the fire had started among those close-packed trees, it would have caught. As it was, it appeared to be a false alarm. This wasn't where the kids were camped out. He had no idea what could have caused the short-lived blaze.

A thick swirl of bitter smoke came at him from above, like a ghostly cloak. He inhaled a lungful and started choking. Surprisingly close, there was an answering cough. A mechanical rasp.

It was not a fire engine.

There was something large in the woods. Paul called out a hello. Something buzzed and screeched, like a chainsaw on rusty metal. He couldn't see anything. He stood still.

None of this was right.

Then there was light. Lots of it, and concentrated. A searchlight beam flashed from treetop height, searing the ground. Bursts of orange flame rose from the earth. Something shone in the woods. Paul was blinking, dazzled by the sunburst, eyes streaming from thick smoke.

Whatever it was was just beyond the top fence. Another blast lit a patch of dry vegetation behind him and swept across the orchard as if following a thick gunpowder trail. A pile of chopped logs, supposedly too green to burn, exploded. Burning sap squirted. He brushed chips of fire from his hair.

He was racked with coughing, and almost blind. He wriggled out of his robe and started flogging the nearest patch of burning grass with it. It was easy to put the grass out, because there was so little to burn. None of the trees had gone up yet, but he knew he couldn't fight the fire on his own. His robe was smouldering. He backed out of the fire zone, skipping over a blackened log, and retreated enough to be able to see the tops of the trees. Up there, something was shining.

A dinosaurian form reared out from the trees with an inhuman screech. A metal carapace bobbed slightly, reflected fires dancing in its coppery-red surfaces. Paul saw three powerful steel thighs and a cobra neck swivelling in search of him, its deadly eye winking. Unmistakably, it was a Martian war machine.

Thirteen

L YTTON HAD FALLEN asleep over a crossword. He woke up, head ringing, in darkness. He'd stretched out on the couch in the small front room of the Gate House before eight. By his digital watch, it was now past ten. He reached for the light switch. The ringing, he realized, was not in his head. He picked up the phone.

'James,' said a female voice. 'It's Susan.'

He was completely alert. The girl from IPSIT was not supposed to associate with him. This must be urgent.

'There's a fire up on the hill. We can see it from the main house.'

'Have you called –'

'Yes. They already knew. The couple at the Pottery phoned it in. The engines are on their way.'

He slipped his shoes on.

'They'll need help,' Susan said.

'Yes. Get Derek and whoever else is still capable of rational thought, and come over. I'll break out some equipment and get the Land-Rover going.'

There was quiet at the end of the line.

'Susan,' he asked, 'is this anything to do with our man?'

A pause, then quietly, 'I don't know. I think so. This could be the start of It.'

'It?'

'It.'

She hung up. He put the phone down. After a moment's deliberation, he fished the keys out of his jeans and had the desk drawer open. The Browning FN High Power was in a chamois bag, tied with a drawstring. He pulled the bulky automatic out, briefly tasted the oil and steel smell of it, and dropped it into his enlarged inside jacket pocket. The gun hung cold against his heart. He left the cottage. The

Land-Rover was parked by the gate. He saw red on the horizon.

In the hall, Susan put down the telephone and zipped up her anorak. She seemed to be the only person moving. A group stood watching her. She tried not to be angry. She'd have to conserve her strength.

'Who were you speaking to?' asked Mick.

'James. We're to go over.'

The chief disciple was displeased. He took his hands from the kangaroo pocket of his apostolic robe and spread them emptily. 'It's not our fire.'

'No. But with this drought, it soon could be.'

Mick's smile was smugness itself. Leaning in a shadow behind the disciple, Gerald Taine wasn't moving either. Arms loosely folded, the big man was relaxed, a karate champion between the ceremonial bow and the first vicious kick. Susan had never been able to read Taine well, but now he was completely shadowed. Janet was there too, not liking Mick but ready to be in with his faction.

Derek barged into the hall. 'Wendy's on her way down,' he said, 'and some of the others.' Several statues moved, joining Derek and Susan's side. Mick still beamed inanely.

'Come on, man,' she said. 'We're not on an island.'

'Have faith, Sister,' said Mick. 'Beloved will protect us.'

She stared into his vacant eyes, wondering how crazed or callous he really was. A little jolted by her eye contact, his long hair started to rise in a frizz as if he were next to a Van de Graaff generator. She snapped herself off before she started to enjoy it, and gave him a mean, knowing smile. Perhaps that would shake him up.

Mick made no motion towards joining the fire-fighting party. But he did nod to Taine, who pushed himself away from the wall, and left the hall. Taine was deferring to the chief disciple as if he were his master. So, Mick had been appointed, or appointed himself, Beloved's Saint Peter. She knew who that made her.

The volunteer fire-fighters were gone. Susan was left with Mick, Janet watching. She tapped a mentacle to a spot between his eyes and gave a slight push. He flinched. That would give him a headache.

Janet stepped back, cautiously alarmed.

Susan left through the main door. As she stepped down to the drive, she heard Mick shout after her.

'Some people are meant to burn!'

After talking to the fire chief in Somerton, Hazel went upstairs and was sick. She hunched naked over the toilet bowl for a minute, stomach spasming, wet hair in her face. When her insides calmed down and there was nothing left to come up, she went to the sink, gargled to get rid of the lumpy taste, scrubbed her teeth clean and washed her face. Then she got dressed in tomorrow's clothes, dug out some thick wool socks she hadn't needed so far this summer, and found the boots she'd brought for walking. Fifteen to twenty minutes, the fire chief had said. She looked out of the bathroom window; all of a sudden, it was too dark to see clearly up the hill. There were flames up there, but she had no idea how big they were. She couldn't make out Paul or anyone else. She went downstairs and filled the kettle; everyone, she knew, would want tea.

'Why d'you wrap a dead baby in clingfilm?' asked the laddish young man whose friends called him Toad.

Teddy didn't know why you wrapped a dead baby in clingfilm.

Toad exploded in a laugh that nearly prevented him from getting out his punch line. 'So it won't *burst*,' he gasped, 'when you *fuck* it!'

Teddy didn't think that was much of a funny – he'd had a stillborn sister, Samantha Rose – but Gary nearly pissed himself, doubling over and thumping the table, and Pam, the redhead everyone fancied, collapsed in giggles.

It was another rowdy night in the Valiant Soldier. Kev came back to the table with his round, and doled out the drinks. The London kids wanted to try Somerset's national drink, but didn't know enough to tell Taunton cider from Calver's scrumpy. Syreeta, the porky woman with the wispy folk singer, asked Teddy what they usually did for entertainment in these parts.

'Drink and telly, mostly,' he said. 'Not like London.'

Then everybody was shouting. Teddy thought it was another fight starting, but it was news of a fire. Everybody was getting up, bumping into tables and each other, spilling drinks, suggesting courses of action, and mainly pushing for the door.

'Ferg,' said the quiet girl, Jessica. 'Ferg's up at the camp.'

In the back of the Land-Rover, Wendy prayed loudly, calling on Beloved to preserve his Chosen. Nobody joined with her, so she shut up and concentrated on silent appeal. She reached into herself and tried to *will* the fire out, as she had been taught. She pictured trees burning like fireworks, then ran the film backwards. Flames shrank, black branches unshrivelled green. A miracle was possible, of that she was sure. Her friends sat with her, tense like paratroops before a drop. Derek was leaning into the cab, talking to James as he drove, sorting out ways of helping the fire brigade. Taine was quiet and purposeful, as always. Woodland equipment shifted and clattered on the floor of the vehicle. Opposite, Marie-Laure smiled serenely, cradling a spike hatchet as if it were the Baby Jesus. Wendy looked down at her lap, and resumed her prayer.

Allison led Ben around the back of the tiny cottage. There was a lot of rubbish around, so she had to be careful not to trip over. She could hear the telly blaring. It was a quiz show, and a pensioner had just won a fridge. She peeked in the front-room window, but saw only two figures lit up by the coloured picture. She slid away, staying close to the wall.

She'd got used to creeping about in the dark during her cat-killing craze. She still had her cheesewire around her ankle, the two cork handles fastened together with a rubber band. Just in case.

She negotiated an obstacle and rounded the corner. Ben was being less careful, but most people didn't notice him. They weren't likely to get caught but, if they were, it'd be too bad for whoever did the catching. Ben was here to settle scores, but he might stay and be her boyfriend. She'd never had a boyfriend before who wasn't scared of her.

Inside the house, a dog barked. Her hand went to the corks behind her ankle, but no one took any notice of the animal.

She'd spent the afternoon with Ben in one of Old Man Maskell's barns, where Ben's bike was hidden. They'd fucked like rabbits, nonstop and all over the place. She could still feel him inside, her jeans chafing where her thighs had been rubbed raw. She'd ripped half the skin off his back, and had grey rinds under her long fingernails. The taste of blood was in her mouth.

Now, they were out recruiting. Ben and Allison had many enemies, so they would take what friends they could get. Round the back of the house, she saw light in the first-floor room. Model aeroplanes poised in mid-dogfight in the window. She could hear metal music, good and loud. That would cover any noise they made. She hauled herself up a drainpipe, on to the sloping corrugated-iron roof of a tool shed. Ben stood in the open in the garde, face turned to a shaggy skull by shadows. Allison reached above her for the windowsill and got her fingers over it. With a soft grunt, she pulled herself up, belly muscles taut as catgut, toes jammed into crumbling dents in the brickwork.

The room was a tip, decorated with pin-ups of naked slags with their legs open and posters of fright-wigged rockers in black leather jockstraps. The boy was on one of the beds, a *Fiesta* magazine held up one-handed in front of his face, other hand working away like a milkmaid's in his open jeans. Allison whistled sharply. The *Fiesta* dropped, and the boy stared in mixed terror and embarrassment at the window.

'Terry,' she said, 'you'm with us.'

He had not fancied another evening in the pub, with Jessica sulking and the Toad pissing off the lynch mob. So he'd decided to stay at the camp with some gear and the cassette deck. He'd hoped Jessica would want to stay behind too so he could get some knobbing in, but she'd surprised him by voting for the pub. They did food, and she wanted a proper meal tonight. So he was left with the fire, which he had to keep going but under control, and the thick paperback of *Dune* Dad had given him last birthday. He'd tried the book several times, and not been able to get into it. He got a few pages further than usual, but still gave up.

By himself, he had barbecued sausages from the cool box. After last night's disaster, he was getting the hang of it. The hot dogs were the first real food he'd had since leaving London. It was quiet up on the hill. He was tired from his day working on the chain gang. They had all got into the festival free by volunteering to help out. Being Dolar's roadies hadn't been enough. He'd been putting up marquees all day, with a group of local lads who had daft accents but made fun of the way he talked. 'Yoo facking cant,' they all said, imitating his London vowels.

He'd decided he liked the country. When he was older, he'd like to get the flash together to buy a cottage somewhere round here. He'd grown some dope plants in his bedroom cupboard with lamps and fertilizer. If he rigged up a greenhouse, he could raise a cash crop and live off the profits. Maybe he could branch out and grow tomatoes and lettuce. He'd been thinking of becoming a vegetarian like his mum one day. With a couple of mates to kick in for their whack, he'd be able to set up a farm of his own. Maybe Jessica would be into moving down. It would do her good to ditch her parents.

Happy from the gear, he'd watched the sun go down. Now, he was searching the fire for new lights. It must be good gear; he'd never had this sensation before.

Then he heard noises. Somewhere nearby, trees were falling. Fuck, he thought, it's the enemy! There was an explosion of light, too, dazzling him. The nearest trees stood out like the bars of a cage. Something was roaring, and someone was shouting.

Shit, he thought.

At Beloved's side, Jenny stirred. She'd been lying with Him for a long time, and He had shared His dreams with her. In her heart, a new flame had been kindled. As she felt it burning, pleasure flooded through her.

Fourteen

THE ARM ROSE in a Fascist salute, heat ray angled down and swivelling like a security camera. Doomed insects spiralled above the carapace. Paul's eyes were drawn to the heat ray, to the LED-like red light where the barrel of a conventional gun would be. As he looked up, he guessed it was looking down at him.

The war machine stepped forwards, body balanced as if fixed in the air, legs advancing in a strange rotary motion. It moved deliberately, assuming a succession of precise postures. It was alien, with a Ray Harryhausen touch. Its image never blurred. The Martians have landed, and their special effects are out of date.

A tree cracked and fell. The war machine stepped out of the woods and stood over him. There was a hiss of expelled steam as it settled, three knee joints telescoping in and locking. When still, it was as dead as a pylon. Except for the red dot.

The light blinked, covered sideways like a snake's eye, and he instinctively threw himself forwards, hoping for shelter under the body of the machine. He crashed painfully into a solid metal leg, and fell. Behind him, there was a wall of instant, intense heat. He half turned, and was flattened by the blast. A flash blinded him, and he heard the crackling of new-started fires.

Flipping on to his back, he looked up and saw the black bulk moving away. He tried to stand, but something heavy and cool swiped him to the ground again. He twisted, and was dragged a few feet. Then he was free of the machine, his face pushed into the grass. A tree fell near him, and his upper body was covered with crumbling foliage. He fought the branches that pinned him down. There were fading sunbursts etched into his vision. He could see only light and dark. A Cinerama semicircle of fire burned in front. He rubbed his eyes, and stood unsteadily.

The worst migraine he had ever had expanded from the base of his brain, filling his head with pain. His chipped tooth exploded in an agony that picked out the nerves wired over his jaw and cheekbones. His head was an anatomical specimen, mapped with lines of pain.

He could see again, enough to keep away from the spreading flames. He had lost his slippers, and his bare feet were messed up. His trousers were ripped and his bare back felt as if it had been flayed. He had rolled over a patch of stinging nettles.

Where was the war machine?

He turned away from the fire and began to run, heading for the woods. He slammed full into someone alive, and felt arms go round his chest, then roughly push him away.

'Fuck!' said someone. Young. London accent.

Paul's eyesight returned painfully. It was a kid, bald except for a central hedge of bright-red hair. He was shaking, staring over Paul's head at something he did not believe.

Paul turned and saw fire through the trees. And the war machine, stepping back into the curtain of flame. It stood out as a monolithic black skeleton for a second, and was gone. Not burned, just gone.

'Fuck!' said the kid.

He had seen it too!

Paul clutched the kid's torn T-shirt with both hands. 'Did you see?' he asked, 'did you see?'

The kid's pupils were shrunk to needle points. 'Fuck,' he repeated, eyes watering. 'Fuck.'

Paul shook the kid, and the kid punched his shoulder, not hard, just to break away. He wore a studded leather wristlet. Right now, he looked fourteen years old.

Then the sirens shrilled, and jets of water burst through the flames. Suddenly, Paul was soaked and standing in leafy mud. There was a lot of shouting, and there were people everywhere.

He had never fainted before.

Fifteen

THEY ARRIVED before the fire brigade. Lytton took care to park on the road, not obstructing the driveway. When the fire engine turned up, he pegged the fire chief immediately and asked what he could do to help.

'Tell you what,' the man said, 'you're in charge of keeping everybody else out of our bloody way.'

'Fine.'

The chief grinned carnivorously. 'We'll see.'

It wasn't as easy as it sounded. People sprang from the ground all over the site like skeleton warriors from dragon's teeth. There was no sense of organization anywhere.

The fire engine had to go slowly up the drive to squeeze past the house. Then it put on a burst of speed and lurched across the garden. It went destructively as far up the hill as it could, finally halting, jammed between two well-rooted trees.

Lytton waved people back, but it was impossible to keep unwanted volunteers and morbid sightseers away. There were several old people in pyjamas and dressing gowns, and as many teenagers as he'd had on his work gang this afternoon. He saw Teddy Gilpin with a mixed group of festival kids, and signed to the boy to come over.

'Teddy,' he said, 'get your lot to form a chain across the top of the garden. Stop idiots from getting up into the orchard and messing the firemen about, okay?'

Teddy snapped off a military salute and went back to his friends, dishing out orders like a little Montgomery. That had probably been a very neat bit of strategy, Lytton thought. If anyone was going to get into trouble, it would be the kids; but, with a bit of authority to weigh them down, they might come through responsibly. Of course, they might also turn out to be disastrously inept.

Near the house, firemen wrenched iron covers off the drains

and fed pump-driven hoses into them. Lytton overheard a hose-unspooling fireman complain about the drought. With the water table low, it was difficult to get enough pressure in the hoses.

There was only one engine for this call, and it was small by big-city standards. It was manned by four efficient part-timers, rugby-club types, and the chief. They appeared to know what they were doing, but they'd be outgunned if this turned into a full-scale forest fire.

Lytton saw flames at the top of the orchard, clawing the sky. He heard a rush of water, and jumped off a thick hose as it unflattened into a rigid tube. There was cheering as hoses started gushing.

'Sir,' said a girl, as if he were a teacher, 'sir, my boyfriend's up there.'

Lytton recognized Jessica. She had spent the afternoon sponging B stage. Miserable about something, she had still done a good job.

'What's that?'

'Ferg. He was up at the camp.'

He couldn't see Jessica's face well in the dark, but knew from her voice she was upset.

'There's been no one hurt.'

'Can we go up and look for him?'

'Not yet. Wait 'til the fire's out, eh? I'm sure he'll be okay.'

She wasn't happy about that, or particularly convinced. 'Someone said a man went up there before the brigade came.'

Before he could think, another car turned up. Its headlights picked out the people standing in twos and threes in the garden. A rumpled man got out, clutching a black bag. The local doctor, Lytton hoped. The fire brigade must have called him in.

A rocket of flame shot into the sky above the hill and crashed down. There was more cheering. The blazes started to go out. It was like bonfire night.

James suggested Susan check out the house. She took Marie-Laure with her, because the sister would hardly be much use for anything else. The verandah lights were on, and there was someone in the kitchen. Susan rapped on the open back door, and stepped in. A pretty, youngish woman looked up from a tray of tea things, startled and fragile. Susan flinched at the woman's poured-out fear, then realized Marie-Laure was standing beside her, hatchet up like a tomahawk. Susan touched Marie-Laure's hand, and the axe slowly descended to hang at her side.

'Hi, I'm Susan Ames. Can we help?'

'H-H-H-Hazel,' stuttered the woman. Hazel was, Susan realized, barely more than a girl. Probably not yet twenty.

'The fire brigade are here,' Susan said. 'They're doing everything that has to be done.'

'I know. I've made some tea.'

'Good idea. Let me help.'

'We'll have to get cups from the pottery. Otherwise there won't be enough to go round.'

She was trembling, near hysteria. Susan hugged her, and she responded instantly, gripping tight, fists fastened to the folds of Susan's jacket. Susan felt the other woman's heart beating near her own, smelled recent shampoo in her hair, and had to shut her mind against the confusion welling out of Hazel's like tears.

'Sh-sh-sh,' she cooed, 'it'll be fine.'

Paul? What had happened to Paul?

Hazel clung tight to Susan Ames, but allowed herself to be led out of the kitchen. From the verandah, they could see the garden. Someone had turned on the lights in the showroom, and the place was like a well-lit playing field.

She felt weak at the knees. Mike and Mirrie would be furious. The fire engine had churned across their lawn, ploughing ruts, crushing completely a forsythia by the kiln shed. (The pots? Were her pots all right?) There was an unfamiliar squelch underfoot. Mud. She'd forgotten about mud. Water was streaming down the hill in rivulets, washing away bare soil and dead vegetation. A surge of earthy, lumpy water rose over her boots. Susan practically lifted her out of the way. And people. There were people all over the place. People she didn't know.

She felt calming waves coming from Susan, and held her as a child holds her mother. Wendy from the Agapemone lunged enormously into view and talked at them both. Hazel shrank against Susan's side. Lots of people were talking, but only Susan seemed to be speaking a language she understood. Wendy finished babbling and went away; Susan kept soothing her, telling her everything would be fine. As long as she listened only to the other woman's voice, she could believe that.

The fire was out now. Smiling firemen were being clapped on the back and making jokes.

'James,' Susan called out to a tall, commanding man. 'This is Hazel. She lives here. She's worried. A friend of hers went up the hill.'

How did Susan know that? She hadn't said anything about Paul. Just thought.

James looked up the hill, peering through invisible binoculars. 'They're bringing someone down now.'

Two black-uniformed firemen, faces camouflaged with soot, came into the light, supporting someone between them. It was Paul, dressing gown gone, head nodding unconscious.

'Doctor,' shouted James, 'over here.'

James and another man went to the firemen and took Paul's weight off them. They seemed glad to be rid of him. Susan left Hazel and helped James lay Paul on the grass. Alone and cold without Susan's reassuring touch, Hazel struggled to keep calm.

'He's just fainted,' said the doctor, his hand on Paul's rising and falling chest. 'No harm done, I think.'

She felt her knees going again, but caught herself in time. 'I'll get a blanket,' she said.

Teddy thought he was doing a good job. He had spread his 'men' – Kev, Dolar, Syreeta, Gary, Salim, Pam and the Toad – in a picket line between two of the Pottery buildings, and wasn't letting anyone unofficial get by. He had particularly enjoyed telling Kev's dad not to go up the hill, and was proud he'd recognized Dr Sweet and let him through unopposed. People were listening to him, following his suggestions, taking orders. Adults, grumpy farmers he'd known all his life, meekly stood back and did what he told them.

He hoped James would be pleased with him.

There were grumbles in the ranks: the Toad didn't want to get his clothes messed up and was prissily jumping from side to side to avoid the streams of mud, and Dolar was too pissed on scrumpy to stand up straight. But mainly they kept together, and Teddy knew that was his doing. He wondered if he might have a chance with Pam. She didn't have a pocket of fat under her chin like Sharon or eyes that glowed in the dark like Allison, and he got the idea she was on the way out with her darkie boyfriend.

She'd smiled at him a couple of times; then again, she'd smiled a couple of times at everyone in trousers.

As the fire went out, it got more difficult to see his line of people. Dolar had definitely fallen over, and Syreeta was moaning at him rather than keeping a watch. He couldn't see the Toad at all. Teddy supposed it didn't matter if the line broke up now. The crisis was over.

This was it, he decided, he'd go over and chat up Pam. He was still a bit drunk, but that was probably a good thing. He talked better when he was drunk. Then his wrist was grabbed and his arm yanked up hard behind his back. He yelled as pain erupted under his shoulderblades.

"Lo, Teddy,' said his brother, mouth close to Teddy's ear. 'You'm playin' toy soldiers, then?'

Wendy had tried to help, but there wasn't much left to do. Susan and James had looked after Paul, and Hazel was wrapped up with that. The fire was practically out before anyone had a chance to do anything. Irritated, she didn't even have anyone to talk to.

Derek was lost somewhere, and she was in the middle of a hostile crowd. She half heard nasty comments and saw several malicious stares. She recognized Jenny Steyning's father, exchanging mutters with some hard-faced men. It was as if they blamed her for the fire.

It wasn't fair. In Alder, they always picked on the Agape-mone. She wished Beloved were here, exerting His calming influence. That would shut up Steyning and his cronies.

She looked in the crowd for Derek. All she found was Marie-Laure, blankly ecstatic, praying in relief at the deliverance.

'. . . just superficial cuts and bruises. I'll clean and dress them back in the house . . .'

'. . . any chance of a cup of tea?'

'. . . it weren't the kids' camp fire. We found that a couple of hundred yards off. They done a proper job, banked it with stones an' all. Must of been the fucking heat . . .'

'. . . never seen no point in this pottery lark. Bloody waste of money, if you ask me. Three pound fifty for that little mug . . .'

'. . . hey, she's one of *they* . . .'

'. . . stripped to the waist and bleedin', he were. Shan't be surprised if'n he's in a bleddy coma . . .'

'. . . anyone seen Danny Keough today?'

'. . . it be these hippies, I'm tellin' ye . . .'

It got darker as she went up the hill. People were just shapes. Where was Derek?

Just as she thought she had gone too far and there were no more people to be found, she almost tripped over a girl squatting in the grass, long hair dark over her face. She wiped her hair aside and Wendy thought she saw the flash of cat's eyes. There was someone else, standing in a pool of black under an apple tree. Someone familiar. A waft of leftover smoke passed by, and Wendy caught the aftersmell of burning, and beneath that the stench of rotten meat. He came out of his shadow and smiled with what was left of his face.

'Hello, Wendy,' said Badmouth Ben, 'long time . . .'

Allison's heart expanded as Ben took the fat woman's chin in his black claw. Ben wanted to teach Wendy a lesson, and Allison was excited, eager to know what the lesson would be. Ben kissed Wendy, leaving smears of himself on her face. He snickered, bright-pink tongue flicking out between black teeth. He spun the woman round and got her neck in an elbow lock. She tugged at his arm, pulling away ragged streaks of leather. He reached inside her shirt and started mauling her fat teats, saying things in her ear. She stopped struggling and shut her eyes fast. Ben started to drag the woman back into his shadow, then let go of her. Wendy fell down and Ben was gone. Allison crept over, feeling a tingle in her bloodless foot. Her cheesewire was wound too tight. She slapped the woman until her eyes were open, leaving angry red marks on her flabby cheeks. Wendy bleated like a sheep. 'Catch you later,' Allison said. 'TTFN.'

In the van, Jessica was all over him, hugging him, wetly kissing him. He didn't want to talk. He didn't want to think. It had been big like a dinosaur, but also like a machine, it had pissed fire on the woods, it couldn't be real because it was from a science-fiction nightmare, it couldn't be walking, burning, *existing*. Finally, after the last stern warning about their fire from the firemen, they had all piled into the Dormobile, and Salim was driving them to the official camp site. Ferg held Jessica, his eyes shut until they hurt, trying to see only the darkness, trying to wipe ten minutes' worth of memory out of his brain for ever.

Beloved let her watch everything on the camera obscura. It didn't work as well at night, and large patches of the tiny tabletop projection were just blackness. But she saw where fires burned. Beloved was unaffected by the fuss. The small, silent people had clustered around the flames like insects. Now, they'd gone away, and the phantom village was still. He took Jenny's hand and touched it to the healed wound above His heart. The darkness imploded, and there was only light. Hungrily, He kissed her.

Sixteen

LYTTON HAD TO stay in the orchard once the fire was out. This was the sort of thing he was in Alder to look out for. Garnett would want a full report. Even if the incident turned out not to have any paranormal aspect, it'd be as well to get it discounted now as to rake literally through the ashes later. Between them, science and bureaucracy could spin this out into a three-month headache.

He took stock of the situation in the garden. Susan was with the doctor from Langport and the young couple from the Pottery. He hoped she could take care of things down here in civilization. He touched an invisible hat brim to her, and she nodded back. The girl was pretty cool for a spook. *Pretty* for a spook, too. Being around her wasn't exactly comfortable, but it was reassuring to think she was on his side.

The firemen were down from the orchard, stowing their gear. Two hoses slithered down the hill in competition as they were reeled in on giant spools, nozzles bouncing. The chief ticked off one of his team for being careless with the equipment, and the man went off to pick up the hoses by their heads and make sure they weren't clogged with grass or earth. His job done, the chief lit up a cigarette and posed, hands on hips, looking up at the steaming patch where the fire had been, waiting to be admired and congratulated.

Most of the rubberneck squadron had melted away, interest evaporated now the fire was doused and they'd enjoyed the opportunity to poke about in other people's business, but there were one or two people milling about in the still-lit-up showroom. He saw Sharon Coram, a lank-haired, dull-faced young girl the lads sometimes called 'the village pump', slip an ashtray off one of the display tables and into a parka pocket. He let it go. He couldn't take care of everything. Still, he'd be careful not to use her in any position of trust on his festival crew.

'Bleddy townies an't got the sense they's born with,' said a harsh voice in the dark. 'Startin' fires an' all.'

'Arr,' came the assenting reply.

Casually, Lytton walked past the two old-timers as they wondered at the foolhardiness of foreigners. They didn't pay him any attention. He strolled up the hill, away from the lights of the house and showroom. After climbing steadily for a few hundred yards, he looked back and saw the Pottery as an oasis of illumination in a desert of dark. He waited fifteen minutes, watching activity die down, people drift away. Then, the showroom lights went off. Headlights shifted, and he heard the last of the vehicles leaving. He'd given Derek the keys to the Land-Rover and instructions to get the Agapemone crowd home. Two lights still burned in the house. It was cool now, almost cold. He turned up his jacket collar. A few months of drought had made him forget what cold was like. He started walking again, letting his eyes grow used to the dark.

He was trudging through mud. There weren't even embers from the fire. He was careful, taking his steps slowly. It would not do to break an ankle or walk into a tree. The gun in his pocket bumped against his chest like a pacemaker. He reached into his jacket and transferred the pistol to his hip pocket. The grip felt comfortable in his hand. He continued to hold the Browning in his pocket. Childish, he knew, but reassuring. No birds sang, but insects sawed the night.

What had happened up here in the orchard? It hadn't been an out-of-control camp fire, and he didn't think Paul had been having an after-lights-out session with an incinerator to get rid of garden rubbish. It had to be Jago, of course. Somehow, it had to be Jago.

Pyrokinesis. He remembered the word from Dr Cross's briefing at IPSIT. Pyrokinesis, psychokinesis, apports, effective hallucination, psychic fallout. Lytton wasn't sure he understood half what Cross had told him about Anthony William Jago. In the last few years he'd learned to be wary of undue scepticism. Giving something a scientific name didn't make it natural. What Jago had could not be calibrated, dissected or exorcized with a Graeco-Latin tag. The man was possessed of . . . powers.

Nearby, at ground level, something groaned.

Instantly: still, listening, gun in hand. Good. The instinct override kicked in when he needed it. It was a long time since his basic training, and he'd had little use for his night skills since.

More groaning. It was someone too hurt to be dangerous. He reluctantly let go of the Browning. He'd have to be careful, or else he'd shoot a hole through his jacket. Or, worse, his thigh. He made his way, half crouched, towards the noise. He could make out someone lying face up, limbs spread as if staked to the ground.

'James,' the body got out, 'I'm done over.'

It was Teddy Gilpin, dark patches – not shadows – on his face. His breathing was noisy and uneven. Froth trickled from his mouth. Lytton knelt and frisked the boy. There were no extra groans.

'No broken bones, I think. What –?'

'Terry. It were bloody Terry.'

'Of course, Terry. Stupid bastard. Can you stand?'

'Reckon so.'

Lytton helped him. Teddy made it to his feet, but sagged immediately. He felt for his head.

'Ohhh, my nut.'

Teddy dizzily tried to stand on his own. He managed it, although he had to paw at the air like a seal to keep steady. One of his eyes was almost closed by bruising, and his cheek was open and streaming. The boy had been knocked senseless.

Lytton gave him a handkerchief. Teddy dabbed his cheek, yelping at the touch, but persisting until the grit was out of the cut. He hawked a lump of bloody phlegm into the linen.

'Did Terry start the fire?'

Teddy thought, then painfully shook his head. 'Nahh, don't reckon so. Wouldn't put it lower 'n him, but he were here well after us. He's in a bloody foul mood.'

'Too right, by the looks of you. Where is he now?'

'Still up here somewhere. With Allison and some crazy biker bloke. He an't got much of a face. They were in it together. They gone off into the woods.'

'Did the three of them beat you up?'

'Nahh.' Teddy's grin shone in the dark. 'That were Terry on his own.'

Lytton tried to make some connections.

'Allison? Is she with Terry?'

Teddy shook his head, grinning again, crusts of blood between his teeth. 'Not likely. Terry's petrified of her. He's bad enough, but Allison's a ravin' psycho loony. She'm the one who kills cats. Terry'll have gone with her 'cause he's too chicken not to do what she tells him.'

Teddy's hands were fists against the cold.

'Do you want me to get you home?'

He shook his head. 'Nahh, we best find Terry 'fore he does somethin' else stupid. I reckon Allison's new bloke is ten times the weird he is.'

'Did you get a good look at this lad?'

'Just enough to make out a fuckin' mess where he ought to have a face. Could've been a mask, I s'pose.'

Lytton wished Susan were here. She might have been able to make something of Teddy's testimony. She was effortlessly intuitive.

'Where'd they go?'

'Where d'you think? Up the hill.'

Lytton looked up towards the wood. 'Okay, let's track them.'

'Sure thing, *kimosabe*.'

Teddy would be all right; he hadn't had daft jokes beaten out of him.

'I just hope you're stocked up on silver bullets, *kimosabe*, 'cause I reckon bloody Terry is turnin' into one o' they werewolves.'

'There are worse things,' Lytton said. Jago's face peered into his mind, and he shivered. 'Come on, we'd better get going.'

There was only one path out of the orchard. It had been used recently. There were wet footprints, which meant someone had come this way since the fire. The woods were a mess up here. Dead trees had split and fallen. Low branches were half furred black with soot.

'This was damn nearly a forest fire.'

Although overgrown enough to be, in some stretches, a tunnel rather than a path, the way was negotiable. Lytton supposed several bodies had been through in the last day or so, swiping too low branches and too thick shrubs out of the way.

He might not be the Lone Ranger, but he was getting well up on his woodcraft. These years in the country must have taught him something, even if only by osmosis. They proceeded with the minimum of noise and fuss, Lytton going ahead, Teddy following.

A scrap of tune went through his head, repeating a phrase from a song, 'In the still of the night . . .' It was late. Nearly four by his watch. The first fingers of dawn would soon be crawling over the horizon. It was also, after this summer of drought and heat, really cold. He was glad now of the sleep he'd caught earlier. The cold seeped through his clothes, reaching for his bones. 'In the chill, still of the *niiiight* . . .' Their breath was frosting.

The path ended. Before them was the Bomb Site, a slight dip in the flat top of Alder Hill, half grassed, half bare shingle. During the Second World War, he understood, a Luftwaffe bomber returning from a raid on Bristol had dumped its payload in the woods, mistaking the hill for a target. Nearly fifty years later, the resultant depression was still called the Bomb Site. Away from the towns and cities, time creeps like a glacier.

'They London kids were camped out here,' Teddy said, 'but they'm gone.'

Opposite the path, there was a house. A wooden structure, built on a platform supported by piles, set into the gentle slope of the hollow. It had a shaded porch, and many of its boards hung loose.

'That weren't here before,' Teddy whispered.

He was right. Lytton had never seen the place, and he had been to the Bomb Site several times before. The house was *old*, something from a Wild West ghost town. It could not have grown overnight like a mushroom.

'Careful. Let's go quietly.'

Lytton stood at the edge of the hollow, in the shade cast by two trees. The quality of the air in the Bomb Site was different, charged with electricity or heavy with an odourless gas. Above, the sky sparkled, inset with diamond chips. The house was as unmoving as a photograph.

On the porch, there was a movement. Wood creaked against wood. A shape bobbed back and forth. Someone was sitting in an old rocking chair. A man. Lytton got an impression of a face leaning towards the light but drawing away before he could get a look at it. The rocking man wasn't alone. A woman, with long hair, stood by the chair.

Lytton had his gun out again. He heard Teddy's curt sucking-in of breath, and signed to him to keep quiet. Stooping low, he advanced into the hollow, taking care to keep his footing on the loose shale.

'Evenin', stranger,' shouted the woman, 'no need to creep and crawl like a snake.'

Lytton's foot sunk into shingles. A fall of jagged pebbles shifted away from his ankle. He stood up straight, foot free, and walked as calmly as possible towards the house that shouldn't be there. The woman stepped down from the porch to look at him. She'd been Allison Conway a long time ago. Now she was dried up and scrawny. Hair still black, eyes still sharp, her face was worn leather, her hands knuckly lumps of arthritis. Lytton would have to be cautious. The strangeness was beginning.

'Welcome, stranger,' said old Allison, exposed teeth rotten.

There was an explosion off in the trees behind the house, and a flashbulb burst of fire. Lytton was flat on the ground, his ears echoing, slithering forward on his elbows toward cover. That had been a shotgun.

Terry. Bloody Terry.

He'd missed by a mile. A shotgun was no use at night, except for close work. And for that, Terry would have to come out of his coward's corner and square up to him. Of course, that would mean he would have to get near enough to be in range of Lytton's gun. He had the Browning out again, safety off.

Shit, shit, shit, shit, he thought. But he was working around a calm centre in his mind. Lytton didn't want to have to shoot a kid, no matter how obnoxious. He didn't want to have to kill anybody. But he'd signed up for life, and he knew what came with the territory. There were things not in the job description, to which he had committed himself when he wasn't much older than the bloody silly boy out there in the woods with his punky rabbit gun. A snake knows how to bite.

Lytton almost made it under the porch. But the shape got out of its rocker and came for him. He thought he heard spurs chinking.

'Cease fire, fuckface!' The words came out of the shape with difficulty, over a sundered palate, through shredded lips.

Lytton hoped Teddy had the sense to make a run for it. This could easily get nasty from here.

He looked up. Allison and the rocker man stood over him. A fist grabbed his hair, and jerked him to his knees. A dead rot of a face floated before him in the twilight, life in its eyes and tongue.

'Pretty fucking ugly, huh? They call me Badmouth Ben, Mr Snake. I'm putting my mark on you.'

Badmouth Ben produced a huge blade – a bowie knife, Lytton recognized – and touched his tongue with it.

'This is so I'll know you later.'

The point went to Lytton's temple, and he felt a tug at the corner of his eye as the icy steel pinpricked him. But his hands were still free. And he had his gun. Lytton jabbed the pistol – now it felt like a toy in his sweat-slick fist – and jabbed the muzzle into the underside of Badmouth Ben's wrist, pushing the knife away from his head.

The shot was muffled by flesh and bone. The bullet burst through the back of Badmouth Ben's hand, raising an eruption of red in the greasily overcooked skin. He let go of Lytton and howled at the pinking sky. Another howl, even more feral, answered from the wood.

Lytton was on his feet, braced squarely against the porch. He drew aim at Badmouth Ben's chest, but the howling man was suddenly gone, twisting into the crawlspace under the house.

He was pulled away. It was Allison, young again, mad as a harpy. He pushed her off. Teddy was skipping along the side of the house, kicking boards. The structure shook and settled. Inside, nails burst from wood. Teddy was whooping. Lytton wanted this over. He wanted to put his gun away, but Shotgun Terry was still out there, whining like a dog, and Allison could still go for his eyes with her nails. The girl hissed at him, and spat like a vicious cat.

There was another blast, and a hole the size of a tea tray appeared in the side of the house. Teddy jumped away from the splintered gap, and gave the wood a V-sign. The house strained and creaked and fell in on itself. A dust cloud rose from the ruin as boards crumbled quickly, a time-lapse film of decay. The dust bubbled a little and sank into the earth.

Allison showed them her teeth and waved claw-fingered hands. Lytton and Teddy stood back, away from her darting scratches, and she looked from one to the other. Her eyes were still alight. Then, with foxlike swiftness, she was gone into the wood. There was no sign of Badmouth Ben in the fast-dispersing remains of the house.

'Terry,' Teddy called out, angry, puzzled. 'I'll 'ave 'ee for this.'

There was no answer from the woods.

Dawn broke the sky. Somewhere, in the village, a dog barked. Even the dust of the house was gone now. There was just the familiar Bomb Site, shingles and grass, a few bits of weathered rubbish.

Teddy looked at him, then down at the Browning, eyes wide enough to show white around the irises. 'Fuck, James, wha'ss this game?'

Lytton had no answer. Self-conscious, he put his pistol away. A tear of blood ran from forehead to chin. He smeared it away.

'Now we go home,' he said.

Interlude Six

H E WAS A foot shorter than Clint Eastwood, but he'd practised that dead look about the eyes. It didn't really fit his thick-eyebrowed, thick-lipped ventriloquist's-dummy face, but it could help get him what he wanted. His clothes were copied faithfully from Jack Nicholson and Peter Fonda in Hell's Angel films, his language picked up from his favourite writer, Richard Allen. His bike began life as a sleek Kawasaki, but he'd jazzed it up. The front wheel was forward and the banana seat back, the handles curved like the Devil's horns and the petrol tanks had red flames painted on them. In the panniers, he packed everything he owned. The bike was more than his home, it was a part of his body.

He heard about Rivendell in the village pub. The old turds were bitching about it in Welsh, but the lads he played darts with and bought pints for translated and embroidered the stories. Rivendell was a hippie hideaway. Girls with no bras, longhairs trying to grow dope. Kids who'd thrown away everything except their stereos and started all over again. Arseholes, basically. They had moved into three adjoining cottages, derelict until they did them up, and played Robinson Crusoe until they had a farm going. The locals hated them, but Gareth, the boy he was talking to, had stories of girls and grass and generosity that made Rivendell sound like just the roost for Badmouth Ben.

That night, while America was celebrating its bicentennial, he slept by the road, a mile or so from the village, hiding his bike behind a pile of slates that might once have been a wall. Before crashing out, he reread a few chapters of *Skinhead*, his favourite book, admiring the way Allen had life sussed. This summer, he could camp in the open as much as he wanted, not even using his sleeping bag. He thrived on the drought that yellowed the country, turning fruit on the bough to clumps of prunes. Dope would be good this year if the Rivendell folk had watered it properly. So far, he'd stayed cool by keeping on the move.

Still, the idea of a real bed with someone else in it, and real food at regular intervals, was getting prettier and prettier by the hour. He'd been from festival to festival, and everybody was saying that was the best summer since 1967. Now, he wanted somewhere to make the summer his own for a while.

At first, the Rivendell crowd were suspicious. He took off and buried his swastikas before tootling up on his bike, but still had to overcome the bad publicity bikers had been getting since the year dot. The hippies gave him wholemeal bread and home-made jam, no butter, and horrible herbal tea, but didn't want to form an opinion until their chiefs had made up their minds. Jeff and Conrad were the chiefs, oldies in their late twenties. He talked to them. Jeff didn't like him straight off, but Conrad was won over by the bagful of mushrooms he had been toting since Stonehenge. He was invited to crash for a couple of nights. The first night, he wound up fucking one of the spares, a tall and skinny girl called Vanda with long eyeteeth and flowers tattooed all up one arm.

Three nights later, he passed round some of his own dope, and took Jeff's girlfriend Nad upstairs. He made her like it. Conrad was well off Jeff now, and had long stoned conversations with Ben about negative vibes. Conrad liked to talk about the old days before it all got fucked up, and Ben knew he could easily handle him if he had to. Within a week, Jeff was gone. Nad took off after him in a beat-up Mini, the only car the Rivendell folk had, and neither came back. Nobody cared much except a fat cow called Wendy, who whined and cried until Ben had to get her away from the others. He belted her where she couldn't show the bruise. She was outraged, a little kid finding out for the first time that not everybody keeps the rules. She looked as if she was going to go red and stamp her feet and shriek, 'It's not *fair*!' Conrad had gone on a long trip now, and Ben knew where there were some more mushrooms. Ben started sitting in Jeff's old place at the table. One night, he had a ceremonial burning of Jeff's album collection.

It was so hot everyone went around in shorts and sandals or nothing but hair. But Ben kept his leathers on, and always wore his shades. He was still cool. He had long, stoned talks with them all, individually or in groups of two or three. It was like taking sweeties from kiddies, finding the weak spots and working on them. He could smell out the long-term relationships about

to reach the boredom and irritation phase. He could spot the
middle-class moaners who were starting to miss inside toilets
and electric fans. Then there were the hard workers who resented
the slackers, the hoarders who didn't share, the girls who didn't
fuck enough. Any group breaks down like any log, along five
or six different grains. Everybody can find something to dislike
about everybody else. But Badmouth Ben was everybody's
friend, his own most of all.

There were arguments every day now, fights, even. Never
actually in them, Ben always got a ringside seat. Conrad got
sick one night while he was tripping, and couldn't keep his
food down any more. Ben thought if he was being fed that
vegetarian crap he'd want to puke it up again too. As a joke,
Ben made Stodge the leader. Stodge needed a lot of advice, and
Ben was pleased to oblige. Fed up with the wholefood produce
they'd been raising or bartering for, Ben sent Chris and Phil
into town to rip off stuff from the supermarket. When Phil got
caught, Ben told the rest to forget about it and act shocked when
the pigs came round. Ben told the constable Phil must have been
keeping the money they gave him for groceries. He hoped the
bastard would go to jail. The constable looked at him in a funny
way, a way very few people looked at him. It was as if the pig
knew exactly what Ben was about, but wasn't going to step in
and do anything because, deep down, he approved. Someone at
dinner that night seriously suggested Chris be given a suicide pill
to take on his next raiding mission, and Ben called them a bunch
of fucking useless kids.

'The good thing about sheep,' Ben said once, 'is that you
can shag them, kill them, eat them and wear them.' Nobody
laughed.

There were fewer of them than there had been when he showed
up. Mostly, it was guys who left. One or two had to be
persuaded to go with more than Ben's favourite tool, whispered
words. The first, Marius, Ben had taken care of himself. He kept
the teeth, planning to have them strung on a bracelet. Richard
Allen would have appreciated it. After Marius, he left heavy stuff
to Chris and Gareth. He was a good hard boy was Gareth, the lad
from the pub, and Ben could count on him to do what he was
told so long as there were girls and grass going his way.

Ben started to make collections, and sent the girls to town to pawn the things he found. When Rivendell ran out of surplus saleables, he sent the girls out to beg spare change from passersby, claiming they were Krishna kids. He had Chris or Gareth go with them to make sure they came back, though. In the early days, one or two of the girls walked away in the night. The ones that were left would stay. He'd had them all by now, even that poor, miserable Wendy. He'd made them like it. But the commune could do with more girls. There was washing and cooking and fucking needed doing. Ben sent Chris, who was a bit of a pretty boy, to Liverpool to hang around the coach station and see if he could scare up some likely gash. He came back with Carole and Tacey, and Ben soon had them in harness.

Autumn was a long time coming. Farmers complained. The local paper ran reports that sheep and goats and chickens were going missing. There was a lot of grumbling, and the pub put up a NO HIPPIES sign, in English and (needlessly) in Welsh. Ben had his swastikas back now, and he started to wear a shaggy sheepskin waistcoat. Despite the heat, he was cool. That Carole turned out to be a right little scrubber, luckily.

Although there were other girls, especially Carole, Ben got off on sticking it to Wendy as much as possible. He couldn't possibly want her for herself, but she was the most difficult, the most unhappy. It was necessary to keep establishing power over her. She'd stopped crying and complaining, and just lay there like a sack of potatoes as he pumped her whichever way he wanted. In the end, fucking wasn't enough and he started working her over. No one said anything about the marks on her face and arms. He frightened her completely and started telling her things. He told her what he'd learned about the others, and how he used it and would keep on using it. He got a bigger charge out of telling her things than he did from anything else he could do to her.

Wendy had a witless boyfriend called Derek. Chris stamped on his hand once, breaking most of the fingers. Despite Ben, Wendy and Derek were together a lot of the time, plotting and scheming like officers in a prisoner-of-war film. They tried to run away, but Stodge, still the school sneak under his blubber, told on them. Ben punished them in front of the rest, cropping their hair with sheep-shears. It was what the French Resistance used to do to girls who slept with German soldiers. They looked

awful, with patches of scalp showing, a few not really accidental
cuts and the occasional long tuft he'd missed. He tried to get
them to fuck in front of the others but Derek couldn't, even
when Ben made threats with the shears. Instead, Ben dragged
Wendy upstairs and stuck it to her until his dick was raw and
she'd given up crying.

Rivendell was a good place for Badmouth Ben, but they killed
him just the same.

It was his bike. Someone opened the upholstery and pulled
out the foam. Ben knew his authority was being symbolically
defied, and took it seriously. When he was younger, he'd
read paperbacks about Hitler and the Gestapo. He knew how
important smart uniforms and imposing machines were to the
potency of the Third Reich. Ordinary men couldn't help but feel
like shit when they compared themselves to the SS in their black
and silver. It made the Nazis like gods.

From Gareth, he learned where there was a garage that could
fit him a new seat cover. He left Chris and Gareth to take care
of finding out who was responsible, and drove off immediately.
It was about to turn cold. Though the sheepskin kept his torso
warm, his extended arms froze.

On some dirt track between two hills that wasn't even a road,
his engine packed up and his bike went over. He skidded a couple
of yards into the grass, and put his knee out. He got himself and
the bike upright, and checked for damage. One of the flames
was scraped off the petrol tank. It was still half full, but when he
opened it he saw things floating inside. Lentils. Hippies wouldn't
let sugar within a mile of them. He swore, and kicked the ground
with knee-length black boots. He couldn't leave the bike here,
and it would be hours to anywhere. When he got back, some
people were going to get seriously damaged.

He took off his helmet and gloves, pain in the back of his neck.
Two people on bicycles came round the hill. Wendy and Derek.
Great. They could push the fucking bike.

'Hey, you,' he said, 'give us a heave-ho.'

'Got a problem, Ben?' said Derek. 'Let's see.'

Ben realized the shit was going to go for him, and braced
himself. Even with his knee out, he could put holes in Derek.
But it was Wendy who lead-piped his head. He felt part of his
skull go concave, and knew he was leaking. He went down,

reaching for his head, probing for the places where the bone would give under his fingers. It started to hurt.

Wendy pushed the bike over on top of him, and his knee exploded again. Petrol slopped out of the uncapped tank and soaked into his jeans and sheepskin. Derek had a small jerrican strapped to the carrying basket of his bike. He gave it to Wendy, and she poured it out. It was like being pissed on by a petrol pump. The stream sloshed against the bike and over Ben. She made sure to pour the last of it out on his face. It got in his eyes, up his nose, into his mouth. He spluttered and shook his head.

Fat, with her head neatly shaved now, Wendy looked like a nutter Buddhist. She had a little box in her hands, a box of matches. The first three broke or went out before she could use them. The fourth didn't. Flame grew along the splinter, almost to her fingers, before she dropped it. She stood back. The fire grew in a ring. The dead grass caught easily. Wendy and Derek went away, but Badmouth Ben had to stay. He was surprised dying took so long.

III

One

THE SKY WAS grey, but pregnant with a blinding blue that would come later. Up even earlier than usual, a good hour and a half before *Farming Today* came on Radio Four, Maskell walked across his lands. He wasn't sure why he had bothered.

Bothered trying to sleep, bothered getting up.

The heat murdered his nights, making his bed a gritty sweat bath, keeping him wide awake beside Sue-Clare as she turned in shallow slumber. It ruined his waking routine, making most of the daily tasks of the farm redundant. His animals needed tending; the merciful attention you grant any dying thing, not the profit-minded nurturing he was used to. If the cows were not milked, their udders would distend and they'd be at risk of infection. But this summer's milk was thin, bitter and unprofitable. Most of it was literally down the drain.

The earth was spongy with minuscule dew and rotting grass. The farm smelled like a stagnant lake. Maskell might have been walking through an alien landscape, the surface of Venus or a stretch of earthquake-raised seabed. He didn't feel the sense of proprietorship that usually came when he prowled his land.

Insects buzzed louder than the beginnings of the dawn chorus. There were a lot of bugs this summer. Something was thriving. The last few weeks had been increasingly frustrating. Everything had been building up inside him, knots tightening. Usually Jethro walked with him on his early-morning tours of the property, but the dog had taken to hiding under his old blanket, abandoning his master. Even before sunrise, Maskell was sweating into his old check shirt. The knees and groin of his jeans were damp, and he could feel droplets trickling down his calves into his socks.

He saw a mound ahead, dun-coloured against gloom-grey grass. A cow, lying down. There was no doubt it was dead. Insects were already there, swarming around its yellow eye bulges. He walked over, stomach turning. White and red froth

hung from the animal's twisted mouth. Its hide was already stiff
and stinking. Standing over the carcass, he looked around and
saw other fly-buzzed mounds. At least seven. More than had
been sick yesterday. He tried to think pounds and pence, but saw
only useless meat. Flies licked the stickiness around his eyes, and
he brushed them away.

If Danny Keough were here, the daft old buffer would be
blaming hippies. Maskell would have to get these dead things
shifted if this field were to be an overflow festival car park.

Last night, they'd tried to watch a James Bond film on video.
Maskell had been unable to concentrate on the exploits of 007.
Sue-Clare had embroidered fiercely throughout the picture, and
he'd found the absurdly simple storyline impossible to follow.
Scene followed scene without logic. People fell from incredible
heights but were unhurt. He wondered if the video people had
got the reels in the wrong order.

A rind of sun hit the horizon, and he was dazzled. The heat
fell upon him like a heavy curtain. As the sun edged higher, light
spilled across the farm. In the next field, Maskell saw a figure,
standing with its back to him. It had long, tangled hair and an
unmistakably feminine curve. Light broke around her and the
shape shimmered, outline indistinct. He called, but she didn't
turn. She stretched out her arms like a scarecrow, as if bathing
in the newborn sun. He assumed she was a Druid come early
for the festival. He crossed a ditch bridge to the next field and
looked for the woman. She was gone.

His fields were separated by ditches, not hedges. Locally,
they were called rhynes. Even if the woman had left the field,
she should be nearby. There was no cover. He walked to the
middle of the field, where he was sure the woman had been, and
found a circle of bare earth. There were no footprints in the soft
soil.

Tired, he slumped to his knees. The heat was pounding down
seriously. Maskell settled on the ground, letting his bottom sink
to his heels, throwing his head back, presenting his throat to
the sun. He felt the earth shifting slightly beneath him. He
was precisely in the centre of his estate. One of Sue-Clare's
crystal-worshipping friends claimed there was a confluence of
ley lines here. He wondered if the stirrings he felt were related
to the invisible courses of power in which he'd never believed.
He shut his eyes and watched light traces darting in the darkness,

imagining the woman he'd seen hiding behind the glowing squiggles.

The sunlight on his face and chest sank in, carried throughout his body by sluggish blood. Quiet heat seeped up from the earth into his legs and blossomed inside him. He was the focus of the field, receiving the feelings of the wounded land. Warmth filled out his penis, and an erection strained his jeans.

Last night, infuriatingly, he hadn't been able to manage. Sue-Clare had worked on him with her hands and mouth for minutes, but nothing had happened. She'd been decent about it, and gone to sleep leaving him hot, flaccid and awake, balls tingling uncomfortably. He'd been furious with himself, and lain with hard-clenched fists and clenched teeth, cursing everything, knot tightening.

He sat up and unzipped his fly, letting his swollen knob out. He waved flies away from his erection. His vision was blurring, grey blobs circling. Painfully hard now, he grit his teeth as his glans threatened to rupture, skin stretched tight.

His father had farmed this land, but before him the family had no history in Somerset. The Major simply made a shrewd investment after the war, and capitalized on the hungry 1950s. Others in the village had ties to the earth that went back for ever. The churchyard was full of Starkeys, Gilpins and Shepherds, with only a tidy corner plot for a couple of Maskells, his parents. But, apart from the Agapemone, his was the largest estate around Alder. He had the most to lose as the land died. He was charged with responsibility for it.

His head swam, and the earth rose all around him, closing over him like a fist. It was rancid and rotting. For a moment, he was panicked, afraid he wouldn't be able to breathe, but the movements settled. He was all right, cocooned in a thin shell of dirt that caressed and cared for him. Clods shaped like lips kissed him, and a tongue of twigs forced itself into his throat, scratching avidly inside his mouth. Pebbles like fingertips gently raked his back, loosening his clothes. He rolled over and stretched, breaking the surface, and held his head up out of the loose, grass-smelling, earth. The land was roiling beneath him, pushing and sucking, cajoling and scolding.

He made love to his land, knob ploughing into a barely moist cleft, arms sunk up to the elbows in the brown mulch. Flies gathered around him, coating his back, filling his hair. He ate dirt, swallowing rich, gravelly mouthfuls. He pressed his face to the ground and, eyes shut, pushed into the earth. He was joined permanently with his land, knob deeply rooted, aching balls planted like vegetables. His genitals sprouted, sending out tubers under the earth. They sought the fertile spots, the tasty eggs that remained despite the death. He felt his entire farm as if it were his body.

The land loved him, and whispered to him. The land was a woman, *the* woman. It told him what he must do. She had old knowledge for him. The future was failing the land, so he must turn to the past. He understood her and responded. He pumped faster, straining his hips, torn skin leaking. Twigs scratched his sides, and he grunted like a rutting hog. He shoved at the earth with the heels of his hands, slapping it with his pelvis, stabbing deep with his knob. He felt himself coming, first in the soles of his feet, then in his ankles, then in his knees. The earth cracked apart beneath him. His knob-end burned like a dying star, and thick, creamy milk gushed from him, seeping into the dirt. Maskell fertilized his fields.

Two

THERE WERE HANDS on her body, gently massaging. Her eyelids, still shut by sleep, moved but didn't open. The hands moved slowly, heavy and warm. She felt as if she were floating in syrup. She was losing sensation. All she could feel were the hands. They were large but soft. They stroked her hair, brushing out her tangles. They swept over her face, smoothing away her features. It would be easy to lie as she was for ever. Lie, and let it all come to her.

She felt a kiss on her forehead. Cool lips thrilling. The hands shaped her clay, wiping her face into a smooth mask. Her eyelids were thumb-erased, burying her eyes. She was in the dark, but it was a comforting dark. Her nostrils closed, and her mouth was kneaded back into clay. She didn't feel the need to breathe.

Gradually, the hands reshaped her face, pulling out a new, longer nose, pinching more generous lips, opening more widely spaced eyes. Fingers eased open her mouth and gripped her foreteeth, forcing them apart, then back into place, overlap gone. She was being changed, but the changes were not just in her face. Her spine stretched as her ankles were pulled, the vertebrae swelling as she became taller, knees popping as her legs elongated. Her stomach drew in taut and her breasts grew heavier. She felt stronger, and flexed her newly soft, newly supple fingers.

Still, her eyes were sleep-glued. She began to hear sounds. There was something that might have been the crash of distant surf, or the dulled noise of an audience applauding. Perhaps seabirds squawking. As a little girl, she'd loved the seaside. Then her parents had moved there and spoiled it. There was nothing drabber than Brighton when the beaches were cold and empty, the sky a wedge of grey through double glazing.

The touch that reshaped her wasn't a disembodied thing. When the fingers were doing close work, delicately pushing up

her cheekbones, she could feel an arm pressing against her. The
hands were a man's. She felt short, stiff hairs on his forearms.
Her skin goose-pimpled at their brush.

How was she being changed inside herself? Would she wake
up more intelligent, a better potter, a stronger person? The
hands Loved her. The hands were not Paul's. Not any of her old
boyfriends'. The hands were new. The touch was withdrawn.
She lay, desolate, alone. Then, fingertips pressed below her ribs,
reaching into her, sharply cold like icicles . . .

Hazel sat up on the couch in the front room, sleeping bag falling
away, the memory of the dream fingers still shivering in her
chest. She was sweat-filmed, heart rapping like a knuckle against
a door.

Somewhere near, people were chattering. She was in herself
again. She felt her face, the same. She slipped a finger into her
mouth, rubbing the overlap between her front teeth. She wasn't
disappointed, really.

She'd gone to sleep late, several teas after brushing her teeth,
and her mouth felt scummy. She'd pulled off her boots and jeans,
and slept in knickers, socks and a T-shirt. Her head throbbed,
but she knew she'd not been drinking last night. Well, one glass
of wine with dinner.

She ran through the whole thing, fast-forwarding, from dinner
till bed. Going upstairs with Paul, the smoke over the hill,
Paul dashing up into the dark, the fire brigade, Susan Ames,
people, noise, damage, tea, Dr Sweet, Paul hurt, more people,
exhaustion, putting Paul to bed, making do on the sofa . . .

She stood up and wriggled from the sleeping bag. It fell around
her ankles like a soggy chrysalis. The front room, gloomily
orange-lit through the roller blind, was a mess. There were
mugs, half-full of cold tea with floating milk clots, clustered
on the coffee table, brown rings on the bright faces of girls
on magazines. The doctor, and some of the firemen, had
smoked, and the ashtrays were full of butts, the stink of
stale tobacco hanging in the air. She'd have to clean up. At
some point someone had turned on the television, and the
news was droning. A government spokesman was arguing
with a weather man in front of a rainfall chart, refusing to
implement emergency measures. She turned the set off. The
house was suddenly quiet.

She padded on thick socks around the passage and found the back door open. There was dried mud on the hall carpets, and the traces of heavy boots. She went outside, feeling the heat of the sun smack her bare legs as she ventured off the verandah.

Tears started from her eyes. Daylight made things look worse than they'd done last night. There were deep wheel ruts where the fire engine had gouged its way over the lawn. Several shrubs were squashed flat or shredded to bits. She saw the black patch up on the hill where the fire had burned. The hose water had all gone, but there were earth clots, imprinted with bootmarks, where the mud had been. They now had the only well-watered garden in the village, not that it had done any good. The hoses had blasted into the hillside, making the orchard look like a strip mine. Mirrie's flowerbeds were destroyed as if a giant boot had come down from the sky. The whitewashed side of the pottery building was scraped where the fire engine had pushed past it. She hoped none of the stock had been damaged. There was a bad smell in the air, oily and smoky with an undertrace of rot.

Looking around by the house, Hazel found the firemen had neglected to replace the iron drain cover. Peering into the black hole, she saw slimy stone and deformed mosses. She found the heavy cover a few feet away, and dragged it back, dropping it with a clang on the oblong hole, shifting it into place with her foot. Her wool-wrapped toes hurt. It hadn't been much, but it was a gesture towards cleaning up. The rest would have to wait. She wondered what she was going to tell the Bleaches. They'd trusted her with the place for the summer, and here it was a battlefield. It was nobody's fault, but she couldn't have blamed them for being upset.

This whole thing – Paul, the Pottery, the country – was not turning out well. Hazel wondered whether she shouldn't chuck it all. The trouble was Mike and Mirrie. They needed someone here until autumn, and had given her a good opportunity. She couldn't pull out early and leave the place empty. If she went, she couldn't expect Paul to stay.

In the house, the telephone rang, very loud. She looked up at the first-floor windows. The bedroom was curtained. Paul was still unconscious. At least, he must have been until the phone started.

She ran inside and picked up the receiver, instinctively gabbling out her parents' number in Brighton, then apologizing and reading the Pottery's off the dial. It was a journalist from a local paper, wanting details of the fire.

'Was it the hippies?' the reporter asked.

Hazel didn't understand. 'It was a fire.'

'Might it have been the hippies, the festival people? Careless with matches? The drought?'

The man didn't seem to be listening. 'It was a fire,' she told him, 'just a fire. I don't know how it got started. There were some kids camping up on the hill, but . . .'

'Hippies?'

'Kids. London kids.'

'Here for the festival?'

'Yes.'

'Hippies.'

Hazel saw how the interview was running. 'The firemen said it was just a fluke. Nobody's fault.'

'But the hippies . . . the kids . . . they had a fire going?'

'I don't know.'

The journalist asked her name and her age, then got back to hippies. 'Were there any drugs, do you know?'

She didn't have an answer.

If you weren't local, you were either rich or a hippie. She and Paul obviously weren't rich, so that automatically made them, if not hippies then hippie-sympathizers, hippie-collaborators. Back in Brighton, hippies were people her parents' age, not kids.

'Do you have an estimate on how much damage was done? For the insurance?'

Hazel couldn't think. The fire, and more particularly the fire engine, had made a mess, but there was little damage that an insurance pay-out could put right. Besides, she didn't know what coverage the Bleaches had.

'It's too early,' she told him. 'I'm just looking after the place.'

He hung up without thanking her.

Hazel got the impression the journalist had written his story before speaking to her. The call just helped him fill in the names. She'd bought the paper the man worked for once, hoping for information about nearby cinemas and music venues but finding only rugby-club members dressed as women for fund-raising revues, weddings, speeding offences, letters of complaint and stories about hippies damaging farmers' property. Paul said this was like the Wild West, where there was a bounty on Apache scalps: if you took in some bloody hair hunks or the love beads from a dead hippie, they'd give you a flagon of cider and three groats.

She heard a clumping and turned around. Paul was making his way down the stairs like an old man, clutching the banister to steady himself. His hair was over his face and he hadn't shaved. He wore shorts, slippers and his dressing gown. He'd lost the cord, and the gown hung open. There was a huge bruise on one side of his chest, purple and yellow.

'Haze?'

He gingerly stepped off the stairs, arms out for balance. She wasn't sure whether to hug him or back away for fear of hurting. The passage was too small for both of them to be comfortable so close.

'Are you all right?' she asked, arms by her sides.

'I don't know. I feel like I've been hit by a bus.'

'The doctor said you banged your head.'

'There was a doctor?'

Paul held his head, pushing back his hair. He looked old.

'He left some pills for you to take, and a number to call. He said to get in touch if you felt any lasting pain.'

'I can't feel anything else.'

'Poor dear.' That was the sort of thing Mum would have said. Hazel bit her tongue.

Paul managed to get to the front room by himself.

'Can I get you anything? Tea? Orange juice?'

He shook his head, and eased himself into a chair.

'The place is a mess outside,' she said.

'Haze,' he said, trying to focus his eyes, trying to be serious. 'Last night, I saw something. Up at the fire, there was something . . .'

'That was the local paper on the phone. They want to blame it on kids. That's typical, don't you think? Blaming kids for everything.'

'Hazel, it was . . .'

She looked at him, and he didn't finish what he was saying.

'Yes?'

'I don't know. It was big, dangerous . . .'

'The firemen put it out, though. It's over.'

'No . . . yes . . . maybe.'

Paul covered his face with his hands and rubbed. She had the impression he wasn't that aware of her. He was trying to talk to himself, not to tell her anything.

Hazel remembered her dream. She could still feel the touch of the hands. She had never had a dream like that before, where she remembered a feeling rather than a picture.

'I'll go over to the Agapemone later and thank them. They came over to help in the fire. See, they're not that bad after all.'

Paul looked at her. 'No,' he said, 'be careful.'

'Paul,' she said, annoyed, 'you can't criticize. They were a help. Just because . . .'

Because what? She lost her train of thought.

'Dangerous,' he said.

'Don't be silly. I can look after myself.'

He almost laughed, almost nastily. 'I'm not sure, Hazel. I'm not sure if any of us can look after ourselves.'

She didn't know what he meant. He didn't say anything more.

She knew she wouldn't work today. The routine was broken. She'd go to the Agapemone. On the walk over, she could do some thinking. When she got back, she'd try to tidy up a bit. By then, Paul should be well enough to help. Although, at that, she was not sure of Paul. This morning, he was different. The doctor had said there was nothing broken, but Paul wasn't being Paul just now, so maybe there was something wrong inside.

'Tea?' she asked again. Paul did not answer. 'Please yourself.'

She stood up and looked around for her jeans. They were balled up on a chair, legs inside out. Pulling them on, she remembered the long legs she had been given in the dream. Long, strong legs, for running, for gripping. Paul leaned back in his chair and looked up at the ceiling. She wondered just how hard the knock on his head had been. She pulled the blind on the front window and let it whizz up, toggle rattling against the windowpane.

The room was sunlit. On the floor, by the coffee table, she saw her plate, the girl plate, lying face down. It was in three pieces, a jigsaw roughly put together. She felt the loss in her stomach, and water leaked from her eyes. Her nose was clogged.

'What is it?' Paul asked.

She knelt by the broken plate and reached out to it. She could not touch it, could not turn the bits over to look at the face she'd drawn. She was sniffling, tears hot on her cheeks. It was not fair! Susan Ames, the woman from the Agapemone, had looked like the girl on the plate. She put a hand over her eyes and felt tears on the insides of her fingers.

'Haze?'

She didn't want to talk. Getting up, rubbing her eyes, she left the room, left the house. Outside, under the cruel sun, she knelt on the dead grass and bawled like a little girl. Her one decent piece of work. Gone. Lost. For ever. Some clumsy fireman, or Paul blundering about, or one of the villagers who'd crowded in. There'd been more than twenty people through the house last night, offering help, asking questions. Just a slip, and the plate was gone.

She wiped her face on the stomach of her T-shirt and tried to stop sobbing. Paul didn't come out to her. She wanted the touch of the hands from her dream. They could put her plate together as new. They could take away the damage, mess and pain. She thought she knew where the hands had come from.

She stood up, dusty earth on her knees, and left the Pottery, wandering, asphalt hard and rough beneath her socks, down the road. She saw the tree outside the pub, dead and gloating. Up on the hillside, she saw the Agapemone. It looked like a calming place to be. She put her hands in her hip pockets and kept her head down.

Three

BELOVED STOOD OVER the camera obscura. The village was becoming crowded. The lower fields, set aside for parking, were filling with vans and cars. Brightly coloured tents sprouted like fungus in the camping areas. There were more moving figures than there'd been yesterday, people about the scale of toy soldiers. They'd been turning up since very early this morning. Some must have been driving all night.

Jenny saw the scorch where the fire had been, a scar on the yellow hillside, a hole in the picture. Beloved leaned into the illusion, and the hill bled on to His face, brown trees covering His cheeks. He smiled, and let His hands wander through the phantom village, rippling houses and people. Beloved was radiant this morning, glowing faintly. He had a definite aura, unnoticeable under natural light but plain in the dark at the top of the house. It made Him look like an angel.

Jenny saw the woman, a stick figure moving like an insect. Coming from the other end of the village, from the Pottery, she was walking quickly, awkwardly. Three newcomers on bikes silently buzzed her, making a skid turn by the old tree, heading off towards the camp site. The woman kept on walking. Beloved stretched out a hand and touched the tiny head, His finger sinking in so her pinpoint face was on His fingerprint.

'Her,' Beloved said, quietly, 'she is Chosen.'

Jenny bowed her head. Unlike some of the other Sisters, she was beyond jealousy. No man or woman could have Beloved all the time. His grace was to be shared with all humankind. He nodded slightly, drawing the tiny woman to Him as if she were on the end of an invisible silk thread. Beloved held His hand, palm down, over her, casting a blot of a shadow. The plain black of the table showed through the vivid image of Alder, an earthquake chasm across the farms and houses.

Jenny raised her eyes, fascinated. It was hard to look away

from Him. Beloved's wounds were leaking again. A drop of blood formed in the centre of His palm, becoming heavier as it filled out, ballooning into a red tear. It splashed on to the table, shining in the illusion. The woman, as if alerted, stepped out of the way of the red rain and walked around the puddle.

Four

HIS THOUGHTS WERE too fast, dizzying away inside his head. He looked at the ceiling of the Bleach sitting room. It had been decorated in the late Sixties, when the Bleaches first came to Alder. Pictures from Sunday supplements had been pasted up in a collage. Faces from the past were frozen, fading slowly. Paul had been picking out people he recognized. George Best, Patrick MacNee, Anouk Aimée, Harold Wilson, Neil Armstrong, Jimi Hendrix. He had always found it relaxing. Now, it was a visual shriek.

The world was smashed like Hazel's plate, and could not be put back together again. At least, not in a way he would be happy with. Reality, he knew, was a consensus, something everyone agreed to accept. Now, someone was trying to force the unacceptable on him.

In retrospect, it was the fish – not the Martian war machine – that had broken the camel's back. That had not been just unlikely, that had been impossible. Paul kept thinking of the fish, the way it sank slowly into the pond, the fruitlike sucker that attached it to the bush. It must still be at the bottom, resting in thin mud, an impossible thing upon the possible earth. How could he have accepted it as natural, then walked away? Fish, he repeated over and over, do not grow on bushes.

This morning, sharp, clean pains were shot like darts from his broken tooth. Furthermore, his ribs hurt, his legs hurt, his face hurt. His mind, however, hurt most of all.

Things that could not be, were.

His head a lump of fudge-wrapped pain, he made his way from the sitting room to the kitchen, then out on the verandah. He couldn't be bothered with tea or coffee. If the world made no sense, what was the point of breakfast?

Hazel had been right. The place was chewed up. She wasn't around. She must have gone off to the Agapemone. Despite everything, it was his duty to warn her off, to prevent her getting mixed up with the cult. Once he'd dealt with the impossible, he would pay attention to that.

He looked at the hill, at the horizon where last night he'd seen the smoke. It was a distinct treeline, under a cloudless sky. If he'd been looking the other way, would any of this have happened? Or would he be worrying now about Hazel's moods, not the shape of reality? Waking up, alone and hurting, in the double bed, his first thought – before it all crept back to him – was that Hazel was gone.

He still hadn't got it sorted out in his mind, but he knew the Martian war machine had been for him. Who else would have recognized it? He sat on the verandah steps, leaning against the sun-warmed stone wall, and held his head. He wanted to take something to dull the hurt in his tooth, but he couldn't afford to fog his mind. He needed to think this through. Anyway, although Hazel said the doctor had left pills for him, she had not told him where they were. He sloshed spittle around the tooth, imagining the pain washing away. Momentarily it helped, but pain came back in an instant.

Everything was changed.

Fish do not grow on bushes. And, worse, Martian war machines are not only impossible, they are fictional.

Almost anything else would have put less strain on his credulity, his sanity. If he'd close-encountered an alien space-craft of unfamiliar design, all he'd have to do was accept a vast body of UFO lore, proceeding from the logical, well-founded position that there was intelligent life elsewhere in the universe to the far-fetched, but not entirely lunatic, notion that such intelligent life was given to dropping by Planet Earth once in a while. If it had been a Tyrannosaurus Rex chomping on poached sheep, he could blame genetic engineers fooling with fossil tissue, guess that radioactive waste from Hinkley Point nuclear power station had seeped into the seabed and revived the creature, or assume a timewarp was operating in the locality. If it had been Lord Lucan, Elvis Presley or Martin Bormann playing with matches, the meeting would be merely unlikely and he could make a fortune tattling to a tabloid. If it had been a transparent Duke of Monmouth clanking chains and crying for his rightful throne, Paul would just have to admit there were such things as ghosts. These weren't positions he was especially keen to adopt,

but all were within the bounds of credibility. After all, the bulk
of humanity subscribed to religions founded on only barely less
unlikely premises.

But a Martian war machine? This wasn't a scientific unknown,
or a psychic phenomenon, or a strange-but-true story, or a
miracle from God. This was something *made up* in 1898,
something that had no existence outside the imagination of
H. G. Wells. Somewhere in the world, you could find people who
believed in ghosts and demons, elves and fairies, the curse of King
Tut, Jesus Christ Our Lord and Redeemer, Whitley Streiber's
extraterrestrial anal molesters, American professional wrestling
matches, the Loch Ness Monster, Bigfoot and the yeti, George
Bush's campaign promises, the characters on *EastEnders*, the
Hollow Earth Theory, Bacon's authorship of *Hamlet*, Ambrose-
Collectors from Atlantis, *The Amityville Horror*, Maradona's
'hand of God' goal, 'double biological' soap powders. The
human race, among its other accomplishments, could persuade
itself, individually or in mass, to believe almost bloody anything.
But nowhere had anyone ever – except briefly over Halloween
1938, when Orson Welles was trick-or-treating – believed in
Martian war machines.

Yet the thing hadn't been ambiguous. It had been what it
was, as real as his pain. His bruises were proof. He could still
feel the jarring impact of the machine's metal leg. It had rattled
his teeth, making his tooth flare. His skin was broken where the
thing had scraped.

Paul experimented with the notion of hallucination. After
all, he'd spent the greater portion of the last few months, the
last five years, thinking about his thesis, and Wells's Martians
were central to his argument. People see what they expect to
see: whether it be the Virgin Mary, dome-headed midgets in
glowing saucers, or the buckskin-fringed King of Rock 'n' Roll.
He could have misinterpreted, seeing something that put him in
mind of a Martian war machine and mentally transforming it
into one.

He held his tooth between thumb and forefinger, trying to
squeeze out the pain.

Seizing on the hallucination theory, he chewed it in his mind:
the Martian war machine had been instantly recognizable because
it was *his* Martian war machine. The *War of the Worlds* movie
substituted Cornish-pasty-shaped flying ships, and the various

illustrations he'd seen on book or album covers weren't quite right. They were frailer, or more rounded, or less mechanical. The thing he'd seen up on the hill was his mental picture, compounded of the author's description and his own detail-filling imagination. The thing appeared to him exactly as he imagined it. For a moment, he thought he had an answer, then he knew he had only more questions.

One of the problems with the novel – although, for Paul, it was a strength – was that Wells never quite explained how a three-legged machine could move. Logically, it would have to be like a one-legged man on two crutches, but that doesn't sound threatening enough. Christopher Priest, in *The Space Machine*, worked out a system involving a spinning-top motion, but that struck Paul as too awkward. The film-makers had just copped out and got rid of the legs. The war machine last night moved naturally, as if having three legs was entirely the usual arrangement and unsteady bipeds were at a disadvantage.

It had been unimaginable. Therefore, he could not have imagined it. It had been real. It had hurt him, it had displaced indisputably real objects, and it had used a real heat ray. Imaginary hallucinations do not start actual fires.

And the kid, the mohican-haired kid, he'd seen it too.

Paul looked up at the fire site on the hill. It was peaceful now, blackened earth and burned-out trees blending in with yellow-leaved bushes and tanned grass.

Paul tried to picture the kid. It was hard to remember anything but his hair, the one detail overwhelming his ordinary face and standard ripped-jeans-and-a-T-shirt outfit. He'd been skinny, and he'd had a London accent. 'Fuck, fuck, fuck,' he had said. He'd pushed Paul, thumping his shoulder. He'd been wearing a black leather wristlet, dotted with studs. The kid had seen the war machine. Two people couldn't share a hallucination. Paul knew he had to find that kid, talk to him. Maybe, if he did, he wouldn't go mad.

Five

DADDY WAS STRANGE this morning.

During the school holidays, they always had breakfast together, Daddy tucking into bacon and eggs because he'd already done a couple of hours' work, Mummy having just yoghurt and fruit juice because she was forever on a diet, Hannah and Jeremy eating cereal and drinking orange.

Today, they all arrived at the table at different times. Mummy was getting breakfast ready in the kitchen, making a lot of noise, when Jeremy, in his pyjamas, came down to the dining room and found Daddy sitting in his usual chair, covered with earth.

It was over his shirt, hands and face. His cheeks were plastered, like an African tribesman's, with lines of chalk mixed in. Often, he would get dirty. Farming, he said, was a mucky job most of the time. But one of the rules of the house was that you washed before coming to the table.

Jeremy was outraged. Daddy was supposed to make the rules, not break them.

'Daddy,' he said, 'you're dirty.'

Mummy had the radio on in the kitchen, and pop music gurgled out. Daddy turned to Jeremy. Egg-white eyes opened in his mask of dry earth.

'Daddy?'

'Here it comes,' said Mummy, stepping in with a tray.

The tray hit the floor and flipped over, scattering bacon rashers and globs of scrambled egg. A plate smashed, and knives and forks skittered on the tiling.

'Maurice,' Mummy gasped, 'what the *fuh* –'

Daddy looked at Mummy, and she made a scared face.

Hannah tumbled late into the room, rubbing sand out of her eyes, yawning. She sat at the table and filled her bowl with cornflakes.

'Daddy, you look silly,' she said, and sloshed in the milk.

Mummy sat down and shook her head. Daddy's clothes were torn. There were streaks of blood in his dirt mask. His jeans were ruined, the fly exploded and filth-clogged.

Daddy didn't say anything. Jeremy backed away.

'Sit down,' Mummy said.

Jeremy didn't want to go near Daddy, but didn't want to go against Mummy either. He pulled his chair back and slid into it, never letting his eyes move from Daddy's brown face. Hannah was eating as usual. Daddy put his hands on the table, and crumbs of soil spread from his fingers. Daddy smiled an Evil Dwarf smile, a line of spit damping the earth around his lips, and his mouth began to open. He coughed, and chunks of dirt came out, burping on to the table.

'What's wrong, love?' Mummy asked, gingerly putting her clean hand on Daddy's dirty sleeve.

'Nothing,' Daddy croaked. His voice had changed, as if his throat had turned to bark and planes of rough wood were rasping together inside him. 'I've put things right with the land,' Daddy said.

Jeremy looked at Mummy. Obviously, no one knew what to do. Hannah finished her cereal and pushed her chair back.

'Sit down,' Daddy told her.

Unsure, she did, stuttering out a 'But . . . but' before going silent and sulking.

'Give thanks, family.'

Jeremy looked down at the tabletop, then sideways at Mummy. Mummy was scared. That made Jeremy scared too. Scared of Daddy.

He saw dirt thick around Daddy's fingers, coating the nails, clodding in between like duck-webbing. There were rootlike tendrils mixed in with the earth, growing out of Daddy.

He looked up. Daddy had taken an apple from the bowl and was eating it. The apple should have been thrown out today, since it was half shrivelled and nobody had bothered with it before. Jeremy was sure there were maggots in it. As Daddy ate, more dry earth fell from his face. It came off in chunks, showing his skin. Daddy was changed. There were boils on his forehead. Red and protruberant, like little bruised apples, they seemed about to break. His face was longer, nose extended, the beginnings of a wispy beard around his chin. He munched the apple down, skin, pips, core and all.

'We must make sacrifices,' he said, reaching for a breadknife.

Mummy flinched, and Hannah was crying. Daddy pulled his sleeve and bared his forearm. The music from the kitchen burbled out, a disc jockey interrupting to read out funny items about the weather from the papers. Daddy stuck the breadknife into his arm. Blood came, but not much. A greeny-yellow liquid seeped out. The blood was just a few red threads in the other, sappy stuff. It smelled like glue. Daddy pulled the breadknife out of himself and put it down. The hole he had made opened and closed like a goldfish's mouth, spewing more of the yellow-green on to the table.

Mummy got up, and Daddy hit her. His arm was longer than usual, and he fetched Mummy a hard thump on the side of her head, lifting her out of her chair, pitching her across the floor. Mummy fell down, chair tangled in her legs, and, although she tried, didn't get up again. There was blood in her hair.

'Now,' Daddy said, 'bow, you heathens.'

Jeremy and Hannah bowed their heads and mumbled. Daddy laughed, not like himself but like the Evil Dwarf. Dopey had come in the night and eaten his brain. Jeremy *knew* this had happened. The Daddy-shaped thing at breakfast was just the leftovers from the meal.

The children looked again. Mummy was pulling herself up, shaking her head dizzily, holding tight to the table edge for balance. She got her seat upright beneath her, and slumped. Daddy had mashed part of her hair, and a bleeding bruise was showing. She opened her mouth to complain, but a glance from Daddy's rotten eyes silenced her. He reached out again, and Mummy flinched, but instead of hitting, he stroked. His fingers smoothed her hair against the gash in her head, and she winced.

Daddy smiled. Mummy was whimpering quietly, like Hannah when she was scolded. Mummy touched Daddy's arm, fingertips probing the wound, dabbling in the honeyish gum. Daddy nodded, and Mummy tasted her finger. Weakly, she tried a smile.

'See,' Daddy said.

Jeremy looked at the shell that had been his Daddy. The boils on his forehead burst, drops of clear liquid dribbling past his eyes. Tiny shoots, bright green like spring bulbs, were emerging from his head, curling slightly in the light. In his smile, his teeth were bright yellow, like corns on a cob.

'Now,' he said, 'what shall we do today?'

Six

'HAZEL?' THE girl was distracted, blank-faced. Her eyes were large, waiflike. 'It's me, Susan. Remember, from last night.'

She'd found Hazel on the private road to the Agapemone, walking and dreaming. Weirdly, Susan saw herself in Hazel's mind, face cracked into three.

'Oh, uh, hi,' said the girl. 'Good morning.'

She wasn't wearing shoes, just grubby wool socks. Bumping into Susan unnerved her, as if she'd met someone she knew only from a dream.

'Good morning. Are you all right?'

Hazel pushed a hand through her hair, scratching her scalp. Susan saw her confusion. She might be in traumatic shock. Then again, she might just be a daydreamer. It was too easy to intuit the worst all the time.

'How's your boyfriend?'

'All right,' she said, without conviction. 'Up and about.'

They were by the side of the road. Usually, there was no traffic. Today there was almost a jam, with carloads of festival-goers turning up early. There were several travellers' caravans, possessions roped to roofs, rickety and battered as an Okie convoy.

'Out for a walk?'

Hazel tried to think. Susan tried to read her. She'd been almost sleepwalking.

'I thought . . . uh . . . I'd visit the Agapemone again . . . thank you . . .'

She saw in Hazel a vacancy, a need. The girl was under pressure, not easy to read accurately. She was just Jago's type, a vessel steadily emptied, waiting to be filled with the faith.

Susan didn't know what to do. Less ignorant of the dangers of the Agapemone than anyone, she ought to try to put Hazel off. But warning Hazel would rip her Sister of the Agapemone

snakeskin. Soothsaying wasn't her style, anyway. That was
why she was Susan Anonymous. She didn't want to end up
like Cassandra, kicked to death.

A biker cruised by, engine protesting, squeezing between the
cars and the verge. Susan and Hazel had to step out of his way.
The boy's jacket-back, with a flaming skull and 'Route 666' logo,
reminded her that Wendy's leather ghost was still around. At
the fire, Susan thought she'd glimpsed him mingling with the
bystanders.

'Well,' said Hazel, 'must be going . . .'

Susan had to try to help the girl. She did not like to interfere,
to use her Talent like a puppeteer. But sometimes it was the only
way.

'See you later,' Susan said, fixing Hazel's eyes with her own,
pressing a mentacle delicately against the girl's mind. She found
it useful to imagine a point between the person's eyes as a tiny
hole, leading funnel-like into their brain, their mind. Susan tried
to plant a seed of doubt, to give Hazel protection.

'There,' she said. 'Goodbye.'

They parted. Susan watched Hazel wander up past the Gate
House. She had not seen James Lytton since last night. She
must talk to him later. She hoped the girl would be able
to look after herself. Hazel climbed the steps to the front
door and pressed the bell button. Susan was reminded of
Psycho. The Agapemone had an attic window like Mrs Bates's
bedroom, but it was blacked out. Beloved was playing with
his Victorian toy. She looked up, imagining neon eyes in the
sky. She wondered how much Beloved saw. If she could sense
what he was, then he must be able to see through her. Of
course, he had disadvantages: he had only Bible stories to
justify his Talent, not years of tests and research. And he was
mad.

She turned and went on her way.

There was an old red telephone box by the pub, opposite
the dead tree, and Susan had a supply of carefully hoarded
coins. There was no point calling from the Agapemone. She
didn't think the phone was tapped, but it was on the table
in the hall and couldn't be used in private. That was one of
the ways Beloved cut his disciples off from their old lives –
parents, friends, ex-partners, whoever. Mick said the Brethren
weren't prisoners, but that might be because Beloved was a

subtle master. Whenever anyone made a call, they had to account for it in a ledger, writing down the number called and the duration. It was one of Mick's systems to keep bills under control. Susan noticed that if anyone did try to call out, Mick – or Gerald Taine or another of the cabal Susan had tagged as the Agapemone's enforcers – would find something to do within earshot.

On the other side of the road, Derek and Marie-Laure – nobody's idea of a dynamic duo – were doing their best to direct traffic, guiding vehicles on to the hard-packed earth track to the parking areas. Susan waved to them, but they didn't notice. They were fuzzy this morning, too, moving clumsily like astronauts or deep-sea divers. The Sister was prayerfully muttering to herself, eyes fixed on the dirt, while Derek was humming a tune Susan could barely remember being in the charts, 'Nights in White Satin'. He waved at her, head empty.

The telephone box was useless to most disciplines because having small change was a rarely granted privilege. Money was held in common, and every penny spent had to be explained. Only James, useful as a free agent, had any petty cash at all. One effect of this was to isolate the Brethren from the community. They couldn't go to the pub for a drink or even drop by the garage and buy a packet of sweets. Her own coins had been smuggled in and hidden. Mick and Taine held regular inspections to track down uncharitably retained private property. In theory even clothes and toiletries were communally owned. There were penalties for hoarding. Karen Gillard once had to take a month's vow of silence because she kept a transistor radio for private use.

Two lads in an open-top car whistled and shouted a 'Hello, darling' at her. Seeing red, she turned to look in their direction.

'While I've got a face,' one of them said, 'you'll always have somewhere to sit.'

Before she had time to fight it, her mind swelled, and *reached* . . .

There were four quiet pops as tyres ruptured. The car settled, hissing, and stalled. Cars behind hit their horns. Children bawled. Susan was embarrassed. She had not meant that, but sometimes she could be surprised. She must be more guarded. Walking past the swearing youths, she wanted to make a smart comment but bit down on it. Let them think it was a freak accident. One of the lads was out of the car, gawking at the flat tyres. He was wearing a Loud Shit T-shirt and had an X of baldness shaved into his head.

She smiled at him, claiming responsibility.

'Witch,' he said.

Seven

'WHAT YOUM DOIN'?' Terry asked.
'Makin' sacrifice.'

Allison held the pigeon in one hand, her other over its head.
The bastard bird was beaking into her palm but wasn't making a
racket any more. She'd taken it from a tree, creeping up quiet and
clutching fast as a lizard. The small body, warm and bony in her
grip, squirted hot shit at her. She held it at arm's length, so the jet
mainly missed. She needed one hand to grip the bird, otherwise
she'd have used her cheesewire. She squeezed the bird's head and
wrenched it off. Blood choked out of the neckhole and the thing
kicked. She held it up and sprayed blood over the ground. She
sloshed some on Terry.

'Watch out,' he moaned.

She held up the squirming pigeon like a bottle, and sucked
blood. Hot and tasty, it ran down her chin like gravy.

'There, breakfast.'

She dropped the dead thing and wiped her face on her sleeve.
The bird's wings wound down and it quickly stopped kicking.
Sacrifice was made. She knew the importance of sacrifice.
Badmouth Ben had explained it to her. He had come to Alder
because of her sacrifices, because of Mr Keough's cats. Sacrifices
made him stronger.

'Gor fuck I,' said Terry, 'that's disgustin'.'

Allison stuck out her red tongue at him, and smeared his cheeks
with bloody thumbs.

'Clown,' she said, 'like your brother.'

Terry was theirs, marked now by blood and deed. In the end,
he'd be proud to be hers and Ben's. He was the first. Others would
come, initiated by blood. More sacrifices would be made. The
boy was twenty paces behind mentally, huffing and puffing to
catch up. This morning, his beard was heavy and ragged. It was
still a kid's bum fluff, but it gave him a beasty look. Ben had

helped Terry change. He wasn't much of an army, but he was a start. He was just stupid enough to fall in step.

'Last night,' Terry said, 'what bloody happened?'

They'd slept out after the hide-and-seek with Terry's brother and Lytton. This morning, Ben had got up early and gone about his business, leaving her in charge. She'd woken with dew on her face, cradled in the bushes, lying in a beaten-flat tunnel that protected them. Terry, clothes tattered, was nearby, snoring mouth wide open. He wasn't used to sleeping in the open. He wasn't close to the earth the way she was.

'Al'son?'

She smiled, and he went quiet. There were secrets he didn't need to penetrate. He was sensibly afraid of her. The lesson, however, had to be reinforced.

She stood near him, licking her lips, and slipped her hands under his shirt, feeling his soft, hairy belly. There was fear in his eyes, but also a little excitement. He thought he knew what he was getting, and raised his arms so she could pull his shirt over his head. She let her hands climb up his torso like thin spiders. She found his pulpy nipples and pinched hard, digging with her long thumbnails. He opened his mouth to shriek, tears welling up, and she quickly kissed him. With a final, flesh-abusing twist, she pushed him away. He was yelping like a dog now, and rubbing his teats.

'Pain,' she said, 'you got to be friends with pain.'

He swore and bit his lips, sucking in air. She brushed the twigs out of her hair and stretched. Terry sat down and complained again, howling like a kid, tears in the fur on his cheeks.

'Come on,' she told him. 'Get up. We'm got places to go, things to do.'

Eight

SHE GOT TO the telephone box just before a hefty, beef-faced man with a tweed jacket. He was standing outside, shifting his weight from foot to foot, chinking change in his hand, looking at his watch. She didn't have to be a Talent to get the message. She dialled the number. The phone was lifted on the third ring.

'Good morning,' said a cheery voice. Feminine but faceless, like a machine. 'Ministry of Defence, Ip-Sit.'

'It's pronounced "eyesight",' Susan said, impatient with silly games, 'and put me through to David Cross.'

'I'm sorry, Dr Cross is in a meeting.'

'Interrupt. He'll want to talk to me. I'm in a call box.'

Pip pip pip pip.

It was an old-fashioned pay phone. You couldn't fill it with money and talk until your credit ran out. The glass was cracked, some squares missing. The directories were shredded and scribbled on, marked with old stains. There was graffiti magic-markered childishly into the list of exchanges. TEDDY 4 ALLISON. GARY IS A POOF. IRGUN ZVAI LEUMI. AGAPEM-MONY GITS. BANNERMAN BURNS IN HELL.

'Interrupt. This thing is eating my change.'

'Dr Cross is in a meeting.'

'Miss, please get him. My name is Susan Ames. Say Susan Rodway. He'll want to talk to me.'

Pip pip pip pip.

She heard empty air, pencils tapping, muffled voices. Then a rattle as an extension was picked up.

'Susie, what is it?'

'David, I'm in a call box. Can you get back to me? The number is . . . shit, it's been defaced.'

She shoved another twenty pence in the slot. The booth smelled as if generations of customers staggering out of the pub had used it as a urinal. The one-man queue was fuming,

reciting 'bloody hippies' over and over like a mantra. If the box
was a public toilet, he was desperate to go.

Pip pip pip pip.

'I've fed this thing enough to call Singapore for an hour, but it
keeps wanting more.'

'What's wrong?'

'It's Jago and Alder. There seems to be a crisis coming. I'm
observing an increase in phenomena. There's some kind of spiral
effect.'

'I have a note on my desk about a fire last night.'

'That may be connected. I'm not sure.'

Pip pip pip pip.

The waiting man knocked on the door and shook a fist. Susan
turned her back to him, but he just stepped around the corner
and knocked again. She let her hair fall over her face and kept her
head down, bracing her back against the door, telephone cord half
wrapped around her.

'David, close this down.'

'I've tried recommending that before, and got nowhere. This
is Sir Kenneth's favourite spook show.'

'I think Jago is becoming more dangerous. There are a lot
of people here. For the festival. I think we could be talking
cataclysm. This thing goes back beyond Jago. I think it goes
back centuries.'

'Susan, you're rambling. We're parapsychologists, not ghost-
busters. Are you well in yourself?'

Pip pip pip pip.

'Fires. They keep cropping up in the history of this hill. There's
a perennial ghost called the Burning Man, and a World War Two
bomb story.'

'Do you still have the headaches?'

'David, this is not about me.'

'When were you last looked at by our people? Have you had
any unusual physical symptoms? Increased poltergeist activity
during your periods? Apparitions? You may be throwing the
experiment out by your presence.'

'David . . .'

Pip pip pip pip.

Her last coin jammed.

'David . . .'

Pip pip pip pip . . . buzzzzzzz.

Nine

FIRST, WENDY DECIDED she just wouldn't get out of bed. Badmouth Ben couldn't get her if she stayed under the duvet. She could still feel where he had gripped her, hear his whispered words, smell his burned-out stench.

Somehow, she'd got back to the Agapemone last night and, with medical help, gone to sleep. She wasn't supposed to have pills, but she'd got some on her last shopping run to Bridgwater and hidden them from Brother Mick. Luckily Marie-Laure, her partner on the run, was only notionally aware of what went on outside her head. She'd bought first aid supplies, slipped the pills in on the tally, then spirited them to the room she shared with Derek, hiding them inside a tampax container to get through inspections. The bottle, evidence of her guilt, was half-empty on the bedside table. She could not remember how many she'd taken. Even with pills, she slept badly. The nightmare started before she got to bed, and it was not over now she was awake. Hard sunlight filtered through the gable window. Dust shapes formed and dispersed in the beams. Derek was long gone.

The pills made her slow. She pulled the duvet tighter. The clock told her it was past eleven. She should have been up for hours. She'd missed the breakfast ceremony. Her sense of community was weak now. She'd come to the Agapemone for that safety, and it was slipping away. Safety, and Beloved. She tried to pray, but couldn't. If Ben was back, she'd have to see Beloved, have to get His help. Only He could face the dead-alive monster. Only He could save her.

'The good thing about a sheep,' she remembered Ben saying, words twisting like little scalpels, 'is that you can *fuck* her . . .'

His teeth were sharp in the remains of his face. He had polished metal studs set into the burned leather of his forehead, cheeks and chin.

'. . . *kill* her . . .'

Bone showed through at his knuckles, but his fingers had been strong, painfully digging in, LOVE and HATE biro-etched blue on yellow into his knucklebones.

'. . . *eat* her . . .'

His eyes were glittering evil olives, horribly alive in his dead face.

'. . . and *wear* her.'

His hands had been all over her, tearing memories from her flesh, memories of Ben when he had been alive.

'Sheep,' he had said to her, 'go baaa-*baaaa*!'

It was too much. She gave up. Ben could come and have her. It was too late to fight. She lay back like a corpse, hands over her chest. She sucked in her stomach and looked up at the ceiling. The windows were tall and thin. Reflections played around the light fittings. She arranged her hair on the pillow, smoothed the duvet lightly over herself, and recomposed her hands. She was laid out, waiting for the funeral, waiting for Badmouth Ben.

Time passed. The electric clock's hands moved silently. She heard the small sounds of the house, traffic outside, far-off voices. She waited. Ben didn't come for her. She shut her eyes and tried to imagine the worst. Then she thought of Beloved. She began to pray like a child, remembering everyone she knew and appealing for the Lord God's mercy on them. She tried to find the Love in herself and dispense it. She tried to order her soul as she had done her body. She wanted to be a pure martyr, to go to the next world as a credit to her Saviour.

Ben's face faded and Beloved's swelled, replacing him. Wendy might be giving in, accepting death, but Beloved would remain upon this earth until His task was accomplished. He was here to suffer and die for humanity. At any moment, she expected the monster to come for her. Nothing. By day, there was nothing.

She got bored. Hot under the duvet, she was perspiring uncomfortably in her thick nightie. Sunlight lay on her hands, burning. She tried to concentrate on prayer, but her eyes kept creeping open. Nothing changed in the room. There were no shadows to shelter Badmouth Ben. Wendy realized she needed urgently to pee. She got up and tentatively stepped towards the door. No clawed hands shot out from the dark under the bed to grab her ankles. Not only did she have to pee, but her sunstruck wrists and hands were itchy. She had jaw-ache from gritting her teeth and an emptiness in her stomach from missed breakfast.

Crossing herself, she went down the hallway to the bathroom, unsteady on her feet from the pills. She remembered the feeling from before. Before Beloved, before Ben even. Then, she'd washed down her pill ration with paper-cupfuls of vodka. She hadn't drunk since she first met Him, in Brighton, in the Adullam. Beloved met all her hungers and thirsts. Still, a vodka – a *small* one – was about what she needed now.

'Good morning, Sister,' said someone.

She looked, focused and smiled. It was Sister Jenny. Wendy bowed and returned the greeting.

'We missed you at breakfast.'

'Up late.'

'Yes, of course. Are you all right?'

The girl was kindly, concerned, but her question annoyed Wendy. Her bladder was distending, growing heavier.

'Of course I'm all right,' she said, pain blooming in her skull, 'why shouldn't I be?'

'The fire. You were there.'

'Yes.'

'My prayers were with you.'

It would take more than this yellow-haired child's prayers to keep Ben at bay. Jenny was smiling, an impossibly pretty doll. She wore a white dress, laced at the neck, that shone. Nothing could touch her. Wendy's legs threatened to give out. She had to get to the bathroom soon, or her bladder would burst, spattering the girl with pee, bile and blood. Jenny came forward, moving as fast as Badmouth Ben, and hugged her.

'We share Love,' the girl said.

'Yes,' Wendy agreed, gently escaping.

She made it into the bathroom, locked the door behind her, hiked up her nightie and sat on the toilet, letting go. Then she looked at herself in the mirror. Her face was puffy, her eyes red, her hair a stringy mess. Shit, she thought, where did the years go?

She had been with Derek since she was eighteen. Considerably longer than half her life. She didn't understand how he could stay so untouched. He followed her lead with tolerable enthusiasm – from university to dropout, from flat to squat, from commune to community, from dope to pills, from politics to religion – but she didn't know if he really shared her beliefs or went along because it was easier. Recently, he'd been eclipsed by

the Beloved Presence, but he had not complained. Atrocity,
murder, addiction, God in the flesh: there was nothing Derek
could not, given a few joints and some records, deal with.

Now, Badmouth Ben was back.

In Wales, Ben had done terrible things to them all. Being
raped was something you could never forget, not one detail.
And she'd been raped a dozen times the long, hot summer. She
remembered her face in the pillow, a wet fold of it jammed in
her mouth as she bit, and Ben heavy on her, fucking her over
and over, making her bleed. That hadn't even been the worst.

The worst was afterwards, when Ben took her into his
confidence and explained how the world was arranged, who'd
suffer next and how. Ben had once threatened to snip off Derek's
cock with sheep-shears. Yet, Wendy didn't think Derek would
be upset to know the man he'd killed was back. He'd probably
offer him a joint and ask how he'd been since 1976, what
festivals he'd been to, whom of the old crowd he'd seen
recently.

She brushed her teeth, throughly sluicing her mouth, and
washed her face. She soaked a brush and ran it through her hair.
She was seeing to her surface self, leaving her depths troubled.
Back in her room, she dressed slowly, carefully, deliberately
putting arms and legs through holes. She picked her meeting
clothes. She tied her hair with a ribbon.

Wendy went downstairs and outside to another monoton-
ously lovely day. From the steps of the Agapemone, she saw
traffic pouring in. She saw the Brethren at work, setting up the
festival. She saw the yellow stretches of the moors. She tried
hard to Love everything.

'Hello,' said a voice, making her jump.

Someone came up to the Agapemone, shading eyes against
the sun. It was Hazel, the girl from the Pottery.

'Wendy, hi.'

'Uh, hi.'

She didn't know whether to shake hands or to hug. She did
nothing.

'I thought I'd come and say thanks.'

They stood on the green lawn, out in the open. Jenny joined
them, walking from the side garden with a basket of swollen
apples.

'Want one?'

Wendy scarfed it down in a few bites. Hazel nibbled hers slowly. Wendy realized the two had never met, and introduced them. They smiled at each other, pretty girls not in competition. Hazel had tanned, but Jenny was milk-pale. She'd been indoors a lot recently, with Beloved.

'Have you met Beloved?' Jenny asked. 'Mr Jago, Tony,' making herself clear.

'No,' Hazel said, adding, 'but I'd like to. Some time.'

'You must,' said Wendy, scenting a possible convert. 'He'll make things clear.'

'What things?'

'All things,' said Jenny. 'It's hard to put in words. But you'll know when you meet Him.'

'I'll look forward to it. Nothing has been clear lately.'

Wendy knew what Hazel meant.

'Have you noticed,' Hazel said, 'that it's like Sunday afternoon? As if it's all over, and there's nothing in particular to do. People are busy, but nothing counts, nothing is *happening* . . .'

'That's the festival for you,' said Jenny. 'Everyone stops.'

'Not everyone,' said Wendy, looking up at the Manor House. 'Look,' she said.

The attic window's blackout curtain rolled up. Sunlight caught the window as it swung open, shooting a dazzling light at them. All three held hands up to their eyes.

'Beloved,' Wendy and Jenny said, in unison.

Ten

LYTTON HAD MADE it home just after dawn, and drawn the curtains against the sun. In bed, he'd fallen asleep instantly, but woke up an hour later, at his usual time, jet-lagged. He needed a new adjective: brain-lagged, life-lagged, dream-lagged? He must rest, recoup. No matter how strange things got, he couldn't let himself be worn out. He willed himself back to sleep, and dreamed of crossword puzzles in vast checkerboard plains, a maze of oxymorons, palindromes and rebuses. In mid-morning, he woke up again, unable to sleep any longer.

Getting up late made it a special day. He should have been out doing more work at the stage areas. There was a note from Derek under his door, chillingly telling him everything was under control.

About last night . . .

He'd been briefed, by Dr Cross in scientific terms and by Garnett in blunter language. Belief was not a problem. He knew he wasn't going mad, he knew what was happening. He couldn't say he hadn't been prepared for this. There *were* such things. Not things, *phenomena*. He'd seen things all along and stayed calm, sane, rational. Last night had just been an extension of what he'd known since he was assigned here. He wouldn't allow himself the luxury of fear.

They called him a spook, but Jago was a natural, explicable thing. Unexplored, barely known, but natural. Dr Cross would eventually write a serious book, and someone else would do a trashy best-seller. There would be articles, TV movies, commissions of inquiry. And Jago would be an accepted part of the changing world, like coelacanths, depletion of the ozone layer or compact discs. They'd find a concrete-and-lead bunker, prison and tomb. Research would go on with less showy subjects. Still, last night had been quietly spectacular. And the phenomena were just side effects.

His Browning was on his desk, where he had unprofessionally left it last night. The door opened and, instinctively, Lytton picked up the gun, tugging the newspaper to cover it. Susan stepped in, and froze. She couldn't see the gun, but she could *see* it.

'Put that thing away.'

He dropped the paper and wrapped the pistol in it.

'Happy?'

'Ugh.'

'It's just a tool.'

The spook came into the small front room and sat down at his side table. Obviously the experiment had escalated enough for her to set aside their standing orders to keep away from each other. They could stop pretending to be strangers and work together. But they'd been pretending so long and had so little contact beforehand that they really were strangers. An intimacy was whipping up around them, and Lytton wasn't sure about it. He'd got used to stasis, and change suggested things were out of hand.

'I've just tried calling David,' Susan said. 'I've recommended shutting the programme down.'

Lytton drank his coffee.

'Any luck?'

'Weird shit. Just weird shit. For a start, the phone was playing up.'

'Jago?'

She put her elbows on the table and her chin in her hands.

'I don't know. It'd be easy to blame everything on Jago. The weather, even.'

She was sweating into her clothes, dark folds under her arms. Lytton found that faintly sexy.

'Did Dr Cross issue a policy statement?'

'Nothing like. He's writing it off as observer error. You know, unstable Talent plus feminine hysteria. What do I know, I'm an anomaly.'

He looked away from the spook.

'Don't worry,' she said, 'I'm not trying to read your mind. It's not like that. I have some extra chemicals in my brain. That's all.'

'I'm sorry,' he said. Usually, Susan was overcontrolled. Today, she was in a funny mood. Kittenish, scared, nervous, flirty, unpredictable.

'I'm not Carrie,' she said, eyes bugging. 'I do tricks, though.'

His *Guardian* unfolded and the gun slowly spun around, barrel pointing to him. Back at IPSIT, he'd seen videotapes of her playing similar games, spinning a top, remote-controlling a pencil, breaking china.

'See.'

The slide, untouched, shot back, chambering a round. Susan giggled.

Lytton knew she could easily work the trigger, and wondered how the gun, without a human hand wrapped around its grip, would kick.

'I used to bend spoons, too.'

He took the gun and put it in its drawer. He felt a slight pull as it tugged away from her influence.

'Have you reported anything?'

'I haven't had time. I can drop things at the police station in Achelzoy as usual. They get to Garnett.'

'David knew about the fire.'

'It'd have been on the local news. IPSIT are keeping an eye on the area for irregularities.'

Sometimes unmarked vans prowled around the village, bland young men going from door to door doing 'surveys'.

'James,' she said, face open, 'are we on our own here?'

He nodded. 'If we need it, we can get backup, but I'd prefer to leave that as a last resort.'

'It might not be enough anyway.'

'What would be enough?'

'An act of God? Maybe.'

He thought she was overreacting. 'Jago can't be that dangerous. He's been here over ten years –'

'Ticking.'

She was serious.

'Dr Cross thinks the two of us are enough to baby-sit him.'

'Uh-uh, James. That's not how it works. David makes recommendations, Sir Kenneth takes it under advisement. Garnett suggests how much cheaper it can be done, and David's suggestions get half implemented. It gets passed to a desk in the M.o.D, where someone who understands tanks or fighter planes but thinks IPSIT is a science-fiction waste of time has to approve a budget. We're what David has to make do with, and we come cheap.'

'I make my reports. It may be slow, but decisions get made.'

'What are we doing? Taking notes? I don't know about you, but I've been left alone. They're letting Jago alone and hoping he doesn't cause too much trouble. And they don't know how much trouble he can cause.'

Susan was frightened. And that pricked Lytton. He knew what he had to, but he did not *understand* the way she did. Even Dr Cross didn't know what it was like to be Susan, and she was the nearest reasonable thing they had to Jago.

She had just demonstrated how easy it would be for her undetectably to murder him. What point had she been making?

'I tried to warn David, but he has his own theoretical parameters and won't adapt to new data. It's not just Jago, it's a lot of other things. I think Jago is a focus for something that's been going for a long time.'

His hair began to rise. It was not fear, he knew. It was Susan. He'd read her file: when she got excited, she gave people near her horripilation. That was mild; under the same conditions Jago could drive people mad. He'd seen the movies: *The Fury*, *Scanners*, *Firestarter*. He wondered how easy it would be to explode a head.

'James,' she said, 'you're the minister's zookeeper. Are you just here for Jago?'

Muscles in his shoulders flinched.

'Or are you here for me, too?'

Eleven

IN DAYLIGHT, the top of the hill wasn't at all ominous. Paul was at the fire site before he thought to be afraid. The Martian war machine was unlikely enough in the first place. That it should revisit the scene of the crime would be really stretching it. He found his slippers, trampled into dried mud, one half-burned. He looked about for the war machine's imprints but only found firemen's bootmarks. The aftersmell of fire was like the miasma around a stubble-burned field.

The climb up the hill, even at a gentler pace than last night's expedition, reawakened pain in his legs and chest. He stopped to draw breath and look around. The area of devastation was surprisingly small when you were in it, barely twenty feet square. If the drought ended soon, it'd grow over within months. Looking out over the moors, he saw convoys of festival traffic converging at the Agapemone.

His lungs working now, he climbed over the stile at the top of the Bleach property and found himself in the woods. He tried to remember how he had run, the war machine behind and above him, and where the kids' camp was.

Stiff, dry bushes crowded in on the path, scratching. After a few minutes' struggle, he emerged into the clearing. It was empty. He was sure this was the place. There was a beaten-flat area of long, yellow grass, with wheel ruts. A van had been parked there. And there was a fireplace, surrounded by a wall of stones. Like a Western scout, he shoved his hand into the ashes. They weren't very warm. He supposed that meant the kids had cleared out last night. Or early this morning, before breakfast. Or had not been very good firekeepers. Or ash cooled quickly.

'G' mornin', Paul.'

He was not alone in the clearing. It was the wild girl, Allison. He had not heard her coming.

'Bit of a to-do last night, eh?'

He nodded. Allison was even wilder this morning. Her neck was stained with something congealing, like old tomato soup. Fringed jacket tied by the arms around her waist like a Red Indian breechclout, she looked leaner, sharper. She had a lad with her; not the face-ache from yesterday, one of the local yokels.

'This is Terry.'

The lad growled and scratched himself. Paul felt hostility coming off him in rank waves. Terry didn't like outsiders. Or he conceived dislikes easily, and let them fester.

'Wasn't there a camp here?'

Allison smiled, eyes shining. Paul still felt uncomfortable around her. She ping-ponged between seeming young and retarded and old and wise.

'Arr,' she said, agreeing, 'they kids from up London. They was frightened off. By Burning Man.'

'What?'

'Burning Man. Nothing but lights in the woods at night, but folks round here are daft. There's an old story 'bout a bonfire and a ha'ant.'

'A ha'ant?'

'Ghosties.' She smirked. 'Ask some of the old 'uns. Fools they be, but they got stories if youm buy 'em a pint.'

Terry looked as if he was about to drop down on all fours and go for the throat like a rottweiler.

'Where did the kids go?'

'Don't rightly know. Camp site, most like. Not fit for the wild woods, up London kids an't. Take they away from their video recorders and tube trains and them an't got a clue.'

'Was there a boy with a mohican haircut?'

'Arr, daft bugger. Wouldn't catch me makin' a fool of myself like that.'

Allison was prowling around, making him shift to keep eye contact. And Terry was skulking. Paul kept shooting glances at him, just in case he was about to turn.

'Burning Man's seen whenever they's trouble. Comes in a cloud of fire. Terry here's great-great-auntie met 'en once.'

Terry grunted and spat.

'Course, they's trouble now, in't there? And last night, they was fire.'

Allison stepped into the kids' fireplace as if it were a paddling pool, her boots sinking into ash.

'Mysterious fire,' she said.

She stood up straight, on tiptoes, and stretched out her arms, hanging her head to one side. In a high, off-key voice, she began to sing.

'Jesus loves me, this I know . . .'

She was nowhere near the, or any, tune.

'. . . 'cause the Bible tells me so . . .'

Terry had a knife out, a grubby penknife with a six-inch blade. He was digging under his nails with the point, flicking free crescent crusts.

Allison could not remember any more words, and hummed, excruciatingly, further into the child's hymn. She kept her cruciform pose, stretching her shirt over her wiry shoulders and chest. She had an athlete's muscles, a runner's or a tennis player's, thin and strong.

Terry came near him, and Paul caught a whiff of animal smell. Trained from infancy to be polite, he tried not to let disgust show.

'Nice knife,' Terry said. 'Sha'ap. Shave with it, if you liked.'

He held it up. The blade was oily, its edge honed. Terry took him by the back of the neck and laid the knife against his throat. The metal was shockingly cold, like ice. Paul thought he'd been sliced open.

'Didn't shave this mornin', did you?'

Terry scraped up over Paul's adam's apple and wiped under his chin, tickling his stubble. Terry had pressed the *blunt* edge of the blade to his throat. The lad folded his knife and put it away. Paul's head was reeling, his heart racing. Allison came alive and stopped keening. She took Terry's hand.

'Le'ss go,' she said, pulling.

Terry went with her.

'Toodle-oo,' Allison said, as they slipped into the woods.

Paul felt his heartbeat slip back to normal. Whatever had just happened, he felt he'd missed the point.

Twelve

'COME IN,' Jenny invited. 'Perhaps Beloved will see you . . .'
The girl took Hazel's hand and pulled gently. Her grip
was dry and warm, informal. Wendy was behind now, bulk
easing her towards the big door Jenny was pushing open.
'Come inside,' Jenny said, smiling.

Hazel smelled the other girl's clean hair, felt her warmth. The
hall of the Manor House was dark but not gloomy. Yesterday,
she'd seen it as a set from an Agatha Christie film. Elegantly
preserved in the Twenties, elephant's-foot umbrella stands
stocked with blunt instruments, portraits of disreputable family
ancestors liable to have sired the missing heir, an old-fashioned
telephone receiver with a knit cord suitable for surreptitious
snipping or stealthy strangling. Actually, the place was tatty,
with mismatched, frayed furniture and too much ground-in
dirt. The phone on the hall table was old, an unstreamlined
black dial model rather than a slim white oval with push-
buttons.

She hesitated, and Jenny's pull became stronger. A suspicion
flared, and she remembered Paul and – strangely – Susan Ames.
In cartoons, characters often had little figures perched on their
shoulders, tiny replicas of themselves, one with a halo, wings,
a harp and a blue robe, the other with horns, a tail, a trident
and a red face. Paul and Susan were angels, holding her back;
Jenny and Wendy imps, pulling her on. On the threshold of the
Agapemone, she felt a swoon brewing in her forehead. Her vision
went in and out of focus.

Weird.

Jenny came close and slipped an arm around her waist, cooing
persuasively, trying to get her into the hall. Wendy laid a heavy
arm around her shoulders. The Sisters formed a single body,
hugging, protecting, cajoling.

'Love,' Jenny said, disconnectedly.

She took a step and paused again, half in and half out of the house. She could feel the cool of the interior, and it was tempting.

Jenny kissed her cheek and said, 'Come on, Hazel.'

She looked the girl in the face. In a shimmer, Jenny's skin was beet red, pointed horns pushing out from locks of flame. Her smile was heavily fanged, and she had a comical goatee. As an imp, she was a pantomime character, appealing and endearing. She licked scarlet lips with a black, forked tongue, and laughed like music.

'It's nothing, Hazel, just a step . . .'

'One foot in front of the other, Hazel,' said Wendy, gently prodding her back with three arrow-tipped fingers.

The brimstone smelled sweet, and she sucked it into her mouth through her nostrils. She picked up a thick-socked foot and put it down on the bristly doormat. Wendy and Jenny pushed gently, and she was inside the Agapemone. The Sisters let go, and she took a few steps on her own.

In the cool, she turned to look at Wendy and Jenny. The imps, fiery hair flickering, stood in the doorway, shoulder to shoulder, arms folded, red eyes sparkling mischievously. Behind was blue sky and bright sun. It gave them a backlit aura. As she watched, the Sisters changed. Their horns pulled in, their skins faded, their tails curled up under their skirts. Their hair began to shine, floating in circles around their foreheads. From somewhere, Hazel heard the delicate plunking of tiny harps and a choir singing 'We Plough the Fields and Scatter'.

Hazel saw the Light. It was around the Sisters as they stepped into the hallway, spreading into the shadowed corner. The Light was warm and welcoming, embracing like clean sheets, supporting like sea water. Hazel felt herself almost float, surrounded by Light. She turned away from the door. A gallery ran around the hallway, gathering in a landing from which descended a wide stairway, banistered with dark wood. The Light was up on the landing, spreading like ground mist.

She had the sweet smoke on her palate and felt it filling her lungs. Light sparks scattered across her vision. There was someone on the landing, in the centre of the Light. Jenny was on the first step, kneeling, her head bowed.

'Beloved,' she said.

Hazel's knees felt weak, and she sank to them. The touch from her dream returned and began to massage her neck and shoulders, slipping inside her T-shirt to ease her aches. The Light swirled, coming to a focus in the man shape at the top of the stairs.

She tried to stand, but could not. Her knees were gone, the muscles in her legs were limp. She saw His face in the Light. She had never even seen a photograph of Him. A picture couldn't have captured the Light. This was Anthony William Jago. Beloved. His face was vast, yards across, and the eyes in it were holes. Through the holes, Hazel saw Heaven. The rest of the face didn't matter. She didn't know what He was wearing. It could be a golden robe edged with fire. It could be a priestly black suit with a dog collar. Or He could be naked, body sweating Light. His was the touch she had felt.

'Hazel,' he said, taking her name into his mouth, rolling it around and breathing it out again, renewed.

She felt herself standing, knees straightening, feet pressing against the floor. Her arms were reaching out involuntarily, drawn to Him. His smile fell upon her like a warm rain.

'Hazel,' He said, 'Hazel . . .'

He touched one hand to His breast, then held it out, palm bright and bloody. She was on the bottom stair, between the Sisters, drawn up towards Beloved. Jenny looked up at her with Love, Wendy with tolerance. Jenny pushed her upwards. Beloved's eyes were closed now. The Light was inside Him. Dressed casually – white shirt open at the neck, black cardigan running thin at the elbows, trainers – Beloved was human enough to be blotchy around the throat, a little hollow in the cheeks, hairline a touch high. The vessel didn't matter. He contained the Light.

She looked away from His face to His outstretched hand. Shining blood pooled in His palm, glittering. Hazel stepped upwards, towards Beloved's hand. The smoke was in her nostrils, mouth and lungs, filling her. She felt the touch again, soothing, teasing, slipping between her legs. A drop of blood fell from Beloved's hand, tumbling slowly towards the carpeted stairs, turning end over end, making shapes. It fell for ever, Hazel's eyes following the plunge. It struck, spattered in a spider shape, pulsed like a hot coal and faded.

Her mouth was dry, and the touch was around her neck, thumbs in the hollows of her throat, working the hinges of her jaw. Beloved stepped down to her, His hand level, the blood rippling. Hazel's knees were still not working. She felt as if she were held by hooks under her arms, body sagging but upright. Her hair was extending in an electric frizz. Her scalp tickled, excited. Beloved brought His bleeding hand near her face, and she looked into the red depths of the M-shaped lake in the palm.

'Beloved,' Jenny said, 'this is Hazel.'

'Sister,' He said, 'welcome.'

The blood in His hand was wine, giving off a rich bouquet. Beloved held His other hand over the wound and dipped a thumb into the pool. Blood lapped up around the thumb, filming it from knuckle to nail. Knowing what was expected, Hazel fingertip-brushed her hair away from her forehead, relishing the tingle. Her eyes fluttered shut, and she let her chin fall to her sternum. She felt the touch. Beloved's damp thumb was pressed to her forehead, twice. He had drawn the sign of the cross slightly askew above her eyebrows. The blood was cool and pleasant, like cream.

'Hazel,' He said, baptizing her, confirming her.

The touch took her chin, lifted her head. She opened her eyes and looked at Him. His eyes were blue and clear.

'This is my blood,' He said.

His wound swelled, and the blood lapped at her lips.

'Drink freely of it.'

Without thinking, she let her tongue slip out and probe the blood. Beloved angled His hand, letting the blood flow towards her lips. There was a definite tang, not unpleasant, and her mouth filled. He let her go, and she wavered, unsteady on her feet, letting the blood creep past her tongue. Inside her mind, there were explosions.

Thirteen

'JAMES,' HE said, thumping the Gate House door. ' 'S me, Teddy.'

James pulled the door open, and Teddy squeezed in. The curtains were still drawn and there was only a table lamp on. Eyes used to the outside glare, he found himself blinking. With the sun behind them, the curtains looked like rough sacking, pinpoints of light stabbing through the weave.

'James, Terry didn't come home. Mum 'n' Dad's gone spare.'

James wasn't alone. A woman was at his side table, drinking tea.

Teddy felt awkward. 'Sorry,' he said, 'if I'm interruptin', sorry.'

James was standing up at the sink, rinsing breakfast things. He still looked tired.

'It's all right,' James said. 'Come in, have tea. You know Susan?'

Teddy shook his head, and the woman nodded at him.

'Hello, Teddy,' she said.

He wondered why he hadn't noticed her before. She was pretty in a young-mothery, teachery sort of way. Chinese cotton trousers that ended high on the calves, loose shirt with flappy breast pockets. Dark hair, fed-up look, bright eyes. Just the sort who would fit with James.

James, hands still wet, was pouring tea for him.

'James . . .'

He didn't know what to say, how to say it.

'I know,' he said. 'If you think about it too long, you'll make your head hurt. Just try not to think.'

'James,' he said, struggling with so many things. 'Youm got a gun.'

James laughed. 'Yes, Teddy.'

'A prop'r gun?'

James nodded his head.

'Like a p'liceman. You a p'liceman?'

'No.'

'What's up with Terry? And Allison?'

He swallowed hot tea, burning his inside to match the outside of him.

'I don't know,' James said, shrugging. 'Best go home and not think about it, Teddy. I'll do what I can for your brother, not that the dirty bugger deserves it.'

'Youm gonna shoot him?'

James didn't answer.

Susan shook her head. 'No one is going to get shot for a while.'

Teddy wondered what life would be like if James shot Terry. For a start, he'd get hit a bloody sight less. And he'd have a room to himself, a bit of privacy. He didn't even reckon his mum and dad would mind much. All round, they'd be better off if Terry did get shot. But that was not a likely thing to happen. That was just something to think about late at night while Terry was grunting in bed, fucking his fist. Something to make funnies about. It was not something that was going to happen. But James had a gun. And Terry was not just bored and making trouble, like in the pub two nights ago. Terry was part of something bigger, along with Allison and her death-face boyfriend. Something scary.

'For once, it's not Terry's fault,' James said.

'It's *him*,' said Susan, nodding sharply towards the Manor House.

'Jago,' Teddy said.

Susan gave him a thumbs-up sign and ticked in the air. 'Right.'

'You have a problem,' James said. 'You were there with me, so you *know* what happened. Imagine how your parents, your friends, would react if you told them. Gary Chilcot would have them laughing at you for years.'

He was right. This morning, Teddy hadn't told his parents anything. They'd been talking about the fire at the Pottery, and Old Man Maskell laying Dad off, and Terry staying out all night doing Lord knows what. There had been no way to tell them anything.

'This isn't your problem, Teddy,' said Susan.

'She's right. We have to stay. It's our duty, and we're stupid about things like that. But you've got a choice.'

'What you talkin' 'bout?'

He saw seriousness in their faces. James was usually confident, in command. Now he was confused. His hair was awry, and Teddy saw he had a tiny bald seam through his scalp. The woman was calmer, but she was still gripping her mug with both hands to stop shaking, the tea almost invisibly wobbling.

'Leave,' said James. 'Just walk away from it. Go to Bridgwater or Taunton, get on a train, go on holiday. You'll know when it's safe to come back. It'll be on the news. Go to relatives, friends. Get a job in Butlin's, beg in the streets, anything. You want money? Here . . .'

James went through his wallet, and dug up four or five fifties and some lesser notes and change. He slapped the money on the kitchen counter.

'Take it,' James said.

'Get Out of Jail Free,' said Susan.

'But . . .'

James was briefly angry. 'Teddy, get out now!'

'Yes,' Teddy said, 'thank you, goodbye . . .'

He scooped up the money and jammed it into his jeans pocket.

'Don't go home. Walk away with what you're wearing. It's safer.'

'Yes. Thank you, James.'

He backed out of the Gate House, letting the door swing shut in his face. The Manor House stood on its hill, silently humming. Even more than last night, Teddy was scared. James and Susan had been scared, and they knew what to be afraid of. That was enough to be terrifying.

There were a lot of people around, for the festival. From a field, Derek waved to him. He was directing customers towards car parks and camping sites.

Teddy shoved his hand into his pocket, burying James's money deeper. It was hot as yesterday, but his bare arms pricked with goose pimples. He walked away from the Agapemone trying not to run, an escaped prisoner strolling past a police station, determined not to give himself away with a panicky dash. He made his way steadily down the hill, against the tide of cars and hikers. He was getting out before the fun started, whetever the fun was. He was leaving James and Susan, leaving his parents, leaving Terry, leaving everyone. Whatever was happening, he wouldn't be around for the rest of it. He shot a sneaky backwards look at the Agapemone, wondering if Jenny were still inside. He was leaving her, too. It was silly to think more about her than his family, but he did.

A pair of the London kids were sitting by the roadside. One was Pam, wearing a midriff-baring halter and microshorts, along with black tights and several black scarves. But the other was Mike Toad, whose blue jumpsuit was dusty and stained after a few nights in his tent. His formerly clean jawline was stubbled, and he looked a lot less happy than the girl.

'Yo, Teddy,' Pam shouted at him, 'where're you going?'

He stopped, but did not know what to tell them. He shrugged.

'You seen a blue 2CV?' Mike Toad asked.

He shook his head.

'You'll never find them in all this,' Mike told the girl.

'They'll turn up.'

Standing still, Teddy felt panic rising. Frightened sweat crept from his hair, slipping down his spine. Every moment he wasn't running away, he was less likely to make it. He imagined invisible spiderwebs shooting out of the Agapemone, coming straight from Jago's brain, descending all around in a sticky tent, pulling people in, not letting them out . . .

'We're waiting for Jazzbeaux,' Pam said, 'my sister. You'll like her. She's dead glam. Like me, but taller.'

'Juicy,' Mike Toad said.

'Dickbrain here has had his tongue out ever since he heard Jazz was due. He's smitten, in love with a dream. Bound to be disappointed when he meets her. She can be a right cow when she wants to. See this . . .'

Pam traced a faint scar that interrupted her red lipstick.

'That was Jazz playing with a razorblade when we were little. Proper sweetheart she was. Like your girlfriend, Allison.'

'Allison's not my girlfriend. She's just –'

'A good friend,' Pam suggested, giggling.

'No, not 'zactly . . .'

'Good job too. Toad here fancies her, but she gives me the creeps. You have to mainline radioactive waste to get your eyes like that.'

'You seen her around this morning?' Teddy asked.

'I think we passed her and your brother on our way here,' the Toad said, 'but I could be wrong. I'm still wrecked from last night.'

Teddy worked out which route to take to avoid Allison and Terry. He didn't want to run into them.

'Hey, you like jokes, don't you?' the Toad said, grinning with unwashed teeth. 'Why do women have legs?'

Teddy didn't know.

'Have you seen the mess snails make?'

Mike Toad laughed. Pam hit him.

Teddy left them arguing, and headed for the main road. The invisible cobwebs stretched out, tugging his back and legs, trying to keep him in Alder. They were weak now. He still had a chance to break free. Goodbye, Jenny, he thought.

Fourteen

As HAZEL kissed His hand, Jenny bowed. Sometimes, it was best not to look directly at Beloved. The Light could hurt your eyes. If you saw things only He was meant to see, your small soul couldn't encompass the knowledge. With His free hand, Beloved caressed the girl's hair. He smiled down on Hazel, quietly accepting her reverence as she knelt, suckling His wound. Jenny felt the Spirit strong in herself, and shared the girl's epiphany. Hazel's head bobbed as her tongue lapped at the hole in Beloved's hand. She made cat sounds in the back of her mouth as she took her communion.

A step below them all, Wendy tried desperately to share the delight. She had not purged herself entirely of the sin of jealousy. She wanted Beloved to herself, resenting the need to share His glory with the world. Jenny found it in herself to forgive the Sister. She'd been with the Agapemone from the first. Each new Sister-Love must seem to eclipse her in Beloved's heart. But Beloved's heart was big enough for all humanity.

Beloved detached His hand from Hazel's mouth and wiped His wet palm on His cardigan. He bent and kissed the girl, the new Sister, on the forehead. She sighed, entire body shaking. Jenny took one of the girl's arms. Wendy, hesistant, did likewise. Hazel stood between them, eyes tight shut, so deep in prayer that her physical body would have to be guided.

'This evening, there will be a Great Manifestation,' Beloved said, 'and our Sister Hazel will be honoured at the altar.'

Jenny felt a sunburst of joy at the news. 'Alleiluya,' she breathed.

'Alleiluya,' Wendy joined in, mouth set in an ineradicable, involuntary pout.

Beloved turned and ascended the stairs, leaving the new Sister to them. Jenny lowered her eyes so as not to follow Beloved's departure with unseemly ardour. Wendy, her own eyes wet with

ambiguous tears, didn't follow her example. When Beloved
had returned to His rooms, they had to help Hazel downstairs
to prepare for her anointment. The new Sister moved like a
sleepwalker, eyes twitching behind closed lids, cooperating but
not participating.

They steered Hazel through the chapel, into an antechamber
where there was a couch. Wendy let the girl go. She'd been
gripping too tightly, leaving fingermarks on Hazel's bare arms.
Jenny manoeuvred the postulant into sitting on the divan, then
lifted her feet and swung her around, gently bending her back
until she was at rest. She arranged the new Sister's hair out of her
eyes, and tugged her ridden-up T-shirt down over her navel.

'Comely girl, isn't she?' Jenny said.

'All are beautiful to Beloved,' Wendy agreed, grudgingly.

Jenny remembered the Great Manifestation that had brought
her into the Agapemone, the outpouring of Love before all the
Brethren. It had been the most beautiful moment of her life,
an intensely personal salvation and yet shared with the entire
congregation. She had not been aware at the time, but now
she wondered whether Wendy had been standing at the back
of the chapel, reciting but not meaning the words, looking
with jealousy upon her as she now did upon Hazel. Imagining
this evening's ceremony, she could understand Wendy's lapses.
Sharing Love was harder than accepting it.

Jenny touched Hazel's soft face and tried to extinguish the
small flame of envy rising in her heart. She Loved the new
Sister, knowing the Great Manifestation would be shared among
all at the Agapemone, and eventually all in the world. Tonight
Hazel would be visited by God in the flesh, and the world
would be nearer redemption by one soul. Jenny thrilled to the
remembrance of the touch of Beloved, the touch of God. Joy
was in the flesh. Love was in the flesh. Purity was in the flesh.

Interlude Five

T HEY DIDN'T talk. Between Shepherd's Bush and Chelsea, darkness came. Roger tried to pay the taxi driver, but the BBC had covered the fare. Knowing they wouldn't run to a tip, Susan gave him a fifty-pence piece. It was too much, but she didn't have smaller change. Irrelevantly, she realized it was years – two? – since she'd seen a ten-shilling note. They'd been phased out. She resented the hours of her childhood wasted on learning pounds, shillings and pence. A useless lump of her memory was filled with old money.

While she fumbled with her wonky purse clasp, Roger stamped upstairs to the flat. He had a right to be murderously angry. Whatever happened, she'd have to go through at least the next hour with him. Having made confession, she'd now have to do penance. It was a long time since she'd been in a church. Did she think she might be unable to step on consecrated ground?

She stood at the kerb for two or three minutes after the taxi had gone. It was January, and cold. Roger had insisted she wear a summer dress to show off her long, now goose-pimpled legs. The yellow-orange dark of a streetlit night made the city look hostile, like the lunar landscapes she'd seen on television during the Apollo missions. It'd be darker later. The flat was above a newsagent's. Most of the daily papers were gone from the racks, but the two evening ones were out. She saw headlines about OPEC and the oil crisis, Edward Heath and the Three-Day Week. A few years ago, man had stepped on the moon; now, the world was falling apart.

At infants' school, they called her Spike. Squashed and lumpy, she was supposed to look like the vicious dog in the Tom and Jerry cartoons. Things changed when she passed the eleven-plus. She was the only one from her old school at the girls' grammar. Not squashed and lumpy any more, she was tall enough to make buying the uniform a problem. At the new school, everyone pretended to be grown up. Pupils in the upper years got into trouble for wearing make-up. Susan put most of her dolls in her bottom drawer and asked for a chess set for her birthday. Able to beat girls two or three years above her, she joined the chess club and stayed after school two days a week, playing. Funnily, she wasn't really good. She just had a knack for guessing correctly what her opponents planned.

At first, teachers called her Rodway and friends called her Susan. A few girls acquired nicknames. Jayne Weald became Jinx when she broke her ankle the third time, playing netball. Colette Vaizey started being called Coal-Hole for no particular reason. And she turned into Witch Susan. One day Miss Robartes, their science teacher, divided them into pairs to take a test. She handed out special packs of cards. Each card had a symbol: a circle, a square, a star, a cross, a triangle, wavy lines. One girl would pick a card, and the other would guess which symbol she was looking at. The test was supposed to gauge ESP. She knew from her brother's American comics that ESP was seeing through things, like Superman with his X-ray vision. Susan was partnered with her best friend of three months' standing, Annette Post. When Susan was guessing, their team scored better than anyone else in the class. Most times she just *knew* what was on the card in Annette's hand.

Afterwards, they started calling her Witch Susan and asking her to read their palms. Everyone wanted to know who their husbands would be. She didn't mind. It was better than being Spike. Miss Robartes brought a friend into school to see her. David, who reminded her of Illya Kuryakin, was a scientist from a university in London, glamorously distinguished and grown-up. Susan was let off a maths lesson to do tests with him. After the now familiar cards (he called them Rhine cards) David gave her small things – coins, a comb, a watch – and asked her to guess what their owners were like. Sometimes she could make up stories easily. She imagined the comb belonged to a grown-up who lived with David. She kept goldfish and got sunburned easily. Sometimes nothing came into her head. David wrote things down, but never said whether he liked her stories or not. At the end of the afternoon, he gave her a card with his address and phone number on it and told her to get in touch if anything strange happened to her. It struck her then as an odd thing to say to someone.

For weeks she went around expecting something strange to happen, but it never did. Once, at break, some older girls made her play the Rhine game with an ordinary pack of cards. As good with fifty-two choices as with four, she was pleased with herself. But some of her friends didn't want to be with her as much as they used to. As a joke, Annette said she must have put a curse on Jinx Weald, and Jinx dropped out of the chess club. One or two in her class were actually scared of her. She started thinking Witch Susan wasn't such a good name. She stopped playing the games and admitted she didn't really know how to read palms. She put David's card in her bottom drawer, along with the dolls and books she'd grown out of, and forgot about it. For a while.

The light in the flat came on. Snowflakes fell like wet ants on her cheeks. She went up and faced Roger in the living room. He pulled off his purple paisley tie, stretching it like a thuggee strangling cord. Gold rings glinted as he flexed his right hand. Her arm and leg muscles were tense. She sucked in a double lungful of air. Her exhalation was loud, her breath frosting in the air like a phantom megaphone. The central heating hadn't come on, its timer shot by the last power cut.

He didn't hit her until she turned on the television. As the *Six O'Clock News* appeared, she rolled with his first blow and fell on to the settee. She held a yellow square cushion over her face, tasting tobacco and dust. She tried to form a foetal ball, elbows protecting her breasts, knees up over her stomach. He pounded the backs of her hands. She clutched the cushion, willing the pain away. His rings gouged her skin. Her wounds stung like bites. He was too furious to think, or else he might have found a way to cripple her. As it was, he could only hurt her, and she could put up with that.

Neither of them said anything. She couldn't get through with words. He had to tire himself out. Each time his knuckles connected, he grunted in the back of his throat. She was nastily reminded of the wordless sounds he'd made the nine times they'd made love. She wished she could have that part of her life back and wash it. He hit her back and head and arms and shins, but couldn't reach anything soft. She looked over the cushion at him, at the way his arms waved while he kicked. She noticed for the first time that one of his Elvis sideburns was longer than the other. He hit her again, aiming for her exposed forehead and eyes. His fist came down above her hairline and skimmed off the top of her head. She buried her face again and leaned forward, pushing him back. He grabbed a fistful of hair. This was really going to hurt.

He stopped and let her go. After a while, even though he didn't call a truce, she lowered the cushion to her lap. They were on television. Roger was at the other end of the settee, cold air between them. His hands bleeding, he tugged at the sticky, red-smeared rings. When one came off, he ouched and plopped it in an ashtray. Droplets of blood rolled like mercury on the matted-in ash. He knitted his mashed fingers, trying to squeeze out the pain.

Four of five years after the card games, they still called her Witch Susan, but didn't remember why. There was no first time. Rather, if there was she didn't notice it. Things around the house started to break. She had a transistor radio in her room that worked most of the time, but got nothing but static two or three days a month. It wasn't until Nett Post joked about the thing having cramps she realized the radio's static patches coincided exactly with her periods. Her stepfather spent too much time on the roof adjusting the television aerial, and they never got as good reception as the next-door neighbours. None of the clocks kept correct time more than a few days, even the electric one in her mother's Teasmade. Long before anything really happened, Susan was sure it was her fault.

At a party in Nett's garden, spoons started bending. It was funny at first, and most of the others thought it a joke. Susan suspected Nett was deliberately giving her bent cutlery until Colette, now in the science stream, suggested they repeat the experiment under laboratory conditions. Nett fetched down an old dinner service and laid out knives, forks and spoons on the garden table. Susan picked a knife and held the neck of the blade between two fingers. Nothing happened. 'Too thick,' concluded Colette. 'Too right,' replied Nett, and they all laughed again. Feeling stupid, Susan picked up a fork. She had a pain in her temples, and the fork bent into a right angle. Susan passed it round. It looked as if it had melted in the sun but it wasn't even warm. Nett gave her a spoon, and the same thing happened. They stopped chattering, and just looked at the bent bits of metal. Nobody thought it a joke any more.

She practised, becoming familiar with the sudden, nauseating headache that came when it worked. She bent, broke or melted

a succession of metal and plastic things. Once, alone, she stood
in the garage with her hands clasped behind her and tied the car
aerial into a knot. It couldn't be kept secret. Her friends told their
families and someone told her parents. She had to do the spoon act
in the living room for them. Her stepfather, the bank manager,
had nothing apt in his repertoire of reactions, and so kept quiet.
Her mother found it highly embarrassing, but couldn't think
of a way out. Susan knew – not felt, *knew* – her mother had
dreaded for years the day her daughter would embarrass the
family. She'd expected Susan to get pregnant, marry a black
man or become a drug addict. Being a mutant was no better and
no worse than anything else, so Susan was inclined to be proud
of it. There were twelve-year-olds in Russia who could beat her
hollow at chess, but no one she'd ever heard of could pick up an
unattached lightbulb and make it come on by thinking electricity
into it.

Then came newspapers, magazines, radio, television. Even
before she was out of school, she was semifamous. She didn't
need a career option, didn't need her O and A levels, didn't
need any of the university places offered her. She hadn't even
had to go on *Opportunity Knocks*. She'd been given something to
do with her life. Somewhere along the way, it stopped being fun.
Nett's family moved away from Guildford, and Susan didn't have
anyone to talk things through with. Most of the other girls found
boyfriends, but her celebrity isolated her. People were afraid of
her again. She looked into her bottom drawer for David's card
but it had been thrown out with other rubbish years before.

Then Roger Breecher took over. Much older than her, Roger
was one of the first to latch on to the story. He quit the local paper
to guide her through the personality jungle. Unlike everyone else,
he wasn't interested in explaining her or proving her a fake. He
positively encouraged her to believe in what she was. He kept her
away from scientists, warning her against rat mazes and electric
shocks. Her parents didn't like him but by then she'd had enough
of them and wasn't inclined to pay attention. If her parents had
liked Roger, she mightn't have been stupid enough to hook up
with him. He set her up in the London flat, which she was expected
to share with him, and went round the publishing houses until a
contract was offered. He did most of the writing of *The Mind
Beyond*.

On television, Roger – bright orange with a green bar over his eyes – was smiling and confident, tackling the presenter's questions with calculated humour.

'It's too early to make promises, Michael, but who knows . . . maybe Susan is the alternative form of energy we're all looking for.'

The studio audience laughed appreciatively. It was the Blitz spirit coming out again. Plucky little Britain gasping for petrol, workforce idle four days a week, getting by with a smile and a song and a cup of tea. It made her wish, not for the first time, she'd been born Italian.

She was talking now, reticent and nervy. Her hair had been done this morning and looked surprisingly all right. People said she was pretty, but she only saw slightly misaligned eyes and bad posture. Whenever she saw herself on television or in magazine photographs, she thought she looked younger than she felt. She was eighteen. She wasn't supposed to feel old. But she was the first to admit she wasn't normal.

She wasn't embarrassed this time, because it was deliberate. She'd set out to make a bad impression. They edited out some pauses and unended sentences, cutting in shots they'd filmed earlier of the presenter nodding and listening. She still came over as vague and unsympathetic. One long, pointless anecdote was totally gone. The editor would want to get to the good stuff as quickly as possible. They left in the bit where she got the title of their book wrong, saying *The Mind Behind*. The good stuff came. A pretty plastic girl in a knee-length lavender dress came on with a tray and put it on the low table in front of Susan. The camera zoomed in. She saw herself looking down at spoons and spinning tops. She picked a stainless-steel dessert spoon and said something stupid. She got a laugh. She balanced the spoon on her extended forefinger. It wobbled. Her hand was shaking, and she couldn't get the balance right for long seconds.

Off camera, Roger said something soothing and inane. The spoon was balanced now. The TV people had dubbed in spooky music. Her other hand came into the frame. With the right forefinger she gently rubbed the neck of the spoon like a sore spot. Under the creepy music, there were coughs from the audience. Suddenly, her fingers twitched. The spoon clattered out of sight. She reached down. The camera pulled back, losing focus, then came forward again. She was holding the spoon, slightly bent. It was a pathetic kink. 'You *bent* it,' said an expert sitting between her and Roger. He was there as a sceptic.

The audience laughed. Roger's orange shaded red. Susan sat quietly, hands (and spoon) in her lap. The prerecorded piece was over, and the presenter was back live, leaning forward to take the viewing audience into his confidence. 'Let's take another look at that, shall we?' It was better than she'd expected. They'd been filming her from several different angles, and they could slow down and/or expand the image like a football action replay. One camera caught her hand under the table, jabbing the spoon crooked against the studio floor.

They had a bit more of her talking, babbling an apology. Then the sceptic was sarcastic. Then it was all over. The presenter made an embarrassed comment, and the newsreader came on to talk about serious things. President Nixon's tapes, power-sharing for Northern Ireland.

The TV went off, and the lights went out. Roger's voice was hard in the dark. 'Another bloody power cut!'

He swiped at her, but she knew it was coming. She pushed herself out of the sofa and moved silently to a corner. Roger was up, too, but he stepped into the coffee table. Something broke.

She was cosy in the dark. She knew where things were. She knew where he was now, where he would be soon. He came for her, animal noises escaping from his mouth. She reached behind him into the kitchen, to the four unmatched mugs hanging from hooks over the draining board and, one by one, made them pop into pieces.

It came now, as it hadn't in the studio. The sickening lurch behind her eyes, like ice cream going to her head, that always accompanied the push. Her hands clenched tight by her sides, she reached out her mentacles for Roger, to stop him long enough for her to get out of the flat. He would be in trouble. The advance was spent. Deals had been made. He'd bought tickets to New York.

It would be a simple disappearance. Rodway was her step-father's name. On her birth certificate, in the Gideon Bible they had given her at school and on her UCCA form, she was Susan Ames. If Susan Rodway was Witch Susan, Susan Ames was damn nearly Susan Anonymous. In September, she could pick a university and read Eng Lit and be safely Susan Anonymous for the rest of her life. Superman had the right idea. If you were going to go through life with powers beyond the ordinary, the first thing you needed was a secret identity to keep the cash-in artists and psychos off your neck.

Outside, she'd know her way in the dark.

IV

One

ALDER HAD changed overnight. The scenery was still out of *The Archers* or *Straw Dogs*, but the country folk were outnumbered by invaders, and the place had turned into a cross between Woodstock, Hollywood Boulevard and Harvest Home.

Looking across from the Pottery, Paul saw the garage crowded with late thirty-somethings in punitive-in-this-heat leather, crushing beer cans and comparing bikes with the enthusiasm of schoolboys seeing whose erection was longest. Allison's facially impaired boyfriend was mingling with them, slapping gauntlets with Demon Scumsuckers from Hell who were probably accountants the rest of the year. Biker women sat on the low wall in front of the forecourt, pulling off boots and jackets to let their bodies breathe. Big breasts flopped under death's-head T-shirts. Without goggles, the women had dusty cheeks and chins like survivors of a First World War dogfight.

Outside the Valiant Soldier, a young man in a flowered waistcoat, open suitcase balanced on his knees like an usherette's tray, offered to sell a selection of controlled substances, liquorice lumps of cannabis resin, an assortment of pills and tabs, vials of suspiciously baking-powdery cocaine. There was nothing in the pharmacy for toothache. Paul told the dealer to ring up no sale, and the slick-haired hustler shrugged, turning his attention to the next prospective customer, a hairy youth with shorts, flip-flops, a headband and a back pocket full of disposable income.

Even before the official start, camp sites were thronging. Finding one kid in the crowd was impossible. Paul spotted a few lads, even a girl, with mohican haircuts – fifteen years after the Sex Pistols' time in the sun – but none was the boy from the woods. The severely spooked kid could have bolted home. Paul wouldn't blame him. Down by the festival site, at the edge of the Agapemone estate, there was already a holiday

air. There were tents and vans in rows, and queues for the
prefab toilets. Food stalls were open, and a fish-and-chip van
from Achelzoy was doing excellent business. Litter was already
underfoot.

He wandered, slightly dazed, among the festival folk. Some
were kids out for a good time, away from parents and holiday
jobs for a week or so. They had clean faces, casual clothes and
clustered in chatting groups, like guests at a freshers' party. Others
were travellers, a semi-medieval nomad community complete
with ragged urchins, the filthiest imaginable dogs and vehicles
with home-made post-apocalypse armour. They were the ones
building cooking fires and scavenging for supplies. Alliances and
subgroups were forming. Paul knew travellers frequently clashed
with festival stewards and security staff, feeling they were the
rightful keepers of the flame for this life style, that their seniority
should be recognized.

Many attendees were caught in time warps. Superannuated
hippies or bikers congregated in knots, telling old stories.
Festival veterans – survivors of Pilton, Reading and Castle
Donington – spoke of Stonehenge before the police moved
in and the Isle of Wight in the acid haze as if those were the
Great Days of Empire. There were isolated examples of every
style cult that had ever been, from goatee-bearded beatnik and
fuzz-faced folkie through dreadlocked white Rasta and fancy-
dress new romantic to squiggle-clothed acid householder and
stripe-clothed skunker. Some were the right age for their
fashions, flowers in grey-streaked hair or punk spikes over
thinning thirties scalps, but most were teenagers who had pick-
and-matched personae from the past. That was post modernism
for you.

They were all loitering, waiting for the party to begin. Badge-
wearing stewards recruited for various jobs, and the big stages
were aswarm with roadies. As a helicopter overran the site,
rumours spread around that a megastar was touring preliminary
to a surprise appearance. The guessing was inclined towards
Mick Jagger or Peter Gabriel, but someone suggested it was Jim
Morrison back from the dead. The chopper circled once and took
off again.

Paul began to get heatstroke. He had come out without
sunglasses, and his eyes were paining him. He scanned the
crowd, looking for a red mohican. Hazel said the kids had

a Dormobile, so he paid especial attention to them. Even that lead did not help. More vehicles arrived all the time. A cheer went up from the field being used as a car park. An open car had just lurched in on four wheel rims. Its slow progress had caused a mammoth tailback. As it was dragged away, the cork was out and traffic moved again. The two youths in the crippled car were arguing, interspersing insults with shoves, and the stewards were trying to pull them apart.

Tempers frayed all around. Two little kids, faces smeared with chocolate ice cream, were having a screaming match while a mother tried to separate them. Marijuana drifted past on a lazy breeze, and a stern youth with a badge and an armband began telling off a dope-smoker not for flaunting the joint but for dropping it on the dry grass without making sure it was out. A skinny naked girl was lying face down on a blanket between two caravans, face covered by dark glasses, trying to ignore the small crowd of peepers. After a while, she gave up and pulled on shorts and a top. Dogs fought viciously, and someone with a guitar struggled through 'House of the Rising Sun'.

He wasn't doing any good here. He decided to return to the Pottery. Hazel might be back, and he wanted to talk to her, to patch something up that would last until autumn. It was hard to get out of the field because there was a clog of people around the gate. Having arrived and set up camp, they were restless from long journeys and wanted to walk around, visit the pub or just see the area.

A ten-year-old in Iron Age clothing came up and said, 'Spare change?' Paul turned his pockets out and found nothing but doorkeys. The child stuck out its lower lip and walked on to the next prospect, clinking its take of the day in a grubby fist, like Captain Queeg clacking his ball bearings.

He looked up at the Manor House, nestled on its hill. Most houses are schematic faces, front stairs for teeth, drive for a lolling tongue, big door for a nose, windows for eyes, and eaves for a hat brim. The Agapemone was too big to be like that, with a rack of windows suggesting a spider's row of eyes, and swatches of crinkly, dry ivy like a veil. It wasn't a face, but it suggested an expression. The Martian war machine hadn't been like a face either, but it had had a similar impersonally nasty look. One of the gabled attic windows caught the sun and flashed. Paul flinched, expecting a heat ray.

Nothing happened.

He looked again, and just saw a nice old house, not particularly well kept. The gate was free, and he escaped from the field. He walked away from the Agapemone, back into the village.

Two

I T WAS important not to let on that he knew. After last night They must suspect he'd seen something, but Ferg let Them believe he thought the Iron Insect was just a dope dream. It was almost exciting, having a secret he couldn't, didn't dare, share.

He sat in the stuffy blue pupa of his tent, pretending to meditate. Outside, a mass of people milled about, shadows shifting on the translucent but opaque walls. Twenty-five different ghetto blasters competed in a guerrilla war. There were voices in the din, just beyond earshot, speaking with each other, conspiring.

Ferg didn't like to be out in crowds. There were too many of Them, watching. They looked like ordinary people, but he'd seen Their true shape. Having glimpsed the truth, he was changed for ever. He couldn't ever be ignorant again. He didn't know what It was or where It had come from. But It was here. It could take human form, or could enslave humans. From now on, he'd have to watch out. He didn't know whom he could trust. He thought Jessica was all right but couldn't be sure. With her mood swings, it was hard to tell. Mike Toad was one of Them. He was surprised he'd ever been taken in. Mike was off with Pam, the new girl, so she must be with Them too. Syreeta was the type to be part of it all, the hostility between her and the Toad a put-on to cover their plotting. Dolar might be innocent, but Syreeta had him under her control. He didn't know about Salim, Pam's boyfriend. Everyone else, the locals, the strangers, the festival people, he could never be sure of, either way. It was safest to act as if they were all in it together. So, it was him – possibly Jessica, just maybe Salim – against the rest.

Behind him there was a mechanical rasp. He flinched, knowing Iron Insect's three-pronged claw was reaching for his neck. Then a human hand touched him. He turned around. It was Jessica. The noise had been the tent's zip being pulled up.

He didn't answer, didn't dare give a story that could be picked apart. Jessica wriggled in, smiling, and knelt in front of him.

'It's sweltering.'

That was true. Despite the shade, it was like a sauna in the tent. Drops of sweat ran on Ferg's shorn scalp. He'd been breathing his own body odour. Jessica unstuck her T-shirt from her chest and fanned air between her boobs.

'Headache,' he said, venturing an excuse.

'Awwww, poor wickle Fergie,' she cooed, pouting, rubbing his forehead.

The press of her against him made him shrink. She kissed him and giggled. He was suddenly not sure of Jessica. She was changing. She pulled him out of the tent, and he felt like an astronaut being pulled out of a sinking capsule in the Pacific, eyes hammered by the sun. They were in the middle of a field of tents. A mini-city had formed overnight, with beaten-down grass pathways, a Mayfair with bright new-painted vans and pavilion-size marquees in neat rows, and an Old Kent Road of patched one-and two-person tents jammed in higgledy-piggledy.

'Isn't that better?'

Mike Toad's empty tent was next door, and Dolar was sleeping in a shacklike shade he'd built against the side of his van. Syreeta was balancing a dented saucepan over a Calor Gas stove.

'We're making tea,' Jessica said. 'Do you want some?'

Ferg bit his lip. If he refused, They'd immediately be suspicious. But if he accepted, he'd have to put something inside himself that came from Them. It was possible there was something in the tea to make him change as Jessica had changed. Two days ago, she'd been a sulk; now she was fawning all over him, trying to pretend nothing was wrong. It could have been something in the tea. Water boiled in Syreeta's saucepan, tiny bubbles agitating around the sides, large burps in the centre.

'Tea?' she asked him.

He nodded a yes.

Dolar was snoring. Or maybe pretend snoring. He had an old straw hat over his face, but could be looking out, eyes alert, through the cracks in the brim. Syreeta slurped hot water into a row of mugs and threw the rest away. It hissed on the ground like acid. Jessica brought him a cup of milky water with a teabag floating in it. He held it, ignoring the scalding heat, and waited his turn with the spoon.

'Pam's off looking for her sister,' Syreeta said.

Salim was sitting nearby. Silently he took a cup of tea. Ferg dumped his teabag into a plastic rubbish bag, and passed the spoon to Salim.

'The Toad went with her,' Jessica added.

Ferg raised the mug to his mouth. He let hot water lap against his lips but did not swallow. It smelled all right, but he knew the extra ingredient would be tasteless, odourless, undetectable. Salim gulped the tea so fast there was hot sweat on his forehead before he'd finished. It was a shame, but there was no way Ferg could have warned the Pakistani boy. Now it was too late. If he had been all right before, he was tainted now. Tainted by the Iron Insect.

'There might be music tonight,' Jessica said. 'The programme doesn't start officially until the day after tomorrow, but there are enough people with guitars and things to get something together.'

Ferg turned half away while the others weren't looking and spilled some of his tea. It sloshed on the ground where Syreeta had thrown the water, and sank into the earth, unnoticed. He felt a twinge of excitement. There was a pleasure in each of his little victories.

Earlier, he had seen the man from the last night, the monster's attendant, wandering around the site, looking for him. That had made him duck into the tent in the first place. The man was gone now. Ferg would have to be careful of him. He was more dangerous than the others. Jessica and Syreeta would be easy to fool because they thought they knew him. The man had been there when he saw the Iron Insect. He knew he knew.

'How's your tea?' Jessica asked, ringing with fake innocence.

He held up his mug and smacked his lips, but didn't drink. Jessica turned away, and he spilled more tea.

'Never tasted better,' he said.

High in the sky, a white helicopter made a slow pass. Everyone looked up, and he dribbled the last of the tea away. The sleek machine purred as it passed. Ferg had been seeing white helicopters ever since he came to Alder, but only now was he noticing them, realizing what they were for, from whom they came.

'Police,' Jessica said. 'Spying.'

'No,' said Salim. 'It'll be the BBC, getting film for the news.'

'Aren't we near the helicopter air base?' Syreeta asked. 'Yeovilton?'

He shrugged. It was impossible to read any markings on the white helicopter. Not that he'd have believed them. The police, the BBC, the Air Force. They'd all be supporters of the Iron Insect.

He touched the empty mug to his mouth and tipped it. A drop of brown moisture ran against his lips, but he rubbed it off against the rim. He put the mug down, and Syreeta collected it. People saw what they wanted to see, what they expected to see. Syreeta and Jessica had seen him drink their cup of tea, and now they'd think they had him.

It was strange to think They were fooled exactly as They fooled everyone else. How long would it be before one of Them made a mistake, talking to him as if he were in on it, assuming knowledge of the Iron Insect's purposes and plans?

The white helicopter lazily disappeared towards the horizon. Its blades hadn't even whipped up a breeze.

Syreeta rinsed the cups out with bottled water and stowed them away. Jessica sat on one of Dolar's wonky folding chairs and picked up a fashion magazine, riffling through the pages as she compared thousand-pound frocks. Dolar pretended to sleep again.

When it started, there must have been few of Them, and vast numbers of ordinary, uninfected, free people. He wondered how far it had gone. Everyone couldn't have gone over, or they'd jump and take him by force. There must be others like him, as he had been, unsuspecting among the Iron Insect's followers. How many of Them were there? One in ten? One in five? Was it up to fifty-fifty?

Ferg was thirsty, throat parched, skin warm and damp. But he couldn't give himself away by getting a drink. He sat down and lit up. The hot smoke didn't help his throat, but he usually smoked a cig after a cup of tea. He couldn't afford to break with routine. Never forget They were watching. He held the smoke in his dry mouth and felt pain in his lungs. Even if he could get a drink, where could he be certain it wasn't doctored? The bottled water was in the van, where Syreeta or one of the others could get at it any time he wasn't around. If he went to one of the stalls selling warm beer and Coke at inflated prices, he had no way of knowing the stuff hadn't been tampered with. Canned drinks should be safe. But he couldn't be certain. They could have taken over factories and be doctoring drinks at source. Maybe drinks had always been doctored. Maybe he wouldn't know the taste of a drink that hadn't been.

The Iron Insect had had three triple-jointed legs, and a body shaped like a wasp's nest. There had been something obscene about it. More than a machine, It had been alive, its metal a hard kind of flesh, the wires and workings arteries and organs. The Thing was like a queen ant, and the people who served It, buzzing around with one mind and one purpose, were workers, drones. Maybe They were usually invisible. Maybe now he wasn't drinking doped tea, he'd start seeing Them everywhere. They might be always striding down Charing Cross Road, scuttling up the Post Office Tower, screwing noisily in Oxford Circus, waiting patiently outside the Houses of Parliament. Unseen masters, attended always by white helicopter catspaws.

He pulled the neck of his T-shirt and a waft of hot, body-scented air rushed up past him. It was getting hotter, and shade was shrinking. He used his hand as a cap-peak and peered up at the sky. It was cloudless blue, the sun an agonizing white blip, impossible to look at. Around him, young people were tanning. A girl walked by wearing only shorts, her chest a Caribbean brown, no strap marks on her back and shoulders. She licked her lips at him, and he knew she was one of Them. He was supposed to look at her dark nipples, not her empty eyes, and be fooled. They thought They could lead him by his dick. His bare forearms prickled in the sun. He kept watching the skies.

Three

'THINGS ARE going to be different from now on,' he told his son. 'No more crying, no more bed-wetting, no more nonsense about the dark. No more Evil Dwarf. Do you understand?'

Jeremy looked up, tears swimming in his eyes, and nodded with shuddery eagerness.

Maskell took the breadknife away from the boy's throat and said, 'I'm proud of you, Jerm. Proud.'

Sue-Clare was in the corner, hugging Hannah as if the girl were a teddy bear.

'See,' he explained to her, 'it's simple when you put things simply. No problem.' He smiled at his obedient son. 'No problem at all. Is there, Jerm?'

Jeremy nodded vigorously, hair flopping. The jagged red line on his throat where the knife had been was vanishing quickly. But the memory would remain, and Jeremy would never again be funked of the dark, or blub like a baby in the playground, or pee the sheets.

Maskell felt better this morning, as if he could shrug off the heat, absorbing its goodness through his skin. His lands seen to, he could take care of his family.

'Come here, women,' he said, stretching out his arms. 'Come,' he said, voice deeper.

Sue-Clare stood, unsteadily, and Hannah escaped from her mother. The girl ran to him. He picked her up, rubbing his face against hers.

'Ouch, Daddy,' she said, in a mock scold, 'your face scrapes.'

He laughed as Hannah put her fat little hand into his hair, smoothing back the moss that grew there.

'Look,' she said, pulling, 'a flower.'

'For you, my Princess Precious,' he said.

Hannah hugged, body warm against his, cradled to him in one arm. The other he stretched out towards his wife, fine tendrils twisting from his hand. Sue–Clare took a step away from the wall, and paused.

'What's the matter, Suki?'

She was hovering, as if dizzy. There was a bruise on her forehead, a cut scabbed over, from when he'd had to put her in her place. That was over and done. She'd learned and now she'd have a treat.

'We can be a family again,' he said. 'I'll show you.'

He snapped his fingers, sap leaking from the knuckles, and whistled for Jethro. The dog lurched unsteadily out of his basket, trailing his blanket. Maskell had been neglecting Jethro, and needed to make amends. The dog was limping, head swollen and discoloured like a large fungus.

'Here, boy,' Maskell said.

Hannah laughed as the dog zigzagged towards them. He tried to yap happily, but his throat was furred inside. The dog was ailing, and Maskell needed to succour him. Balancing Hannah on his hip, he knelt and patted Jethro. Amber eyes opened in the yellow fuzz of the dog's face as his hand curved around Jethro's head, twig fingers sinking into overripe softness.

'That's better,' he said.

His hand sank into the doughy mass, filling the head. He punched through between Jethro's shoulders and sprouted into the dog's body. Maskell's arm grew, fingers splaying inside Jethro. The dog gurgled happily as Maskell gave comfort, tail erect, legs tucked in. He stood again, lifting the weight of Jethro. A tiny branch poked out of Jethro's anus, displacing the dog's tail, and spread into a green hand with flexible fingers. Maskell felt a tingling as the dog collapsed, incorporated into his arm. Jethro was little more than a fur sleeve now, eyes lodged unblinking in Maskell's shoulder. The tail hung from his wrist.

'Good boy,' Maskell said.

His bicep was ringed with Jethro's teeth, inset like stones in a mosaic. His hand was swollen out again, his arm supple and strong. He tickled Hannah's nose with Jethro's tail, and she giggled.

'Oh, Daddy,' she said. 'Sorry, Maurice.'

'No, Precious Princess,' he breathed at her, 'Daddy is all right. Daddy is right.'

Pressing Hannah's head to his cheek, he looked across the room at his woman. He stretched his arm, its new fur rippling, and beckoned with a four-jointed, bud-tipped forefinger. Swallowing air, Sue-Clare walked to him, hands in full view. When she was within reach, he curled his arm around her, pulling her close. He kissed her cheek, feeling her shudder.

'My family,' he said, 'my oak and staff.'

At this moment, everything was perfect. Everything was connected. Cobweb-thin tendrils grew out of him, gently puncturing Hannah and Sue-Clare, feeding his seed into them. His family, his lands and his body were all one, growing together in nature.

'We plough the fields and scaaaatter,' he hummed, 'the good seed on the land . . .'

Hannah took up his hymn, 'but it is fed and waaaaatered by God's Almighty Hand . . .'

She sang on, mixing up the words, but getting the meaning.

'He sends the snow in winter,' he breathed, 'the warmth to swell the grain . . .'

Sue-Clare gasped and shook as she was threaded through, but Hannah – good girl, Daddy's princess – accepted, and appreciated with her child's innocence the miracle of life. Sue-Clare twisted, struggling as she sometimes did to make it more exciting, hands playfully thumping his chest, yellow fluid leaking from his tendrils on to her neck and shirt. He kissed her mouth, mashing tongue against teeth. His knob stood out again, poking through his ruptured fly, a hardwood spear with a creamy tear at its eyehole. His balls were swollen too, grapefruit heavy with seed.

'Suki,' he said, 'now . . .'

He saw her eyes widen as he pressed her down on the rug, pulling her jeans. Hannah was part of this, part of their cocoon, a serene bubble unto herself. She shifted until she was riding him, hanging on his back, arms around his neck, knees clamped to his sides. Maskell remembered making love while Sue-Clare was pregnant, feeling one flesh with his child as well as his wife. Sue-Clare did not fight him as he angled his knob against her, sliding himself in.

'Maurice,' she whispered, 'Jeremy's here . . . Maurice, don't . . .'

Maskell lowered his weight, slipping deeper into his wife, his connection to her swelling as tendrils sprouted between them. Sue-Clare bit her underlip and shut her eyes tight, tears pressed in silence through the cracks. Maskell was fully covering her now, barked elbows against the rug. He didn't need to push with his hips. His knob thrust and swelled, withdrew and shrank, by itself.

He craned his neck, and twisted to look at his children. It was important they learn the facts of life. Growing up on a farm should be educational. Hannah was warmly nestled, stubby fingers working into his fruity flesh. Jeremy stood by the door, eyes wide.

'Come here, son,' he said, 'join us, and be a man . . .'

Jeremy was panicked. It struck some that way, Maskell knew. He had a problem boy.

'It's natural,' he assured the child.

Sue-Clare was with him, riding herself to a peak. Her eyes were open now, clear as pools. Shoots pressed against the scarf that held her hair, and her tan was beginning to crack like young bark, showing green lines. Where their bellies pressed together, they were joined by a sweet-smelling gum that tickled as they squirmed.

'Join,' Maskell said to Jeremy, again, 'then we can watch a video. You'll enjoy that.'

His knob burst, and Sue-Clare received a frothy gush of seed. They were grown together. Father, mother, daughter. Jethro, even. All fertile, all ready to sprout. Jeremy made a decision and stepped towards them. Maskell had a rush of love for his family, for his fields. Everything would be perfect. Then Jeremy turned and shouldered through the door, clattering across the kitchen, out into the open. Doors banged behind him.

Maskell stood up delicately. His knob, now supple and snaky, came easily out of Sue-Clare. Hannah detached from his back as painlessly and neatly as a ripe apple falls. His wife hugged herself on the floor, pulling the rug around her. There were gummy golden tears like syrup on her cheeks, breasts and stomach. Hannah slept, white threads on her face, limbs and stomach swollen like peaches, juice dribbling from her mouth.

He still wore the remains of his clothes, although his boots had long since burst and been thrown away. He picked at the strands of his shirt, matted to him by dirt and natural secretions, and slowly peeled himself. His skin was the brown of healthy soil, his broad chest dotted with green spots where the shoots would come. He tore his jeans with strong fingers and dropped the denim strips on the floor. He was able to stand more naturally now, knees bending properly both ways, the coconutty fur on his calves sprouting nicely.

Naked and perfect, he was ready to follow his errant son, to bring him back to the fold. He kissed Sue-Clare's forehead, patted Hannah and tweaked her nose, and walked through the kitchen out into the farmyard. The honest, enriching smells of earth and shit filled his tunnel-like nostrils.

He couldn't see Jeremy, but the boy was his seed and he had a dowsing rod between his legs. His manhood dangled freely, not stiff with the need to fertilize but loose and comfortable. He held it extended horizontally away from his body, and waited. He snorted warm air. His knob twitched towards the barn. The office. It had once been a loft, now it was an office. The conversion had been a mistake, made during his time of ignorance. Computers and books had no place on a farm. Plastic and paper had no smell. The loft was for bales of warm hay, not dry and dead numbers and records; for prickly coupling with ripe farm girls, not futile wrestling with sums and screens.

Jeremy was up there. Maskell's knob twitched again, a little turgid, slightly painful. He let the rod hang free and strode across his yard.

'Here I come, Jerm,' he shouted, 'ready or not.'

Four

STEPPING OUT of the Gate House with Susan, Lytton was surrounded immediately by demands. Derek was in the forefront with news of a parking disaster. The wrong fields had filled up first, creating a logjam unable to get to the overflow areas. There was a Road Runner-like background beeping from gridlocked traffic. A driver from a hire firm was trying to get a receipt signature for a load of public-address equipment. Sister Karen wanted approval for a test bundle of wet-ink programme sheets before going ahead with full-scale printing and distribution. Kids he'd given positions of minor authority reported back with missions accomplished, neglected or fouled up. There was even a local journo with questions about last night's mysterious fire. Everyone was talking at once.

He sorted the crowd into an orderly queue, and took the easiest problems first, giving orders to surplus people. He told a kid to rustle up personnel and help Derek clear the parking throughways. He glanced over the lorry driver's manifest and initialled it. The equipment was already being assembled by brought-in techies into an ear-abusing pyramid of power. He fobbed off the reporter by claiming that all press statements would be issued by Marie-Laure Quilter, sending him away with his hand-held cassette recorder. As far as Lytton could remember, Sister Marie-Laure hadn't spoken to an outsider in years, and was unlikely to start now.

Karen's programmes looked fine to him. From experience, he knew everything would start an hour later than scheduled, but the timetable was a start. Susan, who was in charge of printing, commended Karen on a good job and they scurried off to the printshop, which was part of what had been the Manor House's warren of garages and stables, to begin mass production. Susan looked back and saluted, mouthing 'later' at him. What Susan said had affected him, but he was back in his snakeskin. Until he received further orders, he should keep on with things as normal. His morning off – essentially, a morning wasted – had probably allowed chaos to descend on the site. More chaos.

As the festival had grown, Lytton had become more important to it. Jago almost never did anything personally except take part in ceremonies of blessing, so someone had to liaise between the Agapemone and the hordes of show-business characters – not to mention stallholders, haulage people, ticket distributors and troublemakers – necessary to keep the show running. A committee, on which Mick Barlowe represented Jago, decided on the line-up and sorted out niceties like scheduling and local accommodation for the performers. Once they'd done their bit, it was down to Lytton to put the plan into action. The festival gave him more leeway than any other Agapemone activity. Complicated, challenging and interesting, it kept him half in the real world, out of the *mondo bizarro* side of the community.

He strode towards a portacabin marked ADMINISTRATION, where a bank of temporary telephone and fax lines had been connected. It was ironic: the Agapemone so limited contact with the outside world that it had to set up special facilities to keep running during the festival. Inside, telephones were ringing and printers chattering. Temporary staff were beavering away.

A troupe of bikers cruised by, booted feet kicking dusty turf, engines snarling. They were all in black trews and jackets with skull, sword, demon and swastika emblems. Lytton felt a shudder creep up his back. He couldn't be sure, but he thought Badmouth Ben was in the parade somewhere, stringy skeleton body under leather, tattooed bones gripping handlebars, growling to match the engine of the machine he'd brought back from Hell. The bikers were through the gates, touring the fields in search of a prime parking space to set up their own enclave, a mini-camp where they could listen to their own music and build their own fires. There'd been occasional trouble with the bike boyos, but usually they proved to be a damp squib, emptying crate after crate of beer and keeping to themselves, swapping stories and joints. The hassles came from 'nice' kids who freaked out on too much booze or dope, aggressive Rastas demanding free admission, or the increasingly tribal and crusty travellers.

All roads to the festival site were clogged with slow-moving traffic. At least the lines *were* moving.

'Oink, oink,' said Gary Chilcot, popping up, 'the pigs are here, James.'

Lytton tutted. 'Only to be expected.'

'They got a couple of cop cars out on the main road, and they're settin' up a tent.'

'Checkpoint Charlie.'

'Yurp.'

'I'd best be neighbourly.'

The narrow side road to the site was passable on foot. Lytton ambled through the gates, passing the booth where a Sister of the Agapemone and some fairly together staff were taking gate money and passing out badges to those who had not prepaid. He checked with Beth, a girl from the village, and she told him not to worry. Hourly, she was locking up the take in a cashbox and having it sent over by a trustworthy gopher to the administration cabin, where Mick would be putting it in a safe. That way, there was no temptation. This year, people could even pay by plastic. A youth with temporary flower tattoos on his cheeks and hair down to his arse was fishing under his tie-dye poncho for a credit card. As the turn-of-the-millennium hippie wondered whether to use Access, Barclaycard or Amex Gold, James reflected that the Sixties had been a long time ago.

He made his way past the line of vehicles. At the main road turn-off, where he had stationed Kevin Conway and a large sign, there were two police officers in shirtsleeves and helmets, standing by a marquee tent. A burly chap in plain clothes drank tea from a thermos.

This was routine. The festival had an agreement with the police that they were not to come on site unless especially requested. But they usually turned up at the perimeter to keep an eye on things. Relations had been strained in the past, mainly thanks to an incident four years ago when the force had been especially requested on the site to investigate some minor vandalism against a car. It had turned out the complainant was a plain-clothes constable with about as much impartiality as the pro-Soviet regime who had 'especially requested' that Russia invade Afghanistan, and, once on site, the police had taken the opportunity to round up the usual suspects, hauling in nuisance-value drugs and drink offenders. Since then, Lytton had been careful to toe official lines and make sure the right local councillors were invited to the opening and closing ceremonies.

He had even tried to get the bishop of Bath and Wells, since the Agapemone was officially a Christian community, but the Anglican Church had a long memory and was still wary of the formerly Reverend Mr Anthony William Jago.

'Good afternoon,' he said to the tea drinker. 'I'm James Lytton, from the Agapemone.'

The policeman spat warm, brown liquid on the dead grass.

'Detective Sergeant Ian Draper,' he said, extending his hand.

Lytton shook. 'Drug squad?'

'We don't call it that.'

'But . . . ?'

'Yes,' Draper said, 'obviously.'

He snapped at a blond constable with an Aryan jawline, 'Erskine, what's our mobile-phone number?'

Erskine coughed it out, and Draper wrote it down with a biro on the back of a business card.

'Here,' he said, handing the card to Lytton. 'If you need us, we're here.'

'Sergeant,' said the other constable, pulling Draper aside, whispering in his ear. He was black, doubtless a delight to the police-recruitment people and a neatly 'political' choice for this duty.

Draper grinned. 'Oh, is he now?'

The constable did a brief aye-aye salute, and left the tent-erecting to signal a battered van to pull over.

'PC Raine informs me an old friend just arrived,' Draper told Lytton. 'Possession with Intent. A hundred hours' community service. Repeat offender.'

Lytton shrugged. The van driver, who was about James's age, complained about being harassed again, but went along with the procedure. While the policemen made a cursory search of the van and Draper patted the driver's pockets, ten or fifteen cars took the turning undisturbed. A lot of people would be passing this way on foot, too. Checkpoint Charlie usually pulled out faces they recognized, then took a flyer on about one in fifty people. Sometimes they were even useful to the festival. Every year they scooped in quivering seventeen-year-olds with a plastic bag of marijuana or a couple of pills, and the poor sods spent the festival in holding cells while their mummies and daddies got long-distance bad-news calls. But Checkpoint Charlie also turned up not a few Carrying a Concealed Weapon cases, confiscating its share of knives and chains. Meanwhile, someone respectable-looking always turned up with a bootload of the drug of the month and spread it around unhindered. Personally, Lytton felt very few illegal substances caused as much trouble as Douggie Calver's perfectly legitimate but lethal cider.

The van passed the inspection, and Draper told his former catch to have a good time.

'See,' he said, 'no trouble.'

'Fair enough.'

'This should be a pleasant holiday for us,' Draper said. 'If the wind blows the right way, we should even hear a little nice music.'

'What wind?'

Draper grinned again, and wiped his sweaty forehead with a meaty, sparse-furred wrist. Draper was ten years younger than Lytton, in his early thirties, but he was already bloating around the neck and belly. He was missing the second button up on his white shirt, the torn hole testifying that it had been popped by his expanding gut. He didn't look like a drug-squad hard nut or a war-on-crime crusader.

A couple of young men in pink and orange shorts and vests sauntered by, arm in arm, whistling the *Dixon of Dock Green* theme.

'Comedians,' Draper said. 'Let's have 'em in the tent, shall we.'

Lytton shrugged.

'You,' Draper said, 'Claude and Cecil, over here . . .'

Erskine, the tallest of the constables, let his hand stray to the handle of his truncheon.

'Good afternoon,' Draper said to the gay couple, flashing a laminated identity card, 'we are police officers and we'd like you to cooperate in a search. If you've got nothing nasty, you've got no problems. Would you care to step into this tent and Constable Erskine will see to you.'

One of the young men swished and said, 'You don't get an offer like that every day.'

Erskine flushed deep red, but held the marquee flap up. The gays, giggling, stepped in.

'Do you tell fortunes?' one of them said in a high-pitched, high-camp voice. 'Madame LaZonga Sees All?'

Erskine followed.

'See,' Draper said, 'perfectly civilized.'

Five

IN VIDEOS, Daddy got annoyed when people being chased went upstairs in tall buildings. 'That's stupid,' he always said, 'when he gets to the top, he'll be trapped.' Jeremy had been stupid. The office was a good hiding place, but the only way out was the floor trapdoor he had come through. There was a wooden door in the wall, for tossing bales, but it was bolted from the outside, because Mummy was worried about Hannah or him falling out of it. If Daddy followed him up here, he'd be trapped. And Daddy would get him.

Something had happened to Daddy, and he'd got Jethro and Mummy and Hannah. Jeremy didn't really understand, but he knew something had been done to Jethro and Mummy and Hannah. If he was caught, it'd be done to him too. It'd be more than a quirting.

The trapdoor had been left open to let draught into the loft. Otherwise Jeremy couldn't have got in. He wasn't strong enough to push it up by himself. Usually, he had to ask Mummy or Daddy to lift the heavy weight if he wanted to go up. He scrunched behind Daddy's desk, trying to be as small as possible. He gripped the trowel he'd taken from the bench in the workspace below. He could see the open trapdoor from where he was. If Daddy came after him, he'd know.

There were no windows and it was dark. Not much light came through the trapdoor. He'd been so frightened of Daddy he'd forgotten to be frightened of the dark. Now, alone under the desk, more familiar fears came back, chewing the edge of his mind. He knew Daddy was outside looking for him. But Jeremy didn't know whether he was truly alone in the dark. The Evil Dwarf could be around somewhere. After all, the Evil Dwarf lived in the dark. Whatever had happened to Daddy must be the Evil Dwarf's fault. Daddy wouldn't change on his own.

His father had put his arm through Jethro as if the dog were made of Plasticene. He had seen Daddy stab Mummy between the legs with his stiff dickybird. Penis. He didn't use baby words now. It wasn't a dickybird, it was a penis. Jeremy had been surprised by his father's penis. He'd seen Daddy in the shower, and his penis had never looked like that before. It had been a length of sausage, not a tree branch.

Jeremy closed his eyes and tried to keep out the dark. He heard planks creaking in the barn, but didn't know whether the noises were natural, the wood noises he'd heard all his life, or signs of the presence of the Evil Dwarf.

The only thing his daddy was afraid of was stupidity. Usually, Jeremy was clever. Now, he felt stupid. Perhaps the Evil Dwarf had started on him while he was asleep, licking the surface of his brain, sampling the icing of his intelligence the way you might lick hundreds and thousands off an ice cream.

He opened his eyes, and saw Daddy's hand resting on the floor, gripping the edge of the trapdoor hole. Jeremy saw in the gloom that Daddy's fingers were long, with wispy vines wound around them. The hand got a better grip, vines shifting, and Daddy pulled himself up into the loft. His head came up first, larger than it had been, antler branches standing out of his forehead, and then his weighty body. Daddy got a knee on the loft floor and rose entirely through the trapdoor.

'Jerm?'

Jeremy's heart was hammering, and he was afraid he'd pee in his shorts. He held his tool up, hoping it was sharp.

'Jerm-eee?'

Daddy's voice was high and whining, cartoon-nasty. Like Lisa's, when she was picking on Jeremy. Daddy knew he was in the loft but was playing a game.

'Now, where can that blasted child be?'

Daddy stuck a stick-finger to his lips, and posed thoughtfully with a fist on one hip.

'Perhaps he's . . .'

Daddy stepped into the dark.

'. . . *behind the filing cabinet!*'

Daddy pulled the cabinet over. Metal screeched as drawers came out, the whole thing crashing to the floor. Jeremy pressed tight against the desklegs. Daddy kicked the filing cabinet, putting a dent in its side with his bunched-together bare toes.

'Nope,' Daddy said, 'no Jerm here. Tut tut tut. What a mess.'

Daddy looked around.

'Maybe Jerm-Jerm-Jerm-Swallowing-Sperm is . . .'

He pulled a shelf away from the wall. Nails wrenched and books thudded around Daddy.

'. . . *up on that fucking shelf!*'

Daddy had said a bad word.

His father held the plank that had been a shelf, and twisted it, dumping more books. Finally, it came free, and he tossed it into the dark. It crashed against something. Jeremy heard glass breaking.

'Obviously not,' Daddy said. 'Not behind the filing cabinet, not up on the shelf. What an elusive little Jerm. Daddy's proud of his piglet.'

Jeremy cried silently, fighting the heaves in his chest. He wanted to bawl and sob but knew it was important to be quiet.

'Maybe Jethro can find his little master, eh? Here, boy. Good boy.'

There was a strangled barking, and the tail stuck out of Daddy's wrist wagged obediently. Daddy hung his head, and talked to his arm.

'Here, Jethro. Go find Jerm.'

Daddy swallowed his tongue and made woof-woof noises. Jeremy was sure the Evil Dwarf was in the dark with them. Dopey must be enjoying his victory. Daddy took a grip on his own shoulder, and snapped his arm off. It came away like a dead branch being wrenched from a tree.

'Go get 'im, Jethro.'

Daddy tossed the arm into the dark, and Jeremy cringed. The arm hit the floor with a thump, then ran towards Jeremy, scraping across planks. Jeremy tried to cram himself against the wall, head bumping against the underside of the desk. Jethro squeezed into the gap and sank his teeth into Jeremy's ankle.

Jeremy screeched, and dropped his tool. Jethro or Daddy's arm or whatever it was couldn't bite deep, but its sharp teeth ripped his sock and scraped skin. It growled, and slobbered into his shoe.

'Aha,' Daddy said, 'looks like we've found us a Jerm, boy.'

Daddy ripped the desk away and threw it across the loft. Still plugged into the wall, the computer thudded down beside Jeremy, plastic and glass cracking.

Jeremy took the dog thing by what should have been its neck, and tried to squeeze the life out of the fur-covered meat and bone tube. Teeth grated against his ankle as he wrenched the thing free. It squirmed in his two-handed grip and felt disgusting. Jeremy threw it at Daddy, and he caught it.

Daddy stuck his arm back on, slightly skewed, and made a fist, gripping Jethro's tail. Even in the dark, Jeremy could see Daddy was changing more.

'Go for the throat, Jethro,' Daddy said. 'Woof fucking woof.'

Beneath the loft was the garage space where Daddy stored the farm's tractor and kept a lot of tools. On the way up, Jeremy had grabbed something from a wall rack. A large trowel, with a foot-long diamond-shaped blade, dusty with dried cement. In his hiding place, he'd been gripping the chunky handle as if it were a magic sword. He scrabbled on the floor for the trowel, and snatched it up again.

'Come to Daddy, Jerm-features,' Daddy cooed, lurching over Jeremy.

Jeremy held up the trowel, blade before his face.

'It won't hurt.'

Daddy bent over, reaching for Jeremy. His long hard penis got in the way, and he had to stand back, fingertips latching on to Jeremy's shoulders, barbs wriggling through his shirt into his skin. Silhouetted against the light from the trapdoor, Daddy's head was changing. His antlers sprouted, developing like the sped-up plant films in TV nature programmes.

Drawing in breath through his teeth, Jeremy angled the trowel so that it pointed outwards and upwards.

'It won't hurt at all.'

Jeremy yelled and thrust, standing up and throwing himself against Daddy. The trowel stabbed against the underside of Daddy's penis, pricking through the green bark, and Jeremy shoved, gouging a curl of skin from the shaft, slicing shallowly into the white wood flesh.

Daddy bellowed and held out his arms to steady himself. Jeremy pushed, and the trowel shuddered out of his father's penis, leaping at his double-fist-sized hanging balls, sinking about two inches into his hard-shelled but mushy scrotum. Shouts filled the loft. There was blood all over Jeremy's hands, green and sappy, not red and slippery. Daddy staggered back, yanking the trowel out of Jeremy's hands, and tripped over the trapdoor. For a moment, he was hung in space over the gap, then he fell bum-first through the hole. Jeremy heard him landing badly, heard things breaking.

It was time to run, to get past Daddy. He bolted to the trapdoor hole, and looked down. Daddy had fallen on the steps leading up to the office. One of his antlers had snapped off, and green stuff was squiring out, dribbling down his face. He was still alive, but he wasn't going to get up soon.

Jeremy stepped down the stairs, one at a time, and edged around his father, speeding up when he was past him. He felt Daddy reaching for his ankle, and ran, hearing his father's fist closing on the nothing where his foot had been. He ran round the tractor, leaving a handprint on its dusty red cowling, into the barnyard. Behind him, Daddy was roaring and struggling.

He looked at the house and saw Mummy and Hannah standing by the door. Behind them was the spindly wreck of a patch of ivy Mummy had encouraged to sweep up over the side of the house. Jeremy thought Mummy and Hannah were leaning against the ivy, letting its creepers twine about their legs and arms to hold them up. Earlier this summer, the ivy had gone from rotten brown to brittle grey, but now it was deepening green, its colour reflected in the faces of his mother and sister.

Mummy waved. He ran away from the house, towards the road. There was a steady flow of traffic being directed by young men in armbands into the fallow field. Daddy had said cars from the festival would be using some of the dry pastures. If Jeremy could reach the traffic, he'd be safe for a while. If there were people, he'd be safe.

Six

When Hazel woke up, she felt different. The comfort of sleep carried over into consciousness. Her pains were eased, her head clear. It was pleasantly cool inside the alcove. High up on the wall was a stained-glass slit window. Coloured shapes hung on the purple curtains, a smudgy back-to-front picture. She tried to remember how she'd got here, but swiftly realized it didn't matter. Everything before the Agapemone, before the Beloved touch, was a fading dream. She'd been born on the steps of the Manor House. What was important was now.

'Sister,' a girl's voice said. The curtain was drawn aside.

Hazel got up and stepped out of the alcove. They were waiting for her in the chapel. Jenny's white dress and blonde hair shone in the twilight. Three other women, faces she recognized but couldn't name, wore different robes, light blue with white edging. Sisters of the Agapemone.

'Alleiluya,' they chimed.

Jenny hugged her, holding tight, pressing her soft cheek against Hazel's face. Hazel felt Love pouring into her.

'You're honoured,' Jenny explained. 'Beloved has chosen you. Tonight there will be a Great Manifestation.'

'Alleiluya,' the women repeated.

'It'll be wonderful, I promise. You'll be a Sister of the Agapemone.'

Hazel nodded, accepting the honour. It was the right, the only thing. For the first time, probably in her life, she knew what she must do, what she wanted to be.

'Let me introduce everyone,' Jenny continued. 'Sister Cindy, Sister Janet, Sister Kate.'

The women smiled when named, and leaned forward to kiss her. Jenny smiled sunnily. She was the perfect angel. Hazel could imagine delicate wings, cornsilk-gold to match her hair, spreading under Jenny's dress, straining to emerge.

'Come with us,' Jenny said. 'First, you must be anointed.'

The Sisters grouped around her like an honour guard, and she was led beyond the altar into a vestry that looked like a Roman bath-house, with marble benches, wooden cabinets and empty nooks for classical statues. There was a sunken pool, dry at the moment, four feet deep, with a shaped stone block at the bottom for sitting on. The windowless vestry was lit by fluorescent tubes.

'Sister Hazel,' Jenny said, 'you've been baptized, confirmed. That was the first step.'

Hazel remembered Beloved's touch on her forehead. She wondered if the sign of the cross was still there, glowing like a cattle brand.

'Simple, wasn't it?'

Hazel agreed.

'Outsiders imagine terrible things, but the Agapemone is founded on simplicity.'

Jenny was trying to put Hazel at her ease. Her hair was loose, and she played with it while she talked.

'The Great Manifestation will be your initiation, not only into the Agapemone, but into its Inner Circle. You'll be one of Beloved's Sister-Loves. That's special. Not everyone gets so far so quickly.'

'You've been bumped up a couple of grades,' Cindy said. 'Lucky girl.'

Hazel was just about following this. The procedure didn't matter, it was the acceptance that was important. Once this ritual brouhaha was concluded, she would at last feel complete.

'Before the Great Manifestation, you must be cleansed in body and spirit. Don't worry. It's symbolic. You don't get scrubbed with lye or anything. Basically, you take a long bath and meditate, think things out.'

'Don't worry,' Kate, roundly pregnant, said, 'it's quite pleasant.'

The women all agreed, nodding and humming.

'I know it seems like dressing up and playing games, Hazel. Beloved believes in ceremony. Rituals channel natural forces.'

Jenny's voice was soothing, persuasive.

'Sister Janet, get Sister Hazel a towel, would you.'

The slender blonde girl, tall and angular with a fringe over her eyes, opened a whitewood cabinet and brought out a full-size beach towel.

Jenny tugged Hazel's T-shirt out of her jeans.

'It's all right,' Hazel said. 'I can manage.'

She took off her T-shirt and wriggled out of her jeans. Then she sat on one of the benches – sort of enjoying the chilly shock of marble – and pulled off her socks and underwear. Janet draped the towel around her.

Cindy – small, smiling and dark-haired – was turning a wheel set into the wall. Under the floor, something gurgled, and water gushed out of a fish-head tap, splashing the bottom of the pool.

'It's luxurious, actually,' Cindy said. 'Beloved believes in comforts of the flesh.'

'Comfort of the flesh frees the spirit,' said Kate. She scattered what smelled like bath salts into the water, raising a slight froth.

'It's natural,' Jenny said. 'Herbs from the garden, mostly.'

Janet was folding Hazel's clothes, stowing them in one of the chests.

'We'll get you a proper dress later,' she said. 'What are you? Five three? Five four?'

Hazel didn't know exactly how tall (rather, short) she was, but that sounded about right.

The water rose, giving off a wonderful scent. Cindy stuck her hand in to check the temperature.

'Fine by me, but you have to sit in it. What do you think?'

The towel wrapped a little awkwardly around her, Hazel bent down and touched her fingers to the water. It was warm, but not hot. She nodded.

'Okey-dokey,' Cindy said, 'that'll do then. Jan, turn it off, would you, or we'll have water all over the floor. Again.'

Janet wrestled the wheel back, and the fish dried up.

'Right,' said Kate, 'let's get you in.'

Janet took her towel. Hazel didn't mind being naked with these almost strangers, although she was usually self-conscious about her body. The Sisters were family. Cindy and Kate took an arm each and guided her to the bath's edge.

'Careful,' Kate said, 'it's deeper than it looks. Step on the seat.'

Hazel dipped her toe, then her foot, then her ankle, into the water. The fine hair on her shin prickled. The Sisters lifted her over the bath and lowered her like an invalid. The water rose, sucking a little, and warmth wrapped around her, lapping up over her body. Her bottom settled on the seat and she leaned back. The shaped stone was surprisingly comfortable. Water came up to her neck and rippled against her chin, the scents of herbs tickling her nostrils. It'd be easy to fall asleep.

'You're comely, Sister,' Jenny said.

'Yeah, dead comely,' Cindy agreed.

Her hair was wet now, floating around her, drifting against her cheeks and shoulders. Jenny stroked it out of her eyes and mouth, smoothing it against her head.

'It'll come after the evening service,' Jenny explained. 'I'm afraid you'll have to skip dinner. You're supposed to fast.'

That was all right by Hazel. She'd been meaning to eat less anyway.

'Beloved will read a short lesson, and you'll be brought to the altar. Be careful, by the way, the altar is an antique and easily damaged. Sister Kate nearly knocked it over during her initiation into the Inner Circle.'

'That was hardly my fault, Jenny. The spirit was moving within me.'

The women laughed. 'Just teasing, Sister,' Jenny assured.

'You won't be familiar with the ritual, but, believe me, your part is easy.'

Hazel was warm all over.

'You'll know what to do,' said Kate, easing her pregnancy with her hands as she knelt by the bath.

Janet had sat down, and was dangling bare feet into the water.

'Just let the spirit come.'

'We're well rehearsed,' Kate said. 'We've all been through it.'

'More than once, in some cases,' Cindy said.

Hazel wondered if Jenny were blushing. The girl pulled her hair over her face, and continued.

'Beloved is the Lord God made flesh. The Great Manifestation will give you proof. Until then, you'll have to get by on faith.'

Hazel nodded, water slopping into her mouth. She understood this was important, but didn't feel it vital she understood everything straight away. If she'd been waiting all her life, a few more hours didn't matter.

Kate cupped a little water in her hand and sprinkled it on her bulging dress, wetting down her stomach.

'For luck,' she explained. 'The baby will be blessed.'

'We share Love,' Janet said.

'We all share Love,' Jenny agreed. 'Tonight will be yours, Hazel. It'll be special, but we all have a part.'

'Alleiluya,' they chorused.

The four faces bobbed over the water, beaming benevolence.

'We'll be with you from now until the Great Manifestation. We'll look after you. Think of us as bridesmaids.'

Seven

ONCE PAUL decided to phone the Agapemone to see if Hazel was all right, it took twenty minutes to find the leaflet Wendy and Derek had left. It turned up in the showroom, weighted down by one of Mike Bleach's ashtrays. A prospectus for stallholders at the festival, it listed three local telephone numbers.

He sat at his desk with the remote phone, and tried to control his breathing. He didn't like tricky conversations on the telephone, and avoided them whenever he could. The first number he dialled was engaged. The second rang twice and fed him through to a series of bizarre, birdlike squawks. He'd called a fax number by mistake. He dialled the third number. It rang. And rang. He began counting rings. After about twenty or twenty-five rings, the receiver was picked up.

'Festival office,' a secretarial voice chirruped, 'Angela speaking. How may I help you?'

'I'd like to speak with Hazel Chapelet, please.'

There was a pause, and Paul heard the girl clicking her tongue to herself, presumably as she ran her eyes down a list.

'I'm sorry, I have no one of that name down here. Is she staff, or with one of the bands?'

'No, she's a visitor.'

Angela tried not to laugh. Paul imagined her looking out the window, seeing fields full of visitors.

'Not to the festival,' he explained, 'to the Agapemone.'

'This is the *festival* office. We don't have anything to do with the Agapemone, really. Your best bet is to call the Manor House.'

'Do you have the number?'

'I'm not really supposed to give it out.'

'It'll be in the phone book, won't it?'

'Yes, I think so.'

'Fine. Angela, could you be a love and save me some time by giving it to me? Please.'

He smiled at the phone, trying to exhude charm down the line. Angela had a nice voice, slightly low with a West Country burr. He imagined a pretty face and sparkling eyes, and concentrated on impressing her.

'Oh, all right,' she said, and gave him a number.

There was no pen within reach, so he scratched it in a soft notepad with the handle of a teaspoon.

'Thank you, Angela,' he said.

'Have a nice festival,' she replied, and hung up.

He waited a full minute, trying to calm himself. He was ridiculously on edge. The war machine had rattled his entire life. He imagined a cooling breeze, but was disappointed by reality. It was another hot, oppressive afternoon. There was a crack in the side of the house and white dust had fallen from it. Probably subsidence. Slowly, he dialled the Agapemone number. A man answered almost immediately.

'Ben,' the voice rasped, as if through a scrambler.

'Ben, hi,' Paul said, 'could I speak with Hazel?'

'Huh?'

'Hazel Chapelet. She's with you at the moment. Tell her it's Paul.'

'Huh?'

Something about Ben's voice spooked Paul. He imagined it went with glowing eyes like Allison Conway's. Come to think of it, her number-one boyfriend – Harley-Davidson's answer to the Phantom of the Opera – had been a Ben.

'Who is this?'

'Ben,' he repeated.

Ben had trouble breathing, and was wheezing into the telephone like an obscene caller. Paul got the impression he was talking with an idiot. He needed someone he's talked to before, someone who'd know who Hazel was.

'Could you get Wendy?'

Ben laughed, sending crackles through the telephone.

'That's what I'm here for.'

The receiver at the other end was put down with a clump.

'Ben?'

Paul heard footsteps. Ben had left the phone off the hook, and was walking away. He heard tiny telephone noises, and the line was cut off. He dialled again, but the number was engaged. Paul felt he'd just been shat on. Again.

Eight

Terry was starting to enjoy himself too much, which was dangerous. He wasn't *Mastermind* material at the best of times, and when he enjoyed himself his brain power dropped below that of the average lump of pond scum. He had no vision, no foresight, no eyesight. Allison would have to keep him in line with some pain. That, he could understand.

They'd been in the crowds, sussing things out. Allison's vision was improving. She recognized the people she wanted. They had an aura, a cloudy jacket around their entire bodies, especially thick over the eyes. It was like a personal atmosphere, held in place by a baggily invisible diving suit. There were potential recruits for Badmouth Ben's army. She'd struck up conversations with a few, sounding them out, puzzling them, planting seeds. Apart from the aura, they were no different from anyone else. That was good. That would help.

By the Agapemone, Allison and Terry ran into a couple of the kids from London, Mike Toad and Pam. They shared cigarettes and listened to some of Mike's jokes.

'How does a Somerset farmboy know when his sister's having her period?'

Allison didn't know, but had an idea she was about to find out.

'His dad's dick tastes different,' the Toad cackled, raising only stunned silence.

His aura was thick and smoky, phantom tendrils wrapped around his head like a scarf. Pam had none, and didn't sense the community shared by the others. Pam thought she was pretty, and didn't notice much. Mike Toad was a fool, but he had potential.

'How do you save a coon from drowning?' Mike asked. 'Take your foot off his head.'

Pam was uncomfortable. Her boyfriend was some sort of nigger. Mike Toad might do very well indeed. He had a hipflask which he passed around. Terry choked on the stinging whisky, but Allison took a burning gulp and let it settle. Handing the flask back, she saw the fog sleeve around her own arm. It was black with silent discharges of violet lightning.

'We're waiting for my sister,' Pam explained. 'She's bloody late.'

Terry was looking at Pam, and there were yellow-green squiggles in his aura. He clenched and unclenched hairy fists, and didn't say anything. Sooner or later, Allison would have to let him cut loose a bit, before teaching him another lesson. He'd already had a dose of the stick; it was time he got a whiff of the carrot.

Pam scratched her short, red hair. Her make-up was perfect, even in this heat, a white mask with a blood-heart of lipstick, eyebrows distinct as a Japanese doll's, black-lined eyes. Her clothes might not look like much, but they were expensive. City girl in the country. Pam would learn. And Allison would be her teacher. She felt like extending one of her fingernails and scraping through the white powder, drawing an X across Pam's face. Then scraping through the skin and flesh, baring a cross of bone and muscle.

Pam shuddered and said, 'Someone walked over my grave.'

'His brother was looking for you earlier,' the Toad said, jerking a thumb at Terry, who grunted.

'They don't get on,' Allison explained.

She remembered Teddy's face from last night, drawn and white and scared. Last night had been weirder than she expected, but a thrill. She was looking forward to nightfall, to more of the same.

'Look at that,' Mike Toad said, spitting, 'the Gestapo have moved in.'

A police constable was sauntering up the road towards the Gate House. He wore a short-sleeved shirt and had a radio clipped to his top pocket. A truncheon shifted like a displaced dick in a thigh pocket as he walked. The copper had a short brush of fair hair.

'Bloody Barry,' Terry grunted, recognizing the man.

Barry Erskine had a reputation for coming down hard on juveniles. Terry claimed he'd been roughed up by PC Erskine outside a disco in Langport. If it was true, Allison reckoned Terry was bound to have deserved the knocks. He was an extreme arsehole when he had a few pints in him.

'I thought they weren't allowed at the festival,' Pam said.

'They aren't,' Allison agreed. 'But the festival is past that gate. This is the approach road.'

'Good afternoon, Master Gilpin,' Erskine said, smiling with his even teeth but not with his blue eyes. 'Still a music lover, I see.'

Terry grinned. He thought he had something that gave him a shot at Erskine. He was wrong.

'Afternoon, constable,' Allison said, a neat and nasty thrill in her water.

Erskine tapped his helmet brim. 'Good afternoon, miss.'

Allison looked him in the face and saw swirls of black radiating from his clear eyes. His aura was like a dark, ragged cloak.

'Just making sure things are nice and quiet,' he said.

Allison and Erskine looked at each other, understanding.

'No trouble here,' she said.

'So I see,' he replied. 'Catch you later.'

He turned and walked away, aura trailing. She should have expected it. Badmouth Ben didn't just want kids and thugs. Allison knew the army would surprise a lot of people.

'Heavy shit,' said Mike Toad. 'Back to the panzer car, PC Plod.' The London boy laughed nervously, impressing no one with his brave show of out-of-earshot defiance. 'What has four legs and a cunt halfway up its back? A police horse.' Mike snorted at his own joke.

'Terry,' Allison said, 'take hold of Mike's ear.'

Terry did. Mike yelped.

'Now, stand up.'

Terry yanked Mike upright, and lifted. The ear went red, and Mike's hat fell off. He made sounds like a patient during an inept dental drilling. Allison was warmed as Mike's pain gulped out of him. Pam raised a perfectly outlined eyebrow.

'That's enough.'

Terry let Mike go.

'Show respect for the law, Toad,' Allison said. 'Everyone needs laws.'

'I think that's Jazz,' Pam said, pointing at a blue car. The door opened, and a girl with a foot-tall black cockatoo perm and a wispy shroud stepped out, upside-down crucifixes and dagger brooches clacking.

Pam whistled. 'Over here.'

Allison looked at the girl and felt warm again. The clouds around Pam's sister were feathery but thick. Another recruit.

'Good trip?' Pam asked.

'Pamela.' The new girl sighed wearily. 'You are a fucking moron.'

Pam laughed.

'Three hours to get to Alder,' Jazz said, accent posh and cruel, 'and two more in a fucking car getting from one end of the village to another.'

Violet flashes danced in front of Jazz's eyes. Under her shroud, she wore a tight leotard. Her face was made-up white like Pam's, with black lipstick and eyeshadow.

'This is Mike Toad,' Pam said, introducing the boy, who was trying to look cool.

'Toad, eh?' She looked him over, unimpressed. 'Why doesn't he hop off and croak?'

The Toad grinned, nervously.

'This is Terry and Allison. They're local.'

Jazz took a cursory look at Terry, then looked right into Allison's eyes. Erskine had seen something, but Jazz got the whole message at once.

'Allison?' she said.

'My sister, Jazzbeaux,' Pam explained.

'Call me Jazz.'

They shook hands. Jazz wore half-gloves and had black-painted fingernails like sharp little shovels.

'Welcome to the West,' Allison said.

'Charmed.'

It was as if Pam wasn't there: they'd ditch her soon, anyway. Her purpose had been to bring her sister into the army. Jazz was like Erskine, like Badmouth Ben. A kindred soul.

Nine

Susan had minions folding the four-page programme leaflets, and gophers came regularly to handle distribution. The system was working. One year, they'd farmed the job out and had the programmes professionally printed a month before the festival. Last-minute schedule changes meant the whole thing had been worthless, and the only way information could be disseminated was by chalking it up on boards all over the site.

'Lots of helicopters passing over,' Karen said.

Susan had noticed that too. She assumed David was having her panic checked out.

'Probably government spies,' the Sister remarked.

Karen Gillard was a left-behind. She'd come to the festival last year, and broken up with her boyfriend when he got off with another girl. Her lift home lost, she'd hung around the Agapemone afterwards. If she had any other life, she never mentioned it. The kind of blonde they had used to call 'bubbly', Karen tried to fit in, but wasn't quite Sister of the Agapemone material. She'd been disciplined for odd trespasses – keeping a radio, holding back money and going to the pub, persistent lateness – and Susan thought she'd probably get it together to leave if she found someone at this year's festival to latch on to. Jago hadn't taken to her the way he did to some of the other Sisters.

The photocopier shook as it retched out programmes. Karen gathered an armful from the tray and passed them to the folding crew. Susan sensed flare-ups at the periphery, and knew things were happening. There was a hotspot out on the moors, perhaps in one of the farms, and the Manor House itself was as vibrant as always, but, despite the thronging crowds, she felt no major agitation. She thought things would speed up after dark. Beloved was gathering his energies, and all things conscious or unconscious around here followed his lead. Another lot of programmes went out, a runner prepared to scatter them to the winds.

'Susan,' Karen said, 'out of paper.'

The photocopier was protesting.

'I'll see to it.'

Changing the paper was a job that defeated Karen, but Susan was supposed to be able to handle it. She scalpelled open a wrapped ream of copier paper and slipped it free. Then she shoved it into the feed tray and jostled, hoping it would settle. She printed an experimental programme. The machine tore the sheet of paper and spat it out in scrambled pieces. Susan swore and slammed the tray again, hoping to settle the paper. This time, it wouldn't even take one sheet. Susan kicked the machine.

'That won't help,' a folder said.

'It helps me,' Susan replied.

Besides Jago, she was the greatest Talent IPSIT had ever assessed. She was the most powerful psychokinetic in captivity. But she couldn't get a photocopier to work.

'Let it cool off,' she said.

Kate Caudle came into the printshop. She wore ceremonial blue and radiated excitement. Susan found her easy to read, like most of the more enthusiastic Sisters. It had a lot to do with sex. She carried Jago around in her heart like schoolgirls carry pictures of their boyfriends.

'Tonight there will be a Great Manifestation,' she announced. 'We have a new Sister.'

Susan did not need to ask who the lucky girl was. Hazel. Karen clapped her hands, and Susan tried to smile.

'Wonderful news,' Karen said.

Ten

H E HADN'T been able to leave the village. With almost three hundred pounds in his pocket, Teddy could go to London, find a hostel, try out for one of those comedy clubs, wait for everything to finish. If he stayed, he expected to get hurt. Terry had hurt him before, and things were changed for the worse. If his brother got to him now, he'd be hurt more than any of the other times. Last night, Terry had started changing, become a thing in the woods that howled. It hadn't even been a full moon.

He'd walked the length of the village, from the Agapemone down past the Valiant Soldier, past the garage. Walking against the tide of traffic and pedestrians streaming towards the festival, it had been slow going. But he still should have got further than the village sign. He'd left the Gate House, talked to Pam and Mike Toad, some time in the morning, and now it was nearly evening. What was it? Half a mile, less? It had been five or six hours. He wasn't sure of the time, and his crappy Christmas-present watch was always unreliable. It told him three o'clock, but he knew it must be past four or five.

He put one foot in front of the other, but didn't go anywhere. People jostled him as they passed. Cars crawled by. It had been hot earlier, and he'd developed a bad headache. Now it was cooling. The insects were out, nipping his face and hands.

He must have stopped and taken rests for hours at a time, but he thought he'd been walking solidly. He'd passed people he recognized, people who recognized him. Gary Chilcot called him over and tried to scrounge some cigarettes, but he didn't have any. Old Man Maskell's funny-in-the-head kid was dashing in and out of places, playing hide-and-seek with the Invisible Man. Jeremy wasn't so bad; last year, in the crèche, he'd liked Teddy's funnies and got on with the festival-goers' kids. It was only local brats who picked on him. Sharon was up on a gate, dress around her thighs, french-kissing a darkie. Jenny's dad was on the garage forecourt, helping Steve Scovelle with the pumps. The guy from the Pottery, Hazel's boyfriend, was wandering around in a daze.

Teddy's feet chafed inside his daps, toes blistering, ankles aching, insteps unsteady. His sweated-through shirt was damp on his back as the temperature dropped. The traffic flow carried him back, like a real wave, back past Mr Keough's cottage and the building site next door, back past the Pottery and the garage, back past the Cardigans', almost back to the pub. It was as if he were walking up a down escalator and had stopped for a rest, finding himself automatically carried downwards again. He'd have tried hitching a ride, but all the cars were going the wrong way, coming in to Alder, not leaving.

His ears were popping. The pain inside his head swelled, pushing at the backs of his eyeballs, throbbing inside his nose, jarring his teeth. The more he walked, the more it hurt. He stopped and rested, slumping cross-legged on the verge. He was out of breath and had a bad stitch. His mouth and throat were dry. He'd missed his dinner. Get up, he told himself, and walk. The greasy grass of the verge was populated. His legs were covered with crawling red ants. He scratched his thighs and brushed insects away.

He got up, knees popping, and felt as if someone had taken a hammer to his head, fetching him a blow under the eye, smashing a cheekbone, lifting him off his feet. This was what he imagined being shot in the head was like. He looked at the dusty wall, and didn't see his own brains and blood dripping from a yard-wide splash. He stumbled a few steps in the gutter. Someone beeped a car horn and yelled, 'Piss-head!'

He stopped stumbling and, very carefully, started walking again. He focused on the backside of the sign that marked the start of the village. Once he was beyond the sign, he was out of Alder, on the open road. It was only a few miles to Achelzoy, and he could catch a bus to somewhere with a railway station.

The front of the sign was fresh-painted, black lettering against a brilliant cream-white background. The backside was dirt-clogged, rusty around the plugs that held the letters on. The sign stayed where it was. Teddy walked towards it but didn't seem to get nearer. The sign should get larger, but it stayed the same size, shrank a little, even. He passed houses, driveways, people. The sign was fixed.

He put his hands into his pockets, feeling the crushed-up notes, and leaned forwards, as if walking into a gale-force wind. He passed the garage and the Pottery again. The sign lurched larger, nearer.

His whole face was throbbing as if it had been pounded against his skull with a meat tenderizer. He ignored the pain. He reached the building site. There were cats in the works, mewling and hissing threats at each other. Pain slipped down his throat, swelling his neck, sliding into his whole body. His leg muscles were stretched, sharp jabs of agony where they promised to snap.

Mr Keough's house was quiet, no lights on yet, shut up tight against invaders. Teddy wondered if the old man had mined his garden path. He hated the festival more than anyone. Teddy wondered whether Mr Keough mightn't have been right. His front door was graffiti-struck. Someone had carved a Jewish star into it, and squiggled in Arabic or Hebrew or one of those languages with sloppy alphabets.

The sign was near now, barely ten yards away. Beyond, it wasn't Alder any more. It was the Achelzoy road. He wondered how his mum and dad would get on. Five yards. He didn't think Terry would hurt their parents, no matter how much he changed. Dad could still take a belt to him. Closer. A yard? They probably wouldn't notice Teddy was gone.

He drew level with the sign, reached out, touched it. The metal was warm from a day of direct sunlight. A thrill coursed up Teddy's arm, through his entire body. The pain lessened. He gripped the sign, pulled himself past, and turned to look at the lettering. ALDER. He was out of the village. He looked back and saw the road running towards the tree outside the Valiant Soldier, splitting there. He saw the Agapemone.

Jenny. Jenny Steyning had barely spoken to him in five years. He should walk on, get to Achelzoy before it was too late for a bus. Jenny in her white dress, seeming to float, golden hair a halo, lips a whisper apart. He should walk. Jenny. Walk.

He stepped past the sign, back into Alder, and it was as if he had stepped off a cliff.

Eleven

FOR WENDY, the Agapemone was a safe haven of order. She knew what she had to do, when it had to be done, how long it was supposed to take. Services and meals were scheduled. Duties came around on a roster. The little unstructured time she had was filled with supplementary committee meetings, organized readings or simple prayer. She recognized that, for some of the Brethren, the Agapemone was a God-given excuse never to think for themselves. Marie–Laure, with her convent experience, probably hadn't made a decision since joining the community. And Derek, whose entire life involved since along with things, thrived on imposed routine.

It was simple to live by the rules, but today Wendy had failed. Having missed the breakfast ceremony, her whole day was out of whack. She had a nervous spurt of sinfulness at the neglect of her duties. At the festival, her special province was the crafts stream; jewellers, silk printers, wood-turners. This morning, she was supposed to have visited the field where the stalls were to be set up, checking that each was in its place according to the prearranged pattern. She hadn't gone.

With all the Brethren about their particular tasks, regimented by Mick or James, Wendy was alone, at a loose end. It was as if she had used an excuse to get out of a PE lesson. Unsupervised, she was free to do whatever she wanted. But she had never known, not as a schoolgirl and certainly not now, what she wanted. She wandered through the third-storey gallery, an empty and rarely used space that ran the length of the Manor House, and let herself out on the balcony.

She was facing away from the festival site, in the shade, looking further up the hill towards the woodland. The festival had spilled around the house, and she could see people exploring the woods. There were marked areas off-limits to the crowds, but the boundaries would become blurred over the next couple of days. A couple of bikers were pissing against a tree. The shade became colder. They saw her and roared drunkenly, shaking cocks at her with feeble pelvic thrusts. They had beards, proper faces. Laughing, they zipped up and went away. Badmouth Ben was out there somewhere, but Wendy felt safe in the Agapemone itself, as if Beloved radiated a protective shield.

Wendy explored her own feelings, mingling guilt with excitement at her bewildering freedom. Derek would be organizing the traffic patrols, shepherding cars and vans. Karen and Susan would be in the printshop, cranking out programmes. James would be bossing the stage crews, supervising roadies assembling the cliff-face of amplifiers. Away from the festival, Sister Jenny would be with the postulant, Hazel, seeing her through her anointment.

Only she had broken the pattern. Wendy wondered whether, without her, the crafts fair was a free-for-all, stallholders smashing each other's merchandise, getting into fist fights. More likely though things had gone smoothly, suggesting all her work really did not do much. Once people signed up for their stalls and plots, all they had to do was arrive with their goods and set up. They shouldn't need a traffic cop.

The Agapemone wasn't like Rivendell. Ben's whispered words could hurt but not wreck. Rivendell had been weak before Ben turned up. The Agapemone was strong. Rivendell had no Beloved. Suddenly, Wendy felt an overpowering kinship with Beloved. She felt closer to Him than she had since the Great Manifestation that had brought her into the Agapemone, since the days – before Kate, Marie–Laure, Janet, Jenny, Hazel – when she was the most favoured, the Sister–Love.

Her duties had been a distraction, absorbing too much attention, preventing her from concentrating on the true purpose of the Agapemone. Liberated, she felt herself back in the centre. Beloved was in His rooms, she knew. She was closer to Him than anyone else, perhaps twenty feet away. Wendy had been His first Sister–Love, the first of the Inner Circle. She'd been among the first in the Agapemone. She took off her band and shook her hair free. Ben might find her. Today she might die, but she would have been first.

When Badmouth Ben died, Rivendell broke up and the remaining members scattered. Wendy held on longer than most, not wanting to disappear immediately after the 'accident'. She and

Derek stayed for a few weeks, while her hair grew out. The police came round, more concerned with discovering exactly who Ben was, so they could notify his next of kin, than in finding out how he'd died. They thought he'd taken a turn badly and his petrol tank had exploded. Now he was dead, everyone realized how little they knew about Ben. No one even knew his surname or where he'd come from.

With Ben dead, Rivendell fell apart, but not before the repercussions and reprisals. Gareth Madoc and Christopher Pringle, Ben's lieutenants, unable to keep up the reign of terror, fell from power. Christopher left and never came back, but Gareth was local and had to stay around. Two weeks after Ben's death, a couple of boys kicked some of Gareth's ribs in and dumped him on his parents' doorstep. Wendy and Derek left after that, hitching for Liverpool.

While they were on the road, the summer finished, a spectacular thunderstorm putting an end to the drought. Stranded out in the open between lifts, Wendy and Derek were soaked. Wendy thought of it as a cleansing of her sins. She'd thought it would be the end of Ben, the end of her fears and guilts.

She looked up at the sky, china blue above the chimneys of the house, and wondered how long they'd have to wait this summer. Eventually, the weather must break. It must rain.

In her memory, the thunderstorm lasted for days, weeks. They travelled the length of the country, clothes plastered to their bodies, emptying and discarding vodka bottles, and ended up on the south coast, in Brighton, where a river was running down the road to the seafront. Washed along in that stream, they reached the beach and stopped running. The only people in sight, where a week earlier there'd been thousands of sunbathers, Wendy and Derek sat down beyond the tarpaulined playground, watching the rain making orange puddles, constantly speckling the sands. They finished their last bottle and rolled it into the waves. Derek gave up eventually and huddled under the West Pier, smoking soggy cigarettes. But Wendy stayed, lying face up like a sun worshipper, rain slapping her face, getting in her eyes, filling her mouth. She felt empty.

High in the sky, she saw a vapor trail. It was a small aeroplane, passing over the Agapemone. She sat down on the balcony, putting the building between her and the plane's sightline. She remembered the emptiness.

Her entire life had been a matter of trying to fill the emptiness. She'd been aware of it since school. She tried to fight. First, she went against parents, teachers, friends. She tried to fill the void with disobedience, thick lipstick, eyeshadow, short skirts, undone blouse buttons, loud music, notes to boys. Her body started getting heavier, her arms and legs chunkier. For a few months, she stood out because she had breasts and wore a bra, but then all the other girls did too. Empty again. She tried working, expending bursts of energy on essays, exams, revision, projects. Her parents and teachers approved, and her reports said she'd settled down. This phase carried her through O and A levels and got her into Essex University, reading geography.

After her first term, as she came to realize what a swot and a virgin she was, she felt empty again. She found Derek in the next room at her hall of residence, surrounded by a haze of dope, listening to his Strawberry Alarm Clock and Jefferson Airplane albums, reading Castaneda and William Burroughs. She tried filling her life with Derek. Then with protests, occupations, campaigns, marijuana, vodka. Her studies became at once difficult and irrelevant. Some of her friends had already dropped out. After a long, serious, mainly one-sided talk with Derek, they followed suit, handing back their documentation to their course tutors. She asked for a notice, explaining their reasons for withdrawing from the university, to be put up in the common room. While children were being bombed in Cambodia, she couldn't see the value of geography.

Outside, they were together but still empty. Between university and Rivendell, there were five or six years of emptiness, wandering, drinking, doping. They tried drugs, politics, mysticism; Derek always following her lead. Rivendell had been a good idea, but it was an Eden that advertised for a snake. Rivendell under Badmouth Ben was a nightmare that had shown just how easy Wendy's previous sufferings had been. The first time he hit her, she wasn't able to believe it. After the fourth or fifth, it became routine. After Ben raped her, she didn't let Derek near her in bed. Only after Beloved's healing touch would she let her boyfriend back into her body. The ghastly thing was that with Ben, she didn't feel empty. While he was alive, she had hatred, fear, the need for revenge, the need to right injustice. Oppression gives the revolutionary a purpose. Watching the bastard burn, she lost her purpose.

On the beach, immediate purpose fulfilled, rain in her face, vodka fug in her head, Wendy felt – as she'd never done when Ben was fucking or battering her – that she might as well die. If she kept her mouth open, she'd drown. The rainwater would fill her lungs. Literally, she would not be empty any more.

There was someone in the gallery, standing quietly in the doorway. Wendy twisted her head around to look.

Beloved.

Beloved found them on the beach. He loomed into her field of vision, rainwater streaming from a wide-brimmed black hat, dog collar white in the gloom, and lifted her, wiping her face with a scarf, kissing her. At once, Beloved was father, teacher, purpose. He was her Saviour. Derek joined them. They were unable to speak. The rain was roaring too loudly, surf thrashing the sand. Beloved radiated His own warmth. Empty, Wendy knew Beloved would fill her.

She realized why she'd been emptied, why Ben had been sent to destroy her old life. She had to begin anew with Beloved, start from nothing, grow from a baby again.

Apparently, Beloved had a Vision, and ventured out into the storm knowing He must find someone, someone who'd be the heart of the community that was already beginning to form. He wore a long coat and elastic-sided boots, shiny with rain. Immediately, Wendy recognized Him for an Angel.

Later, Wendy learned about Beloved. By then, He had broken with the Church. He was living in a tiny deconsecrated chapel, with Mick Barlowe and a few others. He had renamed the place the Adullam, after the Biblical cave in which the unfortunate, the outcast and the desperate took shelter at David's summons. The rain drumbeat the roof, streaming in and running down the walls. The pews had been taken out and most of the windows were broken and boarded over, but there were mismatched cots and chairs for furniture. It was even more primitive than Rivendell, but the feeling of community was unmistakable.

Mick, not yet the composed second-in-command, was totally devoted to Beloved. Beloved fed Wendy and Derek, gave them shelter. After a meal of hot soup and bread, He preached.

'I am come into my garden, my sister, my spouse; I have gathered my myrrh with my spice; I have eaten my honeycomb with my honey; I have drunk my wine with my milk.' He added footnotes, whose meaning would only become clear with time, 'Thus has the Son of Man manifested Himself among us with eyes like a flame of fire.' She was captivated. At last, she felt this was it, that her emptiness was cured, gone, forgotten. In His eyes, Wendy saw the Spirit of the Lord. She found her faith and vocation. Then, in that damp and old-smelling chapel, while lightning struck the sea outside and thunder rattled the walls to the foundations, there came the Great Manifestation. Taken to the altar, Wendy held Beloved fiercely as the Spirit moved within her. He prayed for her. 'Though your sins be as scarlet, they shall be white as snow.' He *knew*, she realized, and felt Love washing over her like rain, cleansing the blood. He forgave her with a kiss. Apparently, she spoke in tongues and had to be restrained. She only remembered a white heat of revelation. When the night was over, she was the first Sister of the Agapemone, the first Sister-Love.

The Agapemone existed before Beloved bought the Manor House. It was a community, not stone walls and a roof. And she was in at its birth. Derek followed her. And others. The unfortunate, the outcast, the desperate. The Adullam became crowded, a joyous place even when it was so cold you had to wear gloves to bed. Beloved found more Brethren. The owners of the site called them squatters and kept trying to shift them. The Adullam was condemned, a mini-market due to be built where it stood. Beloved claimed faith kept a roof over their heads even if it did tend to drop off in bits. Eventually they were scattered in flats and houses all around town, a skeleton complement left in the Adullam to keep occupancy.

Beloved planned an exodus. He announced that the Agapemone would find suitable premises. Everyone contributed whatever they had, whatever they could. Some apostates left rather than part with their worldly goods, but most gladly gave all. Bequests arrived from Beloved's former parishioners in Leeds, from mysterious but doubtless devout well-wishers, from a few elderly ladies in Hove to whom Beloved had been a comfort in their last days. The Agapemone became temporally as well as spiritually wealthy. He was more earthly in those days, taking part in the practical organization of the community. With Mick and Wendy, He set out to find and purchase a home, finally coming upon Alder and declaring the Manor House predestined to be the site. Wendy remembered Beloved wandering into these woods after first looking over the property, and coming across a clearing, barren and shingly, where He took a deep breath and went into a trance. She had to support her Saviour, and let Him gently down. Eventually, He awoke, and the business was decided.

'This shall be our Canaan,' He told them.

Since then, His trances were more frequent. Once installed in the Manor House, the Agapemone ran smoothly.

'This one man, myself, has Jesus Christ selected and appointed His witness to His counsel and purpose,' Beloved preached, 'to conclude the day of grace and to introduce the day of judgement, to close the dispensation of the Spirit and to enter into covenant with the flesh.'

The Great Manifestation became a regular occurrence. The ranks of the faithful swelled. For a while, for over ten years, the Agapemone had been a paradise for Wendy. Then, Badmouth Ben came back.

Wendy stood up, and stepped into the gallery. 'Beloved,' she said, spreading her arms.

He looked at her with compassion, understanding and sorrow.

'We share Love,' she said.

'Love,' He agreed.

He had not apparently aged in over fifteen years. She imagined a hat on his head, water pouring out of the halo-sized brim. She heard the steady beat of rain on sand, the whoosh of surf, the calling of seabirds.

'Beloved.'

She stepped towards Him. He did not move. My Lord, but Beloved was a handsome man. Water coursed down the walls, discolouring the plaster. Wendy looked up. Water was flowing across the ceiling, gathering at the beams and falling floorwards. She took another step, but got no nearer Beloved. The gallery was stretching. Beloved was yards further away. She walked, ran. The walls cracked as the gallery became a corridor. Lumps of plaster fell from boards. Doors flowered like fungus, and lolled open.

'Beloved!'

She ran hard, heavy pain in her heart. There was water in her eyes, and she couldn't see Him clearly. She rubbed her face, wiping away water to no purpose. Shapes came through the doors. Water ran cruelly against her ankles. Her shoes were filled, her feet heavy. It was difficult, pulling her feet out of the icy stream and putting them down again. She tripped and fell, shoulder first, into the running river. There was carpet under the water, squelchy and loose.

Beloved stood, miles away, still.

A filthy seagull, wings edged with oily muck, dove at her, beak thudding against her skull. It bounced away, wings back-pedalling against the wind and rain, and lurched upwards. The bird had stabbed her scalp, and there was blood in the water pouring from her hair.

'Beloved!'

There were people standing over her. Someone stepped between her and Beloved. A girl, thin, with a fringed jacket, long tangled dark hair and shining eyes. Allison Conway. Wendy took hold of the girl's legs, and pulled herself to her feet.

She turned, and saw three, maybe four young people. The nearest was the thick-faced lout James had fired from the car-park crew, Terry Gilpin. He shot a fist into her stomach, and put his weight behind it. She lost her wind and bent double.

Terry looked around to his friends for approval, grunting a laugh. One of them was wearing a soaked panama hat, and looking out of his depth. The other was a girl with a tall hairstyle, a skeleton draped with a black spiderweb shawl, chains around her neck and waist.

Allison put an arm around Wendy's shoulder and pulled her up. 'This the one, Ben?' Allison asked.

The familiar figure pushed its way through the rain, elbowing aside Terry and the others. Water pooled in Badmouth Ben's sunken eye sockets, running down deep grooves where his cheeks had been.

Ben nodded. 'Sheep,' he said, chilling her.

She twisted her neck, looking for Beloved. She could see the far door of the gallery, but there was only darkness.

'Sheep,' Ben repeated, spitting the word out with difficulty through his mess of a mouth. He put his bone-and-scrap hand on her throat, not squeezing but kneading, and ripped downwards, tearing at her blouse. Buttons scattered, and his ragged nails scored her skin. Terry sniggered at her jelly-mould breasts, but Allison shut him up with a slap and said; 'This is *serious*!'

Panama Hat bit his lip and reached out. He pinched Wendy, taking a handful of loose skin from her ribs and pressing it tight between his fingers. It was an experimental cruelty. He laughed in relief as he let go, finally believing he'd done it and nothing had happened to him.

'Happy now?' Allison asked.

Panama Hat nodded and shrugged at the same time, then he stepped away, deferring to Ben.

His patchy flesh shrivelled on to his skull, bone soot-blackened. Wendy saw through the ragged skin, saw how the jawbones locked together, how the shrunken muscles worked.

Ben took a huge knife from a sheath on his belt, balanced it in his hand in front of Wendy's face, and then shook his head, rejecting it. He tossed it away. The taller girl unbuckled some of the thongs at her waist and thigh, and pulled a nine-inch stilletto out of its sheath. She handed it to Ben like a nurse passing a scalpel to a neurosurgeon.

'Fuck,' Ben said, tongue running between his black teeth, wet knife sparkling in the rain.

'Fuck. Kill. Eat. Wear.'

Wendy shut her eyes and prayed.

Twelve

PAUL WAS on the main road again, without really knowing why. That was a lie. He knew why. Hazel. But he hadn't found the mohican kid on his last expedition and didn't want to set out seriously after Hazel, just in case he failed this time too. The Agapemone sat quiet and calm on its hill. Hazel must be there. In Jago's clutches? It was hard not to think of it like that. Clutches. Would she be more annoyed with him was if he barged in there like Eliot Ness and hauled her out? Or would she feel rescued? As it too often was with Hazel, he was in a no-win situation.

Ben's voice had stirred up in him the stomach-twisting panic he'd felt when the Martian war machine loomed out of the woods. It had been the same phenomenon, something totally unnatural, like the fish on the bush.

It was nearly evening. The sun was not down, but the skies to the west were shading orange. The flow of traffic slowed. The people who'd arrived today were settled and the road was passable again. The main road, with pavement on only one side most of the way through the village, was as thick with pedestrians as Oxford Street in December.

Paul ambled towards the Agapemone, trying to feel casual. When the sun set, would the Martians come out? The garden of the Valiant Soldier was thronged. The general feeling was of a lot of people standing around waiting for something to happen.

'Weather's about to change,' someone nearby said, 'storm coming.'

The doom-sayer was shouted down. If it rained now, farmers would sacrifice first-born children in gratitude. And the festival would be a wash-out, with probably the beginnings of a cholera epidemic thrown in.

A monk-hooded young man with Buddy Holly glasses and Doc Marten boots sat on the wall by the garden, picking at an acoustic guitar, baseball cap out for small change. He was singing a strange sort of revivalist hymn.

> 'Don't you mess round with the Moonies,
> Send your guru back to Tibet,
> Ignore those orange-clad loonies,
> My new religion is the best you can get.
> I'm renting holiday villas hereafter,
> Self-catered cabins in the clouds,
> Holiday villas hereafter,
> Book early and you miss the crowds.
> I'm selling front-row stalls in Heaven,
> At a price you can afford,
> Front-row stalls in Heaven,
> Plus a dinner date with the Lord . . .'

The kid scooped up enough to buy a half of bitter. Obviously, he wasn't a candidate for the Agapemone. Paul wondered whether the bulk of the crowd felt the same way. There must be plenty of people only here for the beer, the music, the laughs. But Jago sat up on the hill and got something out of it. Paul didn't doubt that. Front-row stalls in Heaven. Was that what the Brethren were trying to sell Hazel? Most cults ran on fund-raising scams, with tin-rattling foot soldiers required to turn over worldy goods to the master. If that was the deal, the Agapemone was in for a disappointment. As a part-time student, Hazel was even poorer than he was. Of course they might not just want money.

A tall, pretty young woman in a light-blue dress walked by. She wore a pectoral cross. There was no mistaking her. The Sister of the Agapemone looked like a cross between a nun and an air hostess.

'That's not a convent,' someone muttered, 'that's a harem.'

The girl turned. Paul thought she might be annoyed, but she laughed and flounced her dress.

'Miss?' he called. 'Sister?'

She turned. 'Yes?'

He had to ask a straight question. 'Have you seen my girlfriend, Hazel? Hazel Chapelet? She went to the Agapemone today.'

She looked at him, weight on one leg. People made comments, but she ignored them. Looking as she did, she must have had practice.

'Sister . . . ?'

'Janet.'

'Sister Janet. Have you seen Hazel? Brownish hair, eyes. Not tall. Overlapped front teeth.'

The Sister gave it thought, so much so that Paul thought she was stringing him along, imagining this an elaborate pick-up.

'No,' Janet said, 'I don't think I've ever met anyone like that. Holly, you say?'

'Hazel.'

'Hazel? Nice name. Natural. Aren't you the man who had the fire last night?'

'Yes.'

'Lucky escape. The whole county could have burned. No wonder your girlfriend has bolted.'

He was about to tell Janet she didn't understand, but the girl wandered off, whistles following her, walking towards the Agapemone.

He followed her for a few steps, but something grabbed his leg.

'Mister?'

It was a small boy, with grazed knees and a dusty face.

'Mister?'

The child looked up at him, just wanting someone to pay him attention.

'Have you lost your parents?'

The boy wasn't sure, and chewed his thumbnail.

'Well?'

'No.'

'That's all right, then.'

'I've run away,' he said, solemnly. 'My name is Jeremy.'

Paul had the impression he was on the edge of a precipice, toes nudging air, looking down, feeling the ground crumble.

'I'm Paul.'

'I've seen you. You're at the Pottery.'

'That's right. Do you know the girl who lives with me?'

Jeremy nodded.

'Have you seen her?'

Jeremy shook his head.

'It'll get dark soon,' the boy said, 'and the dwarf will come out.'

'The dwarf?'

'Dopey.'

'Why have you run away?'

'Daddy's penis got funny.'

Paul didn't need this extra shit. He didn't even like children much. They were beneath reason and he wasn't sure how to handle that. Kids made him uncomfortable, self-conscious.

'Daddy tried to hurt me with his penis.'

What?

'Jeremy,' Paul said, dropping to a crouch, looking the child in the eye, 'do you know what you're saying?'

Jeremy nodded.

'You're not making up stories?'

Jeremy shook his head. Paul could never tell if children were lying. There was a difference between what was true and what they believed.

'Have you told your mother, your mummy?'

'Daddy hurt her with his penis, and she grew ivy in her hair.'

There must be some weird explanation. Maybe a leftover flower child had dropped acid into Jeremy's Tizer. From what he understood about child abuse, kids who suffered were more likely to lie and claim that it hadn't happened than tell total strangers about it. Jeremy was probably one of those kids who made things up. The story sounded made-up.

'Daddy and the Evil Dwarf are ganging up on me.'

'Where do you live?'

'Maskell Farm.'

'Are you lost?'

'No.'

'Do you want to go home?'

'No,' Jeremy insisted. 'Daddy's there.'

Paul looked around, trying to find someone in authority he could pass the child on to. He had his own problems. Why had Jeremy picked him out? His tooth stabbed pains into his jaw. There were people around, but none of them looked like a social worker or a policeman.

'Daddy put his hand through Jethro and stuck his fingers out his bum.'

'You're making up stories, aren't you?'

Jeremy shook his head violently. 'No,' he said, eyes screwing up. 'I *told* you.'

Paul was losing patience. He always did with children. Their logic was so far beyond him, their demands so insistent.

'What do you want me to do?' he asked.

Jeremy didn't know, really. He wiped his eyes, and gave Paul up as a bad job. He walked away, slowly.

Thirteen

'JESUS FUCK,' said Mike Toad, swallowing to keep from vomiting. 'Jesus, Jesus fuck.'

Allison laid a hand on the boy's cheek, leaving bloody fingerprints. 'Calm,' she said. 'You're no use if you panic.'

'No use,' Badmouth Ben growled.

The Toad was shaking, but got himself under control. Only Allison had known how far Ben would take the sheep-worrying. She'd been prepared.

It wasn't any different from watching her father killing a ewe. Ben did most of the hard work. Allison was mainly there to keep the others from bolting. Terry was excited as Ben fucked the fat woman, knife to her throat to stop her crying, but Allison knew he could lose interest afterwards. He'd have to be watched closely. Pam's sister, Jazz, was a cool case. She popped tablets under her nose and paid attention like a good student, doing what she was told. Only the Toad showed up gutless.

The woman's eyes went empty while Ben was sticking it into her. After the first few blows, she had become compliant. Now she went along with Ben. It wasn't even hurting her any more. This wasn't about pain, this was about sacrifice. This wasn't about Wendy, it was about Ben's army. She turned herself over, presenting her arse to him, and she lifted her hair away from the back of her neck so he could put Jazz's stiletto point between her hackles.

'Fuck,' Ben said, 'fuck, fuck, fuck . . .'

With every thrust of his skinny, flame-etched hips, Ben grunted 'fuck', repeating it until the word lost any specific meaning. Wendy gritted her teeth and tried not to make a sound, but as Ben ground into her, blood slicking between their bodies, she let out an involuntary *baaa*, like a real ewe. It took Ben a long time to finish. This wasn't for pleasure, this was for power.

Allison had Terry and Jazz hold Wendy's arms, more to stop her collapsing than to prevent her from hurting Ben. Mike Toad she let off, and told to watch the door. The Agapemone wasn't quite empty, but they shouldn't be disturbed.

Finally, Ben pulled out of the ewe. He picked up the rag of her skirt and wiped himself, cleaning off her blood and slime. He had punctured her inside, and she was bleeding.

'Terry,' he said. 'You can have a go now if you want.'

Terry looked at Wendy's blank face and bruised body, and spat. He shook his head.

'Don't say you weren't given the chance.'

Ben pulled up his cycle trousers and buttoned his fly. He was relaxed, tongue curled behind his teeth. It was Allison's job to stay cool. Wendy didn't try to cover herself.

'Baa baa, shorn sheep, are you feeling cold?' Allison sang.

Ben gave Jazz her stiletto back, and the girl crouched by Wendy, leotard stretching. She stuck the tip of her knife into the woman's belly and scratched, just cutting the skin, prodding the flesh beneath. Wendy's stomach muscles went tight under their upholstery, and she half sat, jaws clenched with hurt. Jazz had got through to her, woken her up again.

'She should know what's happening,' the girl told Allison.

Pam's sister was really into sacrifice, but was perhaps too show-offy. It might all be a pose, a studied, forced thing, not a natural instinct. She licked blood from her blade and pushed Wendy's head back, cracking it against the floor. She dipped her forefingernail in the spreading smear of blood, and dabbed it in the hollow of her throat like a spot of perfume.

Mike Toad, determined, turned around and ran over. He launched a vicious kick into Wendy's side, dislodging a shout from her.

'There,' the Toad said, 'see . . . there. I can do it, see.'

He was hyped up, jumping with excitement. He kicked the woman again, in one thigh, and picked up his foot to stamp on her face. Allison pulled him away. 'Don't spoil her,' she said, pushing him back towards the door.

Ben had wandered off, towards the balcony. He came back and pressed his teeth to Allison's cheek, a lipless kiss.

'Kill,' he said.

Allison was proud she'd been chosen. This was the most difficult part of the ritual. Jazz offered her knife but Allison had her own methods. She rolled her jeansleg up to the knee and slipped the rubber band off her cheesewire. Her foot tingled as she unwound the weapon. It had been too large for cats. Perhaps she had always known its true purpose. Making fists around the corks, she thread cutting wire between her fore and long fingers, then snapped it tight. She had three feet of thin steel between her hands, edge as sharp and minutely serrated as a blade of pampas grass.

'Lift her head,' she told Terry.

He took hold of Wendy, and got his fingers tangled in her hair. She let out a quiet yelp.

'Careful,' she said, 'you're hurting her.'

Jazz brushed the clumsy man aside and took over, carefully bunching Wendy's hair and holding it to one side. The ewe coughed, and dribbled blood.

'Kill,' Ben said, 'quickly.'

Allison didn't need to be told again. She put her knee on Wendy's chest and slipped the wire under her neck. Jazz helped. She made a loop and noosed it loosely around the woman's throat. Jazz let go, and Wendy's head lolled, neck held off the floor by the wire. Allison gripped the corks like the handles of a chest-expander. She looked into Wendy's face, wondering if this was an important moment for them all.

'Goodbye, lambkin,' she said.

Then she pulled. The wire bit into Wendy's fat neck, and Allison felt her thrashing under her knee. Jazz and Terry had her arms again. Skin parted and wire sank in. Allison felt the noose slicking against corded muscles and held fast. Wendy's eyes opened wide and her mouth puckered tight, tongue forcing her lips apart. Allison kept the noose taut until her upper arms ached.

'Done,' Jazz said.

Allison relaxed and Wendy's head fell, slapping polished herringbone tiles. It was over for her. Allison picked the wire out of Wendy's neck, and avoided the gush of a severed vein. Terry got blood over his jeans. His face was changing shape, hairline creeping down towards the midpoint of his ridge of eyebrow, chin jutting, nose receding. Allison looked at Wendy's dead marble eyes. The woman was gone. Her part in the sacrifice was complete.

'Eat,' Ben said. 'All of you, eat.'

This was the most important part, also the trickiest. No one knew where to start. Finally, Jazz began. She pinched Wendy's ear, and put her stiletto to it. The blade sliced easily at first, but got stuck on gristle. She had to saw to get the morsel, the lobe and half the lower ear, free. Taking a deep breath, Jazz popped the lump into her mouth and began chewing. The raw meat obviously wasn't appetizing, but she kept at it. After too little chewing, she swallowed it down, besting a choke, and grinned, blood between her teeth.

'Delicious,' she said, not meaning it.

Watching, Terry had been psyching himself up. His bum fluff was heavy and dark, stiff beard creeping up his cheeks. His pointed ears were slipping back and up. His lower jaw was sliding forwards, lips dislocated by swollen teeth. He held Wendy's floppy arm like a joint of meat and salivated on it, making animal noises as he rocked his head. With an instantly stifled howl, he sank a mouthful of sharp teeth into the flesh of Wendy's arm. He worried at it like a dog and tore a hunk free, gulping it down. He left a messy patch, edges ragged. The bulging tissue must be fat, Allison thought, the stretched rubbery stuff, muscle. Terry dropped the arm and scurried away, using his hands and feet like a toddler, into a corner. He had a strip of meat in his mouth, and chewed steadily.

'Mike,' Allison said, 'over here.'

The Toad tiptoed across the gallery, clothes still wet from the soaking.

'You bought into the game,' she said. 'Now you have to play.'

He looked from face to face.

'Shit or get off the pot, funny man,' Jazz said.

He didn't want to touch the dead body but had no choice. Closing his eyes tight, Mike Toad picked up the ravaged arm and fastened his mouth over the wound Terry had made. He sucked noisily, and some blood trickled out. He let go and chewed. He had not bitten off much, just a strip of skin, really, but he'd bitten off something and got it into his stomach. Even if he spent the rest of the night puking, that counted for something. Excited at getting it over with, the Toad laughed and shook.

It was Allison's turn. Used to raw meat, she still borrowed Jazz's knife. She cut herself a steak from the thigh and kneaded with her fingers, squeezing out the juice.

'Stop playing with your food,' Mike said, smug confidence creeping back. 'There are people in India starving.'

Allison bit off a corner of her steak. The meat had to be thoroughly chewed before she could get it down. Wendy didn't taste like anything special. She gave half her portion to Ben, and he wolfed it hungrily.

'What now?' Jazz asked.

Ben took the stiletto from Allison and drew a line with it, from the red ring around Wendy's neck to her bulging navel.

'Wear,' he said. 'Fuck, kill, eat . . . *wear*.'

Meticulously, with deft movements, Ben began to loosen the skin from Wendy's upper body, lifting it free of red flesh. Allison was still chewing her meat. Now Wendy was dead, Ben looked thin, scarecrow-framed as if the fat woman had been keeping him going. He'd told Allison he could only stay if people believed in him. Ben laid Wendy's ribs bare, pulling back the skin of her chest like the flaps of a jacket. Allison put her hand on Ben's shoulder, feeling pride in his workmanship, pride in the beginnings of their army. Even with Wendy gone, she would believe in him.

Interlude Four

'TELL VICAR what you told me, JoAnne,' Mrs Critchley ordered her red-nosed daughter, gloved hand twitching in readiness for a good smack around the ear. JoAnne had been crying recently but had stopped now, even if she did have to keep snuffling her nose into a tiny hankie. She obviously didn't want to repeat whatever it was she'd told her mother.

Jack Boothe looked at his curate and mentally shrugged, knowing Tony would get the message. When the young man had arrived in the parish, Jack had joked at the Rotary with Johnny Collins that Tony was the image of Noot, the chinless church functionary in the television programme *All Gas and Gaiters*. Johnny had, a little unkindly, come back by suggesting that Boothe himself bore a resemblance to Noot's wine-bibbing superior. Since then, Tony had wiped away the joke by proving himself unfashionably tireless as a soldier of the Church. Johnny was constantly plotting, only half in jest, to poach the young man to replace his own curate, who was more interested in rugby football than parish work.

A sliver of late-afternoon gold leaked through the window, lining Tony up against the wall as if he were caught in the reflection of a column of fire. The rest of the room was getting a bit dim. Before Boothe needed to say anything, Tony quietly turned on the lights.

'There,' Boothe said, 'that's better.'

Boothe hoped this silly meeting would be over with quickly. He wanted to watch Malcolm Muggeridge on BBC2. He was giving an interview about the Youth Problem. Boothe thought that would be amusing, probably relevant to this current nuisance.

Tony stood by the cocktail cabinet, gently tapping a decanter with a fingernail. The lad had all the bright ideas.

'Sherry, Mrs Critchley?'

The woman looked at him, lips pursed. After a pause, she nodded. 'Thank you, vicar.'

Tony had a glass ready.

'Not from *him*,' Mrs Critchley said, biting down hard on the pronoun. 'I'd as soon take poison.'

Boothe noticed JoAnne surreptitiously shooting a look at Tony, then quickly casting her eyes down. Tony filled a glass anyway, and held it near Mrs Critchley, tempting.

This was absurd. Boothe couldn't believe that with man practically on the moon and the pill on prescription, mothers were still accusing clergymen of 'ruining' their daughters. The trick had been passing out of use when he'd been a curate, and that had been back when the people of Leeds were packing their men off to invade Normandy. He felt like telling Mrs Critchley to pull the other one.

The woman finally overcame her distaste and snatched the sherry out of Tony's hand.

'JoAnne,' Mrs Critchley said, whining. 'Tell vicar.'

The girl shook her head.

'Not with *him* in the room,' Mrs Critchley said, indicating Tony with her sharp eyes.

JoAnne still shook her head. Boothe was sure the girl was frightened and desperate because of her mother's threats, not because of anything else that might, or might not, have happened to her.

The obvious had been ruled out. Boothe had talked in confidence with the girl's doctor, a Rotarian. He confirmed that JoAnne, who'd been brought to see him a few days ago, was, although not precisely virgo intacta, certainly not due for a blessed event. And while her lack of strict virtue might be regrettable, it was not, in this day, really a concern for Jack Boothe. Besides, he doubted that Mrs Critchley, when she was Margie Cox in 1943 and our brave boys were about to go overseas, had been all that different.

'JoAnne,' Tony said, 'what is it? You know you can talk to me.'

Tony was a willowy youth of twenty-six, with hair down to his dog collar and sideburns the bishop disapproved of. He'd been bringing in a younger set to the church. Working in the youth club and on the rec committee, he had had a remarkable success in his attempts to win back the children of the parish from the

Rolling Stones or Manfred Mann or whoever might be this week's instrument of the Devil. Johnny said the curate had 'youth appeal', whatever that was. Tony had been pulling in children like JoAnne Critchley, involving them in the works of the parish in a way Boothe had quite given up on. The lad might have funny ideas, including a love of high-church ceremony that tended alarmingly towards popery, but he'd learn. Boothe consistently sang his curate's praises. When he came to retire, he hoped Tony would be available to take over the reins. The lad was such a bright spark, he'd surely be given a parish of his own within a few years.

'Tell . . . them . . . JoAnne,' Mrs Critchley said, drawing out each word. A regular churchgoer, she was just a little *too* devout, a touch more willing to wield the rod than to use the caress. A good woman, no doubt of that, but unconvincing. She wanted her daughter to atone for her own sins rather than make her separate peace with God.

JoAnne wasn't a pretty girl, but would, in time, have a few years of being oddly attractive. She had large blue eyes behind National Health specs, a tiny freckled nose and a gap between her front teeth. She wore a short dress which alternated yellow, pink and orange like a three-flavoured ice lolly. She had been in the youth club a year or so. Johnny and Boothe called the organization Tony's fan club, remarking on the number of dreamy girls the curate always had trailing around after him, sighing and swooning. They wrote his name in exercise books, embellished with coloured hearts. It was all rather sweet.

Tony knelt down by JoAnne and held her hand. The girl looked up, and a fragile smile erupted. Boothe saw the gap in her teeth. Mrs Critchley had one too.

'JoAnne,' Tony said, 'is there anything you want to say?'

JoAnne shook her head and smiled.

'Boyfriend trouble? How's Robbie?'

'Gone,' she said. Boothe was impressed by his curate's knack of talking to teenagers.

'Is that a problem?'

'No,' JoAnne said, really smiling. 'I chucked him. He were a berk.'

Tony laughed, and JoAnne attempted a giggle.

'And home?' he asked quietly, as if Mrs Critchley weren't there.

'All right, I suppose,' JoAnne said, shrugging.

Boothe looked at Mrs Critchley, and saw a woman who wasn't satisfied but had no choice.

'Mam,' JoAnne said, 'I take it back. Sorry. It were lies.'

Mrs Critchley was more annoyed at being made to look foolish than she'd been at the imagined trespass.

'It *was* lies,' she said. 'You've had enough school to know that. Was, not were.'

'Actually,' Boothe said, 'I think you'll find the correct form would be "they were lies" or "it was a lie", but I don't think it matters. Spoken dialect and written English have always differed, and I understand JoAnne is a good student.'

He had talked with her headmaster, another Rotarian, also. No one could say Boothe did not do his homework.

'Will we be seeing you at the club?'

Tony was using his sparkling eyes on the girl now. It was a real Charles Boyer look, and Boothe envied the young man its effect.

'I hope so,' JoAnne said, eyes sideways towards her mother.

If Tony had been so inclined, Boothe was sure he could have lent meat to JoAnne's stories. It was not the first time this phenomenon had come about, and it must be a source of embarrassment to the young man. Teenaged girls dream, and sometimes believe their dreams. Just now, too many of the girls – indeed, some of the women – of the parish dreamed a sight too much of Tony Jago and his sparkling eyes and silky southern voice. Next to him, most of the local youths looked like apes. The sooner Tony got married, the better it would be for himself and for the whole parish.

'Mrs Critchley?' Tony said. 'Margaret, isn't it?' He shone his face at JoAnne's mother. 'I'm sure JoAnne meant no harm, really.'

JoAnne nodded.

Mrs Critchley held out for a moment, but crumpled. Tony's magic had worked again. Her frown melted and reformed as a girlish smile. She looked a lot like her daughter when she smiled. She even still had the traces of freckles. Tony, JoAnne and Mrs Critchley stood up simultaneously. Mrs Critchley gulped the last of her sherry and mumbled goodbyes. Dragging her daughter, she left. JoAnne let herself be dragged, but looked at Tony with her big eyes until the door shut over her face.

'Another conquest, eh?' Boothe laughed.

The curate shook his head, a little sadly.

'Think of it as a compliment, Tony. You've obviously got star quality.'

V

One

'**N**OW WHAT?'
Allison looked up from the broken doll-woman.
Wendy was a sprawl on the floor, body a large beanbag, limbs
pulled-out empty sleeves. Her eyes open but expressionless, she
still poked out her tongue like a naughty child. Her exposed
ribs, slabs of fat and barely buried muscles made her look like
an abandoned anatomy specimen.

'Allison?'

It was Mike Toad, hat in hands, picking loose straws in the
brim.

'Now what?'

She untied the arms of her jacket, which she'd been wearing
around her waist, and pulled it on. Her face was sticky but she
didn't have too much red stuff on her. On the whole, it had
been cleanly done.

Jazz was relaxed, awaiting further orders. Badmouth Ben
stood by the balcony, back to them, shivering in his new
pink waistcoat. Terry was licking his fingers, getting a long
tongue into the webbing between them. Only the Toad was
really agitated, on the point of panic.

Communion established, they didn't immediately have to
prove anything. Mike opened his mouth to whine again, and
Allison gave the nod to Jazz, who hit him with an open palm.
The slap sounded loud in the gallery. Mike instantly shut up. In
this quiet, out-of-time pause, Allison heard only dimly sounds
from outside. The rest of the world moved in slow motion,
fighting through thick waters, talking in extended growls. She
felt serene, grown-up.

'Should we get rid of it?' Jazz asked, prodding the dead woman
with a pointed boot.

Allison didn't know. She looked to Ben for an answer, and
nothing came. Ben was between the open window-doors of the

balcony, light behind him, faint around the edges. Her boyfriend
was becoming see-through.

'Ben?'

He stood, face away from them, rippling like a disturbed water
surface. Wendy's skin jerkin hung loosely on him, nipples like
badges, blood smears a pattern on the back. Now it was over,
Ben was fading. Wendy had called Ben to Alder. She'd been his
beacon; now her light was out, his grasp was weakening.

Terry sat up on his haunches and draped one arm in his lap,
rubbing his crotch with a hairy hand, extending the fingers of
his other hand and prodding the dead face, making Wendy's
cheeks shake. He sniggered, and slapped the woman. Her face
shuddered, but her eyes were still fixed.

'Stop that,' Allison said.

Terry bared teeth at her. Mike Toad, red handprint on his
face, was smarting, fuming purple flashes in his aura. Jazz
shrugged, bored, and pulled out a pocket mirror. She fixed her
face, powdering over bloodstains, perfecting black lips. Wendy
wasn't bleeding any more, wasn't hurting any more. She was a
lump of nothing, an embarrassment.

'Cover her,' Allison said.

All three ignored her, each expecting one of the others to do
the job. This was not what was meant to happen. They were
supposed to have discipline, be united by what they had done.
Allison repeated the order, looking at the Toad. He was the
weakest. She fixed him with her eyes. Mike's purple evaporated,
and he sweated frightened yellow from his nostrils, mouth and
eyes. Looking around the room, he found a canvas dustcloth,
neatly folded, on a chair. It was about the size of a full-length
portrait. Mike shook it out and let it settle over the dead thing.

Allison wished Ben would tell them what to do next. He
was definitely a phantom now, dimly superimposed on the air,
wavering in an unfelt breeze.

Terry, using his arms like a chimp, scuttled over to Jazz and
touched her, slipping fingers up over one knee, smoothing
her leotard over a long thigh, trying to get a good grip on
her. All the rules had been repealed and he might as well
do what he wanted. One hand still clam-clamped to one of
Jazz's arse-cheeks, he tried to open his fly with the other. His
swollen fingers couldn't work a zip fastener, and he grunted
annoyance.

Jazz didn't fancy Terry. That was obvious. She whirled around, foot darting out in a ballet movement, and connected with his chin. He swallowed a yowl, and was shoved back against a wall. He tried to stand up. Jazz backhanded him across the head and pinned his neck with her forearm, launching short, powerful punches into his stomach and groin.

They were losing control. Allison didn't want to step in. If either Jazz or Terry thought they could take her on, she'd have to kill or cripple them. That would leave her with only Mike Toad, and they'd have to start all over again, from scratch.

'Ben,' she said, to herself as much as to him.

Jazz dropped Terry and kicked him. He was curled up, arms over his face. Jazz wasn't angry. She was professionally hurting the boy. Allison had to admire that. It could be the London girl was more worthy of Ben. That wasn't something she'd expected. She didn't know how she'd handle it.

Allison took a few steps towards Ben. She tried to take his hand, her fingers sinking into cold, misty matter. She found a bony core, and held fast to it. An electric charge, sparking deep inside her body, shot through her into Ben.

Jazz stood back and examined the tips of her boots.

Allison kissed Ben where his lips should have been, tongue pressed past his exposed teeth. She came, violently, and bit her tongue. Her knees failed, but she was kept upright. Ben's solid arm was around her waist. His hand in hers filled out, expanding her fist with muscly flesh. Allison was still coming, climax extended by several peaks, throbbing pain-pleasure exploding from her clit. She could hardly breathe.

Ben was sustaining himself from her. Her muscles twitched like galvanized froglegs. Her eyes fluttered shut, and she kept the darkness in. He held her, tighter. As his arms became substantial, his grip was more powerful. Pleasure like a knife slipped into her, and ripped upwards to her ribs. She was unable to scream, but an internal shriek built up inside her, ululating in gasps, echoing in the vault of her skull.

She opened her eyes, and saw Ben's face fill in.

The others were fascinated, together again, under control. Terry was on his knees like a devoted dog, looking up. Jazz bowed her head in awe. Mike Toad smiled weakly, begging for approval, fear and delight mingling.

Ben let her go. He had to stand on his own. Allison almost staggered, a deep flush on her neck and between her breasts. She was standing on pins and needles. Stumbling, she turned and got her back against the wall.

Ben smiled quickly at her, the flesh around his mouth swarming like Plasticine.

He was still filling out, still growing.

'Hello, bay-beuh,' he said, in a deep, chuckling voice.

'Fuck,' she gasped.

He looked different. His face was redder, wetter, raw, mobile. His wounds were fresher, more a part of him. He was taller too, broader-shouldered. Allison was sure Ben had been shorter than her, now he was just the right size. They fit together perfectly. She leaped at him like a kid, and he whirled her around in his arms, laughing. He put her down, and crossed the room to look down at the sheeted bundle. He was loose-limbed now, lithe and athletic, fast as a snake, powerful as a big cat.

They were all around now, trying to get close, too nervous to touch Ben, but obviously hoping he'd touch them. He did, pecking Jazz on the cheek, tousling Terry's hair, play-punching Mike Toad's chin.

'The world's getting old,' he said, boot resting on the dustsheet, mobile eyes momentarily downcast.

Jazz nodded. Her breath back, she felt strong. Her pleasure was a part of her, a suppleness in the limbs, a fire in her heart.

'We have to clean house.'

Allison understood. It was like knocking down an old slum to make way for a new office building. Before you built, you had to wreck. That was what Ben was here for. That was what they, his army, were. The wreckers.

'Go out,' he said, pointing to the window. 'Be fruitful and multiply.'

Two

OLD HOUSES settle and shake, supports brittle as an old person's bones, and gradually sink into their foundations, façades crumbling slowly, arterial corridors clogging with junk. Susan had been aware of the moods of houses all her life. Even the neat Guildford detached-with-garage where she was born and the temporary flats she'd passed through since had been aging perceptibly. The Agapemone was no different. It might seem like a further layer of Jago's person – his physical form the brain within the larger body – but it was only a house. Much of her affinity with the personalities of houses was projection, her mental translation of unresonant estate-agent's details into something human. Like most of her Talent, it had as much to do with herself as with the external world. Sometimes it was a mirror, throwing everything back.

She stepped into the empty TV lounge. Thick walls shielded her from the outside, but she was rattled by a nearby disturbance. There was nothing she could do but force herself to calm down. The programmes were being distributed by Sister Karen and her elves, so Susan's job for the day was over. Rather, her duties in the Agapemone were concluded; her other job, her snake's job, was a permanent thing, like breathing.

She exhaled slowly, trying to will pain out of her head. This wasn't the traditional haunted house. Beyond the windows – dusty because the cleaning rota wasn't as rigidly enforced as other formalities of the community, not through studied and despairing neglect – was bright sunshine and a large, undisciplined, commonplace garden. Some vegetation was withered, but not in an ominous, doom-laden way. Places are haunted, retaining snatches of their pasts, discharged emotions accruing in corners like dust devils. But this room was dead, beaten and drained. Jago tended to absorb natural residues into himself. Susan had the trick, too. She could moonlight as an exorcist.

In the window seat, back stiff against the padded rest, feet against the opposite sill, she twisted off a child-proof top. She popped a couple of aspirin into her mouth, chewing chalk to powder, salivating powder to paste, sucking paste down. She wondered if she should get something stronger. David occasionally prescribed sedatives to get her through the blinding crises her Talent threw at her when she was menstruating, when she was surrounded by psychic turmoil, when things were really shitty and the face in the mirror looked like Linda Blair. Slowly, the pills affected her, and, Talent dulled, she let her shields slide. The room really was empty. No ghosts. For Susan it wasn't a matter of not believing in ghosts. She knew ghosts were just memories, like Wendy's death-faced motorcycle boy, not survivors from an afterlife returned to pester the living. She did not know what came after death. The ghosts Susan sometimes saw were fading snapshots, carried around by people and places as keepsakes.

Above the mantel of the walk-in fireplace hung a portrait of Beloved, executed enthusiastically rather than skilfully by Brother Phillip, a housepainter with artistic ambitions. It wasn't very good. The eyes were painted to shine but didn't follow you around the room. Unlike truly great or even simply inspired pictures, it was just paint on canvas. Susan couldn't pick up anything from it, not a residue of the painter nor a trace of the sitter. In some cases, these could last for centuries. Susan found Van Gogh originals as impossible to look at as the naked sun, and had been surprised by the wellbeing and serenity that underlay the triptychs of Hieronymus Bosch, terrors of Hell balanced by the prospect of Heaven.

Susan saw the painting as a palimpsest, Jago's face superimposed on a portrait of Edwin Winthrop, now stowed away in the attic, that had hung there before. Edwin had believed in ghosts, table-tapping, theosophy, astral voyaging. Unlike David, he'd been intrigued by mysticism, and tainted his scientific approach with pompous nonsense. Born earlier, Jago might also have gravitated towards the lunatic fringe of psychic research rather than the Church. There were plenty of curious sects and secret cults in the Twenties. Jago could have made one around him, just as he'd fashioned the Agapemone.

Outside were as many people as on a tourist beach at the peak of the holidays. Emotion roiled off them in waves, breaking against the house. The crowd was mainly happy in a sunny late afternoon that had cooled enough to be tolerable. People looked forward to the festival, not too many drunk or stoned, everyone mingling and meeting. Life was fine. Susan gulped whole another aspirin, swallowing phlegm to keep it down. After a day of tightly shielding herself, she was drained. Whatever happened, she was nearly at the end of her rope. She'd have to open up or crack up, and take whatever Jago could unleash. Being near him so long had worn her reserves down. Susan Anonymous was coming apart like a jigsaw. Witch Susan would have to step up and protect herself.

All those years of drifting, of damping her Talent, of trying on and throwing away jobs and relationships as if shopping for a cardigan, of hoping it would all just go away. And two years here, with Jago. That had all been preparation. She knew she wasn't imagining, projecting. This was the crux of her life. She'd be judged by how she measured up to the immediate future. Precognition. That was one of the things she didn't have. David thought it was philosophically, physically and psychically impossible. She couldn't know the future. But she knew that just beyond her sight, enormities waited.

For a while, hiding had been easy. She had found out about aspirin, and how it could quiet her down. At Lancaster University, her doctor put her on the pill to regulate her still-troublesome periods, and that helped too. Her Talent didn't go away, but she learned how to suppress it, how to control it. Graduating in 1977 with a frankly mediocre 2.2, she moved to a succession of provincial towns – Poole, Eastbourne, Harpenden – and short-lived under-achieving jobs. Assistant librarian, typist for a medical publisher, receptionist at a local radio station. Filing, photocopying, making tea. She amused herself imagining ways to use the Talent to make a fortune. She could become a professional gambler and read her opponents' cards from their minds or pop the roulette ball into the right hole. Or she could become a star conjurer, or dowse for gold and oil, or investigate large-scale insurance fraud. Or work as an invisible assassin, pulling triggers without leaving fingerprints. When David found her, she was in local government, processing social-security payments in Loughborough.

IPSIT had just been founded, and David, with ten years of committees and lab-rat tests behind him, was searching for

Talents. He'd followed her career, even tracked her off and
on through her Susan Anonymous phase. He approached her
as she was getting fed up with pretending to be living a real
life. She'd drifted away from her latest boyfriend. Men told her
she was afraid of letting them get too close. Jobs were boring
her and, the headaches becoming crippling, she had a reputation
for malingering. David offered her a chance to be a star again,
but not to go public. Unable to conceal his astonishment at the
extent of her Talent, he called in sceptical colleagues – some
from America and France – to assess her. She juggled objects
and made plates spin, although her telekinesis had peaked in
late adolescence and she was capable of far less spectacular
trickery than she had been as a teenager. Now, her Talent
was intuitive rather than effective. She was a psychometrist,
she could *see* things. After years of anonymity, the burst of
activity was liberating, exciting. She had one or two almost
satisfactory love affairs. She kept herself apart from the other
Talents. She knew the names – Poulton, Kermode, Tunney –
but didn't want to get close. Bringing Talents together was
like putting magnets on the desk: either they clanged tight and
were hard to separate, or they found a soft, tough repulsion
field between them.

In the early 1980s, she was taken to a Sheffield police station
and given a pile of women's clothing to sort through. Skirts,
blouses, shoes. Some were new, some were old and worn. Some
were ripped, some had bloodstains. She was able to sort the pile
into three smaller piles. The new-bought garments that had no
resonances whatsoever. Clothes donated as control specimens
by policewomen. And the victims' leftovers. She didn't see the
murders like a movie flashback, but found the impressions – of
violence, pain and hatred – overwhelming, and was suddenly
able to give details, mostly trivial, about the dead women. David
and the fatherly inspector encouraged her to think beyond the
women and build an image of the man who killed them. He was
a shadow, distorted by his victims' pain, but there were things
she could tell them. He was not 'Jack', the man who'd sent a
tape to the police confessing in a Geordie accent. His name, she
intuited, was Peter, and he'd already been ruled out as a suspect.
The inspector, who obviously didn't think that was much help,
thanked her and she was taken away. Not long afterwards, by a
fluke, they caught the Yorkshire Ripper, Peter Sutcliffe.

Her bottle was empty. She had a finger in, scrabbling for a last pill she had already taken. She'd been eating them like Polo mints. Unbending out of the window seat and standing up, she felt woozy. How many had she taken? She had a huge tolerance, but, even so, there were dangers. Her head didn't ache. Then again, she could feel hardly anything. She couldn't think how much, if any, time had passed.

The light changed. It had been getting dim in the unlit room, shadows expanding as the sun passed to the other side of the house. Now it was as if someone had drawn the curtains and turned on the lights. Not electric light, but the wavering glow of gas or fire. It was warm, but a different warmth, not the heat of the outside seeping through, but heat from a fire keeping out a cold beyond. There was a fire, and Edwin Winthrop hung over it. The furnishings were polished wood and new upholstery rather than jumble-sale aquisitions. There were ghosts, memories of people Susan recognized. Edwin, leaning against the mantel, fire cupped in his brandy glass. And others. The young Catriona Kaye, shorter than she'd imagined, in a pink dress with fringes. Irena Dubrovna, the medium, spilling out of a black evening gown, lifting a heavy veil with a dramatic gesture. This was quite common, although Susan had never experienced it at the Agapemone. A random snippet of the room's past was being replayed. It would pass. Edwin and Catriona began to dance together. Someone played a piano that occupied the space where the television set would be. Susan was more comfortable with these ghosts than with the current occupants of their space. Long dead, or at least long gone, they couldn't affect her, any more than a film on video cassette could touch her or a painting talk back. She was a spectator. The scene began to fade, and the present flooded back. Edwin and Catriona whirled together, coming apart. Susan saw Catriona's face freeze, staring directly at her. Rather, at the place where she was. Knowing it impossible, she imagined Catriona Kaye, briefly and shockingly, could see her. Then the ghosts were gone.

Susan found herself on her knees, head whirling, and put out hands to push away the carpeted floor. Her head, weighted like an anchor, dragged her down. The empty aspirin bottle rolled away. She fought heavy eyelids. Someone stood over her. She recalled Catriona's eyes as she saw what couldn't be there. And she imagined Jago staring, caught, as he was sometimes during her sermons, by a vision of the beyond which he misunderstood as proof of his own divinity. Her eyes popped open even as she sank, and Beloved was there. He raised a foot, and she saw the sole of his shoe. She flinched mentally, her body lagging way behind her mind, expecting the tread on her face, but he simply touched his toe to her chest, a hunter posing with a shot lioness. A thrill leaped from him and electrified her. She jolted, then slumped, shocked asleep.

Three

'Hmmmn,' Hazel said, 'that was nice.'

Cindy, a trainee hairdresser before coming to Beloved, fussed with Hazel's hair and face, as if prettying a doll. They had all felt it. Jenny recalled the transport of her own Great Manifestation, and a deep warmth spread from her heart.

'Just a taste, my Sister, my Love,' she told Hazel.

'It's like hot ice cream, isn't it?' Cindy said.

Hazel snorted a laugh, and her hair shook. 'Not at all, it was . . .'

She had no words. That was all right. Beloved was beyond words.

'It was the Beloved Presence, Hazel. You'll get used to it.'

'I'm not sure about that.'

Ever since her own Great Manifestation, Jenny had known the cycle was drawing to a close. When Beloved found perfection, He would end all things. Looking at Hazel's face, with the slight Chinese turn to her eyes, Jenny wondered if she was perfection. Maybe it had to do with purity of intent, an ability to forget self, to become totally the empty vessel for Beloved's benison. Certainly, Jenny's own thoughts had been too much with herself. Beloved had forgiven, but she remembered the sharp edge of her own disappointment. That had been soothed away in the white-hot intensity of the Great Manifestation.

'There now,' Cindy cooed, arranging Hazel's shining hair around her shoulders. 'That's comely.'

In her dream, Susan was a teenager again, struggling with a difficult lover. It might have been David, as he'd been when she first saw him. It might have been Roger, sucking back spit as he tried to get himself into her. It might have been one of the boys from Lancaster, the slightly younger-than-her feebs she attracted. It might even have been James, unfamiliarly young

and uncontrolled. Her lover's face was shadowed. Bedclothes
tangled between them. He wasn't hurting her, but, despite a
great deal of effort, he wasn't doing anything right either.
She wished he'd slow down or stop. His lips were on her
neck and face constantly. She took his head in her hands and
eased it up so she could see his face. Instantly it faded to
transparency and coalesced with the darkness. But the eyes had
been unmistakable. Anthony William Jago.

They were ten feet from each other, doing different things.
Syreeta was sorting through a box of cassettes looking for
Dolar's demo tape, and Jessica was pretending to ignore him
while she watched him. Ferg was uncomfortable, but didn't
want to move for fear of exciting interest. He was sure Syreeta
was really looking at him, too.

Suddenly, as one, the pair of them looked up and gave an
identical gasp, as if taken by surprise. They looked into the air
at nothing, then at each other. Jessica was blushing and Syreeta
shaking her head. Something had passed between them, a secret
message. He knew it, and boiled inside. Then, together, they
began giggling.

'What's wrong?' he asked.
  'Girl fainted.'
Gary Chilcot was kneeling over a small body, fanning with a
paper plate. Lytton's neck prickled and he imagined the worst.
It was Pam, the doll-like redhead.
  'Should I loosen her clothing?' Gary said, tongue scraping the
grass.
Lytton got close. The girl was breathing, didn't smell of drink,
wasn't obviously wounded and didn't have a syringe stuck in her
arm. He touched her eyelid with a thumb, planning to check her
pupil for dilation. At his touch, her eyes flicked open.
  'She's fine,' Lytton said, not yet sure if she was.
Pam sat up, and put her fingers through her short hair. She
didn't seem to have had anything apart from a nice sleep and
pleasant dreams. The girl looked at him directly, and gave an
unmistakable smile.
  'Fuck,' she said with wonder, shaking her shoulders and
head.
  'She's all right.'

Lytton stood. Pam propped herself up on her elbows and stretched her entire body, cream-pale midriff drum-tight.

'I couldn't half do with a cigarette,' she said.

The family were together again, Maskell joined with Sue-Clare, Hannah and Jethro in the big bedroom, producing fruit. His flesh extended, joining with his wife and daughter, heavy with his seed. Sue-Clare whispered in his ear, occasionally nibbling the lobe, occasionally flicking the inside with her tongue. She was coaxing his seed free. Hannah, wrapped in her ball of moss, sang 'All Things Bright and Beautiful'. Maskell's hand was under his wife's breast, fingers snug against the grooves of her ribs.

'Ssssuki,' he hissed, loving her.

He pulled back to watch her face change. Bangs of tiny ivy shoots around her cheeks shook as she received his seed. Her eyes shut, she caught her breath, held it and, as the blush settled, slowly sighed air out of her lungs.

His vision blurry, Teddy groped his way, using the low walls as a guide. The burning in his head was worse than the worst hangover he'd ever had. Fighting, he stood up and got his eyes open. After a heroic effort, he managed to stand straight. He stared and his eyesight came back. He was not the only one staring. Sharon Coram and the black boy Teddy had seen her with earlier were on the grass verge, wound together like the strands of a rope. They were clothed, but their mouths were fastened as if Sharon were swallowing the boy's tongue, a fakir taking a snake into her stomach. They wriggled against one another, buttons coming free as if the couple were so hot to get down to it they couldn't even wait to take off their clothes. The crowd laughed and made comments, but the performers didn't mind. Stan Budge, who worked and drank with Teddy's father, opened his throat and began, in a boozy bass, to sing one of his annoying folk songs, 'The Village Pump'. Sharon wrenched the boy's head to one side, her hand gripping his dreads, and screamed. Not with pain.

Jeremy couldn't understand it. Beth Yatman, who'd been standing at the gate checking customers' badges, was laughing like a hyena, a deep, full and dangerous laugh that disturbed him.

He wasn't sure what to do. Beth was staggering, and the line of festival people were getting impatient.

'Another loony woman,' someone said.

Beth found this hilarious and almost choked. She fell against the gate and slid to the ground. Her long dress caught on a nail and, as she slid down, was pulled up. Jeremy watched as inch after inch of Beth's dress rucked up, showing more of her thin legs. Someone in the queue cheered. Beth covered her laughing face with both hands. Her dress tore and she plopped on to the dry earth, kicking like a baby. Her dress up around her waist, Jeremy saw she was wearing knickers covered with yellow flowers. Jeremy knew he shouldn't be looking, but couldn't pull his eyes away. He felt slightly sick inside, but also excited. Beth pulled her dress together over her knickers and legs.

'Something in the water,' someone said.

'Don't be frightened,' Jenny told her. 'There's no pain. You'll see. It's like a kiss.'

'The best kiss,' Cindy added.

Hazel was in the centre of a swirl of warmth. The bath was wonderful, soothing all her aches and pains, all her doubts and disappointments. Now, she was embarking on a voyage. An exciting cruise.

'Miss?'

It was the girl Paul had seen earlier, Janet. She was in a dream, standing by the steps of the Agapemone, gently shaking her head.

'Can I help?'

'No,' she said, smiling. 'It was the Love.'

Unexpectedly, without warning, she kissed him. He tensed as her lips brushed his, then felt suspended over an abyss. Janet's kiss became moist, skilled, warm. She withdrew, and laughed pleasantly.

'We share Love,' she explained. It was something he'd been hearing a lot lately, although not from Hazel.

He thought of Hazel, up the stairs and beyond the door. Janet stroked his face, clucking a little.

'There's Love all around, Paul.'

He didn't remember whether he'd told her his name. His tooth spurted pain into his mouth.

The Sister of the Agapemone mimed plucking a grape from a vine and popping it into her mouth.

'Wouldn't you like to drink champagne from the hollow of my throat?'

Again, Paul thought he'd just been out-weirded by a professional.

Allison went first, venturing on to the landing, then down the stairs, then into the hall. The others followed, Terry bringing up the rear, constantly turning to look behind them. They were an army unit. Her body prepared to lash out, she walked down the last flight of stairs and turned towards the front door. It was a long hallway, running the length of the Manor House. It wasn't yet dark enough to have the lights on, but gloom had descended.

She saw the figure standing in the doorway, half in and half out of one of the big rooms off the hall, half his face visible. She made fists and brought them up, ready. The man didn't move. Badmouth Ben was at her side, the others a little behind him. Her arm muscles went tight, and she calculated where to strike first. Throat, then balls, then eyes.

Ben held her upper arm and shook his head. They walked, slowly, down the hall. As they progressed, Allison saw more of the face. It was Jago. He was standing over a woman who lay in a faint at his feet. Ben eased past Allison and stood across the hall from Jago, looking him in the eyes. Jago was in his vicar outfit, reverse collar and black suit, eyes wide and hard. Allison looked from Ben to Jago, and saw similarities in stance and feature. Their eyes were alike, alive in deathmasks.

'What . . .?' Mike Toad began. Allison put two fingers over his mouth, shutting him up.

Jazz was momentarily unsteady on her feet, hips shaking, hands pushing against the fabric over her thighs. She had a belt of silver metal letters tight around her narrow waist, reading SEX DEATH SEX. Allison knew how the London girl felt.

Jago turned from Ben and looked directly at her. The memory of her climax flooded her, and her knees went again. Ben had the front door open and light was pouring in, hurting her eyes. She held herself up and stepped past Jago, feeling his gaze on her back. He was powerful, and his aura filled the whole house, shimmering in and out of sight, a quicksilver halo as delicate and complicated as a butterfly wing.

She got to Ben and he held her up again, supporting arm around her waist. Outside, the sun was setting, staining everything.

Four

T EDDY WAS NEAR the end of the village again. This time, he'd
given up hope and was trudging mechanically. He wouldn't
get past the sign. He'd lost count of how many times he'd
approached this point. The day had gone, the last of the sun
fading from the sky. Traffic had quieted. Evening dragged on.
He was near the garage and the Pottery. Soon, the pull would
come. At first just a gentle tugging, it would become irresistible,
drag him back up the road. After this, he might give up.

Alder was like the jam jar he'd seen on a wall at the Pottery
last night, a wasp trap. It was easy to crawl in, all but impossible
to get out again. Wasps buzzed around, waiting for death. He'd
been walking all day and was tired to the bone, legs limp lengths
of ache, head too heavy for his neck.

The main road was a street carnival. A clown in an oversized
dinner jacket, with a stiff collar the size of a bucket, was doing
magic tricks by the garage, entrancing a crowd that included
Steve Scovelle and Mr Steyning. A little girl – Jenny's litle sister
Lisa – clapped her hands and laughed. Jenny had looked exactly
like Lisa when she'd been that age. Jenny had something to do
with the pull. If Teddy could forget her he might break free.
He remembered her face as she'd been the other night, and tried
mentally to rub out her picture, feature by feature. But memory
kept coming back, like the tide filling marks in the sand.

He looked back up the road, towards the tree. By the Valiant
Soldier, there was a thick crowd.

''lo, Teddy,' said a woman's voice, startling him.

He turned and saw Allison and Kev's mother, standing on
her front doorstep. Mrs Conway had an apple-round face with
a permanent smile like Kev's. She didn't look anything like her
daughter. Allison hardly seemed from the same planet as her
mother, let alone the same family.

'You seen the children today?'

Teddy shook his head.

Mrs Conway tutted. 'Up to mischief, I 'spect. Kevin's a prop'r handful these days. I don't know what gets into 'en.'

Though Mrs Conway expected Kev to be a bit of a tearaway, she refused to believe anything she heard about her daughter. The village monster was still her baby. Although, having known Allison all his life, Teddy couldn't remember her ever being any better. The girl had been born strange, and taken a turn for the worse. He imagined Allison in her crib, glowing eyes in a fat frown, making tiny fists, teething in silence, waiting for the body she needed to grow around her.

Mrs Conway must have been busy all day, because she hadn't yet taken her milk in. Three bottles stood by her front door, and a fourth was on its side, cracked and leaking.

'Cats,' she said. 'I thought we'd seen the last of the blessed creatures, but they'm come back.'

Teddy helped her with the milk, picking up the three unbroken bottles while Mrs Conway cradled the other delicately. She led him down a short hall into the kitchen. She opened the fridge and he popped the milk in. She set the damaged bottle on a saucer, and left it.

'Thank you, Teddy,' she said. 'Can I get you anythin'? Tea?'

Teddy shook his head.

He couldn't remember being in the Conway kitchen before, although he'd been to the house to see Kev. There were framed pictures of the children on the wall, Kev ashamed in a jacket and tie that would get him ribbed mercilessly if the photo became public knowledge, Allison in a black dress looking grown-up and sophisticated, eyes half-closed like a cunning cat's.

'Must be goin',' he said.

Mrs Conway kept smiling. 'You should wait for the children. Maybe you'd all like to go out together, listen to the music.'

At the thought of a night out with Allison, a sliver of ice slipped between his shoulderblades.

'When I were a girl, I used to love they pop bands,' Mrs Conway kept on. 'Bee Gees, Monkees, Blue Mink. Dad said it were all noise, daft old bugger.'

'No,' Teddy said, 'I'd best be off. Be late for tea otherwise.'

'All right then,' she said, 'mind how you go.'

Teddy escaped from the house, half-afraid Allison might be hiding ready to pounce in one of the dark rooms off the hall.

When he got back outside he realized he'd been wrong to worry. Allison was about a hundred yards up the road, coming this way with a group of people. Terry was one of them.

Teddy didn't want another beating. They hadn't seen him yet. Allison and Terry had quite a gang now, enough to do him serious damage. Terry loped behind the others like an old dog. People stayed away from Allison's gang, feeling threat boil off them like sweat smell. It *was* Allison's gang. No matter how awful Ben looked, the girl gave the orders, kept them together.

Teddy considered ducking back into the Conway house and taking refuge. He didn't think Allison would do anything if her mother were around. But he also had a bad feeling Allison could stab him to death in the kitchen, and Mrs Conway would just tut and refuse to see what was going on in front of her, offering Terry and Ben the Mutant tea and sandwiches, while they watched Allison hack chunks out of him with a carving knife.

By Mr Keough's cottage was a half-built house the Starkeys were supposed to be working on. The builders hadn't been in for weeks, so Tina's dad must have run out of money. It was perfect. Before Allison and Terry saw him, Teddy stepped on to the building site and scraped along a side wall, pressing himself out of sight between Mr Keough's cottage and the house shell.

He heard his heart, and thought it must be sounding out like a drum, alerting Terry's wolf-sharp ears. Something furry and stiff writhed between his ankles, hissing. He jolted back against the wall, slamming shoulders against hard brick. Only a cat; it had given him a scare.

'Kitty kitty kitty,' he said, not looking down.

When they were kids, Terry had enjoyed terrorizing Mr Keough's tribe of cats, always dragging Teddy into it. Terry had especially liked letting off rook-scarers – the incredibly loud fireworks Dad used to see off field pests – in the road, and watching the animals whizz like little missiles. The main road was a battlefield for cats, and Mr Keough's platoon had been whittled down by enemy tyres. Also, Teddy guessed, Allison had scored a few kills, passing her work off by leaving corpses where traffic would squash them. It was a van, though, that had done for the boys' faithful pet, Doug Dog.

The cat was gone, but Teddy heard a whining that came from Mr Keough's cottage. Teddy didn't know what it was. It might have been an animal but it might have been human. It was high-pitched and feeble, desperate. He imagined something bigger than a cat, badly hurt. A large dog, crying and drooling. Or an old man, lying face down, making sounds in the back of his mouth, trying to be loud enough to be heard, but incapable of raising anything but a thin, reedy moan.

The light wasn't on in Mr Keough's kitchen. The whining wouldn't stop. It was definitely inside the house. In cities – Teddy heard from his mum – pensioners often died alone, and weren't found for days or weeks, not until the smell annoyed the neighbours enough. That wasn't supposed to happen in the country, in a village where everyone knew each other, where everyone looked out for each other. Mum had a whole speech about cities and how heartless they were. It was supposed to stop Teddy thinking about moving away. In cities, you could be robbed and murdered by perfect strangers. In cities, old people were thrown on a scrapheap to rot. In cities, the air was thick with poison fumes. In the country, you could be robbed and murdered by kids you'd been to school with. And old people still died alone.

'Mr Keough,' he said, as loud as he dared. 'Are youm all right?'

The whine caught itself and gurgled something, trying to make words. It was getting dark. Teddy edged around the cottage into Mr Keough's small, walled-in back garden. There were neglected bowls by the back door, with congealed turds of catfood stuck to them. The concreted-over area smelled like a zoo toilet. By the door was a cat's-piss-yellowing pile of the *Western Gazette*, as high as a bench, threatening to topple.

Teddy wished he had a gun like James's. He ought to be holding it up like a *Miami Vice* copper, inching towards a door he would kick in. It was open a split, darkness beyond. Someone had spray-painted symbols on the door and the back windows. Mostly Jewish squiggles, incomprehensible. But the crude skull and crossbones were recognizable. The whine was coming in feeble yelps now, increasingly far apart, like someone gasping for breath.

'Mr Keough? It's Teddy Gilpin. Youm okay in there?'

The whine was strangled, cut off. He felt his heart stop. The whine began again, frustrated and angry. He breathed again. If it was Mr Keough, at least he was still alive. Teddy guessed how it might have happened. The other night, in the pub, while

Mr Keough was waving his petition, he'd been red-faced and flustered, almost weeping with anger. He'd always had a short fuse, getting heated about the festival, or Terry's stupid antics, or foreign wars. If old people got too steamed, their hearts packed in. Mr Keough could have gone home fuming after his scrap with Terry, and his heart could have burst on him, leaving him paralysed, helpless.

He pushed the door. A sweet, nasty smell seeped out of the cottage at him and he coughed. He stepped on the doormat, and something snapped. Nerves on edge, he ducked towards the floor, mat shooting out from under his daps. There was a thud and the sound of breaking glass. He fell face forwards, hands out to push the floor away. His wrists were slammed, but he wasn't hurt.

What had happened? The door had snapped shut behind him, one of the window panels smashed outwards. Two small hatchets were embedded in the wood, attached to a three-pronged fork which was fixed to a spring in the ceiling. A third axe had come free and shot through the window.

Carefully, Teddy stood, trying not to touch anything. The tripwire or balance plate or whatever had been hooked to the doormat. The kitchen was a lot like Mrs Conway's, only smaller and messier. It had that fried-food smell Teddy knew from his own mum's chips-and-pies-and-fish-fingers repertoire. And there was another smell. He couldn't hear the whining now. The cottage was quiet as a monk's tomb.

A muscle in his thigh twitched. His heart spasmed, ready for a motion-sensitive anvil to fall on his head. He couldn't stay here. He took a step towards the hallway. Nothing happened. Another step. The hallway was dark, and Teddy didn't want to risk a light switch. But he also didn't want to chance his way in the dark. There could be any number of traps hidden in the shadows, waiting to tear him apart.

He made out a switch by the hallway door. In the dark, it was a bump on the wall. On the filthy gas cooker was a heavy frying pan, a film of dust over thick grease. After making sure it wasn't fixed to anything, Teddy picked up the pan. It wasn't a gun but it was reassuringly weighty, and he was sure a thump with its heavy edge would leave a nasty wound.

Standing back from the doorway, Teddy worked the hall lights with the pan. The lights came on and nothing happened.

Except Teddy could hear something trickling, like sand in an hourglass. He held still, waiting, frying pan in a two-handed grip. Then, in the hall, there was a small explosion. And another and, simultaneously, three or four more.

Teddy ducked back into the kitchen, pan up in front of his face.

The noise was the worst thing. It was as if his ears had been clapped by iron hands. It wasn't possible no one outside the house had heard. But they hadn't. Teddy waited three or four minutes, shaking the echo of the explosions out of his head. Nobody came. He recognized the chemical smell of the smoke that curled out of the hallway.

'Rook-scarers,' he breathed.

He gingerly stepped into the hall, and found the exploded cardboard packet by the stairs. He couldn't see how they'd been rigged, but one had triggered the others. There was a sooty flash on the wall and the carpet, but no flame.

The whine came again, a final, energies-gathered cry of pain. Hoping he'd come to the end of the tricks, Teddy went upstairs. The landing lights were on. At the top of the stairs, he found Mr Keough, face grey and soft, a splatter of bloody gruel beneath his head. He was stiff and unmoving, mouth open in a surprised zero. His shirt and trousers were open, showing a blue and tiny slug of a dick. The source of the smell Teddy had been sniffing, he had not been making the noise.

She was in the bedroom, fingers hooked into the blankets to keep her from drifting away. Speaking a language Teddy didn't even recognize, she was barely there. He made out a brown and pretty face and the general shape of a woman, but she was a tattered phantom, lower body and limbs melting into a twist of sheets. There was pleading in her voice. Teddy felt sorry for the creature, whatever she was.

'Do you want some water?' he asked, offering the only thing he could think of.

She knew he was there but didn't answer. Her eyes were solid dots in her indistinct face, burning spots of promise in a thinning mask. He supposed she was a ha'ant. She had haunted Mr Keough. Now he was gone there was nothing to keep her, but she didn't want to leave. Almost for the first time today, he wasn't scared. This thing could hardly do him harm. He was more worried about Allison or Terry. The ghost woman must have been beautiful when full. Her face moved like heavy curtains in a breeze, and he thought she looked a little like Jenny Steyning, with her quiet smile and long hair. As he had the thought, the ha'ant became a shade more substantial, lower body dividing into long legs. She wasn't even wearing a white sheet. Teddy was embarrassed by her nakedness. As she came together, she became obviously female. She was as he had sometimes, in his suppressed thoughts, imagined Jenny must look without clothes.

There was no light on the bedroom, but she had a glow. Her mouth tried to make his name. Teddy shook his head, and she wasn't so much like Jenny any more. She was a stranger, fast fading away. She pointed at him, and he saw her hand was a gun, a ghost-flesh weapon at the end of her wrist, forefinger a barrel with sight, other fingers curled around like a trigger guard. She had the drop on him. Her face was washed away, just a pair of eyes and a smooth curve of silk like a harem girl's mask.

'Believe in me,' she said, in English, in Jenny's voice, begging, 'believe . . .'

Mr Keough had died quickly, by violence. And this ha'ant who had lain in his bed was slowly coughing her half-life away, neglected. The thing was pathetic. The ha'ant's gun kicked, and squirted a cloudy lump. Teddy stepped aside and it splashed against the wall.

'Sorry,' he said.

He couldn't help because he couldn't understand. She must have meant something to Mr Keough, but to him she was ridiculous. She contorted herself, thrusting out breasts like one of the girls in Terry's magazines, a mawlike smile opening up in her no-face. Her head came off at her neck and floated like a slow-punctured balloon, tendrils dangling towards the rupture on her shoulders. Her eyes closed, and only debris was left. The ghost body came apart like tissue paper in a whirlpool, drifting away and melting. A drape that had been an arm swept against his face and curled around his head. Cold and wet, it became a damp nothing.

He had best get out of the cottage and tell someone – James? – about Mr Keough. The front door was rigged up with a battery, but it was easy enough to pick all the leads away and defuse whatever trick Mr Keough had set. His traps hadn't kept out the ha'ant who'd killed him. The whole cottage was faded and forgotten, an old person's place.

He had to find James. He'd know what to do. Teddy took a
last look at the door to make sure there were no fail-safe booby
traps, and wrenched it open. It was twilight-dark out on the road
now, the lamps of the garage and the lights beyond the curtains
of nearby houses standing out.

'You there,' a voice said. 'Sonny Jim.'

Two men, indistinct in the dark, stood a few feet away from
Mr Keough's front door. A torchbeam lashed out, and Teddy
was blinded and blinking.

'Edward Gilpin, unless I miss my guess,' the voice said,
'brother of the more famous Terrence.'

The other man, who was wearing a helmet, laughed.

'And following in the family tradition with a spot of breaking
and entering, I do believe.'

Teddy could make the men out now. One was a police
constable with a face like a shop mannequin, the other a burly
man who flapped a wallet of identification at him.

'My name's Draper,' he said, 'Detective Sergeant Draper. I
expect your brother's told you all about me.' He slapped his
hand with his wallet as if it were a lead-filled blackjack. 'There
are a lot of stories about me, you know.'

Terry had been in scrapes with the police a couple of times,
but Teddy couldn't remember his ever mentioning Sergeant
Draper.

'Taunton Deane's answer to Dirty Harry, they say.'

The constable laughed again. Teddy hadn't noticed the first
time, but it was a scary laugh. There wasn't any humour in it,
like the laughs Terry gave out before he thumped.

'Actually, I think Dirty Harry's a bit of a softie. He ought to
try it on with some real hard nuts, like your bleedin' brother.'

Draper put his wallet in his back pocket and scratched his
neck.

'Let's take a look inside this house, shall we,' he said, 'see if
there might perhaps be one or two things amiss, or a-missing?'

Teddy rolled his eyes upwards, and knew it was all over. No
way could he explain what they'd find upstairs.

Five

A GROUP EMERGED from the Agapemone, clustered as if shooting their way out of a prison yard. They straggled down the steps around him. Still too bewildered by Sister Janet's active tongue to keep up, Paul recognized Allison, wilder even than this morning, and Terry, hanging back like an in-reserve, off-duty berserker. There were others, a gulping lad pulling a straw hat down on his head, a girl with a tall hairstyle and a Morticia Addams facial. And Allison's original boyfriend, Ben. The whole crew unnerved Paul. He felt the memory of Terry's blunt blade at his neck. It was unusual to find such variety in a kid group, he knew. A biker, a goth, a poseur, a grebo and feral Allison. Even in the diversity of the festival, like cult stuck with like. That was the whole point of cults, to be alike, uniform.

Allison saw him, and stretched a smile over her sharp teeth. The goth raised a Fu Manchu eyebrow and fluttered laquered black nails under her chin. The thing these kids had in common was that they were dangerous. Bored and brutal. Everyday evil. The type Paul would have walked past in a hurry with his head down on the Brighton seafront after closing time. They had predator eyes, bloody mouths. Surrounded by the festival crowd, Paul guessed there was no immediate danger. And Allison, he imagined, had some sort of scary soft spot for him.

Beside him, Sister Janet smiled and extended her hands to the kids.

'We share Love,' she said, again.

Allison, blinking in the last daylight, laughed in the woman's face. Janet turned the other cheek, a Christian martyr beyond the reach of cruelty. A Moonie sex kitten, she was probably beyond the reach of anything.

Ben looked directly into his face, his glance a punch in the pit of Paul's stomach. The world did a simultaneous backtrack and zoom, ground falling like an airliner hitting a pocket of turbulence.

'Nice to see you,' Ben said, teeth shining.

He had not seen the boy up close before. At the Pottery, he'd been in heavy shadows. In thinking the biker suffered from a bad birthmark or scar-mottled skin, Paul had been wrong. At some point, Ben had been soaked in acid or burned to death. He wasn't a natural thing. Like the Martian war machine, he could not be, but was . . .

'To see you . . .'

His face was an open wound, slimily red with ridges of exposed bone like tribal scars. And he wore a ragged sleeveless jacket that stank. It was uncured pink hide, falling apart and dripping. Even if he wasn't an Angel from Hell, he could pass for an extra from *Biker Zombie Holocaust.*

'. . . nice.'

Paul looked away, and saw Janet still smiling. She couldn't see anything wrong with Ben. Looking directly at the biker, she appeared to be seeing a normal person. Not everyone saw what he saw, Paul suddenly realized. Everyone saw things differently. He looked back at Ben to be sure, and the dead boy was walking away, followers with him. The crowds parted to make way.

Paul was still shuddering, hands knotted fists, teeth painfully clamped. Somebody was scraping his exposed nerves. As she walked past, Allison reached out and touched his cheek, simpering.

'Can't go on meetin' like this,' she purred, 'people'll say wurr 'n love . . .'

She patted him, and touched a finger to her forehead in salute. Then she fell in step, hair and hips swinging, and walked off with the gang.

A toddler with a smiley-face balloon wandered past. The goth touched a sharp knuckle ring to it and it burst. The child began screeching, but the culprit was gone. That small meanness was almost reassuring, as if Ben's gang didn't have the imagination for anything worse. But Paul wasn't convinced. Wells's Martians. Zombie bike boys. Fish on bushes. There'd be worse.

At the top of the steps, the double doors slowly swung shut. Paul got the impression someone was behind them.

It wasn't night-time yet. Midges filled the sodium-orange sunset, a cloud of flying nuisances. Out on the moors, the last of the red was reflected by the damper ditches. As the sun went down, the moon tugged at the tides, pulling aside the curtain of reality, letting loose monsters.

Somewhere, a Hendrix-head guitar screech sounded out. With the nightfall, the crowd would get noisier, rowdier, wilder. He tasted the last of Janet's kiss in his mouth, and spittle-washed it away.

'Hazel,' he said to himself.

Somewhere inside the Manor House, Hazel was waiting. Even in his confusion, he knew that this time he must stick to his purpose. Now, his mission was important. He'd go in there, he'd find her, and he'd get her out. Before it was too late.

'Excuse me,' he said to Janet, and started up the stairs.

'Paul,' the Sister protested, 'you mustn't . . .'

The doors were unlocked, of course. Ben and Allison had just come out of the Agapemone.

'Paul . . .'

He took hold of a doorhandle and pulled. The door wasn't even heavy. The hall beyond was gloomily underlit in the afternoon. Janet was climbing the steps behind him. He stepped through into the hall and shut the door behind him, shutting the Sister out. Three steps into the Agapemone, the world beyond the door was a thousand years gone. Thick walls, Paul supposed, kept out noise. Outside there were crowds. Here he was alone. It was just a hallway. There was a telephone stand and a heavily burdened coatrack. The carpet was worn through in the middle. A notice board had scraps of paper map-pinned to it.

He was inside. Now what? He expected Sister Janet to follow, to continue protesting his invasion. But she stayed beyond the door. If this was a game of touch, he was home safe. Or else he had strayed into a region so dangerous no one dared follow.

'Hazel?' he said, feeling stupid. He had no idea how to go about searching a house.

One of the doors off the hall was ajar, a bundle on the floor preventing it from swinging shut. He turned on lights, and the bundle became a woman. Not Hazel. Paul squatted, and saw she was breathing. Her face was familiar, a wing of hair over one eye. She was slumped fainted or asleep in the doorway, right hand open, an empty medicine bottle by it. Alarmed, he slapped the woman's face. She mumbled. 'Wake up,' he said, slapping her again. He looked around, hoping for help. He thought he saw someone, a female shape in a long black dress. But she must be just a shadow. He had no idea how many pills the woman had taken. Was she an attempted suicide or a druggie on a bliss trip? She could just have a bad headache and terrible judgement. The woman coughed and dribbled, a hand up to her mouth.

'Hello?' Paul said.

She sat up, eyes opening, then made a face as pain hit her.

'Are you all right?'

'Ugh, no,' she said.

She thumped her head with the heel of her hand, as if it were a faulty radio. She looked at him, eyes clearing.

'Ah,' she said. 'Paul, right?' He was amazed she knew his name. 'I'm Susan. I was at your place last night. I helped Hazel.'

Hazel? Did this woman know where she was?

She thought a moment. 'Here, I think. Last I saw her . . . ouch.'

Eyes closed, she tried to stand up. Paul helped her.

'Thank you,' she said.

'Hazel? What about Hazel?'

'You're here for her. That's the best thing. Paul, get her out of here. Out of the Agapemone, out of Alder.'

Paul couldn't keep up with Susan. She was reacting to things he only thought. She pushed her hair back, stinging her hand on static.

'I hate it when that happens.'

Susan was standing by herself now. She was disconcerting – like a lot of women around here – but he wanted to trust her.

'Hazel will be in the vestry,' she said.

'That's right,' came a male voice. 'But she can't be disturbed. She is being prepared.'

Paul and Susan turned and saw men coming down the stairs. The speaker was fairly unimpressive in a cardigan, with greying long hair. Behind him was a calm-faced bruiser who looked like efficient trouble.

'I have to insist, I'm afraid,' the speaker said. He had a practised voice, like an actor or a politician.

There were other people in the hall, on the upstairs landing. Several women wore floor-length white robes and had cameolike, pretty faces. Somewhere among them, Paul thought he saw again the veiled woman in the black dress. She didn't fit in with the Sisters, who clung together like a timid chorus line.

'Sister Hazel doesn't want to see you.'

Sister? Paul made a fist behind his back.

'Our postulant is at a delicate stage just now.'

Postulant? Paul didn't like the sound of that.

'Who the hell are you?' he asked.

'I am Brother Mick.'

'How come you speak for Hazel?'

The man was unperturbed.

'In the Agapemone, we share Love. We speak for each other.'

'Wonderful, now let *me* see *my* girlfriend so she can tell me she doesn't want to talk to me.'

'Our Sister is not your possession.'

The bruiser was a few steps below Mick, waiting for the order to break him in two. Paul turned to Susan. She shrugged minimally. He was on his own. She was looking away, he realized, at the woman in the black dress.

'Now, if you'd care to leave. We have an important ceremony.'

Susan said Hazel was in the vestry. Where was that? A vestry was supposed to be a room off a church or chapel. In a religious community, a chapel would be an important place. There was only one set of double doors, at the other end of the hall, by the main staircase.

'Brother Gerald,' Mick said, nodding.

The bruiser stretched out a large hand towards Paul's shoulder. He ducked under it. There was no one between him and the double doors, and he was faster than Gerald. He hit the doors hard, and found they opened outwards. Shoulder still jarred from the slam, he grabbed handles and pulled. A rush of incense swept out, and he knew he had the right place. He saw pews and an eagle-shaped altar, stained-glass windows. Arms hauled him off his feet. He kept his grip on the doorhandles. The doors opened wider as his arms stretched. He kicked and was wrestled upwards. Change fell out of his pockets. A girl was praying by the altar, blonde hair pouring down the back of her white robe. Not Hazel. She turned, showing her child's face. Gerald had a good hold on him now and was shaking. The others were grouped around. A pregnant woman was picking at his fingers, trying to get him to give up his grip on the handles.

'This isn't permitted,' Mick was shouting. 'You must not interrupt the Great Manifestation.'

He was pulled loose, and Gerald let go, hurling him at a wall. He hit his shoulder again, and pain lit up his entire side. His tooth shrieked.

'Jesus,' he yelped.

'We must ask you to leave.'

Paul could barely stand. Susan was returning his compliment, helping him.

'Sister Susan, leave him alone,' Mick said. 'He's an interloper. Maybe a journalist.'

Gerald took over, rough hands replacing Susan's helping touch.

'You mustn't disturb the postulant,' Mick said.

Slowly, deliberately, Paul spoke, 'I want . . . to see . . . Hazel.'

Gerald tapped his neck, finding a pain point that sent a jolt through his entire skeleton. Paul saw Susan deciding to be cautious, letting the others surge around her.

Mick was still the spokesman. 'Next week,' he said, offering meaningless compromise, 'when the ritual is complete, maybe Sister Hazel will want to see you.'

Suddenly, this maniac was issuing policy statements from his girlfriend. Gerald still wasn't letting Paul breathe properly.

'I can't leave until I've seen her,' Paul said, without much hope.

Mick nodded again, and Gerald fisted hard and fast at Paul's chest. He gulped and convulsed, pain radiating. His tooth hurt the most. As it throbbed, so did someone in the crowd. His angle of vision was limited, but Paul saw it was the veiled woman. Posed like a Twenties photograph, she stood apart from the Sisters, ignored by them as if they couldn't see her. As the waves of pain broke and washed back, the woman wobbled like a reflection in a mercury mirror, and grew ghostly. When Paul was hurting the least, she was her most solid; when the agony pushed him to the point of screaming, she was a wavering phantom. Gerald took his arm away from Paul's neck and let him go. He pulled in a breath, and the bruiser hit him in the face, a knuckle jamming against his injured tooth. The woman in the black dress vanished altogether, and Paul screeched in fury, knowing the hurt would never end.

Six

THERE HAD BEEN a clown on the garage forecourt earlier, entertaining crowds. Now a thin-bearded singer was irritating them. Even Jeremy could tell he was no good. Kids who'd enjoyed the clown's magic tricks were restless, harassing the singer with nasty comments. Jeremy had sat down quietly on an old tyre and was thinking. This was a good place to be, he decided. For the moment. Now it was getting dark, the lights strung around the garage made him feel safe. There were people all around. Daddy couldn't get him here. Mr Steyning would usually have shut up shop hours ago, but was keeping open because of all the people. They weren't buying petrol any more, but he was selling lots of sweets and drinks from the shop by his office. Steve Scovelle, who helped him with the pumps, was looking after it. Mr Steyning had gone indoors, but his wife was still outside, looking after Lisa, her younger daughter. Jeremy knew enough to stay away from Lisa, who always picked on him.

'Hey, lost kid,' someone said.

It was a man with a funny haircut, an X shaved into short black hair. He wore a shouting-face T-shirt and was drinking from a can.

'Yes, you.'

Jeremy said hello. He wasn't supposed to talk to strangers, but Daddy wasn't supposed to try to hurt him either. All rules were broken. X sat down on the next tyre. He had a friend, a worried-looking man in an army jacket with the collar turned up, and he sat down too.

'Want some Coke?'

X-head offered him his can and Jeremy said thank you. He meant to take only a mouthful, but as soon as the fizz got to his tongue, he realized he hadn't eaten or drunk anything all day.

Only the drink wasn't Coke. It tasted like armpits and Jeremy
guessed it was beer.

'Hold your horses, kid,' X said. 'You'll choke.'

'Ask him if he's got a sister,' X's friend said.

Jeremy nodded at the worried young man.

'And what's her name,' the man asked, 'is she pretty?'

'Her name's Hannah, and she's . . .'

Pretty wasn't a word he'd have used for his sister, although
he had grandparents who did. To them, everything was pretty.
Jeremy was pretty.

'Horrid.'

'Older than you?'

Jeremy shook his head. 'She's only little.'

X laughed. 'Just your type, Ingraham.'

'Yahhh,' said Ingraham, punching X's bare shoulder. X had a
blue tattoo on his arm, a cartoon skunk on fire.

'Bastard,' X said, thumping Ingraham.

'Fucker,' Ingraham spat, grabbing X's wrist and twisting.

'Dick-heaaaad,' they both said together, grabbing each other's
hair, laughing, catching Jeremy in the middle. They let go, and sat
up again. He'd finished the beer. Once you got past the taste, it
wasn't so bad. It made him feel grown-up. He handed the can
back to X, who sucked a drop out of it and licked the sharp
hole.

'Empty,' he said, smashing the can against his skull, grinding
it flat.

'He's mental, kid,' Ingraham said. 'Just out of borstal. You
know what borstal is, kid?'

'For bad boys.'

X laughed. 'Yeah, bad, wicked.'

'He was born to be bad,' Ingraham explained.

'Bad to the bone.'

'What did you do?' Jeremy asked.

'Shoved a hippie's head down a bog,' X said, looking at the
singer.

'X hates hippies,' Ingraham said. 'He's a real skunk.'

'We came here to duff up hairheads,' X said, laughing.

'Only it looks like we're outnumbered,' Ingraham said. There
were a lot of people with long hair in the crowd. One couple, a
boy with a red mohican and a punky-looking girl, really stood out
among all the muslin and beads. They were with the singer.

''Kin hippies don't deserve to live,' X said.

The singer still banged his guitar. A big woman with a purple skirt and a headband swayed in time, shoving her voice in with the man's. She was trying to get the people who were still listening to clap along with the song.

''Kin hippie crap,' X said, throwing the can.

X's aim wasn't very good. The can bounced on the floor near the singer's sandals. The woman with the headband looked at them, frowning like a teacher when kids talked in class.

'What's your name, kid?' Ingraham asked.

'Jeremy.'

'Jermy, huh? Jermy Jerm. How about that, X? We've got a Jerm here.'

'Yo, Jerm,' X head said.

Jeremy didn't like being called Jerm, but thought he shouldn't let X and Ingraham know. He wasn't sure he liked them, but being with them was better than being back home.

Mrs Steyning was standing nearby, disapproving. Jeremy had seen her sharing a cigarette with some people in the crowd earlier.

'You all right, Jeremy?' she asked. 'These boys bothering you?'

Jeremy shook his head.

'We're baby-sitters, ma'am,' X said, politely.

Ingraham looked at Lisa and licked his lips. She wrinkled her forehead.

'Lisa,' Mrs Steyning said, 'time for bed.'

She tugged her daughter's hand and pulled her away. Lisa turned, poking out her tongue at Jeremy.

'Rude cow,' X said, after she was gone.

'Should teach her a lesson.'

'Show her something.'

'Give her a spanking.'

'Goin' for the little 'uns again, Ingraham?'

Ingraham made a fist and pumped his arm, laughing. 'Nahh,' he said, 'that blonde bimbette's more Jerm's speed.'

Jeremy would have blushed, but things were strange this evening.

'Want to give her one, Jerm?' X asked.

Jeremy smiled and said yes, just to go along with them.

'Randy little bastard,' X said, with admiration.

'Stick her,' Ingraham said.

'Poke her.'

'Pork her.'

'Bang her.'

'Bonk her.'

X and Ingraham fell around laughing, arms flailing. Jeremy ducked out of the way. They smelled beery, and weren't responsible for where they hit.

The singer was doing a song about flowers.

'I've had enough of this shit,' X said, getting up. He was wobbly, and shook his head.

The singer's girlfriend was going around with a leather hat, taking small change from the crowd. She wasn't getting much, but a few coins chinked in the hat. She shook it in front of X.

'Thank you kindly, ma'am,' he said, scooping out money, rattling it in his fist. 'Gold,' he said, eyes wild, 'goooold, gooold. Hah hah hah. I'm rich, rich, rich, d'you hear me, rich. Goooold, diamooonds, jooooowels. Hah hah hah. Gooooooooold.'

The woman's eyes went angry. X stopped acting and smiled, all innocence.

'Very generous,' he said. 'Every little helps. A penny saved is a penny earned. Look after the pennies . . .'

The woman held the hat out, waiting for the money back. The singer was strumming chords, looking the other way.

X opened his fist and looked at the coins.

'Ingraham, remember I said I wouldn't listen to hippie shit music if you paid me to?'

He put the money in his back pocket.

'I admit it,' he said, 'I was wrong.'

The woman's fist was tight on the hatbrim, knuckles white. 'Give . . . it . . . back . . .' she said, serious.

X laughed and snatched the hat. He perched it on his head.

'Look, Ingraham, I'm a 'kin hippie.'

He flopped his arms and legs, and made an upside-down clown mouth.

'Hey, oh wow, man, I'm so out of it,' he said, 'heavyyy . . . wowwww, maaan . . . lentils, peace, hair . . . don't step on the drugs, man . . .'

X ripped off and tossed the hat like a frisbee. It whizzed past the singer's head over the fence into the Steyning back garden, lost for ever.

'Woww, I blew my mind,' X said. 'Tangerine apostrophes have stolen my Ultra-brite.'

'Leave those skunks alone, Syreeta,' the punky girl said to the big woman, 'they're just pathetic.'

X clutched his heart, and shouted, 'Stabbed, stabbed, stabbed! Ingraham, old fruit, she said I was – gasp, gulp, the shame, the shame – *pathetic!*'

The girl looked frightened, and clung to her mohican boyfriend.

'Heyyy, punks roooool,' X said to the boy, making a fist and thumping the air. 'Annn-arrrr-kayyy-yehh for the Yewww Kayyy! Gobble my snot and gob in my old aspidistra, why don't you? I go pogo!'

The boy shrugged the girl off and walked away. The singer, still fingering his guitar, hadn't noticed anything. Jeremy wondered if there'd be a fight. Whenever there was a fight in the playground, there was a moment when everyone knew it was going to happen. Kids would be arguing or making jokes or pushing, and it would go quiet for a second or two. Then there'd be a fight, and it would end with crying and a bloody nose. It was usually him bleeding.

'Jerm,' Ingraham said, 'let this be a lesson to you. Don't grow up to be a 'kin hippie. It's that simple. Just say no.'

The woman, Syreeta, went to the singer and stood by him, expecting him to take on X and Ingraham. He didn't. The moment passed, and Jeremy knew there'd be no fight. The singer went away, friends with him.

'Enough for a can here,' X said, patting his pocket. 'I'm here for the beer, me.'

Jeremy had been told not to take sweets from strange men. But he was so hungry he wished these strange men would offer him some. It was so dark now that the other side of the road seemed far away, barely visible in the garage's light overspill.

'Look,' Ingraham said, pointing, 'the filth.'

Across the road, there were policemen outside Mr Keough's cottage. They had Teddy Gilpin with them.

'It's a raiiiid,' X shouted.

'P'lice brutality,' Ingraham shouted.

'Bloody Old Bill.'

'Pigs.'

'Copper cunts.'

'Gestapo jackboot bum bandits.'

X and Ingraham slapped hands, then made German salutes and started whistling the tune they played in war films when Hitler came on.

'Piggies, piggies *über Alles*,' they sang.

One of the policemen, a blond in a helmet, looked across the road, and X and Ingraham shut up. Jeremy wondered what Teddy had done. A constable, a black man, was holding his shoulder.

'Cor,' X said, screwing up his face, 'get a whiff of that! Something's 'kin died in there.'

A smell was seeping across the road, coming out of Mr Keough's place. A fat man came out of the cottage and was sick in the gutter.

'Yo,' X shouted, 'it's the Incredible Puking Pig!'

'Look at that Huey and Ralph,' Ingraham said, 'diced carrots and tomato omelette . . .'

The blond policeman strolled across the road.

'Ello, 'ello, 'ello,' he said, 'what's all this then?'

He took hold of X and Ingraham by the ears, and cracked their skulls together like coconuts. He grinned at Jeremy and saluted.

'Evenin' all,' he said, turning to walk back to the cottage.

Jeremy looked at Teddy Gilpin, and saw the boy was badly scared.

'Fuuuck,' X and Ingraham said, together.

The fat man got up and wiped his mouth. He made a fist in front of Teddy's face but put it in his pocket. The police took Teddy away.

Seven

THE ROBE slid over her skin like a caress, as delightfully perfect as new-washed clothes in soap-powder adverts. It was a floor-length white dress, loosely laced down the front, clinging in the bodice and flowing below, baggy sleeves gathered tight at the wrist, shoulders bare. Cindy helped her with the laces. The Sister pulled her still-wet hair out of the collar and arranged it on her shoulders. She was a bride, ready for the aisle or the honeymoon.

'There,' Cindy said, 'lovely.'

There was a commotion in the chapel. Cindy tutted and turned away before Hazel could work out her brief, dark expression.

'A postulant must be serene,' Cindy said. 'People never learn.'

It sounded like a fight. Someone was banging a door and shouting, screaming. The voice was familiar.

'Don't pay attention,' the Sister told her. 'Make yourself an empty vessel for Him.'

Other people were talking. There were more cries, and some hefty thumps. Sister Cindy winced.

'Tut,' she said, 'silly, silly . . .'

Gerald had Paul against the wall again, and was holding his throat. The big man didn't have to hit again, the fight had already been knocked out of him. Anything the Brother did now was a free extra pain, for the pleasure of it. Paul's tooth was a chip of agony.

'Now,' Mick said, 'if you'd be so kind as to leave.'

Gerald eased up. Paul sucked air over his tooth, biting down on the throb. He held his jaw. Spittle pooled in his hand. He looked at Susan, standing with the Sisters of the Agapemone. She didn't have the body-snatcher smile of the others. He couldn't understand the woman. What was she doing with this crowd? Behind Susan stood the veiled woman, in the shadows by the front door, the light through her from a freestanding lamp making her a sculpture spun of black silk cobweb. The pain in his tooth died slow. As the woman became more substantial, her veil lifted. Her face was in black and white. A creature of the past, she moved silently. Martians zombies, cultists. Now, ghosts. What next?

Gerald prodded him with hard fingers. The ghost didn't see Paul, didn't see anything. He shook the Brother off and tried to stand straight, brushing invisible dust off his shoulders and knees. He was sharply aware he looked ridiculous, the cuckolded husband in farce.

Susan kept quiet and did not interfere. She told herself that if Mick Barlowe tried seriously to hurt Paul she'd step in. But Paul had already been hurt. She was a snake as well as a spook. She had to keep her skin on, not give herself away. James would have done the same. Irena Dubrovna had shown up again. There were other shadows. Her head was still woozy from the pills and Jago's jellyfish shock. Susan felt bombarded.

The circle around Paul was swaying as the Brethren focused on the intruder. It was the beginning of a lynch mob, or a sacrifice. She couldn't distinguish individual minds in the mass. In the rituals of the Agapemone, everyone blended into one entity, all subsumed to Jago. Her headache came back, jabbing her between the eyes like an icepick. Mick came out of the circle and stood in front of Paul.

'Go,' he said, pointing to the door.

A break appeared in the circle, and the Brethren formed two lines, a gauntlet. Karen pulled Susan back and kept her in line. Paul walked slowly past. Susan felt his fury, his confusion.

From the chapel, Jenny watched Hazel's boyfriend slope out. It was part of the ritual, the Brethren purging the postulant of her old ties. Gerald Taine and Marie–Laure opened the doors and held them. Outside on the lawn, there were lights and people. Music drifted in.

Her side was touched, and Sister Cindy was there. And Hazel. Jenny hugged the postulant and kissed her cheek. Hazel hugged back, and saw Paul in the doorway. Jenny felt the postulant tense in her arms.

From the doors Paul saw Hazel, held back by two white-robed Sisters.

'Haze,' he said.

Mick hissed at him, 'So long.'

A stab from his tooth made him wince. He couldn't make out any expression on Hazel's face. She was dressed like the Sisters. She looked younger, more fragile. He stepped forward, and Gerald's arm was in his way.

The man on the doorstep was a stranger to her. But he reminded her of someone. Jenny and Cindy whispered in her ears, soothing, telling her not to be distracted. The Brethren turned, making her the centre of attention. She heard their massed inrush of breath.

'Alleiluya,' Brother Mick said.

'They adore you,' Jenny said.

It was nice to be adored. It gave Hazel a warm, belonging feeling.

Susan was worried Paul would try to fight his way to Hazel. The Brethren could have torn him apart. But he just looked, disbelieving. The girl had changed. The Sisters of the Agapemone might be all sizes and shapes and colours and tempers, but they were the same. That was the scary thing about them. Cindy, Janet, Marie–Laure, Wendy, Karen, Jenny, Kate . . . All masks for a single face. Now Hazel.

Paul stepped through the doors but stood on the step, looking back, appalled. Irena Dubrovna had combined with a curtain, and was a clinging shadow, ignored and irrelevant. Karen pinched Susan's arm and pointed to the top of the stairs. He stood there. Beloved.

'Alleiluya,' the Brethren of the Agapemone said, in unison.

Jago smiled down on his flock.

Hazel's heart nearly burst with Love. Beloved's presence made everything else distant, unimportant.

Beloved's blessing fell upon them. Warmth surged inside Jenny, spreading through her body. Hazel clung tight, trembling.

'Nothing to be afraid of,' she cooed. 'It's only Beloved.'

Marie–Laure let the door go. It swung to, half cutting off Hazel's boyfriend. She ran between the Brethren, towards the stairs, and threw herself face down, full length, on to the floor.

'Alleiluya,' Mick said, standing over her.

Mick looked up at Beloved. Marie–Laure shook, and pushed

herself against the floor. Two of the Brethren came forward and
helped her up, pulling her back into the line. The Sister was still
spasming in ecstatic vision. Jenny understood her, but knew she
must be strong. She was charged with Beloved's Sister–Love, and
had to be in control of herself.

'Beloved,' Kate cried out, 'bless me, Beloved, bless me . . .'

'Beloved,' another voice joined, 'Beloved . . .'

'We share Love,' Kate breathed, arms stretching around Cindy
and Jenny and Hazel. Jenny heard the beating heart of Kate's
child.

'The Great Manifestation,' Brother Mick announced, 'is here.'

Paul, on the step, watched doors close on him, leaving him out
in the cold. He lost sight of Susan, her sane face surrounded
by adoring, beatific smiles. Everyone was looking towards the
first-floor landing.

'Beloved,' they said.

All he could see of Jago was a pair of black-trousered legs. He
had shiny black shoes.

'Alleiluya.'

He looked again at Hazel, in a huddle with a pregnant woman,
another sister and the blonde girl from the chapel. He saw no
recognition in her face. Doors slammed shut in front of his
nose, and he stepped back, overbalancing on the steps. He
wound up sprawled on the grass. Above, the Agapemone was
as impregnable as a medieval castle.

Susan was caught inside. It would happen again. She'd have to
watch. The Brethren swarmed to the chapel, sweeping her with
them. As Beloved, came downstairs, her head exploded inwards,
shards of pain spiralling into the mass of her brain, sparking a
shock in the core of her skull. Turning her head, she saw Jago
arrayed in light.

Sister Kate, Sister Cindy and Sister Jenny lead her to the altar and
left her there. Hazel stood as the Brethren found places in the pews.
Love radiated. Beloved came into the chapel and walked towards
her, hand out. Weak at the knees, she sank, feeling the thickness
of the carpet. Beloved, smiling down, stood over her.

'Alleiluya,' the Brethren chorused.

Hazel waited for Beloved's touch.

Eight

THE GENERATOR kicked over and the lights strung around Tent City finally came on to a huge and sincere cheer. The stars dimmed. Lytton checked his watch. It was well past ten. The generators should have been working hours ago, but the PA team had blown important fuses, giving an impromptu firework display. Lytton was worn ragged by the demands of the day, but couldn't go to sleep. Something might happen, something like last night's incident. The stream of people coming to him with problems had slowed but not stopped. He felt as if he'd been juggling live grenades.

The cider marquee flaps were thrown back and, after hours of unloading barrels and setting up trestles, Douggie Calver – whom Lytton saw lighting a foot-long cigar – was ready to make his customary fortune. Crowds flooded towards the tent.

Lytton had picked up camp followers. Gary Chilcot was hanging around, running errands. And Pam, the trimly put-together redhead, also seemed to have attached herself, groupie-style, to him. Separated from her crowd, the girl was loitering like one of the crèche kids. She was not just hanging around to flirt. Worried about something, she thought of him as protection. Her banter was brittle, not a perfect cover for her nerves.

'Can I get you a drink?' Gary asked.

Lytton thanked him, but said no. His head was scrambled enough. Gary darted off to barge through the queues with his staff badge and screw a freebie out of the tap-girls.

Lytton was oversensitive to trouble, but it was in the air. There'd been a mini-scrap earlier, a couple of crusties trying to push in the toilet queue tussling with a well-dressed muscleman. Battle lines were drawn, allegiances formed, strategies laid. As if there wasn't enough to worry about, a conventional riot could be thrown in his direction. Travellers, dispossessed even of their position on the festival circuit, were spoiling for a major fight,

and any number of factions and individuals – from bikers to local
yeomen – were willing to take up the challenge. The other stuff,
the scary stuff, was always simmering under the surface. Lytton
saw things out of the corner of his eye. Things that, when he
looked closely, weren't there. In the crowds, almost anything
could hide.

For most of the day, Mick Barlowe had been whizzing about
the site, making arrangements, delegating touchy jobs. But he'd
disappeared about an hour ago. Lytton thought that quietly
creepy by itself. On one level, he could understand Brother
Mick; the man's power trip was so transparent. He angled for
position within the Agapemone, raking in a few benefits – like
Marie-Laure Quilter – from his status on the next cloud down
from Jago. But, underneath that everyday grasping egoism
and self-centered bastardy, Mick was still a True Believer in
Beloved's Gospel, and that gave him a crazy, calm centre of
unpredictability and irrationality.

He looked up the hill, and saw light in the Agapemone. From
the stained-glass colours, he could tell the chapel was in use. Pam
said something, trying to make conversation. Lytton didn't catch
it. The girl sulked. As he found himself doing increasingly often,
Lytton looked around the field, listing who was in sight, checking
what they were doing. Beth Yatman, cackling like a witch in a
crowd of admirers, had come down with sunstroke, neat vodka
or pep pills. Sharon Coram was snogging a well-dressed Chinese
boy, egged on by a claque. Jack and Ursula Cardigan, the 'we're
not yuppies' couple who'd renovated the old Graham house,
were strolling around, eating health-food mix out of lukewarm
pitta bread.

There was no sign of Allison, so her gang must be off making
mischief where he could not see them. He was worried about
howling Terry and dead-faced Ben. It was after dark, and that was
their time to play up. It would be useful to have Susan around, to
see if she could divine anything.

Gary came back with a paper pint, already half empty. 'A very
good year,' he burped.

Pam smoothed her skirt and tugged up her halter. In the stretch
of unmarked skin between the two garments, she appeared to
have no navel.

Lytton looked at the Agapemone again. Susan must be inside,
with Mick and the others. He'd seen Derek wandering back

towards the house half an hour ago. Marie-Laure and Karen, who'd been around and active well into the evening, had gone in too.

He checked the field again. Sharon and the Grahams had disappeared. Beth Yatman had quieted down, getting ready to be sick. Pam's friends were in the cider queue, which was degenerating into a free-form standing-around experience.

A duffel-coated troubadour entertained the troops, singing along with his guitar, a song he had announced, sharply, as 'The Ballad of Anthony William Jago'. He must have a grudge, an indoctrinated girlfriend or an emptied bank account. In the early days of the Agapemone, there had been falls from grace, apostates leaving the community. Since then, Jago had tightened up. Almost no one walked away any more

> 'No more sin, no more crime,' the singer sang.
> 'Folks can have a real good time,
> Hell for most, Heaven for some,
> At the Dawn of the New Millennium . . .'

The kid, who had big boots and unfashionable glasses, was better than most, but seemed to be scraping nerves.

> 'I'm gonna live for ever and ever,
> Look at me, folks, ain't I clever?
> I'm gonna reign for millions of years,
> So hip-hip-hooray, and three big cheers . . .'

The doubt that had been pestering Lytton came into focus. 'They're not here,' he said, suddenly.

'Eh?' said Pam.

Lytton shook his head. 'Nothing.'

Everyone had Susan's handbills so the job was done, but the Brethren who'd been distributing them were gone. Wendy and Derek should be here. And Mick. And the others. But the Brethren had filtered out of the crowds and gone home. That gave Lytton a chill. The community's evening meal should have been done with hours ago, and he would have expected the Brethren to emerge and mingle, soliciting donations, spreading propaganda, smiling emptily. It was time he went to the Agapemone, to check in with Susan. He did not want to miss anything.

> 'Tell you the truth, folks,' the singer continued,

'Ain't no lie,
When it comes down to it,
I . . . ain't . . . never . . . gonna . . . die.'

The new-strung lights hissed and a bulb popped, dumping a whole area into dark.

'Excuse me,' Lytton said to Pam and Gary. 'I'll have to leave you two young people to it for a moment.'

He nodded towards the house, and began walking. Gary looked more enthusiastic left with Pam than she did being with him.

'James,' Kevin Conway shouted.

Lytton turned. Kev was waving to him, calling him over.

'What now?'

There was no queue by the gate, just kids milling around. Beth was on her feet again, propped up against a hedge. Kevin was waving frantically. On the other side of the gate, Lytton saw the bland blond face of Constable Erskine, helmet off, Nazi-like and impassive.

'James,' Kev said, 'we've got a problem . . .'

Nine

PAUL HEARD the doors being locked from the inside. Whatever was going on inside, he was shut out. He held Hazel's face in his mind, seeing her not recognize him, calmly standing among the Sisters of the Agapemone. He admitted it. He'd lost her. The realization was as sharp as his jabbing tooth. He stood up, wiping his hands on his jeans.

The Agapemone was closed to him, its thick walls holding in the secrets of Jago's Brethren. Holding in Hazel. Sister Hazel. Paul wondered how he was going to explain this development – and the explanation would be demanded from *him* – to Hazel's family. Her father would automatically blame Paul, and probably take out a contract on him. Patch, he wasn't so sure of. She understood her sister better than anyone. She might even not be surprised. He would tell Patch, then let her break it to her father. That was as good a cowardly way as any to get out of it. Maybe he should call Patch now.

Someone had set up an amplifier and was playing gospel music very loud, shaking a tambourine along with the tapes. People were dancing, throwing themselves in the air like voodoo-worshippers.

How was he going to put it to Patch? Hazel has found God. Hazel has found religion. Not found, caught, the way you catch herpes. Hazel has caught religion. Not one of your High Street religions either, C of E or the Roman Candles. Not even the Hare Krishnas or the Unitarians, the Church of the Latter-Day Saints or the Church of Jesus Christ – Scientist. No, Hazel had strolled past the franchise churches and even wandered beyond the usual cults, the Unification Church, the Scientologists, the Jesus freaks, the Church of Satan, the Church of Elvis . . .

The Agapemone. The Abode of Love. He made fists, and resisted an impulse to hammer on the doors. 'Hello, Love,' he would have shouted, 'Are you at home, Love? Answering the doorbell, Love? Registered letter for Love Divine. Step outside, Love.'

'Lord god,' he said, emptied of feeling, emptied of anger.

He couldn't stand here all night. Paul walked off, elbowing through crowds. Away from the Manor House, he was surrounded by cacophony. There was music in the air, jarring and ill-proportioned. And a hundred clashing voices. And bodies in motion. Someone with a boom-box was playing Loud Shit, loud and shitty. He even recognized the track, 'Heavier'n Osmium, Hotter'n Hell'. People were either fighting around the sound or slam-dancing. Someone collided with him, sorried, and backed off.

He walked into the village. The cider tent was doing bank-holiday business. Walking through the crowds, Paul felt like the Invisible Man. Annoyed with himself, he realized he was crying. He kept to the road, but the festival had overspilled its site and was leaking into the village. There were people all around, dancing, yelling, singing, wrestling.

Someone else rammed into him. 'Watch out, fuckface,' a young voice snarled. A paper carton crushed on the asphalt of the road, yellow-green cider spraying. Paul spread his hands in a shrug and said sorry.

'So you should be,' the young man said.

Looking up, Paul saw the face of the youth he had bumped. His red mohican stood up like the spinal crest of a prehistoric monster. Recognition came like a spark.

The Iron Insect's disciple grabbed, getting a strong grip on his shoulder. Ferg counter-grabbed, catching the man's wrist, trying to push him away.

'Ferg,' said Jessica, 'what's wrong?'

As if she didn't know.

She was putting on an act for his benefit, pretending not to know the disciple. Salim stood quietly by, ready to slip a blade into Ferg's back. Dolar and Syreeta goggled, overdoing innocent bewilderment.

'Last night,' the disciple said, 'the war machine, you saw it? The Martian war machine?'

Ferg trembled and jerked his head forwards. He'd have nutted the disciple, but the man would have steel in his skull. That would be a good way to catch Ferg, to get him to smash his head open.

'He didn't mean to make you drop the cider,' Jessica said.

Ferg hawked and spat in the disciple's face.

'Eeuurgh,' Dolar said, 'filthy beast.'

Jessica took a step back. She was out of it, letting her superior take over the fight. The disciple wiped himself with his hand, cold evil in his face. It was incredible he could pass for human. Underneath his plastic skin, you could see the steel skull. His eyes were frozen crystals, machine fluid pouring out of them.

'Mister, I'm sorry,' Jessica said, still pretending.

Ferg ran. He ran hard, feet lifting up, slamming down. He had to get away. If they caught him, the Iron Insect would get into his brain, sucking his memories.

As he ran, Paul's chest hurt. Gerald had given him a few bruises, and he wasn't used to running, anyway. A twenty-yard sprint to catch a bus left him with a throbbing head and pained ribs. His feet flapped, and he couldn't breathe properly. His cursed tooth twinged. He ran after Ferg, and people ran after him. The girl was following, and a couple of others.

'Gangway,' he shouted at people.

Mostly they'd already been pushed aside by Ferg, so he had an easier time of it. The kid was younger than him, not that much fitter, and badly spooked. And he was slowing down.

'Just . . . want . . . to . . . talk . . .' he gasped, each word a knife in his lungs.

They were in the village proper now. Ferg put a foot wrong and tumbled, skidding on his hands and face. He fell by the dead tree outside the pub and lay there, branch shadows across him. None of the locals or visitors in the crowded pub garden made a move to help the fallen boy. They barely noticed him, continued with their drinking.

'Ferg,' Paul shouted.

He reached the tree and knelt by the dazed boy, helping him sit up. Ferg had cuts on his hands and a scratch down one cheek, but wasn't badly hurt. The girl was there now. Unable to speak, she sank by the low wall of the pub garden and fought to get her puff back. There were others with her: an Indian or Pakistani boy, an old hippie, a woman with a headband.

'What's wrong with Ferg?' the woman asked.

Paul shook his head. 'I don't know.'

'What did you do to him?'

'Nothing.'

'Why chase him?'

He had no easy answer. Ferg, recovered from his knock, kept his mouth shut like an arrested Mafia don waiting for the mob lawyer. This close, Paul realized the boy was scared to the point of paralysis. Holding Ferg's arm, he could feel steel-cord tension in him.

'Ferg,' the girl said, 'Ferg?'

Ferg looked away, face to the tree. Paul realized something else. What Ferg was terrified of. Him.

Ferg looked up and saw the Iron Insect's limbs stretched against the sky. They were coated in gnarled wood, but unmistakable. They curled like fingers making a fist. He knew he was caught. The disciple had him. The others stood around, victorious. It was over. He might be the last human being in England.

'Ferg?' Jessica said, carrying on the cruel game. 'What's wrong?'

He waited to be changed.

'He's in shock,' Paul said.

The girl listened to him.

'Are you a doctor?'

'No, I'm a PhD candidate.'

'Then who gives a toss what you think?'

She was angry, protective. She'd hoped for someone authoritative to explain things to her. She sat by Ferg and hugged, hands curving around his face. He cringed as if she were a Martian, bloodsucking tentacles attaching to his flesh, poison-dripping mandibles tearing his skin.

'Ferg?'

She let go of him, hurt in her face. The boy squirmed against the ground, pulling in his arms and legs and covering his face.

'Last night,' Paul said, 'at the fire, we saw . . . something.'

'You're him,' the woman said, 'the man who went up the hill.'

'Yes.'

'He wouldn't talk about it,' she explained. 'What happened up there?'

'I couldn't tell you,' he lied. 'I don't really know myself.'

The Asian boy looked disgusted and said, 'You too, huh?'

'Very sharp,' Paul told him. 'Me too. If you weren't there, you wouldn't believe me. If you were, you'd be like us. Everything is changed. You can't go home again.'

Up by the Agapemone, people started cheering. Din cascaded down the hill, and the cry was taken up by the people in the pub garden. A smile spread on the old hippie's face, and he joined his voice with the others. The mass emotion scared Paul further. In the moonlight, he saw the outline of the Manor House, stained-glass windows multicoloured pinpoints. He remembered Hazel's eyes as she failed to recognize him, as she was tugged to the chapel.

The girl stood up and began to caterwaul, her joyous, mindless shout lost in the racket. The Asian boy and the hippie woman joined in. Paul saw that in the pub garden even the resentful locals, red-faced and middle-aged, were taking part. The sound was like a football crowd during the slow-motion replay of a last-second winning goal from the home team. The massed voices were a natural force. He was afraid his eardrums would burst. The people were not screaming or shouting or singing. They were not voicing recognizable words. They were opening their throats and making noise. He didn't know how many thousands of people were part of the one giant voice, but it was one sound now, impossible to shut out of his head, impossible to resist.

Paul's mouth was open, and the yell was spewing out. Then he saw Ferg, looking up at him, mouth shut, eyes cool, and the noise did not get past his tonsils.

The Iron Insect's followers chirruped in worship. Invisible but obvious, monsters strode among the crowds, exciting commotion wherever they stepped. Ferg saw them all give in, drop the pretence. Dolar was first, but the others followed almost immediately. Jessica joined in. Then Salim, Syreeta, everyone. The disciple began, but stopped. And Ferg realized he was wrong. The man from the fire wasn't a disciple. He was like him, one of the hold-outs. One of the last real people. The man looked at him. Ferg stood up. The noise of the Iron Insect's worshippers was hideous, louder than any rock concert he had ever been to, louder than a hurricane. The man's mouth opened and closed, but there was no way Ferg could have heard anything he said. He shrugged and held

out his hand. The man mouthed exaggeratedly, and tapped
his chest. Finally, Ferg worked it out. Paul. The man was
introducing himself. Paul took his hand, and held fast. Among
the ranks of the alien-infested, Ferg wasn't alone. He held on
to Paul's hand as if it were the only fixed point in a collapsing
universe.

Ten

S USAN WENT WITH the tide, filing towards the chapel with the rest of the Brethren. Inside, pain was a constant, shutting her senses down one by one.

'We share Love,' said Karen, taking up the phrase that rustled, a meaningless wind, through the congregation.

Brother Derek grinned, and nodded towards the postulant. 'Looks smashin', doesn't she?'

Even if she shut her eyes, Susan could sense Jago. He was nearing, swelling large, blotting out all else. Beloved *was* the pain, a man-sized wound in her mind. In the dark of her head, he stood out like a man on fire, as if her mind were a night sight sensitive to body heat. His heart burned like a candleflame. Tonight, Jago's Talent was active, reaching out beyond himself, dragging his followers into the world he'd made in his own image. It took all Susan's strength to hold still, not to be sucked into Beloved's vortex.

Angels and demons crowded in with the Brethren. Christs in the windows cried red from their wounds. According to David, Jago was a deluded Talent. Nothing more. With powers beyond the ordinary – like hers – and a misguided faith, he was capable of casting himself as his own holy trinity.

She paused on the threshold of the chapel, and looked back. The hallway stretched for a hundred yards, dotted with ghosts. The floor undulated like gentle waves. Taine bolted the front doors and used the big keys in the locks. She thought of Paul, shut out of the Temple, and guessed he was better off. In this struggle, Hazel's boyfriend was a civilian. She was the good soldier, bound by duty. The chemicals in her brain gave her a responsibility, whether she wanted it or not.

Pain burst behind her eyes, and she had to be steadied by Karen, who held her hand, squeezing. Tottering like an old woman, Susan took her place in the front pew, fighting the

explosions inside her. Agony blurted out of her mouth as she
coughed. Karen's hair stood out sideways.

'Sorry,' Susan said through pain, 'not . . . my fault . . .'

'We share Love,' Karen said, smoothing her hair.

The Lord God came into the chapel and strode in glory down
the aisle, Mick and Taine trotting respectfully behind him. Mick
was robed in white, a winged band around his forehead, a brass
instrument he could not play in his hands. Symbolically, he was
the Angel of the Last Trump. Taine's ponytail was undone,
hair hanging to his shoulderblades, and he wore matte black
sunglasses. In Jago's fancy-dress theology, the Brother was
Samson, strongest of the Faithful.

Susan looked for Hazel. Tied up inside like a knot, she knew
she would have to sit through another Great Manifestation. Hazel
was kneeling before the altar, waiting. A lamb, a kid. Oh, child,
Susan thought, child . . .

Jenny looked at Hazel's profile, and helped her fix her hands
together in prayer. Hazel's face, side on, cut in half Sister
Kate's, face to, making one moon-face, noses meeting. Hazel's
exposed eye looked at the altar, while Kate's looked at Jenny. The
combined face was cross-eyed. Hazel trembled, not sure what to
do.

'Bow,' Jenny said, kindly.

Jenny's nose touched her pressed-together fingertips. Kate held
the postulant's hand and stroked her back.

'It'll be all right, Sister-Love,' she said.

'All right,' Jenny echoed.

The temptation to turn to Beloved was enormous. Jenny could
feel His presence as He came down the aisle. She could hear the
Brethren's breath held in awe. She felt the Heat, saw the Light.

She flashed back to her own Great Manifestation, with Janet
holding her hand, the thrill of the Divine Touch, the Coming
of the Light, the acceptance into the community. Only then had
she understood the name. The Abode of Love. She remembered
Beloved's face, filling her field of vision. She remembered
becoming the vessel for His Love, the channel for the redemption
of all. For Jenny, it had been a rebirth.

The postulant was unsteady, uncertain. That was the lot of all
the unsaved, confusion and despair. Soon, Hazel would share in
such wonders. All confusion gone, all despair past.

She knew her part in the ritual, had learned the words by rote, rehearsed them when alone, poring over her school Bible. She remembered how Janet had said her piece when Jenny had been the postulant. Janet's voice had been lovely, firm, perfect. Everything about her elevation had been perfect. It was down to Jenny to give Hazel the gift that had been given to her.

She drew breath, almost bursting with excitement. Kate took the veil, a transparent silk square threaded through with silver, and placed it on Hazel's face.

'Look up,' she said.

Hazel did, and Kate set the veil in place, slipping a circlet around her brow to pin it. The veil sparkled.

To herself, Jenny thought, 'The Song of Songs, which is Solomon's . . .'

Kate turned Hazel around to face the flock, to face Beloved. Beloved shone.

'Let Him kiss me with the kisses of His mouth,' Jenny said, finding strength in her voice, 'for thy love is better than wine . . .'

'Because of the savour of thy good ointments,' Kate joined, 'thy name is as ointment poured forth, therefore do the virgins Love thee . . .'

'Draw me,' Jenny Steyning said, attention split between Hazel and Jago, 'we will run after thee. The King hath brought me into his chambers . . .'

Susan wasn't hurting so much now. Jago was focused on the ceremony, and there was less loose power floating around. She could almost get some peace in her head. Now, the tinnitus was outside. At first, Susan thought the noise was a gale-force wind, battering the old roof of the Agapemone. Then she realized it was a crowd chorusing with one voice. It was as if the whole village, population swelled by the festival, were howling doglike at the moon. In the chapel, the flock were engrossed, hypnotized. If they heard the wailing, they paid it no attention.

'I am black but comely, oh ye daughters of Jerusalem,' Kate Caudle continued, ridiculously, 'as the tents of Kedar, as the curtains of Solomon . . .'

As far as Susan understood, the Song of Solomon got into the Bible by mistake. With its mix of erotic, mystic, dramatic and twaddlesome, it was a natural cornerstone for Jago's self-serving religion.

'. . . tell me, oh thou whom my soul Loveth, where thou feedest, where thou makest thy flock to rest at noon . . .'

Susan looked at Jago, rejoicing in the glory of himself. Central to his church was that he got all the good parts: the Lord God, Ezekiel, King David, John the Baptist, the Messiah. He was Lion and Lamb, Father, Son and Holy Ghost. Handsome and dignified in Old Testament magnificence, he was now Solomon the Wise, the Young, the Virile. Beneath the embroidered robe, he was naked, barefoot to show humility. He stood arms out, the gold and silver threads of his sleeves catching light. If things had been otherwise, Susan thought, he could have lived a perfectly useful, harmless, fulfilling life as lead guitarist of Status Quo. Slowly, solemnly, a churchful of necks craning to keep eyes fixed on him, Beloved ascended to his spot behind the altar, robe rippling and throwing off light.

'If thou know not, oh thou fairest among women,' he said, words familiar, 'go thy way forth by the footsteps of the flock, and feed thy kids beside the shepherds' tents.'

The first time, with Janet as postulant, Susan had been tempted to giggle at the nonsense about shepherds and the Queen of Sheba. But even then she'd known more or less what to expect. It had been hard not to feel sick. And since then, she'd watched Jenny's elevation. Sometimes virgin blood spilled before the altar.

It was a dream, and Hazel let herself go with it. It was draughty in the chapel, her skin goose-pimpled under her thin dress. Her nipples were tight, pleasant knots. The flagstones were ice under her knees.

'I have compared thee, oh my love,' Kate said, 'to a company of horses in Pharaoh's chariots. Thy cheeks are comely with rows of jewels, thy neck with chains of gold . . .'

As Kate spoke, she took a necklace from a wooden box by the foot of the altar. Hazel instinctively dipped her head and the Sister slipped the necklace over her, resting the heavy jewels on her chest.

'A bundle of myrrh is my well-Beloved unto me,' Jenny said. 'He shall lie all night betwixt my breasts.'

She looked up, veil clinging to her face. Everything was beautiful. Candleflames sparkled. A white face in a window shone, moon behind it. Hazel didn't understand the words, but

Love welled inside her, surrounding her, taking in the Brethren, wafting towards the Beloved Presence.

'Behold, thou art fair, my Love,' Jenny said, standing, helping Hazel up too. 'Behold, thou art fair.'

Hazel's knees tingled after so long kneeling. Her robe, pressed into her skin, came free like a sticking plaster. Kate, made awkward by her child, stumbled, and Hazel had to put an arm around her to help her up. Together, the handmaidens stood before the altar. Jenny put her head close to Hazel's and lifted her chin, raising her eyes. She saw the Beloved.

'Thou hast doves' eyes.'

Looking at Him, Hazel saw it was true. His eyes were the gentle, golden, peaceful, wise eyes of doves. Behind, radiating through His robes, phantom dove-angel wings spread wide, the points reaching towards the roof.

'Behold, thou art fair, my Beloved . . .'

This was Love in the Flesh.

The handmaidens stepped back, respectfully. She was alone before the altar, before Beloved.

'I am the Rose of Sharon, and the lily of the valleys,' Jenny continued, 'as the lily among thorns, so is my love among the daughters. As the wood apple tree among the trees of the wood, so is my Beloved among the sons . . .'

This was Hazel's night now. Who stood before the altar was the vessel, the representative for them all, for all the Sister-Loves, for all the Brothers and Sisters of the Agapemone, for all the world.

'. . . stay me with flagons, comfort me with apples, for I am sick of Love. His left hand is under my head and His right hand doth embrace me.'

Having come out from behind the altar, Beloved took Hazel, slipping a hand under her hair, and another around her waist. The memory of His touch was enough to make Jenny falter.

'. . . I charge you, oh ye daughters of Jerusalem, that ye stir not up, nor awake my love, till He please . . .'

Beloved bent His head down and kissed the postulant, touching His lips to her veiled forehead. Everyone felt the pleasure.

'. . . the flowers appear on the earth, the time of the singing of birds is come, and the voice of the turtle is heard in our land . . .'

Jenny had thought when Beloved kissed her at her elevation that she would swoon and be unable to go on. But she had managed. She saw Hazel go limp in Beloved's embrace, and willed strength to the postulant.

'Oh my dove, that art in the clefts of the rock,' Beloved said, lifting the veil, 'in the secret places of the stairs, let me see thy countenance, let me hear thy voice, for sweet is thy voice, and thy countenance is comely . . .'

Hazel's eyes opened as the veil slid off her face.

'My Beloved is mine,' Hazel said, voice clear, 'and I am His.'

'He feedeth among the lilies,' Kate and Jenny said.

Beloved kissed Hazel.

Lips touched her mouth, then fastened. A jolt of pure energy shot through her, and she felt the pleasure would never end. Every muscle tightened, every nerve sang. She convulsed, but He held her close, tongue in her mouth, closed eye next to her cheek. Gently, Beloved withdrew from her and smiled. Her heart was overflowing. She became a true vessel, loose-limbed and pliant to His purpose. He eased her back, lifting her off her feet until she rested on the altar. It was surprisingly comfortable, and fit the contours of her body. She felt a touch at her wrists, and saw her handmaidens had come forward. Jenny and Kate held her tight, keeping her from sliding off the altar. Beloved touched her body, and the Light came down from Heaven, entering into her.

Eleven

IN THE BOMB SITE, a ring of flame burned cold and silent. Phantom fire filled the crater like ground mist, not giving off heat. Allison recognized the fire as an aura of the earth. She experimentally dipped her hand into it and felt nothing. Mike Toad gasped, and she laughed at him.

'See,' she said, wiggling her fingers. 'Magic.'

'Doesn't it hurt?' the Toad asked, bending to peer into waving flames.

She grabbed the back of his neck and rammed his face into the fire, holding his head under for a moment, then let him up again.

'What do you think?' she asked.

The boy was shaking but unharmed.

'There, there,' she said, maternally. 'You know I wouldn't let you get hurt, Toad Boy.'

Badmouth Ben strode past them, wading into the fire. It eddied around his legs as he made for the scraped-bare shingles at the clearing's centre. Ben was still changing. Wendy's skin combined with his leathers so that he seemed to be wearing a poofy pink jacket, stained red in a tie-dye pattern. There were zips, straps and pockets, all made from the sacrifice's hide.

The scream of the crowd down in Alder was like the pounding of waves, a solid thing that would always be there. From the crest of the crater, Allison could see energy currents swirling and throbbing above the village. There were obvious focuses, a main concentration being the Agapemone. Jago, the Lord God, was at the heart of it all. Allison had been thinking about the man in the Manor House, and realized he was important in the scheme. As important as Ben or herself. He had power.

Ben stood in the fire, gazing at the sky. Allison walked to him, entering the flames. Terry on all fours, scrabbling along, and Mike, frightened, fingering his unburned face, came to

the fireline. Jazz, still poised, stepped in, smiled as if paddling
in warm water, and walked through the flame, giggling in
wonderment. She looked back at the others, still hesitating
at the edge. Terry scurried into the burning circle, and the
Toad, giving up, followed him. Terry's back stood out of fire
as he snuffled ground. Ben stood dead centre, where the fire
had burned out and the ground was shining black, speckled
with embers. He looked out over the moors, down to the
village.

She wondered how far the noise carried. To Bridgwater and
Glastonbury at least, perhaps to the Bristol Channel. There were
firefly headlights on all the roads, bringing more to join the
festival. The cry was worship, but also welcome. Terry was on
his haunches, howling along. The Toad also cried out, swept
away by the communion of the scream. He took off his hat
and tossed it high into the sky. It spun like a flying saucer
and sailed off into the woods. The Toad was laughing, his
noise lost in the greater noise. He played an invisible guitar,
one hand stuck above his shoulder fingering chords, the other
worrying his groin. Terry rolled over in the fire and kicked
his arms and legs into the air, shaking his back against the
ground, scratching for fleas. Jazz was fascinated by the flame.
She lay down and let it wash over her, feeling its painless
flicker.

Allison dipped a hand into a flame. Her flesh tingled, but there
was no hurt. The fire was an echo, a ghost. She raised her hand,
and threads of flame ran like mercury in her palm. She drank the
fire, and swallowed. She felt nothing. Terry and the Toad were
part of the crowd, mouths open, adding their voices to the yell.
But Allison and Ben were quiet, enveloped by noise but not a
part of it. Jazz was spared, too. Allison realized the London girl
had a part to play, and was ready.

Jazz sat up, wiping scraps of flame off her face with ring-
knuckled fingers, and paid attention. Ben was facing the two
girls, fire in his eye sockets. He began to unzip and unbuckle his
jacket, unfastening straps on sleeves, belly and chest, loosening
Wendy's leftover skin from his own body as he had removed it
from hers. His jaw dropped and a voice came, cutting through
the scream. Not Ben's voice, but a voice speaking through him,
pouring out of his burned skull like milk from a jug. It was a
cool charm of a voice, and wrapped around Allison like a gentle

snake. She felt the voice in her breasts, in her belly, in her clit, in her eyes.

'Behold, thou art fair, my love. Thou hast doves' eyes within thy locks, thy hair is a flock of goats that appear from Mount Gilead . . .'

Allison saw Jazz was affected too. She crawled on all fours, arse moving from side to side, through the flames. She felt a pang of possessiveness for Ben, but knew she shouldn't question the higher purpose. There was enough for everyone.

The voice continued, meaningless but seductive. 'Thy lips are like a thread of scarlet, and thy speech is comely . . . Thy two breasts are like two young roes that are twins, which feed among the lilies . . .'

The voice entered into her, loving her, fucking her.

'Thou art all fair, my love; there is no spot in thee . . .'

She was at Ben's feet now, face to his polished boots, abasing herself, loving herself, hating herself. To attain perfection, one must first become nothing.

'Thou hast ravished my heart, my sister, my spouse. Thou hast ravished my heart with one of thine eyes . . .'

Jazz was beside her, writhing against the shingles. They both kissed the biker's boots, tasting dirt on leather. The boots were overcooked pork, hard and crusted crackling over bloody meat. Ben dropped his jacket and peeled his T-shirt from his burn-tattooed chest. Allison and Jazz caressed his legs as he freed his belt from its skull buckle and unbuttoned his fly. He skinned his trews over eaten-away hips.

'How fair is thy love, my sister, my spouse. How much better is thy love than wine, and the smell of thine ointment than all spices.'

Ben took the girls by their chins and pulled them upright. Allison trembled at his grip, bone fingertips biting her cheeks. Ben brought them close to him, their faces touched his chest. Allison felt his ribs through papery skin, heard the beat of his heart.

'Thy lips, oh my spouse, drop as the honeycomb. Honey and milk are under thy tongue . . .'

Ben let them go, and they straightened, looking at him and each other. At that moment, Allison loved Jazz, but was prepared, at a nod from Ben, to kill her. That might be a part of the ritual. She didn't know.

'A garden enclosed is my sister, my spouse . . .'

His glance wandered between their faces, and Allison knew she would be chosen. The worst of it was past. Jazz helped her lie down, kneeling and taking her head and shoulders into her lap, stroking her hair. Behind the London girl, flames rose higher, enclosing them like a wall. Faces stood out of the fire like masks. Mike Toad and Terry. Ben kicked off his boots and trousers, and knelt between Allison's legs, his prick stabbing her dirty denim thighs.

'Spikenard and saffron, calamus and cinnamon, with all trees of frankincense, myrrh and aloes . . .'

Jazz's hands locked with Allison's, and they clutched tight. The scream was all around, a background to the voice that sounded in her head. The scream was in the fire. She could see the moon through Ben. He was fading again, thinning without his clothes. Much of his flesh had come away with his leathers, and his skeleton was visible through the transparent stuff of his body. The fire gave him a glow, but made his bones stand out black against orange.

'Awake, oh North wind, and come, thou South; blow upon my garden, that the spices thereof may flow out . . .'

Ben thrust forwards and melted into Allison, phantom prick spearing her cunt, face pressing against hers and passing into her head, body lying heavy for a second, then sinking through her ribs. Allison was bloated, incorporating what was left of Ben into her own flesh. Her clothes bit into her. She fought Jazz, but was held down. She kicked the ground, huge belly ballooning, legs like tree trunks. Then she was shrinking again, clothes easing up. Her stomach writhed, but shrank. Her bones, stretched and cramped, fell back into their proper places. The prick snug in her cunt turned inside out and, with a nerve-pinching thrill, she knew she had absorbed all Ben's power. She opened her mouth, feeling cold night air in her gullet, and shrieked her pleasure.

They were together, in the same space. In her mind, she felt his last moments, seeing a younger Wendy – head shaved – watching with hate as flame gnawed him. She screamed again, her scream ripped from her, passing into Jazz like a sword.

Allison saw her own face bent over her, felt a red-hot wire tight around her throat. Hello, Wendy, she thought, recognizing the other presence inside her. She felt the blast of air in her face,

the surging power of an engine between her thighs. She knew
things, could remember things. There was a great deal of Ben,
a younger, harder Ben. But she had also taken in Wendy, with a
hard focus on her time with Ben – they had fucked, Allison was
shocked to discover – and a suggestive fog for before and after.
Now she was dead and sacrificed, Allison Loved the woman.

Allison – Allison-and-Ben-and-Wendy – stood up, gently
pushing Jazz away. The other girl looked at her, adoring.

Allison knew she was changed physically. Ben was a part of
her. She felt her jeans crotch swell as Ben's prick and balls
coexisted with her cunt. She was male and female. Her prick
was a hard rod of power, her clit a hot coal of pleasure. Hard,
burning scars swarmed on her face. She was everything.

'I have eaten my honeycomb with my honey,' she said, a voice
coming from inside her as it had from inside Ben, 'I have drunk
my wine with my milk . . .'

Above the fire, the patterns of power were clear, sparkling
among the stars, revolving around the node of the Bomb Site.
Terry and the Toad were out of the flames too, faces full and
glowing as if they'd absorbed fire. Jazz stood between them, face
a panda-eyed black-and-white mask of beauty. Allison wanted to
fuck them all. Inside her, Ben wanted to hurt them all. Wendy
went along with them. And the voice still spoke.

'I sleep, but my heart waketh . . .'

Allison took Jazz by the shoulders, feeling stiffly permed
hair against her hands, and brought her face close. Her black-
lined eyes flicked from side to side. Her powder-white cheeks
were pockmarked with tears and soot. She was wearing one
silver earring, a ruby-eyed skull with a sword stuck through
it, a snake twining around the sword and through the skull.
Around her white throat was a clutter of tiny crucifixes, scarabs,
skulls, daggers, angels, ravens, rosaries and eye-in-the-pyramid
emblems. Even a miniature swastika, like the one Allison's
granddad had given her, with inset green paste jewels.

She saw through Ben's eyes and through her own, two images
of Jazz settling to make a third. The temptation and the rival
became a lover.

'Open to me, my sister, my love, my dove, my undefiled . . .'

'Yes,' the London girl said, almost under her breath.

Allison's mouth latched on Jazz's black lips, and she kissed the
girl. Fire closed around them all.

Twelve

'OPEN TO ME, my sister, my love, my dove, my undefiled . . .'

Beloved stood back for a moment, and the handmaidens came forward. Jenny, smiling, tugged at the laces of Hazel's robe, and the garment came apart at the front. Kate opened the folds, baring Hazel's body. His touch had warmed her, so she didn't feel cold. She knew the whole congregation was watching, but she didn't feel embarrassed.

The altar wasn't uncomfortable, although the eagle's wings scratched a little. The handmaidens still supported her weight, keeping her on a sort of seat. The fine hair on her legs and arms stood up. She could see the beams of the chapel ceiling, vines twining ivylike around them. Bunches of grapes hung from the vines, swelling by the moment, dropping juice like rain.

'. . . for my head is filled with dew, and my locks with the drops of the night . . .'

Hazel felt the Love entwining her.

Beloved, face angelic, unfastened His raiment and stepped out of it, moving forward, pressing His body to Hazel's, easing her legs apart, guiding His penis.

For an instant, she was disappointed. So *that* was all there was to the Great Manifestation.

The handmaidens helped, letting her weight fall slowly as Beloved joined flesh with her. They raised her arms around His shoulders, and she held Him. His stomach and chest pressed against her. Her chin rested on His shoulder. He swelled inside her, filling her. It was not a struggle.

Inside her mind, tiny buds of doubt opened. How had she got here? She thought of Paul, of her father, her sister . . . All around her were strangers. Smiling faces, names she barely knew, a man inside her she'd never met. These people didn't know *her*, couldn't understand . . .

Beloved – this calm stranger joined to her – took her head in His hands and looked into her eyes. She almost fought Him, muscles of her arms tightening to push Him away. But He spoke to her. Without words, He soothed her doubts, showed her truth, guided her along the path.

'Alleiluya,' the Brethren sang.

He didn't seem to thrust, but He moved inside her. A drop of sweat gathered between His eyebrows and fell to her cheek like a tear. His eyes were clear, and she could see into them, the future, the past, the beyond.

The Brethren were singing for her, Hazel realized. She hung on to Beloved as her mind expanded and contracted.

She was . . .

. . . loving an angel of flame, rejoicing in the healing fire of His touch. . . . at the feet of a sad-eyed bleeding Messiah, wailing before the cross. . . . lost in the darkness but with a beacon ahead. . . . dancing in a Brighton club, one she'd dreamed of visiting when she was ten but which had closed years ago, impossibly agile and attractive, boys staring at her from the dark beyond the strobe-lit dance floor. . . . evolving into a higher lifeform, body changing beautifully, mind swelling to conquer mysteries, hand becoming a gun that could shoot Love. . . . leaving her mother's womb, swimming in wonder towards the world. . . . leaving her clumsy body, drifting towards a golden field. . . . the Earth, Loved by the farmer who sowed his seed in her, extending pebbly arms to embrace him, to reward his devotion. . . . clay, shaped by her own hands, perfected.

'Alleiluya . . .'

The chapel roof was crumbling and being sucked upwards, like jigsaw pieces being taken away. She saw stars scattered in the night, the cold eye of the moon. Then, there was light. The picture cracked open and the sun exploded, filling the night with day. The skies were blue and white, and filled with birds. The sun grew enormous and burst, its light blotting out all else. The light rained down a fiery gold that splashed and ran like quicksilver. She felt it on her face. The gold glittered, shot through with divine blood.

The arms around her were feathered. Her weight was pulled upwards, lifted off the altar. Her feet dangled in empty air. She heard her own voice added to the song. She was danced in air, her own wings beating nervously, Beloved's with supreme confidence. Still joined, they rose through the chapel, and bathed in the falling light. The gold was deep red now, a red that ran for ever, blanketing the world below. She looked at the face of Beloved, and saw God.

She lost herself, lost Hazel Chapelet. Free of her old loves – the nasty tangle of compromises and competitions and petty affections that tied her to Paul, to Patch, to Dad, to herself – she could join in the greater Love, the Love that would redeem the world.

'If you go away this summer,' Dad had said, 'there'll be tears. He's nearly thirty, and he's not grown up.'

'I have to go away some time,' she'd said back, seeing an escape from the quiet, thickly carpeted house.

At first, she was scared. Among so many, she was alone, easy to overlook. Rivers of red gold flowed through crowds, encouraging the faithful to bathe. Beloved knew even the least of His flock, Loved them with a passionate fire, cared for them, protected them. And she was His sister, His spouse.

'I love you,' Paul had said.

I'm not so sure, she'd thought, saying, 'Thank you.'

She was wrapped tight around Beloved, falling back gently on to the altar. It was soft as a mattress. He was wordlessly caressing her, His face huge, His eyes suns.

'Haze, be careful,' Patch always said, 'you know what you're like.'

No, she always thought, no, I don't.

Now she knew. Now, no longer even able to feel the superiority due her after all these years as the less clever one, she knew all things, understood all things. Paul and Patch were too clever really to *know*, to understand. She hoped she could redeem her old loves, could bring them to the arms of Beloved.

The singing was a joyous scream, and she knew it was hers, her scream in the throats of others. They exulted for her.

'Love,' she said.

Thirteen

A S SUDDENLY AS it began, the scream ended. His hands were over his ears. The noise had been painful. The screamers ceased and looked in wonder at skies only they could see. In the sudden quiet, Paul heard the tiny sounds of night. Standing up slowly, Paul looked to Ferg. The boy shrugged. The hippie, Dolar, had a beatific just-swallowed-an-ounce-of-dope look. Everyone looked into the sky, as if a comet were streaking miraculously past, exploding into multicoloured fireworks. After the scream, the quiet was unnerving. Paul felt he was standing on the thinnest of ice covers, afraid to breathe lest it should shatter and plunge him into the darkness beneath. Finally, he let go before he choked.

Susan wanted to be sick. Karen was holding her hand with an imbecile's grasp. The overflow from Jago's coupling with Hazel was running through the congregation. Even she could feel the warmth inside, hating herself for it. This time, the Great Manifestation had been stronger. She was sure Beloved had levitated a few inches while he pushed himself into the girl. There had certainly been a few lighting effects, and the stained-glass eyes of saints and martyrs had glowed with lust.

It was not finished yet. Usually, Jago managed to wind it up with a pristine climax and withdrew to be wiped down by the handmaids. Tonight, he was grunting softly as he ground away at Hazel, using the senseless girl as if she were a sex doll.

She caught snatches of the bright-glowing fantasy pouring from Jago's head, but, for the most part, her Talent let her see the tawdry truth: a haggard lecher fucking a brainwashed dupe.

She unwound Karen's hand from her own and got out of her pew. Nearby, Jenny was on her knees, smiling quietly to herself, looking with worship at the Great Manifestation. Joan of Arc must have been mad, too.

Jago's hands held Hazel to the altar. Tears flowed from shut-tight eyes as his dick knifed in and out of the girl.

'Alleiluya,' the Brethren sang, over and over. 'Alleiluya, alleiluya . . .'

It wasn't even Jago's fault. He was mad because his people wanted him to be, begged him to be. Letting him play out his Messiah fantasies was a way of keeping his Talent caged. God knows, it wasn't easy living with what they had in their heads. Chemicals in the brain. Sometimes the Talent felt like an alien parasite, edging out the original occupant of the body, taking over. Inside, there was probably a shred of the real Jago.

Susan walked to the aisle, where Mick had stripped Marie-Laure and was trying to penetrate the mindless woman, begging for a response, crying out in his own agony. Cindy and Phillip were spooning, hands held, teenagers in the back row of the stalls. Derek – without Wendy for once – was on his knees, praying, adoring, shoulders shaking. Sister Kate was stroking her pregnancy, pain and happiness mingled in her face. Their eyes all flashed gold and red as the Spirit moved them.

Useless, Susan accused herself.

All her Talent, all her powers, all the things that made her Witch Susan . . . Nothing had helped.

'I'm sorry,' she said, looking at Hazel's slumped, sleeping face.

It was stifling in the chapel, and her robe was sticky, scratchy.

Mick squirted semen on Marie-Laure's belly, never having managed to get inside. He fell, sobbing, on the woman. Reviving a little, she stroked his back, needle-marks purple on her skin. Susan stepped around them, and walked towards the doorway.

She decided. No matter what might come down from the ministry, from David, no matter what James advised, she'd end this.

She looked at Jago, sensing he was nearly through, and his eyes bolted open. For the first time, Beloved, confused and questioning, *saw* Susan, recognized her for what she was. In this moment, he wanted more than anyone else for her to do what she could. Then, his face red, he began to shake. And light erupted all around.

In her arms, Jazz trembled like a bomb on the point of exploding. Allison held her tight. Ben-in-Allison stabbed into Jazz, sinking through their stretched-taut clothes. The fires burned on all sides. Allison felt Badmouth Ben flowing out of her, bursting from their male–female loins, struggling to be born again. Jazz's head had worked a depression in the shingles, and her hair was a shaggy ruin, sharp stones clinging to her goth perm like ornaments to a Christmas tree. Even through Jazz's clothes and her own, Allison could feel heat building up in her, feel the searing where their flesh met. The girl's mouth was open, and she was sucking in fire. It flowed like a reverse film into Jazz's mouth and nostrils, ears and eyes.

Jenny shared Love. Beloved had chosen well, Hazel was truly a Sister of the Agapemone. She was transported to her own Great Manifestation, and sang in joy. For a moment, she was Hazel, and Janet, and Marie-Laure, and Wendy. They were one person, a female embodiment of Love. Then she was herself again, weak from ecstasy, unable to stop babbling. A stage of her elevation was over. It had been very special, very tempting, very rewarding. But now Hazel was the Sister-Love, and she must step back, be truly a handmaiden, truly one of the Sisters. Humbly, she bowed her head. There was light all around. Everything was changed.

In the Keough cottage, Lytton held tight to the banisters. The screaming had stopped, and the house no longer shook as if in an earthquake. The madness had lasted a few minutes at most. Draper had ignored the whole thing, mind fixed on the corpse at the top of the stairs.

'He's not been dead long,' Draper explained, 'and we caught this young bugger slipping out, pockets full of silver candlesticks. He might as well have been wearing a striped jersey, a mask and a black beret, carrying a bag marked "swag". He had over three hundred notes on him. Where'd a no–no like our Edward get that unless he was pilfering?'

'But . . . but . . .'

He couldn't complete the thought.

The whole village had just screamed, Lytton included. He didn't know why, but he'd screamed with the rest, clinging to Danny Keough's banister and shouting like a dying man. He hadn't been the only one. Teddy had screamed too, and the black constable. He was afraid even Danny Keough, stiff on the landing, had joined in. Now it was over, his ears weren't used to it. Everything sounded like the scream.

'This is serious, of course,' Draper shouted.

In her dream, Hazel was happier than she'd ever been. She was
on the beach at Brighton. The sun was tropical, the sea bluer
than the summer sky. Paul was there, laughing and joking. And
her parents, holding hands as they paddled. And Patch, with her
faceless boyfriend, big glasses on, not reading a book. Susan, hair
over one eye, posed for a snap, looking pretend sad. The light was
so strong everything glittered and sparkled like molten gold, but
it did not hurt her eyes. Music was playing, calling everyone.
An open-topped double-decker bus, bright red, drove along the
seafront, party-goers singing and dancing on the exposed deck.
Everyone was around her, laughing, smiling, stroking. She was
in love, but not with anyone in particular. Just in love.

'Fuck me,' X said, 'what was that all about?'
    Jeremy didn't know.
    'Fuck me,' X said again.
    'Yeah,' said Ingraham, 'that's right, fuck you.'
    'No, fuck you.'
    'You!'
    They began fighting. X made a fist and smashed Ingraham's
nose. Blood burst from his nostrils. Then X put his hands by
his side, and Ingraham punched him in the stomach, doubling
him over. X held his gut and straightened up, while Ingraham
composed himself. X crouched and punched upwards between
Ingraham's legs. The boy strangled a cry, and took a moment or
two to get his breath back.
    The policemen came out of Mr Keough's cottage, dragging
Teddy Gilpin, the man from the Agapemone wandering after
them. Jeremy watched X and Ingraham exchange blows, gradually losing interest in the fight even as eyes swelled and teeth
were spat out.

Susan tried to hold on, but the world fell down around her head.
Jago's Talent was beyond even his control now. And it was
loose.

Beloved gently stood back, and His Sister-Love slithered from
the altar, falling in a faint, robes bunching up around her. Jenny
had His towel ready, clean and scented, and she rubbed oils and
ointments from His body. Kate helped, dabbing at Him. His Love

enveloped them. The Lord God was in the flesh, and among the Brethren.

Teddy couldn't explain, not to Draper, not to James. Constable Erskine held his arm up behind his back as school bullies sometimes did, giving him a wrench every minute or so, just to remind him how close he was to pain.

In the street, there were lots of people. People he knew. Sharon Coram, stripped down to a bra and a half-slip, was kissing a long-moustached Rasputin look-alike he didn't recognize. Kev Conway and Beth Yatman passed a plastic container of Calver cider between them.

'Kev,' he said, 'get –'

Erskine gave his arm a yank, and a knob of pain in his shoulder burst.

'Hang him,' someone shouted.

Two skunk lads, observed by a quiet and white-faced Jeremy Maskell, were belting each other silly by the garage forecourt. From a slightly tugged-aside curtain, a pale little-girl face looked down at Teddy as he was dragged into the road. He thought for a heart-stab moment it was Jenny, but it was Lisa. When he thought of Jenny, he preferred to think of her as she'd been when she looked like Lisa rather than as the God-bothered stranger she'd grown into.

'Kick him in the goolies.'

'Looks like your fans are out in force tonight, Gilpin Minor,' Erskine said, pressing his knee to Teddy's back.

'*Hang* him by his goolies.'

Sharon, who'd always been a mean cow, took the trouble to spit in his face, then got back to work with Rasputin, her hands twisting in his crotch-length beard. Kev and Beth had gone away, slipping into the crowd, not wanting to admit they knew him. Teddy supposed he didn't have any parents any more, much less any friends. Erskine wouldn't let him wipe Sharon's phlob from his face. He went quietly, bent almost double, looking up despite the pain in his neck, just in case Erskine fancied running his head into a wall.

James was with the police, but hadn't done anything to stop them. That was the way it always was for Teddy, with teachers and adults. He always ended up disappointing them. The only person who looked him in the face was Jeremy, and the freak kid was hardly likely to be any help. Teddy knew he'd regret not getting out of the village this afternoon.

Susan watched Jago tie his robe about his middle again, putting away his dangling hosepipe of dick. The sickening thing was that, in the end, the Agapemone was just about Jago's dick. The rest was trimming, a religious smokescreen to prevent him suffering guilt. She thanked God he'd never fancied her.

The rest of the Brethren were fixed on their leader now, murmuring Beloved, reciting random scraps of the Song of Solomon. Mick was crying, trying to Love himself. Marie-Laure was beside him, head up for once, quietly contemptuous. Cindy and Phillip still held hands.

Ignored by all, Susan stepped past Jago, taking care not to touch so much as the hem of his garment, and knelt by Hazel. Jenny and Kate were too busy adoring to bother with the postulant, so it fell to Witch Susan. The girl was just asleep, dreaming sweet dreams. She didn't even seem to be bruised by the Great Manifestation. But Susan had no way of knowing how damaged Hazel was in her mind. For the moment, she arranged the robe around her, covering her sacrifice's body. She hoped Hazel was on the pill, or not ovulating. One Jago was enough for the world.

'Hazel,' she said, touching the girl's face.

The others were leaving the chapel, following Beloved's procession. Karen, a weak link, lingered, and came over.

'Help me with her,' Susan said.

'She's blessed,' Karen said, admiring.

'That's one way of putting it.'

As Jago walked away, Susan felt his power dwindle. But she knew it wouldn't dissipate this time. It was outside him, rushing through the whole village, making dreams come true. How long had Alder been waiting for Jago, she wondered, waiting for the fuse to set the explosion? There were individual screams now, of pain and terror. Jago's charade was continuing, with real blood spilled, real people hurt. Soon, she was afraid, the Massacre of the Innocents would start. That would be another role for Jago's biblical CV: Herod.

'She's coming round,' Karen said.

Hazel was murmuring in her sleep, smiling, stretching like a cat. Her eyes slipped open. 'Beloved,' Hazel said.

Susan knew the girl was lost.

*

Terry and the Toad held the thrashing Jazz down as fire poured
into her. Allison straddled the girl, watching the ritual work itself
out. Almost all the fire was in Jazz now. Allison was herself again
in body. She would always have Badmouth Ben in her heart,
but she'd absorbed his flesh completely. It had been interesting
being half a man for a minute, but she wouldn't want to try it for
life.

Auras swirled in the air, clinging like overlapping curtains.
Allison could touch them. Forces in the earth were welling up.
This was a site of power, and it was flowing into Jazz. The goth
should be honoured. She was full of fire now, as hard to touch as
a boiling kettle. Allison stood up and rubbed her burned thighs.
Her jeans were scorched where she'd been straddling Jazz. Terry
and the Toad kept their grips on the girl's wrists, smoke pouring
through their fingers as they yelped with pain.

Jazz's face was scarlet now, fire burning under skin, reddening
flesh like a bulb inside a thick shade. It didn't hurt the girl, but
she found it hard to contain the power. Her legs kicked,
spike bootheels stabbing shingles, and her shoulders wriggled
against the ground. Allison, feeling the Spirit inside her, knelt
and delicately extracted Jazz's stiletto from its sheath. The
instrument was warm, but not uncomfortable to the touch. It
had already been consecrated with blood. Inside Allison, Ben's
breath quickened at the feel of the knife he'd used. And Wendy
flinched, remembering its sharp slipperiness.

There were fires down in the village, and the shouts of a fight.
She knelt again, one knee against Jazz's tight stomach, forcing
the girl's back against the ground. She ignored the burning pain
and touched the tip of the stiletto to Jazz's chest, slicing away the
gauze scarves to rest against the black stretch of leotard over her
ribs where Allison could see the pulse of her heart. The last of
the fire was gone, and Jazz was trying to twist under the knife.
Allison pressed slightly, and the knifepoint scratched a hole in
fabric, drawing a dewdrop of blood.

People ran past Paul, jostling him. Ferg was crouched down by
the wall, arms over his head. Dolar was grinning and holding out
his hands to touch people, some of whom hit him as they passed.
He didn't seem to mind. Ferg's girlfriend was pressed against Ferg,
though he was cringing away from her. The Asian kid and Dolar's
companion were totally bewildered.

'Peace,' Dolar was saying.

There was a boom, and Dolar was lifted off his feet, slammed against the tree. He slipped to the ground, a rose-shaped splatter on his shoulder, seeping into his muslin shirt. He put his hand to the blooming blood and stared it, disbelieving what he saw or felt. There was another boom, and a patch of the tree's black bark exploded, showing orange flesh beneath. A man in striped pyjamas stood in the street, shotgun in his hands. He was trying to reload, fishing cartridges out of his top pocket, muttering something about 'beatnik bastards'.

'Peace,' Dolar burped, hand pressed to his bleeding shoulder.

Paul pushed away from the tree, out of range. The gunman had reloaded, and snapped shut his double-barrelled gun. He yanked both triggers, and there was a flash as the gun misfired. He pebble-dashed the ground with shot and, crying, dropped his weapon, kicking it with bare feet. He clutched his bruised toes and sobbed.

Dolar's smile spread wider. 'Peace.'

Having slept the day away, Maskell awoke under the moon, family about him, erection stabbing the sky. Slowly, he pulled his roots out of the earth, refreshed by the goodness he had absorbed, and stood up. Sue-Clare, Hannah and Jethro stood too, in their places. Something was missing, though, and the gap nagged Maskell. His knob twitched towards the village. He saw fires in the distance, a glow outlining the hump of the hill.

'Jerm,' he said. 'Jerm, Jerm, Swallowing Sperm.'

Jenny and Kate helped Beloved to His room. He was exhausted, drained. It was hard to remember He too was confined for the most part to a body of flesh and blood. The handmaidens laid Him on the bed.

'Come to me, my Sister, my spouse,' He said.

Jenny instinctively slipped towards the bed, pulling covers aside. Then she realized He meant the new Sister-Love.

'Bring Sister Hazel,' she told Kate.

Erskine forced Teddy to the ground in the middle of the road, and pulled his arm back and forth. Lytton tried to protest.

'It's better than he deserves,' Draper said.

There was an audience for all this, shouting advice. Erskine was playing to the crowd, hurting Teddy for their pleasure. Raine, the black policeman, was standing by, doubtful but not enough to interfere.

Lytton felt someone pulling his arm, and turned to see Pam, moving fast. The girl tried to kiss him, tongue pressing past his teeth, almost choking him. He fought free, and she collapsed against him, arms around his neck, anchoring him. Draper and Erskine were fifty yards away, carrying Teddy between them. Then there were people in the way, and he couldn't see them any more. Pam pressed herself against him, cooing endearments. He found her harder to pull off than a multisuckered clam. Every time he detached one of her hands, another part of her would latch on to him. It was a strange dance.

Up the road, a bottle with a tongue of fire flickering from its neck flew out of a top-floor window and shattered against the asphalt, spreading a circle of burning liquid.

Lytton threw himself against the grass verge, pulling Pam with him. They rolled together into a depression, and she was on top of him, kissing his cheeks and lips, pushing his head down. For a moment, he thought of giving in. Then, he fought again.

Kate came for the postulant and Susan didn't fight to keep her. Hazel, floating and smiling, was easily led away. Before she went to Beloved, she said, 'We share Love', and Susan had wanted again to be sick. With Karen, she watched Hazel and Kate go upstairs.

'When the festival is over,' Karen announced, 'I'm leaving.'

'We're all leaving,' Susan said. 'When the festival's over, it'll all be over.'

She promised herself.

X and Ingraham were on their knees, faces and fists dripping, breathing like old men, barely able to inflict each blow, taking longer and longer to work up to the next one. Jeremy was huddled behind the tyres. There was a fire in the road. Fights were going on. The man from the Agapemone had been fighting with a red-haired girl in a shallow ditch. He had won his fight, and was staggering off.

The dry grass of one verge was on fire. Whatever had happened to Daddy had happened to other people. Some of them were even changing. A scary clown stalked past, double-joined legs like stilts, exaggerated face not make-up or a mask. Jeremy knew there was no point in running away. He would just be bringing attention to himself.

Ingraham was lying down now, feebly trying to get up. X joined his hands over his head in victory, then fell forwards on to his friend. In their heap, they lay.

From out of nowhere, Lisa Steyning appeared in a nightie. She pulled his hair, making him ouch, and ran off into the dark, slippers flapping. That was the last thing he would put up with. He scrambled out from his nest of tyres and ran after Lisa's filmy nightie. She was only a girl. When he caught up, he'd smack her face until she bled, and kick her until she cried.

Jessica tried to cuddle him, but Ferg battered her off. She was turning into a whining hag. The invisible invaders had landed, and he heard them clumping through the village. He saw dents in the road where they'd trod, weight cracking the tarmac, crushing the cat's-eyes. Everyone was panicking. They would come for him and Paul soon.

Hazel lay down beside Beloved, content and complete. At last, she belonged. She was Loved for herself as she was, not for someone else's idea of her. She was too happy to sleep.

Allison knew she'd done what she had to. She put the stiletto back in its sheath on Jazz's hip, and stood. The small tear over the girl's heart expanded, pinpoint of blood glowing like molten metal. The tiny bubble was the focus of the fire. She took Terry's hand, and Mike Toad's, and led them back. They stood at the crest of the crater, watching Jazz. She convulsed, face bright red, casting her own light, the blood bubble so bright it was hard to look at. Jazz was swallowing her own aura.

Susan looked down the hallway, and lashed out with her mind. Panels on either side of the door exploded into fragments, which burst outward in a shower. The frames smoked, and she felt petty satisfaction with her destructive potential. Karen goggled at her.

'Abracadabra,' she said, bitterly.

Lisa's nightie stood out, blonde hair streaming down it, as the small shape ran. Jeremy knew he could catch her, even if she did try to get lost in the crowd. Lisa pushed through a gate into the Pottery, and Jeremy followed. The Bleaches had a big garden. He remembered it from a barbecue his parents had taken him to. Lisa had teased him and kicked him when no one was looking. He'd been sent home early for throwing orange juice over her party dress, and she'd huddled giggling with Hannah as Daddy, angry, carted him off to a smacking, no supper and an early night.

It was dark in the garden, but he still saw the nightie. Lisa was heading up the hill, but had slowed down. She was too weedy to want to run all the way to the top. Jeremy was getting a stitch. Lisa stopped still, and turned to look back. He imagined her tongue poked out.

'I'll get you,' he said to himself.

He ran up to her, slowing down, making fists. She walked towards him, and dread struck him down. The blonde wig came loose and was thrown away. The nightie was shucked. He found himself looking at the vacant, drooling face of the Evil Dwarf, and his bladder gave way. Giggling like Lisa, the Evil Dwarf came for him.

Paul knew it'd be safest to get off the road. But there was fighting between the tree and the Pottery. He wondered about Hazel, about how she was. With all this commotion, they couldn't have had time to finish their ceremony. Perhaps she had not been initiated after all. Perhaps she was savable. He bit down, and his tooth flared.

Jazz was inches off the ground now, head lolling back. Light around her throbbed. Allison saw the blood bubble burst inwards, and tried to look away. It was a sudden explosion of darkness, sucking everything into a tiny spot. There was a crack, and a violet discharge that hurt her eyes. Where Jazz had been, there was nothing.

Interlude Three

'AT THE END of the programme, it was in Westminster Abbey, a hundred feet high, with eyes and tentacles and slime and . . .'

'Nahhh,' Reggie sneered at him, 'youm makin' it up.'

'No, it was on the television,' Maurice insisted, 'last night.'

The boys were out on the wetlands, bored. It was August, school weeks away. Reggie was two years older, and his dad worked on the farm. The Major didn't really like him playing with Reggie, and he sometimes wondered himself why he put up with the bulky, sulky, bullying boy. He somehow always ended up wading barelegged through stinging nettles, raising fierce red blotches on his skin that took days to subside. Reggie was often hanging around the farm at a loose end, although Maurice had never been invited to the Gilpin house. There were few children in Alder, and Reggie, because his dad worked for the Major, was the only one who didn't stay away from the newcomer as if he carried the plague. The Maskells had been in Alder a year, since the Major had bought the farm, and they were still newcomers. Maurice's father liked it that way, believing it important that everybody knew their place. 'The rich man in his castle,' he explained, 'the poor man at the gate, He made them high and lowly, and ordered their estate.' The Major liked to stride around the farm, quirt at his side, making sure everything and everyone was in their place.

'Tellyvision,' Reggie said, spitting a lump at a cowflop. 'Load a' rubbish, boy.'

'No,' Maurice said patiently, 'the monster was real. I saw it.'

He had, too, just before the names of the actors came up, and the eerie music he couldn't whistle sounded out, sending a chill straight to the base of his spine. Lying awake last night, with his torch on under the bedclothes, he had decided the Quatermass Experiment was the scariest monster to which he'd ever been exposed. It was worse than the silver robot in *The Day the Earth Stood Still*, worse than the Nazi war criminals Yank Steyning had told him about, worse than the werewolves in the American comics his father had burned. It sat there in the rafters of the abbey, writhing and dripping. Next week would be the last episode, and Maurice thought he wouldn't be able to get a real night's sleep until it had been transmitted and the world was put to rights. He imagined the monster frozen in the abbey for a week, waiting for Professor Quatermass to come and put it in its place. Next week, he hoped, the professor would find some way of destroying the monster, and the world would be saved. If not, then it would be the end of all things, and everyone would be turned into tentacled, many-eyed monstrosities. It was too dreadful to think about. No one would know their place then, because there wouldn't be places any more, or people to know them . . .

'Where'd thic bleddy monster come frum then?'

'The spaceman turned into the monster. Remember the spaceman?'

Reggie sneered. Maurice had been explaining all summer what was happening with Professor Quatermass and the spaceman. Professor Quatermass was a scientist, brisk and dedicated, and he took no nonsense from the soldiers and politicians who got in his way. The soldiers reminded Maurice of the Major, snapping orders and not paying attention, sure everything was in its place while the world disappeared under writhing slime. Reggie pretended he wasn't interested in Professor Quatermass, but when Maurice finished the explanation of this week's instalment, he always asked questions, digging for extra details.

'When the cactus got into the spaceman, he turned into a giant cactus monster.'

'With they tentacles?'

'Yes,' Maurice said, 'lots of tentacles.'

The only time Reggie Gilpin had seen television was the Coronation, when the Major had invited everyone in the village to watch the great event on their receiver. Maurice's parents had the only set in Alder. That day, the vicar and the other farmers had a party afterwards. All the children had stared well into the evening at the bubbly screen with its fuzzy little people. Maurice had been bored rigid by the Coronation, which was just people talking and wandering in and out of Westminster Abbey. If there

was going to be anything in Westminster Abbey, he preferred it
to be a hundred-foot-high monster from outer space.

A herd of cows milled around in the field, stupidly chewing
grass, full udders sloshing. Reggie's dad had been working
steadily over the past few weeks, stringing up wires in the
fields. Yank Steyning, an American who had come over for
the war, helped out, wearing thick cowboy gloves and talking
like Tim Holt. Maurice always wondered when Yank, who'd
married Anne Starkey, would saddle up and ride on like Tim
Holt, vanishing over the horizon on a horse, wandering to the
next town for the next adventure. Reggie's father and Yank had
done a thorough job, but the wires were pretty useless fences.
A cow could easily knock one down. A series of iron poles
held up the wire, which was two feet off the ground where it
wasn't sagging, and they were already sinking at funny angles
into the wet ground.

The Major had told him not to mess around with the wires or
else he'd get hurt. Maurice knew what that meant. Whenever he
did anything his father told him not to, he got hurt. The Major
kept his quirt, which was like a tasselled riding crop, with him
all the time. He'd used the quirt in the Far East during the war.
When Maurice wouldn't go to bed or broke anything or talked
back, his father would tell him to drop his shorts and underpants
and bend over, then he would strap him across the backside with
the quirt, always ten times. It certainly hurt.

'Did they cactus come frum out a' space?'

'No, the hospital where they put the spaceman when he came
back ill.'

'Sounds stupid t'me.'

Maurice didn't quite understand how the cactus and the
spaceman had become combined in the monster.

'I suppose it was the radiation.'

'Like they bomb buggers?'

Maurice nodded. 'Yes, atomic radiation.'

Reggie's upper lip, skilled in the art of the curl, expressed his
opinion of Maurice's stupidity, and he spat again, apparently
hawking a fist-sized gobbet of slime in with the spittle. Reggie
always treated Maurice as if the younger boy were a mongoloid
idiot, but Maurice knew Reggie was near the bottom of his class.
They were at the same school, but when he took his next exams,
Reggie would be going to the secondary modern in Achelzoy,

while the Major had already made arrangements to send him away to the school – the posh school, Reggie called it – he'd gone to himself. That had nothing to do with being clever. That had to do with tradition, the Major had explained to him. Reggie told him that at the posh school, he'd have to do five hours of homework every night and take cold showers at six in the morning. He'd complained to his mother about this prospective torture, but she told him Reggie didn't know anything and was just showing his enviousness.

"Tomic raddyation. Tha'ss wha'ss in they wires,' Reggie said, pointing to the droopy fence.

Maurice laughed. 'Don't be silly. Atomic radiation comes out of bombs.'

'Weren't no bomb got they bleddy spacyman bugger.'

That was true, he couldn't deny.

'That was outer-space radiation.'

'Same diff'rence.'

Maurice was impatient, unable to explain to Reggie why he was stupid. He didn't have all the facts himself, but knew the older boy was wrong.

'If there was atomic radiation in the wires, we'd be dead. And the cows would die too.'

'Not if'n i'ss they slow-type raddyation.'

Reggie didn't even read comics, so he didn't know what he was talking about. But he'd often try to make Maurice angry by arguing stupid things. Once, he'd called Maurice a red, and argued that only communists had televisions. How else were they supposed to get their orders from Stalin in Russia if it wasn't through the television?

They were quite near the wires. Nearer than Maurice's father had said he should go. Up close, he could see the wires weren't nailed to the iron posts, but strung into little loops at the top of each. He thought he could hear humming.

Maurice felt itchy. He wanted to piddle, but the Major had told him not to relieve himself in public. When he was younger, he'd wet the bed a few times and his father had made him lie in it until it was dry, then quirted him.

In the Far East, the Major had been an officer prisoner-of-war, and had to keep up discipline in the camp. He had stories about troublemakers and slackers who let the side down, and how he brought them into line. He had medals and a letter from an important general commending him for spirit and bravery. He didn't tolerate indiscipline in the ranks and came down hard on it. But when Yank Steyning saluted him, he got red-faced and angry, accusing the American of being disrespectful. Yank had been in the war too and had medals to prove it. He hadn't been a prisoner, though; he'd loaded bombers at the airfield in Achelzoy.

The Major wouldn't want Maurice to piddle in the field. Still, he had drunk most of a bottle of pop this morning and not been to the lavatory. He could feel the pop in his bladder, pressing to get out.

'You can hear they raddyation raddyatin',' Reggie said.

'Don't be silly, it's just a fence, that's all.'

'One touch, and you'm be a pile a' they ashes.'

This was another of Reggie's stupid arguments, Maurice could tell. Like the time he said the Bomb Site was haunted by the ghost of a German parachutist who'd come in the war. Or his attempt to convince Maurice that Danny Keogh limped because he had a wooden leg the army had given him. He had persuaded Maurice to stick a pin into Danny's leg to disprove that story. That had been worth twenty strokes of the quirt, with Danny watching quietly while his father did the business.

'It's just wire.'

'Prove it,' Reggie said, quietly.

'Father says I'm not to touch it.'

Reggie's sneer was out loud, a laugh of victory. 'See, 'tis bleddy 'tomic. 'Ven yer red daddy knows it.'

'No, I'm just not to touch it.'

'Then don't touch it, jus' cluck-cluck-cluck chicken.'

'But it's not atomic.'

The wire looked harmless, a dead line hanging like an old skipping rope. It could be jumped over or crawled under. Cows would trample it soon enough, and they wouldn't be turned to ash. Maurice knew the Major wouldn't have anything put up that might threaten his livestock. He was always talking about how much money he'd invested in the farm.

Maurice was bursting. He turned to a ditch, unbuttoned his fly, and took out his knob. He didn't like to with Reggie watching, but he didn't want to wet his shorts and get the quirt.

'Tell youm what,' Reggie said, 'youm piss on thic wire.'

That was one way to settle it. His knob in his hands, Maurice waddled over to a place where the wire sagged almost to his knees. He aimed, and let go. The stream of piddle missed the wire, but he brought it closer, until it touched . . .

There was a steaming crackle, and the worst pain Maurice had ever experienced shot through his knob. Sense shocked out of him, he collapsed.

VI

One

THIS COULD TURN into a rock-'n'-roll riot, even a disaster of tabloid-headlines-for-six-months, hospital-visits- from-the-Prime-Minister proportions. The pre-festival bacchanal was turning into ragged scuffling. A homicidal dickhead was tossing home-made Molotov cocktails into the street. A boy with fluid spurting from a burst eye slammed into Lytton and ran on, hurdling firelines. When the dawn came and the figures were in, this could rack up a kill-count to make an airliner crash or a football-stadium collapse seem a picnic on the lawn.

The Browning was back in the Gate House. Lytton wished it were with him. He'd left it behind because he didn't want the discomfort of it in his waistband all afternoon. Now, that seemed like a beginner's mistake.

An amplified cassette deck was playing the Ramones' 'Rock 'n' Roll High School'. Some were passing buckets around the patches of fire in the road, others were dancing in firelight. Lytton saw Ursula Cardigan jiving topless, warpaint dashes of soot and lipstick on her cheeks. A milk bottle full of paraffin sailed across the road, burning handkerchief jammed into its neck. It burst against a parked Ford Escort, flames spreading over paintwork, fire dripping to tarmac. A leading edge of fire washed down the Ford's body, swarming towards the petrol cap.

Lytton dragged himself over a low wall. He was in a flowerbed in front of a small cottage; he smelled crushed roses, felt thorns scratching, tasted soft earth. Crouching against the dry-stone wedge, he counted, as if timing the distance between lightning and thunder. After fifteen, the Ford's petrol tank exploded. He felt the shudder in the ground. Even with eyes shut fast, he saw the flare, a white blast in the dark. Hot hail fell on his back, and he writhed in his jacket, trying to get the searing shrapnel off him. Heat poured over him in waves. The

small garden was floodlit by magnesium-harsh flames. Someone
screamed and leaped the wall, fire sprouting from back and
hair, slammed against the house and collapsed into a bush, life
shocked free of the body. A sick-making smell of scorched flesh
smoked off the burning person.

Slowly, he got off his knees and looked at the main road. Fires
were spreading, the exploding car having spat hot chunks against
a row of cottages. One of the last thatched roofs in Somerset
was dotted with burning debris, clouds of smoke boiling from
its depths. The amateur fire-fighters had given up and joined
the rock-'n'-rollers, thrashing heads in the firelight. The cottage
front door opened, and a middle-aged woman in curlers came
out, wearing only a pyjama top. Naked from the waist down,
she tutted at the damage to her flowers, and started fussing with
a row of carefully cultivated chrysanthemums, squatting down
to talk to the blooms. She ignored Lytton and the still-burning
body.

As a field agent, he'd never been mixed up in the wet end
of the business before. Montreal hadn't been Belfast, Beirut
or Phnom Penh. This wasn't like his training exercises. This
wasn't like anything.

'Gabba gabba, we accept 'em, one of us! Gabba gabba, we
accept 'em, one of us!' the Ramones sang. 'Gabba, gabba hey,
gabba gabba hey.'

He looked up at the Agapemone, and imagined Jago sitting
with his camera obscura, watching it all, half knowing he had
caused it. Was Beloved pleased with the world he had made?

A boy from the car park crew pogoed too near the fire, his
Bart Simpson T-shirt smouldering. He bopped harder, scraping
at his burning chest with his hands, screeching lost in the music.
He slam-danced into others, spreading fire. People danced in
the flames now, shaking heads and hips like damned souls.
The cassette player was burning too, its music snapped off.
New music, new sounds, flooded in to fill the gap. There was
a heavy-metal bass, overlaid with screaming and the crackle of
flames.

Lytton knew he wasn't immune to the madness. Earlier, he'd
screamed with the rest of them.

'Gabba gabba, we accept 'em, one of us!'

The crowd had taken up the cry from the Ramones song
'Pinhead', the chant from the movie *Freaks*. 'Gabba gabba, we

accept 'em, one of us, one of us!' New freaks joined the dance every moment. The physical fire was petering out, but the spiritual flame was spreading. Kevin Conway and Beth Yatman were dancing close, jumping off the ground and colliding in the air, collapsing, scrambling up, and trying it again. Beth was laughing, long skirt in ribbons like a Polynesian princess's. Kevin had smears of blood on his shirt from his flattened nose. The couple were jostled into the crowd, swallowed by a mass of unrecognizable people. Burned people, dead or unconscious, were kept upright by the press of bodies. Lytton stood at the edge of the throng, his back to a cottage wall.

A wave of movement came through the crowd, stirred by something a hundred yards off. Maybe a thousand people pressed together, pushed to one side of the road. A wave of dancing, stumbling people came. He felt as if a hundred tons of mattress had just swatted him against a solid wall.

The smell of people was overpowering, and there was pressure on every bone in his body. This was how people died in panicking crowds: by inches. Broken bones were painful, but mainly asphyxiation got you, breath slowly squeezing from you. Pain came alive in his chest as his lungs emptied and bodies squashed close around prevented him from filling them again. Faces were pressed close, silent pain exaggerating their features. As you suffocated, you didn't even have the wind to scream. A dozen elbows dug into him wherever he was soft. Caught as tight as the centrepiece of a three-dimensional jigsaw, he didn't know if his feet were on the ground. He couldn't feel below his waist. His back ground against plastered wall. The straining of strangled voices was all around, like the creaking timbers of a wooden ship. There was the occasional pop of a snapped bone, followed by a short, crush-defying yelp.

Slowly, his ribs constricted his lungs. It was as if he'd been mummified with strips of wet leather and left to dry in the sun, all-over wrappings shrinking around him. This, he realized, was how he was going to die. He thought of all the snake tricks he'd learned but never got to use: hot-wiring a car, killing a guard with his bare hands, disposing of a body, making a bomb out of everyday household articles. He thought how promising he had been as an undergraduate, and of how little he had actually done in the years – decades – since then. He thought of all the

women he wished he'd gone to bed with, and they all came
out Spook Susan.

Then, like a miracle, he could breathe again.

The human tide had broken against the row of cottages, lucky
people spilling through gaps into back gardens. Now it was
flowing back again, towards the other side of the road. Another
crush of people, formerly at the back of the press, were being
forced against another set of walls. There was a sudden gasp, and
Lytton's lungs were full. He was sliding down the wall. His back
and hair were white from plaster dust. People all around him
were coughing and choking. He had not been seriously injured,
although his skin must be a bruise-mottled purple. He caught
himself before he lost balance, and stood. Nearby, people who
had not thought so fast were being trampled.

Susan was right. It was time to shut up shop. He listed
priorities. He should get his gun, then he should get word to
the outside. The obvious thing would be to go to Checkpoint
Charlie, wave accreditation at Sergeant Draper, then use the
police radio to call in the IPSIT equivalent of an air strike.
Garnett must have teams of jumpsuited snakes ready, probably
at the Fleet Air Arm base in Yeovilton, to move in and clean up
the mess. The country had had enough disasters and terrorist
atrocities since Lockerbie and Hillsborough to give doctors and
troops experience in damage limitation. Jago could simply be
switched off with an injection.

He fought through to the chrysanthemum-grower's garden,
and stepped over a pile of groaning victims. More than a few
were unmoving, further casualties. There was a tiny alley beside
the cottage, and he shoved himself into it. The half-nude
gardener was still pottering about, ignoring her wounded
guests. She applied a dainty watering can to a small nest of
fire, dousing it with a sprinkle.

Round the back, it was dark. The row of cottages shielded the
fires. Lytton's clothes were wet through. For a heart-stabbing
moment, he thought he was bleeding from a hundred gashes,
then realized he'd had all the sweat squeezed out of him.
Someone, he hoped not himself, had pissed down his legs in
the crush. He scrambled over a back-garden wall of chickenwire
threaded with dry climbers, tumbling into a mushy ditch. There
was a powerful smell of compost. The ground broke rancid
under his hands. This end of the village was just two rows

of buildings either side of the main road. Once you got out beyond back gardens you were either up the hill or, as he was, out on the moors.

If he kept off the road, he could get to the Gate House. Trying to ignore the din, he crawled out of the ditch and, muscles protesting, began to run, crouched low, across fields. There was a scattering of people, even a few cattle, but they mainly got out of his way. Somewhere above a helicopter circled, and he hoped to God that meant this was tugging some bell cords, maybe even shaking the great web of the spook show to such an extent that Sir Kenneth would be hauled out of bed to make a decision.

He circled through the fields and neared the festival site, hoping to rejoin the road just by the Gate House, a short hike away from Checkpoint Charlie. As he got nearer the site, the noise got louder, more boisterous. There was music again, and singing and laughter. It was easy to mistake this whole catastrophe for a carnival. He made it free and clear without incident, and barged his way through a scrubby hedge, hacking the bushes apart with his arms. Scratched and aching, fouled and filthy, he tumbled back into the road.

'Fuck I, James,' Gary Chilcot said, 'youm been in the wars.'

He lay on the verge a moment, struggling for breath again, feeling his bruises tingle. It was preparation for the siege of pain which would, he knew, set in within the hour. He should keep moving, outrun the agony. Faces loomed over him. Gary. And Pam, simpering like a black widow whose husband hasn't quite escaped. Others he didn't know.

Gun, he thought. Get the gun.

He stood shakily, Gary helping. Pam reached around his chest to hug, then flinched away with her whole body when she got a noseful. He stepped free of his support, and looked at the Gate House. The door was open, all the lights were blazing. His Astrud Gilberto tape was playing as loud as the system could be turned up. Bodies moved inside, clumsily crashing into things. He guessed he would be unable to have a quick shower in private and change his clothes before trying to save the world. That was a damned shame.

In his front room, there was an orgy. Sharon Coram was pressed naked between four or five other bodies, mostly male. The group's strenuous activities had displaced all his furniture, shoving desk, chairs and sofa against the walls, knocking over

television and video, and bringing down most of the pictures
on the wall. There was a litter of cast-off clothes and crushed
cider cartons on the floor. Astrud, backed by Stan Getz, was
intolerably loud, rattling his brains with 'One-Note Samba'. The
throaty, whining gasps of the cluster-fuck resounded, along with
the thumping and squelching of their bodies, like the distorted
soundtrack of a blue movie.

An arm snaked around his neck and he was turned. Pam,
overcoming her distaste, put her face to his. As she hugged, his
pain went into overdrive. He was choking, ribs popping out of
alignment. The girl's hand slipped into his fly and groped for
his penis. Pam licked his chin and playfully bit him. For an
eternal second, he had the thrill of an incipient erection, and
lost purpose. He wanted to join the blue movie, to lose himself
in the scrambled flesh, to work his way towards a climax which
would blow off the top of his head. He would join with Pam,
Sharon, the others. They'd become a carnal pool, fucking for
ever, squirting defiance in the dark. Perfume stung his nostrils,
seeping in behind his eyes. Pam's tongue touched his earlobe,
warm and wet.

A shot of agony from his wrenched back killed arousal, and
a gulp of nausea rose in his throat. Finding a pressure point – a
snake trick, at last – he gripped Pam and pushed the girl away
from him. She looked at him, blossom of fear in her eyes, and
stepped back. He made a fist and clipped her on the chin, to
put her out of it. He knew where the knockout button was and
struck perfectly. But this was not an academic exercise, and
she was not dropped immediately senseless. Sergeant Parry, his
instructor, would have given him a Fail. Pam's head lifted and
banged against the door jamb and, groggy, she fell out of the
Gate House, a puppet with half her wires snipped. She was on
her knees, shaking her head, curling into a foetal ball. He would
have preferred a clean stun, but that would have to do. 'Sorry,'
he said.

The desk was up on two legs against a wall, unlocked drawers
spilled on to the floor, adding their contents – pens, pins and
paperclips – to the mess. Part of the cluster began to scream in
noisy orgasm. The pistol was in the one locked drawer. And
the key was in the Mike Bleach teapot on the windowsill. Only
the teapot, along with the potted cactus and the wind-up plastic
alligator with which it had shared the sill, was broken in the ruin

under the bodies. The carpet swirled like a giant water lily under the cluster, trailing bits and pieces in its folds.

Lytton tried to find even the smashed pieces of ceramic, but couldn't. The cluster rolled over, a new team in ascendance, and, like a group of wrestling amoebae, unstuck themselves, then reformed in a new alignment, to begin the sweat-, sperm- and saliva-slick churning all over again. A black girl, abnormally long tongue attached like an umbilical sucker to the belly-button of a bald man, was on top of the cluster. Stuck to her back was the key. It was pressed between her scything shoulderblades, stuck fast by gummy fluid. The bald man was Stan Budge, die-hard enemy of the 'hippie invasion'. Budge was being penetrated by a blue-tattooed white youth, and his red penis was shoved into one mouth or another. The arrangement was generating an odorous heat that made the small front room a greenhouse.

Lytton stepped close and leaned over. Sharon looked up at him from the bottom, teeth bared, but didn't see anything. Her eyes were clouding over, and she was sucking in air through the ring of her mouth. Lytton plucked the key from the black girl's back and backed away from the cluster. It rolled towards him like a juggernaut, legs kicking, arms flailing, genitalia pumping. Pulsing like a complicated organ, it tore itself apart and came together again. There was blood in with the other sticky stuff. He wondered if the cluster was literally fucking itself to death. Apart from Sharon, who was obviously the Queen of Dangerous Sex, none of the components were visibly enjoying themselves.

He shoved the key into the drawer lock, twisting it so hard it bent as it worked. As he pulled the drawer open, the Browning slid down the sloping bottom. Picking up the gun, feeling its grip in his hand, Lytton felt whole again, as if he were drawing strength from the weapon. He relished its weight for a moment, then shoved it into his deep right hip pocket. Leaving the cluster to wear itself out, he left the Gate House.

Pam, feeling her wonky chin, was sitting on the grass, skirt rode up until it was essentially a belt. She looked at him, hurt.

'Sorry,' he said again, and loped off towards Checkpoint Charlie. By his watch, it was just around midnight.

Two

IF THE ONLY THING that frightened Daddy was stupidity, the Evil Dwarf was Stupidity on two stubby legs, a bell-topped dunce's cap on his scraggly head. Jeremy's stitch stabbed his side like a broadsword. Without realizing, he had fallen, and could feel scratchy earth and grass under his knees. His shorts were warm and wet, bunched up and scraping between his legs. One way or another, he'd been running all day. It was well past his bedtime. Just once, he'd have been pleased to go up the stairs into his room in coal-black dark. If he hadn't been afraid of the dark, perhaps things wouldn't have come apart.

He'd always known there was an Evil Dwarf, but never thought beyond the mere scariness of his being an actual thing. He knew Dopey would suck out his brain, but, with the tongue-dangling dwarf getting near, he couldn't imagine what that would mean. Mummy and Daddy had told him Dopey was just a cartoon in a film so many times he'd almost forgotten what was actual and what was not. It was possible he'd made the Evil Dwarf actual by believing in him. That was how some monsters worked. A girl at school who was excused assembly because her parents didn't believe in Jesus said that was how God worked too.

The Evil Dwarf would play with him first. Dopey circled, dancing clumsily, cap-bell tinkling. Jeremy twisted to keep the dwarf in sight, to stop him latching on to the back of his neck, digging for his brain through his hackles. Dopey's tongue – tipped with an orangy blob Jeremy supposed was poisonous – shot in and out like a toad's. The dwarf wore heavy boots with curly, pointed toes. He whistled the dig-dig-dig song from *Snow White*. From his broad leather belt, he took a tiny miner's pick, blade sharp, and licked its length with one slithery pass of his tongue. Jeremy knew Dopey would prise out his eye with the pick, and get that tongue into his skull. There was nothing more he could do. This was the moment he'd always known would come, when the Evil Dwarf got him.

'Stupid,' he said, meaning everything.

The Evil Dwarf was shocked. His watery eyes shook, glints of meanness in blue depths. A single tooth scraped his lower lip. He pulled in his tongue, shoving the last of it into his mouth with fingers like burned-down candles.

'Stupid,' Jeremy said, meaning to hurt.

The Evil Dwarf trembled with a rage he couldn't put into words. His stupidity was like a plug in a boiling kettle, keeping steam in until it exploded. Red blotches emerged on his cheeks like splashes of paint, and his neck swelled until it was the thickness of his head.

'Retardoid, moron, cretin, spastic,' Jeremy said, the worst insults he could think of, the worst that had ever been used on him.

The pick struck out, and sliced whistling past Jeremy's nose. The Evil Dwarf backhanded, and Jeremy had to duck to avoid a triangular flange which would have scraped off his face.

Dopey's mouth worked hard as he tried to get words out.

'. . . *dig dig dig dig dig dig dig dig dig dig dig dig dig dig dig dig dig dig dig dig dig dig* . . .'

With each 'dig', the Evil Dwarf jabbed, pickpoint dimpling Jeremy's skin and clothes but not puncturing.

Up close, the dwarf smelled horrible. His arms and legs didn't work well, his fingers couldn't even hold his pick properly. One hand was a stiff knot that reminded Jeremy of his sister's barbarian doll, who could only hold the magic sword she came with if Hannah used Sellotape. This wasn't what he had expected. Although as mean and cruel as Jeremy had imagined, Dopey was a kid monster, unable to do anything properly, with moods and tantrums, not even capable of controlling his body. He flopped around like Nigel Harris on a trampoline, barely able to keep his balance, let alone get in the air.

Boldly, Jeremy stood up to the Evil Dwarf, fisting his chest. He staggered, incensed at meeting resistance, and Jeremy jeered at him.

'Thickie,' he said, remembering kids at school who picked on him, but whom he left behind in class, his brain racing ahead of theirs. He was supposed to be 'gifted'. That must give him power over this dope.

'Dopey the dope, brains full of soap,' he said, pleased with his rhyme. 'Dopey the dope, dwarf without hope . . .'

The Evil Dwarf began to thump the ground with a gnarly fist. Dwarves were stunted, growth stalled like a broken-down car. The Evil Dwarf was stunted in more than just his body. Dopey was sulking, eyebrows jammed together in a hard ridge over mean eyes, great lumps of snot dangling from his nose. Jeremy wondered what would upset the Evil Dwarf more than being called stupid.

'Shorty,' he said.

The Evil Dwarf howled. Jeremy could see through Dopey now, could see the ground through his smock.

'Knee-high to an ant's little brother.'

Jeremy had got close, so as to dig deeper with his words. He'd forgotten the Evil Dwarf was still dangerous. The pick swung through the air, and jammed into his bare shin. Jeremy screamed, feeling the point grating bone. Instantly, the pain vanished and his entire leg was numb and tingly, as if he'd been sitting on it for a long time.

'Stunted runt.'

Dopey's howl turned to a whine. He tried to pull the pick out of Jeremy's leg, but couldn't get a proper grip.

'Two foot two, eyes like spew . . .'

Jeremy kicked the dwarf, the pick coming out of Dopey's hand as he moved his leg. The Evil Dwarf rolled into a ball like an overturned hedgehog, and Jeremy kicked him again.

A way away, down on the road, there was an explosion, as when a spaceship blew up in a James Bond film, and lots of screaming. A plume of flame shot up in the dark like a firework. Jeremy, distracted, stopped kicking for a moment, and bent to pull the pick out of his leg. It came free easily, and felt good in his hand. As soon as the point was out of him, he felt pain again, and a dribble of blood ran down to his sock.

Dopey's hands pawed his neck, fingers not long enough to get a stranglehold. Jeremy was pulled off balance, and the two, locked together, rolled down the hill. The Evil Dwarf didn't feel actual. His hands and knees were hard and hurting, but the rest of him wasn't all there, as if he were a thin film over mushy stuff. Jeremy was more hurt by the stones they rolled over. When they came to a halt, back in the Pottery garden, the Evil Dwarf was on top. Jeremy still had the pick, and he stuck it deep into Dopey's left side, jiggling the blade. There was a hiss, like a slow puncture, and Jeremy saw alarm in the dwarf's eyes.

'. . . *dig dig . . . dig . . . d-d-dig dig dig . . . d-d-d-d-d-d-d-dig . . .*'

'Die, you cretin.'

The tongue poked out, orange bulb pulsing, and fell in a coil to Jeremy's face, where it slipped on his forehead and came to rest over his left eye. He felt a mild stinging and the tongue squirmed, trying to bring its point to bear on his eyeball. He screwed his eye tightly shut, and shook his head, trying to get the tongue loose.

Drool dribbled down the fleshy rope towards Jeremy's head. The left side of Dopey's face was stiff and withering, substance going out of it. Jeremy stuck the pick into the Evil Dwarf's armpit and tore upwards, ripping through flesh like unbaked dough. The pick burst out of the dwarf's shoulder. An arm hung on threads of white gristle.

His eye was stinging badly now. Jeremy sliced with the pick, and hooked the tongue. It was whipped away, and draped across the grass.

'. . . *dig dig dig dig dig dig dig dig . . .*'

Jeremy stood up, the Evil Dwarf clinging to him with one hand, and shrugged Dopey off. The dwarf thumped the ground, badly out of shape. His parents had been right. The Evil Dwarf wasn't actual. Jeremy could see through him, see the gravel of a thin garden path under Dopey. The tongue slipped back like a snake returning to a hole, but the Evil Dwarf was beaten. The only actual thing the dwarf had brought was the pick. Jeremy knelt, and sank the pick into the Evil Dwarf's heart. It was like scything into thick mud. The pick and Jeremy's hand sank into the dwarf, and he felt a jarring in his wrist as the point lodged in the path. There was a heavy wetness on his hand where it was buried in Dopey's transparent body. He stirred with his fingers, and ripples ran through the whole creature.

'. . . *dig . . . dig . . .*'

The Evil Dwarf collapsed, and was a damp outline on the ground, shimmering like a snail trail. For a second, there was a sighing scream, then just the trickling of the leftovers sinking into gravel and earth.

'I don't believe in you any more,' Jeremy said. There was muck on his hand. He stood up, and gently wiped it off on his shirt. His peed-in shorts were drapes of ice, and he felt he had filth all over his body. It was very dark, but the darkness was empty. The imaginary monsters had been banished. He was stuck with the actual world and the horrors it still presented. His daddy would have been proud of him, if his daddy was still his daddy. He could see flames beyond the house, out in the road, and hear shouting. The Evil Dwarf might be defeated, but there were still monsters, *actual* monsters, prowling in Alder.

Three

A LAMP STRUNG from the central pole cast a bright circle on a wood and metal school chair, leaving the rest of the tent in curtained dark. Constable Erskine shoved Teddy into the chair and produced a pair of handcuffs like a conjurer pulling a rabbit out of a hat. He clinked them in the air.

'Hands by your sides,' the policeman said.

Teddy, who could barely feel his right hand after the arm-abuse he had taken, obeyed.

'Lovely,' Erskine said, and bent down behind the chair. The cuffs slipped around his wrists, biting deep as Erskine fastened them. The policeman stood back to admire his handiwork. Teddy reflexively struggled, and found he had been cuffed to the chair, hands pulled below the seat, chain stretched tight underneath. His shoulders and wrists hurt, and he couldn't get the cuffs free because of the chairlegs. Even if he slipped forward and got loose, he would still be cuffed to the chair, because the tube legs had runners between them.

'Trussed up like a battery hen,' Erskine said. 'Right and proper.'

'Can I have my phone call?'

Erskine laughed. 'Bloody television,' he said. 'We get more people like you than you'd believe.'

'Come on, it's my rights.'

Erskine, teeth shining, stalked around the chair and chuckled.

'That's America, Edward. This is England. Old England, a civilized country. We don't waste rights on steaming heaps of dog dirt, my son.'

Teddy leaned forward, feeling stabs in his shoulders. He didn't have anyone to call, anyway. His parents would have been out of their depth.

'By the way, anything you say will be taken down and may be used in evidence against you. Do you understand that?'

Teddy nodded.

'Out loud.'

'Huh?'

'Say you understand that anything you say will be taken down
and may be used in evidence against you.'

'I understand.'

'That anything I say . . .'

'I understand that anything I say will be taken down . . . and
may be used in evidence against me.'

'Fine and dandy. Oh yes, fine and dandy.'

Teddy was in the Twilight Zone. Erskine wasn't acting like
a real copper. His very white skin had developed stubbly
blemishes, like measles. Erskine cracked knuckles and took a
swing at his chin. Teddy's head shot back on his neck, and his
whole body, the chair with it, tipped over. Erskine caught him,
and kept him upright. Teddy was completely stunned.

'A little insurance,' Erskine said, taking two more sets of
handcuffs from somewhere. He clipped Teddy's ankles, fastening them to the chairlegs so he couldn't even kick.

'Meet the whopper,' Erskine said, unsheathing his truncheon.
'A woodentop's best friend is his whopper.'

There was blood in Teddy's mouth, and his jaw was wonky.
He shook his head, trying to shake the ringing out of it. Erskine
was as cracked as Terry and Allison.

'Now,' Erskine said, slapping the truncheon into his palm like
a German sausage, 'say after me . . .'

'Uh?'

Teddy wasn't following. If he tried to concentrate, his head
hurt so bad he saw flashes before his eyes.

'Say after me, "I confess to the murder of that old man."'

'What?'

Erskine jabbed his neck with the truncheon and lifted up his
head. His blue eyes observed Teddy's face, deep and empty. The
constable had hair so blond his eyebrows were invisible. He had
a fine white scar on one cheek, like a duellist's mark. And a
purpling bruise on his forehead which he kept unconsciously
scratching. He had caught something nasty. Spots were erupting
all over his face.

'I confess . . .' Erskine prompted.

'I didn't –'

The truncheon jabbed again, striking Teddy's collarbone.

'I –'

The pain was so severe, he couldn't even think to speak. Erskine bent down and rapped Teddy's right knee, like a doctor testing for a reflex. It was an explosion of hurt. Teddy screamed and bent over, biting his tongue hard. The pain grew in his knee, seeped into the rest of his body.

'Just confess, and we can use that in evidence against you. That's how it works, sunshine. One more old fart in the world, more or less. Who cares, eh? Just sign on the line, and I'm sure the magistrate will let you off with a right bollocking.'

Erskine did the other knee. Teddy now had matching agonies. The cuffs around his ankles bit as he kicked.

'Temper, temper. Only nancy boys kick, you know.'

Teddy sat up straight, trying not to whimper. Behind Erskine, he thought he saw a face glowing in the dark.

'No need for anything elaborate, Edward. A simple "I did it" will do just as well as a detailed confession. Can you say "I did it"?'

'But I –'

Erskine slapped Teddy's left shin with the truncheon. His knees flared, and new pain joined the old ones.

'You were about to protest your innocence again, weren't you?'

Teddy nodded.

Erskine slapped the other shin. 'Tut tut tut. Naughty naughty. That's cheating. If you say "I *didn't* do it", that's cheating. Not British at all, cheating.'

Erskine straightened up, and licked the truncheon like a little girl being provocative with an ice lolly.

'Lesson number one. It's the words that count, not what you think, not what you mean, not what you feel . . .'

Erskine gobbled the top of his truncheon, giving the leather a quick suck, then took it out of his mouth. A line of spittle stretched and broke, dribbling on the leather.

'I was lying about you getting off easy, you know. Sinful of me to try and entrap a confession out of you that way, but we're all sinners. If you say "I did it", then it's all over, and we throw you in prison for ever. That's all there is to it. Have you ever been to prison?'

Teddy shook his head.

'I thought not. Most people haven't.'

Erskine's grin grew, splitting his face almost from ear to ear. He circled around behind the chair, and talked into Teddy's ear from the back.

'You watch the crappy movies and the TV documentaries, but you don't know what it's like inside. I'll tell you this for nothing, you won't like it, Sunshine.'

Between Erskine's words, Teddy heard the slap of truncheon against palm. He expected a blow to fall every instant, aware of the vulnerability of the back of his neck, the fragility of his skull.

'At your age, you'd be at the bottom of the pile. Prisons are full of bitter, twisted, hard people. All they have in life is making weaker people miserable. And you'd be the weakest person in miles.'

Erskine was breathing hard, excited.

'You might not last a year. They take away your belt and shoelaces and anything sharp you could hurt yourself with, but that just means you have to find some really painful way of topping yourself. You can do it just by swallowing your tongue. Nasty one, that. You puke around your tongue and drown in vomit. You could bash your head against a wall. Takes a lot of grit to do that, to keep on bashing until you've ruptured your brainpan. Forget tunnels or hiding in dustcarts, suicide is the only real way of escaping . . .'

Erskine came round to his front again and, crouching, talked into Teddy's face.

'And to win this wonderful all-expenses paid holiday in HM Hell, all you have to do is say "I did it". You understand?'

Teddy nodded.

Erskine chuckled again. 'Thought you did, darling boy.'

Teddy was not alone with Erskine. In the corner, sitting on a chair like the one he was cuffed to, was the sergeant, Draper. He was the face in the dark. Teddy only saw him when he puffed on his cigarette, the red end flaring and making his face glow for a moment. There was a standing lamp, but it was pointed at Teddy's face. He thought there might be other people around the fabric walls of the tent.

Erskine stood in front of him now. His shirt buttons were undone to the waist, and Teddy saw a white, hairless chest, dotted with spots. He was tapping the bruise on his forehead with the end of his truncheon. Teddy thought the skin might be cracking. Erskine had another bruise, a red cold-sore-like scar, in the valley between his nose and upper lip, shaped like a Hitler moustache.

'So, we understand each other, Edward. My job is to get you to say "I did it". Your job is to try to hold out as long as possible. Because when you lose, it's all over. By the way, you will lose. You can't win. That's how the game works. Shame, really, but there it is.'

It was quiet in the tent, as if the canvas were six feet thick. Teddy spat blood at the ground, coughing.

'Filthy fucker,' Erskine said, cruelly tapping Teddy's shoulder just where it already hurt.

'Say it,' Erskine cooed, mouth up close, close enough to kiss. 'Just for your old Uncle Barry, say it . . .'

Erskine reached into Teddy's lap with his free hand, and pinched his balls, hard. Teddy screamed.

'Bloody racket,' Erskine said, scratching his forehead with a thumbnail. 'Loud enough for Loud Shit, I shouldn't wonder. Real British craftsmanship. No modern electrical equipment wired to the old scrote, dear me, no. No psycho stuff and drugs and disco lights. Nope, just the traditional country-fresh methods that have been handed down from father to son for centuries. Just meat and bone, and the old whopper . . .'

Erskine sucked his truncheon again.

'Seen a lot has the whopper. I killed a Paki with it once. I made him say "I did it", but by then I was enjoying the game so much it would have been a sin to stop. Niggers bleed red like you and me, you know. Quite a surprise. A skull makes a hell of a din when it cracks. Like a gun going off.'

Erskine's bruise was peeling, flakes of skin falling.

'Say it,' Erskine said, from behind, applying the truncheon to Teddy's shoulder again. 'Say "I did it".'

Teddy couldn't say anything. It hurt too much even to think. Draper's face glowed red, like a pantomime demon.

'Say it.'

Whatever he did, Erskine would torture and kill him. In a queer way, Teddy thought it'd be worse for him if he gave in. Erskine enjoyed the game, and would get angry if cheated out of it.

Erskine slipped the truncheon into its sheath, and got to work with his fists. He pummelled the small of Teddy's back, then came around, and began punishing his chest.

'Have you ever seen anyone killed?'

Teddy shook his head.

'I thought so. Not many people have, these days. It's the education system that's lacking. Everyone should see someone killed, even if it's only on video. It wakes you up, makes you understand.'

Erskine's bruise was completely gone, leaving a neat red circle on his forehead. Inset in the raw circle was what looked like a blue tattoo. It was a swastika.

'When I killed the coon, I suddenly understood. It's one thing to know how the world works, another really to understand it. God puts all these wonderful things inside you, inside your head. And it's your job to let them out, to spill them on the ground. If you crack a skull and let the brains out, it's like making an offering. Like going to church.'

Erskine made a knuckly fist and knocked on Teddy's forehead.

'There are wonders in there, waiting to be let out. All the angels, all the devils . . .'

The policeman shoved Teddy's head, tipping him backwards. He felt the chair runners lifting off the ground, and there was nothing under his feet. His centre of gravity shifted, and he felt the chair falling. Erskine shoved again, and Teddy landed hard, his hands pinned under chairlegs, his head rapping against the hard earth. Erskine put his foot on Teddy's chest, and ground in with his heel.

Teddy saw the sagging roof of the marquee, and the pole that held it up. If he bent his head back, he saw the person who'd been standing behind him throughout Erskine's game. It was the black constable. He stood to attention, a line of sweat trailing down from his helmet.

'Give him a boot, Chocky,' Erskine said.

Raine stepped forward and, doubt on his face, kicked Teddy in the head, just above the ear.

'Feeble, Chocky, feeble. Where's that jungle instinct?'

Erskine kicked Teddy in the hip, where it hurt.

'See, give it another go.'

Raine kicked Teddy, harder.

'Magic,' Erskine commented. 'Like riding a bicycle, you never forget once you've got the trick.'

Patches of skin had sloughed off Erskine's bare arms, and he had more tattoos. Nazi insignia, an SS skull surrounded by lightning bolts. He even had a tattooed swastika armband in red, white and black.

'Are you enjoying Uncle Barry's Summer Camp?'

Teddy held still.

'Is everybody happy?'

Teddy looked up. No reaction at all was the best way of surviving.

'We've got a quiet one, Chocky. We'll have to do our best to bring him out of his shell. We can't have our Edward being a wallflower.'

Raine bent down and picked up Teddy's shoulders, bringing him upright. Teddy felt dizzy after his horizontal spell, and his head flopped forwards, chin thumping his chest.

Erskine slapped him to get his attention.

'Wakey wakey.'

Erskine took out his truncheon again.

'Been a funny old day at Dock Green Station,' he said. 'Life's like that, you know. A Paki made a bit of a nuisance of himself. Rum do, it was. Real rum do. We gave him his cuppa char and his sticky bun and took down his statement, then fucking killed the nig-nog bastard with multiple blows to the head. Dear oh dear oh lord, but that was a giggle. Multiple fucking blows to his black old fucking Paki wog nigger coon jigaboo head. As my old sarge used to say, better safe than sorry. They don't have feelings like you and me, you know. Don't have mothers, most of 'em. Don't stand up when they play the national anthem.'

Erskine lashed out, and struck the side of Teddy's head with the truncheon. Teddy felt his ear mashed against his skull, and was sure the bone had broken, that blood was pouring out. The chair tipped to the side, but Raine caught it and kept him upright.

'Say it,' Erskine said, seriously.

Draper had stood up, and walked over. He was still smoking, but his face was red with more than a reflection.

'Steady on, Barry,' he told Erskine. 'Leave some for the lads back at the station.'

'But he's a fucking murderer, sarge.'

Draper shrugged. 'Nobody's perfect. Murderers aren't such a bad lot, you know. Not once you get to know a couple. Lovely singing voices, some of them have.'

Erskine giggled. 'I suppose so,' he said.

'No,' Draper continued, 'there's much worse than murderers. Most murderers you can talk to, have a drink with, go down the dogs with. Murder is an understandable crime. Everybody wants to kill somebody some time.'

Teddy told himself he wouldn't beg for mercy. Draper finished his fag and stubbed it out on Teddy's shoulder. It didn't even hurt much.

'No, if you're talking scum of the earth, you're talking drugs.'

Erskine agreed, nodding.

'Yeah, drugs. That's the worst, Barry. Slimy little shits injecting ten-year-olds with heroin, passing round the crack in kindergarten playgrounds . . .'

Draper took Teddy's shirt collar, and arranged it properly. Then he pulled hard, ripping his shirt open, scattering buttons.

'Search him for drugs, Barry.'

Erskine saluted, and picked up the chair, sliding Teddy off it. He found his feet and hands together, cuffs clattering, and he was dragged along the groundsheet. From this position, he saw the bundle under a canvas sheet, dragged to one side. A pale human arm, ringed with bangles, stuck out. Erskine lifted up the canvas to give Teddy a look, disclosing a couple of boys, throats open and black, bunched together and stacked ready for disposal.

'And here are some I prepared earlier,' Erskine said.

Raine pulled Teddy's body over, making him face upwards.

'Get his belt off and his jeans down, Chocky,' Erskine said. Erskine handed the constable a pair of polythene gloves.

Raine struggled with Teddy's belt, and loosened his trousers. It was difficult, with the chair and the handcuffs, but Raine did his job. Teddy thought this was the lowest it had ever been. Worse than when he was a kid and he'd been spanked on his bare bottom in front of Jenny. He didn't care any more. They couldn't do anything more to him.

'Fuck off,' he said.

Erskine laughed and tugged at the chair, flipping him over, pushing his face to the groundsheet. 'Wrong attitude, Edward. Spread your cheeks now, and don't let out a fart or I'll be giving you a whopper enema.'

Teddy wouldn't have believed there was more pain coming. But this hurt like nothing else. He felt invaded, violated, split apart. Erskine took his time, and was casual about it, rooting around.

'Nothing up here, sarge. Except his brains.'

The policemen laughed. Even Raine.

'The drugs must be on him somewhere,' Draper said, 'or inside him. Sometimes they try to get through by stuffing the drugs into tied condoms and swallowing them. He could have a gutful of cocaine.'

'You want me to search his stomach?'

Raine struggled with the chair and Teddy and Teddy's clothes, rearranging all three into an upright position. Teddy was bleeding from a lot of cuts. He might have had a couple of broken bones, but he was hurting too much to notice.

'I could make the bastard puke,' Erskine suggested, 'and we could sort through what comes up.'

Draper shook his head. 'Just cut him open.'

Erskine delved into a cardboard box, and came up with a serrated Rambo knife.

'We confiscated this from a satisfied customer,' he explained 'Useful little tool. Not up to the whopper, but it'll do the job.'

Erskine grabbed the back of Teddy's hair, and pricked his stomach with the point of the knife. Swastikas were erupting all over his chest like zits. They dripped down from his ears, swarming around his neck, showing up raw on his scalp through the blond fuzz of his cropped hair.

'Barry,' said Raine, speaking for the first time, 'I wouldn't . . .'

Erskine stopped before he thrust, and relaxed his grip, easing away from Teddy. He spread his arms, but didn't drop the knife.

'That's right, Barry,' said a new voice. 'I wouldn't.'

Four

W HATEVER HAD RUN through the village had passed for the moment, leaving creepy calm in its wake. People were standing around, some crying, some stifling hysterical laughter. There were dying fires. Despite the aftermath feel, Paul wasn't convinced the panic was over. This wasn't all that different from the usual hour after a Loud Shit concert. The only thing was that the skunk band weren't due for days. Above, a helicopter circled, lights winking in the sky, blades beating. That made him feel like a specimen under a microscope, observed to see how quickly hostile bacteria would consume him.

Jessica and Syreeta were helping Dolar stand up. The folk singer, not taking much notice of his shotgun wound, still smiled peace at everyone. Ferg was quiet, alert, looking up at the sky.

'They're up there,' he said. 'The Iron Insects.'

Paul knew what he meant, but wasn't sure he was right. He thought the Martian war machine had been a nonrecurring phenomenon, a Sunday-for-one-day-only anomaly. Tonight's monsters would be a different species.

'Someone's up there,' he agreed.

The crowd began to talk to itself. Rumours ran around, trying to explain the collective madness. They were at war, under attack, in a riot, in a dream. Paul was as bewildered as everyone else, but less surprised. Everyone else was catching up with what he'd realized as soon as the war machine stepped out of the trees.

They weren't in Kansas any more.

He had found Ferg, confirmed the evidence of his senses. But that meant little now. Everyone else was seeing things. Different things.

They'd been walking for minutes, apparently without intending to. Paul realized he was going back to the Pottery, the others following him. It was as good a place as any, he supposed. Hazel was locked up tight in the Agapemone, and nothing he could do would secure her release until she was ready to come out or Jago was ready to let her free. Just now, he could not even remember her normal face; he either saw the blank stranger he'd glimpsed in the chapel, or got her mixed up with her sister, imagining Patch's huge glasses blotting out Hazel's distinctive eyes.

People got out of their way. Dolar was trying to get loose of his supporters, but was not steady enough on his feet to keep going without them. Paul guessed Salim, the Asian kid, was quietly going crazy, meditating himself into nothingness to avoid what was going on outside his skull. Ferg, a natural paranoid, was looking around, barely suppressing excitement, seeing invaders in every shadow. Somehow, this group had latched on to him and elected him leader. Ferg was top sergeant, the rest cannon fodder. He didn't know what to do with them, any more than he knew what to do with himself. The only person he'd met today who had any apparent idea what was going on was Susan, and she was back in the Manor House with Jago's Brethren, refusing to stick her neck out. These were hard times indeed if he could think of a woman he first met while she was overdosing as a beacon of common sense.

There was a burned-out car in the road. The asphalt was thick with bodies. From the groaning and crying, Paul assumed they were all hurt or drunk, but he saw unmoving lumps among them and realized – with a queerly detached shock – they were the dead. The corpses looked like people lying down. He'd never seen a dead person before, and they were less of a jolt than the war machine or Bike Boy Ben. He'd always admitted the dead were a part of the world, laid out in rows on the news as a foreign correspondent covered the latest atrocity. Now the atrocity was underfoot.

If the shotgun man had been less hysterical, Paul might have seen Dolar get his head blown off in close-up. Wouldn't that have been a first?

'Unprecedented,' he murmured.

Ferg's ears pricked up, expecting words of wisdom from a fearless leader, but Paul had nothing more to say.

One of the wounded coughed black stuff and shook, turning into one of the dead.

'What happened?' Jessica asked. No one had an answer.

There were dead people at the sides of the roads, without an obvious mark on them, lives squeezed out in the crush. At least

Hazel had been saved from that. Where she was, she was safe from blind fate, even if she could be subject, in his imagination, to calculated malice.

Outside the Pottery, Paul found the child he had spoken to earlier. He was dirtied and drained, sitting on the verge. Another recruit, Paul thought. The boy was clutching a small tool, like a miner's pick.

'Jeremy?'

The kid recognized him, but didn't have the strength to change his dull expression.

'Come inside,' he said, including Jeremy. 'At least we can get washed. Have a coffee.'

Stepping through the gate, which had been opened, was like walking away from a battlefield. Paul had wondered if the rioters would swarm through all the houses, breaking crockery, looting, smashing furniture. But the Pottery was left alone. He turned on the lights in the showroom and saw undisturbed tables and shelves, pots gleaming, slightly dusty, in order, prices marked. The lawn was rutted from last night, and his desk still stood in the middle of the grass, abandoned.

'Find some clothes for the kid to wear,' Paul told Ferg, 'and get him to take a shower. He smells like he's had an accident.'

Ferg looked a question.

'He's okay, he's one of us.'

The boy was satisfied. Paul reminded himself that, although Ferg was paying attention to him, that didn't mean the mohican was any less loony than the rest.

'The bathroom's on the landing, first door opposite the stairs.'

Ferg took Jeremy inside, and more lights came on in the house. Syreeta and Jessica sat Dolar down on an old wicker chair on the verandah, and he started to feel his wound, ouching profusely. Paul saw Hazel's wasp trap was clogged like an insect Black Hole of Calcutta.

He went into the hall, and heard the shower running upstairs.

'There's a T-shirt up here that'll fit the kid,' Ferg shouted down, 'and a pair of shorts that could be belted on to him.'

Paul picked up the telephone, not even knowing whom to call, and heard nothing in the earpiece. He rattled the receiver and tried again. Nothing. So much for outside help. A noise as big as Alder made must be noticed. The fire brigade would be back, and police, ambulances, media.

'We sit tight and wait for the locksmith.'

Out the window, he saw Syreeta bending over Dolar, un-picking his shirt from his shallow wound. He looked up the hill, at the spot where the Martian war machine had appeared. Trees stood unwaving on the horizon. He wondered if all this were a curse that befell those who got too wrapped up with petty problems. Too worried about your thesis, your toothache, your girlfriend? Well, try worrying about *this* . . .

Salim sat cross-legged at the edge of the verandah, staring out at the garden. Paul stepped through the back door and watched Syreeta work. She was taking tiny chunks of shot out of Dolar's shoulder with her fingernails, and he was sucking in breaths with each plucked fragment. In the bathroom upstairs, there was a pair of tweezers he should get for her.

There was a commotion off around the side of the house, and he felt the ground shaking again. He realized, a paralysing twinge shooting from his tooth, that he'd fouled up as a field commander and forgotten to shut the front gate.

Salim stood up on the steps of the verandah, and half turned. Paul just had enough time to identify the noise as hoofbeats before a horse, weighed down by a rider, careered around the house into the garden and reared up, hooves fully a foot above Salim's head. The animal, its rider clinging, breathed steam and kicked the air. Salim caught a blow with his head, and staggered against the wall. Paul tried to hold Salim up, but missed getting a hold on him. The boy, a red dent in his face, tumbled down, legs kicking. The horse's forelegs clumped down, raising divots from the lawn, and foam fell from its mouth. Paul saw the rider was a woman, hair matted with twigs and flowers, skin greenish in the odd light, unripe-apple breasts bare, eyes golden lamps. A little girl clung to her from behind. The green woman was riding bareback and without reins, wearing only the last of a pair of jeans, barbed knees lodged in the horse's flank, hands twisted in the animal's mane. She wasn't a natural thing.

Jessica was screaming, hands stuffed into her mouth. Salim stopped kicking, dent in his head filled with greyish stuff. His eyes rolled up and showed only white. Only their twitching suggested he was alive.

The horsewoman brought her animal under control and patted it. Paul saw her fingers were too long and triple jointed. Her face was a thin triangle, with a pointed chin and stretched cheeks, a

thick widow's peak V-ing into her forehead. She looked like a
large, angry wood nymph, or Herne the Hunter's nagging wife.

Ferg was behind Paul in the door.

'Fuck,' he said.

'Too right,' Paul echoed.

'Jerm,' boomed a voice that sounded out as if through a giant
bassoon. 'Jerm!'

The kid was there, too, a shrunken adult in floppy Hazel clothes,
clinging to Ferg's legs.

Jerm? Jeremy?

Something large and unwieldy came around the house and
shambled towards the verandah. The horsewoman pulled her
animal's mane, and they stepped back a few yards to make room
for the thing.

'Jerm, Jerm, Swallowing Sperm.'

The Green Man was as tall as his wife on her horse, and twice
as broad.

'Jesus fuck!' Ferg said.

The Green Man stretched his branchy arms, foliage rustling,
and roared out rage, his chest-bark splitting as his lungs expanded,
dark-green sap trickling. Ripe ears of corn grew under his arms
like plague buboes. His groin was thickly leafed, a greenwood
spear jutting out of the vegetation. Cactus spines and potato eyes
dotted his calves, tentacles waved from his head, dripping slime.
He looked like the illegitimate offspring of the Jolly Green Giant
and a *Dr Who* rubber-suit monster.

'Daddy's here,' the Green Man shouted, and Jeremy trembled,
one arm around Ferg, the other around Paul.

'Don't let Daddy hurt me,' the child begged. 'Please, please. . .'

Paul did not know if he had enough grit to face this, to see
it through. The Green Man's penis bent like a homing aerial,
then pointed straight at Jeremy's head. It swelled, green veins
thickening.

'Far out, man,' Dolar said, standing up, stepping off the
verandah. 'Look at all the leaves and flowers . . .'

The folk singer stood next to the Green Man, tentatively
extending a hand to touch his vine-covered side.

'It's Swamp Thing, man,' Dolar said. Paul might have known
the singer would be a comics reader.

Even Salim's eyes were not moving now. He was leaking red
and grey on to the flagstones.

'Come away,' Paul told Dolar. 'Slowly.'

Dolar smiled. The Green Man had taken root, tiny tendrils from his splayed feet digging into the earth. But he was none the less dangerous. He fetched Dolar a swipe with one branch, and the singer staggered away, falling first to his knees, then to his face.

'So much for trying to communicate with it,' Ferg said. 'We've got to rig up some electricity, or get some fire going. That should see it off.'

Paul wasn't sure the boy's suggestions were practical.

'Come to Daddy, Jerm.'

Paul remembered what Jeremy had said about his Daddy when they had first met. 'Daddy's penis got funny . . . Daddy tried to hurt me with his penis . . . Daddy put his hand right through Jethro.' That was the last time he discounted anything a child told him.

'Do what Daddy says,' the horsewoman said, her voice musical, lyrelike. 'It'll all be fine.'

'We'll be a family again.'

Jeremy, unconvinced, was clinging very tight.

Five

WE PASS THIS WAY but once, an ex-SAS training sergeant had told him years ago during a four-week course, *so if there's anyone you want to shoot in the head, do so at your first opportunity. No member of this department has ever been prosecuted for murder or manslaughter. You make a mistake, you can always say sorry.* The gist of Sergeant Parry's lecture on Skill at Arms was, there was no point in employing a gun as a threat. On television, anyone who had a gun pointed at him put his hands up and obeyed orders. In real life, the mere sight of a gun makes a surprisingly high proportion of people react like a claustrophobe locked in a broom cupboard, so you have to shoot them anyway to keep them quiet. *People are arseholes, don't expect them to act in their best interests.*

Discounting Badmouth Ben, Lytton had never shot anyone. In Canada, he hadn't even been issued with a gun. And on this assignment, the most he'd got to do with the Browning, before last night, was take it out once a month and, following carefully the instructions in the manual, clean it. Now, he was making Parry – who'd been knee-capped with a Black and Decker drill by the Provos in Belfast and succumbed later to a trauma-induced coronary – turn in his grave by breaking his first rule. He was employing the pistol as a threat.

'Draper,' he said, gun steady, 'have Young Adolf step back.'

The detective nodded to Erskine, who looked like an illustrated Nazi, almost all of his exposed body covered with swastika tattoos, a nine-inch-blade hovering before Teddy's bare chest. If Lytton was going to have to shoot anyone in the head, it would be Erskine. He had already drawn the slide, jacking the first of thirteen rounds into the chamber, pulling back the hammer. He was textbook-ready to kill.

Erskine stood over Teddy, knife in his hand. In the gloomy tent, Lytton couldn't see the policeman's blue eyes, but he thought the madman would probably force the issue before standing back.

Don't bother with any of that Roy Rogers faeces about warning shots or firing for the legs or hands, Parry had insisted. *If you absolutely must talk to the bastard afterwards, give him a bullet in the gut or groin. Take my word for it, he'll be only too pleased to give away all his H-bomb secrets if you promise to put him out of his misery. Otherwise, the safest bet is between the eyes or, if you're a wobbly shot, slap in the chest. With the kind of overkill cannons you lads get issued, six inches either way around the heart doesn't matter much.*

Erskine looked at Lytton, smiling, swastikas crinkled in the lines of his face. He was the image of the Beast of Belsen, his own fantasies shaping him. Jago's constituency must be spreading around the whole village. The state of Teddy suggested Erskine had been beating the boy to death. There were already a couple of corpses in the tent.

Lytton focused on Erskine, aiming the Browning at his chest, but was still aware of Raine and Draper at the extremes of his vision. If he took Erskine, the others would come for him. As policemen, they were trained for these situations. He'd shoot the black constable first, then the overweight sergeant.

Don't think about it, do it.

Erskine spread his hands and stepped back, away from Teddy, out of the circle of lamplight.

'Drop the pig-sticker.'

Erskine shrugged and tossed the knife to the groundsheet. Then he took another step back, canvas behind him shaking a little.

'Not that far,' Lytton said, beckoning with his left hand.

Don't use a gun to make gestures or point at things. That's what you have an extra hand for.

Erskine halted. His truncheon dangled from his belt by its thong.

It wasn't the department's stated policy to shoot British policemen. Then again, it wasn't the Avon and Somerset Constabulary's stated policy to torture and kill teenagers.

'Teddy?'

The boy, slumped and cuffed, bruised and bleeding, groaned. He was still conscious, which would make it easier.

'Fuck, James,' he said.

'Uncuff him,' Lytton said to Raine.

'He's got the keys,' the policeman said, jabbing a thumb towards Erskine.

'Well, get them.'

Raine fumbled with a pouch on Erskine's belt, and the white policeman giggled.

'Careful, Chocky, don't get too intimate,' Erskine said. 'I don't want to catch coon AIDS.'

Raine, whose face was studiedly devoid of expression, flashed angry for a moment, then swallowed it.

'You realize you're interfering with officers in the course of their duty?' Draper said. 'That's a serious offence.'

Raine had Teddy's feet uncuffed, and was bending under the chair to get to his hands. It was awkward for him.

'Possession of an offensive weapon,' Erskine added. 'That's a good one.'

'Breach of the peace.'

'Conspiracy to assist the escape of an apprehended suspect.'

'Blue murder.'

Teddy was free. He stood up carefully, wincing. Tonight, everyone had their bruises.

'The cuffs,' Lytton said. 'Use them, Teddy.'

The boy took the handcuffs from Raine.

'Arrange them around the maypole.'

The central support pole of the marquee was sunk at least a foot into the ground. Lytton had the three policemen hold hands crosswise in a circle around it, and then had them cuffed together. They were satisfactorily cramped, and Erskine was making exaggerated faces at being so close to Raine. 'There's a bloody monkey smell here,' he said. Raine looked away, pretending not to be involved.

'You are making a very big mistake, Mr Lytton,' Draper said. 'Charges will be brought.'

Lytton held up a flap of canvas, and Teddy stepped through. Without saying goodbye, he followed. He'd managed to get through the scene without shooting anyone, and he levered the hammer down. *Remember, no one was ever killed by a dead person.* Of course, Sergeant Parry hadn't met Badmouth Ben. Or conceived of a world with Anthony William Jago in it.

Outside Checkpoint Charlie was a bonfire. A group of kids sat around it, passing a foot-long joint between them. The smell of marijuana wafted towards the drug-squad tent.

Teddy was bent over double, feeling his pains.

'That Erskine's gone fucking mental,' he said.

'So has everybody,' Lytton said.

The police car parked by the roadside was locked. *It's for killing people, not hammering in nails, so don't use it for any purpose for which it was not intended.* Lytton smashed the front driver-side window with the butt of the Browning.

'Vandal,' one of the dope smokers shouted.

'Keep the countryside tidy,' said a girl.

He could hear a woman's voice on the police radio, and bored officers exchanging CB codes and traffic complaints. Lytton jammed the gun into his waistband and got the door open. Sliding on to the glass-strewn front seat, he pulled the radio handset from the dashboard. He found the send button, and pressed it.

'Hello, Achelzoy?'

The woman answered, 'Who's that then?'

'My name's Lytton. I'm in Alder, Checkpoint Charlie. I'm using Sergeant Draper's radio.'

'What are you doing that for? Put Ian on. He's well past report time. I was going to put a query on his sheet.'

'I'm at the fish-and-chip van now, Stace,' interrupted a male voice, 'two cod and chips and a spring roll, right?'

'Hello, Achelzoy?'

'Still here, where's Ian and Barry?'

'Listen, this is important. Who am I talking with?'

'WPC Stacy Cotterill.'

'Who's the senior officer present?'

'Um . . . me? Ian's in Alder, and Sergeant Sloman is on the chip run. There's only Greg Dunphy otherwise, and he's very junior.'

'Ms Cotterill, can you get hold of Alistair Garnett?'

'Who's he when he's home?'

'Fishcake, sausage in batter and chips for Greggie?'

'Garnett. He's been liaising with you. Your station has been a message drop. For IPSIT.'

'Eyesight?'

'Fancy some curry sauce, Stace?'

'My name is James Lytton. I'm working for Garnett. In Alder.'

'Sorry, don't mean a thing.'

'. . . motorway tailback to Shepton Mallet,' said a new voice, 'and we're stuck in it . . .'

'Ms . . .'

'Miss.'

'Miss Cotterill, things are out of hand here.'

'Don't I know it? Complaints all night about the noise. But we've promised not to go on site. They're just kids, and it's only for a week.'

'Mission accomplished at the chippie, Stace. Back in five mins. Put the kettle on. Ten-four, heh heh.'

'. . . be here all bloody night . . .'

'Sergeant Sloman?' Lytton tried.

'Who's this?' the chip runner replied. 'Get off the line.'

'Call Garnett, and tell him to send in the cavalry. If Jago isn't shut down soon, this will blow up.'

'This one of they terrorist hoaxes?'

'Where's Ian?'

'. . . roads are impassable, everyone's gone whacko . . .'

There was a whine, and the radio choked to death. Lytton spun across the frequencies, but couldn't pick up anything. He hoped he'd started the machinery working, even if it was clanking. At the least, Sloman should send a car to Alder to investigate his unauthorized use of the radio.

'Any luck?' Teddy asked.

Lytton shrugged. 'No idea.'

'What's bloody happening?'

'A deluge, Teddy.'

The dope smokers were up and dancing, moving slowly like deep-sea divers. Two girls picked up one laughing man and, after three good swings, dumped him into the bonfire. He didn't stop laughing and rolled off the logs, damping the flames. Several dope smokers had large scorch marks on their clothes. Two guys were rolling another colossal joint, paying minute attention as if they were assembling a bomb.

Checkpoint Charlie was shaking, the point of the central pole wavering, guyropes snapping. The pole lifted up and slowly fell. 'Timberrrr,' the dope smokers shouted, clapping as the canvas puffed out and fell in on itself, a wriggling centre showing where the policemen, hands entwined, were struggling. They might be free of the pole, but the heavy canvas, pinned to the ground by stakes, would keep them where they were for a few minutes.

Lytton knew he'd come to the end of another rope. He would have to look after himself, and whoever else he could manage, until help turned up. Teddy didn't have to be told. They walked away into the milling crowds, deeper on to the festival site. The Browning was uncomfortable against his hip. Everywhere, there were people: sleeping, talking, dancing, scrapping. It was late, but there were hours to go before the dawn. Hours.

Six

JEREMY WAS HIDING behind the two young men, the normal one and the one with the punk haircut. The goodness of the soil rose through Maskell's tubers, feeding him strength. This summer the topsoil was baked dry, but there was always goodness a few feet down. When the land was sick, it was a passing, surface thing.

'Get away from my son,' he told the men. They didn't move, despite his order. He'd have to teach them a lesson, put them in their place.

His knob pointed at the flesh of his seed. If Jeremy defied him further, Maskell would have to lay about him with his quirt. The memory of a transforming shock thrilled in his knob, reminding him of the moment when the spark of the land had passed into him, setting him on his course.

His woman was behind him, their daughter with her, up on Fancy. The family's animals were a part of it. Together, they were Maskell Farm. The land was the most important thing. All served the land. Farm and family, custodians of the soil.

Jeremy pushed past the men, and stood on his own, wobbly on his feet. 'I'm not afraid of the dark any more, Daddy. There's no Evil Dwarf.'

Maskell was pleased that nonsense was over.

'I killed him.'

Maskell bent his head, bark of his neck splitting. 'Come to me, my flesh.'

Jeremy was on the steps of the sunken verandah. The others were holding back, hiding under the eaves of the house. Those he had put aside lay unmoving in their places, one on flagstones, the other on grass.

'It's all right, Jeremy,' Sue-Clare said, voice like a flute. 'We'll be together.'

Jeremy looked silly in a baggy T-shirt that came to his knees and a pair of shorts cinched tight with a belt marked like a tape measure. His hair was wet and he had his hand behind his back, concealing something. Boys were like that – he'd been like that – hiding fat frogs and curious stones and toy soldiers. Maskell smiled, the wood of his face shifting.

The normal man stepped out of his place and said, 'You have a real problem. Something is happening to you . . .'

The man didn't understand anything.

'Something is happening to us all . . . maybe we can get help . . .'

'Jerm, don't listen to this clod, come here and give Daddy a hug.'

Jeremy took a few steps. Maskell felt his son's body warmth. He bent down and made a basket of his arms, sweeping Jeremy up in it.

'There there,' he said, elated, justified, complete.

'*Dig dig dig dig dig dig dig dig,*' Jeremy shouted, taking a sharp implement from behind his back and, with a vicious slice, embedding it in Maskell's chest.

The alien vegetable had the boy in its grip, but Jeremy stabbed it with his pick. Ferg heard the blade's thudding chunk, saw the gusher of green sap splash the kid's face and chest. A roar was born inside the alien and grew, making its entire body reverberate like a giant musical instrument, finally bursting forth from moss-moustached mouth and knothole nostrils. It was a single note, drawn out and echoing. It filled the garden and rose to the skies, to where the invasion fleet must be swarming, locked in an invisible orbit, sensors aimed at Alder.

Jeremy struggled with the invader, trying to tip himself out of its embrace. Paul, there to catch him, fell under the weight of the child, scrabbling away from reaching arms. Ferg dashed forwards to help and pull Jeremy away. They ran along the side of the house, but the alien woman was there on her horse, blocking their path.

Paul stood, and the alien bashed him. The blow didn't strike properly, or else he'd have been as out of it as Dolar or Salim, but Paul reeled under the wooden fist, and fell on the lawn.

Aliens were all over the place. All kinds of aliens. The Iron Insects had been the spearhead. Syreeta and Jessica were

standing back and watching, traitors to the human race egging
the invaders on to victory.

Ferg grabbed the horse's mane. The animal waved its heavy
head like a hammer, and jumped its forelegs off the ground. The
alien woman, attached parasitically to the horse by suckers on
her knees, had her steed under control. She reached and took
Ferg's throat, pulling him off his feet.

The alien woman had him up, side-saddle, before her, and her
twiggy fingers grew around him. He clawed her arm, shredding
green and brown layers. She smiled, horribly beautiful, skin the
colour of a cooking apple, fine antennae wisping up from her
eyebrows into her hair. Her golden eyes shone, alive with liquid
intelligence. The horse couldn't support three weights, and sank
to its knees. Ferg picked a finger away from his throat, and it
snapped like a carrot. The alien woman sang pain, and he was
dropped.

There was an alien child too, covered in cactus spines, hair
a tussle of pampas grass. The creature was grappling with
Jeremy, pressing him to the ground, pummelling him. Ferg
felt a slamming force between his shoulders, and knew the alien
woman had brought him down. It was no use. They were here,
and they were taking over.

Hannah was on top, scratching with point-ended fingers, calling
him names, trying to get past his hands to his face. Her fingers
had become long, sharp pencils, and she stabbed the backs of
his hands with them, wanting to get at his eyes. Daddy always
warned Hannah about her pencils, saying she'd have someone's
eye out one day.

'Jesus makes us shine with a clear, pure light,' Hannah sang,
'like a little candle burning in the night . . .'

The Evil Dwarf had been easy. He wasn't actual. But Jeremy's
sister would never give up, never go away. Sisters didn't. She'd
sworn a pact with Lisa Steyning to get revenge for the time he'd
told on them when they set fire to newspapers in the barn. With
terrible sisterly cruelty, she'd bided her time, plotting. Now
she'd have her revenge.

'. . . in this world of darkness, you and me must shine . . .'

Hands over his eyes, he felt pencil leads stabbing. Mummy
and Daddy made strange noises; everyone else shouted and
screamed.

'. . . you in your small corner, and I in mine.'

Hannah got a good grip on one of his wrists and wrenched hard. His hand came away, and he saw with one eye. His sister smiled down at him, pretty flowers in her hair, sharp chips of wood for her teeth, a thin beard of spines around her throat.

'Gotcha!' she said.

Paul tried to get up, but his tooth wouldn't let him. It had come alive when the Green Man hit him, and now seemed to be a quarter of the size of his body, a solid lump of disabling agony. It hurt like hell, no matter what he did; if he moved, if he tried to stand, the pain multiplied tenfold. The tooth was bigger than his head, weighing him down like a cartoon anvil, a million ants eating away inside the enamel, acid delicately scraping out the nerve. He pressed the ground with his hands, and screamed as the throb expanded. The pain got worse as he stood, but he climbed over it, shutting the explosion behind closed eyes. Weak, he sagged against the wall of the house, and let his eyes fall open.

The Green Man stood tall, hand-tipped branches stretching. As the pain burst inside his mouth, Paul saw the face of the farmer inside the wooden cocoon. He was the puzzled, buried and forgotten seed that had sprouted the monster, bleeding from the pick stuck into his chest. A moment of complete darkness, with the man screaming inside it, it passed, the Green Man instantly growing and reforming over him. Paul realized he knew the man inside the greenery. Maskell had come to the Pottery to replace a Mike Bleach coffee cup, one of a set, that had been broken. He was offhand and squirearchical, but his wife had been pleasant.

That pretty woman, in dark glasses with a navel-revealing tied blouse, was the horseback huntress now, Paul realized. Jeremy and the junior monster grappling with him were their children.

'Maskell,' he said, trying to reach through the shell.

The Green Man ignored him, continuing his yell. There was a scrum in the garden, with Jeremy underneath his transformed sister, and Ferg underneath the boy's mother, all four of them scrambled together. The horse that had hooved Salim down stood by, easing up from its knees. Paul bit on his tooth and dark truth flooded back for a moment. Pain cut through the illusion like a knife. He saw the troubled farmer, lost in himself, blood in his chest hair, clothes gone in tatters.

He ran past the Green Man and hauled Jeremy out from under everyone. The girl scratched his hands, but he kicked her away. The Green Woman stood up, pushing Ferg aside, and her daughter ran to her, arms twining around her waist. They looked at each other, each with a child clinging to them, spies contemplating an exchange of hostages. He wasn't giving Jeremy up. He'd yielded too much ground. It was time to win something back.

'Sue-Clare?' he said, hoping he remembered her name right.

He had. The Green Woman wrinkled her brow, arrowlines appearing around her widow's peak. Her eyes were unreadable nuts of pure gold. Paul bit again, and saw for a moment the streaked, dirty face of the woman he remembered. She wasn't as far gone as her husband.

'You don't have to be like this.'

The Green Woman straightened up, daughter still clinging, and looked to Maskell. She moved with birdlike grace, turning her head with each slight change of eyeline, shifting back her shoulders when she lifted her hands. A golden tear dripped down her cheek.

Mummy had gone funny, but Jeremy was still scared of her. Daddy had changed her. She wasn't all right yet. Daddy wanted to get him, even more than the Evil Dwarf had wanted to get him. Daddy didn't want to eat his brain, but to make Jeremy like him. Once, he'd heard Daddy tell Mummy, 'Thank God I didn't grow up like my father.' Jeremy remembered Grandpa as a strict old man with a white moustache, who insisted on polished shoes and done-up top buttons. Daddy wasn't like that. It was only fair, if Daddy hadn't had to be like his father, that Jeremy not have to be like Daddy. He hid behind Paul.

It was time to end this. Maskell heaved his chest, forcing out the spike stuck into it, and spat the tool away. The mouthlike wound closed as soon as the thing was gone. His women were letting him down, and he would have to step in. It would be painful, but a lesson would be learned. In the end, everyone would be in their place. His knees straining and creaking, he stumped towards his son. The normal man turned, and Jeremy darted behind him again, his back to Sue-Clare. They had Jeremy and the normal man pinned down between them.

'No supper, ever,' Maskell said.

The strength of the land filled him. He only needed his family about him to be complete.

'No videos, no books, no comics.'

The normal man was weak, incomplete. He wouldn't fight.

'No sleeping with Jethro, no pocket money.'

Hannah was a good girl, like her mother. She did as he said, and always took her quirting when she she stepped out of her place. Jeremy was a troublemaking child, always refusing to do what was best.

The punk was standing next to the normal man, Jeremy in the middle. One or the other would do as an example. Maskell was a farmer. He raised crops, and cut them down. Giving death was as much a part of what he did as giving life. He'd sown his seed; now was the time to reap his harvest, to separate wheat from chaff.

Chaff was kids with silly haircuts and torn clothes, snarly faces and scarred knuckles. Kids who knew their place, but never stayed in it. Kids from the cities who poured into the village and shat over the land.

Maskell stood over the three and put his hands on them, pushing the normal man and the punk aside like curtains. He raised a foot and pressed Jeremy down with it, crushing his son to the earth. Jeremy screamed and struggled, but was held fast in his loving father's grasp.

'Now, Jerm,' Maskell said, hand growing around the punk, 'for a lesson. This is what happens to people who don't know their place, to people who don't respect the land.'

His hand had grown completely around the boy's head, leaving slitlike interstices for eyes, nose and mouth. The absurd coxcomb of red hair jutted out through the top of Maskell's fist. The normal man backed away, Sue-Clare's slender and sinewy arms wrapped around him to keep him out of this. The boy screamed, eyes wide. Maskell joined voice with the boy, taking up the scream, turning it into a yell of triumph, calling to the earth to accept sacrifice. Strength flowed down his arm, filling the cage his hand had become. Tubers twined around his head-sized fist, covering the boy's eyes and mouth, leaves swarming thickly. The leaves puffed out where the boy was screaming. Tubers probed the boy's skin, but didn't dig in, didn't burrow. They crept along close to the face, feelers spreading out to make a flesh-and-wood mask that enclosed the boy's head perfectly.

'Don't!' shouted the normal man.

Outsiders were a menace, deadly as a blight, destroying crops and livestock. Danny Keough had been right about that. Each year, more and more outsiders poured into the village, spreading polluting shit, corrosive foolishness. It was only proper that an outsider feed the earth, help repair the damage done through the years.

He held a complete life in his hand, and knew that was actual power, the power of life and death. Maskell's hand grew tight, and his grip began to constrict.

Seven

ALTHOUGH THE GLASS panels at either side were blown, the great door of the Agapemone was still locked, and Taine would have the keys. Fuck this for a game of toy soldiers, Susan thought, jamming her forefinger into the large keyhole, working the tumblers with a *push*. She overdid it, and pulled her fingers away quickly, avoiding the slow explosion of broken metal and wood that burst from the lock. Might as well finish the job, she thought, popping the hingepins and butting her head towards the door. It fell outwards and tobogganed down the steps. Cooler night air swept around her, and she felt a release from the pressure cooker of the Manor House. Jago was about unconsciously to expel her from his sphere of influence, a whale shrugging off a pilot fish. That suited her fine, and she felt the mindwind build up behind her, riffling her clothes against her back, streaming her hair around her cheeks.

The garden of the Agapemone was pandemonium. Splits had opened in the earth and disgorged implike clouds of flies. The insects swarmed among the people, clustering on bodies like parasitical growths. Some were suffering the torments of the damned, some experienced the raptures of the blessed. Close to the house, Jago's fantasies were the strongest, the most dangerous. Things were moving like moles under the ground.

She turned back to the hallway. Karen stood by the stairs, staring at her and seeing a fallen angel. Earlier, the girl had doubted Jago, but Susan's little display of third-degree psychokinesis and children's-party prestidigitation had tipped her back towards belief in Beloved. Nobody loves you when you're a witch.

'Coming?' Susan asked. 'Going?'

'Staying,' the Sister said.

'Your choice, Karen.'

'Share Love.'

Susan shrugged. 'Look after yourself.'

Walking away, Susan had to fight the compulsion to break into a jog, then a run. Then to hurl herself blindly into the night, until she collapsed from exhaustion, as far as possible away from Jago. What the Brethren had been saying was true. These were the Last Days, the cork was about to pop. The whole golden dream would go up in flames and either self-destruct or spread itself across the face of the earth.

The garden pond was a stretch of glittering crystal. A girl Susan had never seen was lying by it, staring at her broken reflection, stroking the surface, tearing her hands on jagged edges. Ribbons of blood rolled along faults, clustering about the crushed pondweed. There was someone under the pond, trapped with the goldfish, one hand stuck out like that of the Lady in the Lake, fingers waving, sometimes making a straining fist.

These were isolated cases, surrounded and outweighed by the tired, stoned, crazed and forgotten hordes. Many were sprawled asleep under blankets or sleeping bags, or stretched out, exchanging dope-fuelled rambles. Beside the noise of their conversation and the various muted strains of self-made music, she was picking up a whisper of mental static that washed around in her head, tickling away at her permanent migraine.

She picked her way between bodies. No one had been hurt here, but she sensed pain in the village, black spots she knew meant death.

A group of kids were chasing a ball of blue flame around the flower beds, sometimes catching it and tossing it like a frisbee. One of them had an ass's tail dangling from a split in his jeans, and donkey ears.

By the Gate House, she found James. He was with the boy he'd told to get out of the village. He hadn't managed to save even one soul either.

'Susan,' he said, 'thank God you're okay.'

'Am I?'

She saw the flash of despair in his face, and read his thought that she had cracked on him.

'I'm sorry,' she said. 'I've had too much to dream tonight, you know? Jago's fucking everything in sight. I mean that most sincerely, folks.'

'It's chaos all over,' James said. 'There must be dozens dead.'

Teddy coughed and bent over. He was badly hurt, nasty bruises on his face and hands.

'What happened to him?'

'Ask a policeman,' he said. 'I've tried to get word to Garnett.'

The blue fireball bounced in the rutted driveway, and the ass-boy leaped past them to catch it, dribbling it like a basketball and taking a shot at the face of one of his friends.

'It'll be dawn soon,' James said.

'You hope.'

Eight

Inside FERG'S head, things were tight. The aliens barged into the school disco just as the smooch track started. Ferg was dancing with Jessica, getting a hand on her bum for the first time, when three of them sat at a table nearby. They had blank faces and zipless leather jackets, dark glasses like shields. As they passed the brown-paper-wrapped bottle between them, he saw their little fingers didn't bend. Jessica's hands were climbing his back as the number got worked up, and he was tongue-kissing her. Fourteen and thirteen and they were only on tongues. Ferg was getting desperate. Everyone he knew did it, or said they did. Jessica was already well covered. He felt the points of her breasts against the Sex Pistols T-shirt he'd got down the market. The aliens were making comments. Since he started having his hair in a mohican, he'd been getting a lot of comments. Use yer head for a loo brush? Big heap medicine, ugh! Think you're hard, do you? Jessica didn't notice the aliens. He wiped her hair back from one ear, and licked her neck. His tongue froze as he saw what he'd uncovered. She didn't have an ear, just a round hole covered by thin, veined, vibrating membrane. Her hand pushed his face away, all her fingers bent but the little one. She shoved him, laughing like a back-masked message. The aliens caught him, pulling him off the dance floor, dragging him through the push-bar exit into the fish-and-old-newspapers-smelling alley by the club. Two of the aliens pinned him to a wall while the third punched him in the face, chest and belly. As the alien's fists went in, his face started to slip, wax mask cracking, peeling away from his lizard skin. Gristle in Ferg's nose broke, and he was wheezing through bloody snot, tasting blood trickle into his throat. While aliens beat the piss out of him, Jessica stood by the exit, watching, thoughtlessly picking patches of skin off her arms, rubbing her itching scales. The aliens holding his shoulders dropped him, and he slumped down hard, doubling up as he puked thin gruel through his ruined nose. The aliens had lead-weighted moon boots under their grey jeans, and they kicked him while he was down . . .

In the pain swirl, he felt his cheekbones crushed, his jaw clamped tightly shut. He was cooped up in Dolar's van, trying to drive, but the dope-smoke between his face and the windscreen was thick as the atmosphere on Venus. He'd been on beer and wine and gear for days, and his body wasn't working properly. His tongue, too large in his mouth, flopped like wet leather. There was a vile taste leaking from his tongue, but his sense of smell was dead and gone. An ache in the small of his back clawed its way up his spine, boring under his shoulderblades, settling around his neck like a collar. He clung to the steering wheel as if it were the edge of a cliff, fingernails torn and bloody. Dolar sang, Jessica complained, Mike Toad told foul jokes, Syreeta criticized, Pam giggled, and Salim, usually quiet, shrieked in agony. Ferg leaned forwards, smoke parting before his face, and got close to the glass, trying to make out the road. The van rolled on, gobbling up white lines. Outside, the smoke was just as thick, although Ferg could see the taillights of the next car winking in the white-grey cloud. They were pressing the upper edge of the speed limit and the van's capabilities, but, bumper to bumper with speeding vehicles, Ferg couldn't slow down. The van was like the middle carriage between two belching steam engines, rushing along the rails towards a bridge that might or might not be standing over a chasm. The cassette player was broken, spewing out loops of brown tape and mangling the theme from *Easy Rider*. Tape was bunching around Ferg's knees, writhing like a worm. Ferg had a bad nosebleed, blood streaming around his mouth. The pressure inside the van was building, and he heard the sea in his ears, pounding brutally against shingles. The sea sound rose, drowning out the others in the van. Ferg bit his tongue, trying to feel something as the breakers became a painful roar. The smoky atmosphere pressed on the sides of his head, and Ferg felt his inner ear inflate like a balloon. The speedometer ground to its fullest extent and broke. The van was bumped from behind, pushed into the car ahead. The pain in his ears was a constant explosion. Something burst, and silence flooded into his head. Liquid trickled down from his earholes . . .

His ears and nose were clogged, as if plugged with gritty wax. Jessica sat cross-legged on the other side of their fire, mouth opening and closing silently like a goldfish's. His paperback *Dune* was burning in with the scavenged firewood, cover shrinking, pages blackening one by one to ash. Jessica had a three-pointed fork stuck over the fire. Fat worms wriggled like live bait on each of the prongs, rudimentary faces tiny but bloated replicas of Jessica's. Mouths screamed without noise as skins crisped to black, parting to reveal bulging pink fat. The trees around crowded over, and mechanical dinosaurs strode through them. An Iron Insect stood at the edge of the clearing, heavy head swivelling, burning searchlight raising hedges of fire among the tents. Jessica passed him the trident and made a sign with her hand, urging him to eat. He raised the forked food, still alive, to his mouth and could not smell the burned flesh. He bit off the head of the first sausage-worm. It was like taking in a mouthful of molten lead. The food burned, eating away his teeth and tongue in a moment, melding his jaw to his skull, flooding his throat. Jessica rolled up her sleeve, pushing her bracelets to her elbow, and thrust her porky forearm into the fire. As Ferg's mouth cooled to deadness, the girl's skin turned black in patches and parted, showing lumpy flesh and muscle underneath. The fat spit silently, and her meat cooked on the bone. Now the wax was over Ferg's mouth too, solid like a welded-on mask . . .

He was stumbling through the woods, fleeing the Iron Insect. He couldn't hear it, but he could feel the ground shake as it took each deliberate, heavy step. Trees got in the way, and he slammed into them, jarring his already wounded head. He'd been hurt badly inside, bones cracked, his brain probably leaking into his broken nose and senseless mouth. There wasn't even pain any more. The ground got steeper, and he had to use his hands to pull himself up. His shaven scalp itched where he'd once had hair. He was climbing now, an almost sheer rockface. The Iron Insect slowed, forced to crunch out holds for its clawed feet before it could lift its weight. Ferg hauled himself up, gripping a well-anchored bush, and lifted his head above the crest of the cliff, chinning the edge. He scrambled over and, exhausted, lay down, looking up at the night sky. A dart-shaped spaceship crossed the grinning face of the moon, tiny drones spurting from it, spiralling towards the earth. From his position, he saw fires all over Alder, hovering aliens hunting and exterminating humans. It was a rout, Earth was doomed. He wasn't alone on the hillside. A boy sat on a rock, watching. Salim turned to Ferg, and moonlight showed a deep hole displacing his features, as if someone had sunk an iron into his face. He painfully hauled himself to his feet, arms extended. A mechanical device, like a spider with blinking lights, stuck to his neck, legs digging beneath his skin. The boy had been brought back from the dead by the aliens. Allison lurched out of the darkness, face chalk-white and gaunt, low-cut and wasp-waisted black shroud trailing behind her bare feet, arms extended too, black fingernails reaching. The zombies piled on to him, pressing him down, forcing his head into position, making him look up at the towering shape of the Iron Insect. The cobra-neck appendage bobbed and pointed at him. The zombies dug into his stomach, freeing his guts, pressing faces to his wounds. Allison held up his liver and took a bite out of it, red dribbling down her bone-white chin, eyes glowing enormous in her cavernous skull sockets. The Iron Insect's antenna was directly in front of him, a few inches from his eyes. There was an aperture in the antenna. He'd seen these things spread fire with their death ray. He tried to close his eyes, but his eyelids were paralysed. A shutter within the aperture opened, and light flooded his vision. His face burned, and his eyes burst . . .

In the dark, Ferg felt the tightening hood around his head. All other senses were gone. His head was getting smaller and coming loose from his neck. In the dark, the aliens swarmed, exulting in their triumph. The alien giant with the killing, crushing hand held fast. There were unseen shapes around him, unheard voices. He felt, but did not hear, the final snap.

Nine

'WHERE'D SHE GO?' Mike Toad asked, shaken.

Allison stood up and brushed herself off. The ground where Jazz had been was finely dusted with chalk. There was a murder-victim outline, but no other trace of the girl.

'Where?'

Allison looked at the Toad, and he shut up.

'Transported,' she said, liking the sound of it. 'As us all shall be.'

The Toad looked doubtful.

''Tis our reward,' she reassured him. 'Faithful will sit at His right hand.'

Terry was on all fours, hairy back burst through his shirt, thick fur all over his face. He was fidgety, gouging the shingle with his claws.

First Wendy, then Ben, now Jazz. With each passing, she was stronger. She was putting aside weights that anchored her to her old life. She was being purified, like the Sisters of the Agapemone. But she was stronger than they, fit to sit by the throne of the lion, not to bleat in the arms of the lamb. Her Beloved wasn't meek and mild but the terrible scourge that swept all before Him away in flame.

On the hillside it was quiet, but she heard the wailing from Alder, wafting up in the still night. The souls of the transported lingered like fireflies. The armies were assembled, and the first skirmishes had been fought. With Ben's passing, she'd won a field promotion. She was now a general, second only to the Beloved.

Mike Toad wanted to say something, but had nothing to say. His aura was sickly, congealing yellow around his heart. He was coming to the end of his purpose. He was becoming one of the weights that must be set aside. Terry howled at the stars. The Toad cringed.

The first pink of dawn showed. Their night on the mountain was nearly over. Soon, it would be time to go among the multitudes and spread the word. But first, she must lose another weight.

'Mike Toad,' she said, pulling him around by his chin to face her, 'tell us a story, tell us a joke.'

He shook his head, and she nodded slowly, contradicting him.

'Youm a funny boy. Make I laugh.'

He gulped. Terry stopped howling and cocked an ear to listen. Allison squeezed, thumb digging into Mike's cheek, nail pressing a crescent of red under his eye.

'Come on, boy.'

She pulled her hand away. Mike swallowed. He knew she meant it.

'No . . . wait . . . right . . .'

She watched him collect himself.

'My girlfriend, right, she's so fat . . .'

Allison folded her arms. Mike was having trouble getting his joke straight in his mind, let alone his mouth.

'Fat, right? Yeah, really fat . . . anyway, she was going through customs at the airport . . .'

Terry was bunching up his shoulders, muscles tense, head thrust forwards. Allison put a hand on his head, fur prickling under her palm.

'. . . and they pull her aside . . . searching, no, looking . . . looking for drugs . . .'

Terry growled in the back of his throat, almost below the range of human ears. Allison felt his readiness to pounce. He was like an Olympic runner on his marks, knees bent, thighs and calves ready to pound ground.

'. . . so they strip-search her . . . they take down her knickers, and what do you think they find?'

Allison didn't think Mike Toad would get very far. He didn't have the legs for it.

'Ten pounds of crack.'

In the pause, nobody laughed. Terry rose, shoulders expanding, fur standing like porcupine spines. Mike turned, looking for the path. Terry's growl dribbled out.

Allison nodded, and Mike began running.

'Fetch,' she said, slapping Terry on.

The boy made it into the woods, and Terry bounded after him.

Ten pounds of crack. Allison thought about it. As the noises of the chase disappeared, she got it, and let slip a low chuckle. Very funny.

Ten

ONCE, AT A PARTY, Paul had seen a steroid braggart crush a tennis ball, rubberized guts exploding through his fingers. When the Green Man broke Ferg's head, his huge fist made exactly the same sound, spurts of red gushing through gaps between leaves and wood. On the verandah, Jessica whimpered. The Green Girl giggled and clapped. A spray of blood struck Maskell's face, standing out day-glo against his green skin. Paul had no more disgust in him. Even his pain had receded to a blunt, constant ache.

Ferg's limp body hung like a dead rabbit from the Green Man's hand, legs trailing the lawn. Maskell's fist still shrank. Everything below Ferg's neck fell, blood gushing from the stump where his head had been. The Green Man opened his hand and scraped his palm on the side of the house, leaving a pink and red patch.

Jeremy, not struggling, was held by his mother and sister. Long dawn shadows stretched across the lawn, light in the sky. As the sun came up, the Green Man seemed more a natural thing. Maskell was obviously refreshed by the light, a carved smile standing out on his face. The bastard must be photosynthesizing. Paul wondered if a ton of Paraquat would do any good.

Jessica ran from the verandah, but stumbled before she could reach her boyfriend. Paul caught her and pulled her back. She was sobbing, mind dissolved. She stopped fighting and clung, pouring tears into his chest.

'See what you've done, man,' Dolar said, still dazed.

Maskell didn't look ashamed, but made no more violent moves. He wasn't rooted, but he was standing straight, waiting for his son. The Green Woman and her daughter brought the boy forward and made him kneel before Maskell, bowing his head. Maskell used his sword-length of penis to tap Jeremy on the shoulders, like the Queen dubbing a knight.

Jessica was chewing his shirt, deep sobs racking both their bodies. Dolar and Syreeta were staring at the whole thing. Salim, Paul realized, was dead. The horse stood placidly, unperturbed.

The Maskell family closed around Jeremy, tendrils twined between them, swarming around the boy, caging him in. The Green Man and the Green Woman joined at chest and loins, ivy creepers intertwining, secreted gums hardening together. Paul still saw Jeremy's expressionless face as his sister forced him further into the middle of the clump. The family put down roots, lawn around them churning as they spread under the earth. The bodies twisted in their foliage, coming together like the bole of a tree, thick bark spreading around them. Jeremy's face was covered.

The sky was red now, an orange light spilling across the village, casting dark shadows. Jessica went quiet and slumped exhausted in a faint. Birds scratched the air in a dawn chorus, but Alder was otherwise momentarily quiet. Dolar and Syreeta approached the Maskell Tree, tempted to touch – perhaps to worship – the green Spirit. Paul heard grass growing. Soon, everything would wake up. The world disclosed would be changed beyond recognition. There was dew on his face.

The Maskell Tree shot up, branches extending, twigs sprouting where fingers and thumbs had been, clumps of fruit swelling. Nourished by Ferg's blood, the foliage looked rich and healthy in comparison with the premature autumn of trees nearby. The horse stood scratching its head against the bark, and stretched up, picking an applelike fruit with its teeth and crunching it down. The tree sighed, its branches stirring slightly, exhaled air reverberating musically through pores in the wood. Paul walked over. The horse was nervous with him near, and whinnied. Dolar and Syreeta were smiling, holding hands.

'Beautiful,' they said. He had lost all his followers to death or surrender.

With the dawn, the tree calmed, individual members of the family melding and losing consciousness. The green-grey bark was mottled red, the last traces of Ferg. Gingerly, he fingertip-touched the tree. It didn't bite him or suck his blood. He pressed his hand to the bark. It felt like any other tree, although he could tell from the curve that he was touching what had been Sue-Clare Maskell's back. He could still make out shoulderblades and the line of her spine.

'Jeremy,' he said. If the boy could hear him, he could not answer. The tree shook a little, a few fruit falling with thumps to the lawn. Paul felt absurd. 'Jeremy,' he asked, 'are you in there?'

Nothing. The tree was quiet, still. Jeremy was another loss.

Tired, he wanted sleep. Even to fall into a dead faint like Jessica would have been an escape. But if he slept, he would miss what came next. He might not wake up. Although he felt as if he had been put through a mangle, his mind was racing too fast to allow sleep to crawl over him.

Syreeta and Dolar were cuddled together, backs to the Maskell Tree, trying to get comfortable, ready to sleep in its shade. Ferg's blood was a bright-red smear on the house, on the lawn. His body lay neglected, a thrown-away, special-effects dummy.

Paul listened. The birds had stopped singing. Everything was calm, as if a multitude had collapsed into the sleepless quiet that was overtaking the hippie couple. Beyond the Pottery, thousands must be lying like them, waiting for the next surprise.

He was sure the seed of it all was the Agapemone. The place where Hazel was.

He wandered away from the Maskell Tree, around to the open front gate. The road was still liberally covered with bodies, dead or otherwise. A few animals picked their way between them. A man in a three-piece suit lay face up in the gutter by the Pottery. Sitting on his chest was a creature the size of a small monkey, beet-red and hairless, with a long whip of a tail, and barbed, webbed hands and feet. It stuck its head up and looked both ways quickly, like a nervous road-crosser following the safety code, then dipped its sharp mouth to the hole it had dug in the body, tearing a chunk loose. The animal had horns, pointed ears and vestigial gargoyle wings. Seeing Paul, the creature squawked in alarm and scurried off as fast as a rabbit, zigzagging up the road, bouncing off cars and walls. He had no idea what the thing was, but he'd seen it in plain daylight.

Across the moors, a sound came. A rhythmic beating, blades slicing through the air. Helicopters. Paul looked at the dots on the horizon, and waited.

Interlude Two

'F RESH EGGS . . .'
The war was working out swell for everyone, Pfc Harry Steyning thought. He'd be grease-monkeying B-24s and chasing skirts for the next couple of years, and Ivor and Bernard would toil draft-exempt down on the farm to feed the khaki masses. None of them would be dodging bullets, unless someone got wind of these late-night exchanges in the woods. Bernard Conway had his shotgun with him, to fend off hungry hijackers. He was disappointed that being a farmboy kept him out of the fight, although not for patriotic reasons. Eyes shining in the twilight, Bernard reminded Harry of his cousin Floyd.

'. . . fresh butter . . .'
It wasn't easy in the dark to match items, but he didn't think Albert Pym would gyp the US Army. He stood to rake in dollars as long as the air base at Achelzoy was running and Colonel Colley had a hankering for more than powdered egg and beans.

'. . . fresh cream . . . tasty, eh?'
Ivor and Bernard stamped heavy-booted feet in the cold, breaths frosting. It was the first really bone-freezing night, English drizzle creeping through his uniform, sinking into his skin.

'Three sides of beef . . .'
The goods were stacked in the back of the jeep, ready to be tethered under a tarpaulin. Harry didn't have to be back on the base before dawn. That gave him time to pay a call on Annie. After this jaunt, he could do with a warm welcome.

'. . . two mutton . . .'
The list was in his head. He knew better than to be caught with an inventory. The brass hats would throw him to the wolves; then he'd be in the guardhouse for black-market activities, sentenced by Colonel Colley, who'd made out the list in the first goddamn place, who'd be getting fat on these eggs and

cream. By the same reckoning, Ivor and Bernard would take the fall for profiteering, while their boss Albert Pym, the big-shot farmer in Alder, sat on his magistrate's bench and tutted at their intolerable behaviour. That was the way it always worked when a kid and Pop had regularly been shaken down by his best 'shine customers, the sheriff and the circuit judge.

'. . . a whole pig . . .'

In the most gentlemanly way, Colonel Colley and Albert Pym had agreed to dispense with the formalities in supplying the officer's mess. Harry, on general-issue rations, would barely get a lick of what he was picking up. He was only ground crew, and this provender was for fly-boys. A waste, really. Most heroes upchucked anything they ate as soon as they drew the first flak over France, or when they tumbled, miraculously alive, back to the tarmac at Achelzoy. The ones who didn't come back presumably wouldn't have given a flying crap what they had for their last supper.

'. . . assorted vegetable produce . . .'

There were advantages that went with this off-the-record detail. The use of the jeep and nights away from the base put him on the inside track with Annie.

'. . . and what's in these kegs?'

Ivor Gilpin grinned and Bernard's creepy eyes glowed. 'Scrumpy, Yank,' Ivor said. 'Cider. Strong drink. Have the roof o' yer mouth off.'

'Swell,' he said. 'Local moonshine, right? You should try the stuff from Pop's still.'

'Cowboy drink, sir?' said Bernard, drawing out the word 'cowboy' with withering contempt.

'Not many cowboys in Kentucky, pal,' Harry said. These people had no idea. To them, America was all cowboys and gangsters. Annie's younger sister Vanessa had asked him if he'd been there when the monkey fell from the big building in New York.

Harry dug out a pack of cigarettes and offered them around. He flipped his Zippo, and Pym's labourers dipped their heads to suck flame.

'Three on a match,' he said, lighting up his own smoke. 'Bad luck.'

'Arr, sir,' purred Bernard, cig ends reflecting in his eyes like firefly sparks. 'So I heard.'

Ivor called him 'Yank', Bernard called him 'sir'. Ivor was
okay, but Bernard reminded Harry more and more of his cousin.
Floyd had raped his thirteen-year-old sister and drowned her in
the creek. After a tri-state manhunt, he'd wound up dead in a
shootout with the FBI. Like Bernard, Floyd had been polite all
the time, but with a slight curl to his lip that made it obvious
he didn't mean it.

'Pop told me that was from the First War. German snipers
could zero on the third light. One for the alert. Two to get the
range. Three, pop, bang, brains in your helmet. Just like that.'

As he snapped his fingers, something nearby exploded. Light
hit first, an eye-punishing flash. Then the sound, then the wind.
Strong enough to lift Ivor and Bernard off their feet, it rammed
Harry against the jeep. His shoulder and hip took the blow, and
pain shuddered through him. For a moment, he thought he'd
been hit by shrapnel. Blast still drumming a Gene Krupa frenzy
in his ears, he heard hail-like patter. Pebbles and earth rained on
them. A foul smell stung his nostrils and he tasted vomit in the
back of his throat. His gasmask was under the dash of the jeep,
strapped uselessly in its case.

His eyes stung as he blinked, unable to get rid of the afterbursts
of the flash. In the sky, he thought he saw a flying cross-shape.
An airplane? It seemed to flit rather than fly, zigzagging like a
bird or a bat, not looming through the air like a bomber. He
couldn't be sure what he saw. Light still lingered on the surface
of his eyes. Harry was coated in dust. Nearby, there was a fire.
Ivor was already on his knees, shaking his head and coughing,
and Bernard was calmly standing, face a mask of earth in which
his eyes shone like neons. They were both okay.

'A dumper,' he said. 'It must have been . . .'

The Germans wouldn't want to bomb Alder Hill. They had
never, despite the drills, even gone for the air base. Harry
guessed the plane was a straggler from a raid on Bristol or
Bath, sagging low and heavy in the sky, no idea where its target
was. He knew from listening to the crews what that was like,
sitting on a ton of potential explosion, looking for somewhere
– anywhere – to dump the load, looking for a light below.

Three on a match. A tiny flame in a blacked-out forest of
dark. Bernard was walking towards the fire, Ivor following. It
couldn't have been Harry's Zippo. The explosion had come too
swiftly after the flame. No bombardier could target and drop

that quickly. From base scuttlebutt, he knew it seemed eternity between targetting and the big bang, that they were lucky to get a single bomb within five hundred yards of the objective.

'Hold up,' he shouted, pulling himself up, 'wait for me . . .'

Hand pressed to his side, he loped after the Somerset men. It could have been a crash, he thought. But they hadn't heard a struggling plane, something he'd have recognized under any conditions. This explosion had literally come from nowhere. Up ahead, Bernard approached an apparent wall of flame and was silhouetted against it. Then he vanished, as if he had walked into a concealed hollow behind a waterfall. Harry waited for the next explosion, as the shells in Bernard's gun blew.

Ivor half turned and sank in sideways, also tugged into the flame curtain. He passed into fire, a distinct line washing across his face. Harry wished he'd brought his gun. He still heard after-ringing and saw dazzling blobs, but was getting over the initial blast. This wasn't like a usual fire. It didn't seem to be burning, and it wasn't giving off smoke or smell. Flames were swelling straight against trees, but leaves and branches weren't catching light. It wasn't even hot. His breath was still clouding.

Harry hoped he wasn't caught up in some Buck Rogers secret-weapon shit. There were rumours around the base about egghead scientists playing with death rays and jet planes. The Nazis were supposed to be developing something that could disintegrate you with sound vibrations the way Deanna Durbin broke glasses.

There was a newly gouged depression in the hillside. The air was thick with soil-tasting dust. The funny fire nestled in the dent, cupped and contained.

'Ivor,' Harry called, 'are you okay?'

He stepped forwards and touched the fire. It burned and stung like regular fire, but he couldn't pull away. He was sucked in, as if the explosion were reversed and everything displaced was violently pulled back, Pfc Harry Steyning along with it. There was a tingling moment of agony as he was jerked through the flame barrier, and he found himself in a new-made clearing, hot shingles under his boots, surrounded by an overturned bowl of white. Bernard and Ivor were there. And someone else. The Somerset men were bending over, examining the figure writhing on the ground.

'Parachutist,' Bernard said.

'Spy,' Ivor echoed.

'Nazzy bugger,' Bernard spat, hawking a gobbet of slime at the shingles, where it hissed.

'Let me see,' Harry said, pushing in.

'Look,' Bernard said, pointing, 'Nazzy stuff.'

The 'parachutist' was a woman, dressed more like Wilma Deering, Buck Rogers's girlfriend, than the daughters of Mata Hari Goebbels was supposed to be infiltrating into Britain. She wore a tight, one-piece flying suit of a dark and sparkly material Harry had never seen before, a bit like opaque nylon. She had black, ankle-high spike-heel boots with silver trimmings and pointed toes, a belt made out of scorched chain-link letters that spelled out SEX DEATH SEX, and enough necklaces and arm bangles for a Dorothy Lamour pagan princess. Her white face was streaked with black where her lipstick and eye make-up had run, her hair a bushy tangle of black twice the size of her head.

'Nazzy,' Bernard said, tugging at one of the woman's necklaces. It came loose, and she murmured in pain as he pulled it away. Harry looked into Bernard's hand and saw a jewelled swastika.

Ivor whistled. 'Cert'n'ly a spy,' he said.

Harry wasn't sure. He didn't think a spy would let a swastika within a mile of them. She'd be more likely to come draped in the stars and stripes. The woman was hurt. Her suit was torn in many places, and she was leaking blood.

Bernard carefully put down his shotgun. His Floyd eyes excited, he undid his belt buckle and slid the leather strip free of his pants.

'Only one way to treat a spy,' he said, his eyes shining.

'Hold on there, fella,' Harry said.

Bernard wrapped his belt around his hand, looping it through the buckle to make a lash. He cracked it in the air. The woman's eyes, embedded in black smudges, opened at the sound.

'We should call the cops,' Harry said. 'Let them have her. She'll have to be interrogated.'

Bernard slapped the belt across the woman's stomach. She sucked a scream into her mouth and half sat up, then collapsed.

'No coppers,' Ivor said. 'Can't say why we were in the woods, can us?'

Bernard slapped the belt down again, on the woman's face. She bled from the mouth. The Somerset man was enjoying himself.

'Deserves ever'thin' she gets,' he said. 'Ever'thin.'

The curtain of flame stuff had dwindled, darkness pouring through. Only a bubble now, sparks danced in it. A bush nearby burned properly, casting firelight over the clearing. Harry heard shouts and commotion in the woods. People were coming this way, calling to each other. The explosion must have been heard all over the county.

Bernard's face was dark with disappointment. He stood away from the woman, and strapped his belt back on. Picking up his shotgun, he pulled the hammers back and pointed the barrels at the woman's head.

Flashlights came out of the night, and voices. Albert Pym's roaring was immediately recognizable as he shouted orders. Annie's father, Wilfrid Starkey, was in the party, nose red with cold, and other farmers Harry knew, Geoffrey Coram, Frank Graham. Danny Keough, fourteen and desperate to be old enough to lick Hitler, tagged along, toting a flashlight for Pym. Wrapped up in enough cardigans and scarves to shape her like a pudding was Catriona Kaye, a trim, middle-aged lady who lived in the Manor House. She had shacked up with but not married a guy who was overseas with the War Office just now. Harry heard she was some kind of spiritualist.

'We'm caught a spy, Mr Pym,' Ivor said.

'I'm not sure –' Harry began.

Pym ignored him and barged through, sticking a boot-toe in the woman's side as if she were a sick sheep he didn't want to examine too closely.

'Had this round her neck,' Bernard said, handing over the swastika.

Pym looked at the swastika, and made a fist over it. 'She must have come from the plane we saw,' he said, 'along with the bomb.'

'I don't think there was a bomb,' Harry put in.

'Nonsense. Look at this place. There's obviously been a bomb.'

'There was a fire here once, Pym,' Miss Kaye said. 'As you know if you'd read your local history. Bannerman's bonfire.'

Pym reined in a shudder. 'Less said about that the better, as well you know.'

This was over Harry's head. Coming to Somerset, he'd seen how like his old home it was, secrets passed down from generation to generation, kept away from outsiders. Families still exchanged the shots and blows of some argument dating back to the Civil War. There were incidents everyone knew about, which were never discussed. Back home, Cousin Floyd was one; here, Miss Kaye's bonfire seemed another.

Danny Keough, a rat-faced kid, was fascinated with the injured woman. There was skin showing through rips in her clothes, but Harry wasn't sure whether Danny was worked up about white flesh or the streaks of red.

Pym was on his knees, roughly examining the woman. She was barely conscious, coughing burps of blood. He struck his hand in her hair, scratching his skin.

'Extraordinary,' he hummed to himself.

The fire was dead now, the cold come back.

'Did you see anything in the sky?' Miss Kaye asked him.

Harry wasn't sure.

'A´ man-shape?' she prompted. 'Burning? Perhaps with wings?'

'None of your ha'ant talk, Miss Kaye,' Pym said. Harry saw at once that Albert Pym and Catriona Kaye weren't kissing cousins. The red-faced farmer, booze-burst blood vessels around his nose, resented having to talk to her. She reminded him of Lillian Gish or Jean Arthur, delicate face surrounded by a wrapping of knit scarves, animated features making her seem younger than she was.

'It's a pity Edwin isn't here,' she mused. 'He'd be interested.'

She pulled off a glove and took the woman's pulse with nurselike efficiency, then felt her heartbeat. She found she had blood on her hand. She didn't look hopeful.

'Miss?' she said, waving her fingers in front of the woman's eyes, 'can you see these?'

'*Spretchen-zee Doitch?*' Pym shouted.

The woman raised her head, neck muscles standing out, blood dribbling from black lips. Her eyes were open and large.

'How many fingers?' Miss Kaye asked, holding up three.

'Fuck,' the woman said, through pain-gritted teeth, 'shit, fuck . . .'

Exhausted, she slumped back.

'Well,' Miss Kaye said, 'English must be her first language.'

'What about this?' Pym said, dangling the swastika.

'That's an older symbol than you think. In magic, the crooked cross has always had a multiplicity of meanings.'

'We should hang her,' said Coram, 'and be done with it.'

'Don't take to her eyes,' said Graham. 'They foller youm 'bout.'

Pym said, very slowly, 'You're . . . under . . . arrest.'

With a growl that rose to a yell, the woman sat up and reached out, grabbing Pym's handlelike ears. She pulled, screaming in competition with Pym, black-lacquered nails digging in. Harry thought to snatch Miss Kaye out of range, and found himself holding the bundled-up woman, feeling bones through her shawls and cardigans. She was a strong little lady, but didn't fight him. The woman in black shrieked like a banshee and ripped Pym, long nails raking his face and clothes. One of his ears was torn. She got to his eyes, and he yelled in furious pain. Ivor and Coram stepped in and tried to get a hold on her, but, wounded or not, she fought. Bracing herself against Coram, she kicked like a chorus girl and sank her silvered boot-toe into Ivor's adam's apple, sending him back, staggering and choking. Shrugging free of Coram with her shoulders and elbows, she attacked Pym again, punching under his ribs. Pym screamed, his face bloody, and scrabbled backwards on his arse and hands, crab-walking himself out of range. She was still shouting pain and rage, expending the last of her strength in berserk frenzy.

Bernard had his gun up and pulled the triggers, but the woman rounded on him, ducking under the blast. A cloud of shot spattered against the trees a dozen yards away, and Starkey yelped, catching some stray fragments in his arm. Harry realized Bernard was lucky not to have killed someone on his side. His load shot, Bernard hit the woman with his gun, and she had it away from him, whirling it against his head. She prodded Danny Keough in the chest with the gunstock, and shoved the kid over. She wasn't steady on her feet, but she was going to fight to the last. Bernard had a pitchfork now, grabbed from Graham, and he stepped in, leading with it, thrusting into the woman's chest. One of the tines bent and broke against a rib, but the others sank in.

The woman collapsed forwards, driving the fork in deeper. Her front was soaked with blood. Danny Keough, too close, got his face speckled red. Bernard got his arm around the woman's neck, hand against her head. Smiling at his butcher's professionalism, he broke her spine and dropped her. Miss Kaye was crying. She clung to Harry, warm in her cocoon of wool. Pym, a handkerchief to his eye, was getting his breath back.

'Gilpin,' he said, nodding to the body, 'get rid of that in a ditch.'

Bernard saluted with the best of them, proud to be noticed. Pym hadn't lost an ear or the eye. He probably just had scratches. And the woman wouldn't be answering any questions.

'Nobody says anything about tonight,' Pym ordered.

The farmers grumbled and grunted agreements. Danny Keough wiped his face with his sleeve, and Annie's father was scratching the shot out of his hand, cursing viciously.

'Private Steyning? You know how important it is to keep mum?'

He remembered the jeepload of black-market goods. 'Yes, sir,' he said.

'Miss Kaye?'

She looked at Pym, expression suggesting she smelled donkey dung.

'No good can be served by raking this over.'

After a long moment, Miss Kaye gave in, said, 'Have it your way' and shoved her way out of the clearing. There was a path to the Manor House. She'd be home before all of them.

Pym was getting his wind again. 'I'll have bottles open at the farmhouse. Conway, you help Gilpin and then join us later. Private Steyning, if you have no more pressing engagement . . .?'

Harry thought of Annie, and decided not to go along with the party.

Pym smiled and Wilf Starkey, handkerchief around his bloody mitt, pretended not to understand. 'I thought not,' Pym said. 'Good night, soldier.'

Ivor and Bernard had the sagging body between them and were dragging it off, pitchfork scraping ground. Harry was amazed how easily everyone was taking this little problem.

Alder worked perfectly, like a military unit, everyone knowing their duty, taking their orders. Except Catriona Kaye, and she didn't have a say in how things were handled. Not being married robbed her of any vote she might have been entitled to.

The farmers were leaving, already beginning to make jokes. Pym, not hurt at all really, was laughing with the rest of them. 'This was the Battle of Alder,' he said, hand ruffling Danny's hair. 'We met the enemy, and we prevailed.'

Harry was left alone in the clearing, hearing shingles cool, waiting for the daze to pass. It never would. He'd seen enough people die in the last year for a lifetime. Shot-up crews, burned-out crews, smoke-choked crews, dead-of-fright crews, lung-frozen crews. He didn't really know what he had seen tonight. Someone had died, but that didn't explain anything. The woman could have been a German parachutist. She had certainly been hostile, and she wasn't like anything from around here. Pym had probably been right. It was best not to talk about it.

VII

One

'I'M SUPPOSED TO be a sensitive,' she said, 'so why don't I feel relieved?'

There were two helicopters coming towards the village, close together.

'I don't know,' said Lytton. 'Maybe your reception's on the blink.'

Teddy laughed, obviously not getting the joke.

It was after dawn. All around, people were stirring. From where they were, they could hear but not see the helicopters. For a precious instant there was mist and dew, but it would burn away like butter on a hotplate. Susan strolled up the road, suppressing a chill. Lytton followed, dragging Teddy like a war hero hauling a wounded buddy through a minefield.

'Perhaps I got through to Garnett after all,' Lytton suggested.

'Perhaps, perhaps, perhaps . . .'

Susan sensed spreading calm, and was perturbed by it. Jago was retreating into himself, pulling in his mentacles. His little paradise could chug over on its own for a while

The helicopters were getting nearer.

The main gate was unmanned. Beth Yatman, swaddled in squaw blankets, was dozing in a makeshift lean-to. If anyone wanted to get in without paying, now was the time to try. Susan walked on to the site. From the gently sloping field, she saw across the moors to the white haze from which rose Glastonbury Tor. It was an Arthurian vista, only slightly marred by the fire-breathing dinosaur flying towards Alder.

'Fuck,' breathed Lytton, almost in admiration. If Susan had been less tired, she'd have laughed.

The helicopters were moving in formation, a giant inflatable monster strung, dangling like a barrage balloon, between them.

It had red lamps for eyes, and puffs of flame belched from its mouth.

Word spread all over the field, and people were sticking uncombed heads out of tents and blankets. By Susan, a youth whose face was thickly scaled, was down on his knees in prayer, iguana wattles of his throat bulging, red crest of horns swelling his temples.

'It's The Heat,' Lytton said.

That made no sense at all. This was one thing no one could blame on the summer drought.

'It looks like Godzilla to me.'

'The Heat,' he repeated, 'not the weather, The Heat. The rock group.'

Susan remembered The Heat. Not quite up there with Led Zeppelin, Frozen Gold or Genesis, but a lot more resilient than Mud, Showaddywaddy or the Bay City Rollers. She'd bought their hit single 'Leaping Lizard' with her pocket money back when she was a witchy pre-adolescent.

'. . . a rock-'n'-roll lizard like meeeee,' she whined.

'Yes,' Lytton said, 'that Heat.'

'Didn't they overdose?'

'Only the drummer, and they have machines to do his job these days.'

Susan looked up at Godzilla and assumed this was the living end. All around, people scrambled, looking to the skies. It was like expecting the Sermon on the Mount and getting Eddie Murphy live in concert.

Something hung out of the helicopters, where the guns would have been in Vietnam. Directional speakers. The unmistakable thrump-thrump-thrump intro of 'Leaping Lizard' was blasting out at the hillside.

> 'I dig surfin' in the sea,' disembodied voices sang,
> 'I dig twistin' on the land,
> My swimming trunks are full of me,
> And my sneakers are full of sand . . .'

People were joining in the words. Some of The Heat must be up there in the helicopters, using power microphones to overdub their old record. Either the crowd was older than she assumed, or 'Leaping Lizard' had filtered annoyingly into the oral tradition. Everyone knew the lyric.

'Please don't ask me why,' a hundred voices choired,
''Cause I don't understand,
But I turn into a monster
When I hear a rock-'n'-roll baaaaaand . . .'

'Is that thing safe?' Susan asked.

Lytton shrugged, appalled. Godzilla bobbed, huge eyes rolling, jaws clamping. The backing vocals (*bop-bop-a-da-bop-bop, bop-bop-a-da-bop-bop, bop-bop-a-da-bop-bop, BOP!*) were coming from its maw through concealed speakers.

'It ain't radiation,
Or an Aztec curse,
Or the end of civilization,
It's something worse.
The music is in my chromosomes,
I never can be free,
Doomed to wander round the world –
A rock-'n'-roll lizard like meeeee . . .'

The Godzilla was overhead now, descending slowly, floppy feet thumping towards the ground, scattering sleepy festival folks. An extended guitar solo abused the air, fuzzing and screeching through protesting speakers.

'Those guys know how to make an entrance,' said an American voice nearby.

'It's just a rip-off of Pink Floyd,' said a cynic.

'Who's this band, Mum?' someone asked.

'I'll surprise the ice-cool cop,' sang The Heat,
'When I eat his car.
Terrorize the high-school hop
And the local bar.
I've got me a master plan,
To rule the world, you see,
I'm gonna make me a master race
Of rock-'n'-roll lizards like meeeee . . .'

Lytton pulled Susan back. One Godzilla foot slapped the ground where she had been, pretend-crushing a hysterical teenager and genuinely crushing an elaborately pitched tent. Mooring ropes were released from the helicopters, and Godzilla swayed forwards and back before settling, anchored by a long,

weighted tail. People in the field scattered like panicking
Japanese extras. The helicopters were climbing now, having
delivered their present to the festival. Susan saw a thin, middle-
aged man with unfettered long grey hair leaning out on a brace,
waving a floppy hat at kids who had not been born the last time
he was on *Top of the Pops*. He lost his hat to the chopper-draught,
and started abusing the guitar slung around his neck, repeating
the solo. Shouting to him for help and an airlift out did not seem
an option.

The helicopters circled, and Godzilla lurched forwards in their
blade breeze, spewing oily flames into the air. Smoke and smuts
fell out of the sky, stinging Susan's eyes.

But what do they do for an encore?

An elegant girl nearby, who had been lying as perfectly
coiffured and made up as Sleeping Beauty on a blow-up
mattress, languidly got up on her elbows. Silk chemise hanging
from her spectacular chest, she opened her startling blue eyes
and saw a fifty-foot, fire-breathing prehistoric monster looming
over her tidy bower. She turned over, silk slip clinging to her
equally spectacular rump, and went back to sleep. Susan envied
her composure, but assumed she was technically insane.

One of Godzilla's legs had a slow puncture. Hissing, it
crumpled like a concertina and the monster listed badly to
one side. Electrical workings sparked and spat in its chest, and
its eyes went out.

'Gangway,' Lytton said, pulling her again.

The slow puncture ripped wide and became a rapid puncture. A last burst of flame coughed between painted teeth, and
sagginess crept rashlike up one side. An arm shrivelled and
deflated, slapping against its collapsing monster hip. A seam
went in its neck, and the head, outside in, fell into the torso.
People all around heckled the glass-jawed monster. With an
embarrassed and embarrassing burp, Godzilla fell down like a
circus tent, heavy rubberized canvas piling up in the centre of the
field, one freakishly still-inflated lizard arm sticking out defiant
from the heap, claws outstretched.

The guitar noise went away. The Heat flew the hell out of the
village. The helicopters became specks on the horizon. A great
booing rose into the sky. The crowd gathered and pounced,
kicking and tearing the monster's remains.

'Like, crazy,' Susan said.

Two

T ERRY THE WOLF had been close on his arse, but Mike had lost
the wereboy in the thick of the forest. The sun was up, but
where he was it was night dark. Gnarled tree trunks were close
together, a tangled web of brambles strung between them.
Thorns tore his jump suit. Low-hanging vines slapped his face,
stinging like bastards. The going was slow and painful, but at
least he couldn't hear Terry rending his way through the growth
after him, slaver falling from his mouth, big teeth swelling. That
kid was one Weird Psycho Fucker from Hell. Terry's teeth and
claws could shred flesh like tissue paper. In the last few minutes,
Mike's panic-making rush of fear – the certainty he was going
to die *right now!* – had evaporated, leaving him with only the
nerve-shredding frustration of being lost in the forest.

Everyone called him Mike Toad, but his name was Matthew
Glover. As a brat, he had told elephant jokes, knock-knock
jokes, doctor-doctor jokes. What's big, red and eats rocks?
Now, it was dead-baby jokes, blackie and Paki jokes, cunt
jokes. Fucking, shitting and pissing jokes. How do you get
twenty queers into a Mini Metro? Cremation. What's a baby
seal's favourite drink? Canadian Club on the rocks. Jokes, always
jokes. He didn't even know why any more. Once, it had been
to make people like him. Now, he told jokes people didn't like,
couldn't like. When he told his zingers, people – especially
girls – were genuinely offended, left the room, never spoke
to him again. Even the the ones who laughed were ashamed,
as if he'd shown them something about themselves they didn't
like.

He was well off the beaten track. He hadn't spent much time
out of London, but still knew these weren't the kind of woods
you were supposed to get in Somerset. The trees were too close
together, brambles too thick. As he fought his way through,
fungus broke under his feet, farting foul odours. If Terry had

transformed into a wild animal, the woodland had transformed into a habitat for Terry.

He'd been knocking around with Dolar for years. They once lived in the same flat in Muswell Hill. The others just put up with him. Syreeta was a fat cow with no sense of humour, and Ferg was on a one-way time trip back to 1977. He hoped the punk would disappear completely, because he might have a go at Juicy Jessica. Mike had never had a girlfriend for more than three weeks. Dozy cunts, the lot of them. Most weren't even good for much of a shaft. Pam had been promising, but got lost in the crowds. Her sister – and whatever had happened to *her*? – was another headcase. Not as bad as Allison or Terry, but still a vicious bitch.

A barbed tendril lashed his face, scratching. Blood trickled past his mouth. The woods were thinning. Sunlight dimly penetrated to the forest floor. Listening, he heard birds – the after-dawn chorus – but nothing else alive. No human sounds, and nothing from Terry the Wolf either. He couldn't get out of his mind the picture of Terry burying his face in the woman they'd killed, and he couldn't get out of his craw the taste of human meat. He'd changed, too. He was blooded.

Jokes just came to him. People would feel the need to unburden themselves by giving him jokes. Sometimes, jokes would literally appear out of nowhere and slip from his mouth, especially when related to a recent news item. What does NASA stand for? he'd asked the day after the space-shuttle crash. Need Another Seven Astronauts. After a stadium fire, how can you identify a Bradford supporter? Dental records. When he was little, he'd had an imaginary friend called Pat. That was where his name started, with Pat and Mike. Sometimes, he thought Pat was the one supplying the jokes. Pat always listened to his riddles, well after he'd pissed off all the adults with them. Who was the skeleton in the closet? A Biafran bank manager.

There was a building ahead, cocooned by trees bending over a red-tiled roof. It was a country pub. The sign hanging outside showed long female legs, with a dress raised far enough to flash red pubic hair. An aroma of beer hung around, getting into Mike's head, making him almost drunk. Outside the pub stood a short, fat man with carroty hair under his derby hat, an emerald-green shamrock pinned to his fully stuffed waistcoat. He had a couple of cans of tartan paint set down beside him, and he was smoking a clay pipe upside down, tugging at leprechaun side whiskers.

'Ahh, Moike, me boy, 'tis a deloight to be seein' you,' said Pat. 'Oi'm just waitin' fer de Queen's Legs to open so's we can wet oor mouths.'

By the time Mike had fought his way up close, the landlord had unlocked the doors, and Pat had pushed into the warm, welcoming dark beyond, beckoning Mike to follow. Beer ran out of the windows and dripped brownly on the wall, staining the white plaster like faecal gravy. Terry the Wolf was after him, but Mike reckoned he always had time for a couple of pints. He barged through bat-wing doors, and found himself in the snug of the Queen's Legs. The pub smelled of tobacco and urine and semen and lager. There were patches of red light in the gloom, and rows of glinting bottles covered one of the walls. At first, Mike couldn't make out anyone in the darkness, just Pat standing against the bar.

'Did'ja hear about de Oirish garden-chair manufacturer comes in here? Patty O'Furniture,' Pat said, laughing.

Pat's laugh was a scraping sound, choking up from deep inside his rounded chest. He had a pint of Guinness up on the bar beside him, another one coming for Mike. The Irishman greeted him like a long-lost friend.

'D'ja know, Moike, Oi was down de Job Centre an' dere was nottin' in de cards fer an honest painter, so Oi walked away. An' outsoide de p'lice station dere was a big sign up wit' a slogan, "West Indian wanted fer rape", so Oi says to mesself, "Dem niggers gets all de best jobs."'

Pat's face split open, and laughter puked from his mouth.

'D'ja get it, Moike, d'ja get it?'

Pat slapped his back, sending him reeling. He laughed like a drain.

'Ya haff ta laff, Moike me boy, ya haff ta laff . . .'

From the populated darkness, laughter came. Mike made out the shapes of drinkers, black shadows outlined red. He smelled their sweat, their drinks. A jukebox, lit up like Piccadilly Circus, was pouring forth *Sinful Rugby Songs*, shouted choruses over a rinky-dink electric organ. Pat poured Guinness into his mouth, letting it flow dark over his chin on to his chest.

'Ah, 'tis a treat, dis Liffey water,' the Irishman said, 'an' 'tis a treat ta drink wit'out bein' disturbed by de terrible,

terrible people dat usually comes in here. Terrible, terrible people.'

Mike held his Guinness in both hands, unable to get a single-handed grip on the glass. It was more like a quart than a pint.

'D'ja hear 'bout de black and sticky dead poet laureate comes in here? Sir John Bitumen. D'ja hear 'bout de 'merican blue fillum star comes in here? Hugh G. Rection.'

A near-nude woman stood behind the bar, watermelon breasts plopped in rolling puddles of lager. She had puckered nipples the size of pancakes and no face. Between her stiff fringe and her chin was a stretch of lumpy dough, expressionless and curdled. She was laughing inside, but it couldn't get out. Her tits shook like giant jellies, rolls of fat under her chin rippling.

'D'ja hear 'bout de mad Russian murderer comes in here? Knocker Bolockoff.'

The background chatter died like a switched-off tape.

'Terrible man,' Pat reflected, 'terrible, terrible man.'

Pat called for another pint. The faceless barmaid hauled on a handle, filling up a bucket with green-yellow froth. As the pump spewed drink, the works gurgled like an old-fashioned chain-pull bog flush. Leaning over the bar, Mike saw the barmaid had an arse the size of a steamroller, enormous cheeks bulging around a tiny, stretched-to-bursting pair of frilled French oo-la-la knickers.

'D'ja hear 'bout de t'ree nancy boys in de Jacuzzi?'

The barmaid plunked Pat's bucket on the bar. He looked into his drink, and saw surface scum clearing.

'Terrible drink,' Pat said, 'but 'tis fer me health.'

The Irishman opened his mouth wide as a letterbox, and tipped the green beer into it. His belly swelled like a toad's neck as the drink went down, and buttons popped from his waistcoat.

'Dey was gropin' away in de bubbles when a dorty great lump o' sperm floats up, an' one o' de pansies says, "Shush me gobbie, but who farted?"'

The gale of laughter came again. Everyone convulsed, laughter blending in with the squelching of the jukebox. The snug was crowded, dark shadows screeching hysterically in every corner, at every table. The red patches had got brighter, but the dark around them was darker than ever. Mike couldn't make out faces.

The barmaid was near Pat and Mike, mammoth breasts on display between the pump handles. Mike couldn't help but look at them. There were acres of white flesh, veined with subtle blue lines, with creases a man's hand could get lost in. Her no-face was shadowed now, and the red light fell only on the breasts.

'Moike, me boy,' Pat said, 'would ya loike to feel a tit?'

Immediately, Mike had an agonizing hard-on that wouldn't go away. His mouth went dry, and he bent his head to his Guinness, sucking up a mouthful of ice-cold stout. He gagged, but kept it down.

The doors opened, and a fiercely bearded cossack exploded into the Queen's Legs, puffy trousers stuffed into the tops of his shiny boots, thick-pelted chest bare, tall fur cap on his head, bottle of vodka in his king-sized hand.

''Tis Knocker Bolockoff,' Pat said, trembling.

Winds and snows roared in around the Russian. He gnashed his teeth, and flames sparked in his misaligned eyes. He slapped a long whip on the floor, and stalked towards the bar with a lion-tamer's tread, glaring at Mike. He began cursing him in Russian. As the red light grew brighter, darkness shrank like a salted slug.

Mike began to recognize the people in the pub. Inchworm-crawling forwards past the Russian's boots was a dead baby, blue face wrapped in clingfilm, forks in its eyes, sharp little teeth in its mouth. And there, by the Ladies', was a legless woman walking on her hands, glistening trail behind her, red vulva throbbing like a hungry wound. And a loose-limbed black buck tap-danced slowly, three feet of tattooed dick stuffed into his jockstrap. They were all laughing at Mike.

He tried to turn away, but the barmaid's laugh had finally escaped and was swarming around him. There was a bloody hole in the middle of her no-face, ragged where the laughter was gushing out. Screeches of laughter came from the jukebox too. An ewe in a black suspender belt and brassiere and a spade-bearded Welshman appeared from a booth in disarray, and added their braying, bawling and belching laughs to the rest. Dead seals, brains spilling, squeezed in among the babies.

Mike looked at the crowd pressing into the pub, and knew he was to be killed. Pushing away from the bar, he ran through the laughter, mirth ripping his skin like fishhooks. Knocker Bolockoff was guarding the front door, long arms outspread

to catch him, so Mike careened past, and slammed into the
door of the Gents'.

The urinal was brightly striplit, white glare bouncing back
at him from all the enamel surfaces. A condom-vending
machine slowly burped rubber johnnies inflated into dick-
shaped balloons. There was an inch-thick lake of still piss on
the floor. It rippled and splashed under his shoes. The light
hurt his eyes. There was a thin window, high on the wall,
paned over with chickenwire-inset glass. Stark messages were
felt-tip-penned on the walls.

THE FUTURE OF THE WORLD IS IN YOUR HANDS. BEWARE
LIMBO DANCERS. MIKE TOAD, EAT SHIT AND DIE.

Mike reached for the window, and thumped. Glass cracked
and bent, but didn't break. The smell rose, stinging Mike's eyes
like teargas.

The door opened, and Knocker Bolockoff, whip thrown
aside, came into the Gents'. His chest heaved as he changed,
bones shifting under his fur, muscles expanding.

The others crowded in. Pat, face red as a beetroot, eyes
squeezed too close together. A farmer's daughter, ping-pong-
ball eyes vacant, bursting out of her too low, too short checked
pinafore. A crèche of dead babies, crawling like maggots,
mewling for bloody milk. A man with a huge vagina in the
centre of his face, displacing all his other features. The sheep,
anus red and bleeding, fury in its eyes. Naked men and women
without faces but with swollen and disproportionate genitals.
Dead astronauts, ferryboat passengers, politicians, football fans.

Knocker Bolockoff bent over as he came for Mike, Terry the
Wolf looming out from inside him. The Somerset werewolf's
face pressed out through the Russian's, snout and fangs emerging
from the gap between Knocker's beard and moustache.

Mike tried to climb the slick wall, and fell. Stinking damp
seeped through his clothes. He slid along the floor, face pressed
into the wet. A moving weight landed on his back, pushing him
down, pulling him along. The taste of piss flooded his throat,
and he choked.

Everyone was laughing. The heavy body on top of him eased
up and turned him over. He felt the wet through his back and
buttocks. Knocker Bolockoff's face was a transparent mask now.
Terry was in control, abundant facial hair streaming away from
angry eyes and red mouth.

Pat gingerly knelt by Mike, watching as the werewolf played with his food. He was changing too, expanding out of his clothes, skin mottling crimson, jagged and grinding teeth forming in his foot-wide mouth. He popped a lump of granite into his gob, and began to chew it to powder.

'Ah, Moike, me boy,' said the Big Red Rock-Eater . . .

Terry's claws penetrated his cheeks, and a killing growl built up in his throat. Mike felt death catch in his throat.

'. . . Oi bet ya feel a roight tit now.'

Three

'THE REVELATION of Jesus Christ, which God gave unto him, to shew unto his servants things which must shortly come to pass,' Jenny read, brass-bound Bible heavy on her knees, as she sat outside Beloved's rooms. 'Blessed is he that readeth, and they that hear the words of this prophecy, and keep those things which are written therein . . .'

This morning, the sun had risen on a changed world. Knowledge had been granted Beloved, and He had passed it to His Brethren.

'. . . for the Time is at hand.'

She set the Bible down, open to Revelations. Standing, she was nervous, unsure. Knees tingling from sitting so long, her whole body felt funny, on the edge of elation. The waiting was nearly over. She still had last doubts to overcome. The bulk of humanity would be cast into the Pit. Parents, schoolfriends, people she'd known all her life. All doomed unredeemably. Only the Chosen would ascend. On such terms, how could she bear to accept her own salvation?

Today, there had been no regular early-morning services. Beloved remained in His rooms with the Sister-Love. His last Sister-Love. Jenny, their handmaiden, waited. She had come close to being Beloved's last and most favoured, but there was no disappointment in her heart. She was proud simply to be the handmaiden.

The Brethren were awake, intent on their purpose. Nothing had been said but everyone knew. Few had been able to sleep. Through the night, she'd heard them. They'd be travelling together, but most had taken the opportunity to be alone with themselves a last time. Jenny imagined she heard their thoughts rustling throughout the Agapemone. Hopes and fears, prayers and curses.

The sun was risen. This was the Last Day.

Mick had gathered most of the Chosen in the chapel, but several had their own paths to pursue, and were by themselves, praying intently, searching for something. From her position at Beloved's door, Jenny saw the stairs and the landings that wound through the house. Marie-Laure was abased two storeys down, forehead to the carpet, arms cast out, wailing. Derek was looking in all the rooms, searching for Wendy. No one had seen Beloved's first Sister-Love since yesterday. Jenny wondered if she'd been transported by the rapture, removed without suffering to Heaven as a recompense for all she had endured upon Earth.

It was hot with a dry heat that grew as if the heart of the house were an invisible furnace. Cracks spread as if the trapped heat were swelling, pushing bricks apart, straining wood. Plaster dust danced in the sunlight flooding from the cupola. Floorboards complained as they stretched. With a gunshot report, a nail burst out of the floor yards along the landing, force spent in the folds of a carpet. Before the elevation of the Agapemone, the community's earthly form would have to be smashed. There'd be resurrection in the flesh, but all the other things would be left behind, destroyed. Jenny loved this old building, but knew it would be nothing compared to the palaces of Paradise.

Jenny knew she was summoned to His side. Bowing, she opened the door and entered. She was surrounded by a formless, sourceless Light and, heart pumping, looked up. A warm breeze – light in motion – spread her hair. Beloved stood by His bed, arrayed in white, eyes aflame. Taller, earthly form transcended, He was complete, the Lord God in all His forms. Father, Son and Holy Spirit; Lion and Lamb; Gentle Saviour of the Chosen, and Righteous Scourge of the Damned; Love Everlasting, Mercy Unknown and Wrath of the Lord.

She sank to her knees as if a weight had settled on her shoulders, bending forwards to present the nape of her neck. Even if she shut her eyes, Light was all around, cleansing her soul. She rejoiced in the Light that was Love transformed. She'd been unsteady, fearful that the Light would be too much for her poor flesh, but, in a calming instant, the cares of her body were washed away and she lost all sense of frailty, standing as if floating, the flame of her heart kindled for ever.

Forcing her eyes open and her head up, Jenny saw the Light was a solid thing, shaped around Beloved like a high-backed

armchair. There was a rainbow about the throne, the Light split
into its elements, then sucked into a mass that was at once black
and white, all colours and no colour. Beloved floated above the
seat, on invisible cushions. He settled, body blending with the
Light. Unconsuming fire burned around Him. The Light, as
pure and delighting as an angel's kiss, didn't hurt her eyes. Jenny
was at the point of rapture.

Hazel was in Beloved's bed, sleeping the sleep of the innocent,
sheets wrinkled over her. She'd become as a little child, Jenny
knew. It was her duty to help Hazel through the battle to come,
to help the Sister-Love stand by the Lamb.

A thundercrack sounded, and the wall beside Beloved's bed
exploded out, bricks showering into the room beyond. Behind
Jenny, the door was hurled off its hinges and over the landing
banister, falling four storeys. The doorjamb splintered and burst,
tearing chunks of wall with it. The ceiling went concave, beams
bending, roof above lifting. Sunlight lanced in through gaps in
the tiles and rents in the ceiling, drawn to focal points within the
throne's back, making a halo around Beloved's head.

Others ventured into Beloved's rooms. Mick, Marie-Laure,
Janet, Kate. All were driven to their knees, crawling forwards
to worship. No one spoke, but there was music – trumpets and a
choir – coming from nowhere, from Beloved, from everywhere
at once. It was like nothing earthly, the music of Paradise.
Behind Beloved, a section of the exterior wall dissolved like
ice in the sun, and Jenny saw tree branches, blue skies, a white
curl of cloud. Sun flooded the room, and was sucked into the
Light. Beloved's halo grew, pulsing like a living thing.

Marie-Laure threw herself forwards, at Beloved's feet, and
babbled in delirium, kissing the throne, face disappearing into
Light. Mick sagged against Jenny, eyes staring, lips drawn
back over his teeth, heart bursting. Janet kept repeating,
'Jesus, Jesus, Jesus.' Jesus H. Christ on a bicycle, Jenny
remembered.

On the floor, seven flames jetted up like geysers from Aladdin
lamps in the pattern of the Plough. Most of the walls were gone
now, the Chosen crowded into the space, those on the landing
pressing close. Beams were broken, but the roof, if it fell, fell
outwards. Beloved kept the debris from crushing the Chosen,
casting it aside harmlessly. Electrical wires stretched in the wreck
of the ceiling, and the shaded lightbulb burst. The whole mess

was thrown out through the gap in the roof, clattering out of sight.

The trumpets sounded, a call to arms. Mick was jolted by Light, and fell, face up, before Jenny. Face red and swollen with blood, rips in his cheeks and around his eyes, he was gone, transported from his body. Just empty meat, he was consumed by Light, the seven flames bursting from his body, every scrap of his flesh gone in an instant.

'Alleiluya,' Jenny whispered.

The floor beneath was as glass. She saw into its depths, where fires were trapped. As the joys of Heaven grew near for the Chosen, so did the torments of the Pit for everyone else. Jesus H. Christ had been kindly, sorrowful for those who wouldn't accept His sacrifice, who wouldn't be redeemed by His Love. They had forged a sword which would be turned upon them. Multitudes would be tormented for ever. The day she first met Jesus, she'd been with Teddy and Terry. They'd burn, tender-heart Teddy as much as tearaway Terry. They had not come to Beloved. She couldn't, even now, envision the damnation of all the world save the Brethren, so she fixed on the Gilpin brothers as the emblematic damned. If she could understand their failure, she could appreciate that of all, the great and the good, the meagre and the monstrous.

At the corners of the throne, shapes formed. A lion, a calf, a man's face, a bird. The creatures worshipped Beloved, singing. The Brethren, schooled in their parts, joined. 'Holy, holy, holy, Lord God Almighty, which was, is, is to come . . .'

The creatures were part of the Light, concentrations of it, taking shape inside the throne, honouring the Beloved. Beloved's face was human, eyes still alive within the balls of flame that filled His sockets. He smiled serenely, humbly proud of His servants. For an instant, His face was a lamb's, seven horns starting from His brows, seven eyes crowding His face. Then He was His human self again, and His Love poured forth.

Marie-Laure was pulled into the Light, vanishing foot by foot into the throne, creatures batting at her with wings. She curled up like a foetus and shrank, Light swirling thick around her. In the heart of the throne, she combined with the creatures of Light. Then she too was gone.

Hazel, innocuously naked, was huddled on the bed, sheet around her, looking on without comprehension, the child who would lead them all.

Jenny stood up and, voice shaking, recited, 'Thou art worthy to receive glory and honour and power.'

Beloved's smile broke into a grin, and Light exploded, swelling to encompass all the Chosen.

Four

INSTANTLY, EYE-ABUSING light flash was followed by ear-punishing boom. Paul's first thought was nuclear. Helicopters had dropped something by the festival site that could easily have been a bomb. Blinking furiously, hands over ringing ears, tooth shocking his jaw, Paul realized at once he was wrong. No blast came to flatten him to the ground, no wave of atomic fire to turn him to spray-paint. His eyes hadn't been melted in his skull, and the boom's echoes diminished, leaving him shaken but not irradiated. The ground had heaved, but he hadn't even been thrown off his feet. The pub sign thumped to the ground, the Valiant Soldier falling face down.

Paul saw the Agapemone, surrounded by people who swarmed like Lourdes pilgrims to the shrine, or sacrifices to the furnace in Moloch's mouth. The explosion had come from the big house, and Paul, shading still-blotchy eyes, looked to see where the damage was. One corner of the building, a tower, was the flashpoint, but it hadn't been an ordinary explosion. Inside the tower, a blob of light was expanding, pushing out through holes in the walls and roof, sending white searchlights into the blue sky. The blot on reality burned brighter than the sun. Sections of the walls and roof had been displaced, but they weren't falling to the ground. They hung in the air as if the explosion were a video image on frame-advance, edging away from the building in tiny jumps. The light inside was different again, a cluster of intertwined glowing clouds, growing organically like a germ culture. As the light expanded faster than the slow explosion, chunks of tile and brick were absorbed, lost inside the blobby glow. The light was unlike any he'd ever seen, as if an expanse of emulsion had been melted off the three-dimensional photograph that was the universe.

All around, people were hypnotized. A girl nearby took off her dark glasses and dropped them, the better to stare. Paul bit

down on his tooth, jolting himself with the clarity of pain, and
scooped up the shades, straining the arm-hinges in cramming
them around his head. The Polaroid lenses damped the glare, but
everything was still harshly floodlit. Paul turned away, realizing
many were intent on looking until their eyes bubbled down their
cheeks. The dead tree that was the central point of Alder grew
burn patches on its dry bark, ready to explode into a million darts
of burning wooden shrapnel. The village was ready to become
three square miles of flame.

His gaze drawn back to the light, he saw things moving inside,
and was sure they were people. A human-shaped ragged shadow
was thrust out beyond the hanging brickery and crumpled into a
wastepaper twist that flared for an instant and was consumed.

Hazel?

She was inside the Agapemone somewhere. He had to try
to get her out before the light filled the whole of the Manor
House. There were people alive inside the light, but he knew
it was unhealthy, knew it held threats worse than death. Ears
recovered from the boom, he heard music. It was coming out
of the spreading sphere. Massed trumpets and an angelic choir.

An ogre with a broad red face and a derby hat sauntered out
of the pub, fixed his ugly eye on Paul, and, in an Irish accent,
asked, 'What's creamy an' shoots out o' de clouds?'

Tendrils of white flame burst from the light and trailed
streamers over the village, falling in ropes to the ground. The
ogre was gone, but his answer rang in Paul's ears. De Coming
o' de Lord.

The noise grew, a choral symphony. Light and dark shapes
danced in the air around the Agapemone.

'Paul,' came a woman's voice, fighting through the trumpets.

He looked. It was Susan, with a few others. They were party-
poopers too, not going along with whatever was overcoming
the multitude.

'Hazel,' he said, 'what happened to her? Is she safe?'

Susan bit her lip and spread her hands. 'I'm sorry. I couldn't
get her out.'

'What . . .?'

'She was all right last time I saw her,' Susan said, answering
his unasked question. 'Alive, at least.'

Susan's sidekicks eased into the garden of the pub. There was
shelter there. Susan pulled Paul, and he followed them. Plastic

kids' toys had melted into primary-coloured pools on the grass. Out of the direct sightline of the Agapemone, they were away from the crowds. Beyond the garden wall, villagers, festival-goers and passers-by all stood in ranks, looking upwards, faces shining with reflected light. Those with glasses threw back twin glints painful to see.

'James Lytton,' said the fit-looking man with a gun in his waistband, extending his hand.

Paul shook it.

'And this is Teddy.' It was one of the locals – face a thinner, cleaner version of Allison's thug friend – and he was limping, half supported by Lytton, obviously battered. His mind had taken a bruising, too, Paul could tell.

'What's happening to them?' Paul asked, indicating the staring crowd. 'And why are we immune?'

'It's partly being prepared in your mind,' said Susan, 'and it's partly pain.'

'Pain?' Paul winced.

Susan nodded. 'You can't think when you're in pain, and you need to think to be taken in by all this.'

'All this what?'

The woman shrugged. 'All this crap, Paul. Jago's mind-crap, that's what's coming down.'

The crowds moved, walking towards the light, sucked in. Paul looked around the corner of the pub. The Agapemone was completely within the sphere of glow. The tower dismantled in the air, rising like a moon rocket. Most of the building was still intact. However, it all glowed, solid walls becoming transparent, light outlining mortar-pattern cracks in the brickwork, in-tolerable bursts through the windows. The lawns outside the Agapemone were a crush of pilgrims, looking up to Heaven.

He had a tooth-twinge, and Susan ouched as if she felt it too.

'I still don't get this,' he said.

'Do you know what consensus reality is?' Susan asked.

'Yes, of course.'

'No, you don't.' She shook her head. 'Not here, not in Alder, not around Anthony William Jago.'

'What?'

'There isn't any consensus reality here. It's been overruled. What we have right now is fascist reality.'

'What's Jago got to do with it?'

'Everything. Jago is a psychic prodigy, and he can put a dent in reality. Everyone has dreams, fantasies, beliefs. Around Jago, they become concrete things. Monsters, angels, whatever. A lot of them are sexual, but it could be anything.'

That made sense, almost. The Martian war machine from his own mind. The Green Man from Maurice Maskell's. Everything else, from everyone else.

'And Jago has his own dreams, fantasies and beliefs.'

Lytton was listening carefully, nodding. Susan was a compulsive explainer, he thought, going around trying to force-feed information into people. He tried to swallow it all, to keep up with her mind-bursting gabble.

'He can turn water into wine, Paul. I've tasted it. And those poor fucks out there are drunk on it.'

Beyond the wall, the tree was thrusting out of the earth, displaced roots cracking the tarmac, trunk swelling like a corpse pregnant with a million maggots. A root burst through the road and whipped in the air, tripping several starers. Paul, Susan, Lytton and Teddy huddled together against a wall. Paul heard a human wailing inside the dead thing.

'Jago is a millennialist, Paul,' Susan insisted. 'A fundamentalist millennialist.'

A section of the tree bark was punched out from inside. It broke like a shield of charcoal. A wiry black arm emerged, six-fingered hand a twiggy fist, and then a head popped out. The imp, red tongue permanently stuck through black teeth, snorted hot coals.

'Jago is your textbook God-bothered fanatic,' Susan continued. 'He believes in the prophecies of Armageddon. And maybe if he believes hard enough, he can make them come true.'

The tree fell apart, and a dozen or more imps, bat-winged and swift, poured out of a hole in the ground, swarming into the air. A belch of brimstone followed. It was a pantomime trick, demons coming out of the stage in a puff of smoke, but it was also real.

'Why here? Why now?'

'He just passed critical mass. It had to be somewhere, it had to be some time. We got unlucky. What can I say, *que sera, sera* . . .'

'How do you know all this?' Paul asked, afraid of the answer.

She smiled tightly, without humour. 'Because I'm a prodigy, too, Paul. And we've been dumped in the same cage.'

A leathery reptile appendage broke the surface like a shark fin, a hundred yards away, and charged towards the pub, ploughing through asphalt, turning aside curls of earth and stone. The underground beast struggled for air, wake spreading.

Lytton propped Teddy against the wall, and pulled out his automatic. He primed it and assumed a shooter's stance, left hand gripping his right wrist, gun aimed at the approaching dirt leviathan.

Eyes loomed on stalks, a flat, wide, several-mouthed head following. With a stereophonic roar, the beast burst from the ground, forty-foot dragon wings extending from a wormlike body, tips scraping houses on either side of the road. It was a superdynamation kindergarten nightmare, a thousand tons of hate wrapped in a dozen acres of fear.

Lytton shot the thing in the nose. The expelled cartridge pinged against a lawn table. A porthole of red explosion appeared in the beast's face, and its eyes dimmed. Collapsing, it became a million gallons of oily substance and splattered over the road, dribbling into the cracks, washing in waves over the garden wall, flooding around their shins and against the wall. As it dispersed, the muck faded into the ground, gone without trace before the echo of its death rage died.

'Feel happy now you've shot something?' Susan asked.

Lytton shrugged.

Paul was happier without the beast around, but it had plenty of kith and kin. The skies were aswarm with winged things, and the ground was covered with creatures that crawled on their bellies. Between mad people and monsters, Alder was going to Hell.

Teddy was curled in a heap by the wall, trying to climb inside the bricks. He'd escaped the easy way, into his mind.

Lytton was obviously Mr Competent with the gun, the local Action Man. Somehow, that didn't make Paul feel much safer.

'What's Jago doing?' Paul asked.

'Trying to end the world,' Susan told him.

He thought about it, trying to swallow with his mind.

'And who ya gonna call?' she asked before he could. 'We don't have much choice, I'm afraid.'

Paul looked at her.

'You, me and him,' she said, thumbing towards Lytton.

'Fuck,' he said.

'Quite.'

Five

HAVING FALLEN asleep on Earth, Hazel woke up in Heaven. It wasn't as she'd expected: an ascent to the clouds, glittering gates parting without a creak, ranks of Angels singing hymns, quiet contemplation and serenity. This Heaven was super-imposed on the world she knew, more substantial by the minute. There were Angels, but they grew inside people, gradually emerging from human cocoons. And there was noise, not music. A wonderful, terrible, beautiful din rang throughout the Light. Every instrument ever created by man was playing at once, full blast, all the saints and sinners who'd ever lived singing the songs of their lives. In the row, it was impossible to pick out single sounds, but the combined music of all the world until now sounded like 'Happy Birthday to You' sung through bullhorns by the massed population of China.

Close by, Sister Janet was caught midway between human and Angel, thick-feathered wings splitting the sleeves of her blouse, halo forming around her fringe, inner light showing in patches through poor flesh. Others had changed without fuss and pain, but Janet found it harder. Her song was a scream. Her bones readjusted to wings, ribcage expanding to stretch her blouse tight, arms fusing with the feathers. Her halo burned bright, fuelled by beams radiating from her eyes and the fissures of her skull. Her scream became a bird squawk, and she flapped wildly, one wing batting away a chunk of brickwork hanging nearby. The chunk floated slowly into the Light, crumbling. Others, full Angels or unaffected, gathered around Janet, trying to soothe, to calm her down before she did damage.

Beloved was unmoved by His disciple's plight. Failure of this test would mean expulsion from the ranks of the Chosen. Hazel, still a newcomer, knew little. Knowing was less important than being, she understood. Last night, she'd become Beloved's Sister-Love, which meant she'd won a celestial contest without even being aware she had been entered. She had the pack-tops and her slogan prevailed, now she was at the right hand of the Lamb. She felt a pulling at her heart, tugging her towards Beloved, towards her prepared role.

Jenny was by her, a robe ready. Eyes fixed on Beloved, Hazel stepped off the bed and into the robe, which Jenny fastened. It tied at the waist and shoulders, but was vented down to the small of her back. To make room for wings. The floor was a soft carpet of Light, like condensed cloud, and gravity wasn't working. Small objects drifted from their places and slowly ascended. Jenny's hair was bobbing in tendrils as if she were floating underwater, bubbles leaking from her smile. The Light was warm, but not hot. As bright as the sun, it didn't hurt her eyes. It tickled her ankles and exposed arms, and sparkled in the air, washing around everything like a liquid one hundred times thinner than water.

From Beloved's face, she could tell her barely remembered old life was over. It might have happened to someone else, and been told to her. She no longer had a family, friends, a boyfriend. She had the Brethren of the Agapemone. She had Beloved.

Janet was airborne, fighting currents of Light, getting the hang of flight. She flapped off, vanishing into the Light, then came back, kicking at the air. She hovered over Beloved for a moment, and then pulled herself up into the sky, rocketing towards her own Heaven.

'The book,' Jenny prompted.

Hazel didn't know what her handmaid meant, but eventually her thoughts came together. Seven flames burned in the floor. They rose into the air like bubbles, revolved in concentric circles, then burst. From the point where the flames met, a book appeared. It fell to the bed, bouncing once on the mattress. Hazel looked to Beloved, but got nothing from Him. She must find her own way, with only her handmaid's cues to guide her. The book looked like a Bible, handsomely bound with gold inlay and tooled leather. It had a shining steel spine, and was locked with seven bands of metal, two at the bottom, two at the top, and three at the side. The bands were welded in place by red lumps of wax, inset into which were ceramic buttons, glazed with symbols she didn't recognize but could have traced.

'The book with seven seals,' Jenny explained.

A knot in Hazel's mind untied, and words came, issued from her mouth. 'Who is worthy to open the book,' she asked, 'and to loose the seals thereof?'

Jenny squeezed her arm encouragingly. She felt as good as she'd done when, at six, she'd remembered and perfectly enunciated her single line in the nativity play, 'I bring myrrh.'

Hazel picked up the book. It was as light as an empty cereal packet.

'Behold,' Jenny said, 'the Lion of the tribe of Judah, the Root of David . . .'

Hazel walked towards the place where Beloved sat upon His throne, surrounded by Light. Once, this had been a small upstairs bedroom; now, it was a vast plain, at once above and upon the Earth. Hazel walked between ranks of Angels, bare feet sinking a little into the thick-pile Light. Among the Angels, she saw the transformed faces of the Brethren. She recognized Derek, free at last of Wendy; Kate, nursing a golden child to her breast; Gerald, purged of his inner violence; Cindy, lost in rapture.

'Thou art worthy to take the book,' she said to Beloved, words pouring from her, 'and to open the seals thereof, for thou was slain, and hast redeemed us by thy blood. And we shall reign on the Earth.'

She spoke as she walked, and distance expanded. Light grew, becoming clearer as it spread. Angels filled the skies to the infinite distance. Among them, Hazel saw Patch, Mum, Paul, schoolfriends, Wendy, boys she'd forgotten. Everyone she'd ever met, so much as shared a bus with. A sea of faces flowed around and above, wings knitting into one mass, haloes linked like a chain, robes flowing together. In her mind, she found more words, 'and the number of them was ten thousand times ten thousand'.

At the foot of the throne, she looked up at Beloved. He seemed miles above her, but she could reach out and touch Him, for she was His Sister-Love. Jenny was by her side, smiling and golden. His wounds opened and shining blood flowed from His feet and hands, streams pooling before His throne, rising to Hazel's knees. She was washed in the blood of the Lamb. She raised the book above her head, its seven seals blinking like seven eyes. Beloved took it, and she was relieved of a huge burden. Hazel and Jenny knelt in the blood of the Lamb and dipped their hands to the pool, feeling the thrill. For a moment, Hazel was Jenny and Jenny was Hazel. Their understandings doubled, they embraced in the pool – now up around their waists – and looked to Beloved, adoring, praising, beseeching.

Jenny took a deep breath, shaking off the fog of rapture, and recited, 'Blessing and honour and glory and power be unto Him that sitteth upon the throne, and unto the Lamb for ever and ever.'

'Amen,' Hazel breathed, proud of her handmaid.

Beloved touched fingers to the first seal, snapped it in two with a pinch.

'Amen,' came a deafening chorus of Angels.

Six

'STOP PLAYING WITH your food,' Allison told Terry.

The boy was a complete wolf now, trussed by the last of his clothes, snout deep in the Toad's open stomach. In the tree-filtered daylight, the blood on the grass and the ground was old and faded, barely even wet. It had been scattered in a fifteen-foot circle.

She had found them a hundred yards into the wood, in a hollow bounded by trees. Mike Toad was half buried, loose earth and dry leaves over his face and chest. Terry was chewing the dead boy, softening gristly scraps for swallowing.

Bob inside, Jazz gone, Mike sacrificed, and Terry a wolf. Of the army, that left her alone.

'. . . and I looked,' Ben said in her mind, 'and beheld a pale horse, and his name that sat on him was Death, and Hell followed with him.'

Terry looked up, around and at her. His wolf eyes were still afraid of her. But that wouldn't last long. Soon, all memory of his earlier life would be wiped, replaced by mindless instinct. He growled through his food, warning her away from his kill.

She left Terry to it, and found one of her runs, a straight pathway, impossible for anyone else but easy for her, leading up over the crest of Alder Hill and back down towards the village, emerging in the gardens of the Agapemone. That, she knew, was where she must go next.

'. . . power was given unto them over the fourth part of the earth, to kill with sword, and with hunger, and with death, and with the beasts of the earth.'

She crouched low and wiggled into her run. The tunnel-like borehole through the undergrowth was well concealed. Beyond the brambles she had cultivated as offputting walls, the close-in branches and bushes were comforting, as if she were safe in her childhood bed, blankets tented around her, toys nestled against her legs. There was a natural earth-and-animal smell. Amid the change, it was comforting to find the familiar.

On elbows and knees, she sped as if swimming through the run. She moved as fast as an animal, low-hanging twigs catching her hair. Under her, the soil radiated a warm aura.

The battle begun, she was called to arms. With Ben gone, she knew to whom she owed loyalty. Her parents always said Jago was mad or a con man. Terry and Teddy used to claim he was a religious fool and an old hippie. Jenny Steyning thought he was Jesus Christ returned. Before she got kicked out of school, she'd heard Tina Starkey's ex-boyfriend allege the Agapemone was a nest of satanic child abusers, and Jago was the high priest of a devil cult. If she'd thought about him at all before this, Allison had considered Jago a threat, almost a rival. They had all been wrong. Now, Allison knew him for what he was. He was her God, if no one else's. Badmouth Ben had been but the palest advance scout. The man in the Agapemone had spoken to her in dreams and through the curves of the land. He'd shown her how to read auras. She wished her granddad had lived to meet Jago.

Outside her brush and bramble tunnel, people were shouting, screaming. She smelled smoke. Fires had been kindled. She licked air, tasting blood. She wondered about Jenny. Allison had known the girl all her life, but never really thought about her. As a kid, Jenny had been careful to keep out of Allison's way. Since she'd joined the Agapemone, they'd barely glimpsed each other. Now, Allison wondered if the light-haired girl was her sister-in-soul, the other half of her dark comma, the white half that completed the yin-yang. Jenny had come to understand Jago, had seen long before Allison that the man was the flame to which she must bow, but they were both Jago's favoured servants.

There were things only Jenny could do for Jago. And there were things that were down to Allison. Last night, she'd killed for Jago. She'd chewed human flesh in her personal communion. She loved Wendy for leading her. Not until she tasted the woman's meat had she truly known her destiny.

There'd be people who'd stand against Jago. He was too pure, too perfect for this world. He'd need someone to protect him. Not someone like Jenny, full of milk-and-water kindness, but someone not stifled by Gentle Jesus Meek and Mild. Someone like her.

She was near the Agapemone now. The knit over growth
above her was thinning out, and light poured into the run.
In the dark of her mind, she saw Wendy, flesh ripped away,
kneeling before Jago and beseeching him, 'How long, oh Lord,
holy and true, dost thou not judge and avenge our blood on them
that dwell on the earth?'

Allison came to the end of the run and stood up, bending aside
two flexible bushes, stepping on to a neat lawn. Half-people
shamble-danced around a corpse which lay amid the croquet
hoops, one shoe off, football-sized lumps bursting out of its
neck. A man kneeling cross-legged with an electric guitar,
turned into an egg-shaped fuzz of fungus, wrung strange chords
from his instrument, fused-together fingers banging against
strings, painful yowls booming from his portable amplifier.

People congregated around the Agapemone. Their collective
aura made Allison shield her eyes for a moment, the kaleidoscope
of coloured glows forming patterns no one else could see or
understand. 'Not yet,' Ben's voice whispered in the crowd noise,
'but *soon*!' The Manor House was a castle of light, a white-hot
jewel set in the green of its gardens. It had become its own aura.
People streamed towards it, pushing into its walls, becoming
part of the building. She saw human shapes inside the walls,
dissolving and dispersing. The Light undulated like a submarine
cliff thick with glowing seaweed.

A naked youth with a long face painted on his chest and belly –
circled nipple eyes, grinning mouth under the navel, malformed
wart genitals erupting through a pubic goatee – ran up to her.
He shouted, 'Gypsy princess, gypsy angel', and tried to kiss her.
Didn't this fool know who she was? She put a thumb in one of
his real eyes and heaved him, shrieking, away.

The ground was shaking, spreading cracks swallowing slabs
of turf and mounds of gravel. Dancers stumbled and dropped
into holes, cries fading as they vanished into the earth. The guitar
player was suddenly sitting on a pillar surrounded by chasms.
He kept flinging his mitten-shaped hands at the strings, a mouth
aperture opening in his face fur to emit a strangled vocal. 'Wild
thing,' he sang, over and over, the chords more agonized, 'Wild
thing, wild thing, wild thing.' Evil-smelling clouds of coloured
smoke rose from the cracks.

Allison walked across the lawns with perfect balance, unafraid
of earthquakes. She was protected as she neared the Light. A

huge shadow fell upon the land, making the Light shine that much brighter. She glanced up. 'The sun became black as sackcloth of hair, and the moon became as blood.' The sun and the moon were both clearly visible, a swarming black ball and a bright red eye-dot. Many panicked and began wailing, fighting, pushing themselves towards the Agapemone. She stood calm, understanding the sky show for what it was. Special effects.

'. . . and the stars of Heaven fell unto the Earth.'

A volley of bright bullets came out of the sky. A wedge of the crowd were struck and fell, bloody or dead. Allison knew she was safe. Steve Scovelle, who worked for Jenny's father, was standing nearby, compulsively wiping his oily hands on his overalls. A shining dart, twinkling as if it were trailing tinsel, speared into his face. Another took him in the leg. He fell, trampled under. The falling stars were bigger now, the size of rocks and boulders. People were smashed down as if by giant fists.

'. . . and the kings of the Earth, and the rich men, and the chief captains, and the mighty men, and every bondman, and every free man, hid themselves in the rocks of the mountains, and said, Hide us from the face of Him that sitteth on the throne, from the wrath of the Lamb . . .'

All around Allison, people were dead or abasing themselves, pleading. As she heard Ben voice the prophecy, she imagined presidents and generals letting themselves into their deep-level shelters, preparing for a holocaust that would reach even them. Missile silos must be open all over the world, swords of Armageddon free of their scabbards. If Jago wanted everything wiped clean, she was sure he'd use the most modern methods as well as the most ancient.

She went round to the front of the Agapemone, persuading the crowd to part, and stood before the stairs. People lay flat, as close together as herringbone tiles, on the front path, and each of the steps was a living person, stretched full across. A moving human road lead to the door. The face of the house was a cliff of light, featureless white. But above the human steps stood the familiar wooden door, lock exploded, side panels smashed. The door hung, held not by hinges but by tendrils of glow. The world might shiver, but the door stayed a fixed point.

'. . . for the Great Day of His Wrath has come . . .'

Allison walked slowly over the screaming path, up the groaning stairs, and stood before the door.

'. . . and who shall be able to stand?'

'Me,' Allison said. 'I shall stand.'

She pushed the door inwards, and entered the Light.

Seven

W HEN THE SKY darkened, Teddy reckoned that was the end
of it. He sat against the wall and waited for the Hand of Death
to grab his goolies.

'Recognize this?' Susan asked the man from the Pottery.

He shrugged.

'"Black as sackcloth of hair, and the moon became as blood,"'
she said. 'Book of Revelation, somewhere.'

Blood rained from boiling darkness. The ground gave way all
round. Something like a red iceberg loomed from one of the
cracks, ripping apart the fence at the end of the pub garden.

'I can only remember the famous bits,' James said. '"His name
that sat on him was Death, and Hell followed with him."'

'That's the one,' the woman said.

Hell was all round.

Teddy didn't believe in Heaven or Hell, normally. His parents
didn't go to church except at Christmas and Easter. In his stream
at school, he had not had to do religious education. He had never
owned or opened a Bible. Christmas was turkey and presents,
Easter was chocolate eggs. The Pope was a Polish bloke in a
white dress, God was the old man with a beard on *Spitting Image*,
and Jesus was a hippie in films they showed on television on
bank-holiday afternoons.

But he recognized Hell.

Angels flew overhead in the red darkness, and devils stalked
below, tridents and swords bloody, hooves gouging earth, bat
wings flapping, horns sharp. Teddy wanted to face the wall and
forget it, but couldn't.

A fat red devil with Douggie Calver's broad face came out of
the Valiant Soldier. Curly goat's horns swept around his face, and
his eyes were cat-slit. He wore a 'Drink Scrumpy' T-shirt and
strained-to-splitting bermuda shorts. The devil stank of cider and
used matches. Talons sliced towards Teddy, but James stepped

under the blow and smashed the devil in the face with his gun,
making blood spout from its ram-nose. James punched him in
the belly, and he was seen off. As he ran, an arrow-ended snake
of a tail dangled between his legs.

Scarlet lightning cracked the daytime dark of the sky. The blood
rain redoubled, turning the ground to fiery mud.

Paul spat out the blood that flooded his mouth. The shower ended,
he was covered from head to foot in sticky red. At last, it had
rained. From the black above, waves of heat came down. The
blood dried to a crust and fell away in patches. He saw Susan's
face mottled with missing jigsaw pieces of clean skin amid the
red. She was scraping clotted filth out of her hair. In the dark she
had a slight glow, an all-over halo.

Revelation was the only book of the Bible he had ever read
all the way through. It was a cornerstone of his thesis that the
imagery of nineteenth-century apocalyptic fiction was adapted
from the biblical original. Now, knowing the prophecies didn't
seem to help. He couldn't get anything straight, and the Bible
had too many tribes and angels and seals and beasts to cope with.
Tribes, he remembered in a mumble, of Judah, Aser, Manasses,
Nepthalim, Levi, Issachar, Zabulon, Benjamin. He wondered if
Jago were picking up sides for the battle of Armageddon, allotting
people to their tribe. He wanted to be left on the bench with the
bespectacled fat kid.

'Susan,' Lytton said, 'how . . . extensive –?'

She answered before he could finish, picking the question from
his mind. 'I don't know. It must be localized.'

'The parish, the county?'

She thought hard. 'I can't tell.'

Above, the black churned. The sun was a hole, sucking
everything in until it was an absence in the sky. The moon,
still not set, was a ball of blood, red as a stop lamp.

How far away were people looking up and seeing this? Were
there people a few miles off who saw plain blue and summer sun?
Or did everyone in the world have the sky according to Jago?

'He's just one mind,' Susan said, 'one vision. His Talent feeds on
all these people, but he can't change the whole solar system . . .'

'Can't he?' Lytton said.

Creatures were fighting in the dark, killing and breaking each
other. Ignorant armies clashing by night.

'Think about it. If the sun went dark, we'd freeze, not boil. The sun and the moon aren't up together. Jago is projecting pictures. He's not really making this happen.'

Something with scythes for arms set about a crowd of devils, slicing and dicing until only jellied demon fragments, still writhing, remained.

'Like I've always said,' Susan insisted, 'it's not demons and devils, it's just chemicals in the brain.'

A gale of demon laughter swept past the pub. A person, piranha imps tearing at flesh, stumbled by, crying out. The victim went down in a pool of flashing teeth, and was devoured.

Paul picked a pebble and bit it with his bad tooth. Sunlight and pain poured in. A man, torn almost inside out, lay in the road. There were no monsters, but there might as well have been. All around, people hurt themselves, hurt each other. As pain receded, dark flooded back.

Inside the tree, the Maskell family were together. Jeremy, closer than ever to his parents and sister, could see through their eyes, feel through their fingers. Even Jethro was a part of it. Their roots were deep in the earth, anchoring the tree to the soil, so the quakes did not affect them. He was safe. Daddy couldn't hurt him without hurting himself. Daddy didn't want to hurt him any more.

It was night again, but a good night, warm and comforting. Protected, Jeremy watched with interest. People who hadn't changed suffered. Over the top of the Pottery, from the topmost branches, Jeremy saw the garage forecourt. People were pulled into the ground as if the asphalt had become a sucking lake of tar. X and Ingraham were up to their waists, going deeper as they tried to get out. One of the petrol pumps was bobbing, pulled from below. With a gulp, it disappeared completely and sticky black slowly filled in the hole. The tar smoked, belching through cracks in its surface.

Lisa Steyning floated as deep as her armpits, a tyre around her, black goop in her pretty-pretty hair. Not panicking like X and Ingraham, she wasn't going under. Jeremy wasn't sorry to see Lisa trapped, but was glad she wasn't sinking. She was mean to him most of the time, but there was something about her – her hair, perhaps – he liked, or thought he would like in a few years, when he got interested in girls. Would have liked, he corrected himself. He would have to be his own teacher, and watch how

he thought. Things were different. His life wasn't going to be
what he'd expected, what his mother and teachers had told him
it would be. Only Daddy had really known, and he had not told
anyone because they'd never believe until it started happening.

It was funny, having a tree as a body, sharing a body
with the others. Hannah's thoughts whispered in his mind,
reciting her times tables. That was Mummy's remedy for
nightmares. Whenever Jeremy or Hannah had bad dreams,
Mummy suggested they go over their times tables – as far as
they had learned them – in their heads, and the evil dwarves
or scary monsters would go away. Times tables, she explained,
were logic. Numbers could overcome the things in the dark.
Mummy had been wrong. Jeremy felt Mummy's love, neat and
safe like a blanket. And he felt Daddy's strength.

On the lawn, Fancy stood, chewing apples that fell from the
tree. The horse had been sick, but was better now.

X and Ingraham had been gulped under. Ingraham was gone
altogether, but X floated face down, the back of his X-shaven
head above the surface, arms outstretched in front of him, the
back of his T-shirt a bubble over the black, the rest of him deep
under. Little flames danced around him.

Jeremy felt the buds of the tree swell. There'd be more fruit
soon.

'She's right,' Paul said. 'It's like there are two pictures.'

Susan felt his pain, sharp and pure. And saw what he saw. It
was no better than what everyone else in Alder was stuck with,
even if the sun was shining and the moon had set. Reality hurts,
she thought.

A demon cavalry officer rode by the pub, in a tight red tunic
with gold piping and epaulettes, a human skin worn *en pelisse* over
one shoulder, tall shako fixed to his head by horns, red-hot sabre
in one elegantly gloved claw. He was mounted on a large locust,
regimental symbols etched into its carapace, saddle perched on
its wing-case. The insect trotted like a well-drilled steed. The
moustached demon surveyed the carnage with all the superior
insouciance of a marshal of France. People fell before the locust,
chomped by its triangular mouth, born down by its shod forelegs.
The officer slashed deftly, detaching heads and arms.

She heard shrieks of panic in her mind. This Armageddon
was the fusion of everyone's dreams and fancies, sucked into

Jago's overwhelming self-belief. His was the basic shape of the drama, but everyone else provided set dressing, worked in their own business. It was a community play, a sprawling spectacle costumed in fancy dress gathered from the back of closets, sets knocked together by DIY freaks with more enthusiasm than skill, variably acted.

The mounted locust was impressive and detailed. But other vignettes were barely sketched in. A cardboard-box robot lumbered down the street, a stiff wire spiral of smoke coming from the flashing light on its head, legs crumpling as it stamped.

Much of the village was destroyed and replaced. A chest-high mountain range had erupted along one side of the main road, throwing back houses and gardens. A black tower, like a large chess castle, stood askew where the Cardigan house had been, ravens circling its battlements, fire pouring from its gutters. Cat-sized red ants surrounded the tower with miniature siege engines.

Susan tried to create an island of calm. She found her centre, and let it radiate. The ground stopped shaking in the pub garden, and light penetrated the dark.

'Susan, is that you?' Lytton asked.

His words shocked her, and she lost it.

'Sorry,' he said.

She shook his apology away, and tried again. It took all her concentration, and showed just how feeble her Talent was next to Jago's. There was now a smooth stretch of pub lawn beneath, garden furniture jumbled up together against the wall. Light descended around them. Teddy shoved himself away from the wall and, unsteadily, stood up. They all looked up at the gap in the night.

Her head was heavy, pain throbbing inside. Her temples hurt, and the entire back of her skull. Still, she'd affected it somehow.

A girl scrambled over the wall, bursting through the curtain of dark, and lay, gasping. She was a redhead, dressed in black, white legs showing through holes in her tights, scrapes on her bare back. She crawled to Lytton, seeking security, and hugged his legs.

'You've found an admirer,' Susan said.

He looked embarrassed. 'This is Pam. She's a nuisance.'

Pam did not speak, just whimpered a little. Another mental casualty.

His wife and children were in their places. And he was fixed to the soil. No matter what strife might rage around, the Maskell Family Tree was safe.

The blood of the boy who'd been sacrificed fed and watered them. Sue-Clare was nestled by his side, head in his armpit, arms wrapped tight around him. The children grew where they should, sprouting branches of their own.

The couple who'd slept in his shade were awake now, presenting offerings. The man found some bananas inside the house and laid them on a shelf that ran around the trunk. They slumped before Maskell, looking up with reverence. Others had joined them in worship. Maskell had a congregation. Everyone was looking for something to believe in these days. He had found nature's path, and it was his duty to let the word spread.

'Show us, oh Swamp Thing,' the man said, 'show us the way.'

Maskell was amused, but didn't reply.

'The sun is black, the moon is red,' the man said. 'Save us.'

'Yes,' chimed the others, 'save us.'

Maskell stretched branches. He wondered what his first demand should be. Most of the worshippers were young men and women who'd come for the festival. But there were a few villagers mixed in. Reg Gilpin stood, naked to the waist, looking up at his former employer. Maskell remembered Reggie from when he was a boy. An electric wire snapped by the house and fell out of the sky, sparking and kicking like an angry eel. The wire brushed the tree, and he recalled the first spark of the soil.

'Come forward,' he roared. 'Bring me Reggie Gilpin.'

Reggie was astounded. He had not recognized Maskell. None of the others knew Reggie, but his reaction gave him away. The worshippers grabbed him and forced him to his knees before the tree, shoving his face into the dirt between the roots.

Maskell's quirt hung from the tree trunk, supple and strong.

He extended arms from his trunk and grabbed Reggie, hugging him to the tree. His quirt whipped out, twining around Reggie's waist like an elephant's trunk, and grew tight. The worshippers gave a hearty cheer as Reggie came apart. Goodness spread on the tree and the ground.

Since he last saw her, Pam had become demented. Luckily, she'd turned timid rather than unmanageable. In the oasis of peace Susan had made of the garden, Lytton hugged the girl like a baby. There was no desire in her clinging, just a desperate need for comfort.

Without consulting anyone, he made a unilateral decision.

'Okay,' he told Susan, 'I'm pulling the plug.'

She nodded, knowing what he meant.

He had twelve cartridges in the Browning, another full clip in his pocket.

'If Jago goes, this all stops, right?'

Susan shrugged. 'Maybe.'

He had been hoping for more positive approval.

'It'd be a start.'

'Certainly.'

He looked at Pam, a frightened child under the streaks of make-up. And he saw Teddy, a broken doll bent by the weight of wonders. There were dead people up and down the street. And monsters.

But could he kill someone? Even to stop all this?

'I don't think he's really alive anyway,' Susan said. 'His Talent has eaten away whatever mind he started out with.'

'I wish you wouldn't do that.'

'I can't help it. You scream your thoughts, you know.'

'Thanks for telling me.'

He imagined putting the Browning to Jago's head, and pulling the trigger until the clip was empty.

'Ugh,' she said. 'Messy.'

He gave Pam to Paul and said, 'Look after her. And Teddy.'

The young man nodded. Pam's tenacious grip was transferred to him.

He hoped he could just walk up to the Agapemone, let himself in and get to Jago without anyone trying to stop him.

'You wish,' Susan said. 'I'm coming with you.'

He did not even have to think his objection.

'You can't do it alone. A Talent could see you coming a mile off. Even a stone-crazy Messiah like Jago. I can engage his attention long enough for you to get near. Then it's up to you. Bang bang bang.'

She made a finger gun and pointed it.

'I'll try,' Susan said, answering some mental question of Paul's. 'Where she is, she should be safe. Once Jago is gone, she should be okay. Everyone should be free then.'

'Let's go,' he said, stepping over the garden wall, back into pandemonium.

Eight

K AREN HAD CHOSEN to become a baby, and was gurgling happily in adult-sized robes, a crown of tinsel perched in the air above her head. Gerald Taine was a full Angel, eagle wings spread behind him, hair flowing to his waist. Derek was in a cloud of multicoloured fog, disco-lit by a swarm of tinkling fireflies. In Heaven, Jenny realized, you were whatever you wanted. She, however, hadn't changed.

'Salvation to our God which sitteth upon the throne,' she said, gazing upon the face of the Beloved, 'and unto the Lamb.'

The Brethren, transformed, chorused, 'Blessing and glory and wisdom and thanksgiving and honour be unto our God for ever and ever, Amen.'

'These are they that have come out of great tribulation,' Jenny said, 'and have washed their robes, and made them white in the blood of the Lamb. Therefore are they before the throne of God, and serve Him day and night in His temple. They shall hunger no more, neither thirst any more, for the Lamb shall lead them unto living fountains of waters, and God shall wipe away all tears from their eyes.'

The Brethren raised alleiluyas, and the Light varied its magnificence. They were wrapped in His glory. Fountains rose behind the throne, Light rainbowing in the sweet waters that flowed around the feet of the Lamb, mingling with the bright blood, flowing down among the Brethren. Kate picked up Karen and gathered her in her arms, together with her own baby. Beloved had opened the book, breaking the seven seals, and set it aside. Below, the consequences raged, as the unrighteous were cut down by unloosed plagues. The chaff blew on the burning wind.

Beloved stretched out His right hand, wound leaking pure Light. He called for the Sister-Love. Hazel, nervous, edged away. Jenny took the girl's shoulders and eased her forwards, up to the throne. Hazel dipped her fingers in Beloved's wound, and the chosen girl's doubts vanished.

'Let Him kiss me with kisses of his mouth,' she said.

Beloved dipped His head, pressing His face close to Hazel's. With their kiss, the Light around doubled its intensity. Jenny, driven back, humbly went on to her knees. Blood and water flowed around her, a brook cascading down the stairways of the Agapemone. She shuffled backwards in the shining stream, and was swept past the ranks of the Chosen, out to the hallway. She'd been chosen by Beloved for her own mission.

The Light wasn't as strong in the hall as in the throne room. The walls of the Manor House were still discernible. The telephone stood on its stand, the lounge door hung open. The veiled, dark woman who was sometimes glimpsed stood in the doorway. Jenny smiled at the lost soul, but she turned away in a flutter of black lace, becoming a simple shadow.

Beyond the Agapemone, the Bottomless Pit was opened up, poisonous smoke seeping out, creatures swarming forth. 'And there came out of the smoke locusts upon the earth, and unto them was given power, as the scorpions of the earth have power . . .'

The front door was pulled from the outside. Jenny spread her hands in welcome. The door open, a rough dark figure was silhouetted, bringing into Heaven some of the chaos of the world below.

'. . . it was commanded them that they should not hurt only those men which have not the seal of God in their foreheads. And to them it was given that they should not kill them, but that they should be tormented five months: and their torment was as the torment of a scorpion, when he striketh a man . . .'

Fringed by Light, the figure's outline was fuzzy, insect-blurred, inconstant, but eyes shone with a watery brilliance. Beyond the Light, a chitinous rattle drowned out the screams of the tormented.

'. . . and in those days shall men seek death, and shall not find it; and shall desire to die, and death shall flee from them . . .'

The figure stepped forwards.

Jenny Steyning stood at the bottom of the staircase, in a blinding white dress with a train that gathered around her feet. Without make-up, her face was her nine-year-old sister's. Very seldom conscious of her own appearance, Allison knew how she must look – with her bramble-tangled hair, luminous eyes and shaggy, smelly jacket – next to Jenny.

'Allison?' Jenny asked, uncertain, peering through the Light at her.

Allison took two steps forwards, nodding. 'Jenny.'

They had never had much to say to each other. Allison remembered being not invited to Jenny's birthday party at primary school, and not caring much. At the comprehensive, they had rarely been in the same class. Teddy Gilpin fancied the girl, but she looked as if she'd break if touched. Besides, she was Jago's. She always had been, from the time the Lord God came to Alder. Now, Jago needed someone else.

Without Jago, their lives might have been different: Allison would be a bruised slag like Sharon Coram, hating herself as much as the louts she fucked; while Jenny would be a young farmers' cheerleader, like Beth Yatman, organizing dances and day trips to Minehead. In a few years, Allison would have turned into one of Alder's solitary mad people, like Mr Keough or her dead granddad; while Jenny would have ended up as Sue-Clare Maskell or Ursula Cardigan, married to a man with property or a business, working one day a week in a charity shop.

Jago had been a saviour for them both. Allison looked into Jenny's face and saw her own reflection, her dark against Jenny's light. She reached out and held the girl, hands on her shoulders. Jenny grabbed back, taking her waist. Neither knew whether to push or pull. Allison knew she could crush Jenny like a butterfly.

'We share Love,' Jenny said.

Allison pulled Jenny into an embrace. 'Sisters,' she said.

'Sisters,' Jenny confirmed.

There was an awkward moment. Allison felt Jenny squirming in their hug and let her go. 'I'm not a dyke,' she explained. 'God knows.'

Jenny smiled kindly and hugged Allison again, quickly and briefly.

'It's all right,' Jenny said, 'the other stuff is all gone. Flesh is old-fashioned. It's just Love now.'

'Love?'

'The Love of the Lamb. Beloved.'

Love was in the Light, but that was only a part of what Jago wanted. First, there must be a scourging.

'He needs me,' Allison said. 'So I'm here for Him.'

Jenny took her hand and led her upstairs. As they climbed, the Light was stronger. They went up more stairs than could possibly be in the house, stairs enough to take them half a mile into the sky. All around, the Brethren sang. They were like Jenny, shining from the inside. At last, having walked and climbed so far the aches fell from her body, Allison was brought before the throne. The girl from the Pottery – Paul's girlfriend – was nestled in Jago's lap. Fountains towered, and Light was made concrete in the throne. Jenny dropped to the floor and humbled herself. Allison saluted, a general before an emperor.

Jenny rose, reciting, 'And the shapes of the locusts were like unto horses prepared unto battle; and their faces were the faces of men, and they had hair as the hair of women, and their teeth were as the teeth of lions . . .'

Jago didn't need to speak to Allison. She knew she was welcomed into the fold. Soon Jago's enemies would try to topple Him. She was charged with guarding His life.

'. . . and they had a queen over them,' Jenny continued, holding Allison's arm, 'the Angel of the Bottomless Pit whose name in the Hebrew tongue is Abaddon, but in the Greek tongue is her name Apollyon.'

Abaddon, Apollyon. The names sounded comfortable, familiar, fitting.

'And in English?' she asked.

'Allison,' she was told.

Jenny, she realized, had just made her Queen of the Earth.

Before the throne were two girls, one light, one dark. Hazel remembered their faces, but it was what had been made of them that was important. Beloved's hand cradled her head, touch funnelling Light into her. Her own memories were faint, memories of a film she'd seen, not a life she'd lead. Other memories crowded in, blotting her out. A city at night, with fire all around, and sirens. London, she thought, during the Blitz. In the north, another city, a sea of faces beyond a lectern, listening to a sermon. A chapel in the rain, with Wendy and Derek. A first sight of the Manor House. The two girls as children, bare knees and big eyes. Her own face, eyes tight shut, with chanting and incense. Beloved whispered in her brain. She held tight to His arms, knowing He'd see her safely through the storm. For a moment, she thought she heard Paul crying out to her to be careful, but his tiny whine was lost in the music of angels. Through His eyes, she saw the earth below, devastated by fire and blood, scarlet seas thick with fish corpses, continents shifting and buckling, a poison star falling into the Atlantic, darkness thickening above the plains of carcasses. But in the Light, the Brethren were safe.

Nine

WITH DIFFICULTY, he managed to get Teddy and Pam into the pub. The boy was on the point of catatonia and probably had a few broken bones. When Paul held up three fingers and asked how many, the boy mumbled 'Jenny', which wasn't helpful or reassuring. The girl was only malleable because she'd been hysterical for so long she was exhausted. She needed to hold on to someone, so he thought it clever to attach her to Teddy, but he hurt when hugged. Finally, she settled for holding the boy's hand with a death-tight grip. Paul installed them in a deep sofa.

The saloon had fewer windows than the public bar, and thus felt more defensible. With Teddy and Pam settled and not in any immediate danger, Paul looked around, hoping not to find anything. If he shut his ears to the din outside, the empty place seemed normal. There was a notice board by the door. The heads of drawing pins reflected the light, reminding him the electricity was still working. There were posters up for a Christmas club and for the local skittles league, plus a bent card from someone who'd lost a cat and was offering a small reward for safe return.

Perched on a bar stool, he was drained. His tooth still hurt, but it was absurd to be concerned with that when he'd seen living people cut up, monsters from a medieval woodcut. He thought of Hazel, and tried to resign himself to never seeing her again, to never putting things right between them. It was impossible that both of them would survive the next few hours, let alone get back together. It was possible no one would survive the next few hours.

There was another tremor, and bottles fell down behind the bar. Teddy drew in a pained breath as Pam pressed close to him. Paul counted the seconds, and, when he was still alive after thirty, breathed again.

What would happen if Lytton killed Jago? Would reality come flooding back, a village packed with injured, insane or dead people? Maybe Jago's dreams could live on after his death, and killing him would end the world. Now, the end of the world was an option he was willing to countenance. At least, it would put a full stop to suffering. In nothingness, his bloody tooth wouldn't torment him any more.

Just for something to do, he poured a tumbler of whiskey, and sipped. The liquid made his broken tooth shriek, allowing actual sunlight to stream into the dark. The reality flash was short-lived. It took more pain each time to dispel the visions. Maybe Jago's dream would finally usurp everyone else's and *become* reality. He drank to the pleasant thought.

He strolled to the window and looked at the chaotic battle. Giant locusts crawled over the dead, six-winged 1950s special-effects horrors with scorpion tails grafted on to their hind parts. His tumbler was empty. He refilled it. No danger of getting drunk. There was enough fear adrenalin and nerve-deadening pain in him to counter a quart of Jameson's.

He couldn't work out how long Lytton and Susan had been gone. Time twisted and contorted around Jago. The black sunny day outside could have been any time in the morning, afternoon or evening back in the real world. Perhaps months had passed since moonset, perhaps only a few seconds.

He started playing with octagonal beer mats, making honeycomb patterns. Bored, he went behind the bar and scavenged. He hoped he'd find something to use in his defence, if it became necessary. All he came up with was a plastic box half-full of shiny drawing pins. Maybe he could scatter them in the path of something barefoot. He pocketed the box, hearing it chink as it slid against his hip.

Teddy was either asleep with his eyes open or in a comatose daze. Pam, tired of being stretched beyond breaking point, was coming round. He offered her a drink, and she shook her head.

'Are you down for the festival?' he asked, for want of anything else.

The girl nodded sulkily. 'I've lost my boyfriend.'

'Snap. Well, nearly. My girlfriend's off somewhere in this mess.'

'We were going to break up after this week.'

'We probably wouldn't have made it through to autumn,' he admitted.

'I think I've lost my sister, too.'

Pam was dabbing her face with a hankie, licking the cloth and then using it to work the clotted make-up away from her eyes and mouth. An ordinarily pretty face emerged.

'Why aren't we mad, like the others?'

'Good question,' he said.

The pub door opened, and Paul saw fear light Pam's eyes. Teddy moaned, his first sign of life in minutes. The saloon door pushed in and an Angel stepped through, wings bent to squeeze under the lintel. Paul recognized Janet, the champagne girl with the quick tongue. She recognized him too.

'Are you saved?' she asked.

Inside the saloon, she spread her wings. They grew from her arms, her fingers turned into lengthy, feathered bones. Her robe hung torn, and her skin shone with an all-over halo.

'Pretty Polly,' she said in a strangled parrot voice.

Pam was smitten, mouth a perfect circle.

Janet turned to the girl. 'Are *you* saved?' She extended a wing and brushed Pam's cheek with feathers. 'It's not too late, repent your sins.'

The girl was torn. She had a choice between the glowing fantasy and Hell on Earth. She threw herself against Janet, and allowed the Angel to fold wings around her. The girl's head rested against Janet's feathered shoulder, wings tight around them like a fur muff.

'Paul?' Janet said.

He shook his head.

'One saved,' Janet said, looking at Paul and Teddy, 'two lost . . .' She backed out of the saloon, shouldering through the door. 'Not a bad score.'

Paul followed, and was in the pub hall when Janet and Pam got to the outside. Pam clung to the Angel's neck. Janet, straining, extended her wings and jumped into the air. He watched them rise, dodging red bat shapes and falling stars, on course for the shining castle of the Agapemone. Pam was heavy, and dangled like an oversize necklace, but Janet's wings were stronger than they looked. The Angel wasn't graceful, but she was air-worthy.

A scorpion-locust scuttled towards the doorway, and Paul slammed the wood into the hole. The sting smashed through the door about a foot above the lino, and wedged, squirting poison. Paul avoided the steaming splash, and hoped the thing was stuck. The sting tugged against the hole, breaking off

splinters and dribbling, then was withdrawn. A locust leg stuck
in through the hole and scrabbled upwards for the doorhandle.
Paul crushed the leg to the door with his shoe, and it went limp,
torn off at the locust equivalent of a shoulder. He could hear the
thing yelling, with a rich Somerset accent, shouting, 'I'll 'ave
'ee', over and over.

Teddy, groggy and shell-shocked, was in the hall too. Paul
didn't agree with Janet. He'd been given two souls to look after,
and lost one. That struck him as a terrible score.

Ten

PROBLEM ONE was getting through the panicked crowds choking the approach road. Waving the gun had no effect on people who'd seen giant bugs and flying women. Lytton fired once, into the air, and the report – which normally caused deafness a mile off – was lost in the clamour. With Susan holding his hand, he shoved, pushed and trampled with the rest, inching towards the Manor House. It was impossible to miss the way even in the unnatural dark: the Agapemone was lit from the inside like a neon novelty.

'I suppose Jago is in there,' he shouted.

Definitely, Susan said, inside his mind.

Lytton shivered. She'd never done that before.

I didn't need to.

Witch.

I read that.

Sorry.

With Susan inside his mind, he was able – forced? – to concentrate. He became single-minded in his purpose to keep her away from whatever else was cluttering his forebrain. Like how often he thought of her recently. Her eyes, especially. Her occasional tight smiles.

I'm flattered, she thought, immediately swallowing it, trying unsuccessfully to keep it from him.

For the first time, just when he had no time to be compassionate, he realized how guarded Susan had to be. She was not really the chilled cynic she seemed; like him, she needed a wall to hide behind.

People began to give them a wider berth, as if an invisible cowcatcher were advancing before them. Lytton saw the road under his feet as the crowd parted, like the Red Sea for Charlton Heston.

'Is that you?'

Yes. Like it?

'Keep it up.'

When the casualties were listed, Jago ought to be lost among the rest of the Js. Lytton had always known being a snake meant, eventually, biting. Now, he didn't have time to think it through. Besides, he hadn't been given a sanction for his wet job. This was strictly a solo decision, taken because of his special knowledge. He hoped he'd never be called to justify his bite to Garnett or the minister.

If it were me, Susan thought to him, *I'd want you to do it. Really. He's not human any more. All the things that count are gone.*

That wasn't what bothered him most. He was afraid Sir Kenneth would want to keep Jago alive precisely *because* he could do what he was doing in Alder. What army would not want to have the Wrath of God on its side? This catastrophe might, within the parameters of the IPSIT project, be counted a success.

They were at the gates of the Agapemone, where multitudes gathered, staring up at the shining house or jostling forwards, seeking admission. The door, unaffected by the light that had seized the rest of the building, hung in space, a heap of faintly moving people on the front steps.

Look.

Lytton followed Susan's direction, and for a moment couldn't see what she meant. Rising out of the crowd was the tree that shaded his own front door, children hanging out of it like agile monkeys.

There's nothing there.

Precisely.

The Gate House was gone, collapsed or torn down. In its place was a Gordian knot of naked bodies. The cluster-fuck had grown, swollen with sinners who'd lost the hope of Heaven and saw no reason for restraint, and Calvinists who believed predestination had won them a ticket to Paradise and their own actions could not queer their passage.

'Fucking Hell,' he said.

That's right. That's exactly what it is. The Fucking Hell.

A head and torso rode the orgy. It was Sharon Coram, greased with bodily secretions, singing out in a continuous coming. Someone turned a hose on the cluster, but water just added to the lubrication. Some components of the churning pyramid only moved because people moved against them. Those at the bottom must have suffocated or been pressed to death. In the end, everyone would wind up at the bottom.

They tried to force their way through the gates, staying as far away as possible from the cluster. It had destroyed his house and was sucking in new people all the time. Lytton thought of things lost for ever, and realized there was nothing irreplaceable. He had not spent his life picking up essentials. He'd miss a few music and video tapes, and some of his broken-in clothes. Otherwise, he'd have junked it all when the job was over anyway.

A middle-aged man attacked the cluster with the hose, sloshing and whipping. He called a halt like an exasperated football referee during a twenty-two man punch-up on the field. He was inveighing loudly against sin and sodomy, lust and lechery . . .

Who is that? he thought.

You don't see him around much, Susan said in his mind. *It's the vicar.*

Arms and legs reached out of the heaving cluster, and the vicar was pulled in, stuck to the surface of the heap of bodies. His clothes tore as he was worked, protesting, to the apex. Sharon was waiting for him, a ravenous queen spider, and her tongue was halfway down his throat in an instant. His lower body was sucked in towards Sharon's momentarily unoccupied loins, and the cluster gave an obscene cheer as he began to respond. In a minute, he was just another part of permanent floating orgy. The abandoned hosepipe spewed water.

Lytton and Susan were through the gateway. Inside the grounds, the press wasn't quite so bad. Able to breathe almost easily, they walked across the lawn to the Agapemone.

'Well,' he said, setting foot on the human steps, 'here goes . . .'

Barbarians were at the gates. Alarums sounded.

'And I stood upon the sand,' Jenny said, 'and saw a beast rise up out of the sea, having seven heads and ten horns, and upon his horns ten crowns, and upon his heads the name of blasphemy . . .'

She looked to Allison, who was ready. The girl saluted Beloved. They knew who was coming, and how he must be met.

This close, Susan was almost doubled with pain, a mass

screaming inside her mind. She forced herself onwards. *Excelsior!*
Jago's unconfined energy rioted, eating away her Talent, spreading frenzy like an infection through the crowds. It had got worse
as they climbed the hill, and it had been bad enough down in the
village.

You'll have to kill him quickly, she thought, *cleanly*.

James understood. All those briefings must have got through
to him.

The knot of sexuality from the Fucking Hell made her uneasy.
A lot of Jago's unconscious problems were sexual, and they
found fruitful soil in people around him. Everyone was screwed
up in the bedroom. Even straight Christianity was founded on
the repression of sexual drives; Jago's brand systemized his belief-
corseted desires into an entire panoply of rituals and practices.

Inside the Agapemone, choirs of angels chorused. Divine Light
throbbed in the walls, and the Chosen raised alleiluyas to His
name.

Sex and God. That was the recipe for an Anthony William Jago.
Take a kid and fuck with his mind, teach him sex is an activity
for sewers and God a bearded bastard who smites multitudes.
Throw in the kind of zealous drive that leads to high office,
extreme wealth and a following of thousands. Then give that
kid the power to destroy a continent. Forget the Talent. It was a
wonder that, after the Jago education, no one had conventionally
ended the world. Beloved wasn't unique in his upbringing, just
in his capabilities.

The hall wasn't empty. Others had ventured in, and stood
about, bewildered. A foil-and-cardboard-skirted Roman legion-
ary was a refugee from some fancy-dress theatre group, thin-
chested inside his Stallone-shaped breastplate. Irena Dubrovna,
the resident echo, was in her doorway, blindly watching. She was
almost solid, another side effect of Jago's mental meltdown. Susan
thought the others could see her too. There were people trapped
inside the walls like flies in amber. By the front door, arms and
legs stuck out like mounted trophies.

'Where?' James asked.

She nodded towards the stairs. The focus was in the centre of
the house. James thumb-cocked his automatic, and began up the
main staircase.

Someone appeared on the landing and charged, fists flailing,
bellowing rage. A gust of hatred came with the man, thumping

Susan between the eyes. The vileness of the unleashed mind made her want to vomit. It crawled and squirmed around him, pouring on to Susan like stinking waste.

Faster than her eye could catch it, James brought up his gun and shot the man in the head. The hate was turned off like a radio, but he kept charging. His body thudded against James, knocking him backwards. They both fell to the floor, carpet wrinkling under them. Susan, relieved at the sudden removal of the man's jarring burst of emotion, helped James get out of the mess and to his feet. The corpse wore the last of a police constable's uniform, his face and hands tattooed with skulls and swastikas, symbols covering every inch of his skin. The last of his hate leaked away, melting into the floor.

'Erskine,' James spat.

He was shaking. He had never killed before, and was having to deal with it. Susan wasn't sure the snake was strong enough for this job. His specialty was surveillance, not assassination. She held him, hand to his forehead, and tried to soothe his worries away, to clean his doubts. *It'll be all right*, she thought, really trying to mean it, *it'll be all right*.

Roughly, he shoved her away. 'Don't,' he said. 'I won't be brainwashed.'

His disgust hurt her, but she was humbled. 'I'm sorry,' she said.

'No, you're not.'

He heard the call of the soil. The land was imperilled. He pulled up roots, and stumped out of the garden of the Pottery. Sue-Clare and the children were still a part of him, just as he was a part of them. Their togetherness gave him pleasure. The tree-worshippers, already organized into a hierarchy, followed at a respectful distance.

'We are your servants, oh Swamp Thing,' said Dolar, who wore a garland of Maskell's leaves around his forehead.

They'd been eating his fruit, and were on the way to becoming part of the family. Dolar had been hurt, and the fruit was making him better. Tiny shoots emerged from his speckled shoulder wound, pea-green boils stood out on his knuckles.

He knew where he should take root. The centre of Alder had shifted, from the Valiant Soldier to the Agapemone. The village should have known that when the old tree died. He was the new tree, and would last for centuries, growing from the heart of the community.

He wasn't sorry Barry Erskine was dead. He wasn't even sorry he'd been the one to kill him. But Lytton was still shaking. If not in body, in mind. And he knew Susan could tell if he was shaking inside. When she slipped into his mind and tried to shape him, he understood how Jago worked on his disciples. And he felt like a tool, like the conscienceless piece of machinery in his hand. Susan was trying to aim him at Jago, groping in his head for a trigger.

Two landings up, the Agapemone no longer even resembled the Manor House. It had become someone's idea of Heaven, walls of white silk billowing gently, marble fountains of warm milk at every corner, air honeyed with incense. Classical busts of Jago perched on pedestals at regular intervals, faces wise, suffering and benevolent.

Susan was close behind, urging. She was homing in on Jago like a plane following a radio signal. Even he felt the force of Jago's Talent. It was all around, like the sourceless light.

Eleven bullets. No, ten. The monster, Erskine, and the pointless warning shot. A spare clip in his pocket.

In Heaven, it was cool and calming. He still heard noise from outside, but very low in the background. Susan tugged his arm and pointed up another flight of stairs. Warily, they climbed again.

Teddy saw claws scrabbling at the frame of the window, then crunching around the wooden bars, smashing the glass. Paul picked up a stool and stabbed at the window like a lion-tamer, shooing away whatever was outside. Teddy covered his face with his arm, and heard the window and a considerable chunk of the wall being torn away. He still hurt, but thought he could probably run if he had to. He'd felt safer with James around. Paul was much more panicky, and had already lost Pam to the winged woman. He choked on dust, and looked again.

'Come on,' Paul said, 'we can't stay here.'

The beams of the low ceiling were creaking threateningly, the whole of one wall gone. Beyond the rubble, Teddy saw large insects fighting over a scrap that had once been alive. Whenever his cracked ribs ground, the insects wavered and vanished.

He got up and, with Paul, ran. With Susan gone, the shell of the Valiant Soldier had turned from refuge to trap. They hurdled the wreckage, and emerged blinking into a dark world lit by a glow from the Agapemone and the bright red of infernal fires. The battle was on the ground on all sides, also in the air. Demon things tore each other. An eight-foot-tall hooded skeleton with an old-fashioned scythe was cutting out the feet from under running people.

'That must be Death,' Paul observed.

A bull-headed beast with the body of a lion and the tail of a lizard charged and bore down upon Death, crushing him to the ground, snapping his scythe, scattering his bones with a worrying shake of his head.

'Great,' Paul said, 'Death is a pussy.'

'Look,' said Teddy, pointing up.'

Between giant bats and rocketing pterodactyls, a set of ordinary lights winked. Teddy heard blades whirring and felt wind on his face. The helicopter hovered as a large searchlight tried to mark out a level spot for a safe landing. Through open side doors, Teddy saw two huddled rows of soldiers, clutching guns, gasmasks on. Paul waved his arms up at the helicopter. A soldier drew a bead and, for a horrible moment, Teddy was sure the dickheaded squaddie was going to put a bullet in Paul's head.

Something with black butterfly wings swished against the rotor blades and was food-processed into a cloud of shreds. The helicopter dipped, the soldier with the gun tipped back into the body. Paul threw himself to the road, hands over his head. Teddy was fascinated by how slowly the disaster happened. The helicopter gently swayed as it turned wrong side up, drifting peacefully down. The seconds dripped by lazily. Two or three people fell out, arms and legs waving for a moment, and broke on the road. The rotors described a circle in the air, the helicopter creaking and complaining, sparks cascading out of its engine. A rotor scraped a wall, and the heavy machine was catapaulted out of Teddy's sight in a screeching cartwheel. It thumped over what was left of the pub and plopped into the dark beyond. An explosion behind the pub knocked Teddy backwards, almost off his feet, and a bright orange cloud expanded, burning his eyes.

The pub was on fire, flames licking the rubble. The pub sign was broken on the pavement, and the corked bottles inside were exploding, flinging burning spirits out in splashes. Teddy looked around for Paul, and thought he'd been trampled under. A gang of leather girls with knives were prowling the area, two on

motorbikes. They had angels tied up and dragging behind them.
One of the girls had a bloody pair of torn-off wings stapled to her
jacket. Not a girl, he realized; it was Mrs Keyte, his geography
teacher.

Fuck, things were out of hand!

Behind him, close, he heard a familiar growl, beginning low
and rumbling lower, spits of viciousness beneath the rasp.

'Terry?'

He turned around, and saw the large shape detach itself from the
shadows. A long tongue touched the floor. On four padded feet,
his brother jogged towards him, wet teeth catching red light.

They entered what Jago must think of as his throne room. It
was precisely the fantasy Susan expected. A choir singing his
praises, women prostrate at his feet, incense-stink of sanctity
thick all around. Jenny, serene in Jago's madness, and a dark,
dangerous girl attended Beloved's throne. The girl in his lap,
mind flickering tinily like a fly in a web, was Hazel. Up at the
top of the house, the curtain walls were fluffier, indistinguishable
from clouds. A pool of light beside the throne afforded a God's-
eye-view of the strife down in the village, a black relief map dotted
with flames, swarming with antlike doomed souls. Her head was
close to critical mass.

'Jago!' James shouted, trying to get the Lord God's attention.

The congregation turned to look, with a craning of necks
and a rustle of wings. Some of the more harpy-like angels
squawked. James and Susan walked down the gold-carpeted
aisle, like Dorothy and friends in the chamber of the great and
powerful Oz. The aisle grew longer, as if they were strolling the
wrong way on a moving pavement. James had his gun tucked
into his jeans, at the back, under his jacket. He wanted to get near
without being torn apart. Tendrils of fear linked their minds,
stretched now to breaking.

'. . . and I saw one of his heads as it were wounded to death,'
Sister Jenny said, 'and his deadly wound was healed, and all the
world wondered after the beast.'

Susan looked beyond Jenny and the other handmaid, beyond
Hazel in the Beloved's lap, and tried to see into the Lord God. His
mind was black, a blank obscured by his Talent. 'You're a very
bad man,' Dorothy had accused the exposed Oz. 'No,' he had
proclaimed, 'I'm a very good man . . .' If there was something

of Tony Jago left in the Lord God, Susan couldn't find it. '. . . I'm just a very bad wizard.' The man himself was another victim of his fantasies.

James was between Jenny and the dark girl now, looking up at the Lord God, reaching for his gun.

'This is a pile of shit,' he told Jenny, drawing the pistol. 'Snap out of it.'

He didn't immediately pull the trigger, and Susan knew they were lost. Jago touched his mind, stayed his hand.

'And he opened his mouth in *blasphemy* against God,' Jenny shouted, the Brethren rising angrily to their feet.

Susan saw at once how James had been written into Revelation. An enormous surge of channelled detestation showered upon him from the Lord God and all his faithful. Jenny was still reciting St John. James staggered back, gunhand jerking as he tried to shoot upwards. He was unable to fire. Susan felt his need to shoot crying out in her mind, but also rising frustration as his wrist and fingers wouldn't obey the commands of his brain. It was over, and they were dead.

'He that leadeth into captivity shall go into captivity,' Jenny said, in an even tone.

The dark girl took James by the lapels and bent him backwards, pressing his shoulders to the floor. The gun slipped away.

'He that killeth with the sword must be killed with the sword . . .'

'. . . here is the patience and the faith of saints.'

Allison had her knee on the Anti-Christ's chest. He was a poor specimen. Their game of hide-and-seek in the woods had given her a chance to gauge his skills. He was nothing. Prince of Lies, Trickster Duke, Pathetic Loser. Allison held the Anti-Christ's chin and kept his head still. She rolled out of the way, to allow the force of Beloved's gaze to fall upon him. She half expected him to shrivel to dust, or to explode in flames. He struggled, weakly.

'Here is wisdom,' Jenny said. 'Let him that hath understanding count the number of the beast, for it is the number of a man . . .'

A circle began to burn on the Anti-Christ's forehead, three commalike sixes twirled together.

'. . . and his number is Six Hundred Three Score and Six.'

*

Paul was swept on a human tide, borne towards the Agapemone.
As the fighting died down, a lemming rush started. Striding on
branches among the crowds was the Maskell Family Tree, a file of
followers trailing behind it like *Hare Krishnas*. Paul was surprised
at how tall it had grown. It had four faces, not counting the eyes
of a dog dotted near its roots. Its worshippers, led by Dolar, were
starting to green. He worked his feet desperately, pumping the
ground, knowing that if he stumbled he'd be crushed. Light was
all around now, banishing the dreadful night, replacing the absent
sun. The house pulled him like the moon pulling the tide.

Beloved stood, and looked upon His fallen enemy. Hazel didn't
understand, but guessed this was the end of a court struggle begun
thousands of years ago. The man with 666 branded on his forehead
was trying not to scream. He didn't look especially evil, but he had
dared to defy Him.

After so long in His embrace, Hazel, set aside, was weak as an
old woman. Jenny stepped in to comfort her and hold her up.

At the end of the aisle stood Sister Susan. She had come before
Beloved's throne with the traitor, and was exposed as a Judas. The
woman was looking about, nervous, expecting an attack.

'Babylon is fallen,' Jenny whispered, 'that great city, because
she made all nations drink of the wine of the wrath of her
fornication.'

Around Susan, the carpet fell apart and shrank from wooden
floorboards. The woman was concentrating. She made fists and
lifted them up. As she did so, Hazel saw nailheads protrude from
the floor. Maybe a dozen of them. The nails popped out of the
floor. Boards twanged as they bent up at the ends. The nails
slowly rose as Susan's fists were lifted. They clustered together
like a flock of tiny metal birds.

'I saw a woman sit upon a scarlet coloured beast, full of names
of blasphemy, having seven heads and ten horns . . .'

The clump of nails began to glow with heat. Susan's fists were
white knots, dotted with blood.

'And the woman was arrayed in purple and scarlet, having a
golden cup full of the filthiness of her fornication.'

Susan opened her fists, and the nails flew towards Beloved.

It was a nice try, but futile. Susan whipped back as the
nails fragmented in the air before Jago's face, spanging

harmlessly against the floor.

If James got to be the Anti-Christ, she was left as the Whore of Babylon. Great. Jago's gospel being Sexism Writ in Flame, she knew that let her in for disproportionate suffering.

'*Babylon the Great, the Mother of Harlots and Abominations of the Earth,*' Jenny screamed, a good little denouncer. Susan tried to remember her as a sweet, funny, confused child. That girl was dead.

'. . . I saw the woman drunken with the blood of the saints, and with blood of the martyrs . . .'

James was bucking, but the dark girl had him pinned down and the Brethren were gathering round. She might be able to make a run for the landing behind her. But Taine was blocking her path, wings outstretched. She shot a mental bolt at him, but he shrugged it off. With Jago around, her Talent was a clip full of spent bullets.

'. . . Her sins had reached unto Heaven, and God hath remembered her iniquities,' Jenny continued, meaning Susan.

Taine grabbed her and forced her forwards, towards the throne of the Lord God. Jago stood over James, sorrow on his face, and glanced without concern at her.

'How much she hath glorified herself, and lived deliciously, so much torment and sorrow give her,' Jenny ranted. 'Therefore shall her plagues come in one day, death and mourning and famine . . .'

Susan felt Jago's mentacles around her heart.

'Hazel,' she said, 'don't believe this.'

Hazel broadcast fear and loathing with the rest of them. Another loss.

'. . . and she shall be utterly burned with fire . . .'

All over her body, flames clung like a garment.

'. . . for strong is the Lord God who judgeth her.'

Susan saw and hated Jago's look of pity and lament. A thousand agonies of fire and insect jaws dragged her deep into limitless night.

Allison picked him up by his head and hauled him upright. Lytton's feet paddled in the floor, numbed and useless. The Brethren jeered him, and things were thrown at his face. Allison led him away from the throne, away from the pool in which Susan lay, through the gauntlet of the faithful. He was punched, kicked and scratched. Hands tore his clothes, ripping his shirt apart, even parting the strong denim of his jeans. They reviled him as an outcast.

Jenny recited, 'And he laid hold upon the dragon, that old serpent which is the Devil and Satan, and bound him a thousand years, and cast him into the Bottomless Pit and shut him up, and set a seal upon him that he should deceive the nations no more . . .'

He knew pleading for life would only encourage the Chosen to abuse him more, but he tried. He called those he had known, and they didn't even turn their heads in shame, instead fixing their gaze on him, pouring out righteous anger at his betrayal. Allison held him up, arm around his waist, and his lower body dragged, legs below his knees trailing through the cloudy floor. If she let him go, he'd plunge through the insubstantial house to be broken on the concrete of the cellar floors.

Janet Speke, magnificently winged, opened her mouth and trilled hate at him. She had just settled into the ranks of the Chosen, bringing someone with her.

'Pam,' he called out, his voice creaking in his throat.

She recognized him, but was afraid to show anything. Earlier, she'd clung to him for protection; now she huddled against the Angel Janet, hiding in her wings. Susan was gone, the presence inside his head shut off. If Pam was here, Paul and Teddy were probably out of it too. He was the last heretic, lunatic in his defiance, unable to accept the One True God, doomed to a despised martyrdom. If he'd shot Jago as soon as he pulled out the gun, he might have had a chance. The reality of a bullet might have pierced the curtains of his Talent.

The Faithful were all around, Jenny encouraging them with her recital. '. . . and fire came down from God out of Heaven. And the Devil that deceived was cast into the lake of fire and brimstone . . .'

He burned inside, a fire kindled in his stomach, flaring in his eyes.

'. . . and shall be tormented day and night for ever and ever.'

Behind him was a solid wall, the Brethren pinning him to face against it. He was hoisted. Something held his ankles and lifted them high, turning him like a clock hand. He dangled, nose pressed to the wall. His feet were tied together, the rope over a hook.

Tormented day and night for ever and ever.

He turned his head, neck muscles complaining, and saw Allison upside down. The girl had long nails in her mouth and an iron-headed mallet in her hand. He recognized a tool from his own kit.

'Allison,' he said, 'make him do it himself.'

'Don't tempt me, Satan,' she said, through the comically fanglike nails.

The Chosen had him against a wooden board. It had been a door, but it was inset into the Light now.

Allison, chaired on Angels' shoulders, was level with him. She held his right wrist and pressed it to a door panel.

'Hold it there,' she told Taine, who was in midair, hovering with occasional flaps. The brother took Lytton's hand and kept it where it was.

He made a fist against the pain to come, and Allison stabbed with a nail between the bones and tendons of his wrist. It was a good eight inches long, and spear-sharp. The point broke the skin, and the nail hung like a heavy tick from his flesh. He didn't even feel it. Then she angled it properly, digging in. A slight tickle turned to grating agony.

'Apollyon serves God, too,' she said, going past him entirely. Whatever the rules were, they'd stay obscure to him.

Awkward on the shoulders of still-human supports, Allison's first hammer blow was clumsy. The nail scraped against a bone, and the hammer slid, thumping against the wood. Lytton screamed, pain blotting everything else. The Light became, for a wavering moment, a peeling and dirty wall. Then, the Light seeped back.

Allison repositioned the nail and gouged deeper with it. It pricked through the underside of his wrist, and scraped varnish.

Oh God, oh Jesus, oh fucking hell, oh . . .

The girl hammered better, and the nail slid through his wrist, embedding itself in the wood. She continued her blows until the nailhead was set into his skin. Blood leaked around it, but she'd been careful not to tear an artery. That would have been too quick.

Tormented day and night for ever and ever.

The bonds of his ankles shifted and, for an eternal moment, Lytton's full weight was on his punctured wrist. As he screamed, he saw the ruin made of reality. A group of mad people in the dingy top-floor hall of the Manor House, surrounded by wreckage, clothes ragged, eyes unhealthy.

Then they were holding him up again, working on his left hand. Allison was better at it now, and sank the nail through wrist and door with only four precise taps. Her face was changed for an instant like a flash superimposition, every time she struck. The eaten-away skull mask of Badmouth Ben grinned over her determined look. She was businesslike about the crucifixion, but he delighted in it.

Pinned, Lytton was left to hang. His face and chest thumped wood, and he felt sweat and blood pouring down his body, clogging in his hair. Allison was lifted higher, and he felt her fussing with his feet, tearing away the rope and crossing his ankles so she could drive the long nail clean through both of them. This would have to take all his weight.

Tormented day and night for ever and ever.

As the Chosen backed away, his body dropped and his wounds tore. He thought he might fall free, and heard the nails straining. His shoulders popped, and he felt air between his chest and the wood, gravity fighting the nails. He tried to make fists, but as the tendons in his wrists and arms grew tight, so the pain increased.

Reality was almost constant now, but no comfort. Jago sat on a chair, not a throne. The Chosen were bedraggled, ignoring their own wounds, hearing a different tune and seeing a different picture. The girl with Jago was a bruised waif, gown hanging open. Jenny was a child in a play, smugly remembering her words. Allison was a scary nut, carried away.

The Light of Heaven couldn't be completely dispelled, even as he was pulled away from it by the slow trickle from his wrists and ankles and the increasing pain in his lungs. Crucified victims, he remembered, mainly died from suffocation as they became unable to breathe. His ribs were sagging, making a funnel too narrow for his lungs.

Tormented day and night for ever and ever.

Each air intake was boiling lead sucked up his throat. Inside his chest, two furnaces stoked. He felt membranes tearing inside him.

He thought he heard Susan calling him, and wondered what came next.

Blood roared in his ears. He couldn't focus his eyes. His heart beat, loud as a drum. It stopped. The torment ended.

Interlude One

W RIGHT, THE piano player, was running through the latest Dixieland tunes, some borrowed, some invented. 'The Okeefenokee Swamp Stomp', 'It's the Thing to Sing and Swing on the Susquehanna Sands', 'If the Man in the Moon Were a Coon'. Catriona hadn't yet got used to the tinkling and clunking of the new music, but Gussie and G-G claimed that Wright, who had been Edwin's sergeant in the war, was an authentic genius of the art.

At the other end of the table, Madame Irena was a spectacle in her black Paris gown, black feathers around lovely throat, jade pendant hanging between pigeon breasts. The medium claimed to be a Serbian refugee, but Edwin had privately established that 'Irena Dubrovna' was born in Holloway as plain Irene Dobson. Parting her veil, Irena sipped iced water. Nothing alcoholic, for she was teetotal. Alcohol would disturb her spirit guide, she had explained in her stage *Mittel*-European accent.

Catriona wondered if any of the men in the company – if *Edwin* – would like Irena for a mistress. Then she mentally rapped her own knuckles for even thinking the word. She never thought of herself as Edwin's mistress. Theirs was an equal partnership, unsanctioned by the hypocrisies of a ceremony neither regarded with anything more than an anthropological interest. He wasn't her proprietor in the way he would be, whether he liked it or no, as her husband.

Edwin was by her side, at the head of his table, lampooning the absurdities of ritual magic to Robert Querdilion. The war poet was attracted to the dressing-up aspects of the occult, which sometimes led him into lunatic company, while Edwin was as committed a debunker as a believer. Convinced there was a plane beyond the physical, he'd devoted years to the assessment of psychic phenomena but was thoroughly scornful of the hocus-pocus of the dilettante seance-hounds and the mumbo-jumbo of the secret-society sorcerers.

She wondered if he was deliberately not looking at Irena, even though her dark-eyed gaze was almost constantly on him. Wright hammered the piano with fingers like chopsticks, playing his own 'Chinatown Child'. Irena's head swayed with the music, a cobra fascinated by the charmer's flute. For a pseudo-Serbian, she had very little Holloway in her.

Catriona refilled her own glass and tasted the claret. Like everything else in Edwin's house, it was impeccable. Casually, his hand rested under the table on her knee. The touch told her she should feel no threat from Irena. With a gulp, she washed away all silliness.

Irena dangled a long cigarette holder in front of Gussie Augustine. Flicking a flame for her from his faulty lighter, he grinned like a clot, and G-G, his flapper girlfriend, made a small, pinched mouth with her bee-stung lips. Her name, Catriona had learned, was Guinevere Guillaume, but she liked G-G. Wright began to play the song he had written for her, 'Century Baby', and to croon the lyric.

> 'Century Baby, dancing in flame,
> Century Baby, too wild to be tame . . .'

Wright was better at tunes than at words. Still, his song fit G-G, fast and light and over too quickly.

Catriona ran through the rest of the company, the rest of the circle. Colonel Eric Trellis, Edwin's old commanding officer, a late Victorian if ever there was, red-faced and arguing quietly about drink and blood-pressure with his robust and overly kittenish wife. Querdilion, a sensitive skeleton in too perfect evening dress, never backward in quoting favourable reviews of *Gas and Barbed Wire*, his slim volume of sonnets. Gussie and G-G, trying everything several times, desperately keen on convincing you they simply didn't care, darling. Poor, poor Tom Coram, a stuttering relic of the war, half his face dappled red, mind working three-quarters of the time. Edwin, who had a penetrating brain no matter how far it wandered down obscure byways. Herself, another century child, hoping the world would grow up along with her. Add half-fraud genius Irena Dubrovna-Whatever and you had an interesting guest list, if altogether too many emotional fluctuations entirely to suit the pure-science experiment Edwin intended. She'd be interested in a study of seances that tried to link phenomena observed not to the spirit world but to the current interrelations of the sitters.

Mary Jago, the housekeeper, discreetly told Edwin the room was prepared. He tapped his glass with a silver knife.

'Madame Irena,' he said, 'are you ready?'

'Of course,' she replied, smile dazzling in the candlelight.

'We should form the circle.'

They got up, and filed across the hall to the withdrawing room. Gussie made a spook joke, and G–G told him, after she'd stopped giggling, to be serious. Catriona saw his point. Madame Irena swanned languidly into the room with an extravagance of gesture that Theda Bara would have found excessive, and flopped into her chosen chair as if it were a throne, her dress a black pool around sparkling pumps.

'Very theatrical,' Edwin said, under his breath.

Catriona smiled at the confidence. They had discussed the idea of seance as theatre, and concluded that the more shadows, incenses and curtains a medium relied on, the less likely she was to be one hundred per cent. The ones who put on the best show always turned out fake. Irena, Edwin contended, was at least a partial exception.

The room had been locked since Madame Irena arrived in Alder. It couldn't have been tampered with. As she sat, Gussie and Querdilion were close on the medium, remarkably convincing as ardent suitors. Edwin had instructed them to be attentive, to keep the woman busy fending them off so she'd have no chance to secrete apparatus about her. During the 1890s craze for table-rapping, false mediums had concealed a variety of devices under voluminous skirts. Irena's clinging sheath of a dress didn't offer much in the way of latitude for such cunning subterfuge. The high-backed chairs were arranged in a circle. They all sat down and joined hands. Gussie managed not to make a joke. Catriona found herself between Edwin and Trellis, contrasting Edwin's powder-smooth grip with the colonel's perspiring paw.

'My friends,' Edwin announced, 'this is a scientific experiment, not a game of charades. I should thank you to conduct yourselves accordingly.'

'Thank you,' said Irena, dipping her eyes, slipping her veil to her shoulders. While Catriona and G–G had bobbed hair, Irena's unconfined raven tresses fell well past her shoulders. No matter what her origins, she carried herself in old-world style.

'Would you dim the lights,' Edwin told Mary. The servant nodded, and went around the room, dropping scarves over the electric lamps.

'Dark is essential, I am afraid,' Irena said, original vowels peeping through her exotic purr. 'The spirits find light a distraction. On the other side, there is no light or dark as we know it, but to communicate with us, spirits must dip a toe into our plane.'

Catriona saw Querdilion nodding intently, thin face set. One thing about the war was that those who lived through it knew a lot of dead people, a lot of potential spirits.

'This place – the house and its surrounding environs – is a focus,' Irena continued, making a tidy tautology, 'a place that holds great attraction for the other side. The barrier between the planes of existence is thin here. A little frayed, you might say.'

Mary stood in the corner, face in shadow. Catriona thought the woman a little afraid of Irena, and wondered what superstitions had been drummed into her. Although from the village, she was an outsider. Her mother had not been married, Catriona understood. She never showed much in the way of emotion, not even with her ten-year-old son, Billy. Her coachman husband, Anthony, had been killed in the war. Despite everything, Catriona usually believed Mary a strong woman, able to bear most suffering. Unlike most of the servants, she treated Catriona without a hint of incipiently gossipy disapprobation. Now, she was silently wary of her master's pursuits.

Irena closed her eyes and swung her head, fall of hair shifting around her shoulders. She didn't make elaborate summoning incantations. She appeared to be probing the darkness inside her mind.

Edwin was especially interested in a local myth about an apparition in the form of a Burning Man. He hoped this seance might delve into that mystery.

Irena drew in a breast-heaving breath, and looked up. Her eyes opened, and she shrieked.

'Don't break the circle,' Edwin said, loudly, his hand gripping.

Irena's scream continued. It was a single note, almost musically pure. This wasn't the spirit voice Catriona had been lead to expect. A child or a Red Indian were more usual. The scream trailed on for as much as a minute, then died. Irena's face changed, and she looked around as if recognizing the room but finding it rearranged.

'This is the teevy lounge,' she said.

Teevy? Teavie? TV? What did that mean?

'What is your name?' Edwin asked.

'Susan,' said Irena, voice different.

'Susan?'

'That's what I said.'

'Have you . . . passed over?'

'If you mean, am I dead? I think so.'

'Only think?'

'I'm not in my body. I was falling into a pool, falling into fire. His throne was burning.'

'Is there anyone here you want to speak with?'

'I don't know. You're Edwin Winthrop, aren't you? And this is Irena Dubrovna?'

Irena's face was subtly different as she spoke with another woman's voice. Her features were unchanged, but her expressions were wrong. They didn't fit on her. She'd not only dropped the Serbian rasp, but assumed a whole new timbre. If an impersonation, it was good. Much better, indeed, than her 'Irena Dubrovna' act.

'You must have Catriona Kaye around somewhere, too.'

Catriona wasn't frightened, but the spirit's familiarity with her was unusual, an argument for her theory of unconscious influence. She looked around at intent faces, wondering which, if any, was transmitting through the medium. Tom's face was hanging, sweat trickling down his brow, jaw twitching.

'Are you in pain?' Edwin asked.

'I was. Now, nothing.'

It was a struggle for Irena to keep talking, as if the spirit were being pulled out of her, and trying to cling on.

'Jago,' she said. 'He must be stopped.'

Mary Jago gasped, and dropped a lamp.

'You may leave, Mary,' Edwin said, sharply.

'But –'

'Jago,' Irena said, face contorted, voice heavy with disgust. 'You may leave.'

Mary picked up her lamp and backed out.

There was a scent in the room, an ozony tang that clung to Catriona's nostrils. She'd smelled something similar at other seances, usually when ectoplasm was manifested.

'G-g-g-ggasss,' Tom said, tears running from his eyes.

'Is Jago there?' Edwin asked.

'No . . . yes . . .'

'Make your mind up,' G-G snapped, frightened.

An electric shock passed around the circle, and Catriona's hands stung. Everyone ouched and yelped.

'Hold fast,' Edwin said.

There was smoke now, choking and thick. Catriona's eyes were watering, and Tom was practically sobbing.

'Hell . . . fire,' said the spirit.

There were lights in the ceiling, red and white. And sounds flooding in through the lights. Explosions, gunshots, shells, shouts, screams, the growl of machinery.

Tom twitched and fell into the circle, hands torn free of those either side of him. The phenomena didn't cease when the ring was broken. Wright held the shellshock casualty, slapping him, trying to pull him back from 1917.

Gussie was shaking Irena, trying to get her to wake up.

'Don't,' Edwin ordered, and Gussie stopped.

There were phantom fires in the room now. The walls and the ceiling displayed moving pictures. Explosions in darkness, and masses of people plunged into lakes of fire. Edwin was on his knees before Irena, holding both her hands, talking into her possessed face. Catriona knelt beside him and tried not to be afraid. The explosions hurt her ears. It was hard to believe the house wasn't falling down around them.

'Go back,' Catriona said.

Edwin was gabbling questions together, asking about his dead coachman, the Burning Man, others he had known in the war . . .

'Go back.'

Susan, the woman behind Irena's face, looked at her for a moment. Their eyes met, across unknown years.

'You're right,' the Spirit said through Irena's lips. 'It's not over.'

Edwin was aghast. 'No,' he said, 'explain . . .'

Susan nodded a salute to Catriona, and dwindled inside Irena. The medium's true face came back. She looked frightened and exhausted. The lights went away and the noises faded. Colonel Trellis, breathing heavily, whipped the scarves from the lamps. Tom was under control again.

'That was a powerful presence,' Madame Irena said, fanning her throat with ringed fingers.

Edwin was quiet, controlling his anger.

'I think we should get some brandy in here,' Gussie said. 'We've all had a bit of a turn.'

He left the room. Catriona looked around, checking everyone. No one was really hurt. All they'd had was a fright. Edwin was at the window, looking out into the dark mirror at the shapes of the garden. She went to him and laid a hand on his shoulder, afraid he'd shrug it off. She had ended the experiment before he was ready. Instead, he put his own hand over hers.

'You were right,' he said. 'She had to be sent back.'

Gussie returned with a decanter and glasses on a tray.

'Mary's gone,' he said, setting down the tray. 'Cook says she took little Billy and ran into the night without more than one bag of clothes. Told her she was off to London.'

'That's best,' Edwin said, pouring brandy for them all.

Catriona gave a glass to Irena.

'Just this once,' the medium said, throwing the liquor into her throat like a professional guzzler.

'What happened?' Catriona asked.

'It didn't *happen*,' Irena said, 'it *is happening*. It won't be over 'til long after we've left this place, if ever . . .'

VIII

Paul was almost up against what had been the walls of the Agapemone, the crowd behind pushing. There were people inside the walls, turning and changing. Near the house, the crowds stood still, looking up in adoration. He fought the flow, allowing people to stream around him, trying to keep a steady footing.

A black man in a police helmet was shot out of the press, making a space Paul shrank into. The policeman, whom he'd seen earlier, had grown polka-dot reflecting sunglasses and foot-wide-at-the-ankle flares. A hundredweight of gold chains and medallions, including his police badge, clumped against his chest. He tried to get up, using the lightwall for support, hand sinking as if pressed against wet clay. From inside, another hand appeared and took a six-fingered hold of his wrist. The policeman produced a non-regulation-issue straight razor and hacked at the arm emerging from the light. Golden blood trickled, a streak against the pulsing wall. People all around eased off, letting Paul step back a few more paces. The policeman was pinned, drawn in. He'd dropped his blade. Light crept around his body like a vertical stretch of water, filling the distended pleats of his clothes, meeting over his neck and knees. The folds of his purple-and-lemon flares stuck to the surface even as light lapped around his shouting face and closed over him. Paul wasn't sure whether the man was drowning or being overcome by transcendental ecstasy.

Lightclouds broke above the crowd, raining down insubstantial but sticky gold spray-thread. Some were on their knees, praying and begging. Many were on their faces under the others, dying or dead. Paul slipped through, fighting where he had to. The crowd was thinning a little. He didn't like to think of reasons for that. Finally, he was far enough back to be able to see the whole of the house. Inside, things were happening. James and Susan should have reached Jago. The upper quarter, where the roofs and gables had been, was swelling like a dome. There was quite a congregation inside the bubble. Paul assumed that was where Jago was.

There was a human shape up there, feet up, head dangling. From the hands and torso, red squirted into the gold, staining the Light. Red grew around the hanged man, filling mortar cracks that had been invisible. It was James Lytton, a burning sign on his forehead, the 666 of the Anti-Christ. Upside down, it was a 999 distress call.

That was what you got for defying the Lord God. The body was tossed out of the light. Arms still stretched, James's corpse seemed to swan-dive into the crowd. He landed nearby, and Paul had to struggle to avoid the knot that immediately gathered to kick and spit and rend and tear. Everyone made it clear how they felt about the dead man's heresies.

The door hung open in the face of the Agapemone. The Green Man grew like a bushy shroud around it, faces in his bark, woman and children, eyes moving. The face of Maurice Maskell, set in an afro of leaves, was carved and stiff, fury knitting brown brows, mouth set in a grim crescent. A pile of the dead littered the stairs. The door itself, splintered and bent, was left over from the old world.

An elbow jammed into his mouth, and pain showed him the dark front of the house as it really was, windows broken and bloodied, corpses all around, mad people shrieking in the late afternoon, Maskell family clumped together in a pained embrace.

Light came back, the skies above starless black. Knowing only that he wanted to be near the centre at the end of it all, Paul sprinted towards the door. He hoped the Green Man was in a dormant phase. He was scrambling up the stairs, bodies rolling beneath his feet, when the branch wrapped around his neck.

Susan was in her own body, lying in a pool, confused and wet. Falling into the Pit, she had fastened on something stretched out in the dark, and found herself in another body, another place, another time. The details were jarred and bewildering, fading as fast as dreams dreamed the instant before waking. She remembered silk against her unfamiliarly ample bosom, heavy hair on her shoulders, tickling feathers around her throat. And two faces; the man, asking questions that baffled and distracted her; the woman, telling her what she must do, what must be done. Irena, Edwin, Catriona. The other place had been uncertain, the people fearful, but there had been a serenity, a calm sense of balance. That was how the world had been before there was an Anthony William Jago in it.

James was dead. And she was thrown aside, left for dead. Jago was working up to the destruction of the world and the creation of an exclusive Heaven for all who followed him.

It must be stopped.

Angry, mentacles stretching out to hold and hurt, she sat up, wet hair trailing down her neck like a ducked witch's, heart thumping like a cannon, defiant shout escaping from her throat.

'Jago!' she shouted.

The man on the throne turned to look at her. For a moment, she had his attention.

Jeremy was uncomfortable so close to Daddy, bound to him by gummy strips of bark, not able to move by himself. Hannah was the same way, fixed to Daddy's other leg. And Mummy was near. Even Jethro was twisted in a basket fixed to Daddy's back. Paul, the man who'd tried to help, was being pulled into the Daddy Tree, creepers and vines twining around him. Daddy was going to hurt Paul. Jeremy felt a thrill in Daddy's quirt and recognized it as the way Daddy felt before he hurt someone. It was funny, feeling what Daddy felt. Jeremy had feelings he couldn't understand, didn't know what to do with. Daddy had been right. Becoming part of the family made him stronger. Muscles in his arms and legs growing wood-hard. Daddy looped a branch around Paul's arm and pulled as if wrenching a wing off a roast turkey. Jeremy didn't want to let Daddy hurt Paul.

The Whore of Babylon had crawled back from the Pit, unconsumed by the lake of fire. This gave Jenny pause. It wasn't in the prophecies. The Whore stood up, foul in her defiance, summoning the demons of the Pit for one last assault on the Citadel of the Beloved. Apollyon, the demon queen who served ultimate good, strode to face the Whore, but was knocked away from the unclean woman by an unseen force.

'Take that, bitch,' the Whore swore.

Apollyon's head twisted, hair waving Medusa-snakes around her. She screamed as the Whore forced herself into her head, tearing and scratching with her witch mind.

'Beloved,' Jenny said.

He stood, towering over His throne, and looked wrath at the Whore. The wanton, seized by the Beloved Glance, was paralysed, and Apollyon wriggled free. She wiped the spittle of her scream from her chin.

Beloved and the Whore faced each other. Jenny felt invisible forces clashing around them as the Divine and the Damned locked death grips. Gasping, the Whore broke the look-lock, turning her head aside, covering her eyes. The harlot was defeated. Utterly.

Jenny chided herself for the momentary faltering of her faith. She found her voice. 'And when the thousand years are expired, Satan shall be loosed out of his prison . . .'

His shoulder lurched out of joint. The more it hurt, the more Paul seemed in the grips of a maddened farmer, not a walking tree. But it didn't matter. Real or not, the Green Man would kill him.

The pain stopped, and the Green Man stiffened. A shape had climbed Maskell's trunk and fixed twiggy branches to his head, pulling and shaking.

Jeremy!

Paul slithered through the Green Man's grip, and had to hold on to prevent himself from falling. Jeremy was wrapped around his father's head, stopping up the bunghole of his mouth. The boy's branches twirled and wound tight about Maskell's head, shoulders and arms. The vines parted, and Paul let himself drop, pushing away from the Green Man so he fell through the door, on to the WELCOME mat of the Agapemone. Shoving the floor with his feet, he sledged on the mat, away from the gaping doorway.

Maskell wasn't fighting Jeremy off, because the Tree was coming apart. Sue-Clare Maskell's head peeled away from her husband's chest, face pink in the green. Paul slammed the door into its hole. The Green Man was too busy with his family to pursue him further. He was home, if not free. Before him, the staircase rose, a stepped spiral disappearing into the light. He began to climb towards Heaven.

Susan understood the torments of the Damned. She faced Jago, and it was worse than she could have imagined. The Lord God penetrated her mind as easily as she would crumble a fortune cookie, and sucked her whole being up in a single swallow, spitting it back out again into the cup of her skull. Physical pain was the least part of it.

She tried, but couldn't get a mental purchase on Jago. It was like trying to hold the core of a nuclear reactor with bare hands. Jago knew all about her – about her Talent, about IPSIT, about her snake duties – and always had. He had never bothered with her. There had been no reason to. Like James, she was never any real threat. They hadn't even irritated him enough before now to be worth the trouble of swatting.

Allison came close, and slapped her cheek. The palm blow was nothing compared to the pain inside her mind. Susan laughed at the petty hurt, and Allison hit her again, in the stomach, with a knuckle-knotted fist. She doubled over as a reflex.

'Whore,' Allison spat.

The Brethren called her names. Whore, harlot, wanton, slut, unclean, filth, shit, dirt, cunt. That didn't hurt either. *Sticks and stones may break my bones, but names will never hurt me.*

Great, Allison thought back at her, *we'll use sticks and stones.*

She fell down, and faces loomed. Jenny and Allison.

'We fixed your lover,' Jenny said, righteous but spiteful. Susan realised she meant James. 'We crucified the Anti-Christ. Upside down.'

That hurt, but only a little.

'Goodbye, Jenny,' Susan said.

The angry saint was struck by her own name. For a moment, Susan saw the girl she had known these last months. Pretty, smart, lost.

'I forgive you.'

Jenny looked the other way, and Allison spat again. She had sticks in one hand, and stones in the other.

As he climbed, the stairs became less earthly. Patched carpet gave way to levels of light. Stained banisters became marbled curves. The air was thinner here, suggesting that angels conversed with helium-strangled voices. The Manor House was still the base, but the construction was mainly candyfloss fantasy. Paul's anger died, fear bubbling in the back of his throat. The noise of the outside dimmed. The faint chinking that accompanied his upward steps was, he realized, the box of drawing pins in his pocket.

His brother was on his chest. Terry dipped his snout and clamped jaws around his neck. Teddy waited for teeth to sink in, to tear his windpipe loose, to puncture his arteries. Terry snuffled and took his snout away, leaving warm wet on Teddy's neck. Terry licked his brother's face with scary affection, eyes shining like Allison's.

Teddy wondered how long Terry's good mood would last. They were occasional, and never stayed long. His brother's weight shifted, and he was able to sit. He experimentally slipped his fingers into the fur of Terry's neck, and scratched in the way their dog used to like when he was alive. Doug

Dog, Teddy called him, which always struck even Terry as comical, although their parents never saw why it was funny.

Terry grinned, showing white teeth and red gums.

As little kids, Teddy and Terry had pretended Doug Dog had his own cartoon series on television. In a funny American accent, Teddy would announce, 'Gilpin Productions Ink Preeeeesents . . . *The Adventures of DOUUUUG DOGGG!* . . . in Super-hypermegadoggovision with Stereoscopic Doggy Farts . . . Innnn *Collar* . . . Tonight's Episode, *Bone Free* . . . Guest Starring Woof Barking, Pete Pinscher and Al Satian . . .'

Terry growled when Teddy's scratching slowed, and snapped at the air. This could not last.

'Down, Doug,' he tried, and Terry's tongue lolled again, steam coming out of his mouth. Teddy kept scratching.

On one landing, Paul found Brother Derek, face painted in psychedelic stripes, crying and hugging something.

'Wendy,' he said, over and over. 'Wendy, Wendy, Wendy . . .'

Paul saw the dead Sister's calm face, and realized it was attached to the black-and-red rag bundle Derek was clinging to. She'd been flayed from neck to waist. The blood had clotted, but she was still leaking.

Derek had found her in a room, and dragged her to the landing. There was a rust-red trail to mark her path.

'She's dead,' he said, gingerly touching Derek's shoulder.

The Brother whirled, and rounded on him.

'I know that,' he mewled, hurt. 'I'm not mad. But Wendy isn't supposed to be dead. None of the Chosen are supposed to die. We're supposed to be judged, every man and woman, according to our works.'

It was impossible that Wendy be judged and found wanting.

'She was a saint. She passed her life atoning.'

Wendy was an empty thing, no longer interested. Derek rocked her.

'This isn't supposed to happen,' he said. 'Not to Wendy.'

'Not to anyone,' Paul agreed.

He left them, aching legs carrying him up more steps. He must be near Jago's Paradise now. He was sure he'd covered Clouds One through Eight.

Allison hit the woman, trying to prevent her escape into senselessness. It was important she be aware of what was done to her. With the Anti-Christ, it had been over too soon. She wouldn't make that mistake again. The Whore of Babylon would suffer all the torments. New torments crowded into her brain, whispered by the last of Badmouth Ben, and her hands were impatient to try them. There was time. As Apollyon, in the service of the Lord Jago, she'd have an eternity.

'I saw the Holy City, New Jerusalem, coming down from God out of Heaven, prepared as a bride adorned for her husband.'

Hazel didn't know where the words came from, but as she spoke, they were true. Spires shot up like skyrockets, cupolas expanded like mushrooms, glittering bridges and walkways spanned turrets and towers, bobbing aircars passed through glass and steel canyons, choirs and orchestras made music in many plazas, saints and angels strolled upon the mezzanines. There were shops, concert halls, schools, galleries, parks, gardens, statues, fountains, trees, ice-cream parlours, band-stands, showrooms, cinemas, discotheques, night clubs, zoos and pavement cafés.

'Behold, the tabernacle of God is with men,' Beloved said, almost quietly, so only she could have heard, 'and He will dwell with them . . .'

His whisper filled the Heavens, and all the faithful heard. Hazel saw her handmaids, Jenny and Allison, on their knees, giving thanks. Even the outcast looked up with worship in her face, a last convert. Their praises rose and entwined around Beloved and His Sister-Love.

'God shall wipe away all tears from their eyes, and there shall be no more death. Neither shall there be any more pain, for the former things are passed away.'

Slowly, they floated down towards the streets. All around, citizens were celebrating. It was carnival. Confetti blew on the warm breeze. Children laughed. Wild animals roamed among the people, letting themselves be petted. A little girl hugged a smiling tiger. A bear with a pink heart in his fur capered in baggy pants, to a tune played by a long-legged mountebank in a multicoloured coat. New Jerusalem bustled around them, market stalls open, musicians and dancers performing, potters and sculptors displaying their wares. Among the pots laid out on a long trestle, Hazel saw her own plate, with the face of the sorrowful woman, made whole again.

The face was that of the outcast, Susan. Her glazed eye stared out, one last tear starting. The tear grew as Hazel focused on it, disturbing her. There were discords in the music of Heaven.

'Behold,' said Beloved, 'I make all things new . . .'

On the stairs, Paul found James's gun, thrown away. He picked it up, feeling cold reality. It was a tool for killing things.

Waves of light streamed around. He held the gun in his left hand and took the box of drawing pins out of his pocket, shaking a few loose. He made a fist over them, and pain showed him prosaic stairs.

He popped the pins into his mouth, and shifted the gun to his right hand.

Upwards and onwards . . .

'I am the Alpha and the Omega,' Jago said, voice like gentle thunder, 'the beginning and the end.'

Susan was on her knees at last, between Allison and Jenny, heart overcome, belief pouring out. Jago was the Lord God, and the Kingdom of Heaven was at hand.

'He that overcometh shall inherit all things, and I will be his God, and he shall be my son . . .'

Susan saw a shaggy figure at the gates of the city, stalking Beloved with a sword of ice. She opened her mouth to warn the faithful, but her voice would not come.

'. . . but the fearful, and unbelieving, and the abominable, and murderers, and whoremongers, and sorcerers, and idolaters, and all liars, shall have their part in the lake which burneth with fire and brimstone which is the second death . . .'

Beloved's face was terrible in His wrath. Red lightning cracked over the city, cellophane skies crackling and crumpling.

The stalker shouldered through the gates and slipped among the Chosen. He was the last of the liars. Susan loved him for it. Ashamed, she kept her silence.

'Come hither,' Jenny said to her, delighted, 'I will shew thee the bride, the Lamb's wife . . .'

Terry was changing back, shoulders growing, hair shedding. Teddy stopped scratching his brother's throat. As he lost wolfishness, he snarled more, became aggressive. No amount of 'Down, Doug' would keep him pacified. While he was wrapped in transformation, Teddy threw his brother, fast becoming painfully heavy, aside, and stood. Terry rolled on the grass, backbone shifting. Teddy ran into the darkness.

Heat was all around Maskell. His sap was swelling, popping and bubbling through his skin. Jeremy, Hannah and Sue-Clare had broken away, and the Light had got too close. He was burning to his roots, the goodness of the soil feeding the fire. The flames ate into him, crumbling his leaves to orange ash, chewing the meat of his limbs. An electric shock shot up through his quirt, striking a killing blow to his heart.

Jenny was a little girl again. Jesus H. Christ smiled to her, blowing a kiss. His bicycle rested against a wall, chrome polished to burning mirrors. Granddad, who had come to Heaven years earlier, was there, a young man in uniform as he had been in the pictures in the family album, dancing with Grandmother Annie, whom she had never even known. Her mum and dad brought round soft drinks in bright-coloured paper cups. Balloons drifted past, and party poppers went off, jetting streamers of harmless fire into the air. Lisa, her sister, ran past, chasing a winged cat, chortling delight. Cherubic servants circulated with silver salvers of triangular sandwiches. Hummingbirds and bluebirds trilled.

Her throat was hoarse, but a sip of the liqueur Mum gave her soothed the pain – the last she'd ever feel – away.

Beloved and His Sister-Love embraced.

Susan, cleaned and redeemed, sat awkwardly to one side, not believing she'd been judged worthy of the New Jerusalem. Jenny had always known the Lord God was merciful, and Loved even his errant children. Allison, a queen of the fay, twirled in her white dress, darkness gone from her. Joyful music was all around. John Lennon sang 'All You Need is Love', strumming his guitar with six-fingered hands.

The hammer was back and there was a bullet in the chamber. Even Paul, who had never held a real gun before, knew all he had to do was point and pull the trigger. The trick was getting close enough to point.

He had been walking through the light, towards the music. When he found the music, he'd find Jago. And Hazel. He tried to think whether he now loved Hazel or not. It didn't really matter. He didn't even know if he was saving a world or destroying one. That didn't really matter either.

Curtains parted, and he was in the streets of a celestial city. It was vaguely Middle Eastern, like a Technicolor bazaar in an Arabian Nights fantasy, but 1930s science-fiction skyscrapers grew above. He heard Beethoven, Bach, Brahms and Mahler conducting their own posthumous works, setting knee-weakeningly transcendental music to bright new words by Shelley, Keats, Shakespeare and William Blake. Happy people rejoiced, in robes of flowing white that could have been classical or futurist. There was little to do in Heaven apart from rejoice. After a while, he assumed, it would get infernally boring.

He wandered through the city, knowing Jago would be its centre. Turning a corner after a mosque carved from Italian ice cream, he bumped into Janet. She didn't have wings any more, but was still an Angel. Smiling, she embraced him with lung-puncturing force, and he clung to the gun, hoping it wouldn't go off.

'We share Love,' she said, her tone suggesting she was willing to share one variety of Love here and now.

Paul gulped, drawing pins rattling against his teeth.

Janet let him go. Paul hoped there'd be a good deprogramming service available for her after this was over. Once she'd been counselled for five years, he might even try to get her telephone number. He saluted her, touching the sight of the gun to his forehead, and she giggled at how silly he looked. He left her rejoicing.

Jeremy watched his father burn, and cried. Daddy had changed, had been mean and cruel, but he was still his daddy, and Jeremy somehow knew none of it had really been his fault. When they were close together, Jeremy had been surprised to find out how much Daddy hurt. They were both afraid of the dark, but of different darks. There was fire all around, and Jeremy was huddled with his sister and mother. As he screamed and shook, Daddy became his old self again, and Jeremy could not watch. He pressed his face to Mummy, and she held him tight, whispering comfort through her own tears. Jeremy could still hear his daddy. As he burned, leaves and branches fell away, showing the actual daddy underneath.

Allison was washed clean in an instant. Her greasy skin cleared up, her hair was newly shampooed and combed out. Her other life had been a dream, and this princess was her true self. There'd been blood on her hands, but it was cleaned away. She was at Jenny's party, surrounded by flattering boys who weren't afraid of her. Soul II Soul was playing. Ben was gone, cast aside like an old snakeskin, no longer necessary. He was outside now, handsome and cool and tall, face fixed, machine gleaming. She drank the cordial of Heaven, and felt she had earned her reward. For the first time, she laughed genuine laughter, feeling it tickle her chest and throat as it came out. As she laughed, she was aware she was coming, gently. The pleasure made her weak, then strong again. Someone brought her a new drink, and she sipped, trying not to giggle.

Paul found Jago in the town square of Heaven, standing on his pedestal, surrounded by a street party. His heart glowed a fond red in his breast, shining through transparent flesh like a billion-watt rosebulb. His own heart kicked as he saw Hazel, robed in white, standing on a pedestal just beneath him, her face turned up to his, his head dipped to kiss her.

The first stab of pain let him see the dusk and the attic.

Then, Heaven was back, stretching into the forever distance, pillars of Light rising, fountains of golden milk spurting. The moon belonged to everyone, the best things in life were free. Happy days were here again, the skies above were clear again. Troubles melted like lemon drops way above the chimney tops. The corn was as high as an elephant's eye.

An Angel handed him a snowdrop for peace, which melted in his hand. He looked around the square. Estate agents owned platinum skyscrapers, bristling with inviting signs. Newspaper stalls sold nothing but the *Reader's Digest*. Burger restaurants were got up like primary-coloured plastic cathedrals. Pearly kings and queens breakdanced in front of the Christian bookshop. The quadruplex cinema was showing *E.T.: The Extra-Terrestrial*, *A Room with a View*, *Three Men and a Baby* and *Steel Magnolias*. A three-storey flag with Jago's face on it was gradually unfurling down the side of one monolith. Paul wanted to puke.

While Jago kissed Hazel, he was not paying attention to the fraying edges of his pretend Paradise.

With his tongue, Paul jostled a drawing pin into his jaw, point up, scraping against his broken tooth. He fixed Jago's place in his mind, so he could walk up and shoot him with his eyes closed. The point of the pin slid into his cavity, nudging the nerve with a brisk shot of agony.

He had a glimpse of the attic as it was, dusty and cramped, tiles smashed away from the roof. It was sunset in the real world. The Brethren were crowded in, bent over, slumped in corners.

It was only a glimpse. The weight of the fantasy was too much. The pain would have to be incredible to give him enough time to get close. As incredible as the pain of a pin jabbed into an exposed dental nerve. Paul bit down on the drawing pin, hard.

The scream distracted Susan from her Heaven of forgiveness. It was a yell of pain and defiance, cutting through the cotton-wool fog that had descended, deadening her Talent. She came alive again, and was in a dark, hot room, with a lot of other bodies. Someone brushed past her purposefully, and his red-hot agony lanced into her.

OH JESUS OH GOD OH FUCK OH JESUS OH JESUS OH GOD OH GOD OH HAZEL OH FUCK OH GOD OH THE PAIN OH CHRIST OH LORD OH MAN OH KILL OH JESUS OH FUCK OH GOD OH HAZEL OH KILL KILL KILL OH HURT OH PAIN OH CHRIST OH LORD OH FUCK OH JESUS OH PAIN OH GOD OH HURT OH BLOOD OH AGONY OH FUCK OH JESUS OH LORD

A doubt troubled Allison, and the admirers melted away. Across the square, she saw Jenny. They were the only two real people at the party. The rest had been mannequins.

Someone was running towards Beloved, towards Jago.

'Stop him,' Jenny shouted.

Soldier ants eating his skin. Hot copper needles in his eyes. Crocodile clips shocking his scrotum. Football-size swellings in his bowels. Ground glass shifting under his foreskin. A hypodermic directly into his heart. Worms crawling tunnels through his brain. A rat burrowing into his entrails. Strips of flesh sloughing off. Vinegar rubbed into all his wounds. His nerves drawn out and plucked like harpstrings.

Jenny saw the last of the apostates run by her, sword in hand, intent upon doing Beloved harm. If his purpose were achieved, then the New Jerusalem would fall into the Pit, and the eternal night would descend.

The pain was so much that he didn't see the reality it tore him back to. Eyes screwed shut, he stumbled across the floor. The pain had its nucleus in his tooth, but spread throughout his body, throbbing in his every atom. He held the gun so tight he was sure it had discharged.

Allison got to him first, and took hold of his arm. He was stronger than she'd thought. She was unable to prevent him lifting up his gun. The weapon went off, incredibly loud, under her collarbone, and she felt a used cartridge tapping her face like a hot coal. Jenny had him too, but he fought with the strength of the damned. A stab of pain pierced her, and she knew she'd been shot. The world revolved and Heaven shrank, darkened, pressing in, strangling her. She tasted blood in her mouth, and felt as if she were transfixed by a bar of white-hot iron.

The painwave broke, and he opened his eyes. Allison and Jenny were on him, tearing his face. He let them. The pain helped. He'd fired once, wild.

Above, perched on an old chair, Jago watched, unfeeling as a statue. Susan said he was dead anyway.

He got the gun up, fighting the full weight of Allison hanging on his arm, and had the barrel pointed at Jago's face.

He thought his elbow would give way, and his arm would dangle useless. Allison would wrestle him to the floor. She was hurt, but the stronger for her pain. Pain brought her close enough to him to drag him down.

He began to pull the trigger. With a slowness that was beyond belief, the hammer eased back.

The pain in his mouth was subsiding, shrinking away. Behind Jago's head, a halo grew. It spread, bringing with it the buildings of the city. He saw the Lord God's heart glowing in his chest, radiating peace and harmony. Paul could not feel the hand holding the gun. Allison crawled along his arm, her grip fastening. There was blood on her chin and in her eyes.

Jago's face, impassive until now, began to crack a smile. The thin line of his mouth curved, flashing teeth. The light grew, and the waves of gold washed around him . . .

Susan saw the struggle at the centre of the square, and tried to run towards it. Paul was in the middle, with Allison and Jenny on him. He had James's gun. Jago was unconcerned, not part of the untidy scuffle, but something was getting through to Hazel.

She was tugged from her pedestal, pulled away from Beloved's side. The assassin struggled with her handmaids. Allison had been hurt, but was soldiering on. Hazel raised a hand to strike him, to push him away from the Lord God. But she saw his face, a face she didn't recognize, and could not land the blow. The ground beneath was snatched away, and she hung in space a million miles up, waiting for gravity to pull her to the jagged ground. The moment was drawn out, and she heard a voice from far away . . .

The warmth was all around, easing his pain. It would have been simple to go with the warmth, to allow the Spirit into his heart. The women holding him weren't fighting now, but soothing, stroking his face. Allison picked at his fist, trying to free the gun from it. Jenny was speaking in his ear, trying to convince him that he was Loved, that the Lord was with him. Jago's heart was a beacon in Paul's darkness, lighting his way to salvation.

He looked along the sight and saw Jago's smile, illuminated by the light from his heart. Without moving his hand, he looked to the side and saw Hazel. She was afraid, and shrank from him. At once, he bit down on the pin and pulled the trigger.

Interlude Zero

H AZEL FLEW or fell through doomdark, kiss sweet on her lips, gunshot terrible in her skull. Cold rushed against her eyes as she followed Beloved. He was ahead of her, tumbling, head in flames. An umbilical ectoplasm stretched tight between their mouths. She touched Him, brushing the hem of His garment. The contact was a sparkshock, bursting Light into her head. Her hand found His, and fire spread to encompass them both. She screamed, but there was no noise. They had lost Heaven.

There were others in the dark, a school like fish, drawn towards a far point. Close to Beloved, Hazel was part of Him, at the centre of the school, warmed by His blazing heart. A greater part of the faithful were along with them. Allison and Jenny were near. Maybe Susan and Paul. They'd all been in the scuffling scrum an instant, an age, before.

A life flashed through her mind, from the kiss-shot towards youth, childhood, birth. She walked for ever backwards, aches massaged from her bones, semen gulped out of lovers with her penis, friends lost and made. She grew smaller, unlearned lessons, shrank into and out of children's clothes, saw Mama rise from the dead. Then, squeezed between Mama's knees, burrowing and kicking into the wombwarm.

This wasn't her life. That was still in her mind, a fragile presence almost crowded out by explosions of alien memory. She was Hazel Chapel, she told herself. A life from London to Brighton, to Somerset. Her hands in clay. Paul, making her laugh without realizing why. She was a woman, not a man, not the Lord God.

Flame rose around them, blotting out the dark. The fire didn't consume, didn't even hurt. Together, they roller-coastered backwards, downwards, spiralling towards a tiny dot.

In her mind, He remembered . . .

While Jenny watched . . .

It was like coming home. Alder, the village was called. The name cool and familiar, enduring for ever. The house was perfect, just as he had known it would be. It made him think of Nana Mary and her stories of being 'in service'. The fear that lived in the house couldn't touch him. 'This shall be our Canaan,' he said. His path written down, it was his duty to follow. There was a little girl watching as the Chosen arrived. He saw her mind, a tiny fire burning on a plain of snow. The day was sharp and cold, and Sister Wendy was tiresomely solicitous. There was another little girl, just out of eyesight, her mind a pillar of ice in the desert. That night, taking his Sister-Love into his bed, he thought of the two girls, and knew they would grow up for him. Their presence confirmed it. The book was opened. This was the place, the place of Armageddon.

While Badmouth Ben died . . .

The Devil had come for him in Leeds, and he was cast down. But faith endured. He did not despair. He could always survive. The Chosen would soon come. He had his spot by the West Pier, opposite the poet who was coming around, and he could fix on minds about him. The hot summer had become oppressive. Knowing which would give him money before he asked, he approached only those. He still wore his dog collar, collected money in a bowl. He felt pity and desire from the women in their sweat-marked print dresses and floppy hats. Women – girls – were all around, in string-and-patch bikinis, browned flesh shimmering in heat haze. Again, he knew which to approach, which to leave alone. Mick Barlowe, the poet, envied his evening successes and joked uneasily, all the while following his own path towards belief, fighting each inch of the way. Under the pier, he took women who were surprised at themselves for surrendering. He opened their flesh, seeking in them a communion with the Lord who had abandoned him. With women in his arms, his flesh inside theirs, he realized the Lord had not truly left. He *was* the Lord.

While Susan vanished . . .

Beyond the altar, faces looked up, waiting, expectant. He reached inside for the words, but none came. His text coughed and died in his throat. A rustle of alarmed talk ran through the congregation. He felt a cluster of closed minds. Finally, he found his voice and began to speak, to pour forth the words that swelled from that dead spot inside his brain, the spot that whispered blasphemies. He spoke of fire and insects and the end of all things. He raged against the Lord, and as he raged, people were fixed to their pews, unable to leave. Windows cracked. He smelled brimstone. He felt the sea of despair before him, knowing that all assembled here were doomed. He spoke about death, and darkness gathered in the Church.

While Jack Boothe tippled . . .

All through the meeting, he felt JoAnne in his mind, replaying the things they had done. She had only told because he refused to come to her again. He must not give in to his flesh. His nana had taught him that young. The flesh was weak, but you must not surrender. JoAnne had been warm, coaxing and eager. She still was. From Mrs Critchley, he was getting an extraordinary mix of shame and envy, anger and desire. The women hurt his mind, tampered with his faith. He would be happier when they were gone and he was alone with placid, peaceful Jack. The vicar was a secure point in the maelstrom, a human embodiment of the faith that had brought him to the Church. While Jack and Mrs Critchley looked at each other, JoAnne looked at him and stuck out her tongue, moistening her upper lip.

While Maurice screamed . . .

His Nana Mary was proud because he would be going to the good school in autumn. He had passed his exam, when everyone else in the class had not. She had raised him by herself, and he owed her everything. He was not like the other children in Brixton, dirty and loud and dangerous. He went to Sunday school every week and paid attention, and he was careful of his appearance. When he thought secretly of Barbara, a girl two years older who lived on the bottom landing, he always punished himself afterwards. Nana Mary rarely needed to punish him any more. He would think of Barbara, who he imagined wore lipstick and kissed boys, for no more than a minute, and then hurt himself. He would take a penny with his thoughts until it was red hot, then pick it up and hold it with his fist. He had penny-size spots in both palms. Nana Mary was proud of him. Jesus was proud of him. After he thought of Barbara, he would try to think of Jesus. His nana would not forgive him his trespasses, but Jesus would.

While Pfc Harry Steyning witnessed murder . . .

'He's too young to understand, poor mite,' Nana Mary said, looming over his crib, talking to her friends, 'Mummy dead under a bomb, Daddy dead in the war, like his daddy's daddy before him. He's all alone in the world. Except for his nana. The Lord should love him. No one else will.'

While Catriona held hands . . .

He was a woman, and he was a little boy. Mary was afraid, with the witch woman in the parlour conjuring unholy spirits and the Lord knew what else. Billy was barely awake, mother dressing him in the dark, shoving arms into sleeves and legs into trousers. The Spirits had spoken to Mary, had mentioned her married name. Her husband, Tony, was dead in Flanders, but he would not speak through a witch. Mother was telling Billy they must run away, go to live in London where father had come from. Mary knew the Bible said thou shalt not suffer a witch to live, and warned against false prophets. Only the Lord could decide life and death. When the witch spoke her name, she knew she must leave. There was a curse on her family in this place, a curse that had made her a fatherless shame. It was time to leave. Billy did not want to go to London. He liked the house. He liked Mr Winthrop and his friend, Miss Kaye. But he would go with Mother.

While Bannerman burned . . .

He was a girl, Alice, and he was Bannerman. And he was an angel, a burning angel, looking down upon Bannerman's betrayed face. They were all in the clearing in the woods. Dancing around a bonfire, coupling in the warmth, a life – Mary – sparking in the girl. His own face, seen through flame. Burning, falling, leaving. Fainter, like a shadow, he was another girl and another man, somewhere else.

Beyond the bonfire, the dark tunnel stretched out for ever.

Hazel was part of Beloved now, along with Jenny and Allison and the others. It was hard to remember herself. She was almost squeezed out, what with Beloved and Mary and Billy and Alice and Bannerman and a growing fan of others, spreading back through centuries.

Throughout all, they were one figure, a burning angel, standing in the woods above Alder, seasons flickering by like shadows, the earth absorbing grass and trees. Clouds rolled backwards. Alder grew and shrank. The swamp encroached, turning village to island. People in old-fashioned clothes were glimpsed. Once, like a flash, the waters were covered with boats, and men with swords and shields battled for a mayfly moment. Before the flash, there was a floating red lake of dead men, afterwards withdrawing armies. Slowly, the island sank under waters, rushes sucked into the bottom mud. All life passed, and saltmarsh turned to sea. And Hazel shrank inside the angel, clinging to Beloved's everlasting, comfortless Light.

Beloved's kiss was bitter, and the gunshot reverberated, louder and louder. She thought of Paul, and was snagged on something, her flight or fall arrested suddenly.

Chapelet. That was her name. Not Chapel. Hazel Chapelet.

Something in her mind tore. The others continued the journey, but she was snatched back. She was, for a moment, her old self. The cord between her and Beloved parted, and she felt herself emptying through it, spilling into the dark to be lost for ever. Beloved hurtled away, dwindling to a spark in the blackness, never disappearing.

She drifted on a while, momentum carrying her, but then the drag at her ankles grew stronger. Behind her somewhere was her old life, its pull irresistible. As she fell backwards, she picked up speed.

IX

S USAN HAD never even thought of flying. She'd levitated objects as heavy as herself, but that always proved a skull-cracking strain and left her with a mental hernia. Now, inside the explosion, she had no choice. Flapping her arms was obviously not going to work, so she extended her mentacles, pushing the ground, hoping for a soft landing. She should do something for the other people in the shower of fire and debris. Sometimes, the weight of the world was on her.

What had happened?

It had nothing to do with her. It was Paul, walking across the room in his armour of pain, James's gun held up. The first shot had gone wild, into Allison. The second had done the job.

She'd been close enough to see the hole in Jago's face. The bullet had been between his front teeth and the base of his nose, blasting apart his upper lip, punching into his skull. The crown of his head, where scalp was beginning to show, had come off in a grey-and-black lump . . .

. . . and there had been the explosion.

Jago could not still live, his Talent could not survive. David had established that the seat of the Talent was the seat of perception. The brain. Thanks to Paul, Jago no longer had a brain. There could be no more than the last scrapings of cranial tissue in Jago's toby-jug head.

Beneath her, orange in sunset and the balloon of flame, were treetops. She slammed into a branch, losing her wind and her concentration. Gravity took over, and she fell. A branch broke under her, snapped end scraping.

The struggling clutch of people around Jago fell too, dropping past, plunging through her attempted mental blanket. She felt Paul's mind, a blot of dental pain, zip by, and saw Hazel, almost floating.

They all came to earth in the clearing, slamming into and sliding along the shingles. Fire rained all around, but did not burn. Susan tried to think away the fire, to quell the heat. Paul's pain slipped out of her mind, and she felt her own. Her ankle complained sharply. It had twisted under her as she came down hard on one foot.

Hopping, she held a low branch, and looked around. They'd been blown up the hill, several hundred yards away from the

house. The fires were collected around Jago and those hanging
on to him. His face was a hole with eyes, and the fire was inside
him. She willed him dead, not sure whether she was exerting her
Talent or praying for divine intervention. Paul lay draped over
a bush, gun in his hand. Allison and Jenny were lumped against
Jago's legs, stunned or dead. Hazel was in Jago's arms, someone's
blood in her eyes. Brick and tile fragments were raining down,
pattering like hail against everything. Jago's head had detonated
like a bomb, blasting a hole in the side of the Manor House.

For seconds, everything was almost quiet, and she felt the fabric
of reality bending around the standing dead man. Far away, vast
and impersonal forces focused on this spot, exerting a tidal pull.
If there had to be a second coming, this was when Susan would
have wanted it.

There was another explosion. Rather, an implosion. In a
fingersnap, Jago wasn't there. His body folded into a straight
line and disappeared, leaving behind a vortex which pulled in
everything around. Hazel vanished like a photograph folded
over, and the others were distorted, elongating towards the
knife slit in reality. Susan felt a wind behind her as twigs, leaves,
pebbles and bits of rubbish were sucked in.

It hurt her eyes to look at the wound where Jago had been. It
popped, and went away. Hazel fell outwards, on to the other
girls. Paul made a grab for her, snatching her away. Dust settled.
Susan was coughing, bringing up bricky phlegm from the back
of her throat. Her head was clear, all ache gone. Anthony William
Jago did not exist.

Allison Conway was cleanly dead, neck broken in the fall. Susan
closed the girl's still-shining eyes, and extricated her limbs from
Jenny Steyning's. She laid the corpse out properly, and wished
she had something to put over Allison's face. Dead, Jago's demon
queen looked young.

'Jenny,' she said, reaching out.

The girl flinched, fuming terror. She thought she was in Hell.

'It's all right. It's Susan.'

That didn't reassure Jenny. The girl was afraid of her. She
clutched a fold of her dress like a comforter blanket and buried
her face in it. Her skirt lifted, and Susan saw bare, scratched legs.
Inside her head, the fires of Hell burned as she chastized herself for
failing her Beloved.

Paul was holding Hazel, shaking her. The woman's head flopped. He spat out bloody drawing pins, and tried to breathe air into her lungs, blowing and pumping. Susan felt Hazel's heart. It was still. She was gone. Paul blew fiercely, hands working her ribs like an impatient lover. Susan still read movement in her mind. She wasn't brain-dead.

She touched a finger to Hazel's chest. Scraping the nail with her thumb, she made a spark. Paul jerked away, owwing. Hazel's heart beat. Once. Twice. Regularly. She was unconscious, but she was back. Paul began crying. Finally, Susan had found a real use for her pilot-light pyrokinesis.

Susan picked up the gun he'd thrown away, as much for the memories that clung to it as for protection. She felt James's hand on its grip, and Paul's. And, touching the still-warm barrel, she felt the last of Jago.

Many things had changed with Jago's passing. There were no more demons, no more angels. The earth was closed, as smooth and overgrown as centuries could make it. The Light had gone from the sky, and the Kingdom of Heaven was vanished. In Alder, dreams no longer came true.

But many things were left over. The Manor House was a slow-burning ruin, people streaming from it. There was a din in the air, the combined pain and confusion of thousands of survivors. And there were thousands of dead.

As Susan came out of the woods into the trampled gardens of the Agapemone, helicopters descended from darkening skies. The army was coming in. A large machine with a Red Cross emblem was settling a comfortable distance from the fire. A civilian chopper dangled news cameras.

She heard gunfire, and shuddered with rage. There was no need any more. Weeping, she hummed 'Ding-Dong, the Wicked Witch is Dead'.

She couldn't remember the last time she had slept.

A little boy grabbed her sleeve and pulled. 'Help my mummy and sister,' he said. 'They've been hurt.'

She left Jeremy with the medical team in the garden. A girl called Jessica, who knew the boy, was looking after him, clinging to him like a toy. Jeremy's mother had a broken knee and a punctured side, but his little sister was just shocked. That was

the most common injury, shock. People sat around, shaking
their heads, not believing what their memories told them had
happened. Already, she'd heard a rumour that someone had
released a powerful hallucinogenic gas. A hippie friend of
Jessica's was nearby, complaining as a doctor tried to set his
many broken bones, calling for a missing woman Jessica said
had not come out of the fire. He had dead leaves in his hair.

While the doctors worked to help the living, soldiers were
tagging the dead, setting them aside. Susan had never thought
she would see so many corpses. The mainly young soldiers were
shaken, but persisted with their orders. Susan tried not to look at
the faces, knowing they would mostly not mean anything to her.
Some she had names for – Gary Chilcot, Brother Phillip, Douggie
Calver – but most were strangers. As she stood by, one of the
corpses, a plastic tab wound round her ankle, sat up and started
complaining at the soldier who was laying a polythene shroud
over her. It was the hippie's friend, and they had a reunion. The
couple reminded her of Wendy and Derek.

A young man in hornrims was playing his guitar by the rubble
of the Gate House, trying desperately to exert a calming influence.
A helicopter had just flown in with nothing but a shipment of
blankets, which were fast being distributed to a crowd of naked,
bruised, bloodied and sex-slimed people. She saw Sharon Coram
wrapping herself carefully, a mad but satisfied smile on her face.
No one was going to call her a slag any more, not after what they'd
just done with her. She had discovered her own power, and no one
could take it away. The vicar was crying and praying while a nurse
put him to sleep with a needle. Other survivors of the cluster-fuck
were shell-shocked, not talking to each other, trying to pretend
it had all been a dream. Susan wondered if a Midwich generation
of babies would come out of the Fucking Hell. The soldiers had
some wind of what had gone on with these people, and a few of
the more callous ones were making jokes. Jokes sat ill with piles
of corpses, but everyone had to cope the best they could.

There were fire-fighters too. They had come in by airlift,
unable to get through the people – and vehicle-clogged roads.
The Agapemone was out and gently steaming, a blackened
chunk missing. The roof was Jago's skull, whole crown blown
away. A fireman emerged from the front door with a girl over
his shoulder. It was James's waif, Pam. She was alive. Susan
was surprised how many people were. Good and bad, wheat

and chaff. Gerald Taine stumbled out of the house, long hair burned away. Cindy Lees, blinking in the helicopter searchlights like a convict caught in mid-escape. A soldier led out a radiantly smiling Sister Janet, impatient with her as she preached the immediate Second Coming of the Lord to the deaf ears of the dark. A doctor was trying to prevent Kate Caudle going into labour two months early, forcing his calm on the bucking woman. Susan waited for the others – Karen, Marie-Laure, Mick, Derek, Wendy – but they didn't come out.

Night had fallen, but the rescue work went on. It would take days to count the living. It would take for ever to identify the dead.

'Put it down, miss,' said the scared eighteen-year-old with the rifle.

It took her a moment to realize he meant the pistol. The rifle was pointed at her, and she nearly laughed. To survive Jago and be shot by a raw recruit with a quivery trigger finger . . .

She laid the gun on the ground, and backed away. Two soldiers, their own guns slung, approached and patted her pockets. The first private kept his rifle on her until she was declared clear by the corporal.

'Are the spooks here yet?' she asked.

Her question didn't mean anything to them. They shrugged, and lost interest.

She was still limping, but felt she should not take up the Red Cross's time. There were gravely wounded people who needed treatment.

'Shit,' a soldier said, rugby-tackling her and climbing on to her body, rolling them both into the roadside ditch.

She realized there had been a shot.

The soldiers were all in the ditch, rifles aimed. The corporal nodded, and went over the top, firing from the hip. Her private drew a bead in the darkness, and fired once.

'Snap,' the corporal said. 'Good work, Woodford.'

They all got up, brushing dirt from their clothes. Her ankle was screaming. Woodford was shaking. The corporal was searching a plump male corpse. He had taken a clunky revolver from the dead man. He found a wallet and dug it out, opening it up.

'Congratulations, Woodie. You've just bagged a copper for the pot. Meet Detective-Sergeant Ian Draper.'

'I had to do it,' he explained to Susan. 'Had to . . . he'd have killed us.'

The corporal dropped the wallet on Draper's face, and the unit moved on. There was a lot more mopping up to do. It was the middle of the night, and the fires were only just out.

She found Teddy by what had been the cider tent. Two soldiers were guarding the barrels from looters, and a tea urn had been set up. Teddy had a plastic cup of cold tea in his hand. There was a field full of similar cases, just sitting, not talking much. A few groups were exchanging, 'What the fuck?' wonderment, and dragging on cigarettes for warmth.

'James?' Teddy asked her.

She shook her head, and Teddy spilled his tea, face screwing up. She bent down and hugged him, encouraging him to cry into her shoulder. She saw beyond Teddy, and met a pair of glittering diamond eyes.

Beside Teddy sat a bulkier, hairier boy with the same face, smiling quietly. His brother. Susan sensed ferocity inside the boy, and saw blood on his face and around his mouth. She didn't want to know what he'd done during the last few days, although it was steaming off him like sweat from a racehorse. She wanted to leave Alder immediately, and never see any of these people again.

'Susan,' someone shouted. She turned away from the boys. Out of the darkness walked David Cross, face like death.

She slept under a blanket in a tent by the main road. The IPSIT team had commandeered material from the festival. The tent had been tie-dyed, and sunlight came in multicoloured. It was well into the day. David had tried to debrief her the night before, jabbing questions at her, trying to get round her exhaustion. She had not slept for days, and a dreamless oblivion crept around her. David insisted she take a shot for her ankle, and the painkiller ate away her remaining strength.

When she woke up, there were radios on, and conflicting news reports filtering back to the site.

'. . . Britain's greatest peace-time disaster . . .'

'. . . friends and relatives can call our relief hot line . . .'

'. . . the effects of the heatwave and of unchecked drug abuse . . .'

'Now we have to ask, should these pop festivals be allowed to continue?' said a spokesman for . . .

She sat up, and her head did not ache.

This morning, her Talent was stronger. Jago must have been damping her. She kept her hands by her sides and folded up her blanket. It was a party trick.

Her hair was gritty, and she was hungry. A nurse, tiny IΦT insignia on her collar, noticed her and came over to force her back down. Susan shook her off and went outside. The heatwave had not broken.

By day, things looked worse.

The dead were under tarpaulins, and she could see the damage done to the village. Several houses were burned level sites, with depressed people squatting in the gardens, and almost all the buildings were broken in some way. The road was cracked and churned, and there were burned-out or abandoned vehicles at the sides. Trucks were towing many away, clearing paths for the rescue teams.

On the garage forecourt, a couple of soldiers gathered around a corpse who was inset into the asphalt, his back, hands and the top of his head showing. They were wondering how the hell that had happened. A little girl who looked like a miniature Jenny sat on a pile of tyres, sucking a lollipop.

Helicopters were coming and going, and there were more troops around, as well as medical people and government men in dark suits. The police were out in force, trying to establish what crimes had been committed and by whom. Some of the casualties had been victims of murder or manslaughter. Susan guessed that would never be sorted out. Culprits would go unpunished, except in their memories. Handcuffed youths were being packed into a fleet of black marias by officers in riot gear. 'That's my son's geography teacher,' said a Somerset-accented WPC as three armoured officers wrestled a profanity-spitting harridan into custody.

David was standing by an undamaged beech tree in a devastated front garden, with an army officer and a man in a raincoat. Only Alastair Garnett would wear a raincoat in this heat.

A large helicopter touched down near where the pub had been, and a party of dignitaries clambered out, security men first with hands in their breast pockets and radio mikes, then a waving, sternly solemn figure in a combat jacket. Susan should have known he would show up.

Garnett scuttled off to press flesh with the VIPs, leaving David
alone.

She stood beside the parapsychologist and told him, 'It's over.'

'Susan?'

'The project is finished, David. I'm walking away.'

They won't let you, he thought.

She smiled, and looked around. She did not even have to see the
chunk to pick it up. She got a hold, and lifted a chip of metal into
the air. It was part of a hinge, a rusting triangle with one shining
sharp edge where it had been broken. It was shaped roughly like
an arrowhead.

David saw the glint of metal, and was surprised.

'Your psychokinetic facilities seem to be on the up again. That's
unprecedented. The Talent should have faded with the end of
puberty.'

She made the chunk vibrate in the air, then shot it through the
beech by David's hand. Bark peeled away from the bright orange
borehole that ran right through the tree.

David was shaking. She brought the chunk around to his face,
and let it hover.

'This is wood,' she said, tapping the wounded tree. 'That's
the Prime Minister's head over there. I'm walking away, you
understand?'

He understood, immediately.

She walked through several checkpoints, unhindered. The
soldiers didn't bother her, didn't even notice her. Another neat
trick.

Witch Susan was dead with Jago. She would have to decide
who she was now.

The road from Alder was crowded with stalled traffic. She
understood the motorcade was a mixture of concerned relatives,
late festival-comers and media types.

Several reporters asked her questions, but she ignored them.

She saw the car from a long way off. It was a black length of
limousine parked by the roadside, pointed away from Alder, as
if waiting to pick up someone leaving the village on foot.

Someone like her.

As she walked past the car, a black-mirrored window rolled
down.

'Miss?' said a voice.

She looked. Inside the car was an old, old woman, sensibly dressed, withered but firm. Susan perceived her strength. She could see the young face under the wrinkles, with bobbed hair and a Twenties mouth.

'I've been waiting a long time,' the woman said. 'I used to live in that village.'

Susan already knew that.

'I knew something like this was coming.'

Car horns honked, but they were ignored by the impatient jam.

'Susan?', the old lady asked.

She admitted it, and got into the car.

'Miss Kaye,' she began, 'you saved my life, you know –'

'I know.'

She leaned back against the upholstery. Inside, the limousine was a bit battered, seats faded. But it was comfortable, secure. There was a nurse with Catriona Kaye, taking up room.

'I'm sorry about Camilla here, but I don't work as well as I used to.'

The nurse frowned.

'I'm a Century Baby,' the old lady said, 'and I should like to see out the millennium.'

Camilla touched a button and the window rolled up, shutting out the glare of the sun. Susan wanted to sleep again.

'We'll talk when you wake up,' the old lady said. 'And then I'll drop you off somewhere.'

Afterwards

THE THESIS was not what he had expected when he first
planned it, but nothing ever was. *The Secular Apocalypse* was
finished, typed and due back from the binders. Next week, he
would submit. And, *viva voce* or not, it would be over. If anything
was ever really over.

To celebrate, he took them out for an afternoon, going to the
aquarium and for a walk along the seafront. The sea calmed Hazel
down, and she could look at it for hours, even in the November
cold. It was late for seaside holidays and there was almost no one
around. Pie shops and arcades were shut up for the winter.

They sat on a bench and watched Hazel playing down by the
tide. She was wearing the black riding helmet she had picked up
somewhere and would never be without.

'Watch out,' he shouted, 'you'll get your shoes wet.'

She turned and stuck two fingers up to him, giggling. He
wondered where she got that from. She was a fast study, and
learned new things every day. The waves foamed an extra two
feet when they came back, and swarmed around her new shoes,
soaking her to the socks. She laughed. There were children –
other children, he could not help thinking – on the beach, and,
despite their disapproving parents, they let Hazel join in building
a sandcastle.

'She's such a happy little girl,' Patch said, squeezing his arm.
'She wasn't at all like that the first time round. She had moods.'

Paul remembered Hazel's moods. His tongue rubbed his capped
tooth. Living without pain was strange.

Hazel treated Paul and Patch as her mother and father,
demoting her real parents to distant, barely tolerated relatives.
It was embarrassing, and awkward in all sorts of ways. The
couple with the sandcastle-building children twittered among
themselves, discussing the peculiar family they had come across.
The father said something about Hazel being 'not all there', and

they grimaced, as if the condition were infectious, liable to spread to their precious kiddies.

The play got boisterous, and Hazel was pushing a little boy. He'd probably said something about her sacred hat. She was very sensitive about it.

'Careful, Haze,' Paul shouted, 'remember you're bigger than them.'

She made a sorry face and laughed again, running off. She'd be back.

'How are the tutors coming along?' he asked.

'Expensive,' Patch said.

'I'll try to get some more money, but . . .'

She pressed against his shoulder. 'No, Paul, I wasn't complaining. It's not your fault.'

He didn't argue.

'Sometimes I try to think of it, and give up. Learning everything all over again, from Cuh Ah Tuh to GCSEs. I wouldn't have the patience.'

Hazel's memory had been wiped like a videotape. She'd come out of Alder newly born. Now, four months later, she was about eight years old, gaining fast.

'She's starting to lose interest in horses, and think about boys.'

Paul shivered. That could be complicated. And Patch knew it.

'It's not easy being an eight-year-old who menstruates,' she said. 'And she's always breaking things.'

Mike Bleach had sent Hazel some modelling clay, and she was sculpting little figures. Maybe she would grow up to be a potter again. Probably not. Very occasionally, Hazel would do or say something that proved she was still the same girl, but she'd been reduced to nothing and now was building herself up in different ways. Her passion for horses was something new. Paul had given in, and arranged for her to have elementary riding lessons on the Downs. She looked like a lady giant among so many plummy-voiced little girls on ponies.

'You know what was over there?' Patch said, nodding to a bright new seafront gift shop.

Paul did. The Adullam. Like everyone in the world, Paul knew a lot more now about Anthony William Jago. The newspapers still wouldn't leave him alone, and there would be a wave of books, films and television programmes breaking soon.

'I took Haze there last week. She wasn't afraid. There was nothing.'

'Of course. Jago is dead.'

He remembered the man with a hole in his face. A hole he had made.

'They never found his body.'

'He's dead. No ghosts.'

'No.'

The Agapemone had proved, at the financial inquest, to be extraordinarily wealthy. However, the Lord God Eternal obviously hadn't felt a need to make a will, and so the estate was tied up in red tape at the Circumlocution Office for the next century. The Abode of Love was run from an address in East Molesey. Its head was Sister Janet Speke, whose lawyers were putting in a very strong bid for the funds. However, even if she did get the millions, she'd find them insufficient to settle the thousands of damages claims still outstanding against the Agapemone. She was in hiding, under multiple death threats, but issued frequent press releases in an attempt to have Jago canonized. She had come over well on *Newsnight*, but he understood her congregation was tiny.

Paul had been interviewed by three authors working on different books about Jago, Alder and the disaster. And researchers from Granada Television, planning 'a major docu-drama' about 'the British Jonestown' which would apportion blame and point the finger of guilt at the government, the police and profit-hungry festival organizers. He'd lied to all of them, as had the overwhelming majority of the survivors. Those who tried to tell exactly what happened – what they thought happened – were under treatment. The rest were like Hazel, mercifully forgetful blanks. The prevailing theory was that some new designer drug had cleaned out their heads, and the tabloids were still hunting for 'Pusher X' who was supposed to have distributed the mindwipe dope. Mrs Penelope Steyning, mother of two 'Alder children', was the chairperson of a pressure group lobbying for more government assistance. Gerald Taine, the bruiser who had thrown Paul out of the Manor House, was awaiting trial for several murders he might or might not actually have committed during the riots. He turned out to be a decorated Falklands veteran who was rumoured to have garotted three sixteen-year-old Argentine prisoners during a lengthy 'interrogation'.

Unable to cope with maybe three thousand faceless corpses, the Press had singled out one of the dead to represent the rest, and splashed Allison Conway's picture, suitably airbrushed into a semblance of dusky glamour, on all their front pages. The chief constable of Avon and Somerset had resigned, the conduct of his force under investigation. Legislation was passing through Parliament, thanks to the tireless lobbying of Sir Kenneth Smart, the member who'd adopted Alder as his cause. Sir Kenneth wanted to straitjacket the organizers of pop festivals, to increase penalties for drug trafficking, and to provide for a permanent emergency disaster force to be kept on standby. And there were inquisitorial committees looking into the affairs of every fringe religious group in the country, from the Moonies and the Scientologists through to the Quakers and the Unitarians. Relatives were still waiting for a decision about compensation. Peter Gabriel, the Heat and Loud Stuff (the sell-out reincarnation of Loud Shit) had done a charity concert at Wembley Stadium to raise funds for the victims of Alder, while a skunk group called Pusher X had cut a 'Live at Alder' album. None of the published lists of the dead mentioned James Lytton, although, to be fair, it was frighteningly easy to get lost in the fine print sea of names. There were more than a hundred unidentified, unclaimed, unloved dead. Paul heard that Edward Gilpin and Jeremy Maskell had lost fathers, but otherwise were trying to pull through. It hadn't rained in the West Country until late August, but now the weather was back to drizzly normal. Last week, Paul had heard someone tell an Alder festival joke.

'Is that woman looking at us?' Patch asked.

'Ignore it,' he said, glancing.

A woman in a hat and coat was leaning against a railing by the gift shop. Paul knew her at once.

He wondered if she'd come to see where the Adullam had been, or to see them.

Hazel came back, out of puff, and Patch fixed her scarf more firmly around her neck, kissing the red tip of her nose and making her giggle. Hazel's breath was a cloud of frost that misted Patch's glasses.

She broke away from her sister and hugged Paul impulsively, planting a cold, wet kiss on his cheek. These were the worst moments, especially when Patch was around. Hazel was still twenty-one on the outside.

'Look at the lady,' she said, pointing, excited.

Hazel had a blue blotch, like a permanent bruise, on her ribs, above her heart. It was her only physical scar from Alder.

When they looked again, the woman was gone.

Wiping her glasses, Patch felt left out of it. She could tell Paul and Hazel were keeping something from her. Sometimes, in bed, quietly, she would try to draw out of him what *really* had happened. Paul was afraid one day he would try to tell her.

'Who was she?' Patch asked.

'She's my fairy godmother,' Hazel said, eyes quickening.

Acknowledgements

The germ of this novel first appeared in 1979, before Anthony Jago founded the Agapemone. The initial, now unrecognizable, idea arose in the Common Room of the School of English and American Studies at the University of Sussex, during conversations with David Cross and Susan Rodway – both of whom have wound up lending their names to characters certainly very different from themselves – and has stuttered almost to life at several times over the last twelve years. So, forgive me, but the list of people who need to be thanked is annoyingly long. First, a credit to Charles Mander, author of *The Reverend Prince and His Abode of Love* (EP Publishing, 1976), who drew my attention to the nineteenth-century story of the Agapemone, which – in historical actuality – was founded in Spaxton, Somerset, in 1846. The Great Manifestation, as described here, was the chief sacrament of the Reverend Henry James Prince's community, although without the psychokinetic fireworks, and post addressed to 'the Lord God' was duly delivered to Mr Prince.

This debt to an individual leads to another to an organization. In 1980, I was involved in the production of Charles's play based on the history of the Agapemone, produced by Sheep Worrying Theatre of Bridgwater, Somerset. This group later staged my own *My One Little Murder Can't Do Any Harm*, which first took me to the invented village of Alder and introduced the characters of Edwin Winthrop, Catriona Kaye and Irena Dubrovna. Thanks are due to the cast of that production for adding flesh to my 1920s flashback people: Dave Butland, Kevin Freeman, Sally Grieve, Pat Hallam, Elizabeth Hickling, Susannah Hickling, Dave Kieghron, Tim Mander, David Newton, Councillor Brian Smedley (who also wrote the music for the various original songs that crop up throughout this text), Catriona

Toplis. Various people connected with Sheep Worrying also deserve nods for being around in Somerset in the 1980s, notably Angela Leeman and Andrew Napthine for taking me to a muddy Glastonbury Festival in 1982, Alex Luckes and Jon Lyon for being there when Brian stood on Burrow Mump and declared himself King of Wessex, Eugene Byrne, for numerous small points of detail, plus Lynne Cramer, Alan Gadd, Ed Grey, Rob Hackwill, Rodney Jones, Sarah Marks and Robin Tucker for being in various incarnations of Club Whoopee, and for all past and present members of various incarnations of Sheep Worrying Enterprises from 1980 onwards. And, of course, my parents, Bryan and Julia Newman, who own and run the Pottery, Aller (drop in and buy a coffee set) which is the physical inspiration for the Pottery, Alder.

Other, major, debts incurred during the writing of *Jago* are owed to Bryan Ansell, Clive Barker, Iain Banks, Scott Bradfield, Anne Billson, Saskia Baron, Dave Bischoff, Monique Brocklesby, Faith Brooker, John Brosnan, Steve Caplin, Ramsey Campbell, Yer Man Dave Carson, Richard Combs, John Clute, Stewart Crosskell, Meg Davis, Phil Day, Elaine di Campo, Alex Dunn, Malcolm Edwards, Dennis Etchison, Chris Evans, Fiona Ferguson, Jo Fletcher, Nigel Floyd, Chris Fowler, Carl Ford, Neil Gaiman, Kathy Gale (the editor, not the secret agent), Steve Gallagher, Gamma, David Garnett, Lisa Gaye, John Gilbert, Charles L.Grant, Colin Greenland, Guy Hancock, Judith Hanna, Phil Hardy, Antony Harwood, Will Hatchett, Rob Holdstock, David Howe, Kate Hughes, Maxim Jakubowski, Stefan Jaworzyn, Vanessa Jeffcoat, Nick John, Alan Jones, Neil Jones, Steve Jones, Mr Juicy-Juicy, Roz Kaveney, Leroy Kettle, Mark Kermode PhD, Garry Kilworth, Nigel Kneale, Karen Krizanovich, Joe R. Lansdale, Steve Laws, Samantha Lee, Laurence Lerner, James Litton, Amanda Lipman, Nigel Matheson, Paul J. McAuley, Professor Norman McKenzie (who was certainly not expecting things to turn out this way), Tom Monteleone, Mark Morris, Cindy Moul, Colin Murray, Sasha Newman, Peter Nicholls, Phil Nutman, Julian Petley, Linda Pickersgill, David Pirie, Terry Pratchett, Humphrey Price, David Pringle, Dave Reeder, Steve Roe, Nick Royle, Geoff Ryman, Clare Saxby, Adrian Sibley, Dean and Sally Skilton, Cathy Smedley (gurgle gurgle), Brian Stableford, Christa Stadtler, Alex Stewart, Janet Storey,

Kim Newman

Dave and Danuta Tamlyn, Jax Thomas, Steve Thrower, Tom Tunney, Lisa Tuttle, Karl Edward Wagner, Maureen Waller, Ingrid von Essen, Lucy Parsons, Mike and Di Wathen, Susan Webster, Chris Wicking, John Wrathall, Miranda Wood and Jack Yeovil. Finally, I'd like to thank those who've requested they remain anonymous but who provided the bulk of Mike Toad's jokes, including one David Roper told me about Andrew Lloyd Webber that was too vomitous even for Mike to use in print.

Kim Newman,
Crouch End,
March 1991

POCKET
B O O K S

Also by Kim Newman

THE BLOODY RED BARON

1918. Dracula returns . . . Expelled from Britain, Graf von Dracula is commander-in-chief of the Armies of Germany and Austria-Hungary, but Lord Ruthven, his former disciple, remains Prime Minister of Great Britain. Such is Dracula's desire for power and domination that it leads to WWI. Caught up in the conflict that follows are Charles Beauregard, hero of *Anno Dracula*, Edwin Winthrop a young intelligence officer, Kate Reed, a radical vampire journalist, the resurrected Edgar Allan Poe, and the infamous Baron von Richthofen - feared flying monster.

Over the Western Front the living and the dead become embroiled in a war of ancient magic and modern science, of oppression and freedom. And as the Baron increases his score, the workings of nations and the struggles of individuals intersect, climaxing with a battle that takes place in the air and in the hearts of men.